Robert G. Barrett was raised in Bondi where he has worked mainly as a butcher. After thirty years he moved to Terrigal on the Central Coast of New South Wales. Robert has appeared in a number of films and TV commercials but prefers to concentrate on a career as a writer. He is the author of *You Wouldn't Be Dead for Quids*, *The Real Thing*, *The Boys from Binjiwunya-wunya*, *The Godson*, *Between the Devlin and the Deep Blue Seas*, *Davo's Little Something* and *White Shoes, White Lines and Blackie*.

ROBERT G. BARRETT

LES NORTON'S BACK IN

AND DE FUN
DON'T DONE

PAN
AUSTRALIA

As usual, the author is donating part
of his royalties to Greenpeace.

First published 1993 by Pan Macmillan Publishers Australia
a division of Pan Macmillan Australia Pty Limited
63-71 Balfour Street, Chippendale, Sydney

Reprinted 1993

National Library of Australia
cataloguing-in-publication data:

Barrett, Robert G.
And de fun don't done.

ISBN 0 330 27447 3.

I. Title.

A823.3

Typeset in 10/11 pt Times by Post Typesetters Pty Ltd
Printed in Australia by McPherson's Printing Group

This book is dedicated to a fine young gentleman named Chris Widdows. I don't know about my books, but I think we could all take a leaf out of Steady Eddy's.

A MESSAGE FROM THE AUTHOR

After eight books I feel it's about time I enclosed a note of thanks and appreciation to my readers. Not only for the kind words in the street or wherever and the support that keeps me out of the dole office and away from the clutches of the Arts Council. But for giving me the opportunity to do something I enjoy, which in turn gives other people enjoyment. I don't think anyone can ask for much more than that. I also get the best letters from some of the best people all over Australia. From people like the young bloke doing time in Pentridge who said I had 'resurrected his sense of humour' and caused the screws to check his cell, wondering why he was laughing so much. To people like the forensic squad detective in Sydney who said my books were 'dead set addictive' and offered, on behalf of himself and his colleagues, to help me with any research or technical data I might need. From women like the lady academic in Queensland who sent me a narrative analysis on one of my books and is now threatening to do a thesis. Her last three words about the book were however, 'I loved it.' To the young lady from a country town in Adelaide who said, quote. 'You're the best wrighter I have ever wred.' This letter is amongst my favourites. This was when I knew I'd truly made it as an awther. I honestly do my best to reply to every letter. Unfortunately, sometimes a few get lost between the top of the fridge, my dressing table and the pigpen I like to call an office. Subsequently now and again replies can sometimes be a long time in coming. But I do my best and to those people that write, don't think your letters aren't appreciated; they are. This is one of the main things that make it all worthwhile and after reading them it convinces me of one thing. The people that read my books are about ten lengths in front of the poor mugs that ain't. Thanks again.

Robert G. Barrett.

While a little light music eased softly out of the car radio, Warren Edwards kept his eyes on the road as he nosed his red Celica tightly but effortlessly through the lunchtime traffic along Gardeners Road, Mascot, towards Kingsford Smith Airport. Sitting alongside him Les Norton was drumming his hands on his lap while every now and again he'd glance absently out the window at the monotonous, flat houses and streets of Mascot, which were looking even more monotonous and flat on a bleak July morning. It was miserably cold outside the car, with a bitter sou'wester blowing, and Warren was dressed appropriately — dark green corduroy trousers, brown woollen jumper and desert boots. Norton on the other hand was wearing just a white T-shirt, jeans, joggers and a thin, black, cotton jacket. Where Norton was heading would be much hotter than Sydney in mid-winter. Much hotter indeed.

As they pulled up at a set of traffic lights, Warren temporarily moved his eyes from the other cars and, shaking his head, turned to Norton.

'I still don't believe it,' he said. 'I still definitely don't fuckin' believe it.'

Norton shifted his gaze from the surrounding shops and houses. 'What don't you believe?' he asked, a half-arse smile flickering about his dark brown eyes.

1

'You in America.' Warren had to smile now. 'Those poor bloody yanks. They won't know what's hit them.'

'What are you talking about, you little prick?' chuckled Les. 'Them seppos'll love me.'

'Yeah,' nodded Warren, as the lights began to change. 'Just like Mom's apple pie.'

'Exactly,' grinned Les, giving Warren a light slap on the shoulder. 'Just like Mom's apple pie.'

'Yeah. After Manuel Noriega, Saddam Hussein and Colonel Gaddafi have all taken turns pissing in it.'

'Get out, you cunt. They'll be rapt in me.'

The whole thing had come about by accident, or a mixture of the usual Les Norton good luck and bad luck. Things were still travelling along the same at the Kelly Club, or the Sydney Harbour Bridge Club, as George Brennan now liked to call it. Les and Billy took it in turns keeping an eye on things while Price and his cronies played cards, drank piss, plotted and schemed or whatever, generally till around one in the morning. A fair bit of water had flowed under the bridge since Norton's escapade on the Gold Coast. It took about a week to drive back to Taree with DD. A week of non-stop porking, piss and pot. When they arrived at Taree it was a completely different scene, however. DD's mother had tried to kill DD's panel beater father; the whole family had taken sides and were either on bail for assault or trying to get bail, and Les figured DD running around in the middle of all this heat, trying to flog an overnight bag full of dope, was a lay down misère to get busted, and him along with her. So Norton left the girl of his dreams in the small, north-coast town where she came from and headed back to the relative peace and quiet of Sydney. That's showbiz, mused Norton. Or c'est la vie, as they say in France.

Now it was business as usual; winter, football, a bit of graft at the club and plenty of time to pursue other interests. The boys got a good laugh out of Norton's Gold Coast tale, especially Eddie, but as life went on that soon became past tense. Then one Friday night at the club Les allowed himself to be shanghaied into going to the races

2

the following day with Price. Eddie managed to get out of it, so did George and Billy. But that particular night Norton hadn't been tap dancing fast enough, so he got lumbered into spending Saturday afternoon at Royal Randwick.

Norton didn't mind a bet at the TAB, but he hated going to the races; especially with Price. You went with Price and once he got a few drinks in him and a bit of a roll on you never knew what was likely to happen. This particular meeting was no exception to the rule. One of Price's horses got up at 5/2 by a short half head. Les wasn't all that confident so he only had $200 on it. Price, however, won a bundle; as did all the punters he'd tipped off. Les was $500 in front, but walking back to the members' enclosure Price bit Les for another $500 he had snookered away. Thinking it was for a bet or something, Les absently handed Price the $500 then watched horrified as his boss started rolling Norton's money into balls and flinging it to the cheering punters. Price probably thought Les had won a bundle too, and in the melee between the screaming punters, Price half full of ink and the AJC committee jumping up and down at Price's shenanigans, Norton knew his chances of retrieving his $500 were skinny to the point of collapsing from anorexia. To make matters worse, after the meeting Price dragged Les to a function at a nearby hotel where they were having a raffle at $250 a ticket to raise money to send a battling jockey's young daughter to America for a heart operation. First prize was three weeks in California, return trip with Qantas. Disneyland, San Francisco and Las Vegas. And if you didn't buy a ticket, whether you wanted a holiday or not, you were regarded as a mean, miserable mug. So rather than be classed as a mean, miserable mug Les bought two tickets. Price was astounded and Les couldn't quite believe his luck either when Gladstone Gander Norton won first prize.

Oddly enough, Les wasn't all that rapt in his win. Things were going quite well in Sydney; the football season was in full swing with some great games on TV to settle back and watch in comfort and warmth. LA had been hit by an earthquake, along with San Francisco; there looked like being some massive summer race riots in LA; and everybody he'd spoken to who had come back from Disneyland said it was just a big Luna Park, only you queued up for about an hour to get on each ride. Still, Les had won the trip overseas and he couldn't get out of it; if he sold the ticket he'd look like Captain Mingy and if he didn't take the trip he'd look like an ingrate. Or both. Somewhat perplexed, Norton was figuring out his best plan of attack when about a week later an idea struck him.

Around eighteen months ago Tony Nathan the photographer had introduced Les to an American down at Tamarama Beach. His name was Hank Laurel and he came from a place called Siestasota in Florida, which was a coastal town on the opposite side of the state to Miami. His father was an art dealer; Hank was in Australia thinking of buying aboriginal art while doing some kind of photographic assignment on Sydney for a yank magazine to help pay for the trip, which was how he came across Tony. Hank was in his early thirties, about five feet ten, average build with thinning sandy hair and a lean, jowly face that reminded you a little of a grainy Gary Cooper. He was going to stay at Tony's flat for a few days, but Tony had some bird called Big Red coming round. So rather than have Hank get in the way while Tony played chasings with Big Red, Tony asked would it be okay if Hank stayed at Norton's place. Hank didn't seem too bad, for a yank, so Les said okay. Hank stayed at Norton's four days and nights and both Les and Warren found him to be a bit of a pain in the arse, but a tolerable one, and they kept getting a laugh because they'd bag the shit out of him and most of the time Hank never knew what was going on. Naturally the first thing they did was nickname the town Hank came from 'Sepposota' and it still took Hank a while to wake that Australians called Americans 'seppos'. Short for septic-tank: yank. Then, if they'd take him anywhere or anyone

4

called round, they'd introduce him as Laurel Lee. Hank thought this was because of the Southern general, Robert E. Lee. He'd never heard of Laurel Lee the singer. Of course everybody else had and thought it was a great joke. Hank being a yank, naturally this all went straight over his head. He'd clomp round the house in the boots and leather jacket he'd got in Mexico, oblivious to the insults the boys were heaping on him. Les and Warren wouldn't have poked so much shit at Hank, only he came out with the most ridiculous statement the first day he stayed there.

They'd all risen for breakfast around the same time and, when they'd finished eating, Hank lit a cigarette at the kitchen table and casually began tapping the ash into his coffee cup. Les and Warren looked at each other for a second or two before Les spoke.

'I didn't know you smoked, Hank,' he said, with brittle politeness.

'That's right,' answered Hank. 'And I don't eat tofu either.'

Les and Warren looked at each other, barely able to keep a straight face. It was a toss up who was going to belt him first. Warren spoke.

'Well, I don't know about fuckin' tofu, Hank,' he said, 'but if you don't piss off with that cigarette I'll jam this piece of toast, along with that cigarette, right up your arse.'

'You heard him, Marlboro man,' added Les. 'If you want to smoke, out the back. If you don't like the idea, you know where the front door is. And the bus stop's just down the road.'

Hank kind of looked at the boys in disbelief. Being an American, he probably thought he was doing the two Australians a favour by staying there. But the boys had very abruptly put him in his place and told him that if he didn't like the idea he could fuck off. He wouldn't be missed. He muttered something under his breath then clomped out the backyard and finished his cigarette. Hank took his place after that, realising he was staying there as a favour to Tony, not as a guest of honour. He didn't smoke in the house and he didn't bother coming on with the 'macho man — outlaw from the South' shit any more. But after his 'tofu' statement the boys couldn't help but rubbish him and America all the time and treat him like a wombat on wheels in general.

The funny thing was, the more the boys would treat him like shit the more he used to pal up to them. Maybe Hank was into self-flagellation or sadomasochism. Or maybe he was just a sucker for punishment. One night he even seemed to believe it when Warren told him that God made Americans just for Australians to poke shit at.

Hank went back to America, but he always kept in touch. Warren had a word processor in his room and replied to his letters now and again. But for every letter Warren would send, Hank would send six, plus a couple of T-shirts occasionally, or a baseball cap. Hank always said in his letters though that if ever the boys wanted to come to America they were welcome to stay at his place. His family had heaps of money and he owned two big houses not far from the beach.

Around the same time Les won his trip to America another letter arrived from Hank and Norton got an idea. He couldn't get out of this trip to the States but he wasn't at all keen on going to LA. What about a trip to the South? After meeting Crystal Linx and hearing her talk 'suthin' and listening to all that Zydeco music, the idea had entered Norton's head. And New Orleans, Baton Rouge and all that was more or less just up the road from Florida, according to the map Les had been studying. Plus another place that had been playing on Norton's mind for a different reason altogether wasn't far from there either. And the bloody movie had just come up on TV the other night, making it almost an offer Norton couldn't refuse. So Norton got in touch with a mate of his who was a Qantas flight attendant and, following his friend's advice, went to the Qantas Travel Centre at Bondi Junction, where he quite legally and properly changed his flight to a three-week open ticket to the

United States. He'd arrive at Tampa, Florida, then fly out around three weeks later with a four-day stopover in Hawaii. It cost Les roughly an extra $500 with his travel insurance. He rang Hank in Siestasota to say he was on his way. Hank sounded happy as all get up over the phone and said he'd pick him up at Tampa Airport. All Les then had to do was fix up his visa and pack his swag. Which was how Norton found himself in Warren's car with his VISA card, $7000 US in traveller's cheques, a couple of bags and on his way to catch the Qantas 1.55 p.m. Thursday flight to Los Angeles.

Naturally, being the school holidays, the air refuellers put on a strike, so Norton's flight was held up half an hour and instead of flying non-stop to LA they'd be stopping in Fiji to pick up fuel. But the girl at the desk assured Les he'd still get there on time for his connecting flight to Dallas, Texas, and the next one to get him into Tampa, Florida, at midnight Thursday their time. He had plenty of time for a cup of coffee before the plane left so he and Warren found a cafeteria where you got your own, a table next to the window and sat down for a bit of a mag before Norton left. Les had said all his goodbyes the night before at the club. All he really needed was a lift out to the airport. Three weeks in America wasn't as if he was going off to join the French Foreign Legion for ten years.

'Well, what do you reckon, Woz?' smiled Norton. 'I leave here Thursday arvo, fly for about twenty-four hours or something and still get there Thursday night. Not bad, eh?'

'Yeah. Terrific, Les.' Warren looked evenly at Norton. 'Just remember what I was saying, though. I reckon Hank's a bit of a nut. Some of those letters he sent me were weird.'

'I know,' agreed Les, 'I read a couple. But like I said, Woz, it's a soft landing. It's not like I'm stuck in the middle of nowhere, trying to find a cab and a hotel. I got a bloke picking me up at the airport, a place to stay and he'll probably show me around.' Norton shrugged. 'And if he gets too punishing I'll just piss off. I'm not short of chops.'

7

'Yeah, I suppose that makes sense,' nodded Warren.

'Besides, who wants to go to LA and fuckin' Miami? This Siestasota could be alright.'

'You mean Sepposota,' chuckled Warren.

'Yeah, right.' Norton had to laugh. 'Poor bloody Laurel Lee. He could be an awful Beechams at times, couldn't he?'

'Reckon. We soon pulled him into gear though. Christ! Didn't we used to put some shit on him?'

'The outlaw from the South.' Norton shook his head, reflected into his coffee for a moment then looked evenly at Warren. 'I've only met a few yanks, Woz, and you've been there a couple of times. They're not all as dopey as him though, are they?'

'No. But there's some weirdos over there. And they all think they're living their lives on TV.' Warren smiled at the puzzled look on Les's face. 'Ahh, don't worry about it,' he said, raising his cup of coffee. 'Have a good time. Get over there and give 'em heaps.'

Norton raised his coffee cup too. 'How about I just do my best to give Australians a good name?'

'Knowing you, Les, you'll probably put all that good work Paul Hogan's done back about twenty years. Or more.'

'Get out, you cunt. They'll be rapt in me.'

They had one more coffee each then it was time to go. Les thanked Warren again for running him out to the airport; Warren wished Les a safe trip and a good time, saying he'd see him in about three weeks. They shook hands and the next thing Norton was through the security check and seated on Q Flight 21 to Los Angeles.

Despite all the joking with Warren, Les wasn't all that keen on his holiday in America. Anybody else taking their first trip overseas, armed with plenty of money, would probably be jumping up and down in the one spot. But not Norton. He was quite happy to see the rest of the winter out squirrelled away in his nice warm house at Bondi. Americans he'd met, with their loudmouth, know-all attitude didn't turn him on at the best of times, and the bloke he was going over to meet wasn't a close friend by any means. The closest thing to a wrap you could put on him would be to class him as a tolerable, possibly likeable dill, who had been the object of their derision and who was repaying Les a bit of a favour. Oh well, thought Les, at least the other part of the trip he had planned could be interesting; if he went through with it.

Norton was still a bit lucky though. The two seats alongside were unoccupied so he had plenty of room to spread himself out. After they were airborne and he'd finished some orange juice and a bit of a snack he'd been served Les had a rummage through his overnight bag. He was travelling fairly light. Just his travel documents, two Cherry Ripes, a couple of magazines, a Walkman and six tapes he had made up, and a book, *Parliament Of Whores*, by an American writer, P.J. O'Rourke. Les figured it might be a way of boning up on a bit of American culture. Norton wasn't a great reader at the best of times, but he knew after the last book he read this would be a snack. The book he'd finished was called *The Holy Blood and the Holy Grail*. Billy Dunne, of all people, had insisted he read it. It was a documentary; a 600-page brain crusher written by two professors and a journalist. Les had to get Warren's dictionary to understand half the words in it and it almost gave him headaches at times reading it. Once Les got into it, though, he could hardly put it down and towards the end he even left a couple of parties to go home and finish it. The authors had written the book almost by accident. The journalist had started off trying to find out how, at the turn of the century, this unknown French priest, getting around $20 a year wages, had managed to build a huge library almost as big as a castle, a mansion for him AND his servants, pave all the roads and rebuild half the houses in the small village where he lived in the South of France. And live a lifestyle comparable to Michael Jackson. It turned out he was blackmailing the Vatican because by deciphering the headings on old gravestones when he had nothing to do, then digging up the floor in an old church, he'd found out

9

what actually happened to good old Jesus Christ when he was supposed to have died on the cross. Evidently J.C. baby kicked on a bit longer, knocking out about half a dozen kids around France and Spain before he decided to trip upstairs to see his dad. The priest didn't kick on all that much though. Even though he'd never had a day's sickness in his life, and was renowned for his health, he died mysteriously at thirty. The journalist and the two professors had found out the little priest's secret and had written a fantastic book about it. Though not such a fantastic book if you were a Catholic or a priest, thought Norton when he finally finished it. Les settled back and began flicking through P.J. O'Rourke; and Les was right. After the other one, this was like reading a Little Golden Book. Though a hell of a lot funnier.

Having never travelled overseas before Norton couldn't say if the flight was good or bad; it was like a domestic trip only bigger with more flight attendants. Whatever it was, it wasn't all that enjoyable. They gave you plenty of snacks and things to keep you happy and the Lamb Apricot dinner was nice, but it hardly touched Norton's sides. Consequently his stomach was rumbling most of the time and he was glad he'd tossed the two Cherry Ripes in his bag. The stopover in Fiji for fuel took close to an hour and a half, and another half-hour out of Nadi one of the rear toilets blocked up, leaving you with two giant Henry the thirds to stare at if you had to use that particular brasco. Les was in a non-smoking section but a team of hard-core smokers, just a few seats behind, managed to smoke enough cigarettes for everybody else on the plane, so there was a continuous wafting of smoke coming from the rear all the way to Los Angeles. Fair enough, he had plenty of room due to the empty seats alongside. But two mongrel kids behind him cried, put on tantrums and tried to kick the back of Norton's seat to pieces till they ended up falling asleep two hours out of Fiji and about ten minutes before Les was going to choke the pair of them along with their empty-headed parents. So much for the flying fuckin' kangaroo, mused Norton, in between dozing off and reading snatches of P.J. O'Rourke. At least the drinks were free. Norton was just about to put his Walkman on and see what he had when his journey took a sudden and dramatic turn.

There wasn't a bomb on the plane and they didn't get hijacked by Muslim terrorists. A head flight attendant came up, introduced himself as Greg, said he was a friend of Tommy Butterworth's and did Les remember him. He was about thirty-five, with dark hair and a moustache. Les stared up at him for a moment. It was a party about a year ago. Greg had fallen over, cutting his hand pretty bad, and everybody at the party was either too drunk or out of it so Les ran him up to St Vincents. Les had bumped into Greg around the traps now and again after that and always joked about how his drinking hand was.

Greg suggested that if Les didn't want to watch the movie he could come up the front and have a few drinks; which probably meant he could drown himself in it if he wanted. This sounded like an absolutely splendid idea to Norton. The movie wasn't all that hot and it was a good chance to stretch his legs. So before long Les found himself in a galley towards the front of the plane with a couple of off-duty flight attendants who were friends of Tommy's, nibbling little snacks and munchies and all pouring Jackies and Coke down their throats and exchanging drunken jokes and stories like they were expecting the plane to crash at any moment. Subsequently Norton was able to sway back to his seat reasonably drunk and crash out for the remainder of the trip. So after a few hours' sleep, a Farmer's Omelette, coffee and a bit of a clean up Les was too dazed and puzzled to know whether he was jet lagged, hungover or what when they began circling the smog-shrouded, freeway-jammed wastelands of greater Los Angeles around 1.00 p.m. California time. The only thing Les did know, but couldn't quite come to grips with when they touched down and he adjusted his watch, was that it looked bloody hot outside and it was still Thursday afternoon. Doesn't time crawl when you're having fun? he mused, rubbing the stubble on his face.

11

They all started to file off the plane to the polite smiles of the flight attendants when, after winter in Sydney, Les noticed a burst of heat coming from outside. Then Les noticed something else. As they started walking up the ramps and corridors everybody seemed to start walking faster, and faster, and faster. Norton got swept along with the mob and by the time they went along one corridor and into another they'd almost broken into a sprint. What the fuck's going on? thought Norton. Was there an earthquake warning? Is there an impending riot? No one said anything getting off the plane. They scorched up another corridor; Les screeched round a corner, almost blowing the sole off one jogging shoe, and into a huge enclosed area where he stopped dead in his tracks. The only thing he could compare it to was Grand Final day at the Sydney Cricket Ground. There were literally thousands of people from all over the world, crushing themselves and their hand luggage into countless queues to get through immigration and customs. Somehow Les got swept into one queue and stood their gaping. Christ! I'll be here for a month, he thought. People pushed, shoved and argued. Voices boomed out over intercoms in English, Spanish and Japanese. Airport officials — blacks, hispanics, asians, whites — wearing uniforms and badges roamed the queues, ordering people around in weird American accents like nothing Les had heard on TV or in the movies. Now and again a customs official would appear out of nowhere with a sniffer dog and let it run and jump across the passengers' bags. Still dazed and now a bit spun out Norton shuffled forward in his queue and tried to switch off to the heat and bedlam around him.

He'd managed to stuff up one of his immigration forms so he had to fill it out again. But the customs official was quite friendly.

'From Australia, eh?' he sort of smiled.

'That's right,' answered Les.

'Going down to Florida to see the "mates", are you?'

'Yeah, something like that,' said Les, returning the man's smile.

The official banged a stamp on his passport. 'You have a good one.'

'Thanks, mate.' Les pocketed his passport and walked off, wondering whether he should have said that.

Now all Les had to do was pick up his luggage from Baggage Claim 18. It wasn't hard to find; Les just followed the numbers through the melee till he found a mob of forlorn-looking Australians crowded around an empty conveyor belt that just kept going round and round and round. Some bloke in a crumpled white shirt, sitting on the edge of the conveyor belt, looked up and caught Norton's eye.

'The fuckin' hatch is stuck,' he said, his voice tinged with despair and frustration. He looked too tired to be angry. 'I've been sitting here nearly half a fuckin' hour.'

'Christ!' replied Les. 'I'm supposed to pick up a plane to Dallas.'

'Hah!' answered the bloke. 'Join the club. I've missed my plane to Chicago.'

Norton looked at his watch. 'Shit!'

'Yeah. Shit!' nodded the bloke.

After about twenty-five minutes the luggage started to dribble through. Norton's blue canvas bag dribbled through about fifteen minutes later.

Getting through customs was barely a formality, but between the kindly air refuellers' strike in Sydney and the hatch jamming on the plane Les missed his connecting flight by about twenty minutes. Oh Christ! he lamented. I knew this would happen. I just fuckin' knew. It was no big deal, though, according to the woman at the Delta Airlines counter, just behind the customs desk. She re-routed Norton via Atlanta then told him to toss his bag on the conveyor belt behind him. Norton did as he was told.

'Now where do I go?' he asked.

'Out that door there,' pointed the woman. 'Turn left, and it's about a half-mile to your right. You can't miss it.'

I will though, thought Norton. 'Thank you, miss,' he said, and stepped outside the terminal.

If it was hot inside, out on the street seemed like a blast furnace. Norton couldn't tell where he was, either.

Strange noises, strange cars going everywhere, strange voices and even stranger heads. Gripping his overnight bag Les set off in search of Delta Terminal 25 and his connecting flight to Atlanta. To his surprise Les found it without much trouble; he even managed to find a money exchange and without too many stares exchange some traveller's cheques for just on a thousand dollars cash. The flight didn't leave for another thirty minutes; Les figured he might as well be on the plane, sitting down reading and relaxing, as wandering around the terminal. It was no different from boarding a domestic flight in Australia. He showed his ticket at the desk, next thing he was inside some massive plane, the ceiling almost as high as St Mary's Cathedral, seated on the aisle somewhere in the middle. All Norton had seen of LA was a crowded, hot, sweaty, hazy, confusing blur. Settled back in the aircraft's cool interior Les was now able to relax a little and check out the heads on the seppos.

The whites sure had some strange melons. They looked like Australians, but there was something different about them Les couldn't quite put his finger on for the moment. Maybe it was all the different T-shirts and caps most of them wore. Les didn't notice any Mexicans or hispanics or whatever they called themselves, but there was quite a number of blacks who all either looked like Little Richard or Whoopi Goldberg. The flight attendants were mainly women but there were two black men among them who looked big enough to form a rugby league scrum on their own. But for their size they were that polite and obliging as they showed people to their seats that Les found it almost confusing. The plane began to taxi slowly for take-off, the seat-belt sign came on, the flight attendants went through their crash drill while the pilot spoke softly over the intercom in a southern drawl.

'This is Captain Calvin Breuer. On behalf of our Atlanta-based crew we'd like to welcome you aboard Delta Flight 376. LA to Atlanta. Y'all have a nice trip.'

Wah, thank you, Colonel, Norton chuckled to himself. Ah'd sho be obliged.

The plane took off and Norton began leafing through the Delta inflight magazine. Before long one of the huge black stewards appeared, pushing a trolley along the aisle.

'Would you care for a beverage, suh?' he said, turning to Norton.

'Yeah righto,' answered Les, studying the On-Board Amenities list. 'I'll have a can of Pawberry Punch thanks.'

'Certainly, suh.'

It was some flat, purple-coloured drink made from pulped up cherry cocktails and it tasted like shit. Ohh yuk! grimaced Les. How crook's that? Norton placed the can and the plastic drink container on the fold-up tray belonging to the empty seat on his left and stared into space for a minute. He was going to read some more of his book, but decided it was more fun just staring into space. Not reading, not thinking, not sleeping. Not doing anything. Just staring ahead. After an eon or so Norton finally started thinking again. Only two thoughts. Just, where the fuck am I? And, have I got another nine-hour plane trip in front of me or do I go through another time zone? What the . . .?

Norton was still staring into the cosmos when the smell of hot food began wafting from somewhere out of the time tunnel. One of the female flight attendants appeared pushing a trolley. She asked did Les want beef, fish or chicken? Norton went for the chicken, and a can of . . . Dr Pepper. He also asked what time it was now in Florida. The girl told him and Les put his watch forward three hours. He now didn't have a clue what time it was in Australia or how long he'd been travelling. Les shook his head and started on his first taste of American airline food. The chicken was wrapped in bacon and came with rice, green beans and a salad with something called Ranch Dressing for you to slop on it. It definitely wasn't the best feed Norton had ever had. The drink this time was the same purple-coloured, glazed cherry-tasting shit as before, only it had gas in it. Still, Norton ate nearly all of the meal then put what was left on the tray next to him

15

and resumed staring into space. He was still staring into space when they landed in Atlanta at around 10.30.

Norton filed off the plane to pick up his connecting flight to Tampa, Florida. Although he still didn't have a clue where he was and he was still half dazed, Les felt a lot happier knowing he'd arrive on time and hopefully so would his luggage and Hank'd be there to meet him. After Los Angeles, Atlanta was easy; not unlike getting off the train at Bondi Junction and going up the escalator, only everybody climbed aboard a shuttle as well that took them to the other side of the terminal. It was when Norton got off the shuttle that he saw his first full-on black soul brothers and sisters.

There were about ten of them, men and women in their twenties and thirties; four had just arrived on some other flight. And these cats weren't just black. They was blaaaaacckk. Their hair was either braided, shaved, beaded or clipped and shaped like a lot of little black hedges. Even though it was night time they all sported mirror sunglasses to go with the gold plating, one lot wore baggy pants, shirts, hats and dresses of orange, red, yellow, amber and colours that bright you couldn't miss them if you had cataracts on your eyes an inch thick. The others had on black cotton tracksuits and caps with big white Xs on them. Might be a brand of beer mused Norton. White X. As he walked past, it was all weird handshakes and boogie jive.

'Yo! Mah man. What's happening?'

'Hey, brother. What it look like?'

'Yo. What's happening, blood?'

'Shit man. Gimme five.'

'There it is, mah man. Lookin' good.'

'Yo!'

'Hey!'

'Outasight.'

'What's happenin' brother?'

'Yo!'

Get down, thought Norton, as he continued to stroll past. And don't bother getting back up again, you bunch of wallies.

Somehow Les managed to find his connecting Delta flight to Tampa; a much smaller and narrower plane. Les was squeezed in between a woman of about fifty and a girl on the aisle of about fourteen, wearing a Camp Hoocha-kookaboochee or something T-shirt. They took off and all Norton got this time was orange juice, which was all he wanted. The two either side of him picked up on Norton's accent and a bit of polite conversation followed. The woman lived in Tampa but had been working at Atlanta, managing some office; now she was going home for a week. The girl came from Tennessee; she was going to meet her grandmother then she was off to summer camp somewhere in South Florida. Les told them he worked for the Australian Space Industry and was being trans-ferred to Cape Canaveral for a year.

'Oh, you're a rocket scientist?' drawled the woman.

'That's me,' replied Norton sincerely. 'Les Von Brawn.'

'Wow!' said the girl.

Before Les had a chance to tell too many more lies they landed in Tampa, the last part of his trip; and right on time. He filed off the plane into another shuttle to finish up standing next to another baggage claim, watching the empty conveyor belt go round and hoping to Christ his one lousy piece of luggage had come through. Knowing my luck, thought Les pessimistically, it's probably gone off to somewhere like Hog Slop, South Dakota, or something. Norton nearly fainted when his bag was one of the first ones off. Well, I'll be stuffed, he smiled to himself. Somebody up there does like me. And when did I ever doubt it? Now let's just hope fuckin' Hank's here, he thought, as he picked up his bag. Les started peering around the baggage claim area and at the people around him when who should come walking towards him wear-ing dirty jeans, just as dirty white sneakers and a tatty blue floral shirt but Hank, a twisted kind of smile on his face.

'G'day, Hank,' grinned Les, dropping his overnight bag and offering his hand. 'How are you goin', mate?'

'Hey, Les. How are you doin' there?' answered Hank.

17

'Pretty good. Jesus, I'm glad you got here.'

'No real problem.'

They shook hands and Les quickly checked out Hank.
It definitely wasn't the same Laurel Lee who had stayed at
Norton's house. Although it had only been about eighteen months ago, Hank had changed noticeably, and it
wasn't just the wispy moustache he'd now grown. In
Australia Hank had been heavier, his face fuller. Now he
was lean, his face gaunt and grainy and his thinning hair
was now on the verge of evaporating completely. For the
middle of summer Hank had no colour about him at all
and for a thirty-year-old he looked closer to sixty. Norton
had been on a plane about twenty-four hours, he'd had
bugger all sleep and needed a shave, yet standing next to
Hank he could have passed for his son.

But it was Hank's eyes. They were literally spinning
around in his head. They'd catch Norton's for a brief
moment then dart from side to side, but were always
looking down at the ground. Les couldn't help but be
reminded of a caged rat. Christ! he thought. I think I've
got a live one here. He looks fucked. And I think it's all in
the head too.

'My car's out here.' Hank gave a curt nod of his head
and started walking through the other people. He didn't
offer to help Les with his bags.

'Yeah, righto,' answered Les, and tailed him out
through the automatic door.

It wasn't all that cool inside the terminal, but outside
was like a sauna; there was not a breath of wind and the
heat literally hung on you like a blanket. Shit, thought
Les, it must be thirty bloody degrees and ninety per cent
humidity. Hank's car was a black Dodge utility, or pick-
up as they're called in America. It looked to be in
reasonable condition, a bit of chrome round the wheels
and twin copper exhausts at the back. Les threw his bags
in the back.

'Shit, it's hot,' he said.

'You think this is hot,' Hank half sneered 'this is
nothing.'

'Oh?'

Norton walked round the front and went to get in the driver's side, forgetting that Americans drove on the opposite of the road and their steering wheels were on the opposite side also. It was a harmless mistake and Les gave a bit of a self-conscious smile. Hank looked at him as if he was some kind of moron. Les walked around, got in the passenger side and looked for his seat-belt.

'Where's the seat-belt?' he asked, noticing Hank wasn't wearing one either.

'They don't work. I don't use them anyway.'

'Oh.' They started to drive off and Les wound the window down to let a bit of breeze in.

'Leave the window up,' said Hank. 'I'm gonna put the air-conditioner on.'

If there was one thing Norton wasn't rapt in it was air-conditioners. They were a good idea alright, but they were generally noisy and there was nothing like them for giving you colds. 'Yeah, alright,' he replied reluctantly and wound the window back up.

The air-conditioner rattled into life and at the same time Hank lit the first of a string of non-stop cigarettes. However, this time it was different. Les was in Hank's car and Hank's company. And this time, if Les didn't like it, he was the one who could piss off. Which was fair enough. Nonetheless Norton wound the window down about a third. If Laurel Lee didn't like it Les was going to tell him to go fuck his boot anyway. So far Hank hadn't asked Norton how the trip was, how he felt, was he looking forward to his holiday in the States? Kiss my arse — nothing. Norton was going to say something, but he was trying to concentrate on his surroundings. Not that there was much he could make out in the darkness. He just seemed to be speeding along the wrong side of the road along some super freeway built up over water. That was all Norton could make out: some enormous inky bay, reflecting a full moon and some stars. Finally Hank decided to open his mouth.

'How's Warren?' he asked.

'Good,' replied Les.

'The sonofabitch never answers my letters.'

Norton felt like saying, Well, if he answered every one of your letters, Boofhead, he'd have word processor meltdown. 'He's been busy. He's got a fair bit on at work.'

'You never write.'

'Yeah, well, you know me,' said Les. 'I'm flat out writin' a grocery list.'

Hank sucked on his cigarette and seemed to think for a moment. 'How's Tony Nathan? He never writes either.'

'Tony's going good. He's powering at the photography, making plenty of money. He's probably been busy too.' Christ! thought Les, I hope I don't have to keep kidding to this wally the whole time I'm here.

In spite of Hank's generosity in picking Les up at the airport and giving him a place to stay, and Norton promising himself he'd come to America with an open mind, Les found himself already building up a resentment to the American. It wasn't just cigarettes; although Les disliked them, he wasn't that big a nark. There was something else again that he couldn't quite put a finger on. Hank didn't answer and the expression on his face never changed. He just sucked on his cigarette and kept driving. Norton had a feeling he shouldn't say it, but he did. Shit, he had to say something. Inside the car had all the atmosphere of a derelict spaceship.

'So, ah... how's things going with you, Hank?' he asked.

That was all Laurel needed. It was about an hour and a half's drive from the airport to Siestasota and Les got a non-stop whingeing, moaning, litany of woe for the entire journey, accompanied by a non-stop stream of cigarette smoke.

First up, his dumb-ass bitch of a girlfriend, who'd been working for him, had fucked up his business, leaving him broke and now bankrupt. On top of this she left him for some jerk, asshole faggot originally from New York, just because the jerk, asshole faggot had money. But he was a creep and she was the one suffering now and it served her

20

right, the dumb bitch. His father, the art dealer, had died; which Les would have known if he'd read his letters. Just before he kicked the bucket, though, a gang of thieves, probably the Mafia, broke into the gallery and stole all the paintings and anything else they could get their hands on, including the carpets and the light fittings. This left his old man destitute overnight because none of it could be insured, and more debt for Hank. The local cops were useless jerks, so was the FBI; they were all conspiring with the Mafia to split the loot. So Hank hired a private eye. But he turned out to be a jerk also. Now the cops wouldn't even answer his phone calls. The bank was threatening to foreclose on the house he shared with his mother, but it served her right anyway because she was nothing but a drunken old pain in the ass who got in the road anyway. The rest of his family were all dropkicks and had turned against him just because he'd got into a bit of debt. His sister was a snooty bitch who'd married a jerk and who thought of nothing but herself and her family. His brother was the same, so he didn't talk to him or his family. Because of them he had to front the taxation department next week, which was staffed with nothing but more jerks who'd moved down from New York; then he was contesting the will because anything his old man might have had he left to them and why should these assholes get anything, let alone everything. Siestasota wasn't the place it used to be because of all these assholes moving here from interstate and everywhere else and what America needed was a good revolution. Blow all the assholes away. The magazine knocked back the story he did while he was in Australia too; but what would those faggot, asshole publishers in New York know anyway? Then there was the creep who moved into the house next door; he was a jerk like the rest of his neighbours.

By now Norton was staring ahead into the steamy Florida night, hardly believing what he was hearing, and trying to switch off. But he couldn't. Hank might have been a goose at his place; now, he was the most miserable, whingeing prick Les had ever come across. And he'd travelled halfway across the world to meet up with the moron. Not only that, it wasn't as if he could say, Well it's been nice talking to you, Hank, drop me off at the next corner and I'll catch a cab home. He was stuck with the pain in the arse. Norton shook his head in disbelief. And what was I saying earlier? Somebody up there still likes me? Hah! What a joke. No, I can't really blame him, I suppose. Fuckin' Warren. That's whose fault it is. The little cunt. Why didn't he tell me to read more of this prick's letters?

Hank flicked another cigarette out the window and eased up slightly on his tirade about the same time he turned right off the freeway. Norton thought he saw a sign saying Siestasota County. It seemed like another freeway, only there were now houses and other buildings on either side of the divided highway, or whatever it was. It reminded Les a little of Parramatta Road, but about four times as wide and completely flat. They pulled up at a set of lights and for some reason Les unconsciously went to put his foot on the brake and change gears. It seemed funny when there was nothing in front of him.

'Well, Hank,' said Les, not meaning to sound laconic, 'it looks like you've been having a bit of a bad trot, mate.'

Hank looked at Les for a second, then his eyes seemed to dart all over the place. 'A bad trot? Goddamn!'

'Well, you know what I mean.' Despite himself, Les suddenly found it hard to keep a straight face.

They ground on through the night; Hank lit another cigarette while Norton tried to figure out this absolute prick of a situation he'd unexpectedly found himself in. It was a bit of a worry. 'Anyway, Hank,' he said, giving the American a friendly slap on the shoulder, 'how about letting me buy you a beer? Is there a pub or something near your place?'

Hank looked at his watch. 'It's almost one-thirty. Everything closes at two.'

'Oh!' Norton's heart sank down around his ankles.

'There's booze back at my place.'

'Yeah. It's just that I'd love to shout you a drink for picking me up at the airport. That's a bloody long drive in this heat. It was more than good of you. And it is my first time ever in America. I'd like to celebrate a bit. Plus catching up with you again, too.' A drink back at your place'd be great, thought Norton. Especially the conversation. But if I don't have a drink right now and get out of this bloody car and have a mag to someone, even if it's only the local mule, I'll end up necking myself. 'Come on, Hank. We've got nearly half an hour. My shout. Just for old time's sake.'

Hank took a huge drag on his cigarette then let it out slowly. 'There's a bar on Main Street. It's on the way to my place, I suppose.'

'Beauty!' Les gave the American another friendly pat on the shoulder, then eased back in his seat and breathed a quiet sigh of relief.

Hank followed the road they were on, then turned right into one not quite as wide, which was flanked by low-rise office buildings, restaurants and shops with cars angle-parked in front. Near what looked like a book shop he backed his pick-up in against the footpath or sidewalk or whatever they call it. By angling his head around, Les could see a bar with 'Toby's' painted across a window next to a double glass door. Hank got out and slammed the door; Les just had time to stash his bags on the front floor, along with his jacket, and catch up with Hank as he went straight inside.

There was a long wooden bar as you walked in, a dining area down the back, a DJ stand and a small dancefloor to your left near a few chairs and tables and some cubicles. It had that ambient, old-style bar look about it Les had seen in about a hundred American movies and TV shows. Bad luck there wouldn't have been more than six people in there, counting the barmaid. So much for Thursday night in swinging, downtown Siesta-sota, thought Norton. Still, it was a nice enough looking place and twenty years on Devils Island would have been better than another ten minutes alone with Laurel Lee.

'Righto, Hank,' said Les slapping his hands together.
'What'll you have, mate?'

Hank shrugged and straddled his arse across a stool.
'Beer.'

The barmaid was about thirty, fairly attractive with
straight auburn hair. Although it was almost closing time
she had a pleasant smile on her face; more than likely
because she was bored having to talk to the skinny drunk
at the end of the bar and it was something to break the
monotony.

'Righto,' Norton returned the barmaid's smile. 'A beer
for me mate there. And I'll have...' Norton's smile
turned into a grin, 'a margarita.'

The barmaid looked at Les for a moment then began to
grin herself. 'Coming right up.'

The drinks took barely a couple of minutes to arrive
and Norton was impressed; even though he hardly had
time to make a big fumble with his wallet so he could
avoid talking to Hank before they came. The barmaid put
Hank's beer in front of him; Les handed her a twenty. As
she went to the till Les turned to Hank and held up his
drink.

'Cheers, mate,' he said, trying to stop his stomach from
heaving. 'Good to see you again.'

Hank raised his beer like he had a broken collarbone.
'Whatever.'

Les took a monstrous slurp on his margarita. It was
delicious; the salt bit his lips and the whole thing hit the
spot nicely. He noticed Hank took a lengthy pull too and
guessed it might have been a while since Hank had his
mitts on a nice cool one; especially a shout.

The girl brought back Norton's change, put it on the
bar and continued to smile at Les. 'Are you Australian?'
she asked.

'Yeah,' answered Les, a little taken back. 'How'd you
guess?'

'The accent.'

'Christ!' exclaimed Norton. 'I only said about five
bloody words.'

24

'That's all you need, big guy,' winked the girl.

Les threw back his head and laughed out loud and the rest of the margarita disappeared down his throat. 'Well, if that's the case, good lookin', while you're standing there doing nothin' I'll have another one of those please.' Les placed his empty glass on the bar and turned to Laurel. Laurel shrugged again. 'And another beer for . . . him.'

'You got it.'

While he waited for the next round to arrive Les had a slew round the bar, partly out of curiosity, mainly to avoid having to talk to Hank. There was just some skinny bloke in a Bud-Lite T-shirt under a TV at the end, a couple three stools down and another couple in a cubicle by the dancefloor. From out of the dining area a huge black man appeared, wearing jeans and a Toby's T-shirt, and carrying some ashtrays and what looked like paper napkins. Les tossed him a wink and got a happy enough smile in return. The drinks arrived. Les thanked the girl and took another massive slurp.

'So how do you like the United States?' asked the barmaid.

'It's great,' answered Norton. 'One of the best places I ever seen.'

'Hey, isn't that nice?' The girl was genuinely pleased. 'How long have you bin here?'

Norton glanced at his watch. 'About an hour and a half. I just got off the bloody plane at Tampa.' Les watched the barmaid put her hand over her face as she tried not to laugh. 'So what's your name anyway, sweetheart? You're certainly friendly enough.'

'Trudi.'

'I'm Les.' The Queenslander held up his drink. 'Nice to meet you, Trudi.'

'You too, Les. You don't seem like a bad bloke yourself . . . mate.'

'Good on you, Trudi.'

Margarita number two went down pretty smartly, so Les ordered another one, then a whiskey sour, as he raced a big wooden clock at the end of the bar that kept ticking towards two. So far Hank hadn't grunted more than about three words, preferring to smoke cigarettes, act macho and drink the free beers in front of him while Les nattered away with the barmaid.

It turned out Trudi had moved down to Florida from Baltimore with her husband about two years ago. Baltimore was just below New York. At the mention of New York Les smiled to himself as he looked at Hank's reflection in the bar mirror and saw his face go about as sour as the whiskey Les was drinking. Even though Florida was terribly hot in summer, continued Trudi, winter was lovely; especially not having to walk around up to your waist in snow at times.

'So what brings you to the States, Les?' enquired Trudi, getting a kick out of watching him ripping into his whiskey sour. 'On vacation are you?'

'Not really,' said Norton. 'It's more a business trip. Like a working holiday.'

'Oh?'

'Yeah. Back in Australia I'm with the NTCRC.' Trudi looked puzzled, even the skinny drunk at the end of the bar started to earwig. Hank still sat there like a stale bottle of piss. 'The Northern Territory Crocodile Racing Commission.'

'Northern Territory?' Trudi looked puzzled. 'I think I've heard of Sydney and Melbourne. And somewhere called Perth.'

'It's up the top end of Australia. Place called Darwin. I'm over here to buy some breeding stock. I'm taking some alligators back with me. We're gonna cross breed them with the crocodiles and see how they go.'

'You have crocodile races back in Australia?' Trudi stared at Les.

'Bloody oath! It's a big business back home. The annual Darwin Cup's worth nearly half a million dollars. We get crocodiles come from all over Australia.'

'Crocodile racing.' Trudi shook her head. 'How do you get those big, mean critters to stay on the track, or whatever?'

26

'We use koala bears as jockeys.'

Trudi's mouth swung open. 'Those cute little things with the big ears? My god! How do you get them to ride on those big monsters?'

'Easy,' said Norton. 'They got little saddles and whips. And helmets and goggles. Hey, don't worry about koalas. They're tough little bastards, I'm telling you. They hang on to trees alright. Same with crocodiles.' Norton started making jockey motions like he had a whip in his hand and was holding onto the reins. 'Only thing we have to watch is the cheating. There's a bit of that goes on.'

'Cheating? In a crocodile race?' Trudi shook her head again.

'Yeah.' Norton looked serious. 'Only last week we had a racing scandal, and a big inquiry. We caught one of the jockeys using a battery. Had it hidden in his whip, the little bastard. But we were on to him; we knew he was cheating.'

'My God! What happened?'

'The crocodile won by five lengths. But the koala got electrocuted.'

'Oh, my God! That's awful.'

'Yeah,' nodded Norton sincerely. 'If you can't trust a cute, cuddly little koala bear, who can you trust?'

The clock hit two. Hank briefly caught Norton's eye as he got off his stool and headed for the door. Norton drained his last drink and put the glass on the bar, leaving about six dollars next to it in one dollar bills and quarters.

'Well that was truly delightful, Trudi,' he said. 'Exactly what I needed. But now I have to leave. My handsome prince is waiting outside with a pumpkin coach drawn by six white mice.' Just a little unsteadily Les turned towards the door where the big black bloke was standing next to a cigarette machine.

'Hey!' called out Trudi. 'Are you gonna come back and have another drink with us before you go back to Darwin? Saturday nights are good. We have a band.'

Les looked at the big black bloke, who was about three

inches taller and at least ten stone heavier than Les, and smiling feinted a left rip at his massive stomach. 'Ain't nobody here big enough to stop me.'

The black bloke flashed back a white grin that was almost as big as he was and opened the door for Norton. 'You have a good one, brother.'

As Norton stepped through the door he stopped and gave Trudi a wave. 'See you later, alligator,' he called out boozily.

Hank was sitting in the pick-up, smoking a cigarette, with the motor running and the lights on. Pleasantly numbed from six stiff drinks in about half an hour Les swung inside on top of his gear in a better frame of mind to cope with the seppo. They took off in silence and about two miles back onto the highway Hank spoke.

'That was one of the stupidest things I've ever heard. What made you come out with all that crap?'

'It's ... I say, it's called having a joke, boy. You do know what a joke is, don't you, Laurel?' The drinks hadn't helped the sarcasm that had been building up inside Les either.

'I sure know what being stupid is when I see it.'

Tomorrow, thought Les, staring ahead into the night. I'll get a good night's sleep tonight. Then tomorrow, after I've let this prick show me around a bit, I'll hit him right on the chin and break his jaw then move into a motel or head over to Miami or something.

'Back at my place,' Hank took a big drag on his cigarette and gave Les a super smug look, 'I'll show you something that ain't stupid.'

'Yeah. Like what?' Norton couldn't stop himself laughing. 'A photo of you at your senior prom, wearing a white sports coat and a pink carnation?'

'You'll see and feel something you don't see in Australia.'

I can't wait, thought Les. He was going to sling off some more but changed his mind and just wound down the window.

They drove on pretty much in silence with Les still

absolutely clueless as to where he was; all he knew was that it was still dead flat and they'd come about ten kilometres. Or six miles in seppo talk. Hank turned off the main road onto a smaller one, then another. Now there were vacant lots and single-storey homes that reminded Les of holiday houses on the north and south coast of New South Wales, only there were no fences and they all had double garages and huge driveways. There also seemed to be more trees and behind some of the houses Les could see what looked like ponds or lagoons shining a murky silver in the moonlight.

Hank turned left through some trees and they crunched up a long driveway to pull up in front of a rickety carport with a lopsided roof hanging over some car beneath. There was a single-storey house to the right with a light on over a verandah out the front that still reminded Les of a holiday home. A narrow path led from that house to a smaller one about thirty metres away that had an extra storey built on top; it too had a light left on and even from that distance Les could see the paint was peeling off and weeds grew up to the front door. All round were trees with this creepy-looking grey-green fern hanging off them, which Les later found out was called Spanish Moss. It might have been the night and the oppressive heat, it might have been the Spanish Moss in the moonlight, but the whole place had this eerie, necessitous look about it. Hank got out of the car, undid his fly and did a great piss on the driveway. Well, that suits me, thought Norton, and got out and did the same. Hank finished first and started towards the larger house.

'This way,' he said, without waiting for Les.

'Yeah, righto,' answered Norton, and took his time finishing.

Les picked up his bags and walked into the house, trying not to make too much noise. There was the usual small hallway when you entered, a loungeroom to the left and another room to the right with a large wooden table and some old chairs around it. The house was nothing too flash, lots of paintings on the walls, bric-a-brac sitting on old cabinets and a few scatter rugs on the yellowy brown carpet. Somewhere ahead light came from another door; Les headed towards it and found a fairly large kitchen with windows facing on to what looked an enclosed verandah. There were more doors to his right and a passageway that was a laundry. Light came from another doorway at the end of a shorter passageway; Les walked towards it and found what evidently was his room.

It was a fairly large, dimly lit room with carpet — and not much else. There was a single bed against the wall as you walked in; opposite was a long, low table with a lamp on it, a fan, an ancient ghetto blaster and just plain junk. There were a couple of old lounge chairs, another low but smaller table in one corner and that was about it. No dressing table, no wardrobe, not even an overhead light fitting. Just a sliding glass door and a flyscreen to the left as you walked in, left open to get the non-existent breeze or air, and another door in the far corner. The rest was just junk; mainly old wooden frames that looked like they could have once held paintings.

Hank stood in the middle, looking round like it was the Presidential Suite at the Sydney Regent. 'Well, what do you say?'

'Great,' answered Les, sweat already dripping from his chin. His bags dropped on the floor along with his arse. 'Bad luck I can only stay three weeks.'

'You got a bed there, a lamp, the fan works. That sliding door leads out back and this is your bathroom.' Hank opened the door in the corner. There was a shower, toilet and sink; the white tiles looked reasonably clean but it smelled of stagnant water.

'Nice,' nodded Les, as Hank closed the door. Christ! he thought. How do I find myself in these spots? Long Bay wasn't much worse than this. And at least it was cooler.

'Now let's go and have a real drink.'

Les had a last look round his sumptuous lodgings and followed Hank out the same way they came in. I imagine another margarita would be out of the question, mused Norton.

There were a few night sounds as Les crunched along the narrow path to what was obviously Hank's section of his family's rambling estate; though what Les was mainly concentrating on was the bloody heat and flicking Spanish Moss out of his face. Laurel Lee's house reminded Norton of a weekender down the south coast alright. The south coast of East Germany. The front door stood warped and splintering in the dim light just above it, there was a large window and curtains to the right and a smaller window to the left, which Norton surmised was the kitchen. The place was all a sickly orange and white and looking at it from the outside it was hard to imagine that it once was new. All it was now was faded paintwork, grime and dry rot. Come and stay at my place any time you're in America, you guys. I own two houses and my family's got heaps of money. What did Price, the wise old owl, say the night before Norton left? Don't even believe half of what yanks tell you. They're full of bullshit. No wonder his boss was a multi-millionaire and looked twenty years younger than he was.

Hank unlocked the front door and inside was just as tatty, only it was musty as well. There was a kitchen to the left, cluttered with pots and dishes, a grimy sink, a grimy stove and a rusting fridge. The rest of downstairs was just one big room with bare floorboards, except where a landing walked up one step to a curtained off room in the right corner. A set of stairs led left from that up to what looked like the master's magnificent bedroom and lavish toilet facilities. A dusty, noisy air-conditioner, whining away at the top of the stairs, did manage to bring the temperature down a few degrees. There were a couple of daggy animal skins pinned to the walls, two or three paintings and as far as home decorating went, that was it. The only noticeable comforts were an old three-piece lounge sitting between the door and the far wall as you walked in, a small-screen TV set sitting on a dusty, wooden cabinet full of old books, and a coffee table with a telephone on it. Les noticed a locked cabinet against one wall and beneath this a table holding what looked like a home mincer. Norton stared at the handle on it for a few seconds; he knew what it was but couldn't think for the moment. There was no stereo in the room, no pool table and definitely no cocktail bar or cabinet.

'Well? What do you say?' asked Hank.

'Wonderful,' nodded Les. 'Who lived here before you did? Elton John?'

Hank turned on the TV and went into the kitchen. Les sat down on the lounge. The sound was turned down but you still couldn't tell what was on because the reception was mostly a purple blur. Norton stared at it for a few moments, looked around once more, and shook his head. Where am I again? America or Ethiopia?

Hank returned from the kitchen with a bottle of tequila. Norton grimaced and felt his mouth go dry. After all those lovely frozen margaritas in that little bar I know just what this is going to taste like. Shit. With or without the sip, lick, suck. It wasn't even a good brand. A cheap-looking label, slapped on the bottle under a rusty cap, said Gusano Rojo de Oaxaca, and the worm lying at the bottom looked like half of someone's appendix. Yuk!

Hank dropped it on the table along with two tumblers. 'Wait till you try this, pal. It's from a village right out back of Mexico.'

'Terrific.' Norton was beside himself. 'I'll bet it's even got old pieces of Mexican foreskins and labia in it. What did you pay for it? About two bucks a crate?'

Hank poured two half tumblers full of the urine-coloured liquid. 'Down the hatch, buddy. Badlands style.'

Les watched as Hank threw the tequila down his throat as if he was Wyatt Earp drinking Red Eye at the Last Chance Saloon. His beady eyes spun round even more crazily and he looked at Les. It wasn't a friendly drink; it was a silly bloody challenge. Norton picked up his tumbler, looked at it for a second, then did the same. It tasted like Brondecon and kerosene. Norton screwed up his face and hoped his tastebuds would forgive him. 'Ohh shit! That tastes like goat's piss.'

32

'That figures,' said Hank. 'Offering you pure tequila is like casting pearls before swine.'

'Yeah. And me shouting you those nice cold beers was like giving strawberries to pigs. You wouldn't have a beer in the fridge, would you?'

Hank ignored Les and poured another two tequilas, obviously getting a kick out of Norton's displeasure. 'Now I'll show you something else.' Hank took a key, walked over to the cabinet on the wall, unlocked it and swung open the doors. 'There,' he said, glowing with pride and smugness. 'What do you think of these? You don't see anything like that in Australia.'

Norton turned around on his seat. The cabinet was full of guns; four pistols and three rifles all racked horizontally. That was what the thing was on the table — a hand frame for reloading your own bullets. Hank took one of the pistols from the cabinet and handed it to Les like it was part of the crown jewels and he was showing some poor goose something he'd never seen before and the poor goose should be suitably impressed.

'That's a .38 Walther PPK. That's my baby. Go on, handle it. It's not loaded.' Hank gave a little sneer. 'It won't bite you.'

Norton took the gun and held it. It felt snug and comfortable in his hand. It was a good gun alright, but nothing to get a fat over. 'Yeah. That's ... nice, isn't it?'

'Nice,' Hank sneered again. 'And this is a .45 Smith and Wesson. Go on, take it. See what a gun feels like. You poor aussies with your piss ass gun laws. You don't know what you're missing.'

Yeah, thought Les. About ten thousand people a year not being shot; including women and kids. Les held the gun for a few seconds then laid it down next to the Walther; compared to the other gun it was noticeably heavier. 'Yeah. That's ... great, too.'

'This is what's called a Forty-five Peacemaker.' Hank lovingly stroked the next gun and handed it to Les.

It was some huge, heavy, long-barrelled revolver; like you'd expect to see Wyatt Earp pull out after he'd been drinking Red Eye at the Last Chance Saloon. 'What can I say?' said Les, and placed it on the table with the others.

'And this is just a .22 Browning.' Hank shrugged. 'It's a woman's gun. But it fits nicely inside an ankle holster.'

Les had a feel of the .22. It was all stainless steel and shiny and compared to the others it was just a baby. Though just as deadly. 'Yeah, good,' nodded Les, not trying to look too bored, and placed it on the table too.

'Now this.' Hank took down a junky, black, military-looking weapon. With his eyes almost glowing, he hit a catch somewhere behind the rear sight and a tubular folding stock swung out. 'This is an FNC Assault Rifle. Three-round burst capability or rock and fucking roll if you want.' Hank swung it around at waist level for a while before handing it to Les.

It wasn't all that heavy for its size, with a forty shot, curved magazine underneath and a pistol grip at the back. Les stood up and played soldiers with it for a few moments too. 'Yeah, fabulous.'

Hank replaced it in the rack and handed Les another rifle. 'This is an M14. Betcha ain't seen nothin' like that before, pal.'

Norton cradled the gun in his hands and shook his head. What could he say? The last time he'd seen one of these it was shortened and worked over and he'd shot three terrorists with it. And if it hadn't been for him and his brother saving the dopey president of the United States and getting rid of the terrorist's nuclear missile, Hank and the rest of his dopey, gun toting, seppo mates'd probably be at war. You fuckin' know-all seppo prick. Then, looking at Hank watching him, a sudden and dramatic thought hit Norton. And even though it was going to burn Norton's arse unbearably, a little tact and diplomacy were now going to have to be the new order of the day.

'Yeah, that's great, Hank' nodded Les. 'You've sure got a great gun collection.'

Hank's grainy faced dripped self-opinionated conceit. 'I knew you'd be impressed.' He put the M14 back on its rack. 'This one here's called a varmint rifle.' It was a long-barrelled, bolt action thing with a telescopic sight. 'I can put a bullet square through the centre of a dime at a hundred yards with that baby.'

'I'm sure you could,' said Les.

'Tomorrow I'll take you shooting out at the target range. Open your eyes up a bit more. Give you a whole new experience.'

Oh great, thought Les. That's all I'm gonna need tomorrow in this heat with half a hangover. Surrounded by a bunch of rednecks firing guns off in my ear. 'Okay. Sounds good.' Then Les just wanted to get away. Away from Hank, his guns, his fuzzy TV and his shit tequila. It was time to put on a bit of an act. He blinked a couple of times and started to sway on his feet. 'Hey, mate,' he said, slurring his words a little, 'I might have to get to bed. I'm rooted. I think this jet lag's just started to hit me.'

'That and one good shot of tequila.'

'Yeah, you could be right. You might have to finish that other one for me.' Les blinked again. 'Well, I'm gonna hit the sack. What time are we going shooting tomorrow?'

'I'll come over and get you at ten.'

'Okay. I'll see you then.' Norton hesitated at the door. 'Did you say there was a beach around here? I wouldn't mind going for a swim tomorrow too.'

'We'll go for a dive in the afternoon. After we've been shooting.'

'Okay. Well, I'll see you tomorrow. Thanks again.' Hank didn't reply; Les let himself out. Although it was still punishingly hot and steamy, it was a pleasure to be on his own again for a while and look up at some stars. Halfway back to the house Les stopped for a leak and a think while he gazed up at the cloud-scattered Florida sky.

Norton was still thinking when he was lying back on his bed in the darkness, after he'd turned on the fan, switched off the light and stripped down to his jocks. Hitting Hank on the chin and breaking the know-all bastard's jaw,

35

pleasurable and all as it might be, was going to have to be put on hold. Although Hank was no doubt as weak as piss underneath, you could bet he'd put a bullet in Les if he did smack him one. Probably a whole clip. Then more than likely get away with it as self-defence; who knew what the gun laws were in America, especially Florida? But there was more to Hank than just the way the flip fattened up showing off his silly bloody gun collection. Laurel Lee was homicidal, suicidal and that far back in the doghouse you had to feed him with a catapult. He was dirty on the world; that was obvious when he mentioned the letters as they were driving here. He had no money, no girl, no job and you could bet the lemon had no friends either. But in his own peanut brain he was firmly convinced it was everybody else's fault bar his. He was also convinced the world was conspiring against him. And at the same time, by his rude, abrupt attitude, he was also convinced he was doing the world and everybody else around him a favour just by being there. And those were just his good points. Christ! thought Les. What if Hank is a full-on, bell-ringing, yo yo? What say his mother doesn't live here? What say she's dead and he's got her mummified in one of these rooms? Bloody hell! I've travelled halfway across the world to have a holiday with Norman Bates. Jesus! I'll be watching the shower curtain when I have a tub in the morning. But Hank was a whole new ball game to Norton. Les had never come across anyone like him before, because back in Australia pricks that carried on like him got a whack in the mouth and a boot up the arse. And they kept getting it till they woke up. They did in the circle of friends Norton hung round with anyway. Les shook his head in the darkness. No, Hank was a loose cannon, and he was going to have to remove himself from the prick's company very carefully. He'd still be able to sling off at the flip. Hank was just a mug who left himself open for the verbal riposte all the time, and Les wouldn't be able to help himself there anyway, even if it was like bashing up the same drunk all the time. But belting the dill on the jaw was definitely out of the question. Then what about when he got back to Australia, and they asked him about his holiday, and Les told them he was only there two days and he'd jobbed the bloke he'd gone over to meet after staying at his house? Norton was in a no-win situation. Still, there were more ways of killing a cat than choking it with cheese, as old Grandma Norton used to say. I wouldn't mind meeting this ex-girlfriend of Boofhead's. Wonder what she'd have to say?

Suddenly the whirring of the fan seemed to be getting further and further away. Well, yawned Les, what about my first trip out of Australia? What a fine mess I've landed myself in, Ollie. I wish I was back in bloody Australia. Despite himself, Norton gave a little chuckle. One day away and I'm homesick already.

Next thing the noise of the fan disappeared altogether, and Les was snoring softly.

Haven't we landed yet? What the bloody hell's going on? The sound of aeroplane propellers woke Les. It was daylight and it wasn't propellers; it was the fan still whirring away on the other side of the room. Norton blinked up at the ceiling and it all started to come back. Yeah, I've landed, alright. And I know where, too. Christ! Les blinked a couple more times then swung his legs over the edge of the bed and stared at the floor. He didn't feel all that bad; a little tired but no hangover. A check of his watch said it was getting on for eleven. S'pose I'd better clean my choppers. Norton got his shaving-kit from his bag and plodded into the bathroom.

The first thing he noticed was that the light switches clicked in the opposite direction, and then that the toilet bowl was almost full to the brim with water. Well what a dopey idea, Les thought, as he peed away, watching it gurgle and splash. Fancy having a dump with a whole heap of Henry the Thirds sitting right under your date. He pushed the lever and watched the water spiral away like a whirlpool. Glad I don't feel like one. Next, there were no taps; you pulled one lever up for water and another from side to side to regulate hot and cold. Well I sure bloody don't want hot water, thought Les, as he scrubbed away. He got it, though — a great mouthful — and it tasted like it just came out of the nearest swamp. Norton shook his head and stared at the unshaven face in the mirror. Welcome to America — digger. You have a good one.

Now, what's on today? thought Les, as he climbed into a pair of shorts, Tooheys Blue T-shirt and joggers. Shooting this morning, then swimming this arvo with Indiana Laurel at the Temple of Gloom. Les had no shortage of T-shirts; he'd thrown about ten in his bag to give to Hank and his mates as a bit of a friendly gesture. I reckon I'll still have them when I leave, Les smiled to himself as he tucked a Tooheys Blue one into his shorts, because I imagine any friends of Hank's would be on the endangered species list and shit for brains sure ain't getting one. He stopped in front of the sliding glass door for a moment to stare out at the backyard, if that's what it was. There was a house next door on his right and about a hundred yards away past a clearing through some scrubby trees Les could see a dark, murky-looking lagoon, or piece of swamp or whatever, lying languid in the heat. It wasn't the most awe-inspiring sight so he went straight into the kitchen.

There was a soft light still on and coffee on the stove; Les helped himself to that and to the fridge as well. He found some sweet-tasting orange juice, bread, cheese, tomato and other odds and ends with strange brand names and made himself a couple of sandwiches. The coffee was very good. Les was contentedly chewing and slurping away while he stared out into the backyard when he heard a woman's voice behind him.

'Oh, hello. You must be Mr Norton?'

Les turned around, his mouth still full of coffee and sandwich. It had to be Hank's mother. He hadn't mummified her body after all. She looked about seventy, a little short, a little frail, wearing a white shirt and white slacks, with her grey hair in a tidy bun on her head. She looked like a typical mother, but she spoke very slowly and as she did she tilted her head to one side and held her finger and thumb under her chin in a demure, almost theatrical manner. Mrs Laurel had class about her even if her dill of a son didn't.

'I see you managed to find everything alright?'

'Mmmphhh!' answered Les, gulping down coffee and sandwich. 'Yes. I hope I didn't wake you up or anything. I saw the coffee — and it smelled that good I couldn't help myself.'

'Oh, that's quite alright. You just make yourself at home.'

'Thanks. Anyway, I'm Les. You must be Mrs Laurel.'

The lady took Norton's extended hand and gave it a gentle squeeze. 'Well, it's a pleasure to meet you, Les.'

'You too, Mrs Laurel. And I promise I won't get in your road or make a mess.'

'It's a pleasure to have you here, Les.' Mrs Laurel gave Norton a bit of a shaky once up and down. 'Hank told me all about you coming. He said you'd be staying here for two weeks, then you were going to New Orleans.'

Norton stared blankly at Mrs Laurel while she studied him. New Orleans? Shit! What did I say to Boofhead over the phone? They'd take a trip up there and Les would shout the expenses? Christ! Wouldn't that be a fun trip? 'Yes,' he nodded vaguely. 'Something like that.'

At the mention of the word 'Boofhead', who should come clomping into the kitchen wearing dirty jeans, an old grey T-shirt and desert boots but number one son. Mrs Laurel smiled at Les and just looked at Hank. 'Well, I'll leave you to it.' Before Norton had a chance to reply, she was gone.

'What did she want?' asked Hank.

'Not much,' answered Norton, taking a sip of coffee. 'She just said good morning. I think she lives here.'

Hank's eyes spun around the kitchen for a while before arriving on Les. 'Well, are you ready?'

Norton nodded slowly and took another sip of coffee. 'Can you just give me five minutes to press my hunting jacket?'

Captain Rat's eyes spun around some more. 'I'll be out front,' he muttered and disappeared.

Norton didn't particularly hurry finishing his coffee and sandwich and cleaning up after him. He took his time getting some money, his roosters cap out of his bag and cleaning his sunglasses too. There was no way Hank was going to leave without him. Hank was going out to play shoot-em-up-bang-bangs and impress the mug from Australia no matter what. Or is 'jerk' the more appropriate word, mused Les? Hank was looking predictably sour, though, when Les walked outside and climbed into the pick-up. He was reversing around before Norton barely got a chance to close the door.

They rumbled down the driveway and Hank turned right. They'd travelled about quarter of a mile along some wide street, and Les was checking out the houses, when he suddenly grabbed Hank's arm.

'Hey, Hank! Stop the car! Quick!' Before Hank knew what he was doing, he hit the brakes and Norton was out of the car, straight up a driveway and checking out something that was leaning against a sign saying Garage Sale.

Inside the double garage was just the usual display of second-hand rubbish; T-shirts, furniture, books, tools, etc. The only outstanding feature was the elderly couple sitting there who had to be the owners. They were the ugliest, most sour-faced pair of bastards Norton had ever seen. With their miserable, lumpy, seppo heads they reminded Les of those awful dolls you buy squashed up in jars.

'You pair of dropkicks want fifty dollars for that bike out the front?' said Les.

The male doll-in-the jar nodded his lumpy head. Before the ugly dropkick knew what had happened he had a fifty dollar bill in his hand and Les was wheeling the bike towards Hank's pick-up. It was just a blue, flat, frame thing with straight handlebars and ten-speed gears; but it was solid and the brakes worked good. Norton had spotted it out the corner of his eye. He tossed it in the back then climbed in the front as Hank took off, almost completely spun out. You would have thought Les had just committed some atrocity.

'What do you think you're doing?' he demanded. 'And what did you get that pile of junk for?'

Norton gave an indifferent shrug. 'To ride on. What do you think I got it for? All these flat roads, that thing'll be a piece of piss to get round on. I can see the real America.' Plus get a bit of exercise, and it's a good excuse to get away from you — shithead. 'Haven't you got a ten-speed? Me and Warren have back home. So's Tony.'

'What would I want a goddamn bike for?'

'Ride along road. Go to village. See other natives.'

They turned into a wider street then onto some highway big enough to land a 747 on. Hank stared ahead, sucking on his cigarette, then turned to Les for a second. 'I can get a bike if I want to.'

'You should,' replied Les.

'I just might.'

'Good. Make sure it's got a bell.'

After that it was more freeway and off-roads through swamps for about thirty minutes, then Les heard the target range about half a kilometre before they pulled up. *Blam! Kapow! Boom! Blam, blam, blam! Kapow!* They got out of the pick-up, Hank took two metal boxes from the back and handed Les a pair of ear-protectors. You needed them — it sounded like the battle of Dien Bien Phu. Les put them on as Hank nodded for him to follow.

It was a shooting range about two hundred yards long, full of paper targets hung between wooden poles. There was a hill of dirt behind to stop the bullets and a row of benches in front. Alongside the benches was a path with a white line painted down the middle that led to an office. Standing, or seated around the benches, were about twenty gun-crazy seppos in Elmer Fudd caps blazing away with anything that fired bullets, made lots of noise and could be held in your hand. *Blam! Blam! Kapow! Blam! Blam! Blam!* Les decided to act dumb.

Hank directed Les to stand behind the white line while

he went to the office and bought two paper targets and a couple of bright orange stickers, which he put on one side of the targets. Through his ear-protectors Les heard a siren hoot then a voice over a PA system saying something about how it was now a non-fire zone or some bloody thing. Everybody put their weapons on the benches with the clips out then went and checked or changed their targets. Hank told Les to come and help pin theirs up. Les did as he was told. Back at their bench, Hank opened up the two metal boxes; one was full of bullets, the other held the guns. Laurel put the Walther and the .45 in front of Les then set himself up with the Peacemaker. He briskly showed Les how to load the two guns and aim, probably hoping and expecting Les to make a complete dill of himself. But you don't have to be Daniel Boone to stuff ten or so bullets in a clip, slide back a cocking lever and pull the trigger. Not after Eddie Salita's shown you a number of times.

They stood behind the white line, another siren hooted and the voice crackled over the PA that it was now a free-fire zone, then everybody stepped back to their benches and started blasting away again.

Les missed the weight of the silencers they used in Eddie's underground shooting room; still, the Walther went off okay. It fired a little to the right, but after sighting in on the orange markers Les had no trouble ringing eight shots round the bullseye at twenty metres or so sitting down. The .45 kicked back and up, as Norton expected, so he laid the barrel across the block of wood on his bench, gripped the barrel with his thumb and forefinger and remembered what Eddie said: 'You don't pull the trigger. You squeeze it, gently. Just like your girl's tit.' After sighting up on the orange sticker, Les managed to put another eight bullets in a short straight line right across the circle of holes around the bullseye. Les put the guns on the bench after that and watched Hank. Laurel Lee was all concentration, aiming and firing as if his life depended on it; and probably so he could show Norton up. Around him the rest of the mob, in their Elmer Fudd caps and cammies, were blazing away as if they were defending the Alamo. Norton walked down to a drink machine next to the office and got a can of Grape Crush, which tasted alright for a change. When he got back a new team had moved onto the bench next to him. It was a bloke about forty and three kids, the oldest of whom would have been eleven. Dad unpacked the gear and away they went. *Blam, blam, blam!* Then Dad pulled out a huge stainless steel Magnum; even with Les's ear-protectors on the noise was almost deafening. He sat and drank his Grape Crush till the hooter sounded and they all went out to check their targets.

'I've never fired one of those things before,' said Les. 'How did I go?'

More interested in his own target, Hank looked briefly at Norton's. 'You managed to get a couple near the markers and that's about it.' Hank gave a shitty sort of laugh. 'Apart from that, you missed the target altogether.'

'What about that black part in the middle?' Les watched Hank's eyes spinning around as he stared at Norton's target. 'You're supposed to get them all in a circle, aren't you? I managed to do that with the little gun. But the big one just seemed to keep firing in a straight line. Looks neat, but.' Norton gave a little laugh. 'It's still good fun though — ain't it?'

Hank muttered something about Les still not grouping his shots correctly, then stormed back to his bench. Les followed him and away they went again.

After about thirty minutes or so it wasn't boring enough; it was also starting to cloud over and thunder was rattling ominously across the sky. One of the kids at the next bench said something about someone using a big gun upstairs, which Les didn't think was a bad line. Who said seppos didn't have a sense of humour? Hank kept firing steadily away with his Peacemaker, playing John Wayne or whatever. In between breaks he'd scrabble around on the floor for his shells like an old chook. Les knew if he didn't do something they'd be there all bloody day, so he started shoving clips of bullets in the guns and blazing away with them two at a time till there was hardly enough of his paper target left to throw at a wedding. Finally Les laid both guns on the bench, with the clips out, like a good gun freak, and waited patiently. Eventually Hank reached for more ammo.

'Hey! Where's all the goddamn bullets?'

'I don't know,' shrugged Les. 'I think we've run out. Fuckin' good fun, though, ain't it?'

'Jesus Christ!'

'Don't worry.' Les went for his pocket. 'We'll buy some more.'

'You can't buy bullets out here.'

'You can't? Ohh shit! What a bastard. Wait on, maybe some of these people might sell us a few bullets.'

Hank's eyes looked like they were going to spin out of his head. 'Ohh, for chrissake!'

This time around Les thought he might give Laurel a hand to pick up the empty shells; they were nearly all under Les so he didn't have far to reach. They retrieved their targets, Hank threw his in the garbage tin, Les folded his up into a tiny ball and put it in his pocket, saying something about what a great souvenir it would make. There was more thunder, and it started to rain as they packed up and walked back to the car. It had to be almost a hundred per cent humidity now and the sweat was running down the stubble of Norton's face and dripping from his chin. Despite the heat, though, the atmosphere in the pick-up was quite cool, even if Laurel didn't have the air-conditioning on.

'Well, that was tops, Hank. I never had so much fun in my life. We'll have to do it again some time.' Hank muttered something under his breath and took a heavy drag on his cigarette. 'So where are we going now?' asked Les.

'Home.'

'Good.' Norton gazed up at the sky. 'I can get my bike out of the rain.'

They drove back to Swamp Manor more or less in silence. Hank said he had to make some phone calls for about an hour, by that time the rain should clear up and they'd go diving at some place called the Keys. Norton figured out Hank wasn't doing him any favours; after his latest trauma Captain Rats probably needed a swim himself, or at least cooling off. They crunched up on the driveway next to the sagging carport. Hank stormed off to his part of Swamp Manor, ignoring Norton's offer to help oil the guns, so Les got his bike from the back of the pick-up and put it on the front verandah, then went to his room to sort out his next move. He decided to unpack a bit more gear to try and make his miserable sweatbox a little homelier. He hung up his shirts and jeans and spread out a few T-shirts. Hank had mentioned he lived by a beach so Norton had thrown in a pair of hand webs and mini jet fins. Norton's overnight bag had straps on it to double as a small backpack; he put them in it, plus a towel, and then changed into his Speedos. Les had just finished sorting out his tapes and was playing with the automatic telephoto lens on an instamatic camera he'd brought when a thought occurred to him. He hadn't had a crap since he left Australia, and didn't feel like one. Les was blocked up. Between his body clock, the heat, a bit of nerves and all that airline food his system was all out of kilter. And it would stay that way if he didn't do something. Les fiddled with the camera for a few moments more, then not wishing to get around feeling like he had half a housebrick jammed in his stomach walked out to the kitchen. Les didn't find what he was looking for in a bottle, it was in a paper carton, the same as a 500 ml milk one back home, and was under the sink. Les got a cup of hot water together, shovelled in two tablespoons, and down the hatch. It tasted like chewing a burning tyre. Les was expecting that and had poured an orange juice chaser. Fuckin' Epsom Salts, cursed Les, as he swilled more orange juice round his mouth to get rid of the taste. Whoever invented that shit? He swilled more orange juice, shook his head in disgust then went back to his room to read more P.J. O'Rourke and wait to see what happened. After a few pages his stomach began to rumble ominously like the thunder out at the shooting range. A few more pages and Captain Rats stormed in.

'Well, are you ready?'

'Yeah, righto,' replied Les. He put down his book and followed Hank out to the pick-up.

Hank opened up an old plastic shopping bag he had in the back and handed Les a perished pair of flippers and a scratched and battered facemask. 'You have been diving before?'

Les nodded. 'I brought a pair of fins with me.' He had a look in the ancient shopping bag. 'Where's the snorkels?'

'You don't need a snorkel.'

'I don't? We are going skindiving, aren't we? At least that's what you told me.'

'If the water's dirty you don't need a snorkel.'

Before Norton had a chance to suggest that even if you're swimming in sump oil snorkels do come in handy, Hank was in the car with the motor running. Norton got inside and was about to say something but changed his mind, deciding to take another tack. As well as being a twenty-five-carat prick, Hank was obviously mentally unbalanced. Why not knock the flip off balance altogether? And without having to risk hitting him on the chin. Captain Rats could be broken: unmercifully. Les let them get about a mile or a kilometre or whatever it was down the road — with the Americans not into the metric system Les didn't know where he was half the time — then asked Hank the question he knew Hank was dying to be asked.

'Jeez, this is a top car, Hank. You sure don't get 'em like this in Australia. It goes like the clappers. What kind is it? You had it long?'

After that it was easy. Hank vroomed through the traffic, exactly like a would-be, good ol' boy from the South, driving a black pick-up truck, should, while he showed and told Les how good his pick-up was. Even with Laurel Lee playing *Smokey and the Bandit* and the constant stream of cigarette smoke, Norton was just about able to switch completely off. They zoomed in and out of the traffic along these monstrous roads, surrounded by monstrous cars driven by monstrous seppos with equally monstrous heads; generally about one seppo to an air-conditioned vehicle. On either side of the road it was all fast food restaurants and drive-in stores, each with more parking space than Bondi Junction bus depot. There were no buses, no pushbikes, and scarcely a pedestrian in sight. Now and again a pick-up with wheels twenty feet in diameter would pull up alongside, driven by some gum-chewing seppo in an Elmer Fudd cap, and naturally Hank would have to have a go. They turned left onto a bridge across a wide strip of water and came off into narrower roads now surrounded by houses, trees and blocks of flats. Hank turned left again and through the flats Les could see a shining expanse of water, which he recognised from the map he had in Australia as the Gulf of Mexico. A row of touristy shops and restaurants appeared that reminded Les a little of Rose Bay in Sydney. He was looking at the shops when Hank pulled up at a 7–11.

'I want to get a pack of cigarettes and a Coke.'

'Righto. I might have a quick look in that shop there. I need a pair of thongs,'

Hank locked his precious car and took the keys. Beauty, thought Les.

The shop Norton had spotted was a typical surf–dive shop; air-conditioned inside and full of T-shirts, boardshorts, diving gear, etc. Nothing was cheap, especially the silicone facemasks with side vision and the latest snorkels that didn't let water in. Norton paid cash for one of each and left with his receipt and a, 'You have a good one.'

Hank was seated in the car, opening a packet of Winston, with what looked like a plastic bucket of Coca-Cola and ice sitting on his lap, when Les climbed inside. 'Did you get your thongs?' he said, with half a sneer on his face.

It was then that Les noticed Hank was barefoot. It was

at least ninety-five outside and the roads were hotter than stove lids. Poor Laurel. As well as being filthy on the world, he was filthy on himself. 'No. They didn't have any in my size.'

'So what's in the bag?' Les opened it up. Hank's face twisted up even more. 'You bought a snorkel?'

'Yeah, they were on special. Anyway, if I don't need it I can always throw it away.'

Hank shook his head in disbelief. He muttered something without looking at Les and they drove off. Les gazed impassively out the side window. Yes, I've sure got a live one here.

Hank turned off down some side street surrounded by blocks of flats and trees, then pulled up at the bottom where the road running along the water stopped at some houses. There were no natural rocks, just granite blocks sitting on a narrow strip of sand. In front of the blocks, a broken concrete pier jutted out about twenty metres. The sea road to the left had blocks of flats on both sides and beyond Les could see a gleaming white beach that ran for about four miles surrounded by more high-rises. It reminded Les a little of Surfers Paradise. To the right was a channel running past the homes built out to the water's edge. Apart from a couple of small bays and more high-rises in the distance this reminded Les of Sydney Harbour. Only it was a bigger expanse of water. Les also noticed quite a strong current running towards them.

'We'll swim north,' said Hank, getting out of the car. 'Look for snook.'

'Snook?'

'They're big black fish. They'll come right up to you if you dive down just out from the rocks and sit there. The goddamn state won't let you spear them. But I'll come back tomorrow when the tide's right if they're there. I know a guy with a restaurant.

'I'll keep my eyes peeled,' promised Les.

They started getting changed when Hank eyed Norton's webs and jet fins. 'What are those stupid things?'

48

'I like to play Creature from the Black Lagoon,' said Les, opening and closing the webs a few times.

'You have to use them, do you?' Hank's lip curled again.

Norton was going to say something about how you do if you want to swim quicker and easier and how Hank should try moving into the twentieth century and see how he liked it, when several powerboats roared past, full of girls in bikinis and flashy-looking men all doing it in style — champagne, music, gold chains, the works. The noise of the motors almost deafened you as they howled by, leaving a wake big enough to swamp a surf-boat.

'Goddamn tourist New Yorkers,' cursed Hank. 'God, I hate the noisy sonsofbitches. They fuck the whole beach.'

That's not all they're fucking either, Les chuckled to himself. 'Yeah. They're enough to give you the shits alright.'

Hank locked the car and then clambered down across the rocks and sand; naturally Les followed. After they had washed their facemasks and got their flippers on they dived in and started swimming against the current.

Hank wasn't lying when he'd mentioned dirty water; you were lucky if you could see six feet and the water was that warm you could have put tea bags in it. But it was water and it was still wet and it got rid of the sweat and felt bloody good. Just what Norton needed. They plodded along against the current with Hank floundering around having to stop for air every now and again. Armed with all the new technology, Les was doing it cosy, diving up and down just having a good time. The facemask fitted like a glove, the snorkel was almost miraculous and the fins and mini flippers made Norton feel like the creature from the black lagoon. After ten minutes of plodding along behind Hank Les felt like a Ferrari stuck in first gear in traffic. In the dirty, choppy water Hank wouldn't know what was going on so Les decided to put his foot down; or at least his feet. The fins dug in, so did the jet fins and Norton took off like a big, red torpedo. Even against the current he was just powering. After a five minute burst, Les stopped in front of some rocks and looked back. He'd gone past a little bay and about five hundred metres back he could see Hank still floundering around towards the sheltered little bay. The burst through the water felt good and Norton's lungs were pumping. But the strain had a noticeable effect. A ripple of pain and wind suddenly went through Norton's abdomen. Yes, he mused. I think I'll be saying goodbye to an old friend any tick of the clock now. He watched Hank for a couple more seconds then turned round and swam easily off into the current.

Les kept close to the rocky shoreline; dirty, warm water, there could be something else besides snook moving around here, he mused. Still, I have to see what Captain Rats is on about. Les began diving up and down next to the rocks: there was a surprising number of fish for so close to a populated area. Lots of little ones would flitter amongst the rocks then larger, tropical looking ones with colourful stripes and wide flat bodies. Les swam out a little further from the rocks, took a good, deep breath, dived down about fifteen feet into the warm gloom and held onto the rocks. He didn't quite shit himself, but he got quite a start when these long, black fish swam right up in front of his mask and sat there, their fins and tails just moving in the current. They were at least a metre long and looked exactly like New South Wales Whiting; same shape, same long mouths only scaly black. They floated in front of him quite calmly then disappeared when Les came up for air. Well I'll be stuffed. Norton couldn't quite believe his eyes. He floated, kicking in the current for a minute or two then dived down and held onto the rocks again as he popped his ears. Another four Snook swam up and floated right in front of him: one had to be at least five feet long and two feet wide. Again they swam slowly off as Les floated to the surface. No wonder the authorities won't let you spear them, he thought. With gun crazy seppos around like Captain Rats it'd be a slaughter. I could've caught those ones with a plastic fork.

Another two powerboats roared past towards where they'd left the pick-up and further back Les could see Hank, his head bobbing up and down as he swam against the current. Norton was kicking easily, half laughing at Laurel Lee doing it tough only because he was such a flip, when the pressure of the dives along with the sudden power burst hit him. This time an extremely violent pain went all through Norton's system; an old friend was definitely on the move. Norton was just about to pull down his Speedos and say goodbye when an evil glint appeared in the brown eyes behind the new, silicone face mask. Les swam out from the rocks a little, watched Hank for a moment or two as the convulsions went through him, then, judging the current pulled down his Speedos and squeezed. This was a ripper. Les floated there and let it all go; the relief was unbelievable. Les opened his eyes and watched the four old friends, all brown and shiny, drifting rapidly south in the current. They were bobbing nicely along and Norton was thinking how well they packaged their airline food when another attack hit him. This one was more a gigantic, hot spurt that almost moved Les through the water as if he were jet-propelled. It rose to the surface and followed the four Bondi Cigars in the current like a brown lumpy cloud. Now feeling about a stone lighter, Norton pulled up his Speedos, dived down into the current beneath the old friends and swam like buggery back to Hank. Scooting along with the current, Norton almost pulled up with a screech he was going that fast; he stopped just outside Hank keeping the American between him and the shore.

Hank had just surfaced and was spluttering around probably wishing he had a waterproof cigarette. 'So how's it going?' said Norton. 'I haven't seen any of those Snook. Have you?'

Hank slipped his facemask on top of his head and scowled. 'Those goddamn New York assholes in their power boats. The sonsofbitches scare them away. Fuck them!'

'Yeah, I was just thinking the same thing. Noisy bastards.

51

They're a pain in the arse alright.' A movement in the current bobbing towards them caught Norton's eye. 'So what do you want to do, Hank? You're running the show.'

Hank was about to say something when turd number one, about the same size as a Fijian banana, hit him straight in the mouth. Hank spluttered, screamed and cursed and grabbed at his face when Henry number two hit him, crumbling and spreading all over his hands. Hank cursed and shrieked some more and thrashed in the water like he'd been attacked by a swarm of sea wasps.

'Hank,' yelled Norton. 'Are you alright? What is it mate?'

'What is it!' screamed Hank. 'It's fuckin' crap.'

'Stone the bloody crows. I don't believe it.' Les had a quick look to the left. 'But if it is. Duck, mate. I think there's more.'

Hank was still cursing and wiping shit from his face and hands when he was enveloped in a thick brown cloud. He howled up at the sky, and grabbed at his face mask. But it filled up with shit spreading into his eyes as well. Hank was literally in the shit, deep and shallow. He tore his face mask off and still cursing and gagging swam into the quiet little bay. Les gave him a bit of start then drifted up near him and watched as Hank flopped around wiping shit out of his eyes and from his hands, face and neck.

'It's those bloody New Yorkers, mate, you can bet your life,' said Norton. 'Dirty, smart arse bastards in their powerboats. They piss and shit everywhere.' Les slipped his mask on top of his head and sniffed at the air. 'Yeah. Bloody pastrami on rye. You can smell it.'

Hank was in a terrible state; and it wasn't South Florida. He was fuming. He spluttered and gagged some more as he tried to clean the horrible, stinking, clinging mess from him. 'Goddamn!' he swore at the top of his voice. 'I hate those motherfuckers!!'

'Yeah. I don't blame you,' agreed Les. 'They're enough to give you the . . . shits alright.'

'Aarrghh!! Christ!!!'

Norton floated easily in the waist-deep water for a few moments. 'So what do you want to do now?'

'Go back to the goddamn car.'

'Fair enough.' Norton was about to put his facemask back on but stopped. 'Hey, you know, I just thought of something, Hank.'

'What!!?'

'I'm glad I bought a snorkel now.'

Back at the car Hank was still an extremely disturbed patient. He ranted and raved and didn't see the funny side of things at all. Somehow they managed to get changed and into the front seat; Hank had got rid of most of the crap but there was definitely still a hint of Edgar in the air. Norton wound down the window and did his best to sit quietly while Hank shoved a Winston in his gob and lit it.

'So where to now, mate?'

'There's a shower on the beach.'

Les nodded approvingly. 'Not a bad idea. Get the salt water off.'

They drove off slowly along the avenue that ran alongside the water, to where it doglegged round to the main road, and past the shops to the start of the beach Les had noticed earlier. As Hank pulled up for the traffic Les turned to him.

'You know it doesn't smell all that bad.'

'What are you talking about? It smells like shit.'

'Yeah,' agreed Norton. 'But it ain't all that bad. I mean, I'm not trying to say the person who that shit belongs to could get around thinking his shit didn't stink, but it's that close it doesn't make any difference to me. You know what I'm saying? You smell alright.'

'I don't know what the fuck you're talking about, you jerk.'

'Sorry, mate. I was only tryin' to be friendly.'

The shower was a wooden platform that dribbled and ponged away next to the mandatory parking lot about as big as the Sydney Showground. It sat just up from the beach, which was quite wide and had the finest white sand Les had ever seen; it was almost like powder. The hard sand at the water's edge looked about two hundred yards wide from water to beach front, and Les noticed several people on pushbikes. He commented to Hank that pedalling along the beach on a bike looked like a bit of fun; Hank seemed more interested in another cigarette after he finished showering so Les didn't pursue the matter. It was sunny and blisteringly hot but a massive black cloudfront seemed to be moving in from the Gulf of Mexico. While he waited for Hank to finish his smoke Les watched the clouds, and two families of Americans flopping around under the shower. They were the fattest heaps of shit Norton had ever seen. One mother made Roseanne Barr look like Princess Di and one father could have been John Candy's stunt double. They're certainly not starving round here, thought Norton, as they finally drove off.

Les didn't quite know what to say to Hank as they were driving home and Hank wasn't saying much. Norton had had enough fun with the poor goose for the time being and if he wanted to get out for a few cool ones it might be an idea to start buttering Hank up, galling and all as the idea was. Les suggested that if he wanted to go out that night Les would shout, pay back Hank for all his wonderful hospitality and the cost of the bullets Les had used. Norton had money coming out his ears and he wouldn't miss slipping Captain Rats fifty bucks or so. Besides, he was such an arse he'd probably only drink cheap beer and tequila. Hank grumbled and moaned and carried on like a good sort about his business commitments, then said okay. He had a lot of phone calls to make but he'd call in on Les at 9.30. That pretty much suited Norton.

When they pulled up next to the old carport Les took his watch from his overnight bag and was astonished to find it was getting on for seven. The sun was still high in the sky and apart from that ominous cloud build-up moving across it still seemed like just after lunchtime. Where did the day go? thought Les.

'Hey, Hank,' said Les, as they got their gear from the back of the car. 'Do you have daylight saving in Florida?'

'I don't know,' answered Hank. 'I guess so.'

Norton stood and watched Hank's back as he walked

to his house. He was going to say something, but what could he say after that? 'I'll see you at half past nine, Hank.' Les shook his head a couple of times and went inside.

Norton had a cup of coffee and made himself another cheese sandwich. That was plenty; between the Epsom Salts and the heat he didn't feel like eating. After cleaning up his gear Les was sitting on the edge of his bed about an hour later, staring into space and still trying to get over Hank's last statement, when an almighty thunderclap shook the old house. Les couldn't remember ever hearing one that loud, it sounded like it was just above the roof. A few minutes later it started to rain. Just a few drops at first, all as big as pears, then the rest of them, till it was a roaring downpour. The rain thundered down on the roof and in about five minutes all the guttering had filled up and water was gushing over the downpipes in great shimmering silver cascades. It was quite beautiful and Les stood at the sliding glass door almost mesmerised as he watched it tumbling down. By now the humidity had climbed to what felt like 150 per cent. Norton's T-shirt was soaked and sweat was stinging his eyes as it ran down his forehead, across his unshaven face and off his chin. Stuff this, thought Norton. He stripped down to his Speedos and ran outside underneath the nearest over-flowing drainpipe.

The fresh rainwater was cool and absolutely beautiful as it splattered over his head and body. Les even ran inside, got his soap and razor, and had a cold shave and a scrub up. There was an old wire chair just outside his back door. Les put that under a downpipe and sat on it, laughing like a loon as the rainwater splashed over him and formed rivulets in the backyard that turned into tiny streams and ran down to the swampy lagoon Les had noticed earlier. Now this is really living, cackled Norton, the rain seeming to wash away his cares as well as all the sweat. I can't see them arresting you or shooting you in this state for having a free shower in your backyard. Besides, isn't this what freedom and democracy and all those guns I saw earlier are all about? He took a mouthful of water and spat it up in the air as the rain still pelted down. I wonder what Captain Rats is doing right now? Probably inside playing with his guns — and his dick. Norton spat another gobful of water up in the air and let it splatter back down on his face.

An hour or so later Norton had towelled off and was lying on his bed thinking and plotting and scheming about what he was going to do regarding his present accommodation and Captain Rats. The rainstorm had eventually blown over, stars began to appear and the only noise now was the sound of water gently dripping from the trees in the darkness outside. It was a tricky one, mainly because Norton, as well as not really having a clue where he was, didn't know a soul either. Only rabbit brain in the other house, and he was about as much use as a jackhammer in a lifeboat. Still, you never know, he thought. Tonight he might meet someone he could communicate with. So there were more important things to think of for the time being: like what was going to be his evening ensemble. Or what did Les have that wasn't too crushed to wear out? You could bet wherever Hank took him they'd probably have dress regulations: no jeans, T-shirts, joggers, etc. Which was about all Les had that was wearable. But you can't keep an old country boy down. Les found an iron in the laundry and about ten o'clock he was dressed in a pair of black cotton trousers, a grey Western Suburbs T-shirt with a Magpie on it, a black cotton shirt open at the front and black moon boots. That ought to have it covered, he figured. Collar and shoes to get in and if another storm came up he had a T-shirt on underneath. Well, I forgot to throw a Spencer in, thought Les, as he checked himself out in the bathroom mirror and daubed on a little Tabac. Earlier he tried to get the ghetto blaster to work that Hank had kindly left in the room for him, but it was about stuffed, and when he did get it to work you could barely hear it. So he sat in one of the chairs, reading P.J. O'Rourke till Hank arrived. Just before ten, Captain Rats appeared in the doorway; he was wearing an unironed, blue floral shirt, dirty jeans, no socks and an old pair of sandshoes half done up because each one only had half a lace. Norton had seen blokes dressed better working in wrecking yards. Looks like we're going to the Taxi Club mused Norton, closing his book. I didn't know they had one in Siestasota.

'You ready?' asked Hank.

'Yeah,' answered Norton, giving Hank another once up and down. 'Listen, I got a spare pair of shoes if you want. They'd probably fit you.'

'These are alright. They're comfortable.'

Norton was going to suggest there was some string in the kitchen and he'd found an iron, but before he knew it they were in the pick-up and on their way.

'So where are we going?'

'I got a couple of places in mind.'

You have a mind? mused Norton, as they turned onto the main road. 'Listen, Hank. To save a lot of mucking around, here's fifty bucks. Take that for petrol and get a few drinks.'

Hank looked at the money for a second then put it in his pocket. He didn't bother to say thanks, just smoked his cigarette and kept driving.

They didn't say a great deal after that and Norton didn't feel like asking Einstein any questions on quantum physics. It might have been night, but Les was certain they drove over the same bridge back towards the Keys. He saw a glimpse of ocean then they cut back somewhere, finally turning into the parking lot of some roadhouse. Les glimpsed a sign out the front saying 'Sandbar'. They left the car out the back and walked across to some kind of enclosed beer garden. There were people around and music coming from inside. At the gate was a bouncer in a T-shirt and jeans and a bloke next to him in a shirt who could have been the manager. It was three dollars each: Les paid.

Inside looked alright. A small bar on your right as you walked in, a large lounge with a bigger bar to the left, a band and a small dancefloor. There were more chairs and tables outside near the front entrance and a doorway off to the right suggested another drinking area. T-shirts and jeans were okay but Les was by no means overdressed. It looked about equal numbers men and women, all fairly neat and tidy, but somehow different. Then Les remembered you had to be twenty-one to drink in the United States, which not only kept out the eighteen-year-old drunks, but the sixteen-year-olds on borrowed IDs as well. So most of the punters looked in the twenty-five to forty range; not super conservative, but no drunken yobbos. The band was playing a good drop of rock 'n' roll.

'Well, what'll you have, Hank?'

'Tequila. Straight up.'

Am I a mind reader or am I a mind reader? Les went to the bar, ordered a tequila for Einstein and a margarita, and along with the drinks got a big smile from the girl, worthy of a substantial tip. Les returned with the drinks and suggested they move out the back a bit where there was more room. Hank grudgingly agreed, so they moved to the other bar facing the band, near where it elbowed round to a servery facing outside. Hank dropped an elbow on the bar and took a slug of tequila; Les sent down half of his margarita in one go. The band finished their song just as Les finished his first drink. He nodded to Hank, got a nod back, so Les turned to the bar behind them and ordered another tequila for Hank and a Corona with a piece of lime. Hank gulped his first drink, took the other, then looked at Les drinking Corona and his lip curled.

'You got lime in your beer?'

'Yeah,' nodded Les.

'You look like a tourist.'

Norton looked at Hank and blinked. This time Les couldn't help himself. 'Hank, I know this is going to come as a bit of a shock to you, but I am a fuckin' tourist. If you don't believe me, there's a passport in my bedroom and an airline ticket that says I'm here for three weeks.'

Norton was about to add more when, of all things, the

band started playing Midnight Oil's 'Beds Are Burning'. And a red hot version. He nodded to the band. 'That's an Australian song, Hank. From an Australian band. That's where I'm from. Australia. Remember?'

Hank tried to look cool. Les looked at him for a second then turned to the band. Ahh, fuck the idiot. What's the use? Norton got into his Corona, with lime, and the music.

Besides the members of the band Les was probably the only other person there who knew the lyrics, so he started singing and boogying along. The punters around him could see he wasn't just some drunken dill but a bloke simply having a good time. Especially three pairs of fairly attractive girls. One, a blonde with bangs under her chin, seemed to make eye contact. Les gave her a wink and she smiled back.

Hank had moved to the corner of the bar, propped his arse on a seat and lit another cigarette while he moped over his tequila. Fuck him, thought Norton. He seems happy enough and he's got money. Mine. Les waited till the band finished their song, then after cheering and clapping went to the bar and ordered another margarita and a Wild Turkey sour. He hardly had time to pay for the drinks and knock off half his margarita when the band ripped into INXS's 'Don't Change'. Les couldn't believe it. In no time Norton was getting down and dirty à la Michael Hutchence with just a smidgen of Daddy Cool thrown in as well. The band ended their bracket on that one, Les whistled and clapped and caught the blonde's eye again. She was only a few metres away, so Les decided he might as well finish one drink, sashay over and say — g'day. She could only tell him to piss off.

However, there was no open hostility when Les walked over. 'I don't wish to be rude,' he said politely, 'but I caught your eye a moment ago. You're not Bronhilde Peachdale, are you?'

'Excuse me?' said the blonde. Up close she wasn't too bad. About twenty-seven, pert nose, nice lips and hazel eyes. Her bum could have been smaller but she had a nice

59

crumpet jammed into the front of her Levis and she was stacked fairly well under a yellow top. Her girlfriend looked similar, only she had brown hair and her face was a little grainy.

'You're not with the Florida Fisheries Department? I'm a meteorologist, out here from Australia studying hurricanes, and I was at a lecture in an office on Main Street. I thought I met you there.'

'No. I'm Lori. I'm a secretary with a law firm out on North Jefferson.'

'Oh. I'm sorry.'

'Hey, I thought he was Australian,' said the girlfriend.

'Why's that?' asked Les. 'Can you smell me already?'

'No. The T-shirt. My brother used to play rugby at college in Idaho.'

'So what's your name anyway?' asked Lori.

'Les.'

'Les what?'

'I don't know,' shrugged Norton. 'Les said the better I s'pose.'

It didn't take long and Les started getting on famously with the girls. He had to slow up a few times so they could understand him, but they liked his accent, it was 'kinda cute', and Norton's half boozy sense of humour. Lori originally came from Cleveland; she'd been in Florida three years. Her girlfriend was Connie; she was a local and worked as a secretary for the US Customs Department. Lori and Connie believed everything Les told them and laughed at any joke he cracked: no matter how corny. Les bought a round of drinks; another bourbon sour for him, vodka and cranberry juice for Lori and just a Bud Lite for Connie. The girls didn't want to do too big a job on themselves, and they were leaving soon as both had to be up fairly early in the morning. But seeing as Les was such a sweetie they'd hang around a little longer.

'So who are you here with?' asked Lori.

Who am I here with? Shit! In the sheer exhilaration of talking to two normal friendly people, Les had forgotten all about Captain Rats. A quick glance towards the bar

60

said he was still there, drinking a tequila, smoking a cigarette and looking his usual bored, morose self.

'I'm with that bloke at the end of the bar in the floral shirt.'

'Well, why don't we join him for a short while before we leave?' said Lori. 'Is he an aussie?'

'No. He's American. And he's a bit of a wombat.'

'A wahmbat?' said Connie. 'What's a wahmbat?'

Les shook his head. 'Come over and you'll soon find out.'

Les introduced Hank to the girls. Hank gave them a very cool once up and down, like a good ol' boy with black pick-up should, then blew a great cloud of smoke in Connie's face. The girls didn't want another drink; Les got a margarita for himself and a tequila for Hank. When he turned back from the bar Hank had the girls engaged in a conversation, it was that good all three of them were completely speechless.

Connie caught Norton's eye as he handed Hank his drink. 'I think I know what a wahmbat is.'

What could Les do? He nodded impassively then tried to spear her into Hank while he pissed in Lori's pocket for as long as he could. Before long, Connie's face looked like she'd strained a hernia and she was doing everything but jangle her car keys in Lori's face and fire distress flares. Les decided he'd better start tap dancing a bit quicker. He suggested to Lori that seeing he was in town chasing weather balloons for another three weeks, what about giving him her phone number? Lori thought this was a splendid idea and wrote it down just before Connie dragged her bodily out the door. With a smile they wished Les a good time, ignored Hank, and left quite happy.

'Well, what do you reckon, Hank? They weren't a couple of bad sheilas?'

'You think they were good?'

'Well, I'm not saying they're good I'm just saying they're not bad.' Les took a belt of his margarita. 'Shit! What did I say?'

'That Connie was a bitch. And she's a customs narc.'

61

'Go on, eh.'

The band was still on its break. Les sipped his drink and checked out the punters. They were a fairly happy lot, the place had a good atmosphere and there was no shortage of girls on their own. Shit! he thought. How would you like to be here with Woz, or a couple of mates from down the beach, instead of pea brain? Wouldn't you have some fun? Les looked at Hank sucking smoke into his lungs. Well, at least I'm getting drunk. Or, if not, I'm doing a great impression of it. And I don't have to drive.

'What's next door?' asked Les.

Hank shrugged. 'A disco, I think.'

A disco you think, contestant number one. Let's see what's in the envelope. 'Do you want to go and have a look?'

Hank shook his head. 'I'm fine here.'

'I might go and check it out while the band's still on a break.'

'Go for it.'

Norton downed his margarita. 'If I'm not back by the end of the month, tell Qantas to cancel my return ticket.'

Les turned and left for next door. Would Hank piss off and leave him stranded? Les thought as he stepped across the empty dance floor. Hardly. In Hank's estimation Les had jumped from Category A to Category B. Where Les was once just a mug — like everybody else in the world — now he was a mug with money. There was more where that fifty dollars came from. And Hank had access to it. Plus a lot of free drinks. Les was not only a mug, he was now a jerk. You think so, boofhead? Norton chuckled to himself as he walked in the disco. For a few lousy dollars I've got you by the nuts, Laurel Lee baby. In fact it could be quite funny how you finish up before I head back to Australia. Shit for brains.

The disco was pretty much like any other. About the same size as the bar next door, a spinning mirror ball, a DJ playing what sounded like Kool and the Gang; although with mostly wooden panelling and the rock posters on the walls it looked more like a good bar with a

62

dancefloor than a full-on Saturday Night Fever disco. It was a little over half full, plenty on the dancefloor; pretty much the same sort of crowd you'd see in a touristy bar in Sydney, but possibly a little older. They all seemed to be having a good time without getting into it all that much. I'm definitely going to have to cut down on my drinking, mused Les as he went to the bar. Yes. Cut down the nearest cane field and make me a case of Bundy. He ordered two Pina Coladas and immediately drank one.

She was another blonde. A better sort than Lori, same length hair, wearing faded blue jeans, a denim shirt and white cowboy boots with aerobics written all over her. Especially her backside. She was standing at the end of the bar with a girlfriend, a homely-looking redhead with shiny, shoulder-length hair, wearing white 501s and a white top. Ma'am, you just gotta be from Texas, thought Les. Which was the first thing Norton asked her when he walked over. What have I got to lose? he thought. She can only throw her drink over me, kick me in the nuts and tell me to piss off back to bloody Australia.

'Excuse me, miss,' he said, slowly and as courteously as a gallon of mixed drinks would allow. 'You're not from Texas, are you? You know, the big state up near New Mexico where all the yellow flowers come from?'

The blonde blinked at Les, turned to her girlfriend for a second, then nodded. 'Yes. Why?'

'Your father hasn't got a ranch just outside of Dallas, has he?' The blonde shook her head. 'Your name's not Mercedes Lamont?' The blonde shook her head again. Norton made a kind of futile gesture. 'Ahh, well, I've made a blue. I'm sorry. It's just that you're a swap for this Texas bloke I met's daughter.'

The blonde sipped her drink and gave Les a bit of a once up and down. 'Where are you from?'

'Australia,' smiled Norton.

'I know where that is,' said the redhead. 'It's near Germany.'

'No,' said Norton. 'You're thinking of Czechoslovakia. Australia's a big island down near New Guinea.'

'Oh.'

This time Les thought he'd be a wealthy racehorse owner, over in America looking at breeding stock, which was how he met the rancher from Texas. The similarity between the blonde and the rancher's daughter was... absolutely uncanny. It was hard to believe two girls could be so attractive and so alike. The blonde did come from Texas, some placed called Waco; she worked on a marina out on the Keys and she'd been in Florida two years. The redhead worked in real estate, also out on the Keys; she came from Denver and she'd been in Florida a year.

'So what's your name?' asked the blonde.

'Les.'

'I'm Lori.' Norton gave a little blink. 'And this is Genevra.'

Norton raised his glass. 'Nice to meet you, girls.'

Les liked their accents, especially Lori's slight Texan drawl, and of course the girls loved Norton's. It was just 'so cute'. Naturally Les had to slow down now and again and repeat things, and drop off with the Australian slang, but that all added to the fun. They also loved it when Les bought them a margarita each, which was to be their limit as they both had to go to work in the morning. But they didn't mind when Les said, stuff it, let's have another one, and bought three more. Norton might not have been a wealthy racehorse owner, but the way he was tipping and throwing money around he was doing a pretty good impression of one. Lori even dragged Les up on the dancefloor to some track she knew and Les was right about aerobics; Lori sure knew how to shake her money-maker and what she lacked in style she more than made up for in energy. Norton was getting down alright too, and seeing the next track wasn't a bad one either they ripped into that as well. Naturally, same as in Australia, the old mates' act applied when Les got off the dance-floor. Genevra was getting Lori home safe and sound before some bloke, no matter how nice he was, got her drunk and took her somewhere and gave her a right royal porking, even if that was what she wanted in the first place. But would Lori like to go out with Les while he was in Florida looking at horses for the next three weeks? Sure. That sounded like a great idea. She wrote down her phone number and Les kissed the tips of her fingers when she put it in the top pocket of his shirt.

'Well, goodnight, Genevra,' said Norton, as they got their bags. 'Nice to have met you.'

'You too, Les. You have a good one.'

Norton couldn't help but have a last look at Lori's backside. 'I'd be rapt,' he said with a smile and gave her a wink. Lori smiled back — not at all demurely.

Well, what about Lori? thought Les, as he watched them leave. Nothing wrong with her. He finished his drink: now what? Then it struck him. Oh yeah. Back to Captain Rats. What a thought. Still, I'm getting to find these places and meet people. So try to be nice. Norton grinned to himself. I don't think it's going to be for that much longer.

The band had started, Hank was still at the bar — this time he had a beer in front of him: a Coors. He looked absolutely no different and Les figured it would be pointless asking him what he'd been up to.

Hank noticed the sweat on Norton's Magpie T-shirt. 'So how was the disco? Cool?'

Les wiped at some sweat under his chin. 'No. Actually the air-conditioning in there's stuffed.'

'Serves you right.'

'The music was good, though. I love Madonna.' Les turned to the bar. 'You want a drink?'

Hank gave a slight nod. 'Tequila.'

Les ordered the drinks and while he was waiting put Lori's phone number in his trouser pocket next to the other Lori's. Air-conditioned or not it was still quite warm so Les ordered another Corona. He downed almost half in one go while Hank took a hit of tequila followed by an unsmiling mouthful of beer.

'We'll go somewhere else,' he said.

'You don't like it here?'

'It's starting to fill up with celery-pickers and preppies.'

Les followed what Captain Rat's nutty eyes had temporarily landed on. There were some Mexican- or Cuban-looking blokes near the dancefloor, standing next to some people wearing ironed shirts and laces in their shoes.

'Celery-pickers and preppies, eh?' Les took another mouthful of beer. 'If you say so.' Ahh, what the fuck? thought Norton. Go and have a look somewhere else, I suppose. I can always come back here. 'So where do you fancy going?'

'There's a place downtown called "Club BandBox".' Hank gave Les a crooked sort of smile which was most unusual, almost like he had something up his sleeve. 'You'll like it there.'

'Okay. You know your way around.' Les took another glug of his Corona and lime. 'I'm just a shitty fuckin' tourist.'

They finished their drinks in comparative silence then left.

They cut back over the bridge and seemed to be heading along some other massive road into town. Les had the window down, trying to get some air, and was wishing he'd never bothered wearing a T-shirt; the neck and back were all soaked with sweat and in the heat and humidity of a summer night in Florida it felt like a blanket. Les was thinking of taking it of and leaving it in the car when he recognised Main Street again. Hank cut past it onto a road that led straight into a large, modern, high-rise hotel complex surrounded by blocks of home units built up alongside the harbour. It was all glitter, marble and smoked glass, neon lights flashed and out the front was the usual monster parking lot, only this one was dotted with palm trees. Hank found a space in the carpark, locked the pick-up and Les followed him across to what looked like a shopping centre full of restaurants, bars, boutiques, etc. There was a marble fountain out front and uniformed security guards keeping an eye on the crowd. Behind them a set of escalators went up two floors. Hank nodded for Les to follow and they took the escalator to the first floor. It was more shops and restaurants looking out over the harbour and just round from the escalator a small queue of people were entering a double glass door dotted with posters for bands. Above the door a red and black neon sign said 'Club BandBox'.

'In here,' smiled Hank. 'I'll pay the cover charge.'

Norton gave a double blink and nearly tripped over. Am I seeing and hearing things? I think I'd better cut down on those margaritas. It must be all that salt.

They joined the queue and a few people fell in behind them. When they got to the door, Hank propped, the usual smug smile on his face. There were two bouncers on the door — a solid white bloke in a BandBox T-shirt, and a monstrous black man in a grey suit. The white bouncer gave Hank a severe once up and down then shook his head. The black bloke seemed more interested in Norton. He looked at Hank for a second or two then said something to the white bouncer.

'Okay,' said the white bouncer, not looking at all happy, 'I'll let you in this time. But next time wear shoes, okay?' Hank still propped at the door. The smile disappeared and his jaw dropped. 'Well, come on buddy,' said the bouncer in the T-shirt. 'Are you coming in?'

'Yeah, what are you doing, Hank?' said Les. 'There's people behind us.' Hank almost fell through the door with Norton behind him. As he staggered over to the counter to pay the five dollars cover charge Les stepped back and waited, chuckling to himself.

It wasn't hard to figure out what was going on. Hank deliberately picked this place knowing they had dress regulations and they wouldn't let him in looking like B.O. Plenty. Les twigged there was something in the wind when Captain Rats smiled, twice, then offered to pay the cover charge. This would have effectively stuffed up Norton's night and they would have had to go home, where Les could've watched TV and drunk cheap, shitty tequila at Hank's house or gone and sweated the night out in his own room. But they'd got in; only because of the big black bloke in the grey suit. Les was looking at the person in question who was standing barely a metre away. He wasn't just big, he was an absolute monster. At least six feet six and twenty stone, with a huge bony head sitting on a neck as thick as Norton's waist. He saw Les staring at him and flashed an infectious white grin.

'Hey man. Are you Australian?'

'Yeah,' nodded Les. 'Why's that, mate?'

'That T-shirt,' said the man-mountain. 'Rugby. Man, I played that shit at college for a while. That's one helluva game. Broke mah goddamn collarbone.' He looked directly at Les. 'You play rugby?'

'Yeah.' Les nodded again. 'In the forwards. Second row mainly. I suppose you play gridiron?'

'Yeah, man. Used to play tight end for the Dolphins.'

'I'd believe that,' grinned Les. 'Christ! I'd hate to tackle you front on, you big bludger.'

The big man gave a bit of a laugh then seemed to concentrate on Norton's T-shirt. 'Hey, just what is that man? Wests. The Mag-pahs. Hey, that's one bitchin' T-shirt.'

'Yeah, that's them, mate,' said Norton. 'Wests. The mighty Magpies.'

'Mag-pah. Man, I like that.'

Les looked evenly at the big man for a second. 'What do you mean, you like it?'

'That T-shirt, man. I like it.'

'You mean you want it?'

'No, man, I don't want it. All I's sayin' is, I like it.'

'In other words, you want it, don't you? Well, here you are. Take the bloody thing.' Norton started taking off his shirt. 'I'm not gonna fight you over a lousy bloody T-shirt. You're too bloody big.'

'Hey, man. Be cool. I don't want your T-shirt.'

Before the big man could argue Norton had his shirt off and handed to the bouncer in the T-shirt, his Wests T-shirt off, folded and handed to the big man; he was glad to get rid of it. 'There you go, mate,' said Les, tucking his shirt in. 'Take the clothes off my poor back. Leave me to freeze. I don't give a stuff.'

The big bloke looked at the T-shirt in his hands and the huge grin flashed back. 'Hey, man, what can I say? I dig that.'

'That's okay, mate.' said Norton. 'Thanks for letting me in.'

'That's cool. Listen, man,' the big bloke came right up to Les, 'I owe you one, brother. Anybody give you any shit, you come see me.'

'I'll do that. What's your name anyway?'

'Harris.'

Norton shook the big man's hand. 'I'm Les, Harris. I might have a drink with you later.'

'No sweat, brother.' Harris winked. 'Les.'

Norton let Harris get back to bouncing then turned to find a scowling Hank pocketing some change and glaring at him. Norton returned Hank's scowl with a silly grin that dripped blissful ignorance.

'Hey this place is alright, Hank. You come here all the time, do you? Fuckin' ripper.'

The foyer was all red and black with red and black check lino. There were more rock posters on the walls and a big poster of Superman behind the front desk. The foyer led to a short set of stairs on your left that took you to another level and the start of a bar at the top of the stairs. The dancefloor was on your right with another bar in the distance and another set of stairs leading to another bar above them. Built into the wall facing the dancefloor and the upstairs level was a stage for bands, though tonight was all disco. There were heaps of spinning lights and lasers and a big red and green neon sign saying Club BandBox. Hank seemed to get reluctantly swept along with the crowd and Les followed him up the stairs on the left. The top level was chairs, tables and booths, red and black or black- and white-checked walls, and plate glass windows looking out over the harbour. A waist-level partition with a chrome railing ran round the upstairs level to stop the punters falling over where it overlooked the dancefloor. There were TV screens built into the ceiling and on one wall was a giant video screen showing a

69

chimpanzee in a karate outfit sparring with some bloke. The upstairs bar was bigger than Les expected; it circled round almost to the booths on the far left wall. The bar staff were happy and busy, spunky-looking waitresses cruised around in ripped T-shirts and lycra bicycle shorts; from out of nowhere a girl in a nurse's uniform walked past carrying a tray bristling with test-tubes full of different coloured liquids. The punters were about the same age, size and shape as the ones at the first place, walking or standing around, with others, both men and women, seated at the tables drinking jugs of beer — or pitchers as the yanks like to call them. Norton liked what he saw. Club BandBox was about three-quarters full, the punters were clean and tidy, there was no shortage of girls and on the dancefloor it was back to back and bumper to bumper, and raging.

'Hey, nothing wrong with this place, mate,' beamed Norton. 'It's tops.' Hank didn't say anything. Les clapped his hands together. 'Well, while you're in a generous mood you may as well shout me a drink in your favourite watering hole. I'll have another Corona thanks, mate. With a slice of lime too — if you don't mind.'

Hank's eyes spun around crazily and this time Les thought they were going to take right off and join the mirror ball on the ceiling. Instead, he seemed to shake a little then turn on his heel and went to the bar behind him. It hasn't been a real good night for you, has it, Captain Rats? mused Les, trying not to laugh as he moved away from the bar a little and checked out the punters. First you got lumbered with the cover charge, now you're actually in a shout. But think of the good side. You wouldn't have got in here if it hadn't been for me. Before long Hank returned with a Coors and a Corona.

'Thanks, mate,' said Norton, taking his beer and a swallow almost at the same time. 'Cheers.'

Hank took a mirthless pull on his beer. 'That was a damn fool thing you did back there at the foyer.'

'What's that?'

'Giving that nigger your T-shirt.'

'Yeah?' Norton looked surprised. 'I thought he was a mate of yours. Didn't he say something to you when we walked in? He didn't seem like a bad bloke.' Les gave a grudging kind of nod. 'Yeah, I suppose you're right. It was a bit uncool. But that's just me, Hank. It's my nature. I can't help giving things away. Anyway, it's only money. It's not an arm or a leg. Or a T-shirt,' Les added with a laugh. 'And who gives a fuck? I brought that much with me I'll be flat out spending it anyway. So come on. Finish that so I can get you another one.'

Les went for a snakes and was pleased to find the urinals were the same as in Australia. One thing that did surprise him in the toilet though was a travelling barber, selling aftershave, hair gel and trims for the macho poseurs; and he was making a living. Les returned, finished his Corona then got Hank a beer and a tequila and another margarita for himself, telling Hank when he handed him his drinks he might go for a stroll and check the place out. Hank shrugged, found a seat at the bar away from the other drinkers, lit a cigarette and plotted how he was going to get some of that money out of Norton. Les ambled through the punters towards the stairs leading down to the other side of the dancefloor, knowing exactly what Hank was thinking. I'll tell you something, Laurel baby, he chuckled to himself, you'll need more than Epsom Salts.

This time it was a tall, almost striking brunette, with dark features and eyes that matched her dark, shoulder-length hair. Like Norton she was dressed all in black — shirt, slacks and shoes — only she had on a black vest as well, pinned with silver jewellery and knick-knacks. Les spotted her standing near the bar just across from the stairs, sort of boogying quietly around yet oozing energy as she did. She had a wiry, lithe body but didn't look like an aerobics princess; her shoulders were too broad and there was something else about her. The girlfriend was also a brunette and apart from having shorter hair and being a little plumper she looked very similar. She was wearing jeans and a kind of blue and white striped sailor's top. The sailor wasn't moving around, she was standing with a drink, tapping her fingers on her handbag. They looked the type of women that if you tried to front them with some stupid pick-up line you'd either get your head bitten off or be told to go to the shithouse, very smartly. Unfortunately Les didn't have the time to think up some cool, knock 'em off their feet line. Besides he was too drunk anyway.

'Listen, Johnny Cash,' he said, walking straight up to the brunette in the black vest, 'I'm a hypnotist with a circus and I just finished work. That's my excuse for being all in black. What's yours? You look like a rolled up umbrella.'

The brunette gave Norton a cool, but inquisitive, once up and down. 'Did you say something about a circus?'

Les nodded drunkenly. 'Yeah. I'm a hypnotist. What's your caper?'

'I'm a trapeze artist,' answered the brunette evenly. 'I'm down here to start work with Carmichael Brothers. I've only been here two days, and I've never seen you before.'

'What did the pork chop say?' asked the girlfriend. 'He's a hypnotist?' She looked at Les as if she was getting ready to swing her handbag. 'Don't you have to have a brain and be able to speak properly to be a hypnotist?'

'You're not with any circus,' sneered the brunette. 'Get lost.'

Norton the cool swinger suddenly found himself going over like a fart in a mini-sub. He'd sort of tried to be a bit clever and the brunette had belted him straight to the boundary. He couldn't have tried a worse approach. She was a trapeze artist alright, that was the energy and poise Les had noticed about her, and up close you could see the muscles in her shoulders and neck. No one would bother to make up a story like that, not on the spur of the moment. Norton was completely stuffed and if he didn't start tap dancing a bit quicker, and smartly too, he'd make a complete dill of himself.

'Alright,' he said defiantly, 'you don't believe me. I'm also a mind reader. I'll bet I can guess your name.'

The brunette gave her girlfriend a bored look then turned back to Les. 'What?'

Norton stared at her and blinked a couple of times. There wasn't a great deal he could say. 'Lori...?'

The girlfriend seemed to glare at him. 'How did you know my cousin's name? She only got here from Chicago yesterday.'

Norton grinned roguishly. 'I told you,' he said, 'it's all part of the act. Back in Australia they call me Lesto the Magnifico. There ain't nuthin' I don't know.'

The girls had their chance, but by then it was too late. In about two minutes they were holding a fresh drink each and Norton was pissing in their pockets, their handbags, their shoes and anywhere else he could find a spot. Lori was a trapeze artist. Siestasota was an old circus town going back to the turn of the century, some circuses were still based there, while other cabaret acts refitted and organised their tours from there. Lori had just come down from Chicago where she had been working in a cabaret. That finished, she was now touring the mid-west with the circus she mentioned. Lori had also been a champion gymnast at college and represented America at the Olympic Games, winning a silver medal. Under closer inspection Norton certainly believed that; Lori was one fit, strong woman. If she decided to belt you one you'd stay belted. By the same token, if she porked you, you'd know you'd been porked too. The girlfriend was her older cousin Nadine. Nadine came down from Chicago ten years ago, she was divorced, had two kids and owned a house about five minutes away by taxi; if that. Club BandBox was handy and a good venue to see a band now and again and possibly bump into interesting people; even if it was only a stupid bloody Australian like Les trying to pass himself off as a hypnotist. It was a good thing he had a sense of humour and didn't mind shouting a drink. Or their words to that effect.

This time Les thought he might try another tack; throw in a little bit of the truth. He and a mate owned a bar in Sydney, the Kelly Club, named after Ned Kelly the bushranger. He and his partner used to play football, which was how they got the money to buy the bar. He'd met Hank in the bar and that was how he came to be in Siestasota. He was only staying with Hank two or three days then he was getting a place on his own. After that Les was holidaying in America, checking out bars and nightclubs, and if he saw any good ideas he'd take them back to good old Oz with him. It was all tax-deductible anyway; a business trip. Norton threw down another margarita and said he just loved taking care of business.

The girls didn't mind a drink and Les wouldn't let them pay for any. In no time Nadine had downed three solid Jack Daniel's and Coke, Lori easily gargled her way through three margaritas, Norton lost track of how many he had. Lori said the only reason she drank so many margaritas was because of the salt; coming from up north she wasn't used to the heat and they helped to retain the body salts. Although she added a bit of a wink with this story, Les agreed with her wholeheartedly. He wasn't used to such a hot, sweaty climate either, which is why he was drinking them two at a time. Plus in the crowd it was a big hard to juggle four. As well as a drink, the two brunettes from Chicago didn't mind a laugh either. Norton told them a few anecdotes from Australia, but he got the most laughs just telling them about poor silly Hank.

'Yeah, for a while there,' said Les, 'I thought all bloody yanks were as silly as him. I was ready to ring Qantas and get the next plane home.'

'Oh no,' said Lori, seeming to eye Norton very intently over the top of her drink. 'You'll find most Americans are okay.'

Norton eyed her very intently back. 'I'm sure, given time, I will, Lori,' he smiled. 'I know I'd like to find out.'

Norton had a couple of dances with Lori, who had a funny style on the floor. It was all energy and arms and shoulder moves, something like a boxer working out on a speed ball. Les just boogied around as best he could to the unknown disco schlock, but Lori could see that the red-headed boy from Down Under was a pretty fit dude as well. He grabbed Nadine and speared her onto the dance-floor too. She was a little more conservative. But when the DJ threw on Madonna's 'Hank Panky' and Les started jitterbugging with her, she was stoked and went for it like a Mohawk Indian after a big win over the Cavalry.

Les got on absolutely splendidly with the girls and didn't want to leave; not while he had a pocketful of all those silly little bits of green paper to spend. But Nadine had to make a move soon, the babysitter couldn't stay all night. Les said it was probably about time he got back to Boofhead as well. Would Lori like to come out with Les, visit a few bars and restaurants and help him with a bit of work-related research while he was in Siestasota? Maybe. But she'd only just got here herself and she had rehearsals and other things to attend to at the moment. However, they were coming back here on Sunday night to see a band. How about meeting her up here? A few more drinks, a bit more dancing. See what happens. That sounded alright to Norton. So rather than hang around, burning out his welcome, Les thanked the girls for a good time and for putting up with him, gave them both a bit of a quick cuddle, then said goodbye and headed back to where he'd left Laurel, stopping at the bar upstairs on the way for another margarita.

Hank was in the same spot Les had left him, only he was talking to a friend. Norton didn't walk straight up, he hung back for a few moments and was able to catch the last bit of Hank and his mate's conversation. His friend was a tall, dark-haired bloke in a mustard-coloured shirt and brown trousers. Hank didn't appear to be saying a great deal. His eyes were spinning around worse than ever and he looked to be too busy sweating to talk.

'Hey, I'll be back to see you alright. It's been over three months now. Three fuckin' months.'

'Just another two weeks, for chrissake.'

'You said that a fuckin' month ago. What the fuck do you take me for? Santa Claus?' Hank mumbled something under his breath. The 'mate' gave him an extremely severe once up and down. 'Okay. You got another two weeks, and I'm gonna come see you. You know what I'm sayin'?' Hank nodded his head slightly. 'Hey, look at me when I'm talkin' to you. You got two fuckin' weeks, then I come see you. You got that?'

'Yeah, I got it.'

'Two fuckin' weeks. You dumbass prick.' The 'mate' glared at Hank for a second. 'And you better fuckin' believe it too.' Brown trousers left to join another man and two good-looking women.

Hank still hadn't noticed Les standing amongst the other drinkers. He still had that caged rat looked about him, but as soon as brown trousers left he started to get that half, smug smile on his face again. Even though he was pretty pissed, it didn't take Norton long to put two and two together. Laurel had come across a ghost, and not a very happy one at that. But the ghost was still a jerk as far as Laurel was concerned and he could still go shit in his hat.

'So how's it going, Hank old mate?' leered Norton, appearing out of the crowd. 'You ready for another drink?' Les had a fairly good idea what the answer would be.

'Let's get out of here. This place is a dump. It's full of jerks.'

'You know, Hank, I was just thinking the same thing.'

Hank finished his shot of tequila, dropped the glass on the bar and as usual abruptly turned around and walked off without waiting for Les. Norton sculled the rest of his drink and fell in behind. In a way it suited him — although the place was still jumping and there were still plenty of girls around, he'd drunk enough margaritas to salt a bullock hide and his face looked like David Jones's city window at Xmas time. Hank had to slow down for the crowd between the bar and the railing round the dancefloor, and as Les caught up an evil smile crept over his shining face. Well, what do I spy with my little eye? Just sticking out from the back pocket of Hank's grubby blue jeans was the folded up fifty dollar bill Norton had

76

given him. Norton recollected him stuffing it in there as he was driving the car. Norton looked to the left, looked to the right, and in about a microsecond had it extracted between his index and middle finger, rolled in a ball and shoved down the side pocket of his black trousers. Well aren't you just a good bloke, Hank? he sniggered to himself. Or is it a 'good ol' boy'?

At the top of the stairs Norton caught the eye of some frumpy-looking blonde in a black Tampa Bay Buccaneers T-shirt. 'G'day, Lori,' he grinned. 'How are you goin'?'

The blonde gave Les a double blink. 'Where do I know you from?'

'College,' answered Norton.

'Fort Lauderdale?'

'No. Wagga Wagga. Look after yourself, Lori. See you next time I'm up here.'

One of the blonde's even frumpier girlfriends tapped her on the shoulder. 'What did that guy want, Lori?'

The blonde shook her head. 'He said he knew me from college.'

'Yeah?' The girlfriend's eyes followed Les going down the stairs. 'Hey, whoever he was, he was kinda cute.'

Norton was laughing and shaking his head at the same time. Onya, Lori. What do they say? 'Only in America'?

'Hey, mah man! What's happenin'? You leaving already?' Harris was all smiles as Les came through the foyer.

'Yeah.' Les nodded to Captain Rats storming out the door. 'I don't want to, but I got to. That bloke's giving me a lift home. I don't even know him all that well. I only met him tonight.'

'I can soon get you a taxi if you want to stay. That guy looks like a panhandler,' offered Harris.

'No, that's alright, mate.' Les gave Harris a wink and a smile. 'But I might come down on Sunday night and have a look at the band. You gonna be here?'

'I surely am, brother. And you just come straight on in, have a drink on me. I owe you one, mah man.'

'Righto, you're on. You want another T-shirt?'

The huge grin returned to Harris's face and he stroked his chin. 'Wouldn't mind one for my little brother.'

'Okey-doke,' said Les. 'I'll bring you down a Penrith Panthers one Sunday night. Now gimme five, baby.'

'Heh-heh! You got it, man.'

Harris gave Les five and the Queenslander's arm was still quivering from the shock when he caught up with Hank in the carpark.

The drive home didn't even get off the ground as far as conversation went. Hank seemed to be in deep thought as he hunched over the wheel, morosely dragging on another cigarette. Norton was doing a bit of thinking too; after a while he spoke.

'Jesus, Hank, I had a grouse time tonight. Especially that last place, it was fuckin' unreal. I'm glad you got us in there.' Hank just kept driving and smoking. 'The funny part about it, it cost me fuck all. I'd be lucky if I spent three hundred bucks. It costs you nothing to have a good time over here.' Hank turned to Norton for a moment and blinked. 'Tomorrow, though, I might have to cash some more traveller's cheques. Can you give me lift up the bank?'

They pulled up for a set of lights and Hank looked at Les for a moment like he was Bugs Bunny suddenly stumbled across a carrot patch.

'Sure,' Hank nodded casually. 'I have to go up to the office in the morning. You can come up there with me first.'

Gee. Thanks for the invitation, thought Les. 'Okay. What time are you going up there?'

'Nine. Sharp.'

'Righto.' That would probably be about ten-thirty I'd say, mused Norton. You want to have me hanging around in that stinken hot room, half asleep with a hangover, for a couple of hours first. But I'll have a shower and a nice breakfast instead.

They finally pulled up in the driveway. Les thanked Hank profusely for a wonderful night; Boofhead muttered something about he'd see Les in the morning, and trudged off to his house. Les was unfolding the fifty dollar bill and laughing quietly when he saw Hank stop near his door for a piss. Not a bad idea, thought Les, and did the same thing.

Around him the Spanish Moss hung gracefully from the trees like shreds of fine lace, painted silver by moonlight, which was softer than the night breeze itself. Above him countless millions of stars resembling tiny diamonds twinkled daintily from a cobalt sky, occasionally to be hidden by the gentle clouds drifting slowly across the heavens, quieter than a dream.

However, Norton wasn't particularly into romance or poetry that night. All he knew was that it was hot, he was drunk, and it was somewhere to have a piss.

Les cleaned his teeth, stripped to his jox and was lying on his bed in the humid darkness, thinking. Thinking whether it was worth thinking or not. It sure had been a nutty day, and not a bad night either. Has anyone seen Lori? he chuckled. Yeah. Take your bloody pick. Now that's something worth thinking about. Especially the daring young brunette on the flying trapeze. Norton let go a cavernous yawn. But not tonight. Not in this stinken heat. Besides, I'm too bloody drunk anyway. Despite the heat, the humidity and the noisy fan, Les drifted off quite easily.

Les blinked his eyes open around nine. In spite of all the booze he'd literally poured down his throat the night before he didn't feel too bad; nevertheless, after a cold shower, just to be on the safe side, he took a couple of tablets called Tylenols that he'd found in a red bottle in the bathroom. Norton hadn't been thinking about a great deal while he was under the shower, only that he was still lost in the middle of nowhere and he had another exciting day in the Florida heat with Einstein. He threw on a Red Back T-shirt and shorts and was in the kitchen with his head stuck in the fridge when he heard a familiar woman's voice.

79

'Oh, hello, Les. How are you this morning?'

Norton slammed the fridge door shut and turned around, feeling like a burglar caught robbing a safe. 'Oh. G'day, Mrs Laurel.' He noticed she was still wearing a blue silk dressing gown. 'I didn't wake you up, did I?'

'No. I've been up some time. I was just about to have something to eat. I imagine you're hungry too?'

'Well, yeah. I am a bit.'

'Then why don't you let me make you some breakfast?'

'No. There's no need for you to go to all that trouble, Mrs Laurel,' protested Norton. 'I can grab a bit of toast and coffee.'

Mrs Laurel waved a motherly finger. 'You're a guest. So you sit down and let me make you breakfast. I have to anyway.'

Norton smiled and put up a very weak defence. 'Okay, Mrs Laurel. It's your house. You're the boss. I'll set the table.'

Norton knew what Mrs Laurel wanted besides food. An ear. Two would be even better. So while Les was setting the dining room table he let her go and got the guts on the family — what a dropkick Hank was, her husband dying, the break-in, Hank's ex-girlfriend Laverne and more. But it was well worth it. In no time Mrs Laurel had whipped up chilled sliced fruit, orange juice, scrambled eggs with pepperoni sausage, hash browns, unbelievable coffee, plus toast, and other odds and ends. Les ripped in. While he was stuffing himself Les said how they went diving at the Keys the day before and how they'd got out on the drinks last night and they were going to Hank's office that morning. While they were gossiping away, the phone rang. Mrs Laurel answered it, spoke for a short while then resumed her seat.

'That was Laverne. She wanted to talk to Hank but his phone wasn't answering.'

'Maybe he's still asleep?' suggested Les.

'Only from the ears up, Les.' Mrs Laurel slapped some blueberry jam on a piece of toast and downed it with a cup of coffee. For a frail woman in a hot climate she wasn't bad on the tooth.

Les helped her with the dishes and found he was warming up to Mrs Laurel; after Hank she was a class act. Norton said he wanted to buy some orange juice and things himself and found out there was a supermarket complex up the road. He didn't quite understand the look on Mrs Laurel's face when he said he didn't need a car, he'd just bought that bike out the front. Mrs Laurel said she had a map of Siestasota somewhere, she'd find it and leave it on his bed. They'd almost finished the washing up when who should come storming into the kitchen, same dirty jeans, different T-shirt, but Hank, looking anything but happy. There was a kind of weird silence. No 'Good morning' or 'Lovely day outside, how is everybody this morning?' It was like a pall of gloom had descended on the kitchen. I can't imagine why he's even more miserable than normal, mused Norton. He's had plenty of sleep.

Les wiped his hands with the teatowel and looked at his watch. 'Nine o'clock already. Doesn't the time slip away? Must be that daylight saving.'

Hank's eyes spun round to Les for a brief moment. 'Well, what are you doing?'

'Helping your mother wash up,' answered Les rather nonchalantly. 'We just finished breakfast. It was nice too. We had fresh orange juice, scrambled eggs, spicy little sausages . . .'

'Laverne rang, Hank,' interjected Mrs Laurel.

Hank glared at his mother. 'What did that bitch want?'

'She'd been trying to ring you. She wants to see you about something. I told her you'd be at the office.'

'You what!!? Oh, for chrissake. Why did you tell her that?'

Mrs Laurel gave the sink a last wipe and straightened her dressing gown. 'I don't really know, to be honest, Hank. I guess it just seemed like a good idea at the time. Goodbye, Les. I'll leave that map on your bed.'

'Thanks, Mrs laurel. And thanks for a lovely breakfast. It was absolutely delicious.'

'Any time, Les. You're more than welcome.'

Mrs Laurel disappeared again, leaving Les and a fuming Hank shaking his head. 'I don't goddamn believe it. How can anybody be so stupid?'

Norton opened the fridge to get another glass of orange juice. He half looked at Hank. 'She probably thought the same thing when she had you, Hank.'

'What was that?'

'She said, it wasn't far from here to the bank. You still going to give me a lift up? Money, Hank. Cassshhhh. I need some.'

The mention of the word 'money' wounded Hank. He'd searched all through his house and nearly torn the car apart for the last hour looking for that fifty. But it got him mobilised. 'Yeah, we'll go there on the way to the office. I'll be out the front.'

Hank disappeared also. Les sipped his orange juice and tried to keep a straight face. After a while he gave up and took the rest of his drink into his room.

The bank was called Sun, sitting on some intersection about a mile across in a carpark that would have fitted Uluru. Getting another $500 was no great drama. Les flashed his driver's licence, got a laugh out of the plump woman teller, then went back out to the pick-up sitting in the heat. They took off again, heading away from the house and town. Norton still didn't have a clue where he was as everything was still dead flat and spread out with nothing to take a bearing on.

They took a left at some road and Les turned to Hank.

'Y'know, I was thinking, mate. Fifty dollars ain't much for all the trouble you've gone to for me. What say I make it an even hundred?' Norton took out his wedge and peeled off the same fifty dollar bill he'd given Hank the night before. 'There you are, mate.'

Hank took the fifty, nodded, and put it in his pocket. Les looked at him for a moment then stared out his window, blinking. What am I gonna do? He's put it in the same bloody pocket.

Hank's office was a white stucco building in a low-rise warehouse complex built alongside a swampy-looking lagoon, landscaped with a few pine trees. A short walk round the corner from the parking lot, Hank opened up a mirrored door next to two mirrored windows, bent down to pick up some mail and they stepped into a pall of hot, stale, dusty air. Hank closed the door and Les looked around; Double Bay it wasn't. The front room had a false ceiling, scruffy grey carpet and doubled as the office. There were a few shelves round the wall on your left with bugger all on them and a couple of items of cheap cane furniture. To the right was a desk, a chair and a few chipped grey filing cabinets. There was a fax and coffee machine that didn't work, a phone and answering service that did and a golfball typewriter that looked like Jack Nicklaus had belted it through Meadowbank and the US Open. Hank dropped the letters on the desk, sat down and switched on the answering machine. One short, garbled message came through that Les couldn't understand. He also couldn't understand why Hank brought him up there. Probably just to annoy him. It wouldn't be to impress him; it was a dump and all that was on the shelves was a few Mexican-looking dolls and a dozen or so stuffed alligators about two feet long, only instead of green they were white and when you turned them over they had a Confederate flag on their stomachs. Maybe Hank's in the Klan, thought Les. No, that wouldn't be right. Einstein wouldn't be able to spell KKK.

'I might see if I can find a glass of water,' said Les. Hank nodded without looking up.

An open door from the office led straight into the warehouse. It too was dusty and stale and smelled of neglect; the only difference was it was twice as hot as the office. There were bigger shelves round the walls, all bare, a carpeted, metal table in the middle for packing on and a roller door and chain at the back. Flattened cardboard cartons were either stacked or lying around the floor amid shredded paper, rags and other waste for packaging. One match said the one small fire extinguisher on the wall next to a clock that didn't work would last about two seconds if it ever got going. It was a dump. There was a toilet and sink, however, which wasn't too filthy. Les found a cup, cleaned it and was wandering around sipping a second glass of water when he heard the front door open and a woman's voice. Les approached the doorway to the office and held back against a rack of shelves. Hank appeared to be in an argument with a pixie-faced brunette who had just dumped a pile of letters on his desk. She was tall, quite attractive, a neat body and neat short hair, and was wearing a T-shirt and cut-away jeans. Her voice had the same twang as the bloke who put the heavies on Hank in Club BandBox.

'For the last goddamn time, Hank, I do not want you to use the condo as an office address. How many times do I have to tell you? You dumb prick. I'm not telling you again.'

'Oh, for chrissake, Laverne, what's wrong with you?'

'Hey. It's not what's wrong with *me*. It'll be what's wrong with *you* if Ricco finds out. He'll have your ass, you dumb shit. And, frankly, I think it would be a good thing. The condo is not for letters or phone calls. You got that, Hank — you jerk.' Hank seemed to be muttering something as he fiddled around behind his desk while the brunette glared at him. 'Now, where's this aussie guy you said was coming out here to stay with you? I gotta see this.'

Norton figured this might be as good a time as ever for him to enter stage left. Nonchalantly sipping his cup of water, he stepped into the office and caught the brunette's eye. 'Hello. How are you?' he smiled. 'You must be Laverne?' Norton offered his hand. 'I'm Les.'

The brunette gave Norton a very healthy once up and down and a double blink. 'Well, nice to meet you, Les,' she said, giving Norton's hand a squeeze.

'You too, Laverne.' Norton thought he might as well lay on a little charm. 'Hank's mother told me a little bit about you. But I didn't think you were this pretty.'

Laverne seemed to stare at Les. 'You're staying at Hank's place?'

'Yeah. I got a room near the kitchen. It's ... okay.'

Laverne now seemed to be thinking as well as staring. 'How long are you here for, Les?'

Norton shrugged. 'About three weeks.'

'Three weeks. Staying at Hank's.' Laverne's eyes narrowed. 'Les, I don't hardly know you but I'm going to make you an offer you can't refuse. And you can do me a favour at the same time.' She took two keys on a ring from her bag. 'Hank. There's the keys to the condo. Take Les out there.' She dropped the keys on the desk and turned back to Les. 'You can have my condo for the three weeks you're here, Les. Look after it and I don't want anybody in there but you. You got that, Hank? Put Les up in the condo. You'll love it, Les. It's in a nice area and it's got a pool. I'll call out there and see you.' Laverne snapped her purse closed, looking like she didn't want to be in Hank's company any longer than she had to. 'Okay, I'm out of here, Hank. And remember what I told you. Dummy.' She gave Les another smile. 'I'll be seeing you, Les.'

Norton was a little bewildered. 'Yeah. See you, Laverne. And thanks.' For bloody what, he thought.

Hank didn't bother to say goodbye. Laverne disappeared out the door. Norton decided he'd better find out what was going on. He knew if he didn't ask, Hank sure as hell wouldn't tell him.

'What's all this about a condo, Hank? What the fuck's a condo? A car? A caravan?'

Hank tried to look busy with some letters. 'It's a dump. It's out towards town. A crappy apartment.'

Norton knitted his eyebrows. Condo, apartment, letters, pool? 'Hank, are you telling me Laverne's given me the use of a flat while I'm here? With a pool?'

'It's a dump. She wanted me to live there. The pool's about as big as a bath tub. It's full of chemicals and everybody pisses in it.'

'I don't give a fuck if the local circus takes the elephants up there and washes them in it. It couldn't be any ... At least let's go and have a look at it.' Norton couldn't

85

believe his luck. Hank's ex evidently owned a home unit somewhere and Hank was using it as a mail drop. She could have felt sorry for Les, knowing what a prick Hank was, so she'd let him stay there to keep an eye on the place and sort of kill two birds with the one stone. Whichever way, it meant getting out of Swamp Manor and freedom from Captain Rats.

'I can't just drop everything and take you straight over,' said Hank. 'I do have a business to run. Besides, I thought you wanted to go riding along the beach?'

'Well, yeah,' shrugged Norton. 'But it ain't that important.'

'I'll get a bike and come with you. I said I could if I wanted.'

'Please yourself.'

'I'll get a bike this afternoon. And we'll go for a ride on the beach.'

'Okay. Then we'll go and have a look at that condo, or whatever you call it. When do you want to leave here?'

'As soon as I clear this up.'

This took about an hour of Hank trying to look like he was doing something and Les shuffling restlessly around in the heat, but still pondering his good luck. Bad luck he had to stay sweet with Boofhead so he could get the keys and a lift over. But not for much longer. Then he could dump the idiot for good. Eventually Hank picked up his keys and turned on the answering service.

'So where are we going now?'

'Bike shop.'

'I know a good one down by Centennial Park.'

They left the office and before long were once again whizzing along huge roads and highways full of huge cars. Watching him sucking on another cigarette, Les was trying to figure Hank out once more. Why bother buying a brand new bike unless you can absolutely afford it? Just to show Les he could if he wanted? And also, if he was so sour on the world, why bother inviting someone over to stay with you? Hank was a nice nut alright. Along with his lift not going to the top floor, Laurel Lee only had one oar in the water as well. They turned off the road at some fairly large, modern-looking bike shop. It was all glass front and tiles, with rows of gleaming, brand new bikes in the window set in the mandatory monster car-park; only this time there were ample trees and shade. Hank pulled up under a tree and switched off the motor.

'Come in,' he more or less commanded.

Norton shook his head. 'It's alright. I'll wait in the car.'

Hank's eyes went into turbo drive again. 'What do you mean, you'll wait in the car? Come inside and have a look at some decent bikes, for chrissake.'

Les shook his head again. 'What do I want to look at bikes for? I already got one. I'd only be wasting my time.'

'You're not coming in?'

'No. I'll sit here and watch the punters. If you see a good pair of tiger skin lycra bike shorts in my size give me a yell. I might change my mind.'

Hank glared at Norton as if he couldn't believe that Les would not only have the audacity to think for himself but almost disobey an order. He muttered something and stormed into the bike shop.

Nice try, Laurel baby, thought Les. But you're going to have to get up a bit earlier than that. Yeah, I come in and it's, Oh Les, I got a cheque coming next week; alright if I put this on your VISA card? Or, can you give me the cash till next week? Sorry, Hank. Besides, I've already given you a hundred, haven't I? Norton sat patiently in the pick-up and waited. Half an hour later Les was thinking of trying to work the car radio when Hank came out of the shop wheeling a light blue bike, with one five-speed gear lever. It had high, wide handlebars, a big soft-looking white seat and looked like a girl's bike. Well, there goes my fifty, surmised Norton. I'd say he's put that down and got on the murray for the rest.

'That looks alright,' lied Norton, getting out of the car. 'What did you pay for it?'

'Three hundred and fifty,' replied Hank, trying to look cool. 'It makes that pile of junk you bought look pretty sick.'

Norton checked it out. It didn't look too solid and when Les came to the brand name he gave a double, triple blink. Painted on the frame was, Villawood Stylemaster. Designed in Italy for Clive Masters. Clive Masters was an Australian businessman who split Australia for America owing millions of dollars in debts. One of his last capers before he fled was bikes. He sold hundreds of them and they nearly all fell to pieces. Somehow Masters had got to America along with his shonky bikes and had started distributing them. Lucky yanks. And poor silly Hank had flummed one. If he so much as ran over an apple core lying on the footpath or hit an ant it'd probably fall apart.

'You know what brand it is, Hank?'

Hank sounded very matter-of-fact. 'It's a Villawood. Italian racer. Clive Masters is the designer. Hey, I don't buy shit.'

'You're a genius, Hank. I only hope I can keep up with you.'

'I sure as hell won't be dragging ass once we hit that beach.'

'And like Deirdre and I always say. Have a lovely weekend.'

'What are you talking about?'

'Nothing, Hank. Nothing at all.' Norton watched Hank carefully place his 'Italian racer' in the back, shook his head, then got in the front.

They drove back to Swamp Manor to get changed and pick up Norton's bike. Les got into a daggy pair of training shorts he'd thrown in his bag, daggy sneakers, a T-shirt with no sleeves and an old sweatband; nothing he'd worry about losing or destroying. Although the condo thing was on his mind, Les was now looking forward to this pedal along the beach. He needed a good hit out and it might be a bit of a perv too. Plus, even if the water was murky and warm a swim after would be good too. For once Les thought he'd be on time and he was waiting outside for Hank next to the pick-up, his bike in the back. Hank arrived wearing a shirt, shorts and an old baseball cap.

'We off?' said Les.

Hank nodded. 'Let's go.' He lit a cigarette and before long roads and bridges had gone past in the sunshine and they were at the same beach where they'd had a shower. Not a great deal of conversation went down, but at times Les got this weird feeling Hank was almost trying to be civil. Maybe he was worried his meal ticket was about to flutter out the door.

Hank parked the car under some pine trees, near an entrance to the beach. They got their bikes from the back and started pushing them along a sandy trail between more trees; again Les couldn't believe how fine and white the sand was. The beach looked bigger than before too. When they came to the end of the trail, there was about a half-mile strip of sand to their right, on the left was at least five miles of dead flat sand, five hundred yards wide, before some flat rocks at the end. Another two hundred yards of dry sand sloped up towards the high-rises and buildings that ringed the beach. Between the punters either lying on or walking along the edge of the dry sand were shallow tidal pools hundreds of yards long. A gusty wind was coming straight in from the Gulf of Mexico, chopping up the water and pushing in a sloppy, chunderous two-foot wave the entire length of the beach. Somehow it reminded Norton of a cross between Surfers Paradise and St Kilda.

'Well, what do you reckon, Hank?' said Les. 'We head for those rocks?'

Hank gave a weather eye and adjusted his baseball cap. He got on his bike, nodded, then like John Wayne leading the troops out of Fort Bravo started pedalling off towards the rocks in the distance.

Norton couldn't believe how easy it was belting the old bike along the beach. The tyres were hard and dug in, it had heaps of weight and once you got it into top gear it skimmed across the firm wet sand like it was jet propelled. Norton hit the brakes and skidded all over the place. Look out America, he laughed to himself. Here comes Les Norton. BMX Bandit.

89

Hank, on the other hand, was pedalling slowly along like an old primary school teacher taking herself to church on Sunday. He wasn't even in top gear and already he was doing it tough, plus he didn't appear all that keen to get his shiny new 'Italian' racer splashed with salt water. Les watched him for a few moments then turned around and cruised up alongside.

'So how's it going, Hank?'

'I'm doing just fine,' puffed the American, wobbling along in second gear.

'Yeah. That's good.' Norton pedalled along with him for a while through and around the people walking along the beach, but it didn't take long to get punishingly boring, present company included. 'Well, I might have a bit of fun. I'll catch up with you towards those rocks.' Hank didn't reply as Norton slowed up and let him get a few yards in front.

Okay, thought Les. It's mug lair time. Let's see what this fifty dollar special can do. He threw the old bike into top gear, stood up on the pedals and zoomed past Hank like he was standing still. In no time Les was again whizzing along the beach, warm wind in his hair the tyres crackling and hissing almost musically as they zipped across the hard moist sand. There was a scattering of people walking past but spread out enough so you wouldn't hit them. A little kid ran up on Norton's left, Norton veered right, straight into a few inches of water washing across the beach. The old bike screamed across the incoming wave, spraying sea water in every direction and all over Les. Norton roared with delight as it splashed across his face and sunglasses. After that, Les just pedalled faster and faster, straight across every little wave rolling up along the beach, spraying more water everywhere. It was great, and nobody seemed to give a stuff. Les criss-crossed the beach then zoomed up onto the dryer sand where he'd noticed those tidal pools. They were luke warm and about a foot deep. Norton went through them like Wayne Gardner, and any people walking or sitting nearby got doused. He flogged the bike through the pools, along the beach then down the rise from the pools, flat out into the sea. The bike stopped dead in about a metre of water and Les would have done himself an injury only he flung himself over the handlebars to land flat on his back in the ocean, just managing to save his sunglasses as he did. Laughing like a loon, Norton picked up his bike from were it was lying in the water, climbed aboard and got going again. Norton was making a complete dill of himself and should have been thoroughly ashamed. He wasn't: not in the least. While he was making a fool of himself, though, Les had been keeping an eye on Hank. He was back about half a kilometre and the rocks were a little closer than that in front now. Dripping with water, Les again turned back and pulled up alongside Hank. Boofhead's face was starting to get a bit of colour up, and it wasn't from the sun.

'So how's it goin', Hank?' asked Les.

'I told you,' puffed Hank. 'I'm doing just fine.'

'Yeah. It's heaps of fun ain't it? I told you to get yourself a bike.'

They pedalled along in silence, winding in and out of the punters. Hank seemed to be taking it all very seriously instead of just getting out and having a bit of fun. Norton got the feeling Hank was a bit allergic to any strenuous exercise. Despite their slow pace, Les noticed the rocks at the end getting closer.

'Hey, Hank,' he said. 'Can your bike do this?'

'What?'

'Hang in there, Charlie Brown, and I'll show you.'

Les took off his sunglasses and pedalled past Hank up the slope near the tidal pools, where he sat on his bike for a moment waiting for the water to recede. As soon as there was a washout, he jumped up on the pedals, slipped the old bike into top gear and belted down the slope across the wet sand, and with spray flying everywhere rode straight into the surf again. As soon as the waves hit, he jumped up, put one foot on the handlebars, another on the frame, then 'hung five' for about a second before somersaulting over the front of the bike onto his back. It wouldn't have been enough to earn you a place in the stuntman's Hall of Fame, but it was definitely enough to get you thrown off the beach for being a complete dill. Les picked himself and the bike up out of the water, shook the water off, then pedalled back to Hank.

'There you go, Hank,' said Les, water still dripping everywhere. 'That's called a wombat-hang-five-with-tuck. Come on, let's see you have a go.' Hank ignored Les and pedalled along, trying to look as if he was above doing anything so stupid. Norton grinned at him. 'Yeah, I thought so, Hank. You mightn't be a tourist, but underneath you're just another yuppie with a new toy.' Les shook his head in disbelief. 'Fair dinkum. What am I gonna do?'

They reached the rocks, which turned out to be just an expanse of crumbly sandstone running out into the water and off into the distance. There was a concrete pathway and above this a few walled-off houses with cactus plants and the odd stumpy tree in the front overlooking the ocean. Hank rested his bike against the wall; Les did the same and without taking his clothes off jumped straight in the ocean to flounder around in the water while Hank floundered against the wall trying to get his breath back. Les flopped around, checking out a number of names carved in the sandstone. It was sort of nice, but it could have been a beach in Saudi Arabia it was that hot and the water so salty and tepid. Les would have killed for a cold, freshwater shower. A number of punters strolled past, taking in the sea breeze. There were definitely no fit-looking bikini girls like Norton was used to back at Bondi, and the politest thing Les could say about the men was that none of them looked like they were starving. In fact, surmised Norton, if a famine ever hit Florida they'd probably eat each other. After a while Hank looked like he was ready to leave, which meant Les had to go also. They mounted up, with Hank once more leading the platoon and Les bringing up the rear. They'd got about a mile or so with Hank wheezing and Les playing 'splashies' along the water's edge, when Les turned around to see that Hank had got off his bike and was pushing it across the dry sand. Hello, thought Les. John Wayne's horse has gone lame and he's going to have to shoot it. He pedalled back and stopped alongside Hank.

'What's up?'

'I want to go to the store.'

Another trail led up from the beach, they followed that to the street then pedalled along till they got to the main road and a small shopping centre, stopping outside a mini-supermarket. Inside, the air-conditioning felt like the Steppes and there looked like millions of different brands of cold drinks. Les would have been content to keep going and have a drink when they finished, but he ended up with a bottle of something called Lime Gatorade. When he got outside Hank had a can of Coke in one hand and a cigarette in the other. It was something Les had never seen or experienced before — getting some exercise and having to stop in the middle while someone had a cigarette. He drank his Gatorade and stepped back to escape the fumes.

'That was a good ride,' said Hank, very matter-of-factly. 'I always knew I still had it.'

'Yeah, you ride like the wind,' said Les. 'Only because your bike's a lot better than mine.'

Hank sucked in a lungful of smoke along with a supercilious smile. 'You noticed, huh?'

'How could I not notice? It was almost poetry in motion.'

They eventually finished their drinks and headed back to the beach.

They pedalled along, Les still ripping it up near the water's edge and Hank plugging along further up towards the dry sand. The Coke and a cigarette seemed to have sparked him up a bit somehow; he was going a bit faster and Norton got this feeling Hank was planning something. Les was a few yards in front, after splashing through some more water, and was about to take off again when suddenly Hank tore past him in top gear like a man possessed. About fifty yards ahead was a pool of water a few feet wide that some kids must have dug. There were a couple of sandcastles on either side of the pool and a wall of sand around the edge a few inches high. Hank went for it. Hey, go killer, thought Les. Hank burst through the first wall okay and tore through the shallow water: Norton was impressed. With water spraying out on either side Hank got up on the pedals to crash through the opposite wall. He was going like a rocket too and looking good. But as he hit the other tiny wall of sand the front forks snapped, the handlebars dropped and Hank sailed over the front. He did a quick somersault and finally landed on his back in a tangle of arms and legs. He was lucky he didn't break his neck. The bike fell back into the pool, the front wheel all buckled up and the back wheel still spinning like a wobbly roulette wheel. Norton screeched to a halt alongside Hank. Unlike the American's, Norton's face was jubilant.

'Mate,' said Les excitedly, 'you did it. A full-frontal-wombat-with-tuck. That's got to be one of the ballsiest things I've ever seen. You're no yuppie, Hank. You're a fuckin' thrillseeker. What made you decide to do it? You made mine look pretty tame too, I have to admit.'

'I didn't try anything,' hissed Hank. 'The fucking front forks broke.'

'What? Bullshit! That's a Clive Masters Villawood.' Norton looked astounded. 'I don't believe it.'

No doubt about it, though, Hank's bike had collapsed just like the ones Les read about back home. Hank's $350 Italian Sports Racer was a lemon. Another Australian had shit on him. Hank was on his hands and knees, covered in wet sand, still trying to figure which way was up. Les laid his bike down and went to give him a hand up. As he did, Les couldn't believe his eyes. The same fifty dollar bill was in Hank's back pocket and had edged out. Les looked at it again, looked at the sky for temporary forgiveness then removed it the same as he did before and put it in his pocket as Hank rocked unsteadily on his feet.

'So what do you want to do now, Hank?' asked Norton.

'My bike's still going. Can I give you a lift?' For some weird reason Les started singing an old Rolf Harris song. 'Did you think I would leave you lying, when there's room on my bike for two...'

Hank's eyes spun round, his whole body seemed to quiver. 'I don't need a goddamn lift!'

Hank picked up what was left of his bike and began trudging back to the car. Les pedalled alongside him for as long as he could, offering his condolences, before finally heading back to the pick-up where he could have a good laugh in peace.

Hank eventually arrived, scowled at Les, then threw what was left of his bike in the back and climbed in the front.

'Where to now?' asked Les.

'Back to that goddamn bike shop.'

'I should jolly well think so too.'

When they got there the goddamn bike shop was closed. Till Tuesday. Norton thought Hank was going to go completely under this time, he was ranting and raving that much. Back in the car his face looked like an eggplant.

'Can you believe that?' he fumed, when he finally stopped shaking enough to light a cigarette.

'No,' answered Les. 'It's got me stuffed. I thought in America shops opened around the clock and it was all service.' Les watched Hank dragging on his smoke. 'Still, when it's all boiled down, it does serve you right, mate.'

'What do you mean, serves me right, you jerk? The fucking front forks on that sonofabitch snapped!'

'Fair enough. But all's I'm saying is, you shouldn't have bought some fancy wog brand of bike.' Les nodded to the back of the pick-up. 'Look at mine. Roadmaster Star. Delaware Bike Company USA. I wouldn't have bought it if it had of been some wog thing. While I'm here I'll be buying American, mate. It pays dividends.'

Hank sucked more smoke into his lungs and let it burst out again. It hadn't been a very good day, either for the pocket or the ego. In fact, if they'd have taken every rotten day Hank had ever had and stacked them one on top of the other, it's doubtful they would have made a day as rotten as this one.

'So where to now, mate?' asked Les.

Hank sucked in some more smoke and hit the ignition. 'Home.'

'You're the boss.'

Norton didn't say a great deal on the way home. There wasn't much he could say. Though he did mention that if Hank wanted to go out for a drink somewhere that night Les would be only too happy to shout. Hank muttered something along the lines of he'd think about it. It had been a great day for Les. Watching Hank buy that shonky bike then go on his arse was almost as good as watching him get covered in shit. He was the original Sad Sack, no doubt about it, and no wonder his girl left him and he had no mates. But Les also had that condo, or whatever they called it, to check out. He doubted if Hank would want to go over there this afternoon, the mood he was in, so he'd have to leave that till first thing tomorrow. But Les would be there, even if he had to go by pushbike or walk.

By the time they got back to Swamp Manor Hank looked rooted, both mentally and physically. He had a sand rash across his chin, on his knees, down one shoulder and around his elbow. Les could see his arse and back was aching and though he tried to hide it Hank was limping when they got out of the car. He muttered something about Les calling over to his house at nine. Norton watched Hank limp off home with what was left of his bike under his arm and tried not to laugh. It was impossible. Norton guessed that if they did go out that night it wouldn't be for very long.

Norton got his bike from the back of the pick-up, found a hose near the front verandah and washed all the sand and salt water off it, giving himself a good hosing while he was at it. The sun was still high in the sky and, unlike Hank, Les was still raring to go. There was nothing to do hanging around Swamp Manor in the heat. Why not belt down to that supermarket, get some more exercise and a few goodies while I'm at it?

Mrs Laurel had left the map on his bed in a large envelope with what looked like four travel books. Les spread the road map of Siestasota out on his bed. The place didn't look all that big, just spread out, and the main roads seemed to be in some kind of grids. The bigger roads were marked with numbers: 301, 75, 41, 780. Where they'd gone diving and cycling was on a long narrow spit, the Gulf of Mexico was on one side and the mainland side was called Siestasota Bay. Les could pick out the bridge they went over: Hockney Point Drive. Main Street was down there and back to Tampa was that way. Uh huh, thought Les. Siestasota shouldn't be hard to get around. Mrs Laurel marked where the house was and how to get to the supermarket. It only looked about two blocks away. Les got some more money, put on a sweatband, threw the map in his backpack and, wearing the same damp clothes, pedalled off towards the supermarket.

He went past the house where he bought the bike in the first place, got onto another road, then onto some monstrous one that led in the direction of the supermarket. It was still dead flat with vacant lots, an orchard here and there, a few stores, a couple of Texaco garages and not much else except housing estates or homes with 'old glory' or the odd Confederate flag flopping on a pole outside in the non-existent breeze. There was no one around, no buses, no other bikes, just huge cars and trucks all coming at him on the wrong side of the road. The footpath was deserted and almost as big as a road. Les stuck to it but the traffic roaring past still put the wind up him and he wasn't looking forward to the day he'd eventually have to hire a car and get in amongst it. After a while Les realised why Mrs Laurel had given him that odd look when he said he didn't need a car to get to the supermarket because he had a bike. He'd been pedalling like mad for over twenty minutes and it was still nowhere in sight. A block, or one of those grids on the map, was about five miles long. But it was all easy going, Les enjoyed the exercise and you didn't have to worry about pedestrians. Finally the supermarket, called Kash 'n' Karry, loomed up on Norton's left; all he had to worry about now was crossing the road. Every road at the intersection looked about twenty lanes wide, jammed with cars going everywhere they shouldn't, and there was no way Les could figure the lights out. He pressed the 'Walk' button, but you'd have a beard down to your knees waiting for it to change. Evidently pedestrians in Florida were regarded as some sort of feral pest. Rather than take his life in his hands, or grow old waiting for the lights, Les got off his bike, chanced a break in the traffic, then holding it with one hand sprinted like Gunsynd across to the supermarket.

It might have been just another suburban shopping centre by Florida standards, but compared to anything in Australia it was huge. There were video stores, clothing shops, drugstores, other shops and an endless array of restaurants and fast food shops all set round a parking lot that would have held the Solomon Islands. Huge, over-weight Americans, wearing shorts, T-shirts and Elmer Fudd caps were either getting in or getting out of huge, overweight cars or walking round the shaded part of the shopping centre stuffing themselves with hot-dogs and ice creams or with their faces jammed in what looked like plastic buckets full of soft drink and ice. There was a bike rack outside the supermarket with three or four bikes chained to it. Not having a chain and wondering if there might be someone in Siestasota who needed his old pushbike more than he did, Les took it inside and leant it against one wall next to a drink vending machine.

Inside, the supermarket was equally massive and air-conditioned enough to make snow. The staff, wearing candy-striped shirts, tiny red bowties and red Elmer Fudd caps, were all smiles and looked ridiculous. A can of soft drink cost thirty-five cents in the machine; Les found a dime and a quarter, got a can of Grape Crush and joined the other shoppers moving along aisles long enough and wide enough to hold the South Australian Grand Prix. The aisles were stacked floor-to-ceiling with an unending variety of food and just about anything you wanted. Now what do I need? mused Les. Just some cereal, milk, orange juice, maybe some sliced ham and something to make a salad. Norton found the cereal section and stood there blinking like Scotty had just beamed him down to the wrong planet. Forget about your simple old soggies like Corn Flakes and Rice Bubbles. Sure, they were all there. But what about something with bran in it? Certainly. What would you like?

Double Pecan Bran, Grape Bran, Wheat Bran, All Bran, Some Bran, Oat Bran, 30% Bran, 50% Bran, Raisin Bran, Nut Bran, Multi Bran, Raisin Crisp Bran, Raisin Nut Bran. Cinnamon Nut Bran, Blueberry Bran, Crunchy or Non-crunchy Bran, Almond Bran, Banana Bran, Triple Bran, Organic Bran. Bran Bran, the baker man, stole a pig and away he ran.

Milk? Well of course you're going to need milk. Slim Fast, Vitamite Imitation Low Fat, Lactoid, Liquid Coffee Mate, Mocha Cooler, Irish Cream, Hazelnut, Amaretto, Half 'n' Half, Light 'n' Lively, Vitamin D, Multi Vitamin, 1% Low Fat, 2% Low Fat, A-Plus, Non-Fat, Acidophilus.

Something to put on your lettuce, tomato and cucumber? No worries, mate. Peppercorn Ranch, Honey Dijon, Honey Sesame, Caesar, South-Western, Catalina, Blue Cheese, Chunky Blue Cheese, Cucumber and Onion, Mexican Pepper, Louisiana Cajun, Russian, Country French, Honey Mustard, Paul Newman — how did he get here? thought Les — plus others, and all in Lite, Low-Cal, Oil Free and Cholesterol Free. And if you wanted something to slop on your chops or sausages there were at least three million kinds of sauces, from Texas Best to Tennessee Sunshine, Hickory Smoke to Bayou Shrimp.

Orange juice? Why drink plain, boring old orange juice? Why not Orange Cranberry, Orange Strawberry, Orange Banana, Orange Banana Blueberry? Apple Cranberry, Grape Apple, Apple Chantilly, Guava Cranberry, Raspberry Cranberry, Mountain Cherry. White Grape, Dark Grape, Pink Grapefruit, White Grapefruit, Prune

Juice, Clamato. You don't want fruit juice? Try some cordial. Stompin' Banana Boy, Fruity Bubble-gum, Boppin' Betty, Forest Fruit Punch, Hawaiian Fruit Punch, Juicy Blue. And as for that Lime Gatorade Les got down the beach, here it was in every flavour on the planet — plus it came in Low Cholesterol, Low Fat, Low Sodium, Low Salt, how low can you go? Power Burst and Gatorade Lite. Norton was going to buy some bread and butter, but when he saw two signs in front of the half-mile long butter cabinet saying, 'Whipping Butter' and 'I Can't Believe It's Not Butter', he went into a tailspin. Beam me out of here, Scotty, for Christ's sake.

Norton finished up with a packet of Corn Flakes, a carton of plain milk, orange juice and a packet of Hickory Smoked, US Prime Georgia Ham Steaks. Something called Buffalo Wings caught his eye so he thought he'd indulge in a carton of those from the hot food bar and another can of Grape Crush, which Norton got into while he sat outside in the heat and checked out the punters. The Buffalo Wings turned out to be chicken wings in some kind of hot orange sauce that felt like liquid sugar soap. He ate most of them, turfed the rest, then pedalled back to Swamp Manor.

The orange juice was pretty good and Les was glad he bought two containers because in the heat half the first one went down in one go. The ham was quite tasty too. Les made a sandwich thick enough to chock a Neptune bomber, washed it down with some of Mrs Laurel's delicious coffee, then feeling more than contented retired to his sumptuous quarters.

After a lengthy shower Les found he was a little more tired than he expected, which he put down to the sun and heat on top of two fairly long bike rides. Plus one monstrous ham sandwich sitting in his stomach. While he was getting cleaned up Les had a bit of a think; but there wasn't all that much to think about. With any sort of luck he'd be out of Swamp Manor in the morning and the earlier the better. So if he didn't have a late night it wouldn't worry him all that much. Just as long as they went out somewhere for a while and had a few drinks. Les figured Hank wouldn't be feeling all that chipper either, though he wouldn't admit it to Les. But they'd go out — especially with Les paying. Wonder where we'll go this time, thought Les, as he ironed a pair of jeans. Bet we don't go to Club BandBox. When he finished his jeans, Les ironed the dampness and wrinkles out of the fifty dollar bill he snookered off Hank and slipped it on top of his wedge. S'pose I got to give the poor bludger something for letting me stay here, he chuckled quietly. Before long Les was looking and smelling okay in his jeans and a white, Emu Bitter T-shirt. He left the lamp on in his room but stopped for a moment at the front door of the house. There was a light on in the loungeroom and light coming from underneath a long wooden sliding door in the far wall, plus the sound of a TV. Les figured that would be Mrs Laurel's bedroom, which was why he didn't see all that much of her. She'd have it air-conditioned and probably stay in there as much as possible to keep away from Boofhead. Les mightn't miss Swamp Manor and Hank, but he'd miss Mrs Laurel. She was a real sweetie and had a ton of class. When I get a car I might call out and see her, bring her a little present. Next thing Les was knocking on Hank's door. He heard a voice grunt something and let himself inside.

Hank was seated on the lounge, wearing the usual chatty jeans, an unironed yellow shirt and sneakers, smoking what was probably his two hundredth cigarette while he watched the last minutes of some old Steve Martin video on his stuffed-up TV. He didn't acknowledge Norton's presence so Les carved a space through the cigarette smoke, sat on the lounge opposite and watched the video finish. An incident in another Steve Martin film Les had seen, not the one Hank was watching, made Les chuckle. It was about a fireman with a big nose or something.

'Yeah, he's a funny bludger alright, that Steve Martin,' said Norton. 'A comic genius just like Woody Allen. And a good family man too.'

Hank's eyes spun briefly towards Les like he was denouncing him. 'He's not a comic genius. He's not even in the same realm as Woody Allen!'

Les had to think for a second. 'Shit! Did I say that, did I? I'm sorry. I was just voicing an opinion. It won't happen again.'

'Steve Martin's not a comic genius.'

'No, you're right. I was completely out of order. In fact, when I think about it, Steve Martin's a complete and utter arse. He's about as funny as spending three days on a swamp with Norman Bates.'

Hank glared suspiciously at Les. 'Who?'

'A bloke I know back in Australia.' Les watched as Hank got up to remove the video and thought how lovely it would be to boot him straight up the arse. 'So what are we doing... knackers.'

Hank sat back down and finished his cigarette. 'There's a bar on Main got a band. We'll have a look there, then I have to take a trip across town. I'm not having a late one. I got things to do tomorrow.'

Les nodded through the fumes at Hank. 'Suits me. I want to have a look at that condo tomorrow. Get it out of the road early. What time do you want to get going in the morning?'

Hank seemed to look a little oddly at Les. 'Around nine.'

'Give yourself time to have another three-bagger.'

'What?'

'That'll give me time to have my bags packed.'

Hank shook his head. 'We'll go and have a look at the place first.'

Norton immediately sensed Captain Rats was playing some weird game of cat and mouse with him. Go along with it though. It's only for one more night. 'Yeah okay. I'd hate to think I was moving into some dump — especially after this.' Hank's expression didn't change as he sucked on his cigarette. 'Oh, before we go any further, I reckon you would have used a bit of juice and that today. So here's another fifty bucks.' Les pulled out his wedge and handed Hank the freshly ironed fifty dollar bill. 'There you are, mate. Straight out of the bank. And you needn't worry, there's plenty more where that came from.'

Hank almost snatched the crisp, shiny fifty out of Norton's hand. His eyes spun round as he looked at it, almost as if he was examining the serial number. This time he put it in his front pocket. Bugger it, Les cursed to himself. I'll have a hard time getting it out of there. Oh well. For a second Les thought Hank was going to say thanks. Instead, he stubbed out his cigarette and got to his feet.

'Let's go.'

'Okey-doke.' Norton dutifully fell in behind and tailed Hank out to the pick-up, laughing quietly to himself as he watched Hank trying not to limp.

Norton didn't say much as they were driving along; there wasn't a great deal he could say. Holding a conversation with Captain Rats was like trying to talk Hitler into changing his battle plans. He was the greatest know-all Les had ever come across, even for a yank. There was no doubt about that. Now you weren't even allowed to have an opinion when he was around. Les was still curious, however, as to just how big a prick he actually was. While they were driving along Les thought he'd give Hank a kind of 'travelling ink blot test'. They sped in and out of the traffic, past the houses and shops, before stopping at another set of lights. As they did a shiny maroon car pulled up alongside. It had tinted windows, lots of chrome and the way it was chopped off at the boot reminded Les of an overblown Volvo.

'Gee, that's a nice car,' said Les. 'I wouldn't mind getting one of those to run around in while I'm over here.'

Hank moved his cigarette and leaned over to see what Les was looking at. 'You call that a good car? It's a pile of junk. Every jerk from out of state drives round in one of those.'

'Really?' answered Norton. 'Oh! Well, I won't bother getting one of those then.'

They got a bit closer to downtown, the roads got a little narrower and they had to slow up for a line of traffic. Les spotted a rambling kind of two-storey house on the side of the road with well-kept trees out the front and gables on the windows; it was nothing special, but the way it was painted brown and yellow made it stand out from the others and gave it a certain charm.

'Hey look at that house over there, Hank. Isn't it a ripper? All those nice gables and trees.' Les shook his head in sham admiration. 'I could handle living in a nice place like that.'

Hank sneered and blew smoke towards where Les was looking. 'You call that a good house, do you? It probably belongs to some nigger pimp.' Hank shook his head disdainfully. 'I should take you down the Keys one day and show you what a decent house looks like.'

With a sardonic smile spread across his face Les turned to Captain Rats. 'Would you really go to all that trouble for me? Gee, you're a good bloke, Hank.'

Congratulations Boofhead, Les smiled to himself. You just passed the ink blot test with flying colours. You are a twenty-five carat, 110 per cent prick. No, I'm wrong there. A moll up the Cross once told me that pricks are useful. You're a dead prick.

Next thing they'd pulled up in Main Street, outside some shops and restaurants not far from Toby's bar.

They left the car and walked a short distance to a place called Gator Man's. It was a two-storey bar that took up most of the corner, frosted glass windows wrapped right around the corner and across the front was painted 'Gator Man's' in green and red. The awning showed a cowboy and an alligator wearing ten-gallon hats, arm in arm having a drink together. As you stepped inside there was a smallish bar on your right, tables and stools, a small dancefloor with a set of stairs next to it, more tables and stools and a bigger bar down the back. It was very nicely done out with lots of lamps and mirrors, giving it that classy, old style ambience Les had seen in movies about New Orleans. The best thing, though, was the band. They were called the Platinum Tones — four piece, all white in their thirties and howling. The lead singer had short, neat blond hair and rimless glasses and looked like a school teacher, but that was where the resemblance ended. He might have looked a little square, but he shook like a jelly, wriggled like a snake and sang rock 'n' roll like Norton had never heard, while behind him the band scorched out every note tighter than Scrooge McDuck's money belt. The punters were a good style of people, crammed onto the dancefloor, seated at the tables or standing around tapping their feet. There was no shortage of attractive women. But girls nor not, Les would have stayed just for the music, the place was jumping. Despite being straddled with the biggest lemon in Florida, Norton's mood changed the moment he walked in the door.

'Holy bloody shit!' he exclaimed, as the lead singer whipped out a harmonica and let go some licks that singed your eyebrows. 'How good's this?'

Hank gave a cool, almost uninterested shrug, which Les just about expected. If the Rolling Stones were on stage with the queen mother out front topless and juggling chainsaws he'd have done the same thing. Les was a little curious as to why Hank, being such an egg roll, would want to come to a place as bopping as this in the first place. He probably wanted to but never had the money — or the company. And Les was both. For a short time, yes, thought Norton, as he reached for his pocket.

'So what'll you have?'

Hank gave another cool shrug. 'Beer.'

Les stepped through the punters to the smaller bar near the front door. The barmaid had frizzy blonde hair, a red, Gator Man's T-shirt and a nice wide smile that got even wider when Les spoke.

'One beer thanks — any bloody thing in a glass'll do. Plus a nice bourbon sour and a frosted margarita.'

'Youuuuu got it, buddy,' smiled the girl.

The delicious drinks arrived, accompanied by another smile; Les left a good tip, picked up his two drinks and joined Captain Rats. Hank saw the drinks in Norton's hands and his eyes started to spin round in a sort of paranoid disbelief.

'Yours is on the bar,' purred Les. 'I couldn't carry three.'

Hank's eyes spun around some more before he stormed over and got his beer. By the time he got back, Les had demolished his first delicious in three swallows and was doing pretty much the same thing to the margarita.

While Les was slurping into his second drink, the lead singer removed the remote microphone, the lead guitarist did the same with his Fender and they went for a stroll among the punters, ending up in the street out the front. It was great. The two of them were strolling around, shoving the mike in people's faces, while back on stage this scorching rock 'n' roll was still thundering away from just a bass and drums. They got back on stage to the roar of the crowd and continued to scorch their way through some more good rock 'n' roll, while Norton continued to scorch his way through some more good drinks. Gator Man's was nicely air-conditioned but the music couldn't help but make you get a sweat up; Les lost count after margarita number six and bourbon sour number four. He bought Hank one more beer then let him get his own after that. Hank bought a couple of drinks but didn't bother getting Les any. Whoever thought up that saying, 'Wouldn't shout if a shark bit him', surmised Les, definitely must have had Boofhead in mind at the time. Eventually the Platinum Tones took a well-deserved break to more tumultuous applause, and much drunken whistling and stomping from Norton.

'Shit! How good were they?' said Les, still clapping away. Hank, who hadn't bothered to applaud, gave another noncommittal shrug and said nothing. Les told himself he'd be cool and not let Hank get under his skin. But with a sudden rush of tequila and whiskey pumping through him he just couldn't help himself, especially after music like that. 'Hank,' he said tightly. 'Is there anything, apart from that dopey pile of guns you got back at your

106

place, you do like?' Hank's eyes spun around everywhere except at Norton, but he didn't say anything. 'Don't answer right away, Hank,' continued Les. 'Think on it for a while. There has to be something. In the meantime, I'm going for a look upstairs.' He took a slurp of his drink and let his eyes run around the bar. 'Do you think you'll be safe down here on your own for a few minutes, Mel? There's a lot of girls around.'

Hank gave another shrug. 'I'm cool.'

Norton tipped down the rest of his drink. 'Yeah. Like a fur coat in a bushfire.' He put the empty glass on the nearest table and walked towards the stairs.

This is being done to me deliberately, thought Les, as he trotted up the carpeted staircase. Back in Australia I would have slowly choked that goose to death. But now I'm learning to be more tolerant. I'm going to become a better person. Lovely Les they'll be calling me after this. He momentarily glanced upwards. That's if I make it through the night. And the fuckin' morning.

When he got to the top of the stairs Les stopped dead and gave a double, triple blink. One word couldn't describe it. It was classy, plush, opulent and just plain beautiful. One half was a restaurant and bar, the other was just like a huge drawing room in some old, turn of the century mansion. The furniture was fully restored, old Chesterfields and beautifully carved and varnished mahogany or redwood chairs and tables. Tasselled lampshades sat in the corners and soft lights clung to the walls, gently reflecting onto huge, gilt-edged mirrors set round the walls and two exquisitely carved marble fireplaces. Paintings and old photos hung between the mirrors or round the walls and floor-to-ceiling glass-paned doors hung with blinds or red velvet drapes overlooked the street. More tastefully carved dressers and conversation tables were placed carefully around a beige carpet, which was that thick and soft they probably hired a green keeper to look after it. It was like stepping back into another era, into something ... Les couldn't seem to think of for the moment. So he just stood there blinking.

'Like it, do you?'

Norton turned slightly. Standing next to him was a tall, well-built man in his early thirties wearing a light blue shirt. He wasn't hard looking, but he had a square jaw and a confident smile with short, curly brown hair going a little prematurely grey near his ears.

'Like it?' replied Les absently. 'Mate, it's the bloody grouse.' He turned to the man talking to him. 'What, are you the owner, are you?'

'No, I'm the manager.'

Les shook his head in wonder and curiosity. 'You know, this place reminds me of something. But I can't bloody think what.'

'A brothel?'

Norton snapped his fingers. 'That's it. I mean ...'

The manager smiled. 'That's what this place used to be. The most high-class brothel in Southern Florida.'

'Fair dinkum. Jesus, I'll tell you what, mate, it's something else.'

'Used to be called the Siestasota Gentleman's Club. The rooms were upstairs. The girls used to sit around here. Senators, judges, high rollers from all over Florida. This is where they'd come to ...' the manager grinned, 'shall we say ... enjoy themselves.'

'Well I'll be fucked,' said Les unconsciously.

The manager chuckled. 'No offence ... mate. But you'd've been safe. Even with your best dress on.' Norton had to laugh. 'So what are you drinking?'

'Well I ...' shrugged Les.

The manager caught the dark-haired barman's eye. 'Give this guy whatever he wants.'

'Hey, thanks, mate.'

'Our pleasure. Take a look around, I'll probably see you downstairs.'

The manager disappeared; Les ordered a frosted margarita. It came in a brandy balloon big enough to hold a dozen giant carp, and was unbelievably delicious. Shit, this must be that 'suthin hospitality' I keep hearing about. Les took his time finishing his drink while he checked out the paintings and photos of old Florida, moving very discreetly among the clientele. For a second he flashed back to the Kelly Club. Jesus! Wouldn't Price and George love to see this place. After a while he reluctantly went downstairs and rejoined Boofhead.

Hank was standing in the same place, drinking another beer, sucking moodily on another cigarette. Standing among the other clean-looking punters he looked like he'd come to collect the empty bottles.

'So how've you been while I was away, Richard Gere? Still got your cherry?'

Hank's eyes spun all over the place as he took a monstrous drag on his cigarette and tried to ignore Les. There were two girls sitting on stools at the table next to them; both brunettes around thirty, one had on a blue polka-dot dress, the other a black top and a blue skirt. They were no oil paintings, but they looked happy enough and Les was in one of those moods where he would have put a mag on with a deaf parking cop.

'How are you goin' there, girls?' he said, more out of friendliness than trying to chat them up.

'We're doin' just fine, thanks,' answered the one in the black top.

'That's good,' said Les. 'I ain't going too bad myself. In fact, I'm just going to the bar to fill up. Could I have the pleasure of buying you two young ladies a drink?'

The two girls blinked at each other for a second then turned to Les. 'Okay,' said the one in the black top again. 'I'll have a Wild Turkey and dry.'

'And I'll have a vodka and clamato,' said the other.

'I'll be back quicker than a mother-in-law's kiss,' winked Les.

Norton returned with the girls' drinks, plus two more margaritas for himself. He almost wasn't going to get Hank a drink, but changed his mind and got him a beer, leaving it on the bar. As he placed the drinks on the table Les nodded to the bar. Hank muttered something under his breath before he went over and got it. Fuck you, you big tart, thought Les. I don't even feel like shouting you a drink, so the least you can do is get off your fat arse and get the bloody thing.

There was a quick 'cheers' as Les clinked the girls' glasses. 'So where are you from, girls — if I may be so rude as to ask?'

'Indiana,' replied the one in the polka-dot dress.

Norton took a thoughtful slurp on drink number one as Hank returned with his beer. 'Indiana? Don't they call people from there "hosers", or "hoosers" or something?'

' "Hoosiers",' said Black Top.

'Yeah,' nodded Les. 'That's it. What's it mean?'

Black Top gave a funny sort of smile. 'It's kinda short for "Who's ya". Hoosier momma. Hoosier poppa. You got it?'

'Yeah, I'm with you,' Les laughed happily. 'We got a place like that back home. It's called Tasmania.'

'Hey, I know that place,' said Black Top. 'That's where that little guy on the Bugs Bunny show comes from. The one with the huge mouth.'

'That's him,' said Les. 'Aaarrhgloogarharghgrrr-gloogh! Raaabittt!'

'Hey you're not bad!' laughed the girl in the polka-dots.

'I come from an old showbiz family back in Australia,' said Les. 'Va-veer-va-va-veer! That's all, folks.'

Black Top took a healthy slurp on her Wild Turkey. 'So what's your name?'

'Les.'

'I'm Lori. And this is Bobbie-Sue.'

Norton gave a double blink. 'Well cut me legs off and call me Shorty. Pleased to meet you, girls.'

Suddenly the girls seemed to notice Hank, standing next to them like a Lowes dummy. 'Who's your pal? Is he an aussie too?'

Les gave Hank a boozy once up and down. 'No. This is Vinny Luarali. Also known as Vinny the Bike. Vinny's from New York. You know what I'm sayin'. Hey, Vinny. Say hello to the girls.' For some reason Les found himself slipping into the bit of New Yorkese he'd picked up from Crystal Linx. Unfortunately it was going over with Hank like an attack of gout. He turned away and blew smoke towards the front door. 'Hey, Vinny. What is this, huh? Look at me when I'm talkin' to ya. Make yourself a san'wich. Have a glass of milk. You know what I'm sayin'?'

'He doesn't look very happy,' said Bobbie-Sue.

'No. Vinny's got things on his mind,' said Les, completely pofaced. 'He's down here from New York to do a hit. On a guy called Clive Masters. Ain't that right, Vinny?'

That, unfortunately, was enough for Hank. His eyes spun, his body shook, and his face seemed to go a funny colour. He threw down the rest of his beer and dumped the glass on the girls' table. 'We're leaving.'

'We are?' said Norton. 'What's wrong with here? Beautiful girls to talk to. Great music. Fantastic drinks. And we're loaded. You sure you're not an egg short of an omelette?'

'I told you. I have to take a trip across town. I'll meet you at the car.' Hank disappeared out the front door.

'Vinny the Bike,' said Lori. 'Vinny the Schmuck'd be more like it.'

'Christ! Where did you find him?' asked Bobbie-Sue.

Norton shook his head. 'Under a big wet rock at Tamarama, I think. I wish I'd bloody left him there.' Les downed margarita number two in one swallow. His eyes spinning, he reached across and gently pecked both girls on the cheek. 'Well, ladies, look's like Uncle Les has got to hit the toe. Maybe I'll see you down here again?'

'Okay. Nice talking to you, Les. You take care.'

'I'll sure do my best. See youse.'

Out in the car Hank's face looked like Charles Bronson's after they'd shoved a lemon in his mouth and squeezed it in a vice for about half an hour. The engine was running and he was sucking morosely on another cigarette. Norton figured that if he let Hank know he had the shits it would probably brighten up his miserable existence. The best way to get under Boofhead's skin would be to take the opposite tack — even if it did burn his arse. Gator Man's was one of the best little bars he'd ever been in. And it wouldn't have taken long to trade the two hoosiers in on something else. There was no shortage of good style women there. Not counting the fantastic music as well.

'Well, I'm glad you got me out of there, Hank. Those two sheilas were starting to give me the shits. And the band was alright, but it was too fuckin' loud.' Hank crunched the pick-up into gear and took off up Main Street. 'So where are we going now?'

Hank let go a burst of smoke through gritted teeth. 'I told you. The other side of town. Almond Crescent.'

Les clapped his hands and rubbed them briskly. 'Sounds alright to me. Any good bars over there? I might let you shout me a drink.'

They took a right on Main, Les thought he saw a sign saying 789. Next they were zipping along a palmtree-lined boulevard, past a marina full of boats bobbing gently in the moonlight, then over a bridge a lot longer and lower than the other one, finally coming out onto a circular park full of trees and gardens with streets full of shops and restaurants. In the soft glow from the street-lights and the shop windows it all looked very swish in a Double Bay, Toorak kind of fashion, except there were no high-rises. As they went anti-clockwise round the park they passed a busy bar, or nightclub, nestled among the other shops. The front was a wide open pair of folding glass doors with another large glass door on the right. Across the awning, written in white on blue above some little white waves, was 'Reggae Mambo's'. There were about a dozen or so people sitting at white plastic chairs and tables out the front and plenty of people inside. As they went past Les thought he heard a band playing.

'Hey Hank! That joint looks alright,' he said eagerly.

Hank didn't reply. He rounded the next corner and pulled up where the shops ended and the houses and flats began. On the opposite side of the road were more shops and further down, towards where the circle exited back towards the bridge, a genuine blue and white police car, the red, white and blue lights slowly blinking across the roof, had pulled a car over. A genuine American woman cop in a black uniform was flashing a torch over the car while her genuine American cop partner stood very watchfully close by. Bloody hell! thought Les. Warren was right. It's just like in the movies.

He watched as Hank took a long envelope from the glove box. 'You fancy having a drink at that bar round the corner?' he suggested.

'Maybe,' grunted Hank, as they got out and locked the pick-up.

'Suit yourself,' replied Les. 'It's just that it's giving me the shits having all this money and not being able to spend it. I mean, how would you feel?' Norton smiled to himself as that last sentence hit Captain Rats like someone had just thrown a Bowie knife in his back.

They walked over to some sort of gift and bric-a-brac shop. There was a mailing slot in the door just above the ground; Hank painfully bent down and slid the envelope into it. Hello, thought Les. Don't tell me someone actually owes prick features some money. Lord have mercy. Or could it be the other way round? Whatever it is, I don't think I'll bother to ask. Hank took a last expressionless look at the gift shop then started walking towards the corner. Hello, thought Les again. Looks like we're going for a few cool ones after all. Golllly!

Reggae Mambo's looked pretty good up close. It was all different shades of blue on white with a little mauve thrown in, with plenty of shrubs and ferns and colourful flowerbeds dotted with tropical plants all along the footpath. The crowd was orderly and dressed very casual but neat and was maybe a little younger than Gator Man's. Whatever it was, it had a noticeable, laid-back, holiday atmosphere about it. Christ! mused Les. Hank might be a shocking bloody dill, but through him I haven't been to a dud joint yet. A balding, barrel-chested bloke in shorts with a thick New York accent was checking IDs next to a small counter selling T-shirts on the way in. He gave them both a smiling once up and down; Les winked and smiled back. Inside were more chairs and tables and booths set under soft neon lighting and indoor plants. There was one long bar on your left, a kitchen behind that and a band playing country and western down the back in front of a fairly crowded dancefloor. Right of the bandstand a corridor ran down to the toilets, to the left was a fire exit. There were plenty of girls, a happy atmosphere and there was nothing wrong with the music being belted out either. Shit! thought Les. I'd better not start having too good a time or shithead'll probably want to leave. Ahh, fuck it. What am I gonna do, stand around looking as miserable as him?

'Put your money away, Hank,' commanded Les. Not that Captain Rats had the slightest intentions of producing any. 'I'll get them. What d'you want?'

'Tequila. Straight up. And a draught too.'

'Certainly, Mr Bond. Twist of lemon. Shaken not stirred.'

Les squeezed in between some people standing or seated round the bar and ordered his customary whiskey sour with a margarita chaser; Hank's beer arrived in a plastic mug this time and he didn't have to be told to come over and get it. They found a space a little towards the front door where Les knocked over his whiskey in about three good gulps. It was then that he realised why he was getting so roaring drunk: drinks in America were at least twice as strong as drinks back home. Well, God bless the United States of America, thought Norton, as he got rid of his empty glass and attacked delicious number two. Conversation with Captain Rats was limited to periods of brooding silence interspersed with cigarettes, so Les checked out the punters around him. There were several nice-looking girls, especially two black ones in mini-dresses; the blokes all looked very Joe College. Three tall blokes talking to four good-looking young girls at a booth near the wall caught his eye and Les thought he could detect an upper-class British accent drifting across the room. Delicious number two didn't last very long, Les grunted something to Hank about going down to check

114

out the band, got a cloud of silent cigarette smoke in reply, so he got himself another two margaritas and drifted down the front.

They were three piece with a drum machine, long hair, T-shirts and jeans, called themselves No Cents At All and played good, toe-tapping rock 'n' roll with a strong country flavour. Les boogied around on his own while he attacked his two drinks, checking out the band and the punters on the dancefloor; the girls seemed to get around okay but most of the blokes danced like they had a boiled egg jammed in their date. The band belted out the last words of a song. Les caught something about, 'We're two of a kind, workin' on a full house.' Then they paused between numbers. The lead singer dropped his guitar to one side and spoke into the mike with a twangy, mid-western drawl.

'Okay. Attitude check time.'

And the crowd all screamed out, 'Fuck you!'

'Attitude check.'

'Fuck you!'

'Attitude check.'

'FUCK YOU!!!'

'Yeah. And fuck Club BandBox too,' said the lead singer.

Well, I wonder what that was all about? Les laughed to himself. Must be some private joke among the natives. He watched them slip easily into another song, hung for a while, then drifted back through the crowd to Hank. He was his usual happy, vibrant self and fitted in with the neat young punters around him like a drug squad copper at a Nimbin music festival. Les had to talk about something: but what?

'Good band,' he finally said. Hank gave his usual non-committal shrug. 'I thought you'd like them,' said Les.

'I didn't say I did,' answered Hank.

'Didn't you? That's funny. I thought I saw the dummy's lips move.'

Les would have liked to have continued the conversation, but a curtain of nicotine silence seemed to slam

115

down between them. He got another two margaritas instead.

Norton had just finished his first drink when he heard a girl's voice next to him. 'So what do you know about emus?'

She was about five foot three, dumpy, had a pert face under short brown hair, was wearing a white T-shirt and baggy blue shorts. Her face was shiny with perspiration and she spoke with a soft Texan drawl. Les had to think for a moment then he realised she was looking at his T-shirt.

'What do I know about emus?' For some reason Norton's boozy mind flashed back to Randwick Races and all the punters scrambling round as Price rolled his money up and tossed it into the crowd. 'If I hadn't of been where they hang out in the first place, I wouldn't be stuck here with the world's greatest pelican.'

The girl looked puzzled. She didn't understand a word Les said, accent or not. 'Say what?'

'Sorry, sweetheart. I was thinking about something else. Actually, it's a brand of beer back in Australia.' Les gave her a quick once up and down while he tried to get his bearings. 'So what makes you ask anyway, you cheeky little devil?'

'My uncle runs an emu ranch back in Amarillo, Texas.'

'Yeah, that'd be right,' nodded Les. 'I saw something on the news about it before I left. They're having a lot of trouble with rustlers, of all bloody things. And all the farmers are running round with guns, just like the old wild west. Touch mah emus, pardner, and ah'll fill you full o' lead.'

'Hey, you better believe it, buddy. My uncle got hit twice. Them funny-lookin' critters are worth big money. They're like gold.'

Les shook his head. 'Bloody hell! And to think I got the dopey-looking things running wild all round my place.'

'You have? What, big ones?'

'Big emus at my place? Are you kidding? One walked into a garage up the road the other night and they shoved a hundred gallons of petrol in its arse before they realised what it was.' The girl just blinked. 'Well, fifty gallons anyway. It was only a young one.'

That was about all the suave, sophisticated Norton charm that was needed. By slowing down a bit when he spoke, which wasn't hard considering how drunk Les was, he was able to get a mag on. Her name was Terri, she'd been in Siestasota two years and worked in a restaurant around the corner as an assistant chef, which Les surmised meant kitchen hand. From the way she was sucking into the mug of beer she was holding and from her attitude in general, Les tipped her to be one of those pissy tarts that buzz around bars half picking up blokes, half full of shit. He told her he was a racehorse trainer back in Australia, he was in Florida for three weeks on a working holiday. He was here for a good time not a long time. Terri was with the four good-looking young girls who were talking to the three English blokes whose voices Norton had picked up on earlier. On closer inspection Les noticed the girls were better looking than he thought. They were also wearing little tops with a picture of a parrot wearing sunglasses and 'Havana Joe's' in red across the front. It was another restaurant round the corner and they all came down for a drink every night after work. Les was more than a bit keen at first; however, there were two ways of looking at this. He could go over and monster his way among the poms, but he was that drunk he'd probably only make a dill of himself; besides, they looked like they were splashing up and having a good enough time without him anyway. Also, it was odds on that if Hank saw him having a good time he'd come over and stuff things up completely. You could also bet Boofhead would want to go home soon the way he was still limping and moping around; when he bent down to put that letter in the door Les didn't think he was going to get back up again. And even if he did finish up with them, what was he going to do? He was more than a bit tired himself when it was all boiled down. He'd see them down here again and next time he'd probably have his own flat and car. Norton was right on both counts; Terri was just a

117

common camp follower. By the time he'd told her he'd catch up with her again, some other bloke had caught her eye and she left to join him. Then as Terri left, Hank loomed up on his left.

'I want to get going. I have to get some gas.'

'Gas?' retorted Les. 'What are we going home in? A hot-air balloon?'

'I have to get to the gas station before it closes.'

'Oh, my God!' drawled Les. 'You mean to say they don't have an all-night gas station in Sepposota? Oh my God! That's awful. Just awful.'

'Not where I can use my card,' sneered Hank, like he'd just scored a perfect squelch on Les.

'What about the fifty bucks I gave you? Don't tell me you've blown that already?'

Hank finished the last inch of his beer. 'Finish your drink. I'll see you out at the car.'

Welll, so much for Saturday night in Sepposota, burped Norton, as he watched Captain Rats storm off out the door. Ahh well, who gives a stuff? It can only get better. Les finished his drink and left. He was tired, drunk and busting for a leak anyway.

The conversation on the way home didn't reach any great heights. Les didn't expect it would, so he just rocked back and forth in a drunken mellow haze as they headed back out over the bridge, before pulling into some garage, or gas station.

Hello, thought Les, as he watched Hank slip a credit card into the bowser and start filling up, I've got a laugh on the seppos. Petrol's ninety-eight cents a litre, US. Then through his bleary, boozy eyes he saw it was ninety-eight cents a gallon. Which was closer to twenty cents a litre. And I've given that prick, how much? A hundred and fifty dollars? He could've filled the tank ten times over for that. The bastard, Norton grumbled to himself. And there's no chance of me getting that fifty back tonight either, it's right down the front of his jeans. Les was distraught.

Although his heart was nowhere near in it, when they

got back to Swamp Manor Les thanked Hank profusely for another wonderful night out; they'd have to do it again some time. Hank muttered something about how he'd see him in the morning and limped off to his place. Oh well, thought Les, as he piddled and splashed away beneath the stars and the Spanish Moss. A hundred and fifty bucks and a few drinks for three nights' board and accommodation ain't too bad I don't suppose. Hang on. It wasn't that much, was it? Les was still debating on this after he'd cleaned his teeth and was lying on his bed. Ahh, who gives a stuff? It's only money. It's not an arm and a leg.

Although it was hot and uncomfortable, before he knew it that old black cloud rolled in and Norton was snoring gently.

The face looking at Les in the mirror the following morning wasn't quite the face of a well man, and the stomach beneath it didn't feel like a greasy feed of bacon and eggs either. Nevertheless, he managed to get cleaned up and, after dropping another two Tylenols, climb into a pair of shorts and the same T-shirt as the night before, then wander into the kitchen for a feed of orange juice, coffee and cereal — especially some coffee. Norton was leaning against the bar in the kitchen, trying not to make too much noise or mess, when Mrs Laurel walked in wearing her dressing gown.

'Oh, hello, Les,' she said pleasantly. 'How are you this morning?'

Les nodded his head slowly. 'Not too bad thanks, Mrs Laurel. How's yourself?'

'I'm fine thank you. Would you like me to make you some breakfast?'

Norton shook his head even more slowly. 'No thanks, Mrs Laurel. I'm not very hungry.'

'Oh? Are you sure?'

'Positive, thanks. To tell you the truth, I had a bit to drink last night.'

'Oh!' Mrs Laurel smiled. 'Did you go out with Hank?'

119

Les nodded again and Mrs Laurel's expression seemed to change. 'Did you . . . have a good time?'

Les half smiled. 'I don't know about anybody else, but I did.'

Mrs Laurel tossed her head back slightly. 'Well good for you, Les. You're quite an amazing man.'

'And you're quite a lovely woman, Mrs Laurel,' replied Norton, returning her smile.

Mrs Laurel poured herself a cup of coffee and together they had a bit of a mag. Les told her he was going over to check out Laverne's condo and he might be moving out. Mrs Laurel looked genuinely disappointed. She was going to stay with her daughter for a few days later next week, Les had to promise he'd call in and see her before he left for home or wherever. Les said he would. They were chatting away and Norton's headache had all but gone when who should come stomping into the kitchen wearing his usual daggy jeans and T-shirt but the loving son, looking his usual cheery self. His eyes spun suspiciously round the kitchen, as if Les and his mother shouldn't even be there together let alone be having a pleasant conversation, before they briefly settled on Les.

'Well? What are you doing?'

'Nothin' much,' shrugged Les. 'Just having a bit of breakfast. What's it look like I'm doin'? Trying to bun your old lady?'

Hank blinked for moment. 'I'm going to the office.'

'Okay. You mind if I don't come with you? I don't particularly feel like hanging around in the heat. Interesting and all as it is up there.' Hank blinked again. 'What time'll you be back?'

Captain Rats shrugged. 'Around twelve.'

'Okay. Then we'll go and have a look at that condo. If you don't want to, just give me the keys and the address and I'll catch a cab over.'

Hank seemed to think for a second. 'I'll be back at twelve.'

'Alright. I'll see you then.' Hank turned and stormed out; a few seconds later Les heard his car revving. 'Do you know that bloke, do you, Mrs Laurel?'

'I'm not all that sure, Les,' replied Mrs Laurel. 'I think he lives down the back somewhere.'

They chatted away for a little while longer before Mrs Laurel retired to her air-conditioned bedroom-cum-study. This left Norton pretty much to his own devices, which weren't a great deal in the heat. He got his Walkman out and was going to lie on the bed and listen to a few tapes, but changed his mind. There was a slight breeze, some shade and an old wire chair just outside his back door. Les dropped his Walkman back on the bed, plonked his backside out in the garden and decided to read some more P.J. O'Rourke or maybe bone up on a bit more US culture.

Norton was chuckling away at P.J.'s satirical style when a quick movement in the trees caught his eyes. It was a pair of squirrels. They were grey and black with bits of white; very tiny with big, shiny ink black eyes. They made hardly any noise as they darted between the leaves and branches, just a brisk scurry among the shadows every now and again. Les had never seen squirrels before and was thinking how cute and inoffensive they looked when a couple of thoughts struck him. One was some dopey redneck yank he'd seen on TV before he left home bragging about his squirrel gun. Squirrel gun? Les screwed his face up. Why the fuck would you need a gun to kill those poor little things? What bloody harm are they doing? Then he thought of a gun book he'd glanced through at Hank's. It showed another boofheaded seppo wearing a ten-gallon hat, holding a Magnum in one hand and some poor little animal about as big as a canary in the other, and looking into the camera like he'd just taken Pork Chop Hill single handed. The flip. Then Les flashed onto some signs he'd noticed as they were driving around the beach area of Siestasota. BIRD SANCTUARY. NO SHOOTING. ANIMAL REFUGE. NO GUNS ALLOWED. Right in the middle of town almost. That would be like seeing a similar sign at Neilsen Park or on top of South Head. Norton and his family had blasted their share of pigs and rabbits and feral pests. But these ratbags seemed to want to shoot anything that moved. Then he thought of those three kids out at the target range. The right to bear arms, eh? Even if you're ten years old. Les shook his head as Chip and Dale disappeared onto the roof, their long fluffy tails waving in the air. Oh well, whatever turns you on, I suppose. And it's their country not mine. At least when they're shooting the animals they're bumping a few thousand of each other off as well. Like that dope in New York state that shot his mother in his backyard. He thought she was a deer. God bless America.

The human smile button returned; Les heard him pull up, put his book down and walked out the front he was that keen to get going. But he still had to try and act a little casual. Laurel had just got out of the car when Norton buttonholed him.

'So what's doing, Hank?'

'I got a couple of things to do yet.'

'Fair enough. I'll wait here for you.'

A couple of things took over half an hour. Les was expecting this so he got his sunglasses and the rest of one carton of orange juice and drank it next to the car while he waited. Hank finally appeared and they took off for the 'condo' or whatever it was. All the way over Norton couldn't help but wonder why the hell he just didn't pack his gear and take it with him in the first place and save a trip.

The place was called Greenwood Estate, 4701–4771 Manatee. Which was all Les saw on the fifteen-minute drive over; a couple of small shopping centres and mile after mile of walled-off housing estates full of home units and townhouses set along these massive wide roads. Old glory was flapping out the double front entrance next to a wooden sign painted green and white. Hank turned left onto a speed hump, then it was more speed humps and parking spaces like they'd driven onto Rose Bay Golf Links, only they'd walled it off, tarred most of it over and filled it full of townhouses. It was all yellow and black stucco concrete and well-kept gardens. As they drove past, Les noticed a couple of caretakers in blue shirts and jeans moving around next to a row of dumpbins near a toolshed. After about half a kilometre of parking spaces big enough to land the space shuttle, half full of cars almost as big, Hank pulled up in one that said 405, near a sign saying '4771 Block'. Flat 405 was down a small hallway, past another unit and beneath a set of wooden stairs. Hank unlocked the door and Les went weak at the knees.

It was fully carpeted and furnished with pastel-coloured furniture and matching wallpaper with paintings and mirrors round the walls. There were tablelamps everywhere and a glass table and chairs sat under a mini-chandelier next to a bar separating it from a modern kitchen. It was bright and sunny with a TV and a small stereo and someone had left the air-conditioning on. A short hallway led to a huge bedroom with a queensize bed, chairs, tables and an en-suite. A spacious bathroom was just across the hall. But best of all, when Les wandered back into the loungeroom there was a curtained off, enclosed verandah and about thirty metres behind that across a patch of well-manicured lawn was a swimming pool; twenty-five metres long, sparkling crystal clear in the sun and not a soul in it. There was a brown wooden cabana, a whole lot of bulky banana chairs, seats and a few tables, and that was about it. Les turned to Hank, trying to get some words out, when Captain Rats started putting on a drama.

'Have a look,' he ranted, and banged on a wall. 'These places are built like shit.'

'Yeah, I have to agree with you,' replied Norton, still a little stunned. 'So in that case why don't we drive like shit back to your place and get my gear. I'm moving in.'

Hank seemed to ignore Les. 'What's this goddamn air-conditioner doing on?'

'What do you think it's bloody doing? Laverne's probably...'

Before Les got a chance to finish, Hank had found a screwdriver and started pulling a duct covering off the wall near the floor while he babbled on about what a

123

dump the place was and how it was almost ready to fall down. Les decided to let him play his little game while he checked the rest of the place out. There was tinned food and bread in the cupboards, milk and butter in the fridge alongside several large bottles of soft drink and a dozen bottles of Coors Cutter. The deep freeze was full of ice and on a shelf above was a bottle of vodka and two bottles of bourbon. There was everything you needed to clean up with, sheets and pillows on the bed, soap and towels in the bathroom. I know what this is, thought Les, as he looked around the fully appointed condominium. It's my reward for saving the president. Hank's ex must be in the CIA. They knew all along. God bless you, Laverne, wherever you are. The phone worked also, because Boofhead rang up some air-conditioning mob and put on another drama. Les had a look in the duct at what he was raving about. Around the air-conditioning unit was a narrow metal tray with about an eighth of an inch of water in it.

'Look at the thing,' he said, getting back down on his knees. 'It's full of goddamn water.'

'Hank, you know what that is?' said Les. 'It's a fuckin' drip-tray. That's what it's there for. Jesus, you ought to know what a drip-tray is. They named them after you.'

Hank muttered and cursed while he screwed the cover back on. Norton waited as patiently as he could, watching as Hank played his little mind game. 'You finished fucking around, have you?' Hank fiddled in the last screw. 'Good. Now let's go back to your place and I'll get my gear.' Hank mumbled something else as he put the screwdriver back in the kitchen. Next thing they were driving back to Swamp Manor.

Les still could scarcely believe his luck; all he had to do now was get rid of Captain Rats and he was sweet. But not too drastically. How about just dragging him out of the car, jamming his head under the back wheel and driving over it? Naturally, back at Swamp Manor, Hank had important things to do. Les threw his stuff in his bags and put his bike in the back of the pick-up. He knew he had plenty of time but he couldn't help but put the bustle on as he hastily tidied up his room and gathered up all his travel documents and money. He wanted to put as much distance as possible between himself and Swamp Manor in as short as possible a time. Mrs Laurel's car was gone, so he didn't get a chance to thank her and say goodbye; but he'd be back. He got his other carton of orange juice from the fridge and the rest of his food, threw it in a paper shopping bag and waited out at the car. Hank eventually appeared. Driving back to the condo Les didn't quite know what to say. Go and get yourself well and truly fucked, Hank, you wombat, would be the most appropriate thing. But when it was all boiled down, if it hadn't been for Hank, he wouldn't have got the condo in the first place.

'Well that was a stroke of luck,' he said. 'Getting that place.'

'You call that lucky?' retorted Hank. 'The place is a dump.'

'Yeah, I guess you're right,' answered Norton, slowly shaking his head. 'But it'll have to do till something better comes along.' He half smiled at Hank. 'Of course if I get sick of it, I can always come back to your place — can't I?'

Back at Greenwood Estate Hank actually helped Les with his overnight bag while Norton got the other one and wrestled his bike out of the pick-up and onto the enclosed verandah. Within a few minutes Les had his orange juice in the fridge, his bags on the floor in the lounge and Hank standing next to them like a stale bottle of piss. Just outside the back door the swimming pool was sparkling in the heat.

'Well, what's doing, Hank?' he finally asked.

Laurel's eyes spun around as if he was still full of his own importance and Les would be stuffed without him. 'Well, I have to get going. I've got things to do.'

'Good,' answered Les. 'So have I.' Like have a swim, have a feed, play my tapes and hope to Christ you find where you left your flying saucer and fuck off.

'So what are we doing tonight?'

We? Les shook his head. 'I don't know,' he shrugged. 'I'll call back and we'll go for a drink.'

'Yeah righto,' answered Les reluctantly.

'I'll see you about eight-thirty.'

'Half past eight?!! It doesn't get dark till fuckin' near ten.'

'We'll go to a dark bar,' smirked Laurel.

'Yeah alright,' answered Norton slowly. Hank turned to go and had his hand on the door knob. 'Hey, Hank. Aren't you forgetting something?' Hank blinked round the room as Les held out his hand. 'The keys.' Hank's eyes spun round again for a moment before he fumbled the two keys out of his pocket. 'Thanks,' nodded Les. The door slammed and he was gone.

Norton stared at the door for almost half a minute, then fell down on his knees with this delicious grin on his face and started praying towards the swimming pool. He still couldn't quite come to grips with the good fortune that had just landed in his lap. It was like getting out of some gaol and having a giant carbuncle lanced at the same time. A pall of absolute, miserable gloom had been lifted from him and now he had this as well. Gratis. It was that good Les didn't know where to start. The first thing he did was get his two bags and empty them out, throwing the whole lot all over the bedroom floor. Then, after planting his wallet, passport and traveller's cheques, he stripped down to his Speedos, grabbed a towel and almost tore the back flyscreen door off as he charged out to the swimming pool.

Between the condo and the pool was the cabana, with an outdoor shower, toilets and more signs on it than Parramatta Road. No eating, drinking, smoking, splashing, laughing, rubber floats, swim flippers, etc, etc, etc. Shower before swimming, pool hours 10 to 10. Doesn't say anything about guns, thought Les. I'm allowed to go shooting. The shower was on the opposite side to the pool. As he splashed around under it Les noticed about an acre of well-kept park, with a large pond and a fountain in it, running off towards the walls of the next estate. Several lizards and the smallest frogs Les had ever seen scampered round the rocks and gardens and a couple of turtles dived into the pond, disappearing beneath the murky water in a tiny cloud of even tinier bubbles. On the opposite side of the cabana one of the signs said NO DIVING. Fair enough, nodded Les approvingly as he dropped his towel onto a table; then he ran and somersaulted into the pool, landing with a splash like a depth charge exploding.

After sitting in the heat all day, the water wasn't cold or even all that refreshing, but it was beautifully clean and it was definitely wet. Les dived down to the bottom of the deep end and swam underwater to the shallow end, dived and splashed around and just plain dug it as the water seemed to wash away the sweat and any troubles he might have had. The water wasn't over-chlorinated and didn't sting your eyes that much. Les started doing laps, a few freestyle, a few breaststroke before just lying on his back and floating. He could still hardly believe it; this was the last thing he was expecting. He spat some water up in the air and winked a quick smile of thanks towards the sky. How does that song go? he smiled to himself. 'If my friends could see me now.' All huddled round their heaters and I'm in a swimming pool. How droll it is.

Les floated and swam about for what seemed like hours, then got out and went back to the flat, where the first thing he did was turn off the air-conditioner. They're alright in shopping centres, but you get too dependent on them. Besides, Florida in summer couldn't be any worse than Dirranbandi. Fifteen minutes after the air-conditioner stopped it was pretty much like Darwin. Oh well, who gives a stuff? thought Les, as he hung his Speedos on the verandah and wrapped a towel round his waist.

Coors Cutter. Non Alcoholic Beer. Norton took one from the fridge and sampled it out. It tasted okay and went down very easy; just left you feeling sober and a little cheated somehow. Norton glanced up at the bottles of bourbon. Mmmhh. A little early in the day to start

getting out of it. Walking round the flat with his bottle of
Coors, Les was like a kid in a toy shop; he didn't know
where to start first. After Swamp Manor and putting up
with Captain Rats, it was a quantum leap into luxury and
idyllic seclusion. The stereo wasn't all that big and the
speakers sitting on top of the cabinet that held it and the
TV weren't all that big either; but they were big enough.
Among the mess in his bedroom Les found his tapes.
They were mostly Australian bands, some were rock,
some a bit more laid back; number five was laid back, if
Les remembered correctly. He slipped the tape on and
smiled to himself as he adjusted the graphic equaliser.
Right again. 'Send the Divers Down', an oldie but a
goodie by Australian Crawl.

Norton got another bottle of Coors, sat on the lounge
and sipped it as that track ran into 'When the River Runs
Dry' by Hunters and Collectors, then 'Have You Ever' by
the Moonee Valley Drifters. Ahh, how sweet it is. Les
wasn't getting anywhere near drunk or even a glow up,
but he was getting relaxed and thinking it wouldn't take
all that many Coors Cutters to get you bloated up. That
side of the tape finished, leaving Les staring into space
feeling very, very pleasant indeed. Now what to do? Well,
I could tidy up that mess in my room. Or, better still, I
could lie back on that big comfortable bed and just close
my eyes for a few minutes. Maybe even have a little nap
till Prince Charming gets here at half past eight. Yeah,
he'll be here at half past eight, thought Les, as he walked
to the bedroom. That's just to have me sitting around all
dressed up, and he'll lob about ten. He must think I'm as
dopey as he is. Norton laid his head back and couldn't
believe how soft the pillows were and how comfortable
the bed was; just behind him the slightest breeze was
coming through the half-open window. Then a much
happier thought occurred to him. If he was right, he had
half a chace to meet Lori, the daring young girl on the
flying trapeze down at Club BandBox tonight. But with
Boofhead in tow? Maybe he could sool him onto her
cousin? Doubtful. There wouldn't be a sheila in the world

that desperate. No. Les was going to have to get rid of Hank. But how? Norton had a little chuckle to himself as he started to drift off. Somehow he didn't think it was going to be all that hard.

An horrendous clap of thunder rattling across the sky woke Les. He blinked round the room for a few moments before he realised where he was and what was going on, then looked at his watch; it was well after eight. It was just as hot as ever and still light outside, although despite the rain pelting down it didn't appear as heavy as yesterday's storm. Norton watched the rain splattering into the swimming pool and figured that was the place to be, especially with all that lightning around, and with a mask and snorkel on so you could watch yourself being crisped. Still feeling a little groggy he climbed into his Speedos, walked out to the pool and just fell straight in. The facemask fogged up with the heat, but it was fun flopping around in the pool, watching the rain drops hit the water and doing a few laps while he woke up and got a little exercise at the same time. He rolled over on his back and watched the rain splattering into his facemask, duck dived around, having a good time in general for a while, then got out.

Back inside, he showered and shaved in the sparkling clean, fresh-smelling bathroom, got into a pair of jox, then made a cup of coffee and a sandwich and almost tap-danced happily around the kitchen while he played the other side of the tape still sitting in the stereo. It cut out about the same time as the storm eased and after cleaning up what little mess there was Norton once again found himself looking up at the bottles on the shelf. Bourbon and Coke, Mr Norton? Bubbly not flat? Certainly, garçon. Next thing Les was standing in the loungeroom with the biggest glass he could find — half full of ice, half full of George Dickle and Diet Pepsi — staring down at the TV set. It wasn't as big as the one at home and sitting on top was a kind of box with buttons on it that he guessed must be for Cable TV, whatever that was. He switched on the TV, pressed a button on the box and a red, digital display lit up. Les pressed some more buttons, numbers appeared and things started coming up on the screen. He got a movie in Spanish, a yank politician being interviewed by some dude in a pair of braces, the weather in Skunk Gut Missouri, a doco on fly-fishing in Haemotosis Nebraska, and, lo and behold, the Budweiser fights. Two Mexican lightweights getting into it hammer and tongs.

'Ohh yeah! Go the boys,' exhorted Les. He took a giant slurp of his drink then settled back comfortably on the lounge to watch the fights.

If the fights were good, the Budweiser Girls were even better. Ten of the best sorts Norton had ever seen in his life. They porked around the ring in high heels and cutaway bikinis, shaking their boobs and throwing up more growl than a pride of lions, vying to see who was going to be Miss Budweiser Ring Girl. The last one off was a tall, horny blonde, stacked like a timberyard.

'Hi. I'm Lori. I'm from New Mexico. I like tropical fish and I want to be a brain surgeon.'

'Yeah, I'll bet you do,' cackled Norton. 'As soon as they can find one small enough to fit inside your silly bloody head.' The George Dickle was starting to go down well.

The next fight finished early. Some Mexican calling himself the Fighting Clown, because he also worked in a circus, flattened some tall skinny bloke from Idaho. He didn't just knock him out, he poleaxed him, and they were showing the replay. Les was watching one of the most sizzling, short rights of all time when there was an abrupt knock at the door. Now I wonder who this might be? smiled Les. Has Prince Charming arrived? It must be half past eight already. Les sipped his drink while he watched the replay again and took his own sweet time answering the door. It was Hank alright, wearing jeans, a half-ironed floral shirt and desert boots; he looked almost tidy. Les gave him a brief smile, he looked positively irate when he saw Les still in his jox, then got worse when Norton sat back down on the lounge, casually took another mouthful of bourbon and resumed watching the television.

'Well, what are we doing?' demanded Hank.

Norton sort of shrugged. 'I don't know what you're doing. But I'm watching the Budweiser fights. They're alright too.'

'Well, are we going out?'

Les sort of shrugged again. 'Ohh yeah. Watch the fights for a while. There's no mad hurry, is there?'

Hank stood there, his eyes spinning somewhere between Les, the TV and outer space. Norton kept watching as the next fight started. Out the corner of his eye he saw Hank go to the kitchen and return with an ashtray. He was about to plonk his arse down and light up when Norton looked up from the lounge. When he spoke, his voice was very slow, extremely polite but very calculated.

'Oh, Hank, would you mind doing me a favour?' Boofhead blinked at Les. 'Would you wait till you get out to the car before you have a cigarette?'

Hank's face coloured, his eyes went totally spare this time and the wooden cogs inside his head seemed to be disintegrating. It was one of the strangest sights Les had ever seen. He muttered something under his breath that sounded like 'weird' then stormed straight out the door, slamming it behind him. Well, how about that? smiled Les. Looks like sookums didn't like being told to eat his vegies. That was easier than I thought. Les took another slurp of bourbon and resumed watching TV.

The first round finished, Les was about to get another drink when the door opened and in burst Hank. Norton looked up, a little surprised. From across the other side of the room he could smell cigarette smoke on Hank's breath. Rather than wait a few minutes, he'd run outside like a big silly sheila and had a smoke just to show Les he sort of would if he wanted to. Les could hardly believe it.

Captain Rats stood glaring at Norton, his face almost purple with outraged disbelief. Norton couldn't have looked more comfortable lying back on the lounge sipping his drink, completely absorbed in the fight. Hank could have been in another galaxy.

'Well, what are you doing?' he almost shouted. 'Are we going out or what?'

'Ohh yeah. S'pose so.' Les sipped his drink without looking up from the TV.

'Well, I'm going now.'

Norton slowly turned around and replied just as slowly. 'Well, fuckin' go.'

That was it for poor Hank. His eyes spun around crazily as his circuits completely overloaded. He glared at Les for about half a second then turned round and raced out the door, slamming it behind him once again. This time Les got up and locked it.

Well how easy was that? smiled Norton. I knew the goose would come in. But what a dill. I've met hundreds in my time, but he's got to be the best by a country mile. The outlaw from the South. Wish I'd have booted him fair up the arse. Anyway, the idiot's gone and I suppose while I'm up I'd better get myself another delicious. And I might make this one a celebratory one.

The fights eventually finished. Les switched off the TV and played side one of the tape again. Well, what am I going to do? he thought, as he sipped his drink and looked through the verandah window at the swimming pool all lit up now. It's kind of sad really. I'm lost and alone in the U, S of A, got no one to have a drink with and no one to give me a lift into town. Sniff, sniff! Then Norton's craggy face lit up in a grin. But I'll bet they got taxis in this joint.

The phone book was next to the phone on the kitchen bar. Les was about to look under 'Y' for 'Yellow' when he noticed some business cards on top of the book and next to Laverne's phone number and address. There was one for the air-conditioning company, one for a TV repair shop and among the others was a white one with 'Keys Limousine Service. Direct to Car Phone' and the number. Written down the side in biro was 'Joey'. Les hit the buttons; the ring at the other end was a lot slower and flatter than back in Australia.

A voice with a strong NY accent answered. 'Yeah. Keys Limos. Hullo.'

'Is Joey there, please?'

'This is Joey.'

'How y'goin', Joey? Listen mate, I need a limo at. . .'

Half full of ink, Norton started to rattle off the address and phone number, plus his name, when Joey interrupted. 'Hey, hey. Hang on there a second, buddy. Slow down. You're gonna have to run that by me again. I can't understand you.'

Norton dropped his voice back into second gear and managed to get it all across. 'How long before you'll be here?'

'I'll be there twenny minutes.'

'Good on you, Joey, old son. I'll be ready and waiting.'

Twenty minutes was plenty of time for Les to iron a red, hangout, Hawaiian shirt and his jeans, give his hair a detail and roll up the Panthers T-shirt for Harris. In one of the cupboards he found what looked like several blue plastic milkshake containers. He filled one almost to the brim with bourbon, Pepsi and ice and was casually sipping it while the tape played when there was a polite knock on the door. I reckon that's my man, smiled Les, and opened it.

Joey was about five nine, dark hair, wearing a black sports jacket and blue tie. He was a good style of a bloke with a hint of both hardness and streetwise humour in his eyes. He gave Les a bit of a once up and down as if he didn't quite know what to expect.

'You Norton? The guy wants a limo to Main?'

'That's me,' winked Les. 'I'll be with you in a sec.'

'Hey, take your time. I'll be out front.'

Les didn't take his time turning off the lights and locking the place up, but he did take his drink. Joey was just outside, holding open the back door of a dark blue Cadillac stretch limousine. It was all lit up and shiny and looked like the Fairstar on wheels.

'You know Gator Man's on Main Street?' asked Les.

'Hey, do I know Gator Man's? I'll have you there before you finish your drink.'

'You think so?' said Norton, piling into the spacious back. 'Well, you'd better go through a few red lights, Joey, cause I put 'em away pretty smartly.'

It took about fifteen minutes to get to town and Les was able to get a bit of a boozy mag on with Joey. Joey did come from New York; Les told him a bit about Australia and how he happened to be in Florida. Despite the language barrier they managed to communicate and have a laugh while Les sat back and slurped his drink in air-conditioned luxury. Wonder how much this bloody thing is going to cost me? he mused. Probably about fifty bucks. Anyway, who gives a stuff? Whatever it is, it ain't enough. Still, it wouldn't be bad to have that last fifty I gave Hank. Les chuckled sardonically. Gee, I wish he was here. I miss him already.

They stopped outside Gator Man's, Joey held open the door, Les clambered out, still holding about a quarter of his drink. 'Hey, you're not wrong, Joey,' he smiled, giving the ice a rattle. 'So what do I owe you, mate?'

'That'll be twelve bucks.'

Norton's jaw hung open as he gave the driver a double blink. 'How much?'

'Hey, twelve bucks. What, you got your hearing aid jammed in your ass?'

Les shook his head. 'You're kiddin'.'

'Kiddin, schmiddin. Just gimme the twelve. That's a ten with a two. You know what I'm sayin'?'

Norton juggled his drink, fished out a twenty and handed it to the driver. 'There's twenty dollars. And don't even dare to offer me the change, you low mug.' Now it was the driver's turn for a double blink. 'Twelve lousy dollars to come halfway across town in a stretch limo. What sort of a peasant do you take me for? Now get out of here before I report you, you miserable-looking dropkick.'

Joey looked at the twenty for a second before stuffing it in his pocket. He closed the door and put his arm around Norton's shoulders. Les felt like a punter walked off the street straight into Arthur Daley's car yard.

'How long are you in town for, buddy? Les . . . is it?'

By the time Joey drove away Les had three more business cards and instructions to ring any time day or night, anywhere, in any condition; they'd be there in minutes and Norton would be looked after like he was the president. Onya, Joey, Les laughed to himself as he stuck the cards in his pocket and waved the limo off down Main Street. Now that he was more relaxed and didn't have to keep following behind after Boofhead Les noticed Gator Man's was on the corner of a town square or mall. There was a band playing in the open opposite and a squad car with one cop leaning against it keeping an eye on about a hundred or so punters. The cop looked up as the limo drove off and couldn't help but notice Norton. Les thought he'd go over and put his head in; if the cop said anything about drinking he'd simply plead tourist and drop it in the nearest bin. Les crossed the road.

The mall wasn't all that big, just a couple of skinny trees and a few concrete flowerbeds in a tiled square surrounded by shops and restaurants and that was about it. The band was just plain bloody awful, long hair, black vests and singlets, playing some sort of heavy metal with a female store dummy in a purple leopard-skin mini propped in front of the speakers. The crowd didn't look much better. Guess this must be that 'poor white trash' I keep hearing about, mused Les as he stood near the front of the squad car.

'So how's it goin', mate?' he asked the cop.

The cop looked just like on TV. Magnum, mace, all black uniform, black hair and flashing white teeth. 'It's not goin' so bad,' he replied, one eye on Norton, the other on the crowd.

'What's it, something special or just a band playing?'

'Just a band playing. They'll be finished in about an hour.'

Les took a slurp of his drink as they butchered a few bars of some other unfortunate song. 'I bet you'll be sorry when they've finished?'

The cop turned to Les, chuckled for a second and flashed him an understanding smile. Norton finished his drink, dropped it in the nearest bin and wished the cop a good night. After getting a 'you have a good one . . . mate' in reply, he walked across to Gator Man's.

135

Gator Man's was just as crowded as the night before and the band was just as good; probably better. Les got a margarita and a Jack Daniel's sour from the same barmaid who seemed to remember him and joined the crowd. He didn't know a soul in the place, didn't have much idea where he was for that matter and didn't give a stuff. One thing Les did know, as his bourbon sour disappeared down his screech, if he was going to meet Lori at Club BandBox he'd better take it a bit easier on the drink; he was starting to roar just a little.

Nevertheless, Norton managed to roar his way through another two margaritas as the band bopped away on stage and did their thing going through the crowd again. Les didn't want to leave it too late getting to Club BandBox but the Platinum Tones were such a hot band and Gator Man's was such a good bar, making sensational drinks, he had to put his head in for a while. I think I might spend a few more nights in here before I leave sunny Sepposota, mused Norton, as he demolished another margarita.

The band took a break and although there was no shortage of good-looking women on the hang Les decided to split. Outside, the street band was still murdering songs in the mall, despite the police presence. After the band in Gator Man's, Les felt like borrowing the cop's Magnum and shooting all four of them, starting with the lead singer in the black vest. A yellow cab cruised past, Les flagged it down and clambered inside. Club BandBox wasn't far across the other side of Main Street; the fare was five dollars. Les gave the driver ten dollars then skipped through the punters and up the escalators.

There was a bit of a mob standing round the front waiting to get in. Harris was on the door. He caught Norton's eye at the back of the crowd, opened the door, made a bit of space among the punters and beckoned Les straight through, closing the door behind him.

'G'day, Harris,' said Les. 'How's things, mate? Alright?'

'Hey, Les, mah man,' grinned Harris. 'What it look like, brother?'

Les gave Harris a bit of a friendly slap on his massive bicep. 'What's it look like?' echoed Norton. 'Well, it looks a bit like this.' Les pulled out the Penrith T-shirt from where he had it tucked in his jeans. He opened it up and handed it to Harris. 'There you are, mate. How's that?'

Harris looked at the T-shirt and his huge white grin seemed to get bigger. He beckoned to another black man wearing jeans and a Houston Oilers T-shirt standing by the front desk. He wasn't as big as Harris, but close enough with a broken nose and scar tissue round his eyes.

'Hey, Otis. Dig this. This the T-shirt the man from Australia said he gonna bring you. Say hello to the man.'

Otis took the T-shirt and his face lit up like Harris's. 'This T-shirt for me? The Panthers. Man, ah dig that shit.' He looked at Norton. 'Hey, what can I say, man?'

Les shrugged. 'Just thanks'll do, mate.'

'Hey, you got it.'

Harris introduced Les to his young brother, who it turned out was a boxer and a pretty good one too, having fought at Caesar's Palace a few times. Les tried to think if he'd seen him on Sky Channel at one time; he also tried to think what it would be like getting hit by someone that big who knew how to put them together. Extremely jarring, to say the least. They had a bit of a mag for a while, each getting a laugh out of the other's accent and mannerisms. Watching the way people looked at the two brothers or spoke to them as they went past, Les seemed to get the idea that they were the men in Club BandBox.

'Well, I might go inside and have a bit of a look around,' said Norton.

'Yeah, you do that, Les,' smiled Norton. Norton's shoulders were wide, but Harris's monstrous arm went round them quite easily as he motioned to his young brother. 'Sometimes we get a few uncool dudes in there. Anybody give you any shit, I'm here and young Otis be watching yo ass too.'

'That's a fact, Les,' said Otis, folding up his T-shirt.

'Thanks, fellahs,' answered Les. 'But I'll be okay. Actually, I might be meeting a sheila inside.'

Norton pointed towards the girl collecting the money at the desk and got a gentle push in the back from Harris that almost propelled him to the stairs running up on the left. Well, that'll do me, thought Les. I can have a look around from up there and try and spot the lovely Lori. Les weaved through the punters and up the stairs.

The place was pretty crowded and the dancefloor beneath almost packed. The black DJ was hitting the punters with a bit of disco and up on the bandstand, if Les wasn't mistaken, was the equipment belonging to the same band at the Sandbar, only with bigger speakers. There was no shortage of girls and the mob looked fairly cool in a casual sort of way; not quite 'Miami Vice', more '21 Jump Street'. Shit, smiled Les. I'm going into TV mode again. He looked over to where he'd met Lori and her cousin on Friday night, but they weren't standing there. Oh well, thought Les. This still looks alright anyway. He was sort of manoeuvring himself back towards the bar when he heard a voice behind him.

'Well, well. If it isn't Lesto the Great. The wonder from down under.'

Norton turned around and there was Lori sitting where the bar cornered round towards the back of the club. She was wearing jeans, a cut-away maroon top and a sleeveless Levi jacket; she looked just as foxy and her long dark hair just as shiny as ever. On her right was an empty bar stool and a handbag sitting on the bar in front of it.

'Well, I'll be buggered,' grinned Norton. 'If it isn't the girl on the red velvet swing. What's doing, digger?'

'Not much. Just sitting around listening to the band, seeing who might show up.' Lori gave Norton a wink. 'It's good to see you, Les.'

'Yeah, you too, Lori.' Les made a bit of a gesture. 'So how long have you been here?'

Lori shrugged. 'About an hour.'

'I would have been here earlier, but I called into Gator Man's on the way.'

'How was that?'

'It was good.' Norton was about to elaborate when

138

through the crowd came Nadine wearing jeans and a short-sleeved, purple, Utah Jazz sweatshirt. She'd obviously been to powder her nose and smiled both with pleasure and relief when she saw Les. 'Hello, Nadine. How are you, me old china?'

'How am I? I'm just fine. What about you?' Nadine took her seat. 'We didn't think you were coming.'

'You missed me that much, eh?' chuckled Les. 'But I'm here. And might I say how delightful it is to find the two best sorts in Sepposota looking as swish as ever.'

Nadine caught her cousin's eye. 'I don't know what he just said, but I think that's a compliment.'

'Oh, he's such a smoothie,' said Lori. 'I'm sure it must be.'

'You better believe it.' Norton clapped his hands together, happy to find Lori in the place. 'So what's been doing anyway, girls?'

'Not much,' shrugged Nadine. 'What about you? How's your goofy buddy?'

'Me?' Norton tossed back his head. 'Christ! You wouldn't believe what's been happening to this poor lost tourist.'

'Well, why don't you tell us about it?' said Lori.

'Okay,' nodded Les. 'But only on two conditions.'

'What's that?'

'We move round the bar a little, so I can sit my big Khyber down. And you let me buy you both a drink.'

Nadine winked at her cousin. 'Sounds fine by me.'

Lori winked back at her cousin then smiled up at Les. 'Me too.'

There was an empty bar stool next to Lori, so they wriggled round the corner a bit, away from the people walking past, and Les sat down. After a quick consultation he ordered three margaritas. When they arrived the barmaid smiled and shook her head; Les gave her ten dollars anyway and left some more money on the bar. After that the drinks just kept flowing. Les paid for some, some were on the house and it was almost a repeat of Friday night, only better. Les told them some more about

Hank and what a wombat he was, about meeting Laverne and moving into the condominium, even about Joey the limo driver and giving him the twenty dollars. Les cracked jokes while the girls laughed and got drunk. Lori said how she'd been training with the circus and suggested Les come down and get up on the trapeze; he'd probably look good in a pair of satin tights. Les said he'd rather stick his head in a lion's mouth, if they could find a lion with a mouth big enough. Nadine said the only training she'd been doing was chasing her two horrible kids round the house with a baseball bat. They got even drunker, the band came on and started playing quite a few Australian songs in with the others. Les said if the girls didn't have a dance with him now and again he'd sit at the bar and sing the lyrics. After three bars of Norton murdering 'Beds Are Burning' Lori and Nadine took it in turns dancing while the other watched their bags and seats. The night was a hoot.

Before long they were all starting to roar. Harris and Otis would walk past now and again; they wouldn't say anything, just look at Les, shake their heads and smile. Well, how good's this? thought Norton. The band had taken another break and Les was sucking on another margarita while the DJ played some more disco when he noticed Nadine looking at her watch every now and again. Hello, he thought to himself again, this time not quite as pleased. Here it comes. The old wind up. Time to go home to the kids. Goodnight, Les. Thanks for a wonderful time. We'll probably see you up here again. Oh well, not to worry. It's still been a top night, and I'm here for another three weeks yet. Despite being a trifle disappointed Norton kept smiling.

'Well, Les, you sweet gorgeous thing,' slurred Nadine, 'I have to go.'

Norton gave her an understanding smile. 'I can appreciate that Nadine, my sweet little sugar glider. It wouldn't look too good those poor kids of yours wondering where their mother is, and she bowls in pissed out of her brain on cheap tequila.'

'It's not quite . . . like that,' hiccuped Nadine.

Les was going to say something else when one of the girls he'd seen earlier in the nurse's uniform selling shots walked up carrying a handbag and a set of keys. Although she was wearing jeans and a Club BandBox T-shirt there was no mistaking the pixie blonde face.

'You ready, Nadine?' she asked. 'If you can stand up.'

Nadine rocked to her feet and picked up her handbag. 'It's all his fault. He's a bad influence.'

'Gee. And all the time I thought I was being a good bloke.'

'I'll see you when you get home, Lori.' Nadine smiled at the look on Norton's face. 'It's alright, Les. I'm getting a lift home with Lilla. She finishes her shift early on Sunday night.' The nurse smiled briefly at Les as if she was tired and keen to get home. 'So I'm leaving my cousin with you.'

Norton turned to Lori. 'You're not . . .?'

Lori shrugged. 'Not unless you want me to?'

'So you look after her, Mr Les Norton from Australia. Now where did you say you live again?'

'Where do I live? Shit!' Les had to think for a moment. Then like a big, silly, honest kid he pulled a piece of paper out of his jeans, unfolded it and put it on the bar. 'There it is. Mum wrote it out for me before I left. I was supposed to pin it on my shirt.'

Nadine blinked at it for a second or two then kissed Les on the cheek. 'Goodnight, Les. I'll . . . see you after, Lori.'

'See you, Nadine. Night, Lilla.'

Lori's cousin gave them one last boozy smile before her girlfriend dragged her away and they were gone, leaving Norton and Lori to work out the rest of the night between them. As well as not being able to believe his luck again, Les felt great; drunk but not in the least bit tired. That training on the bike and in the pool, getting rid of Hank, and a sound sleep in the afternoon washed down with about 2000 margaritas and other mixed drinks had him jumping out of his skin. And he remembered Lori saying she'd been training hard with the circus too. The way she hit the dancefloor and glistened, Les didn't doubt her. This could be a very interesting evening, with a little more luck. He moved his stool a little closer and took her hand.

'Well. Here we are, Lori, me old mate,' he said, looking deeply into her eyes. 'Drunk again.'

The beautiful trapeze artist nodded. 'I'd go along with that.'

'It's your cousin's fault. Christ! I thought I could put them away. She leaves me for dead.'

'Nadine. When that girl gets a roll on — stand back. But, God! I can't remember the last time I saw her laugh so much.'

'Yeah. Well, it costs you nothing to laugh. That's what I always say.'

'That's . . . a pretty good saying.'

'Would you like another drink?'

Lori gave Les a solid slap on the arm. 'My bloody oath. Isn't that another one of your Australian sayings?'

'Close enough, mate,' smiled Les.

Norton was about to order when he heard a horribly familiar voice from just behind him.

'So how's it going?'

Norton looked around and couldn't believe his eyes. It was Hank. He looked half full of ink, his eyes were spinning around as usual and being half tidy he'd somehow managed to get in. No matter what he looked like he was the last person on earth Norton wanted to see.

'What do you want?' Norton was incredulous.

Hank took a drag on his cigarette. 'I figured you'd be in here. I was driving past so I thought I'd call in, have a drink with you.'

Les groaned and shook his head. 'Ohh, thanks.'

Lori seemed to wake what was going on. She gave Hank a boozy once up and down then turned to Les. 'This isn't . . .?'

Norton jerked his thumb towards Captain Rats. 'Yeah. This is Hank.'

Lori didn't bother to introduce herself. She just stared at Hank. 'You're not the jerk went diving and all the crap hit him in the face?'

'Yep. That's Hank.'

Lori started to crack up on her bar stool, Hank's eyes spun around and sitting next to her Les started laughing too. However, underneath, Les felt like grabbing Hank by the throat and choking him. He couldn't believe the mug turning up here. Not that there was much chance of him stuffing Norton's night up, but you could bet he'd hang around like a bad smell and do his best. And Les thought he'd got rid of him. Again he was in a no-win situation, because if he belted Hank he'd probably make a dill of himself in front of Lori and everybody else. But as Les sat there an idea formed in his evil mind. There just might be another way of doing this. If a couple of cool cats were as hip as Les hoped they were. In the meantime, just suck Hank in and bag the shit out of him. That would be fun, no matter what. Lori brought her head up off the bar and Les ordered two more margaritas and a beer for Hank.

'There you are, knackers,' said Les, pointing to it on the bar. 'Get into that. And while you're at it, tell Lori how you like riding your bike on the beach. Martin Vinnicombe.'

Lori spluttered into her drink. 'Ohh yeah. Tell me all about your Italian racer.'

After that it was just rubbish Hank night; Les had given Lori plenty of ammunition earlier and being a woman she didn't need any help firing it. Hank just stood there and copped it, eyes spinning as he dragged on his cigarettes and beer. The more they poked shit at him the more he copped it, in silence. Les knew he was a glutton for punishment, but this was completely absurd. Lori even offered to light one of Hank's cigarettes, but she'd lost her Italian racing cigarette lighter. Plus, she didn't smoke. Nevertheless, even though it was priceless bagging Hank, Les was still wishing him to the shithouse. Finally after all the non-stop laughing, Lori put her hand on Norton's leg.

'I have to go powder my nose.'

'I think I understand,' winked Norton.

Lori headed for the Ladies, leaving Hank standing next to Les like the proverbial stale bottle of piss. Les stared at him but didn't feel at all like getting a mag going. Suddenly one of the wooden cogs inside Hank's empty head seemed to click into gear. He put his beer on the bar.

'I'm going to the John.'

As usual, Hank turned and abruptly disappeared into the crowd. Les watched him sourly for a second or two then caught the bargirl's eye and asked her if she'd mind keeping an eye on their seats and the money for a minute. No sooner had she said yes than Les got up and walked out to the foyer. Harris was talking to his brother and noticed the look in Norton's eye when he walked over. Now it was the big Queenslander's turn to put his arms around someone's shoulders and play Arthur Daley.

'Listen, do you blokes reckon you could do an old mate a bit of a favour?'

Harris and his brother were very understanding, they were also quite amused at Norton's request, and Harris was impressed too when Les discreetly slipped him a hundred dollars. He was back on his seat, getting into his drink, when Lori returned and sat back down. She picked up her drink and they clinked glasses.

'So what do you think of Hank?' asked Les.

'My God! What a jerk. And you let that moron stay at your house back in Australia?'

'Yeah,' nodded Les. 'Dunno bloody how. Anyway, when he comes back just humour the poor mug. I reckon he'll hit the toe soon.'

'Hit the toe?'

'Yeah. Shoot through like a Bondi.'

'Bondi?' Lori looked even more confused. 'Isn't that where you live?'

Les smiled and patted her on the leg. 'Don't worry about it, Lori. It's all sweet.'

Well, I suppose it costs you nothing to be nice, thought Norton, as he watched Hank arrive back from the toilet. He stood more or less between Les and Lori with his back to the dancefloor below, lit another cigarette and took a mouthful of beer. Lori was shaking her head slightly as she looked at him.

'So where did you go earlier?' asked Les, his voice dripping with false mateship.

Hank shrugged. 'I had things to do,' he drawled. 'Went to a club out on Bennington. Saw a blues band.'

Yeah, I bet you did, thought Norton. 'Alright, was it? Did you have a good time?'

'Yeah. It was neat.'

Lori gave Hank a boozy once up and down. 'Hey, Hank baby. Did you meet any nice — sheilas — out there?'

Les shook his head as he watched her cackling into her drink. Shit! Just what have I started here? he thought.

Lori ripped a few more into Hank, while he stood there in silence sucking on his cigarette and another beer Les bought him. The wooden cogs inside his peanut mind seemed to be grinding around as if he was searching for the perfect squelch to demolish both Les and Lori for all time. Before he had a chance to get it out, an hispanic-looking couple walked past. The man was wearing black pleated trousers and a silver shirt and looked hard as a rock; with his broken nose and the scar tissue around his eyes he reminded Les of the two Mexican lightweight boxers he'd seen on TV earlier. His girlfriend had flashing dark eyes and teased black hair over a whippy figure squeezed into Levis and an orange T-shirt cut low in the front. She was walking ahead and as she went past Hank she made sure she bumped him hard enough to spill his beer; some on her, most of it on him. Captain Rats's eyes went spare. He glared angrily at the beer on his shirt then at the girl.

'You goddamn stupid bitch,' he howled.

'Hey, what's it with you, asqueroso? You did it.' The girl glared back at Hank as she wiped a few drops of beer from her T-shirt.

'I did it?' Hank howled even louder. 'Why, you dopey fuckin' whore . . .'

The boyfriend kind of glided in between them. 'Hey, cateto. You don't talk to my woman like that.'

145

'Fuck your broad. And fuck you too, you celery-picking sonofabitch.'

'And fuck you too — gringo.'

That's when Les knew the man was a fighter. The boyfriend dropped slightly and came up with a left hook, as only Mexican boxers can, that hit Hank right under the ear. Poor Hank's knees went, his arms flew back and the look of utter disbelief on his face suggested it was probably the first time anyone had ever given him a well-deserved smack in the mouth. Before Hank had time to drop or do anything, the boyfriend doubled up with another left hook. This one landed flush on Hank's nose, hard enough to knock him back over the railing and down into the punters on the dancefloor. Which wasn't quite according to plan.

Les had gone over to 'his old mate' Harris and told him that the mug from the other night was in here annoying him and he wanted him thrown out, discreetly but painfully, and the more things that got bruised and broken the better. Les knew they couldn't really do it, but the lazy hundred bucks would soon find someone in the crowd that could. In a free enterprise country like America, cash and the right connections can get you just about anything. So they'd organised for one of Otis's boxer pals, who needed a dollar, to give Hank a rather severe slap. They'd then come over, pick up Boofhead and toss him out, making sure he got a few more bruises as they did. That was the idea anyway, but the little Mexican had a punch like a kick from a mule.

With a flailing of arms and legs, Hank came sailing down onto the packed dancefloor, taking about ten punters with him when he landed. When they got up, some of them started punching and kicking into Hank, then before they knew it, on a hot steamy summer night in Florida, they were punching and kicking into each other. Harris and Otis came trotting up the stairs as planned expecting to throw Hank out. Instead there's a gigantic brawl starting on the dancefloor. And like they say on the TV commercials — that's not all. When Hank's beer went flying it splattered over some beefy redneck's girlfriend, and the glass hit him in the head. She kicked the Mexican girl in the leg and the redneck boyfriend, being twice as big as the Mexican bloke, started on him with the help of about five of his redneck mates. So as well as the brawl on the dancefloor, they had this to contend with too. And it was spreading already as a couple of the Mexican's pals jumped in to give him a hand, and anyone else who wanted could join in as well. There didn't seem to be any shortage of players.

Harris left Otis with the Mexican, to try and sort things out with the rednecks, and charged downstairs into the dancefloor, along with the rest of the bouncers. But it all seemed too little too late. Shit, how good's this? thought Les, as he watched a big fleshy redneck break a pitcher of beer over Otis's big black head. The broken glass cut Otis okay but it definitely didn't faze him. Otis spun round with an uppercut that nearly put the redneck's jaw up through the top of his head. Norton watched fascinated as he hit the deck out cold and blood and bits of teeth started bubbling out of his mouth. Bloody hell, Otis. I couldn't have done much better than that myself. Then the brawl really got going. Otis was snotting blokes left, right and centre as they'd snipe him from all angles, and even though the Mexicans were copping plenty they were dishing it out splendidly; especially the one who started it in the first place. Every time he hit someone he either drew blood or smashed something. The women weren't bad either. One jumped on the Mexican girl's back while another punched her and bashed her on the head with the heel of her shoe. The Mexican girl grabbed whoever was on her back's arm and bit a great piece out of it; even among the noise and shouting and the disco music still pumping in the background her scream of pain hung in the air like a thunderclap. Two big rednecks crash-tackled Otis, scattering chairs and tables, drinks and people everywhere. Then a few of the brothers jumped in to help Otis and started swapping punches with the rednecks. The rednecks just seemed to be drunken

147

brawlers, but what they lacked in skill they made up for in size, numbers and thuggery. If the fight upstairs was getting into top gear, down on the dancefloor it was spreading like the proverbial Blue Mountains bushfire. They were all into it; including the black disc jockey.

Norton sat back against the bar in a state of amused disbelief bordering on outright laughter. It was a buzz to be right in the middle of a monstrous brawl that he had nothing to do with. He might have organised it, but he sure didn't start it and there was no one in there he knew so he had absolutely no intention of jumping into it. The way the beer pitchers were flying around that's all he'd need on his holiday. About four hours in hospital the following morning getting pieces of glass dug out of his head while some doctor put stitches in. Les was just an innocent bystander. Sort of, anyway.

Les watched a redneck smash a stool over some black guy's head, almost decapitating him, as a pitcher whizzed past his face and smashed into the bar mirror, shattering the bottles stacked there as well. He put his arm around Lori, who moved in against his shoulder. Another pitcher came sailing over the bar, followed by a chair that had the bar staff ducking for cover by now. Les was kind of bemusedly thinking how their drinks were still intact when one of the Mexicans pulled out a switch-blade knife. He didn't muck around, he shoved it into the nearest redneck's ample stomach right up to the hilt. The redneck howled with pain and anger as thick dark blood started bubbling over his hands. The Mexican slashed another redneck before a bigger one broke a pitcher and rammed it into the side of the Mexican's face, almost slicing his ear off. Even when people went down there wasn't much room to fall because more people were fighting, cursing and wrestling among the blood, spilt drinks and debris on the floor; and quite a lot of them were women. Shit! thought Les, as another Mexican pulled out a switch-blade. Knives, broken bottles. I got a pretty good idea what they'll be pulling out next.

'Listen, Lori,' he said urgently, 'this ain't gonna get any better. I reckon we'd better piss off.'

Lori was getting a bit worried herself but she didn't quite understand what Les said. 'Are you saying, am I pissed off? Yeah. This is goddamn awful.'

'Well, do you want to leave?'

Lori's eyes widened as she watched another redneck's arm get opened up by a knife. 'Les!' she yelled, above the screams and curses. 'I never thought you'd ask!'

Norton scooped up his notes from the bar, downed what was left of his margarita — it was just too good to leave — and started leading Lori through the melee down the stairs to the foyer. There were a number of couples leaving and uniformed security guards with their batons out charging in. The band had jumped up in front of their instruments and equipment while beneath them the dancefloor continued to erupt in more violence. Despite the seriousness of it all, this made Norton laugh like mad. Because underneath the battle raging on the dancefloor Hank was somewhere on the floor getting the shit kicked out of him. And if that wasn't worth a laugh nothing was. It was definitely worth a hundred dollars. Next thing they were out the door and going down the escalators as about half a dozen cops in riot gear came charging up.

'We'll go straight back to my place,' suggested Les. 'It's okay there. Plus I got some drinks and there's a pool.'

'Sounds fine by me,' replied Lori. 'How do we get there?'

'Air-conditioned luxury — with a bit of luck.'

When Joey the limo driver dropped Les off and gave him his cards, Les said he was going to Club BandBox and he'd probably be leaving before closing time. Joey said he sometimes parked there under some trees near the front. He'd keep an eye out for him. More squad cars, their sirens wailing and lights flashing were pulling up out the front when Les led Lori past the fountains. Sure enough, there was the limo, backed in under some palm trees with Joey leaning against the front. He spotted Les walking over and waved.

'Hey, what the hell's going on up there?' he said, as Les approached.

'Nothing much,' replied Norton. 'Just a few blokes getting stabbed and their heads kicked in. A sort of quiet riot.'

Joey looked at Norton and smiled. 'Did you start it?' he joked. 'Come on. I bet you had sumptin' to do wit it.'

'Not me, mate. I had better things on my mind.'

Joey noticed Lori and he gave a silent whistle. 'And just who is the beautiful lady?'

'Exactly that, Joey.'

Joey opened the back door for Lori. 'Good evening, ma'am,' he said graciously. Lori smiled back as she stepped inside.

'Back to where you picked me up on Manatee,' said Les. He gave Joey a wink just before he climbed in over Lori. 'And you needn't go through any red lights.'

'Slow and steady it is, sir,' smiled the driver, and closed the door.

Lori was on Norton's left, she smiled, possibly a little impishly, and eased up against him. Les draped his arm around her shoulder. 'Well, I'm feeling pretty good, Lori,' he said. 'I wonder how Hank's feeling right now?'

'Yeah, I wonder,' chuckled Lori. 'Wow! I didn't quite see it all start. But that little Mex sure pasted him.'

'Then it just kicked on from there. Serves him right anyway, spilling his drink over that girl. She seemed quite nice and he started paying out on her. The goose.'

'He had a scuzzy mouth alright.'

Les smiled down into Lori's beautiful dark eyes. 'That's one thing I'll say about you, Lori, my sweet little mint pea. You ain't got a scuzzy mouth. In fact, I'd say you've got one of the sweetest little mouths I ever seen.'

'You think so?' invited Lori, running her tongue over her lips.

'I'd go so far as to hazard a guess.' Well, thought Les. I'm not here for a long time, just for a good time. He looked at her for a moment then kissed her.

Norton was right; Lori did have a sweet mouth and an

150

even sweeter tongue. After a few moments she parted her lips some more and it flicked out like a tiny pink flame to be met by Norton's. Not a lot at first, then things just seemed to develop. Les placed his hand in the small of Lori's back and drew her to him. Her skin was as smooth and firm as polished brass and the muscles around her shoulderblades rippled under his fingers with an exquisite, almost panther-like strength. Even her neck was firm and sinewy but lovely to run his hand and tongue over every silken crevice. Les couldn't remember a woman with a body like this. She was wearing no bra, though you would never know. Her breasts weren't all that big but they just sat there when Norton cupped them in his hand and the nipples sprung up like they were spring loaded when Norton massaged them delicately with his fingers.

It wasn't long and Norton was starting to come to the boil; so was Lori. She ran her hand under Norton's shirt and across the hardness of his stomach. Lori must have liked what she felt also. Instead of undoing his shirt she ripped the buttons open and started scrabbling at the hairs on his chest and around the back of his head. That's alright about the shirt, Lori. It might be worth ninety dollars in the shop, but I got it for twenty-five in a pub. Les slipped his hand onto Lori's crutch and began stroking gently. They more he stroked the more Lori spread her legs till they were both somewhere between the back seat and the floor of the limo. Lori's breath was coming in short sharp gasps and Norton was seriously thinking of slipping out of the headlock she had on him, whipping off her jeans and giving it to her on the back seat when the limo rocked to a halt and he heard Joey's voice.

'Hey. You in the back. We're here.'

'Huh?' Norton's head came up and he blinked around like he was coming out of a trance. 'What'd you say?'

'4771 Manatee. Ain't this where you live . . . sir.' By the time Les figured out what was going on Joey had come round and had opened the back door. Les climbed off Lori and somehow they both managed to climb out of the limo. The driver looked at what was left of Norton's

151

Hawaiian shirt and somehow managed to very discreetly smile just with his eyes. 'Did I tell you about our extra service returning lost buttons? I don't believe I mentioned that to you . . . sir.'

'No,' heaved Les. 'You didn't. But I'll take your word for it.' He fished into his jeans and came up with about fifty dollars in drawings of Jackson, Lincoln and Washington. 'Listen, I might be needing you later on to take the young lady home.'

Joey took the money and looked at both it and Norton lovingly. 'I won't be far. In fact, I am going to do another couple of jobs. Then I will wait right here till you and the lady have finished whatever it is you are finishing. Goodnight, sir. Goodnight, ma'am.'

'Yeah. Goodnight,' croaked Lori.

Inside the condo there was absolutely no mucking around. Les hit the loungeroom light and wouldn't have minded just one drink, but the glow burning in Lori's onyx eyes said different.

'The bedroom's just down there,' pointed Les.

'Good.'

Lori didn't need any help at all getting her clothes off. Les barely had time to get out of his jeans and what was left of his Hawaiian shirt when he got a glimpse of a sleeveless Levi jacket and a pair of delicate white knickers with a blue trim sailing across the room, and Lori was on the bed with her legs apart and he was on top of her licking her neck. As well as just one drink, Les would also have liked a little more foreplay; Lori's body was something else and Norton would have loved to run his filthy rotten hands all over it. Her legs and arms were sinewy, her shoulders and neck firm, her stomach was as flat and hard as a billiard table with the most delightful wisp of silken pubic hair running up to her navel. Les had been to bed with fit girls and others into aerobics, but never with a full-on athlete. Especially a trapeze artist. This was something to drool and salivate over. Unfortunately Lori just wanted to get into it. So get into it they did: with all hands to the pumps and all guns blazing.

If Norton was just a little reticent starting, Mr Wobbly was more than keen to get into the action; he was all puffed up and his nasty little head was throbbing and pounding at the door. Les had no trouble slipping in. Lori's ted was nice and firm, but all the work he'd put in on her in the back of the limo had her a bit like a washing machine someone had dumped a whole packet of Rinso into; she was bubbling over and foaming everywhere. Nonetheless, she gave a squeal of delight, which soon turned into one continuous fervent moan as Norton slipped through the gears, a little like whipping his bike along the beach. That was one of the two things helping Les for a good romp in the sack. The bike riding had pumped his thighs up, so he had no trouble thumping away, and the 2000 or so margaritas he'd drunk had slowed his mind down just enough to stop him blowing his bolt too soon. Norton seemed to go for ages. After a while, though, Lori's moaning and groaning and thrashing around while she attacked Les with her tongue started turning him on. It was time for the grand finale. A triple, reverse somersault with the trapeze artist, and don't worry about the safety net.

From among the pile of clothes on the floor, Les grabbed a Merv Hughes, Test Series T-shirt and tenderly gave Lori and himself a bit of a clean up. This time Lori gave a kind of muted scream as Norton got Mr Wobbly where he wanted to be and slipped into gear again. Norton's face just twisted up in the most excruciating agony, it was hurting that good. He lifted her legs up, dug his thumbs into her rock hard calf muscles and, like a good Queensland boy, gave it everything he had for Australia, including what felt like both his kidneys and part of his spine as he emptied out. He got a glimpse of Lori's face in the light through the window and there was no doubt about it, she was literally screwed cockeyed.

Some time later Norton's heart stopped trying to thump its way out of his chest and he was able to poke his tongue back inside his mouth from where it had been lolling against his cheek. Lori's eyes had gone back to normal and the lovers were sort of cuddled up against each other with nothing between them except Merv Hughes's moustache.

'Well, Lori,' said Les, 'I don't know about you, but I reckon that was pretty bloody good. I'm just about knackered.' Lori kind of mumbled something and moved in a little closer. 'You know, I don't mean to skite, but do you know the reason I'm such a good root?'

Lori's eyes opened up a little. 'A good root?' she said evenly. 'Does that mean, a good screw?'

'Yeah.' Les could feel Lori looking at him. 'It's not because I'm so fit, or my star sign, or anything like that. Before I left Australia I studied the Al Bundy Sex Guide. *How To Be a Dynamite Lover and Give Your Wife Multiple Orgasms*.'

Lori stared at Norton for a while, then started to smile as the joke sunk in. After all, she was an American. 'Les . . . whatever your name is, if Al Bundy gave Peg one like that just once in every six episodes, she'd get a job, start wearing decent make-up and take up cooking lessons.'

Norton couldn't help but glow a little. 'You reckon?'

'I'd guarantee it, Les. Or . . . fair dinkum. Isn't that another one of your weird Australian sayings?'

Norton gave her a nice kiss on the cheek. 'Yeah. Close enough.'

If either party wanted to avoid sleeping in the wet spot it would have been pretty tricky, the bed was just one big one. Les suggested there was a pool just outside, you weren't supposed to use it after ten, but if they kept quiet they could have a swim. It was unlikely anybody would say anything. Stiff shit if they did. Lori kissed him and said he just kept getting better all the time. The pool wasn't all that lit up, why worry about swimming costumes? So apart from one towel between them they went skinny dipping.

The water in the pool was absolutely delightful and had just the slightest hint of chill about it. They slipped in quietly, kept their voices down, and just swam and duck dived around, getting all the sweat off them and just freshening up in general; there was still a fair way to go before they'd sober up, however. Les couldn't help but float round at the side of the pool and perv on Lori as she snaked through the water. She had a figure, especially her backside, that would make a Trappist monk start singing in the shower. Before long, Mr Wobbly began to get nasty ideas again. Les floated across and decided to help Lori over the waves. She gave him a quick kiss or two but a toss and shake of her head said no for number two. Yeah, thought Les. Typical yank. All full of piss and wind. However, Lori had to get home. She didn't particularly want to come rolling in at all hours of the morning in front of her sister and the kids, looking like the wreck of the Hesperus. Plus there was an auntie lived there too so a bit of decorum was needed. And lunchtime tomorrow she was going to Orlando for the rest of the week for her work. Not to worry, Les baby. She'd be back Friday. Fair enough, thought Norton, and helped her out of the pool.

Back inside the condo Norton, ever the gentleman, suggested that if Lori didn't want to get her Levis and that all wet she could put his Hawaiian shirt on and he'd throw in the beaut Merv Hughes T-shirt for a souvenir. Lori was stoked. Norton climbed into a pair of shorts and another T-shirt, found a plastic bag in the kitchen for Lori to put her stuff in, and with just her knickers on and Norton's Hawaiian shirt round her they went outside. Sure enough, there was the ever faithful Joey sitting patiently in the limo. He smiled knowingly when he saw them walking over, got out and opened the back door.

'Still enjoying your stay in Florida, sir?' he said.

'Yeah,' replied Norton. 'It's tops. The natives are very friendly.' He turned to Lori.

'8754 North Ewart,' she said, and got inside.

'You heard the lady,' said Les. 'And Joey,' he added quietly, 'get stuck at as many red lights and caught in as much traffic as you like. Let the meter run right over. You dig?'

'Like my mother was a shovel,' winked the driver.

Les climbed in and Lori cuddled up to him. Joey was on the ball straight away; it took him nearly fifteen minutes to reverse out the carpark and negotiate the speed humps through the estate. Before long Les and Lori were in a bit of a lover's embrace. Norton was keen to see Lori when she got back from Orlando, she replied that if Les looked on the kitchen table he'd find her phone number. This touched Les and he told Lori that if she didn't give him a decent kiss goodnight, decent enough to last him almost a week, his poor heart would surely break. Lori didn't seem to mind and slipped her tongue inside Norton's mouth. She also didn't mind when Les started rubbing her stomach and boobs, though she did seem to mind when Les started stroking her ted again. But before long it was too late and the washing machine started bubbling over. Next thing, Les had his fly open, her knickers pulled to one side and was easing the evil Mr Wobbly in.

Lori half pushed him away then she gave a little jump and said, 'Oowahh!'

8754 North Ewart was a nice white single-storey house with two palm trees, a light above the verandah out the front and a car in the driveway. Joey eased up and turned off the lights. Les and Lori made their last goodbyes; even if she did heartily enjoy the ride home she seemed a little self-conscious, so Les didn't have to walk her to the door. However, he waited in the car till she was safe inside, blew her a kiss and got a wave back, then she was gone.

'Righto. Home, James,' yawned Norton. 'And don't spare the horses. Just wake me when you get there. I'm rooted.'

Joey caught Norton's eye in the rear vision mirror and smiled. 'Does that mean you're fucked, buddy?'

'You better fuckin' believe it, mate,' answered Norton.

Les was half asleep when they rocked gently to a halt outside the condo; before he knew it Joey had the back door open. Les blinked at the soft lights around him, gave Joey another fifty dollars, patted him on the shoulder and thanked the driver for looking after him. Joey looked at the money and shook his head.

'Buddy, before you go, do you mind if I just shake your hand?'

'No. Not at all,' smiled Les. 'I reckon I deserve something for tonight's effort.'

Back in the condo, Les managed to clean his teeth and have a leak without falling head first into the bowl, then get his clothes off and flop onto the bed. The sun looked like it was coming up and for some odd reason Les started wondering what time it was back in Australia. Would he be getting up at midday or just before midnight? Shit, I don't know, he mumbled to himself. Christ! What a way to treat your body. Or your body clock, or whatever. As he drifted off, a tiny whiff of Lori's perfume rose up from the sheets. Yeah, what a way. Heh, heh!

Despite the gallons of booze he'd poured down his throat, Norton didn't feel all that bad when he surfaced around noon. Must have been all that 'exercise' last night, he smiled to himself as he cleaned his teeth. I've sweated all the toxins out of me. He still wasn't feeling one hundred per cent as he fiddled around in the kitchen making a cup of coffee and drinking orange juice and figured the best way to get rid of any remaining cobwebs could be a splash around in the pool. He got a towel and stepped out the back door into the customary, open-air, Florida sauna bath.

There were only two other people in the pool, a woman doing some sort of aquarobics at the shallow end and a man on a banana chair puffing a cigar while he read a magazine. Les nodded something to him then quietly dived in and started swimming around. It wasn't the same without Lori and it wasn't all that cool, but it was good enough. Christ! What a funny old night, Les smiled to himself as he started doing a few lazy laps. Was that Lori a fit woman or what? And what about poor, silly Hank? Even if I did feel crook today I don't think there's any way I could be as crook as him. Though I might put Club BandBox on hold for the rest of my stay here. That's if there's anything left of the place.

After a while he towelled off, went back inside and drank the rest of his orange juice. That's what he was going to need, he mused, as he tossed the empty container in the kitchen-tidy. That and a good feed of home-cooked vegetables. If he remembered right when he was driving out with Hank there was a small shopping centre not that far away. A pedal up on the bike would get rid of any remaining toxins, plus he was also going to need some more of those funny little pieces of green paper everyone seemed to love so much in America. He got into the same old training gear he'd worn when he went riding on the beach with Hank, got his bike from the verandah and with his backpack on turned right out the front of the estate and set off for the shopping centre.

Belting along the dead flat footpath was a piece of piss, just punishingly hot, that was all. Again there were no pedestrians. Apart from the cars whizzing along the road, the only other sign of life Les spotted was a girl jogging with a Walkman, whom he almost barrelled as she turned around. The shopping centre was about three miles from the estate; a bank and a garage on one corner and a medium size supermarket complex set in a parking area on the other. Despite walking in, dripping with sweat, Les was able to cash some more traveller's cheques without any drama, even get a pleasant smile from the girl over his accent. After pedalling like a maniac through a break in the traffic, Les made it safely to the other corner, where there was a post office, hairdresser's, travel agency and a number of other shops set round the supermarket, and of all things an Amish restaurant. There was a soft-drink machine just inside the supermarket; Norton decided to get a can of 7-Up and check out the punters before he did the rest of his shopping.

There were a few people coming and going, or getting in and out of cars, but the Amish were the best. They were a funny-looking lot. Old men with quaker beards, wearing black hats, white shirts and black pants held up by old-fashioned braces, riding round on these three-wheel bikes. The women wore crinoline dresses and aprons with what looked like coffee filters on their heads, and not a trace of make-up. They seemed friendly enough, though; if Les made eye contact he'd get a bit of a smile and he'd smile back. Les was contentedly slurping on his soft drink when the fattest, ugliest bloke Les had ever seen in his life pulled up in a car and climbed out. He had the usual Elmer Fudd cap stuck on his head and wore a massive pair of grey pants held up with braces. His paunch was that big it almost dragged on the ground in front of him and he had to swing his arms and his paunch from side to side in a kind of rhythm so he could walk. He reminded Les of the bloke in the Monty Python film, who blows up in the French restaurant. Only this bloke wasn't comical. He was that grotesquely fat he almost made Norton sick. With almost a morbid fascination Les watched him enter the supermarket, then come back out with some groceries and drive off. Shaking his head almost with disbelief, Les watched the car disappear, then got his orange juice, vegies and a few other odds and ends, slung his backpack on and pedalled back to the flat. One of the first things he did when he got there was have another swim; it seemed hotter and more humid than ever and if Les wasn't mistaken another cloud build-up was coming in from the Gulf of Mexico.

A feed of fresh vegetables might have been a good idea, but cooking them wasn't. Five minutes after he'd got the electric stove going and the water boiling, the flat was like an oven and Les was almost tempted to turn the air-conditioner on. He decided to tough it out. The vegetables were a disappointment too. They looked alright in the shop but they tasted flat and nowhere near as good as the ones at home. However, after dolloping them with butter and some yellow sauce called Louisiana Cajun Dressing, Les was able to spice them up a bit and get them down with a few glasses of orange juice. After he'd cleaned up Les made a cup of coffee and thought about what he should do and how he should organise himself now that he'd finally got rid of Hank the wank. A phone call to Laverne to thank her and tell her what was going on might be a good idea. Norton found the number near the phone and dialled. A man's voice with another strong New York accent answered at the other end.

'Hullo?'

'Yes. Could I speak to Laverne please?'

The voice hesitated. 'Who's this?'

'It's Les. The Australian bloke. I'm staying out at the flat... the condo.'

The voice sounded a bit suspicious. 'Hang on. I'll go get her.'

A few moments later a woman answered. She sounded just as wary as the man.

'Hullo? Who's this?'

'Hello, Laverne? It's Les over at the condo.'

'Oh Les.' Laverne gave a bit of a laugh. 'Ricco couldn't understand what you were saying. How are you doing?'

'I'm okay. I just wanted to ring and let you know I've moved in and all that. It's terrific. Thanks a lot.'

'Oh don't worry about it. You're doing me a favour keeping an eye on the place. Just keep Hank out. When did you last see the jerk? Is there something wrong with the air-conditioning there?'

'No. It's as good as gold. But... that's another reason I rang you, Laverne. I sort of... told Hank to piss off last night.'

'Oh.' Laverne seemed to pause for a moment. 'I thought something like this might happen.'

'Yeah. I don't want to sound rude or anything, Laverne. But he's got to be the greatest wombat I've ever met in my life.'

'You noticed, huh!'

'Noticed? Christ!'

'So hey, are you alright? Have you got enough food? We'd better come over.' For all her brashness, Laverne sounded genuinely concerned about Norton's wellbeing.

'No. I'm okay. I got a bike. I can get around alright.'

'A bike? In this heat. My God, you need a car.'

'Yeah, I intend to hire one. But I'm okay. Don't worry about it.'

'No, we'll come over. Just hang on for a moment, Les.'

'Hey it's ...' Les waited on the line for a minute or so, thinking how nice Laverne sounded over the phone.

'Les, I'll tell you what we're gonna do. Ricco and I will come over tonight around eight. And you can come back here for dinner. Ricco wants to barbecue some burgers.'

'Laverne,' protested Norton. 'There's no need for you ...'

'Hey, it's okay, Les. Ricco wants to meet you anyway.'

'Alright, fair enough.'

'So we'll see you about eight.'

'Okay. Thanks, Laverne.'

'Bye, Les.'

Norton stared at the phone for a moment after Laverne hung up. Well, isn't she a number one babe the way she was worrying about me? And now I'm going round for dinner. Then Les found himself shaking his head. How would a girl like that go out with a prick like Captain Rats? Either she's got a heart of gold, or she's related to Mother Theresa. She's right, though. I do need a car. Especially if I'm going to ring those other Loris and have a good look around the place. I'll hire one tomorrow. Maybe the mysterious Ricco might be able to help me out there. So what will I do till eight? Norton drummed his fingers on the bar. I know what I can do. Clean that mess up in my room before they get here. Les got a bottle of Coors Cutter from the fridge and started doing exactly that.

He had his gear half stowed away and was happily pottering about when he noticed something was missing. His brand new Walkman with the graphic equaliser and super bass he'd bought at the duty free shop before he left Australia. Shit! Les cursed to himself. I know where the bloody thing is too. Back on the bed at Swamp Manor. I must have tossed the sheets over it when I bolted out of the joint. Bugger it! That means when I get a car I have to go back around there. Still, I only have to see his mum, and I promised I would. I can avoid shit-for-brains. Les started to laugh. He'll probably be in hospital anyway.

Les finished tidying up then washed a couple of T-shirts in the bathroom and hung them over some chairs on the verandah. All of which was pretty exhausting work, so he went back out to the pool for a while.

After he'd towelled off and was walking round the flat with a large glass of orange juice, Norton started eyeing the paper bag with the road map and travel books in it Mrs Laurel had loaned him. He was going to have to take them back with him when he went round to get his Walkman. I wonder what's in them anyway, thought Les, as he picked them up off the dressing table and put them on the bed. Might give me something to read. It was then Les realised he hadn't read a newspaper, turned on a radio or watched the news on TV since he'd been in America. Christ! Who knows what's going on? We could be at war or anything. Governments might have fallen, Europe could be in turmoil. And most important of all, which league teams are going to make the semis back in Australia? I just pray Balmain isn't among them. Even thousands of miles across the seas Norton could hear George Brennan laughing at him if the Tigers got up and his team missed out.

There were four books. Two small thin ones on Hawaii and Panama. The other two were almost like novels, only full of pictures. One was about Mexico. The other one made Norton's eyes light up.

'Bloody hell!' he said out loud. 'Jamaica, mon. Jamaica.' One of the reasons Les came to Florida was because Jamaica was just a couple of hundred miles away, if that. The James Bond movie *Live and Let Die* had been on TV not long before Norton left. There was 007 running up and down on the backs of alligators as he rescued the usual glamours and took on the evil SPECTRE, or whoever the baddies were, and gave them a severe thrashing single-handed. But apart from that the place still looked alright and back in Australia in the middle of winter Norton could just picture himself strolling around Harry Belafonte's 'Island in the sun'. Snorkeling in the crystal clear, blue waters. Walking in the moonlight across golden beaches with some dusky Jamaican beauty on his arm. Drinking rum among happy, smiling people, listening to reggae music while they all smoked joints of ganja as big as corn cobs. Way to go. But there was more to it than that.

Old Grandma Norton, Isabelle, or Bellah, as everybody on Dad's side used to call her, was always babbling on about the Nortons in Jamaica and how there was a famous poet in the family. No one took that much notice because old Bellah didn't mind a drop or two of the cooking sherry now and again. But Grandma would get a roll on, especially with a few drinks under her apron, about how one mob of Nortons went to Jamaica and the family had roots there; as well as a heap of money. Yeah, Grandma, they'd all say. As far as Les was concerned, apart from a brand of motorbikes, Norton was just another name; some mob of convicts arrived in Australia and that was that. But old Bellah was adamant there was more to the Norton bloodline than that, and even after she was gone it always stuck in Les's mind what old Grandma might have been on about. Especially the money. Bless her dear old soul. He looked at the three pretty little kids on the blue cover of *Seekers Guide to Jamaica*, settled back on the bed and started flicking through the pages.

The book was more than just a travel guide. It went right back to the Caribs, the Arawaks, Christopher Columbus, pirates. The British takeover in 1655, the slave trade. Right up to full nationhood in 1962, Rastafarians, reggae music and ganja the sacred herb. All the places looked choice. Negril, Ocho Rios, Kingston Town, Savannah-La-Mar. Les read on. But what Les was looking for should be in the back index. It was, just like old Bellah said and just like the song. Montego Bay. Les flicked back into the book right onto Rose Hill, the Great House built by Moulton Eduardo Darius Norton in 1681. And not far away was Sweet Ginger Hill, built by Stanley Moulton Eduardo Norton in 1720, where the famous poet Elizabeth Norton Blackmore was born.

'Holy bloody hell!' Les looked around the room as if he expected there was someone there to share his excitement. 'Elizabeth Norton Blackmore. Old Grandma was right.' Les shook his head. 'Well, I'll be buggered.' Les read on avidly. If his grandmother was right and this was the same family of Nortons, he'd accidentally traced his family tree back to the sixteenth century.

The book said how Rose Hill Great House had been restored and was open to visitors for a fee. But Sweet Ginger Hill was now owned by Billy Ray Dollar, the American country singer, and was off limits to the public. Dollar and his wife got held up in his house by bandits one night armed with machine guns, but he still made periodic visits to his Jamaican hideaway. Scenes from *Live and Let Die* were shot not far away. The book went on about how the Norton family made their fortune out of sugar plantations and running slaves. Elizabeth had a brother, Eduardo Xavier Norton. They both lived at Sweet Ginger Hill and brother and sister were very close. Eduardo had a fallout with the family, took on religion and moved to a place called Dredmouth, not far from Sweet Ginger Hill, where the family built him a manse. A 'manse'? What the fuck's a 'manse'? thought Les. The book then said it seemed strange that after their fallout the Norton family, notoriously tight-fisted, would build Eduardo a manse. Les had to chuckle. Notoriously tight-fisted. That's the bloody Nortons, alright. Old Bellah sure knew what she was talking about. It was rumoured Eduardo was involved with pirates, including the equally notorious Black Beard and Anne of the Indies. There was more rumour and mystery about buried treasure, and it was said the clues to where it was buried were in one of Eduardo's sister's most famous poems. There was more mystery surrounding the Nortons around Montego Bay; voodoo, witches, ghosts, etc. Then Eduardo disappeared during a violent storm one night, the same night a pirate ship, the *Cimarron*, was sunk with all hands in 1770. Elizabeth left Jamaica for England not long after her brother Eduardo disappeared, where she married

164

another famous poet, Davidson Blackmore, though she always retained her maiden name. Elizabeth intended to return to Jamaica, but died from pneumonia before she got the chance; she was in her early forties. The Norton family was a famous family in Jamaica and the name lives on, though all the original descendants went back to England not long after slavery was abolished, or are buried in the walled family burial ground that overlooks the ocean beneath the Rose Hill Great House, about twelve miles from Montego Bay. The book then went on about other things around Montego Bay, like Stewart Castle, Flint River, Fort Charlotte. But Les kept flicking back to the part about the Norton family, especially Elizabeth, Eduardo and the manse, whatever that was. There was definitely some mystery and romance or something there; not counting the ghosts, buried treasure and whatever. Bloody old Bellah, Les smiled to himself. And all the time we thought she was off her trolley or it was just the piss talking. Bless her dear old soul.

Les took another look through the book, then lay back on the bed and had a bit of think. Old Grandma. Wouldn't it be funny if she was right? It sure looks that way. No matter what, I'm going there. Jamaica is definitely included in the holiday. I've got another two weeks or so of luxury and cruising around Florida, then I'll go over there for a week or probably a fortnight. In fact, if I like it, I might even stay longer. No matter what, it'll be a buzz just looking around the place. Christ! Wait till I tell the folks when I go home for Christmas. The old man'll shit himself. Les started to read a bit more, then realised it wasn't getting any earlier. If he was going to get scrubbed up and make a phone call before Laverne and her boyfriend called round he'd best get his finger out. Les was about to make a move when a violent clap of thunder rattled across the sky. It made him jump and turn towards the window. Outside, it had clouded over. There was more violent thunder then it started pissing rain again. I don't believe this, muttered Les to himself. It's worse than the Kokoda Trail. Surely it's not like this every day during summer?

Eventually the storm cleared up and the late afternoon sun came out about the same time Les was standing in the kitchen wearing his jeans, a freshly ironed brown check shirt and looking at the two phone numbers he'd fished out of the mess when he cleaned up his bedroom. Now, which one is Lori the shipwright or whatever? I think it's this one. Les dialled and waited a few seconds.'

'Hullo?'

'Yes. Could I speak to Lori please?'

'This is Lori.'

'How are you, Lori? It's Les, the Australian bloke. I met you at the Sandbar on Friday night.'

The girl seemed to think for a moment. 'Oh yes. I remember you. Hey, how are you? How are the weather balloons going?'

Weather balloons? Oh Christ! This is the one that works for the law firm or whatever. 'Yeah, right. The weather balloons. It's funny you remembered. They're going alright. I only had to blow up two hundred today. My lips are stuffed.'

Lori chuckled over the phone. 'You're a funny guy, Les.'

'You wouldn't say that if you could see my lips. I think my kissing days are over.'

Les nattered on to Lori for a short while. You never know, he thought. The other one might brush me and this one wasn't too bad. She'll do for a trade-in till the other Lori gets back from Orlando. He told her he'd moved into a condo out on Manatee and was getting a car. Would she like to go out one night when he was settled in some more? Lori was keen. Les nattered on politely for a while longer and was about to say goodbye.

'Oh, Les,' said Lori. 'There was something I wanted to ask you.'

'Sure. Go for your life.'

'You're a meteorologist?'

'Am I bloody ever. I got the lips to prove it.'

'No seriously, Les. This weather lately. Do you find it unusual?'

166

'Unusual? I don't know about unusual. It's bloody hot, it's humid and it rains every bloody afternoon. You don't have to be a meteorologist to know that.'

'It's just that some friends of mine were saying Florida was due for a bad cyclone soon. The weather's never normally as stormy as this in summer. And someone else said there was a big cyclone building up somewhere. Is there? You should know.'

Les thought for a moment: about what, he didn't know. 'Alright, Lori,' he prevaricated, 'if I tell you this you promise you won't tell anybody?'

'No. Never.'

'Well, there is a big cyclone building up. That's one of the reasons I'm over here. In fact, when I see you, I'll show you some printout sheets from the computer. But you're not to tell anyone. The Australian government would have me shot if they thought I caused a panic. You understand?'

'Yes I do, Les. Oh my God!'

Norton finally said his goodbyes, shook his head, then looked at the other phone number. What am I now? A racehorse trainer. He dialled again.

'Hullo?'

'Could I speak to Lori please?' he said carefully.

'Just a minute. I'll get her.'

A moment or two later came a familiar Texan drawl. 'Hullo? This is Lori.'

'G'day, Lori, you little yellow rose of Texas. It's Les. The racehorse owner from Australia. I met you at the Sandbar on Friday night.'

'Oh. Hi, Les. I remember you.' Lori sounded pleased to hear from him. 'How are you? We were only talking about you at work today.'

'Fair dinkum?'

'Yes,' Lori gave a little chuckle. 'Fair dinkum. There's some aussies own a boat out at the marina. They come from a place called Mal-bourne. You know it?'

'Yeah. Know it well. Are they nice people?'

'Oh yes,' said Lori happily. 'They're nice people. Hey — no worries.'

167

Now it was Norton's turn to chuckle. 'Hey, I think I know where you're coming from, Tex.'

'So how have you been, Les? It's so nice to hear from you.'

'To tell you the truth, things are going pretty good. What about yourself?'

Lori the Texan didn't mind a chat. She filled Les in on life on the marina, aerobics, a part-time job she had at a movie theatre, etc, etc. Les told her he'd moved into a condo, he hadn't bought any horses yet, he was hiring a car tomorrow, America was great and he was looking forward to seeing some more of it.

'So anyway, Lori, I should have this car tomorrow. I was wondering if you're doing nothing tomorrow night, would you like to come out with me? Have a nice meal, show me around Siestasota? Anything you like. What do you reckon?'

'I reckon that sounds like a great idea, Les. I ain't got nothing on tomorrow.'

'Okay. I'll call over. Give me your address, I'll get over there alright. I got a map.'

Lori seemed to think for a moment. 'Listen, Les. I think it might be best if I came and got you. Besides, don't you aussies drive on the wrong side of the road?'

'No, we don't. You do.'

'I'll still come and get you though.' Lori seemed definite about this.

'Well, okay. If that's alright by you?'

'Manatee's not far from here. Then maybe we can go out in your car. At least this way I know I'm going to get home in one piece.'

'I take that as an insult,' sniffed Norton. 'But okay. If you insist.'

Les wasn't going to argue; it couldn't be creamier. He gave Lori his phone number and address, chatted on for a while longer then said he'd see her around eight-thirty tomorrow night. Both parties were looking forward to it.

Well there you go, smiled Les, rubbing his hands together after he'd hung up. A nice night out with a nice-looking girl, a good feed somewhere, then see if I can drag 'the whacko from Waco' back here. Back here? She's gotta come back here to either pick up her car or drop me off. Then it's up to the old Norton charm. Les winked at himself in one of the wall mirrors. Go get 'em, killer. Les poured himself another glass of orange juice and was once again contemplating his luck when there was a knock on the door. He took a sip then answered it.

'Hello,' he said cheerfully. 'You must be from the Salvation Army. Just a moment and I'll get you something.'

'Hi, Les,' said Laverne. 'How are you?'

'Couldn't be creamier,' beamed Norton. 'Won't you come in?'

'Les,' said Laverne, as Norton closed the door, 'this is Ricco.'

'G'day, Ricco,' said Norton, offering his hand. 'How are you, mate?'

'Good day, cobber,' answered Ricco in this horrible affected cockney accent as he pumped Norton's hand. 'How are you goin' there . . . mate?'

Norton winced. 'Nice to meet you too, Ricco.'

Ricco was in his thirties, as tall as Les, though not as well built, with neat brown hair combed straight back off his forehead, and was good-looking in a hard, street-wise fashion, something like the limo driver. He wore tailored grey trousers and an expensive black shirt and shoes. A gold chain hung round his neck and a thin gold watch sat on his wrist. He was well manicured and cologned and for someone just about to have a backyard barby looked more like he was going to see a Broadway play. Laverne looked as pretty as before and happier in a pair of blue shorts and a blue and while polka-dot top. They sat down on the lounge next to the door, Les sat opposite; if Les was giving Ricco half a check out, Ricco was sure doing the same thing to Les.

'So,' said Norton, smiling from one to the other, 'you're the dopey bitch that stuffed up Hank's business? And you're the jerk from New York she left him for just because you've got more money?'

Laverne and Ricco exchanged kind of bemused glances. 'Yeah,' nodded Laverne. 'That's us.'

'Yeah. That's us,' echoed Ricco expressionlessly.

'Well, it's nice to meet you anyway. Can I get you a drink or something?'

'Stay there.' Ricco got up and helped himself to a Coors from the fridge. While he was there he had a look around then turned on the air-conditioner; half for comfort and half to let Les know who owned the place. He settled back on the lounge and took a swig from the bottle, looking evenly at Norton the whole time. 'So what's been happening, Les?' he said, in a nasally thick, New York twang.

"Not much, mate,' shrugged Les. 'I only just moved in.'

'Been quiet, have you?'

'Like a mouse wearing slippers.'

'That's not what Joey Hubcap told me.'

'Joey Hubcap?' Norton looked at Ricco for a moment. 'You don't mean the limo driver, do you?'

'Yeah.'

'Oh! Well, yes I did have a girl back here last night. But she was a decent type. Not just some moll I picked up.'

'Hey, I don't care if you brought a two-bit hooker back here. But just don't bullshit me with this quiet. You know what I'm sayin'?'

'Well, I didn't quite mean it like that, Ricco. I just didn't want to start up with a big come on about all the sheilas I've been getting and all the piss I've been drinking. But if your mate Hubcaps said I had a pretty good time,' Les smiled and winked as he matched Ricco's even stare, 'he definitely wasn't bullshitting you.'

"Hey, don't sweat it. Joey said you were aces.' Ricco raised his bottle.

'So what happened between you and Hank?' asked Laverne.

'Hank? Well, it's a bit of a shame, Laverne. But Hank and I had what's called "a parting of the ways".'

Les told them a few things about Hank. Mainly what a miserable lemon he was and you couldn't even have an

170

opinion about anything, let alone tell the flip anything. How he bagged the condominium, put on the drama over a cigarette, pissed off then followed Les down the Club BandBox and started a fight. Les had previously arranged to meet Lori down there and he managed to drag her out in the middle of the brawl; which was one of the reasons he brought her back to the flat, to settle the poor girl's nerves.

'My God!' gasped Laverne. 'That was on the news. Four people got shot. There were stabbings. The whole place got trashed. And you're saying this was all Hank's fault?'

Les nodded sincerely. 'Yeah. I told you he was a ratbag.'

By now Ricco had finished his Coors without once taking his eyes off Norton. 'Okay,' he said, 'if I'm gonna cook these burgers I guess we'd better get going.'

'Righto, I'm ready to go.' Les got to his feet. 'Give us your empty bottle,' he smiled down at Ricco. 'I'll stick it in the garbage tin.'

Les locked up the flat and they trooped out to Ricco's car; Ricco drove a brand new, dark blue Mercedes with tinted windows. After opening the door for Laverne, Les climbed in the back and settled into a cocoon of opulence and comfort that smelled of air-conditioned sterility.

'You hungry?' asked Ricco, as he started the engine.

'Yeah. I'm a bit peckish,' answered Les.

'We're having burgers and salad. I make great burgers.'

'Sounds alright to me. And thanks for inviting me over. I hope I haven't put you to any trouble.'

'No trouble at all.'

They turned right out the front and started heading towards where Les went shopping earlier. Before they reached the supermarket corner Norton turned to Laverne.

'Laverne,' he hesitated a little, 'this probably isn't any of my business, but I have to ask you. How could a girl as pleasant and good-looking as you go out with an idiot like Hank? Was he blackmailing your family or something?'

171

Laverne smiled. 'No, it wasn't quite like that. I don't know what the jerk's told you.'

As they drove on, Laverne told Les a bit about herself. She'd moved down to Florida from New York about two years ago after getting a divorce. She was lonely, she met Hank on the rebound and sort of went out with him for around six months; then she had a hard time getting rid of the idiot. As for stuffing up his lousy business, she tried to help him, but, as Les knew, he couldn't be told anything and completely stuffed things up himself. She never left Hank for Ricco. He came from New York also, they knew each other back there, and, like her, Ricco had also gone through a divorce. They bumped each other in a shopping mall in Siestasota, then things just started to happen and they had been together for almost a year now. From the way they exchanged glances and the way Laverne had her hand rested on Ricco's leg while he drove Les got the picture. All that was missing was a big purple heart hanging between them with an arrow through it, and if Laverne was suffering leaving Hank for Ricco she certainly wasn't showing it. She owned the condo, which she'd bought with Ricco's help, and lived with Ricco. Hank had been using it as a mail drop because he was on the skids and owed money everywhere. For some reason she liked Les the minute she saw him and knew what he'd be going through stuck out at Swamp Manor, and he was doing her a favour staying there and keeping an eye on the place till some people moved in next month.

Les, for his part, told her the truth about himself. Where he lived in Australia, what he did for a living, how he met Hank in Oz, and how he happened to be in Florida. He didn't say how he organised the fight in Club BandBox, but he did say he had plenty of money with him and if she wanted some rent while he was in the condo she was more than welcome, to which both Laverne and Ricco politely told him to stick it in his ass. Next thing they were driving down a wide street full of expensive-looking homes and they pulled up in Ricco's driveway.

The house was big and white but before Les could get a good look Ricco hit a remote button and the double garage door swung up and they pulled up inside next to what looked like a two-tone brown Ford LTD. Ricco hit the remote again and the garage door swung back down.

Norton gave a double blink as they stepped up from the garage into the kitchen; Ricco acted indifferently but he noticed Norton was impressed. The kitchen was about half as big as Norton's house. Super modern in black, red and silver, high ceilinged with a cooking island in the middle big enough to land a helicopter gunship on. The stove was one of those ultrasound ones Les had seen on 'Beyond 2000'; it caught his eye along with a small espresso coffee machine sitting on an alcove in one wall.

'I'm goin' out to fire the barbecue,' Ricco said to Laverne. 'You wanna show Les the rest of the house?'

'Alrighty,' answered Laverne. 'Then I'll start on the salads.'

Ricco disappeared through some doorway and Laverne showed Les around, pointing things out in a kind of sing-song, gameshow host voice. 'This is the lounge. This is the main bedroom. Here we have a bathroom.' The place was about as big as Price's; but where Price went more for antiques, Ricco's place was more like a mini museum of modern art. Abstract paintings and murals hung on the walls, strange-looking marble and bronze statues sat on smoked glass tables and reflected in some walls which were entire tinted mirrors. It was all pastel colours, the carpet throughout the house was a light blue and smoother than a bowling green. There were five bedrooms; the main one was done out in an Asian style with a futon, waterbed and a monster screen TV. Chandeliers hung from the ceilings, a set of marble steps flanked by two onyx statues led up to the massive front door. Everything reeked not only of money, but class and good taste as well. A couple of steps led down from the loungeroom to an oval-shaped swimming pool enclosed in green mesh, something like a trapezium; beyond that, manicured lawns led up to bush and trees and a distant lagoon. Ricco was down one end of the pool area, pottering around over a barbecue, and Les could smell and hear the faint sizzle of hamburgers cooking. At the other end of the pool Les had to smile. Several long-tailed lizards were outside clinging to the green mesh, being eyed off by a red and green parrot, about twice as big as a kookaburra, sitting on a stand. It looked across at Les and gave a kind of soft squawk that seemed to be telling Rico there was a stranger in the place.

Les smiled and gave it a bit of a wave. 'G'day, mate. How are you goin' over there?'

'So. Do you like the house?' asked Laverne.

'Yeah, reckon,' replied Les honestly. 'It makes my place at Bondi look like a bark humpy.'

Laverne looked at Les expressionlessly. 'I might start in the kitchen. Why don't you go talk with Ricco?'

'Okey-doke.'

There was a table and chairs laid out near the barbecue area and a fridge built into the wall next to it. Ricco was sipping on a bottle of something called O'Doulls while he stood guard over his hamburgers with a metal spatula.

'Well, Ricco,' said Norton, 'this is definitely a nice place you've got. It sure doesn't look like you're starving.'

'I'm a millionaire,' replied Ricco, without looking up from the six hamburgers sizzling on the barbecue.'

'Yeah? Good on you,' said Les.

'My wife made me a millionaire.'

'She did? That was nice of her.'

'Yeah. I used to be a multi-millionaire. Now I'm just a millionaire. It was real nice of her, the bitch.'

'Touché,' chuckled Les. He watched Ricco for a moment deftly flicking at his hamburgers. 'What's that you're drinking?'

'O'Doulls non-alcoholic beer. I should have offered you one. They're in the fridge. Help yourself.'

Les wiped some sweat from his eyes. 'Okay thanks. In fact, that's what I need. I've been drinking piss since I got here like it's going out of style.' Les helped himself to a cool and frosty one. It was something like the Coors

Cutters, only with a richer taste, and went down quite easily. 'So if you don't mind me asking, Ricco, what do you do for a quid?'

'What do I do for a quid?'

'Yeah. What do you do for a living? I mean, you don't drive a Mercedes and own a place like this changing tyres at the bus depot for sixty bucks a day.' Les took another swig of his beer. 'You seem like a pretty interesting sort of bloke. Tell us a bit about yourself — if you want to. If you don't, I'll mind my own business.'

Ricco seemed to hesitate for a moment then flicked at one of the hamburgers. 'Yeah, why not?' he said.

His name was Ricco DiCosti. He grew up in New York and made all his money from a string of pizza shops he owned, which he sold when he got his divorce. He then moved down to Florida. He now owned a coffee shop south of town at a place called Salmo that kept him going. He talked about running with street gangs in New York, his Italian wife had his two kids in Palm Springs, etc, etc. Most of it was pretty mundane stuff, yet all the time Les had this feeling Ricco was holding back. Somehow he didn't seem the kind of bloke who'd spend too much time with his head stuck in a pizza oven or running around tables in a coffee shop; and he knew about Norton's movements before he'd even met him. But Ricco was interesting enough in a terse kind of fashion and his thick 'noo yoik' accent and mannerisms were quite amusing, even if some of his one-liners fell a bit flat, which didn't stop Les from laughing at them as if they were funny as all get up. Next thing Laverne started piling plates of salad and things on the table.

She'd made a ripping Caesar, plus a cucumber and sour cream and a couple of others along with some more nibblies. It was quite a good spread, especially for three people. Ricco put the hamburgers on their plates, telling Les how good they were going to be and all the ingredients he'd put in them. Then Les remembered 'burgers' on the barby in America were a kind of ritual; that was another thing Warren had told him before he left. But they tasted pretty good sitting on two slabs of focaccia with lettuce, tomato, some kind of cracked pepper, Dijon sauce, and washed down with O'Doulls, while Laverne washed hers down with three large glasses of white wine. Finally Les wiped his mouth and said they were definitely the best 'burgers' he'd ever eaten in his life, not that Ricco needed to be told that. Laverne started to clean up then they moved into the kitchen just as the rain started to tumble down outside.

'You like a good cup of coffee, Les?' asked Ricco.

'Yeah. I don't mind one at all,' replied Norton.

'Wait till you taste this.'

Les watched, fascinated, as Ricco started fussing around with the espresso coffee machine. It hissed and steamed and gurgled; a few minutes later Norton had a cup of coffee sitting on the black tiles of the cooking island next to some cream and sugar. Ricco's burgers were pretty good, but his coffee would have taken gold at the Olympic Games. It was sensational; thick with a creamy brown head, as good as anything you get around Haymarket in Sydney. This time Les was one hundred per cent genuine when he commended him.

'Jesus, that is a bloody good cup of coffee, Ricco. I wish I could make it as good as that.'

Laverne, who'd been a bit quiet, suddenly piped up. 'You gotta be a made man to make coffee as good as that,' she giggled, obviously a bit piddly from her now fifth glass of wine. Les gave a kind of mystified half smile, Ricco didn't seem to see the funny side of it at all and Laverne appeared to look a bit sheepish. A kind of brittle silence hung in the air for a moment and Les thought it might be a good time to switch subjects.

'Ricco,' he said, taking a sip of coffee, 'can you offer me a bit of advice?'

'Sure. What's your problem?'

'I'm going to rent a car tomorrow. Where do you reckon's the best place to go?'

Ricco put his cup back on the saucer. 'You want a car?

What sort of car? You want a big car? A small car? What kind of car?'

Norton shrugged. 'I dunno. Just a Ford or a Chevvy. Something to get me round for the next couple of weeks.'

'What are you doing tomorrow morning round eleven?'

'Nothing.'

'I'll call round, pick you up. I got a buddy out on Greenwood. We'll get you a car.'

'You will...?'

'Hey, I said I'd get you a car. You got a car.'

'Shit! Thanks.'

Ricco seemed to sum Les up again then for the first time a noticeable smile seemed to flicker round his eyes. 'Hey, I like you, Les Norton. You're an alright guy. You got style. You got class. What are you doing this Thursday?'

'I don't know,' shrugged Les again. 'I got nothing planned.'

'You want to go boating? I got a boat. I'll show you round the Keys.'

'That sounds alright. Okay, you got me.' Les took a thoughtful sip of coffee. 'Listen, Ricco, you don't have to go to all this trouble for me — even though I appreciate it. The condo, a nice meal, helping me out. I mean, after spending four days with Captain Rats it's all a bit too much.'

'Hey don't sweat it, Les. Like I said, you're a good fella.'

Les seemed to think for a moment. 'Yeah,' he agreed. 'There's probably worse blokes round than me.'

They chatted away, over nothing much in particular, while they finished a second cup of coffee; most of the time, though, Norton once again couldn't believe his luck. Ricco was going to help him get a car then take him for a boat ride out on the Keys, which sounded tops. Ricco might have been a bit terse or abrupt at times, but he wasn't short on hospitality; a marked contrast to Hank. Finally Ricco said he had things to do early tomorrow morning and he'd like to get going if Les wanted a lift back to the condo. This suited Norton admirably. During the drive home he once again couldn't thank them both enough for their generosity and friendliness.

'Okay Les,' said Ricco, as Norton got out of the car at the condo. 'I'll see you here tomorrow morning. Eleven sharp.'

'Alright, Ricco. I'll see you then.'

'Goodnight, Les.'

'See you later, Laverne.'

The rain had eased and a few stars were appearing from behind the clouds, but it was still oppressively hot. Whether it was the humidity, or the food or what, Norton didn't know, but as he opened the front door of the condo he found himself yawning. Inside it was fairly warm too, but clean and fresh, unlike the stuffy mustiness at Swamp Manor, so he once again didn't bother about the air-conditioning. After a glass of orange juice Les got stripped down to his jocks and lay back on the bed with a table lamp on and the book about Jamaica sitting on his chest. Before he opened it Norton had a think about something Laverne had said when he commented on how good Ricco's coffee was. 'It took a "made man" to make it that good.' And while Les had acted oblivious, he noticed Ricco's stony reaction to his girlfriend's bit of a private joke. If Ricco was a 'made man' he'd taken the oath of omerta and was a member of some New York Mafia family. That's what he was being guarded about. Ricco definitely had strong Mafia connections and who knew how high up he was? Though not to worry. He seemed to like Norton and you couldn't ask for better than to have someone like that on-side while you were stopping for a while in America. Then Les had to chuckle to himself. The more he thought about it, the more Warren was right. It was all getting to be like some scene out of a movie or on TV. That house with the pastel colours could've been from an episode of 'Miami Vice'. Ricco was straight out of *The Godfather*. And their love affair had lashings of *West Side Story* or could have been scripted by Neil Simon. What did some English singer say about America? You watch TV and think how totally unreal it is. Then you step outside and find it's just the same. Oh well, I'm here now and that's it.

Les started to read the book on Jamaica, flicking straight to the photo of Rose Hill Great House at Montego Bay. It was like some old Georgian mansion or a French chateau set on lush green lawns with trees in the background. A long, wide set of sandstone steps flanked with wrought iron bannisters led up to a huge courtyard propped up by about a dozen sandstone pillars and arches. There were two more storeys of white stuccoed sandstone built above and back from the courtyard. Judging by the number of gabled windows that were bigger than doors Les estimated there would have to be about thirty or more rooms. A grey tiled roof sat on top and there were more massive windows set in sandstone walls down the sides. The courtyard was surrounded by a wall of chest-high marble columns, the huge front door had two equally huge marble columns set on either side with a marble arch and shelter set above. Yes, mused Les, I'd sure say old Moulton Norton wasn't short of a dollar back then. Of course labour wasn't very cost intensive back in those day. Instead of sick pay, holiday pay and a 17.5% loading, you got a good whipping instead. He was reading about a mob of slaves who escaped and were called Maroons, which came from the Spanish word *cimarron*, and meant wild, and their leader Cudjoe, who with his two sub-chiefs Quao and Cuffee caused the British no end of trouble back around 1670, when Norton's eyes started to close. He switched off the table lamp and drifted into a sweaty, but pleasant sleep.

By the time Les got out of bed the next morning then got cleaned up, made a cup of coffee, pedalled up to the store for more orange juice, had a long swim followed by a late breakfast, then sat around picking his toes while he thought about a few things and got into a pair of shorts and a clean white T-shirt, Ricco was knocking on the door. Ricco looked as neat and dapper as ever in a pair of white trousers, tan loafers and a maroon shirt hanging out.

'You ready to roll?' he said shortly, not bothering to come inside.

'Yeah, mate,' answered Norton. 'I'll just grab me licence and some chops.'

Les got his wallet and locked up the flat. Next thing they were safe from the blistering heat inside Ricco's air-conditioned Mercedes and had turned left outside the estate towards downtown.

'Where are we going?' asked Norton.

'About a half-dozen blocks from here to my buddy Vinnie's place. You'll like Vinnie. He's an alright guy.'

'Is he from New York too?' asked Les, knowing he needn't have bothered.

'Yeah. We grew up on the same block.'

And went to the same reform school too? I wonder what Vinnie's other name is? Vinnie the Fish? Vinnie the Ox? Vinnie Three Fingers?

Les was pondering on this and what scene in which TV show or movie he'd be playing today when two bumper stickers on a big grey pick-up truck caught his eye. There was a Confederate flag on the window and it was driven by a good ol' boy in a black, ten-gallon hat. One sticker said, 'God, Guns and Guts Made America. Let's Keep All Three'. The other said, 'Will the Last American to Leave Miami Please Bring the Flag?'. Yes, thought Norton. Today's scene is either *Smokey and the Bandit* or 'The Dukes of Hazzard'. Norton was thinking on this when they pulled into some sort of caryard.

There were around forty cars sitting there, all big American gas guzzlers with prices on the windscreens and bunting and advertising much like any place you'd see along Parramatta Road. A single-storey brick office with tinted windows sat out the front among about a dozen palm trees. From the roof a number of American flags fluttered slightly in the hot wind and above the flags was a

sign in red and white: BIG V. CARS AND RENTALS.
A monstrous, dark green Cadillac sat out the front of the
office and leaning against it, smoking a cigar as big as a
tin of tennis balls, was a tall, barrel-chested man with a
paunch and short black hair receding in the front. He was
wearing a blue shirt, open almost to the waist, matching
blue trousers and shiny black shoes.

'Hey, Vinnie,' said Ricco, as they got out of the Mercedes. 'How are you doin'?'

'Hey, Ricco,' smiled Vinnie. 'What do you say, buddy?'

'Vinnie, I want you to meet Les. Les, this is Vinnie.'

'G'day Vinnie,' said Norton, offering his hand. 'How
are you, mate?'

'Hey Les. Nice to meet you.' Vinnie's massive paw
wrapped around Norton's and gave it a vigorous crunching. 'So you're the aussie guy wants a car?'

'Yeah. Ricco said you might be able to help me.'

Vinnie turned to Ricco and made an open-handed
gesture. 'Might be able to help him. What is this, huh?
Come out back, Les. I got just the car you need. I got you
a T-bird. Straight off the lot.'

'A T-bird? That sounds alright.' Norton was curious.
He was also dubious. Straight off the lot probably also
meant straight off the street — in some other city.

'You wanted a car,' shrugged Ricco. 'I got you a car.'

The car was an iridescent grey Ford Thunderbird with
rounded fenders and bonnet that made it look more like a
Mercedes. It was only two doors with four pillared
windows, but it was bigger, shinier, and newer than
anything Les had ever driven. Vinnie opened the door
and Les got inside. As he sat down an alarm started,
which Vinnie explained was for the seat-belt that somehow or other seemed to automatically slide up and down
above the driver's side window; Les clamped it on and the
alarm stopped. The interior was all plush grey velvet you
sunk into, with power steering, power doors, power
brakes and power every bloody thing else plus a scanner
radio cassette stereo with four speakers in the doors. The
only thing wrong was that the steering wheel was on

the wrong side and the rear vision mirror faced the wrong way.

'So what do you say, huh?' said Vinnie.

'Yeah. It's a beauty,' answered Les. 'She'll do me. What's the damage?'

'Come inside out of the heat and we'll do the paperwork.'

Vinnie's office was nicely air-conditioned and fairly plush. There were indoor palms, paintings and mirrors on the walls, some bamboo furniture, and lounges with green and white bamboo patterned wallpaper all round. A shiny wooden counter sat in the front and behind that stood a door with PRIVATE on it.

'You want a soda?' asked Vinnie, as he disappeared behind the door in a cloud of blue cigar smoke.

'Yeah righto, thanks,' replied Les.

Vinnie returned with an O'Doulls for Ricco, a 7-UP for Les and a Lemon Crush for himself along with the paperwork.

'You'll like the T-bird,' said Ricco. 'They're a good car.'

'Yeah. It looks alright,' nodded Les, taking a sip of 7-UP.

Vinnie's chunky fingers soon had the paperwork filled in, explaining to Les about insurance, AAA, Auto Club and one or two other things. He checked Norton's passport and driver's licence, along with his VISA card. All up it took about ten minutes and came to $210 for a week including the insurance, with an option for another week or more if Les wanted. Les signed on the dotted line quite happily.

'There you go,' said Vinnie, handing him the keys. 'It's all yours. Bring it back here when you're finished. Or I'll get someone to pick it up.'

'Unreal, Vinnie. Thanks a lot. You too, Ricco.'

'Hey. Any time,' shrugged Ricco.

'There ... is one other thing you could do for me, Ricco,' said Les, a little slowly.

'Sure, what's that?'

'Well, I've never driven a car on the wrong side of the

road before. How about coming round the block with me a few times while I sort things out? You mind?'

Ricco shrugged and half smiled. 'Sure, why not? I'm a thrillseeker. Then you can drop me back here. Hey, Vinnie, if you hear a bang from up the road somewhere, don't sweat it. That'll be me teaching Grandma Duck here how to drive in the big city.'

'Hey, if I hear a bang coming from you, Snake,' answered Vinnie, pointing his chunky index finger at Ricco then curling it, 'it don't necessarily mean it's coming from no car wreck!'

Vinnie and Ricco laughed at some private joke then they followed Les out to the T-bird. Les got behind the wheel, stuck the key in the ignition and the big car hummed into life quieter than a Swiss watch. Ricco got in beside him, Vinnie gave the roof a tap then disappeared back into his office in another cloud of cigar smoke. Les slipped the T-bar into drive, eased the car cautiously to the edge of the busy road and waited for a break in the traffic.

'Hey, Ricco,' he said. 'What did Vinnie mean when he called you Snake?'

Ricco gave a cold laugh. 'That was just a name they had for me back in New York. Ricco the Snake.'

'Oh. And what about Vinnie? They have one for him?'

'Yeah. They called him Vinnie-Sawn-Off.'

Vinnie was around five ten, and at least fifteen stone. Definitely no midget. 'I think I get the picture,' said Les, and slowly turned along the roadway.

It wasn't as bad as Norton thought it would be. He made a few turns at the lights, both left and right, zipped in among the traffic, even overtook a few cars; the roads were that wide you seemed to have all the time in the world to avoid any trouble. The only real blue was a couple of times when Les went for the blinkers and got a windscreen full of water and the wipers going instead. As well as the steering wheel being on the wrong side of the car, the indicators and that were on the wrong side of the steering wheel. But it didn't take Les long to get his act together, and the big car went like a charm and kicked back into second nicely when you tromped on it; Norton was actually looking forward to dropping Ricco off so he could start fish-tailing it and lay a bit of rubber up and down these monstrous great roads.

'So how you doin' there, Grandma Duck?' asked Ricco. 'Think you can handle it without wetting your pants too much?'

'Ohh yeah,' grinned Les. 'By the time I'm due to fly home I should be alright.'

'You know where you are?'

'Yeah.' Norton had a quick look in the rear vision mirror and around him. 'Vinnie's is back that way about two miles. The condo's over there. And we're heading towards Main Street.'

'Hey, you're doin' just fine.'

'I stayed up till three o'clock in the morning studying a road map.'

Ricco looked at Les as if he didn't know whether to believe him or not. The way Les had his mouth set suggested he shouldn't.

With his arm out the window catching the breeze, Norton nonchalantly drove on for another couple of miles or so towards what he thought must be downtown. There were more shops and apartment blocks; there was even the odd feral pedestrian walking around. Shit, what are they doing on the loose? thought Les. Do the authorities or the National Rifle Association know they're around? That's the fourth one I've seen. They're almost in plague proportions. Anyway, I suppose I'd better get Ricco back to Vinnie's. He looks happy enough, but I don't think he's all that interested in a guided tour of beautiful downtown Sepposota.

Norton pulled up for a set of lights with about half a dozen cars behind him and the median strip on his left; Ricco was gazing absently out his window at the car alongside him. Les noticed a tall, skinny, black man in jeans and a white, hang-out shirt standing near the lights on the median strip. He had a black baseball cap with a white X on it jammed on his head above a pair of mirrored sunglasses and seemed to be gazing around waiting to cross the road. Norton was almost about to give him a nod and wave him across when the black man lurched off the median strip, pulled a pistol out from under his shirt and stuck it in Norton's face.

'Get out of the car, you white motherfucker!' he screamed. 'Or I'll blow your goddamn head clean off!'

Norton gave the black man an incredulous double blink and shook his head. 'What?'

'I said give me the fuckin' car, you honky sonofabitch, or you're a fuckin' dead man!'

Norton was too stunned to be scared or shocked, even with the barrel of the gun about two inches from his face. From the corner of his eye he saw Ricco move and heard him speak.

'Hey, spade, you want the car? Then suck on this, you black nigger fuck!'

That was when Les figured out why they nicknamed Ricco Snake. In about a second flat he had whipped a small revolver out from under his shirt, reached across Les, stuck the barrel in the black man's left eye and pulled the trigger three times. It didn't sound all that loud, just an incredibly rapid '*bangbangbang*', but enough to make Norton's ears ring slightly. A strong smell of cordite hung in the car, the black man's eye pulped and began to ooze down his cheek and his other eye flickered momentarily then rolled back in his head, lifeless. He dropped his gun in Norton's lap, staggered back onto the median strip then collapsed on his back as if someone had kicked his legs from under him; blood started to burble out of his eye socket, one arm flopped across his chest, and that was it. The lights changed to green so Norton decided to drive off. Not too fast, not too slow, a bit like Grandma Duck, if anything. Just another day in America.

A little further on he turned to Ricco. 'Nice bit of shooting, mate. I hope my head wasn't in your road?'

Ricco's face was florid. 'That dumb, nigger fuck.

Who'd he think he was? Take my car and make me get out and walk in the heat. Fuckin' jig gink.'

'Yeah. Well, I don't think he'll be needing it now. You soon sorted that out.'

'Sorted that out. Hey,' Ricco made an expansive gesture, the gun still in his hand, 'you want I should have made nice with him?'

'No, no. Not at all. You did exactly the right thing.' Les nodded to the gun. 'What did you use anyway?'

Ricco rested the gun on the palm of his hand. 'Just a .22. They're the best. You know what I'm sayin'? All the heroes like Magnums and .45s. All they do is blow brains and shit all round the place. You stick this in their eye or behind their ear and — *pop*! It just rattles around inside their head, scrambles up their brain and it don't leave no mess. I like a neat hit.'

'Yes, I can see that. Quick and efficient too, I might add.'

Ricco's face suddenly creased into a smile. 'Hey, you're pretty cool yourself. You just drove off. No panic, no big deal. You got class, Les Norton. I like you.'

'Good. Let's just hope no one got the licence number.'

'Nahhh! Who'd give a flying fuck anyway? Just one less crackhead, nigger piece of shit.'

'Yeah, right. Who'd give a fuck? Just one less nigger.' Norton shook his head. 'Which way back to Vinnie's? Back that way, isn't it?'

'Yeah. Take the next left at the lights.'

Norton drove silently along, with one eye on the road, another on the rear vision mirror and another on Ricco, till he came to the caryard. He didn't bother going inside, he just pulled up off the road with the motor running to let Ricco out.

'So what do you want to do with this?' he asked, nodding to the gun still sitting in his lap.

'Hey, what have we got here?' Ricco picked up the gun and examined it. It was some sort of machine-pistol, a bit like Hank's Beretta. The magazine was in the handle and underneath the barrel was a small folding metal grip that incorporated the trigger guard. Stamped along the side was VASP-75. Cal. 9x9 MM. 'A fuckin' Visser. Wonder where that nigger got this?'

'I don't know,' answered Les. 'He probably saved up enough green stamps. But it's all yours. I don't want it. And it's got your dabs on it, sport. Not mine.'

'Okay, I'll take it. I know a guy could use this.' Ricco got out, shut the door and walked round to Norton's side of the car with both guns tucked under his shirt. 'So don't forget Thursday. I'll be round about ten-thirty and we go boatin'. Then I'll show you my buddy's joint at Salmo. Might have a meal after.'

'Alright, Ricco. I'll see you on Thursday. So long, mate.'

Ricco tapped the roof and Norton drove off; he might have been acting cool, but he'd driven about three miles and his adrenalin was still pumping before he worked out he was going the wrong way. He wasn't quite shitting his pants, but wouldn't it be lovely if some concerned citizens got the number and a description of the car. You didn't shoot people in broad daylight and just leave them lying on the side of the road, surely? Then again, this was America. Maybe you did. And there was a chance the car was, if not hot, extremely tropical. If Norton got pulled over his holiday in Florida could last quite a bit longer than two weeks. Somehow he managed to get his bearings and find his way back to the estate. Not driving like Jack Brabham, but not quite driving like Grandma Duck either.

Back inside the relative safety of the condo Les had his head in the fridge wishing there was something in there a bit stronger than 'Colorado Kool-Aid'. But a bottle of Coors would have to do. He ripped the top off one, swallowed half in about one gulp then sat down on the lounge and had a think. Any doubts he might have had about Ricco being in the Mafia were now dispelled. He was a hitman alright, and a bloody good one too. Not to mention hot-tempered and a bit psycho. Then, on the other hand, if Ricco hadn't of shot that X-head, or whatever he was, there was a good chance he would have shot Les anyway, he was that crazy. What a nuthouse. He'd got rid of one gun-happy galah and fallen straight in with another one. Only this one wasn't some flip trying to impress him. He was a full-on Mafia professional, who kept his mouth shut, didn't say 'nuttin' to nobody', then just went out and did it. And he was going 'boatin'' with him on Thursday. Les swallowed some more beer. In the meantime the best thing to do for the rest of the afternoon would be to stay home. If somebody had taken the number any flak would go straight to Vinnie's caryard first. And that was all he had wanted to do, hire a bloody car. Suddenly Les felt like jumping on the next plane and going back home. Though he'd only been away six days, it was beginning to feel like six weeks. But wouldn't they give him a nice bagging back at the club if he did? Especially George Brennan. Norton stared into the bottle of beer and felt more than a bit homesick. He always knew Australia was good, but he didn't know it was that good. Still, he had Lori to take out tonight and that could be quite interesting. Things could be worse. He could have been stuck back at Swamp Manor with Captain Rats. Les finished his beer and went for a swim; a long one.

Which was how he spent the afternoon, alternating between the pool, P.J. O'Rourke, the book on Jamaica and the road map of Siestasota, while he played a couple of tapes — just like any normal person relaxing on their annual holidays. This time he turned on the air-conditioner too; finishing up with pneumonia or the flu couldn't be any worse than some gun-crazy seppo shooting him. Later in the afternoon it started to rain again so Les dozed off for a while to the steady patter of the raindrops and the rumbling of distant thunder. So apart from nearly getting his head blown off earlier it wasn't a bad sort of an afternoon.

Norton was up, showered and shaved and in a pair of shorts, feeling pretty good. He was also hungry and now looking forward to dinner with the blonde from Texas. He had plenty of time before Lori arrived so Les thought he might have 'just the one' bourbon and diet. He wasn't sure of the driving laws in Florida but he'd feed Lori some bullshit line about how he couldn't handle the American road system, that way she could drive. Les took a couple of slurps of his cool one and despite his earlier apprehensiveness now started to think how clever he was. He walked over to the TV set and was about to see what he could find by pushing a few buttons and dials when there was an abrupt knock on the door. Hello, thought Les, his apprehension starting to come back. I wonder who this is? It's too bloody early for Lori. Still holding his drink, Les opened the door and couldn't believe his eyes.

It was Hank, in his customary grubby jeans and a chatty grey T-shirt. But a very dismal-looking Hank. He had two black eyes, stitches in his chin, and his jaw and mouth were swollen. One arm was in a leather sling, his other forearm rested on a metal crutch and one ankle was in a cast. He was kind of standing side-on to the door. No matter how he was standing he was the last person Les was expecting to see, or wanting to for that matter. Norton was that dumbfounded he was almost lost for words as he gave Hank a quick once up and down.

'What do you want?'

Hank's blackened eyes briefly caught Norton's then once again began darting all over the place. 'I was driving past so I thought I'd call in and see what you were doing.'

'What am I doing?' Les couldn't believe his ears, much less his eyes. 'I'm going out. With a girl.'

'The same one you were with the other night?'

'No. A different one.'

'Oh. Then you don't want to go out for a few drinks?'

Les shook his head. 'Look, to be honest, Hank, I'd just as soon stick on my own from now on. You know. Go my own way, do my own thing. Or let me put it to you another way, Einstein. You're probably the most miserable, know-all cunt I've ever come across in my life. I'd have more fun rolling in dog shit or being holed up in a contagious disease ward than I would going out with you. People queue up to hate you. An artificial flower would die on you. Even your own shadow keeps away from you. You pick fights in bars and about the only thing you can accomplish on your own is BO. I can't kid to you any more, Hank. You're an arse. And don't ask me to invite you in. Laverne told me to keep you out of the place. So did Ricco.' Les took another sip of bourbon and diet.

Hank blinked a few times and the wooden cogs inside his head clonked round a couple of notches. It was a pathetic sight, as if he was looking for sympathy. 'So what do you want me to do now?'

Christ, thought Les. What have I got to do to get rid of this prick? 'I don't know. And to be honest I don't give a fuck either. But I'll tell you what you could do: Why don't you try shooting yourself?' Hank blinked around again. 'No, I mean it. This place is full of guns. You love guns. Why not shoot yourself?' Norton was half joking and half fair dinkum. But he was starting to have a bit of fun. He took a sip of bourbon and tried not to laugh openly at the look on Hank's bruised and battered face. 'Or look at it another way, knackers. You've got no money, no girl, no job and no friends. You're thirty and you look closer to sixty. You live in a wooden shack on a swamp that you wouldn't breed greyhounds in, and the bank's going to repossess that. So things aren't going to get any better. Plus your family can't stand you. Not even your mother. I've only been here for a few days and you definitely don't ring my bells either. So think about it, Hank. You'd probably be doing yourself and everyone else a favour. Just stick a gun to your head and pull the trigger. You'd probably love it. And you couldn't miss. You're a good shot — better than me. Plus you've got a heap of guns. If one doesn't work, try another. Use all kinds of different bullets too. You'll get it together sooner or later. Even a dill like you. What do you reckon, Hank? Grouse idea or what?'

Norton was expecting some sort of a stupid reply or a 'get stuffed' or whatever. Instead, Hank blinked around, huffed something under his breath and limped off. Les watched him for a moment then closed the door, went to the kitchen, and put some more ice in his drink. He was sort of half laughing to himself, but still quite incredulous. Christ! What about that idiot turning up? I thought he'd be half dead. Or hopefully a hundred per cent dead. I know what's keeping him on his feet though. Pills. And plenty of 'em. What a bloody moron. Anyway, I reckon that's got rid of him. Bloody hell! If he comes back after that I'll piss on his leg. Guns or no guns. Then a thought struck Norton. Shit! I still got to go out to Swamp Manor and get my Walkman. But that's only to see his mother. I should be able to avoid Captain Rats. He took another sip of bourbon and went back to the TV.

All Les could get was the same programs as before and this time the sport was American baseball, which didn't turn him on all that much. He threw another tape on and ironed a clean pair of jeans and a blue, button-down collar shirt. He was enjoying another bourbon and diet, and King Biscuit Boy's 'Blue Light Boogie' was fading into Canned Heat's 'Red Headed Woman' when there was another knock on the door. This one was carrying a small denim handbag and a much better sight than Hank. Much better.

Lori was spray-painted into a pair of Levis, black cowboy boots and a kind of white pleated shirt that fitted her exactly where it was supposed to and was undone enough in the front again to show exactly what it was supposed to oozing out of a lacy white bra. She gave Norton a pouty smile. 'Hi, Les. How are you?'

Norton's eyes sprung out like two party whistles. 'How am I?' he replied, giving her a monstrous once up and down. 'Don't worry about how *I* am. How are *you*? And come inside before you get arrested for being so good-looking.'

'Oh, Les. You're such a sweetheart.'

'That's me,' agreed Norton. 'Sweet li'l ol' Les.'

Lori came inside and Les closed the door. 'Hey, this place is really nice. Who owns it?'

'I got it through a friend of a friend. It's mine till I leave.'

'I love the furniture. And those paintings.'

'Yeah, it's pretty schmicko. Got a nice big pool out through there too.' Lori had another look around then sat down on one of the lounges. 'So can I get you a drink or something? All I got at the moment's bourbon and vodka. Or Coors Cutter.'

'A vodka and orange would be nice.'

'Okey-doke. No worries.'

'Yeah,' smiled Lori. 'No worries.'

Les went to the kitchen and started pottering around with a glass and some ice. 'Did you have much trouble finding the place?'

'No. I only live about fifteen minutes away.'

'Christ! I got lost about ten times trying to find my way home,' lied Norton. 'I'm glad you called over. I'd've probably got to your place around midnight. You would have starved to death waiting.'

'I figured that. So we'll go out in my car.'

'If you want to.' Les handed Lori a drink and watched her take a sip.

'Mmhh. That's nice.'

They chit-chatted away about nothing much in particular; Lori seemed more interested about life in Australia and listening to Les talking than telling him about life in Florida on the marina. Les blathered along, feeding Lori the first line of bullshit that came into his head, while he checked her out along with the odd corny joke or two. Lori lapped it up and giggled away as she sipped her drink. Norton liked making her laugh. She had a hearty Texan one and every time she did laugh her tits nearly fell out the front of her shirt. They had one more drink then decided to make a move.

Of all things, Lori drove a maroon VW beetle in fairly good condition. Les pointed out the car he'd hired and offered to take it if she wanted to. Lori checked the T-Bird out and said her bug was more fun. This suited Norton admirably. Lori's car stereo was pretty good, with a graphic equaliser, but all she had was one old Diana Ross and the Supremes tape. As they scooted through the traffic with 'The Happening' bouncing out of the speakers Norton tried to figure out what TV show or what movie he was in tonight. If he'd put a floppy hat and some lovebeads on Lori it could have been *Alice's Restaurant*.

'Hey, where do you fancy going for a feed? asked Les. 'I'm a nice, ill-mannered lout. I haven't even picked a place out.'

'You like seafood, Les?'

'Yeah. I'm on a seafood diet. I see food and I eat it.'

'We'll go to Vinnie's Stone Crab Corner. It's nice.'

'Sounds alright. It reminds me of my favourite song back home.'

'What's that?'

'Don't wait up for the shrimp boats, Mum. I'm coming home with the crabs.'

Lori shook her head. 'I don't think I know that one. But the food's great, plus it's got atmosphere. All these Mafia types that have retired to Florida go there. It's quite funny. I've been there a few times.'

As they zipped through the night traffic something struck Norton as curious. 'This Vinnie. Is he the owner?'

'Yeah.'

'What's he look like?'

'Oh, a little under six feet, about two hundred pounds, black hair receding. Got a gravelly kind of voice. Why?'

'Oh, nothing Lori,' shrugged Les. 'Nothing at all.'

They seemed to be heading towards a different part of town, over a smaller bridge alongside an unfamiliar bay or harbour with the odd shop or restaurant on the side of the road or nestled on the corners. Diana Ross was warbling 'Where Did Our Love Go?' when Lori turned off the road, down into a dusty parking lot, and pulled up. There was an expanse of brackish water on one side with a few trees, mangroves and parkland around. The restaurant was single-storey white timber, built out over the water, with an enclosed verandah out the front covered in vines and bright-coloured flowers. Above the front was a red and white sign saying 'Vinnie's Stone Crab' next to a couple of American flags; parked out front was a monstrous green Cadillac. The front door was sort of upholstered red vinyl; Les opened it for Lori and they entered.

Inside it was fairly well lit, the furniture was mainly solid wooden benches with small, checked tablecloths. Lanterns and fishnets hung off the ceiling above white timber walls dotted with soft lights, paintings and US travel posters. It was about two-thirds full with the usual hubbub of people eating and waitresses in blue shirts, jeans and grey checked aprons darting around the tables and in or out of a kitchen in the far corner. There was a fair size bar near the door and a small desk. Les was about to ask Lori if she'd booked when he heard this familiar gravelly voice behind him.

'Hey, hey, Les! What 'cha doin', huh?'

Norton turned around and Vinnie was getting up from a table of four other men. This time it was white trousers and a yellow silk shirt with pink and green parrots on it, and jutting out from his jaw was the familiar cigar like a French loaf. He grinned and made an expansive gesture with his arms.

'So what brings you here, Les?'

'I dunno,' shrugged Norton. 'Someone said the food's half alright and you wash the plates on Tuesday night.'

'The food's alright and we wash the plates. What the fuck! Come here, you aussie sonofabitch!' Vinnie wrapped a hairy arm around Norton's shoulder and gave him a squeeze, then he spotted Lori. 'Hey. Who's the lovely lady?'

'Vinnie, this is Lori. Actually Lori just happened to pick your restaurant. I didn't even know you owned it, mate. Lori, this is Vinnie.'

'Hey. Pleased to meet you, Lori,' said Vinnie, oozing genuine politeness and manners to make Norton look good.

'You too . . . Vinnie,' replied Lori. For some reason she appeared a little nervous.

Vinnie snapped his fingers at one of the waitresses; she looked like a tall version of the mouthy barmaid in 'Cheers'. 'Bernice, I want you to look after this guy. See that he gets the best table and the best service. You treat him like number one. You know what I'm sayin'?'

'Sure, Mr Rizzitello.'

Vinnie put his arm back around Norton's shoulder and got close to his ear. The smell of his cigar was that thick Les could taste it. He was half laughing when he spoke. 'Hey. Ricco told me what happened today. He reckons you're the coolest sonofabitch he ever met. That nigger was gonna ice you and when he whacked him you just drove off like nothing had happened, with the prick's gun still sitting in your lap. Grandma Duck.'

Norton shrugged. 'The light had turned green. What was I going to do? Sit there like a stale bottle of piss holding up traffic? Besides, Vinnie. I always drive like Grandma Duck.'

'You crazy sonofabitch. Enjoy your meal.' Vinnie gave Les another squeeze then went back to his table full of heavies.

Bernice led Les and Lori to a quiet secluded table overlooking the water. There was a marina next to the restaurant full of boats gently bobbing up and down in the moonlight and although the restaurant was pleasantly air-conditioned the window was open just enough to let a pleasant breeze in and any smoke or fumes out. Their waitress put down the menus, which doubled up as bibs you tied round your neck. Les was about to check what was on them when Lori spoke. She seemed even more nervous now and it sounded worse because she was trying to keep her voice down.

'Where do you know Vinnie from?' she tried to whisper.

'I hired a car from him and he's helping me find some horses.'

'You're doing business with Vinnie Rizzitello?'

'Yeah,' shrugged Norton. 'What's wrong with that?'

'Does he own the condominium?'

'No. His mate Ricco does.'

'Ricco?'

'Yeah. Ricco DiCosti.'

Lori gasped. 'You're doing business with him too?'

'Sure. What's wrong with that?'

'Do you know who those guys are?'

'Yeah. Vinnie's got a caryard, and Ricco runs a coffee shop down Salmo.'

'Les, they're Mafia. They wash all the illegal money down here. They take it to the Bahamas and bring it back in again.'

'Okay. So they're in the laundry business. What's the big deal?'

'Les...'

'Hey, I thought you said you liked it here because of all the funny Mafia types from out of town that come in.'

'Yes. But I didn't think...'

'Hey, Lori, listen to this cause I ain't gonna tell you no more. You're here now, so shut your goddamn mouth, eat your goddamn meal or I'll have your goddamn head blown off. You know what I'm sayin', huh? Look at me when I'm talkin' to you. You want Mafia? You got Mafia. Okay? Huh? Huh? Huh?'

Lori looked very quizzically at Norton. 'Les, do you know what you're doing?'

'Do I know what I'm doin'? Of course I know what I'm doin'. I'm orderin' a meal in a restaurant. Alright already. What is this, huh?'

Lori continued to stare at Les. 'Are you sure you're an Australian?'

'As Flo's pumpkin scones.'

'And you're in Florida to buy horses?'

'That's right. I'm looking for Phar Lap.'

Lori stared at Les for a moment, then her eyes dropped down to the menu. 'Yes. Alright then.'

Although Les was having trouble keeping a straight face, Lori didn't appear to see the funny side of things at all; not even Norton's ridiculous attempt at a New York Mafioso accent. So he thought he'd better put her straight. He kept forgetting Americans aren't noted for their sense of humour, especially when it comes to someone giving their leg just a gentle tug, let alone pulling it good and hard. He ordered two frozen margaritas, which arrived quite promptly, and while they were going down he told her about his involvement with Ricco and Vinnie. It was sheer coincidence, through the ex-girlfriend of Hank, the gun-crazy ratbag he'd met in Australia who'd invited him over. This seemed to go over fairly well while the frozen margaritas went down very well indeed. Then Bernice gave Norton the wine list.

There were French, Italian, Californian reds and whites, etc. Les studied them for a moment then went for a Don Cesar, Blanco Rioja 1968, Bin No. 15. If Norton's memory still served him right it should have been a crisp white wine with a rich, pear aroma that left a nice fruity aftertaste in your mouth. It was indeed. Yes, Viva España, thought Les, as he took a sip from his glass and winked a big smiling yes at Bernice.

Les waffled on a bit more about Ricco and Vinnie and Hank. He didn't say anything about getting Hank belted in the nightclub and he sure as hell didn't mention the mugger. As for Ricco and Vinnie being Mafia heavies? Was Lori sure she hadn't been watching too much TV? Lori now didn't appear anywhere near as nervous as when they first sat down, she wanted to know more about Ricco's home and how Vinnie operated his caryard. There wasn't a great deal Les could tell her there, but he started to get this feeling Lori was weighing him up and that her whole attitude had changed. The wide-eyed dumb blonde that had knocked on his door earlier had suddenly developed, if not a hardness, then a noticeable firmness around those wide, hazel eyes. Les suddenly found it a little curious, and the way she was slipping questions at him almost gave him a sense of déjà vu. But he put it down to the kind of silly adulation Lori had for the 'funny Mafia types' she had spoken about earlier who frequented the restaurant, then when she walked in and it turned out her date knew them she got it right between the eyes. A bit of a culture shock maybe? Though why did she seem so convinced Ricco and Vinnie were laundering money? Rumours? Or did she read it in the papers or see it on TV? Not that it would surprise Les if that was their caper. Vinnie the white shoe car salesman and Ricco the pizza man? Yeah, just like Les was a wealthy Australian horse trainer. Anyway, who gives a stuff? By now Les found his stomach starting to rumble something fierce, so he decided to order.

Bad luck they were too early for the stone crab season that went from October to May; but there were plenty of other tasty-looking things on the menu. Les opted for a dozen Atlantic clams on the half shell with a garlic, salsa sauce as an entree, then Pincho de Mariscos looked okay for a main. Lori had a Linguini Marinara then Croquettes de Mariscos. Norton reckoned they should have a Caesar salad and garlic bread as well; Lori reckoned that wasn't a bad idea either.

'Coming right up,' said Bernice.

A bit more Blanco Rioja went down, then the first of the food arrived on the table. Norton's clams were in a wicker basket, steamed among all this spinach or seaweed, and didn't ring his doorbell all that much. But once you got them out of the shell then drowned them in salsa sauce and stuffed them into your face with garlic bread they were okay. Lori didn't complain about her linguini; it was nice and creamy, heaps of clams and oysters and things in it with your own pot of nice bitey parmesan cheese. The Caesar salad was spot on and enough for ten people. The entrees and more wine went down quite well until the rest arrived. Norton's main was spot on. Shrimp, scallops and grouper on skewers in a hot, but not too hot, Cajun sauce. It was tops. Lori wasn't complaining either. Her pink shrimp and crabmeat croquettes were cooked to perfection, accompanied by heaps of Key lime mustard sauce. All up, not a bad chomp.

Lori said she didn't feel like sweets and Norton

couldn't have fitted any in either without bursting; but they did finish with two lip-smacking, flat white coffees. Les wouldn't have minded lingering a bit over another margarita and pissing in Lori's pocket a bit more, and was a little surprised when she suggested they leave.

'Okay,' he said, and caught the waitress's eye. Bernice came over and smiled. 'It's alright. Mr Rizzitello said it's on the house.'

'Oh!' Norton was genuinely surprised. The expression on Lori's face didn't appear to change.

'Did you enjoy it?'

'Yeah. It was the bloody grouse.'

Bernice's smile seemed to get wider. 'Then you'll have to come back here again.'

'Yeah. For sure.'

Bernice disappeared and Lori got to her feet; so did Norton.

'Well, that was nice of my old mate, Vinnie,' said Les.

'Yes. Wasn't it,' replied Lori, a little shortly. Next thing they were heading for the door.

Vinnie was still engrossed in conversation with his friends, Les stopped at the end of the bar and caught his eye. Lori kept her back to them. Vinnie looked up and made a gesture with his cigar.

'On the house,' Norton heard him say, as he tried to shrug a thank you, and gestured to his pocket. 'On the house,' Vinnie repeated, then waved him to the door with his cigar and went back to his friends.

Bernice had the door open for them. 'Goodnight,' she smiled.'

'Yeah, thanks a lot,' said Les, and slipped her fifty dollars.

'Well, thank you.'

A few moments later Lori was gunning the VW and they were heading back to the condo with Diana Ross warbling 'Stop. In the Name of Love' in the background. Lori didn't say a great deal on the way home, though she seemed to be thinking fairly deeply. Les was starting to think American women's mood swings were on a par with some Australian ones he'd come across in the past and had a feeling there wouldn't be any playing hide the saus that night when she dropped him off back at the flat. He was more than a little surprised when they pulled up and he asked her, more out of manners than anything else, if she'd like to come inside for a nightcap and she said yes.

'So what do you feel like?' asked Les, switching on the light in the kitchen.

'Just another vodka and OJ,' replied Lori, placing her handbag on the bar. She lifted one leg behind her and began rubbing her foot. 'Hey, I might have to use the john.'

'Yeah, go for your life. It's down there on the right.'

Norton started fiddling around in the kitchen, getting glasses and ice and that together. The vodka was on the shelf next to the bourbon, Les put the bottles on the bar. Lori's handbag was in the way so he moved it along a little. It wasn't all that big but the bloody thing weighed a ton. Les picked it up again and dumped it back down on the bar with a solid *clump*! What the . . .? He had a quick look towards the bathroom, and even though it's completely frowned upon in the best of circles, opened Lori's handbag. There was a black revolver in a black leather holster, with a black wallet next to it. Norton opened the wallet. It had a blue and silver shield on one side with a star and a building of some kind in the middle. On the other side was a photo ID, something like a New South Wales driver's licence. It said, 'Special Agent Lori V. Benshoff. United States Department of Justice'. The hair was a little darker, the face not as made up, but it was definitely Norton's Texan girl Lori. The whacko from Waco. That was all Les needed to know. He put her bag exactly where it was, moved the bottles along and let out a long silent whistle.

There were about eight million different types of police in the United States, from county sheriffs to campus police, the FBI to the DEA and the Secret Service, who enforced everything from drugs to protecting the president. The US Department of Justice, along with the FBI, the Office of Financial Enforcement and the US Department of the

Treasury went after counterfeiters, gold smugglers, stock exchange rorters and anything to do with crimes against the American currency. It fell into place in about two seconds. Lori was an undercover agent with the Department of Justice. By sheer coincidence again he'd fluked her and she'd fluked him. His invitation to dinner was a chance for her to have a snoop around where the mob ate. Bad luck it blew up in her face when she walked in and Les introduced her to one of the bosses. Her working on some marina, that would give her a chance to watch boats coming and going. And what she knew about Ricco and Vinnie she didn't get from watching TV or reading the papers. Then there was the way she started slipping questions at Les during the meal. A sense of déjà vu? Hah! When they'd finished eating, Les was almost tempted to say he didn't wish to sign a statement without seeing his lawyer. Ricco and Vinnie were laundering money and Lori was keeping an eye on things hoping to make an arrest. Once again Les, through absolutely no fault of his own, had found himself in a potentially dodgy situation. On one hand he'd taken an undercover cop into a mob meeting place. On the other hand he'd almost blown her cover by introducing her around, and it wouldn't take her long to find out Les was no racehorse trainer. He had form back in Australia and she could make up her own mind from there what he was doing in America and how he happened to be staying in Ricco's condominium. It was indeed a dodgy situation. Not that this meant he couldn't try and pork her. If anything, it made Les more determined. He was just going to have to be very careful, that's all. Les had the drinks sitting on the bar when Lori came back and stood in front of him. Whistling softly, he concentrated for a moment on topping them up, then smiled up and pushed her vodka in front of her.

'There you go, mate. How's that?'

Lori picked up her drink and took a sip. 'Very nice, thank you.' She took another sip and put her glass back on the bar.

Norton clinked her glass and smiled. 'Thank you, Lori.' He took a mouthful then put his glass back on the bar near hers. 'No, I mean it, Lori. That was terrific of you to pick me up and drive me around tonight. I feel a bit weak not being able to take you home.'

Lori gave her head a bit of a toss. 'Don't worry about it.'

'Okay. But it's still not the right thing to do. Anyway, I'm here for another couple of weeks, maybe we could do it again?' Les smiled. 'Next time I'll drive.'

'Alright.' Lori took another sip of vodka. 'That sounds good.'

'Lori, that has to be the best news I've heard all night.' Lori had her hand resting on the bar. Norton picked it up and gave her fingertips a delicate but very affectionate kissing.

Lori gave a little squeal of surprise, almost as if Les had hit her funnybone, but didn't pull her hand away. 'Ooh! You're a bit of a devil, Les.'

Norton kissed her fingers a moment or two longer, then gently placed her hand back on the bar. 'You're right. I'm nothing but an animal,' he apologised. 'I'm sorry, I just couldn't help myself. It must have been that filthy Spanish wine. Forgive me.' Lori laughed and gave her head another toss. 'Anyway,' said Les. 'Are you in any hurry to get home?'

'No . . . not really. But I can't stay out too late.'

'Fair enough. Well, why don't we go into the lounge? I'll have a quick snakes myself then I'll put a tape on of some good aussie music and we'll have a mag.' Norton indicated the lounge nearest the door. 'You sit there, and I'll sit opposite.'

Lori seemed to sum things up quickly but carefully. 'Okay,' she said, and picked up her drink and handbag off the bar.

She put them both on the coffee table and eased comfortably down onto the lounge. While he was in the bathroom Les splashed some cold water on his face. He found a laid-back tape when he came out, slipped it into the stereo then sat opposite Lori and took a decent pull of bourbon. Lori seemed to be checking him out pretty intently from the other side of the coffee table. Les let her go for her life as 'Under Your Strangle Hold' by the Sidewalk Swingers cut into James Reyne's 'Any Day Above Ground'.

'Hey, this isn't too bad,' said Lori.

'Bloody oath! We're talking land of the Southern Cross here, woman.'

Lori sipped her drink and moved her head easily to the music. If she was worried about anything she certainly didn't show it. Then again, what did she have to worry about? She was a cop, she had a great big gun in her bag next to her and if Les got out of line she'd pull it out and blow his head clean off his shoulders.

'Listen, Lori,' said Les. 'I saw you rubbing your foot earlier. Are you having trouble with your feet?'

'Ohh, tell me about it.' Lori rolled her eyes and unconsciously grabbed her right foot. 'They give me hell at the best of times. And last week I had to go and twist my damn ankle.'

'Well kick your boots off, Tex, and I'll give your poor old feet a rub.'

'You'll what?' Lori looked at Les a bit oddly.

'No, I mean it. Come on, John Wayne. Take your boots off and I'll rub your feet for you.'

'I don't . . .'

'What are you worried about? You got something on your mind?'

'No.'

'Well what's up?'

'Nothing. I . . .' Lori was a little hesitant, then she gave a kind of shrug. 'Alright then. Why not?'

'Stick your foot up on the coffee table. I'll clear the things out the road.' As Lori kicked her boots off and placed her right foot on the coffee table, Les moved the drinks, along with her handbag. He picked it up once, felt the weight, gave Lori a suspicious look then picked it up again. 'What the . . .?' Lori started to come to life on the lounge but before she had a chance Les opened up her handbag, had a quick look, then dropped it back on the coffee table with a thud. 'There's a bloody gun in there,' Norton was horrified. 'What the bloody hell's goin' on?'

Lori sort of glared at Les, but her cover was blown again. 'I ...'

'Do you mean to tell me you had to bring a gun with you just to go out for dinner? Christ! This is unbeliev-able!' Norton's face paled; he was shocked to the core. 'Jesus! I get away from one gun-crazy wombat and finish up with another one. Fair dinkum. Is it that bad over here that a young girl can't even go out at night without carrying a bloody great gun in her purse? This is unbelievable.'

'Les, it's not what you think.'

'No. I don't want to know.' Les gestured with his hands and shook his head in amazement. 'It's just that back home we don't have people running around with guns all over the place. Not to go out for a bloody meal.' Norton sat back on the lounge, took a great mouthful of bourbon and continued to act the mug from the bush; or Australia. 'Christ! This place is a nuthouse.'

Lori decided to go along with the gag. 'Yes, you're right. It is getting bad over here. And you're lucky back in Australia. It's just that I was worried about ... carjacking.'

'What?' Norton screwed up his face.

'Carjacking. Muggers wait at the lights or wherever, then jump out with guns and take your car.'

Norton's face was pure disbelief. 'You're kidding? You mean hoodlums can come up in broad daylight or what-ever, and just order you out of your car? That's unbelievable.'

'Yes it's awful. Just awful.' Although she managed to hide it, Lori was a lot happier now. She had Norton's measure without blowing her cover, so she decided to keep playing him along for a jerk. 'Actually, there was an attempted one today. A black guy got shot not far from here.'

'Yeah. What, was it on the news? I haven't read a paper or listened to a radio since I been here.'

'Yeah. It was on the news.' It was a perfect call for Lori to keep stringing Les along, yet somehow she couldn't help going into cop mode. 'We . . . They think it was a self-defence thing, though it looked more like a Mafia hit the way the guy was shot all neat and clean in the head. But it's not usually the way the mob does things. They don't leave bodies lying around. They generally bury them or dump them out at sea. And the guy was a known junkie. It was a funny one.'

'Ohh yeah. Real funny. Let's just hope they catch the people responsible. That's bloody terrible.'

'Hah!' Lori gave a short, scornful laugh. 'Fat chance of that. No witnesses, no gun, no nothing. And it's the sixth shooting for the week.'

Really? thought Norton. Isn't that encouraging. And it's only Tuesday too. 'Oh well, maybe they'll catch whoever's responsible. And let's hope they do. In the meantime, could you do me a favour?'

'Sure, Les. What's that?'

'Would you mind taking your bag off the coffee table and keeping it on the lounge next to you? Those things unnerve me.'

Lori smiled; she could hardly believe Norton's naivety. 'Okay.' She reached over and picked up her handbag then took another sip of vodka and orange.

'And you can put your foot back up on the table. I'll still give it a rub for you if you want.'

'You will?'

'Yeah, why not? I said I would. If I don't you'll probably shoot me now.'

'No, I don't think I'll do that.'

Lori relaxed and placed her foot back on the coffee table. She wasn't going to knock this back, her feet were genuinely killing her; and Les had to be the sweetest square who ever lived and breathed. Norton felt like saying, Yeah, stick your big, flat, smelly walloper's feet up on the table for me to rub, I don't mind. It's just part of

205

the shit poor mugs like me have got to go through to get a root. But changed his mind. Actually, Lori didn't have big, smelly walloper's feet. When Les removed the white, ankle-length cotton sock, with the little red hearts on it, it was quite okay; clean, nicely trimmed toenails and dusted well with talcum powder. Les looked at it for a moment, noticing the slight swelling round the ankle, rubbed his hands together vigorously to get the Kirlian energy and some warmth going, then wrapped them around Lori's ankle and instep and squeezed, gently but firmly.

'Is this your crook angle? The one that's hurting?'

'Ohh yeah,' Lori moaned softly. 'Is it ever.'

'I thought so.'

'But God! that sure feels good.'

'I thought it might.'

Norton had huge strong hands at the best of times. He gripped Lori's ankle, pressing it as he gently rotated her foot for a while then put both thumbs in the ball of her foot, pressed a bit harder and started massaging. Lori let out a groan of delight, closed her eyes and settled back on the lounge; the way she was moaning and sighing and wriggling around Les thought she was either going to cough in her rompers or break wind right in his face. He rubbed her foot a moment or two more then stopped.

'There's something missing,' he said. 'Don't go away.' Lori opened her eyes; before she had a chance to say anything Les was back from the kitchen with a bottle of virgin olive oil and a tea towel. He dripped some oil on his hands, rubbed them together again and smiled at Lori. 'Now, where was I?'

Norton tore into Lori's feet with a vengeance. He massaged and kneaded her insteps and soles, rubbed her sweet little toes, ran his fingers in between them, got his fingers into her heel and her Achilles tendon. Lori was moaning and sighing one minute, purring like a kitten the next. Les put more oil on his hands and put extra work in on her bad ankle. His hands were getting a bit stiff an the end but Norton was getting a kick out of listening to Lori giggling and sighing and watching her arch her back on the lounge with her eyes closed.

'Well, I got to take a breather,' said Les. 'Or have a drink anyway.' He gave his hands a wipe and took a lengthy slurp of bourbon. 'So how was that?'

'Ohh Les.' Lori half opened her eyes. 'That was unreal. What can I say?'

'I give good hand, don't I?'

'Do you what. You should charge by the hour.' Lori reached across and took a sip of her drink also.

'Yeah I know.' Norton looked at Lori thoughtfully over his bourbon. 'You know what half the trouble with your feet is?'

'No. What?'

'Those jeans you wear. They're too tight and they're cutting off the circulation to your legs.'

'You really think so? You could be right too. Sometimes they do feel awful tight.'

'They're killing you. What you should do is take them off and let me give your legs a bit of a rub too. Get the circulation going.'

Lori looked evenly at Les through half-closed eyes. 'Oh, you think so, do you?'

'Bloody oath, woman. I wouldn't tell you a lie.'

'And just how are you going to rub my legs on that coffee table?'

'I wasn't thinking of the coffee table.'

'Where then?'

'What about on that great big queen-size bed in there, that belongs to this co called Mafia boss you're having yourself on about?'

Lori looked at Norton and seemed to think for a second; next thing tiny chuckles started to ripple across her shoulders. She tossed back her head, laughed out loud then came round and sat herself down on Norton's knee; eyes wide open now and looking devilish. She put her arms around Norton's neck and Les kissed her on the chin.

'What an absolutely fabulous idea. I think I like you, Les Norton.'

Less pressed his hand into the small of Lori's back and kissed her again. 'Buggered if I know why.'

It didn't take Lori long to get her clothes off. Whether she was madly keen to have a wonderfully romantic evening with Norton or whether she just wanted to be able to skite one day to her cop pals about how she screwed some aussie guy on Ricco DiCosti's bed, Les didn't know and he didn't particularly care. By the time Lori was down to a pair of skimpy white knickers with tiny red hearts, just like her socks, Norton was down to absolutely nothing except Mr Wobbly all pumped up and rearing to go. He lay on the bed alongside her and started massaging her thighs and backside with one hand while he rubbed the back of her neck with the other and started kissing her. Lori's lips were absolutely delightful, even nicer than her feet, and her tongue was as sweet as honey. Les kissed her lips and face, ran his tongue lightly around her neck then started kissing her breasts and nipples. Lori dropped her tongue in his ear and Les felt as if a tarantula wearing ballet slippers had just run up and down his spine. Lori's kissing got steamier and she began scrabbling her fingers through Norton's hair. Les slid his right hand up from her thighs and began massaging her breasts; there was still some oil on his hands and between that and their moist bodies her breasts yielded wonderfully, filling even Norton's huge hands. He rubbed and caressed her some more, while Lori started to moan and press herself against him, then he moved his hand down and started stroking her ted. Lori was starting to juice up now and under her knickers if felt like several slices of succulent Queensland paw-paw and was probably just as sweet. Les slipped his hand inside her knickers and let his fingers do the walking, mainly his middle one, through her silken, neatly trimmed pubes, then moved Lori's legs together and slipped her knickers off. Lori opened her legs and Les went to work with his finger, rubbing it across her clit and poking it inside as far as he could. Lori started to moan louder, almost sobbing with hunger; it was music to Norton's ears. Then the evil Mr Wobbly started growling and throbbing like a Bertram inboard wanting to take things over. Les spread Lori's legs and got in between her, she grabbed his dick for a second then let go. Les lifted her legs a little then Mr Wobbly put his head down and began burrowing away. Poor Mr Wobbly, he almost broke his neck. Lori had the tightest ted Norton had ever come across. They were both pumping out body fluids and lathered up enough to slide out of the county, but Les was having all the trouble in the world getting in. He arched his back, pushed and shoved while Lori moaned and groaned, checked to make sure he was in the right hole, but to no avail. Norton had about an average dick, bigger than some, smaller than others, but the way Lori was squawking you'd have thought she'd jumped into the cot with Johnny 'The Wad' Holmes. Forget about a mouse's ear: this was like a pencil sharpener and all muscle. Les couldn't figure it out. Maybe when Lori was in the gym doing aerobics she'd been doing bench presses with her labia it was that hard.

'Listen, Lori, I got a great idea,' gasped Les.

'What's that?' gasped Lori.

'You get on top.'

'Okay.'

Norton lay back on the bed, held Lori under the ribcage while she rested her hands on his shoulders and lowered herself down. Before long, she had part of Mr Wobbly in, shaking her head around and squealing as she started going up and down like a chook trying to lay a square egg. Norton's face was a wrinkled mask of pain. There wasn't all that much going in, but it felt like there was a hand inside Lori's ted and it was trying to tear his knob off. Lori started going faster and faster, Les just screwed his face up and thought, I'm doing this for Australia. Finally she managed to rub her clit against Norton's dick long enough and with a howl like a werewolf blew her brains out. Les went off about the same time, then lifted Lori up and laid her gently down alongside him. It wasn't a bad sort of 'sexual finale', but it definitely wasn't Norton's idea of a good root. Though it wasn't Lori's fault, or Les's. For a good night's porking with Special Agent Benshoff you'd need a forty-four-gallon drum of Vaseline and a dick like a sardine.

Les got a towel, wrapped it around them and kissed Lori as if she was a cross between every Mills and Boon book ever written, the *Kama Sutra* and all his dreams come true. Okay, so she'd used him just as a sex object so she could tell Ricco on the day of the arrest that she'd done some heavy bonking on his bed, but she was probably a good woman underneath. Besides, she was still a cop and it would be best to keep her sweet rather than just throw her up in the air then throw her out the door. Not that Norton had done anything, but he had been a witness to a killing, the car was just out the front and if something did turn up and Lori had the shits with him, well, hell hath no fury like a woman from the Department of Justice scorned. Norton gave her back a bit of a rub and suggested that if they were quiet they could sneak out and have a quick swim. Lori said yes.

They slipped out the back door and skinny-dipped quietly around the pool, washing away the sweat from the evening's sexual activities in steamy southern Florida. Les didn't make any sexual advances towards Lori, just swam round the pool and gave her the odd kiss now and again. Lori gave Les the odd kiss too and told him her ankle felt unbelievably better, Les was quite a guy. Norton shrugged and tried his best to look modest. Back in the condo Les slipped into a T-shirt and a pair of jeans while Lori got changed. He made two more drinks, small ones and raised his glass when Lori walked out and sat down on the other side of the bar again.

'Well Lori, what can I say? That's one of the best nights I've ever had. I'd like to see you again, only we'll take my car — and next time you can do my feet,' he added with a laugh.

Lori smiled and tinkled the ice in her glass. 'That sounds like a good idea. But I've got a bit to do this week.'

'Ohh yeah. You work at the pictures of a night don't you? The movies, or whatever you call them.'

210

'That's right, Les. You remembered. Yes, so that doesn't help things much.' Lori looked at Les over the top of her drink. 'But maybe next weekend. Say Saturday?'

'You've got me. If I can wait that long.' Norton picked up Lori's hand and started kissing her fingertips again. Lori sipped her drink and let Norton go for his life. 'Well,' said Les, placing her hand back on the bar, 'I suppose you'd better get going. Don't want you arriving at the marina half asleep and falling in the water.'

'I'll be okay.'

'If you do look like drowning, give me a yell and I'll be straight over to give you the kiss of life.' Les reached across the bar and kissed Lori full on the lips and slipped his tongue in her mouth for a second. 'Just like that.'

Lori giggled and finished her drink. 'You're crazy, Les. You're sweet. But you're still crazy.'

'I told you, it's that Spanish wine. It just seems to bring out the passion in me. Les gave her a wink. 'Come on, I'll walk you out to your car.' He pointed to Lori's handbag still sitting on the lounge. 'Don't forget your grenade launcher.'

Les got Lori into the VW and kissed her goodbye. He'd give her a ring through the week and she had his number if she wanted to give him a call. Don't forget Saturday. Goodnight, Les. Thanks for a lovely evening. We'll see what happens. She drove off and Les could faintly hear Diana Ross warbling 'Come See About Me'. Les went inside the closed the door.

He made up what he could of the bed, cleaned his teeth then turned off the lights and flopped down on his back. It wasn't long before he was sweating again. Although he was starting to get used to it now and at least there were no mozzies. It had been a strange old day. In a true sense he was lucky to be alive. Finding out what Ricco and Vinnie were up to was more or less expected, though not necessarily needed. But what about porking Constable Plod? And who said things were always bigger in Texas? Norton laughed to himself. Won't that be a yarn for Billy Dunne and the boys when he got back home. Now, what's on tomorrow? Ohh yeah. Souvenirs for Billy Dunne and the boys back home. Christ! How many T-shirts have I got to get? Warren wanted about eight. Les was thinking on this and one or two other things when before he knew it he'd dozed off again.

Les was in the kitchen about ten-thirty the following morning, after getting himself a bit of breakfast; it was too hot to bother cooking anything so he just had some fruit and a bit of toast and coffee. He was kind of looking forward to the day, tooling around Siestasota in the T-bird with no Hank, no Ricco, nobody to annoy him, just doing his own thing for a change at his own pace. Norton had got out of bed earlier and because it was still so stinken hot and just to be dirty on himself he decided to take the bike up to the little shopping centre to pick up some things: milk, more orange juice, etc. This had him sweating like a pig as usual when he got back, then a long swim and a few sit-ups and a cold shower afterwards had the big red-headed Queenslander feeling pretty good. He was sitting at the bar, sipping a large orange juice and ice, half looking at his map of Siestasota and half thinking about the previous night. Secret agent Benshoff, eh? he chuckled to himself. Wasn't that a bit of a funny one. Though I don't think Mr Wobbly's seeing the funny side of it this morning. He looked like he fell off a motorbike without wearing his leather jacket and helmet. And what about Ricco and Vinnie, the Mafia money men? What a nice quinella. And you can throw in Captain Rats for the trifecta. May as well add Constable Plod and make it the quadrella. Christ! Can I find them! About the only decent people I've met here have been the girl on the red velvet swing and her cousin. And she won't be back still Saturday.

Les sipped some more orange juice and looked at the map again. According to it, there was something called Siestasota Square Shopping Mall, about five miles to the right out the front of the estate going towards Salmo. Yes, thought Les, that looks alright and I think Hank's mother mentioned something about it being a good place to shop. I can go out there, get all my T-shirts and junk. There's a post office up at that shopping centre. I can get a box from somewhere and send it all home, save me lumping it around. Then after that I might take a run over to that St Almonds Circle or wherever it was I saw that funny country band. That looked very Double Bayish over there. One never knows what choice goodies I might pick up just for Uncle Les. And I might shout myself a nice lunch while I'm there. Les clicked his fingers. Then later on I might go out, say hello to Mrs Laurel, and pick up my Walkman. He finished his orange juice and rinsed the glass. Well, no use hanging around here like a stale bottle of piss. It's a lovely day outside and I got places to go, things to do and people to see. Norton slipped into a clean pair of shorts a clean white T-shirt, got his wallet and VISA card then locked up the flat and went out to his car.

The power windows were a great idea. This meant you had to be in the car with the ignition on and the seat-belt warning light banging in your ear while you tried to find the switch to wind the windows down and the inside of the car was like a bloody pizza oven.

'Jesus fuckin' Christ!' Norton cursed out loud. 'What a cunt of a fuckin' idea! Don't tell me it's gonna be one of those days.'

He got all four windows down, then put them all back up again and shoved the air-conditioning on full before he dissolved. After a few minutes he felt a bit better, the breeze coming out of the dash was quite refreshing on his face and at least the steering wheel didn't quite burn all the skin from his hands. Norton kicked the motor over, backed out and began diving over the speed humps around what seemed like the neverending parking spaces of the estate. Although he was a bit loath to admit it, the big car still felt good to drive. There was a skinny black bloke wearing sunglasses and jeans shuffling around dragging a broom behind him. Les gave him a smile and a wink and got a wave in return. Les got to the roadway and pulled up for a break in traffic when a thought occurred to him. He'd forgotten to bring any tapes with him and the T-Bird had a four-speaker stereo. Oh well. Let's see what's on the local radio stations. I haven't even bothered tuning into the one inside the flat yet. He switched it on, hit the scanner button at the end and turned up the volume. Next instant the entire car filled up with raunchy fiddles, twanging guitars, a honky-tonk piano and some good ol' boy wailing.

'Don't fall in love with me, darling, I'm a rambler
Though you are the sweetest sweetheart in this world.'

'Holy bloody shit!' beamed Norton. 'How good a track's this?' He listened for a few moments, tapping his feet and grinning, while he waited for a break in the traffic, then zoomed across the median strip, fish-tailed the T-Bird right towards Salmo and put his foot down. No worries at all. If you were driving in Australia. Norton was roaring down the wide open road to the fiddles and slide when he noticed not far in the distance a whole roadway full of huge American gas guzzlers coming towards him — rapidly.

'Oh Ker-iste!' he howled, his eyes like two big donuts as his face went white.

There was no time to muck around. He tromped his foot to the floor, the T-Bird kicked back to first, and Les tore right, back across the median strip, the sump and diff scraping across the grass, before he bumped and banged his way onto the correct side of the road. The car landed and Les shoved his foot down again to beat the other approaching cars before eventually slowing down, his heart thumping against his ribcage in time to the drums and honky-tonk piano still pounding out of the speakers.

'Bloody Hell! How close was that!' he swore out loud again. At least I know what the scene from today's movie is. *Smokey and the Bandit Meet the Wombat from Down Under*. The other traffic caught up and Les drove along looking straight ahead as if nothing had happened and not wanting to catch the eyes of any other drivers because he did feel like a nice wombat.

'Yeah, that was Travis Tritt and "Don't Give Your Heart to a Rambler". You're tuned to 88.5 WRIV. All country in the big country. And let's put some more drive in your country and more country in your drive. Here's Boy Howdy and "Thanks for the Ride". It's 11.15 and ninety-eight degrees on a steamy summer day in beautiful Siestasota Florida. Weatherman says more rain late this afternoon with possible thunderstorms.'

The next track was even more twangy and country and being an old country boy at heart Norton dug it. He checked the numbers on the scanner and made a mental note to set the radio to that station when he got back to the condo. So after his initial brush with death on his first lone forage out on the highways and byways of America, Les settled down and cruised along past more walled estates, fast food outlets and small shopping centres, listening to country and western music while he kept his eyes open for the shopping mall. The tempo slowed down a little to a bit of 'lonesome cowboy' stuff by Alan Jackson and Confederate Railroad; but it wasn't any worse than some of those wailing George Michael and Barbra Streisand pop ballads he had to endure at times back in Australia. Before long Siestasota Shopping Mall loomed up on his left.

There were traffic lights and signs everywhere, built over a bay in the media strip. Les pulled into the left, waited for the lights then took a right into a parking area about as big as Kakadu without the lily ponds and the Magpie geese. Norton couldn't guess how big the shopping mall was, it was just plain huge. Two or three storeys, brown coloured and modern, flags fluttering, cars and people everywhere, including police cars. He had very little trouble finding a parking space. He locked the T-Bird then walked through an entrance between a movie theatre complex and a couple of restaurants.

Inside was much like the plazas and malls back in Australia, only bigger, busier, a greater variety of shops and possibly, because it was so punishingly hot and humid outside, better air-conditioned. Norton wandered along past the busy shops till he came to a rest area full of takeaway food outlets set round a kind of raised up dais with a green and white tiled fountain, surrounded with flowers, gurgling happily away beneath a wide sunroof. Near this was a coloured layout on a black background listing all the shops and facilities. Les walked over and checked it out to make sure he'd be able to find where he'd left the car and see where everything was. The mall seemed to be built around four department stores: W.C. Penneys and Sears Roebuck at either end of one arcade. Zeniths and Foleys at the end of the other and all the variety stores, restaurants and whatever set in between. Les gave it a good perusal, then, like any normal mug tourist with more money than sense, set off to see what he could find and how much he could spend; and waste.

Norton's little piece of plastic worked like a charm. The shops were only too pleased to take his money and he managed to knock off about two grand in about as many hours. He bought four pairs of Levi 501s in different colours for about a third of the price in Australia. He got Nike Jordans and Reebok pumps for Eddie, Billy and George's kids. Les must have bought at least twenty T-shirts with everything on them from the North Carolina Tarheels to Notre Dame the Fighting Irish to the Florida Gators. He bought caps for baseball, basketball and gridiron, even some for fishing and powerboat racing, plus some Harley-Davidson gear. Nearly all the T-shirts were for the team back home. But one he did get for himself. It was blue with a frozen margarita on the front and 'Margaritaville' written across the chest. That was Norton's and there was no way they were going to get that off him. He got a pair of tan Rockports and some socks. Everything still seemed about a third of what it would cost back home, so Les figured the more he spent, the more he saved. After three trips out to the car, Les attacked the department stores. He got several button-down collar denim shirts, which were about a quarter of the price back home, and the quality seemed good. Les was curious how the yanks could make them so cheap.

216

But under closer inspection they were made in either the Dominican Republic or Mexico. Yes, just like home, thought Les. He bought some striped, button-down collar shirts and ones with other colourful designs on and noticed these were all made in the US; though after sales tax they weren't any cheaper. The service in the shops and department stores was something else. The staff were genuinely polite and obliging without the full-on, antiseptic McDonald's blurb. They all seemed to love Norton's accent and each purchase was followed by a pleasant smile and a, 'You have a good one.' I bloody well ought to, mused Les. It's costing me enough bloody money.

After his third trip out to the car Les was sitting in the food area, munching on three mini-hamburgers and a can of Mountain Dew. There were heaps of gooey, spicy things to eat, from tacos and slices of pizza to shrimp melts and chilli burgers. But what Les missed most was the Asian takeaways like back home. He would have given his left niagara for a Soya Sauce Chicken or a Gow Gee and Noodle Soup. But the mini-hamburgers were okay and he was saving himself for a decent feed over the other side of town. After the last mini-burger, Les decided on a nice cup of genuine American-style coffee then he'd sit back for a while and observe the heads on the seppos.

He found a top little coffee shop called 'Ernie's Coffee & Tea'. Inside was coffee from all over the world and a small, open-air counter for takeaways, or 'to go', as the yanks like to say. There were two friendly women and a happy little guy all wearing red and white striped aprons. The little guy was gay with this cheeky, witty personality and you couldn't help but like him. Les hung back for a while, making out he was choosing, while he listened to the guy and nearly cracked up at some of the things he was coming out with. Especially when one typically dilettantish yank, dressed like Gordon Gekko, came up and ordered coffee and muffins with raspberry jam.

'Are those raspberries fresh?' he demanded.

217

'Yes,' assured the little guy behind the counter. 'I went out in my little bonnet and apron and picked them first thing this morning.'

'Okay, well, I'll take two.'

Les ordered a flat white, which was absolutely delicious, and, still chuckling, sat down in the rest area to watch the American punters.

There were an odd-looking lot. Mostly whites, with big heads, big guts and big arses. If they weren't eating ice creams, they were chewing pizza or hot-dogs with their heads once again stuffed in a plastic bucket of soft drink. They nearly all wore Elmer Fudd caps, shuffling around with their hands in their pockets and their shorts hanging down round their fat arses. Families would walk past, Mum, Dad and the kids all wearing matching floral or checked outfits. Then Les noticed the parochialism in the clothing. All the T-shirts either had something to do with Florida on the front or Siestasota or the United States. This struck Norton as a little odd. You'd barely see locals walking around Sydney wearing Sydney T-shirts, or Bondi Junction wearing Bondi Junction T-shirts. Maybe in the football season you'd see a few with 'Roosters' or 'Parramatta' or whatever on the front. And you'd rarely see an Australian walking around Australia with 'Australia' splattered all over his T-shirt or jacket. Australians went more for T-shirts from other countries; either as souvenirs or to let their friends know where they've been. Maybe you were judged as a 'pinko commie faggot' if you didn't walk around the US wearing a T-shirt with 'USA Basketball' or 'I Love America' on the front and a flag stuffed in your date. And they all seemed to have these sing-song voices like they were reciting poetry. 'Hi there. How are you? You're looking really great. I love your hair.' Hickory-dickory-dock. The-mouse-ran-up-the-clock. 'Ahm leavin' on vacation tomorrow. We're goin' to awrheegon. Bekkie-Sue wants to see her folks.' Little-Bo-Peep-has-lost-her-sheep-and-doesn't-know-where-to-find-them. But it was their skin. That was the thing that had been sticking in Norton's mind from the time he got on that plane in Los Angeles. It was smooth, sort of oily-looking, and they all looked as if their faces were covered with Glad-Wrap. Even the freaky-looking kids about fourteen and fifteen running around with their Elmer Fudd caps jammed on their heads back to front. Les stared and sipped his coffee. It was fascinating, boring, humorous and ridiculous all at the same time. The yanks all ate takeaway food, had takeaway bodies and lived takeaway lives. All wrapped up and ready to go. Have a nice day. Miss you already. Then two security guards walked past doing their rounds, wearing guns, clubs, handcuffs and bullet-proof vests. Ahh yes, thought Norton. Welcome to America. You have a good one, and freeze, motherfucker, or *bang-bang-bang*, I'll shoot.

Les finished his coffee and drifted back towards the car. He still had St Almonds to visit yet, and he hadn't even put a dent in his VISA card. As he walked past another sports store he noticed a bookshop. He had nearly finished his P.J. O'Rourke, so he thought he might go in, have a bit of a browse around and maybe pick up something else to read. There was a plentiful variety of books and even these were cheaper than in Australia. He was looking through a few novels when he noticed a section entitled POETRY. For some reason Les drifted over. Right at the very front was a book of poems by Elizabeth Norton Blackmore. Hello, Norton smiled to himself. What have we got here? It was only a fifty-page book, called *The Great Poets*, and on the light blue cover was a painting of Blackmore wearing a white, buttoned to the neck, dress. Norton's smile got wider when he noticed she had red hair and a fairly square jaw. Inside were more photo plates from old paintings of England and one of old Moulton Norton wearing frock coat and breeches. A bit of a tingle went through Les when he noticed old Moulton had red hair, red muttonchop sidelevers and a red moustache. The small book was $15.95 plus tax, Norton paid cash and flicked through it as he walked out to the car. Although Les was somewhat excited coming across a book of his alleged ancestor's poems, it was too hot to sit reading it in the carpark, so he laid it on the seat next to him, intending to read it over a few drinks back at the flat that night, and proceeded to St Almonds Circle.

It was about a twenty-minute drive and in the daytime the place did look very Double Bayish; mainly restaurants, boutiques and up-market men's shops and other souvenir or knick-knack shops all set in an uneven circle, or radiating from it around the park just down from the bridge. Les recognised Reggae Mambo's and got a parking spot near the shop where Hank put the letter under the door. It was oppressively hot as usual when he got out of the air-conditioned car and Les cursed himself for starting to get used to it as he flicked some sweat from his eyes. Shit! This is getting to be tough going. But when the going gets tough, the tough go shopping. Where to first? I reckon these shops round here, then I'll work my way back.

The shops were all nicely air-conditioned, the staff were friendly and the quality of the clothing was good. But a bit of a rip off. Some neatly patterned silk shirts caught Norton's eye, until he turned over the price tag. One hundred and ninety-nine dollars plus tax. Yeah, that's all you need, mused Les. Two hundred bucks for a shirt and either some drunk rips it off your back in a fight or some dopey sheila walks past you in a bar, waving a cigarette around, and burns a hole straight through it. He ended up buying some T-shirts with tropical fish and manatees on the front and a Johnny Rebb cap made out of blue denim. The rest of the stuff didn't turn Les on all that much. It was nice, but just a bit too pricey, even for this mug tourist.

Then Les found this shop that looked more like a big grass hut stuck out in the jungle. The windows were full of artificial palm trees, toy monkeys, lions and tigers and other oddities. It was called 'Jungle Jennies'. Canned laughter was coming out of some hidden speakers, lights were flashing on and off and as you walked in the door, a sensor alarm set off the most lecherous wolf-whistle imaginable. Inside were all manner of novelty things

220

from T-shirts to hats, drinking mugs to whoopee cushions. Walking around the shop was an attractive, dark-haired woman in black leotards carrying a monkey in her arms; the way it had its arm round her neck and she was petting it you would have sworn the thing was real. Norton browsed around for a while, wondering what he was going to waste his money on, when he saw them and just stopped dead in his tracks. They were sitting in front of a jukebox that was playing Bill Hayley and the Comets' 'Shake, Rattle and Roll'. The All Star Frog Band. Five little green plastic frogs, counting the lead singer, up on their own little stage with their own little light show. They were like those plastic flowers and Coke tins on legs that you put in front of a set of speakers and they move in time to the music. Only these were five frogs about six inches high, and they were going for it. The lead singer made Mick Jagger look like he was going in for a hernia operation. Norton, being a man of discerning taste and vibrant wit, was absolutely fascinated.

'How much are they?' he asked the girl behind the counter.

'Forty-seven dollars, plus tax.'

'Give me four,' said Les. 'No. You'd better make that half a dozen.'

While the girl was getting them together Les sprung another tasteful little item among the novelty ashtrays and things on the counter. Another little green frog. This one was rubber, with a huge grin across his face, his little arms and legs spread apart and this giant, monster cock sticking out in front. On the box it said, 'Genuine Florida Horny Toad'.

'And give me six horny toads too,' said Les.

'You got it,' said the girl. 'And, might I say, you're a guy that knows what he wants.'

'That's me,' answered Les, still looking at the massive wozzer on the little frog. 'I'm a class act, sweetheart.'

Absolutely delighted with his purchases, Norton strolled back to the car and placed them in the boot along with the rest. Now, what about that nice feed I promised myself? he thought. Though I'm buggered if I'm all that hungry in this heat. I might have a snack at that Reggae Mambo's. It looked half alright. There was a shaded, vacant table out on the footpath. Les ordered an O'Doulls, which he demolished rather smartly, so he ordered another one plus a Lime Garlic Grouper Cozumel and a side salad. This turned out to be a fillet of grouper, marinated in lime and garlic, sprinkled with cracked black pepper, grilled and served with more garlic mayonnaise. It was pretty good, so was the salad and the coffee after and it wasn't a bad way to finish the day, sitting in the shade, watching the seppos walking or waddling past. Satisfied with his day's effort, Les left some money on the table and drove home to more fiddles and slide.

Back at the estate Les noticed the same skinny black guy he'd seen earlier working on a lawnmower outside the caretaker's shed. He stopped the car, got out and walked over.

'G'day, mate,' he said pleasantly. 'How are you goin' there?'

The black caretaker looked up from what he was doing, looked at Les, then kind of blinked around him, seemingly a little mystified at someone actually giving him the time of day let alone being pleasant. Norton had noticed everybody on the estate appeared to act a little self-important and probably treated the caretaker just like a caretaker. And a nigger one at that.

'How am I going?' he replied. 'I'm doing just fine, thank you.'

'Good on you,' said Norton. 'Listen, mate, I was wondering if you might be able to do us a bit of a favour?'

'Sure. I'll see what I can do.'

'Well, I've bought a whole lot of T-shirts and junk and I need a box or something to put it in, so's I can send it all back home.'

'Hey, where's home, brother?'

'Australia,' said Les.

'Australia. Shit! I thought that's where you might have

bin from.' The black guy stood up and had a good look at Norton through his sunglasses.

'Yeah. The dreaded,' answered Les.

'And you need, like, a — cardboard box?'

'Yeah.'

'I'll see what I can do for you, brother.' The caretaker headed for the door.

'And while you're there, can you have a look, see if you got some tape and a marking pen?'

'No problems, brother.'

'Good on you, mate.'

Les could hear the caretaker rummaging around inside. He was back out in a few minutes with a big white fruit carton, a roll of wide masking tape and an Artline marker.

'There you go, brother. That do you, man?'

'Reckon. You're a bloody beauty, mate.' Norton was rapt and went for his pocket. 'What do I owe you, mate?'

The black guy made a gesture. 'That's cool, man. Don't sweat it.'

'Fair enough. But here you are. Get yourself a drink anyway.' Les gave him a twenty.

'Hey. Much oblige, brother.'

'No worries,' said Les, picking up the carton. 'What's your name anyway?'

'Jerome.'

'I'm Les, Jerome. Pleased to meet you.'

Jerome shook Norton's hand and grinned. 'Damned if I ain't too.'

'I'll leave the pen and that outside your door when I'm finished.'

'Any time brother.'

Jerome pocketed the twenty and went back to his lawnmower. Norton threw the carton on the back seat and drove round to the condo.

Inside, with a Coors Cutter in his hand and the radio playing, Norton couldn't believe how much junk he'd bought. But there was more than enough for everybody, including family and friends, and it all went into the

223

carton alright. He packed the T-shirts and jackets around the cartons holding the frog bands so they wouldn't break and when he strapped it all down with masking tape the carton was as solid as a rock. All Les had to do then was address it to himself then take it up to the nearby post office. He did that after dropping the pen and what was left of the masking tape at the door of the caretaker's shed.

The post office was about two doors from the travel agency and Les was a little surprised to find it was run by an Amish couple in their fifties. It was musty and kind of old-fashioned looking. But if the post office was old-fashioned, the two Amish looked like they'd just come straight from the sixteenth century. Sober black clothes on the man, the woman wore this ankle-length, crinoline dress with a white coffee filter on her head and their skin looked almost grey. They reminded Norton of those reproductions of old Rembrandt and Titian paintings from school. Both of them were polite and efficient, but unlike the other Amish, they were the most sober, unsmiling people Les had ever come across; almost as bad as the two lemons he'd bought the old pushbike from. The only thing funny about them was the husband was going bald and he had his hair plastered across his scone in a giant smother and it looked like two slices of mouldy, burnt toast araldited to the top of his head. Norton nearly had to have his arsehole araldited back in when they weighed his package and told him the postage. Over $200 US. Les paid with a very shaky hand.

There was a liquor store close by; Les thought it might be an idea to stock up and replace what he'd consumed so far — he also felt like a drink after having to fork out $200. As usual there were more brands and types of booze than Les had ever seen before ... there were six different types of bacardi alone. Les knew he'd be in there all day once he started picking and choosing, so he got four six-packs of Corona, two bottles of George Dickle soft drink and a bag of ice. Back at the car he was laughing to himself and thinking the owner had robbed himself, but

224

when he checked the receipt Corona was a dollar a bottle and the bourbon, which is about forty dollars a bottle in Australia, was thirteen dollars including tax. Christ! thought Les, as he started the engine, it's a good thing I'm only here for another two weeks or so. Otherwise I'd be donating my liver to the Powerhouse Museum when I get back home.

Back at the condo, Les packed the beer and ice away, turned on the radio again and was thinking that apart from blowing two hundred on postage it hadn't been a bad day, shopping and checking out the yank punters. There were still a few more things he wanted to get so he'd do it again. It was also good just cruising around and taking his time with no silly bloody Hank to annoy him. Norton was about to attack a Corona when he changed his mind and put it back in the fridge. I know what I'll do, he mused. I'll go out and see Mrs Laurel and pick up my Walkman; without my breath smelling of booze either. He checked where they lived was on the map then decided to ring and say he was on his way; he didn't have Mrs Laurel's number but he had Hank's. A smile spread across Norton's face when it didn't answer. Looks like Captain Rats isn't home. Good. That means I don't have to talk to the prick. I can have a nice cup of coffee with his mum and a mag, then stall. Les snapped his fingers. That's who I should have bought a little present for. I will before I leave. He locked up the flat and headed for Swamp Manor. It had started to cloud over and Brooks and Dunn were twanging their way through 'My Next Broken Heart' when Les crunched up in the driveway.

Norton's initial smile faded to a sneer when he saw Hank's pick-up under the battered carport and no sign of Mrs Laurel's car. Ahh shit! he cursed to himself. How's that for timing? Boofhead must have just got home. Norton was no happier when he knocked on the door and saw that the house looked like it was all locked up. Ahh shit! Norton cursed to himself again when he remembered Mrs Laurel telling him before he left that she was going to visit her daughter or something for a few days during the week. That means I've got to go and knock on Captain Rat's door. I'll bet she's probably given him the thing to give to me and he deliberately hasn't so I'd have to make a trip out here. The fuckwit. Les had half a mind to give it a miss and buy himself another Walkman. Ahh! I'm bloody well here now. I should only have to talk to the dill for a few minutes, even if he does start playing his usual stupid fuckin' games. He strode down the pathway through the Spanish Moss and buzzing insects, knocked on Hank's door and waited. Despite a good loud knock there was no answer. Les knocked again: louder. Still no answer. He's probably in there having a three-bagger.

'Hey, Hank,' Norton yelled out towards the top windows, 'stop playin' with your dick and get down here and answer the door. You Beechams bloody pill.'

Still no answer. Les had a look around then knocked again.

'You in there, Hank?' he yelled out. There was still no answer.

Ahh, what a pain in the arse, cursed Norton again. I wonder where the imbecile is? He put his hand over his forehead and took a peek through the loungeroom window. It was dark and gloomy inside, but if Norton wasn't mistaken there was someone sitting back on the lounge asleep. It looked like Hank. Les rattled on the window; the figure didn't move. Yeah, he's probably pissed or full of painkillers, thought Les. Bugger it. I suppose I'll have to go in and wake the cunt up. The door was unlocked; Les opened it and stepped inside.

Despite the light behind him, it took a second or two for Norton's eyes to get accustomed to the gloom. It was Hank asleep on the lounge alright. In fact it would be fair to describe him as being dead to the world. His eyes were closed and he was slumped to his right, his right arm still in a sling. His left arm was sprawled across the lounge, his hand open, and sitting on the lounge, just in front of his fingertips, was the Walther Les had used at the target range. On Hank's left temple, just near his eye, was a blackened, congealed hole with some powder burns around it. The other side of Hank's head had a rather large piece missing and that part was splattered across the back of the lounge in a mixture of scalp, bone and bits of grey-looking stuff all surrounded by dried, rust-coloured blood. The hole in the left side must have pumped a bit of blood for a few moments before oozing out because some had soaked into Hank's lap and a couple of rivulets had spread out across the floor. Between the rivulets was a single, spent cartridge. How long he'd been dead was anyone's guess.

Norton stared at Captain Rat's body for a few moments and if not actually horrified, he should have at least been a little shocked. He wasn't. After the scene with Murray and the six terrorists, Les swore nothing would ever shock him again. Instead, Les found it somehow amusing; laughable almost. Norton knew Hank was a bit psycho, though he considered him more of a flip than anything else, and when he told him to go shoot himself Les meant it as a sardonic, sarcastic joke really. Les's gross insult to finally get rid of him. But trust Captain Rats to take his advice to the letter. On the other hand Hank was like a stupid big kid at times. Could there be a bit of nyeh-nyeh-nyeh-nyeh-nyeh, I'll show you Les, thrown in? Well, he certainly had. Now what?

Framed in the light from the open door Les stared at Hank's bruised and battered face, pale at the best of times, now looking almost pale blue, and for once Norton was completely stumped for words. What could he say? Nice bit of shooting, Hank? Glad to see you took my advice, Hank. Now you can cut down on your smoking. Have you seen my Walkman anywhere, Hank? Les knew it was wrong, but he couldn't help laughing. He'd met some dills in his time but Hank took the cake, and the blue ribbon as well. Shaking his head slowly, Les put his hands on his hips and looked around the room, just in case his Walkman was sitting there somewhere or maybe a suicide note. There was nothing, and if anything the place looked more gloomy and depressing than ever. But good ol' Hank had gone out in style. His own man. No note, no nothing. Those jerks he'd left behind weren't worth wasting his time on anyway. Onya, Hank. You're a bloody beauty, thought Les. Or at least you were.

Then Les saw it sitting on top of the TV and his face lit up in a grin. But he couldn't do it, could he? Not much he couldn't; and what a souvenir. Norton walked over to the TV, picked it up and examined it. Yes, it was definitely the same fifty dollar bill he'd given Hank folded neatly in half. He folded it again and looked at Hank. At least Les now had something he could say.

'Well, Hank. I don't suppose you'll be needing this any more? Will you, mate?' Norton slipped the fifty in his pocket, took one last quick look at Captain Rats then left, closing the door softly behind him.

Norton didn't think about much on the way home. The sky had started to blacken and flashes of lightning were streaking across the sky among the rumbling claps of thunder. He made it back inside the condo just as the heavens opened up. The humidity was almost unbelievable now and streaks of perspiration were soaking across Norton's face and T-shirt. He turned the air-conditioner on and the radio then got a bottle of Corona from the fridge and took a good long pull, swallowing almost half the bottle. As Les burped he reflected into the bottle and something else struck him as funny.

'Look at that, Hank,' he said out loud. 'No bloody piece of lime. At least I don't look like a tourist.'

Norton didn't feel in the slightest bit sorry for Hank. He didn't raise his bottle in a toast to the dear departed. Norton was having a beer because it was stinken hot and he was thirsty. As far as Norton was concerned Hank was where he belonged and very soon Les would be outside having another swim in the rain. In fact, if anything, Hank should have shot himself sooner and Les would be in LA or Las Vegas or maybe even back home drinking Eumundi lager and watching the football. At least I will be in another couple of weeks or so, mused Norton. He took another swig of cold beer then sat down on the lounge to listen to the radio. Les was about to kick his

Nikes off when he stopped and screwed his face up. There was some congealed blood on the toe of one and a little around the heel of the other.

'What the...?'

Then it struck Les. When he was being half smart and had walked over to get the fifty dollar bill sitting on the TV, he'd stepped in Hank's blood, more than likely leaving a couple of footprints. This meant that when Mrs Laurel came home and found her loving son's body she'd have to ring the police, and even though it was an apparent suicide there'd be some sort of a forensic examination. They'd find the footprints, which would show someone had obviously been walking around in there. Who? And the only person who had been anywhere near Hank recently that Mrs Laurel would think of would be that nice Mr Norton from Australia. Who was now staying in Ricco DiCosti's condo, the Mafia money-mover, where he'd already been half pie grilled about it by Special Agent Benshoff from the Department of Justice. So there was a chance Les might get a knock on the door, possibly by the weekend, from the local wallopers. Great. But I only went there to get my Walkman, officer. Then why didn't you report what you found to the police? I was meaning to, honest. But I was a bit confused. And how come your fingerprints are all over the gun too, Mr Norton? Maybe you did it and put the gun in the deceased's hand, Mr Norton? You are an associate of Mr DiCosti and Mr Rizzitello. That's already been established by Agent Benshoff. Are you helping them launder money and the late Mr Laurel found out? Shit! cursed Les. All over a lousy fifty dollar bill. Norton wasn't being paranoid, but he just didn't know what these local redneck southern cops might think. He finished his beer then washed the blood from his Nikes in the bathroom. When he got that off, Les made sure there was none on the carpet and even ran out in the pouring rain and checked to see there was none in the car. Satisfied everything was in order, he got into his Speedos and went for a long swim in the rain; if nothing else, it at least had a cooling effect.

The rain kept up after Les got out of the pool and got dried off and into a clean T-shirt. If anything it got heavier, which suited Norton in a way. He wasn't in the mood for going out, he didn't feel like chasing a root, he didn't even feel hungry. He just felt like staying home and getting half drunk. He wasn't down in the blues so much; Les just had the shits more than anything else with the way things were turning out. He thought about ringing Laverne and Ricco and telling them what had happened, but changed his mind. He'd be seeing them tomorrow, maybe he'd tell them then. Les got another Corona and drank it while he watched the rain pelting down onto the estate as darkness began to fall, then he made himself a rather large delicious and slurped on that to some more country and western music.

After a couple more drinks Norton got sick of the radio so he switched on the TV to see what he could find. He got the last of some American sitcom he'd never seen before then a station promo saying to keep tuned for the Clint Eastwood movie, *Thunderbolt and Lightfoot*. That'll do, thought Norton. I've seen this thing before yonks ago, but it's not a bad old flick. I'll watch it again. A couple more drinks later and Les was half into the film. Clint Eastwood had been chased out of the church by George Kennedy and was on his merry way with his partner in crime to get the anti-tank-rifle and snaffle the rest of the loot. Then Norton couldn't figure out whether he was getting drunk or there was something wrong with the film. It was like half the dialogue was being cut out. Was it the electrical storm outside? No. He was watching cable. Finally it dawned on him. Any words that were remotely blasphemous were being zapped out. Even 'damn, 'bastard', 'shit', 'sonofabitch'. Let alone the juicy ones — the frucks and crunts. This was the South; the Bible Belt. Good, God-fearin', nigger-lynchin', Jew-baitin' Christian folk. Glory Hallelujah and praise the lord. What a fuckin' load of shit, thought Les, and what a weird fuckin' country. You can buy all the guns you need then go out and shoot anything that moves. The place is awash with heroin and cocaine. There's a serial killer in every town or some prick standing on every corner with a gun waiting to steal your car. Yet you can't see a tit or hear someone say 'poop' on TV. Les shook his head as another word got zapped out. God bless America.

He watched the end of the movie, more out of drunken amazement than anything else, then turned the TV off and left the radio off as well. Half revved up from the booze, he decided to read his book on Jamaica and cross reference it with his book of Elizabeth Norton Blackmore's poems. According to the book on Jamaica there was a clue to buried treasure in there somewhere, supposedly in one of her poems. Les poured another drink and started reading. An hour later he was drunk, tired and absolutely buggered if he could find any connection between buried pirate gold or whatever and poetry. The poems and the prose were probably some of the most beautiful ever written. But to a Philistine like Norton the words meant sweet bugger all. And if there was any connection, it was either a myth handed down through the years or you'd have to be Albert Einstein to work it out. I mean, have a look at this, Les mused drunkenly and tiredly to himself.

I raise my weighted soul up solemnly,
As once Delphinia her cryptic urn.

How could you make any bloody sense out of that? And what about this load of utter edgar?

That heartless perfection which thou lentst her,
To so affront man's darkest deeds in different times,
Reach up thy divine countenance amongst
    transfigured friends,

Fair dinkum. How could you make anything out of that bullshit? The bloody stuff doesn't even rhyme. Here's a good one. Short and to the point of absolute nothing.

How do I love thee? Let me count four ways.
Confronting you directly, my beloved, I see all four at
    once,
Yet 'tis for this very reason I canst see the ten,
A heartbeat to the left or right and I see all four again,

231

Though the last love may be obscured,
And 'tis indeed the last love I treasure most, my
dearest,
This is a love we both did share and shall ever treasure,
Our laboured love. The last love at the manse.

Norton slammed the book closed in disgust and took a slurp on his last drink. What a load of bollocks. He looked at Blackmore's portrait on the cover and shook his head boozily. I hate to say this, ol' Betty baby, but I think you were playing with your ted when you were writing this stuff. Ferociously. But then again, maybe you were before your time. In this new age of sexuality, if it's okay for Madonna to get her photo taken fiddling with herself, I suppose it was alright for you to play a bit of one-finger panty polka too. But on the other hand, if I get caught having a bit of strop, I'm a wanker. Fair dinkum, Betty. I don't know what to think. It's all very confusing; especially when bourbon's only thirteen bucks a bottle. Les finished his drink and put the glass in the sink. I do know what I do think though. I'm drunk, I'm tired and it's time I went to bed. Norton cleaned his teeth, then turned out the lights and did exactly that. Outside it rained for a little while longer then stopped and the stars reappeared.

The phone ringing around eight-thirty the next morning got Les out of bed. He'd woken up about half an hour earlier, feeling a little seedy, and couldn't be bothered getting up, so he lay there, half dozing, half thinking about different things. This holiday in America just seemed to be getting weirder and weirder. When he walked out and picked up the phone it was Ricco.

'Hey, Les. How are you doin'?'

'Not too bad, Ricco,' Les answered, a little thickly. 'How's yourself?'

I'm feelin' great. You ready to go boatin'?'

'Yeah. What time are you gonna call around?'

'I got a couple of things to sort out and I'll be there at ten. You gonna be ready?'

'Yeah. If I'm not out the front, just knock on the door.'

'Okay. I'll see you at ten.'

Yeah, righto, thought Les, blinking slightly at the phone. Do I pack a rod, or bring a violin case? I suppose we'll have a shoot-out with the coastguard or something this time. The way things are going, nothing would surprise me. And the way I feel I couldn't give a stuff either. Les poured himself two large glasses of orange juice and went for a swim.

Outside it was hotter than ever. There wasn't a breath of wind or a cloud in the sky and the heat seemed to shimmer in the air, almost distorting your vision. Christ, Les muttered to himself as he trudged across the back lawn. Peter O'Toole didn't do it this tough in *Lawrence of Arabia*.

There were four people in the pool; Les ignored them, threw his towel on a chair and flopped straight in. Again the water was wet and clear and that was about it. As far as cooling you off went, if a Bondi iceberg fell in he'd end up with third degree burns. But again it was cleansing enough and a few laps along with a few duck dives in the deep end got rid of the sweat along with the cobwebs. Les climbed out, got under the pool shower for a while then retreated from the heat back inside the condo. By the time he'd made some coffee and a sandwich, swallowed more glasses of orange juice then washed some T-shirts in the bath and hung them from the rafters in the verandah it was almost ten. He got into a plain white T-shirt and shorts then threw some things in his backpack just as there was a knock on the door. Les turned off the lights and the air-conditioning and stepped outside.

'G'day, Ricco. How's it goin'?'

'I'm doin' just fine.' Ricco was wearing neat blue shorts and lemon-coloured T-shirt; sitting on his head were a pair of Bollés. 'You lookin' forward to a run out in the gulf?'

'Yeah. It's sure bloody hot enough,' said Les. He locked the door and they walked towards the car.

'Vinnie tells me you had some good-looking broad out his joint on Tuesday night. Who was she?'

'Just some sheila works on a marina. I met her when I was out with Hank one night. Her name's Lori something-or-other.'

'Uh-huh.'

'Funny thing. I didn't even know that was Vinnie's restaurant. We just fluked it.'

'Vinnie put a good rap on you. Said you were aces.'

'I don't know about that,' smiled Norton. 'But the food was aces. It was great.'

'Yeah. Vinnie does a good meal. Maybe you'll see her again and the four of us can have dinner?'

'Yeah okay. That'd be good.' Yeah. Real good, thought Les.

Laverne was sitting on the front seat of the Mercedes wearing baggy white shorts, a pink tank-top and sunglasses. She smiled broadly when she saw Norton.

'Hi, Les. How are you?'

'Pretty good, thanks, Laverne,' replied Norton, climbing in the back. 'How's yourself?'

'I'm fine.' she swivelled round and continued to smile at Les. 'Ricco tells me you're becoming quite a ladies' man. One at the condo on Sunday night. Another for dinner at Vinnie's on Tuesday. You're a regular Julio Iglesias, aren't you?'

'It's just my boyish Australian charm,' smiled Les. 'But I still haven't come across one as sweet as you yet, Laverne.'

'Oh you're such a kidder, Les.'

Ricco hit the ignition. 'I'd better move the car before the wheels get stuck in all this bullshit.'

'Yeah,' agreed Norton. 'There's a bit of it around.'

They turned right out the front of the estate and headed along the same wide road that took Les to the shopping mall the previous day. Laverne waffled on, asking Les had he heard from Hank, what he'd been up to and who was his latest squeeze. Les said he hadn't heard from Hank — which was true — and he certainly didn't mention Lori was a cop. As they went past the mall he pointed out that was where he went shopping before he drove over to St Almonds Circle. He made a joke about the frog bands but didn't mention buying the ones with the big dongers. Ricco had the radio tuned softly to some middle of the road station, so it was polite conversation and polite muzak as they drove further south. Despite the easy, air-conditioned banter while they cruised along Ricco seemed a little pensive. Even Laverne would go quiet now and again. Maybe Les was imagining it, but he seemed to pick up a funny vibe in the air, as if there was something going on between them and they weren't letting on. Whether there was or not, Les didn't let on, he just chattered away as they headed further south now on some monster freeway full of trucks and cars going past what seemed like an endless row of stores and takeaway food shops dotted with the odd supermarket or shopping centre. Ricco spoke just as a sign loomed up on the right saying Salmo.

'My coffee shop's just a bit further on. I'll show you.'

'Righto,' nodded Les.

They drove about another mile or so and Ricco slowed up as they went past a small block of shops separated from the freeway by parking bays. There were a few shops, including hairdressers and some sort of hardware store, and set on the approaching corner was the shop. It wasn't all that big but it was neat and modern-looking, painted mostly black, white and brown. A half-dozen glass tables and wicker-backed chrome chairs sat out the front with some potted palms underneath a candy-striped canvas awning. A sign in black sitting above the awning said 'Ricco's Rendezvous'. It said the same on the windows next to a white cup and saucer with steam rising off it. The place seemed to have a certain style and class about it as they drove past, but no customers sitting out the front. Les didn't notice any through the glass door either.

'Yeah, that looks alright, Ricco,' said Norton, watching it disappear out the rear window. 'If the coffee's as good as what you made me the other night, you should do alright.'

'It gets me a living.' Laverne and Ricco exchanged a wry look when he said that. 'You're gonna have to come down for a cup. You think that stuff at home was good, wait till you try the specialty of the house. Riccochinno I call it. Make the blind see, the lame walk and the deaf and the dumb hear and talk.'

'Sounds pretty good,' laughed Les.

'You come down tomorrow around lunchtime and I'll do you a chinno and provolone with yucatan pickle on Cuban bread. You won't know what hit you. You'll be ringing your buddies in Australia telling them to get their asses over here fast as they can.

'Okay, Ricco. You got me for coffee around lunchtime tomorrow.'

Another mile past the coffee shop Ricco turned right at a sign saying Wharf Road. The road was narrower and seemed to be mainly warehouses or nautical shops. They got to where the road stopped at the water and Ricco pulled up and switched off the motor. They seemed to be surrounded by massive concrete and wooden storage sheds built over a concrete wharf or docking area. They got out of the car and Ricco took an ice-box from the boot. When he opened it to move the ice around Les noticed half a dozen bottles of O'Doulls, the same of Millers Lite and two bottles of white wine. A fair-haired guy in a pair of white overalls with 'Salmo Marine' on the back came over, said something to Ricco and pointed. Ricco motioned for Les to follow him. Offering to carry the ice-box, Norton followed behind along a walkway and down some steps. He was expecting a marina jutting out over the water with boats bobbing up and down all moored alongside. Instead, when he looked into one of the monstrous concrete sheds, there were dozens and dozens of huge powerboats and cruisers stacked up on the walls, almost like bottles in a wine cellar. Parked on the concrete floor was the biggest forklift Les had ever seen, holding up a boat at least fifty feet long ready for stacking or putting in the water. So that's how it works, surmised Les. They stack and store your boat for you then when you want it they drop it in the drink for you like a rubber ducky in a bath tub. Very convenient. Ricco's boat was tied up almost at the bottom of the steps. It was the full-on 'Miami Vice' special: or close enough. About thirty-five feet long, painted gleaming white with a black and tan trim and more chrome than Elvis Presley's Cadillacs. The seats at the rear were a plush, padded black, the front had a half cabin underneath with a chrome rail running round it all the way back to the bridge or cockpit. A white spoiler arched over the back and behind it were two shiny black 125 HP Evinrudes. There was no name, just a number. D601-L49.

'Nice boat,' said Les.

'It gets me around,' replied Ricco casually.

Les stepped on board and stowed the ice-box under a seat as Ricco and Laverne did the same with the two carry-bags they had. 'What do you want me to do?' he asked, looking around him.

'Nothing,' answered Ricco. 'We can handle it.'

'Righto.'

Norton made himself comfortable on one of the seats and wiped his sunglasses with his T-shirt while Laverne and Ricco cast off the two lines holding the boat. Laverne sat opposite Les while Ricco settled down behind the controls. He hit a button and the twin Evinrudes rumbled into life in perfect unison. Ricco let them idle for a minute or two then pushed the throttle forward a fraction and they moved off smoother than honey on a slice of hot toast.

Norton sat back, toffing it up a little, and tried to figure out where they were. Ricco turned right once they left the docking area and they seemed to be going slowly along what looked like a wide, flat river. But from what he remembered of his map Les figured it would be another inlet among all the keys, as this part of Florida seemed to be dotted with shallow keys and inlets or mangrove-covered sandbars sticking out of the water. They rumbled along past a pole with a sign saying 8 MPH and now there were huge houses built on the water's edge with their own private jetties or surrounded by either parkland or private property. A bit further on a huge white boat loomed up on the right with 'US Coastguard' painted along the side in black and a wide orange band painted round the hull with the coastguard seal on it. The stars and stripes hung off the stern and the whole thing bristled with cannons and machine guns. Les was glad he was only joking about getting into a fire fight with them. With all that armament, not counting what was below, you'd last about two minutes. Ricco didn't say anything as they went past the patrol boat, but Les noticed him turn round and give Laverne a wink.

They cruised on a bit more, finally leaving the inlet and entering a long narrow bay; there was shoreline off to the left and right and in front of them was a long skinny spit, or key, with an inlet going through it. The water was a kind of soupy blue-green, there still wasn't a breath of wind and when Les looked up to the sky he now noticed a band of thick grey clouds moving in from the north. If it was hot earlier it must have gone up another twenty degrees; Norton's T-shirt was soaked. Laverne got some block-out from one of the bags and began spreading some on herself and Ricco. Not a bad idea, thought Les, getting some Coppertone out of his backpack, plus his blue Roosters cap. Slip, slap, slop. Me no fry. No, just fuckin' dissolve if I don't get one of those beers out of that ice-box and into me. Next thing they were through the inlet and heading into a huge expanse of calm green water.

'This is the Gulf of Mexico,' said Ricco. 'I'll cruise out there for a while then we'll come back the other side of town through the Main Pass.'

Norton was about to say 'aye-aye, Captain' or something when Ricco hit the throttle and the boat took off like it was jet propelled, throwing Les sideways as it almost leapt straight out of the ocean. The Evinrudes dug in again, Les grabbed his hat and moved further back in the seat with his back to the stern.

It was a buzz and a half because Norton had never been in a boat as powerful as this; the big craft literally skimmed across the water with the spoiler keeping it down. There were no waves, just a few tiny swells, so they didn't make any gigantic leaps, but there was plenty of noise as the ocean rattled and banged beneath the hull. Behind them the twin Evinrudes roared power, spreading a creaming, foaming wake across where they'd been. Well this is alright, thought Les, the wind howling round his ears as they headed out into the Gulf of Mexico. I could think of worse ways to put in an afternoon; and it looks like getting better. Laverne went to the ice-box and got Ricco an O'Doulls so Norton thought he might do the same, only he took a Millers. While he was there he also opened a bottle of riesling for Laverne. Half the bottle of Millers went down in about one swallow, making Les let out a massive burp which was hidden by the roar of the motors. He sat back and sucked on his Millers while Laverne and Ricco got into some sort of a conversation. They weren't quite ignoring him, but whatever they were talking about seemed, if not deadly serious, at least important.

Whatever, Les didn't take too much notice. He sat back, demolished the rest of his beer and enjoyed the breeze as they blasted out into the Gulf of Mexico. After the amount of booze Norton had had the previous night, the one can of lite beer had put a bit of a head on any that was left in his system and he was starting to feel a little blissful as well as refreshed. So blissful in fact that he thought he might be a rude guest and help himself to another Millers: without even bothering to ask. Not that Laverne and Ricco would have noticed anyway, they were still deeply engrossed in their head-to-head and checking charts and watches. Norton left them alone and concentrated on his surroundings. The first thing he noticed was that they were a bloody long way out from shore. Also, that thick dark band of clouds he'd noticed earlier had got darker, spreading right across the horizon and, even though the sun was still out in force, was covering the sky rapidly. Ricco drank more O'Doulls and continued to rocket into the gulf. As far as friendly conversation went and pointing different things out to a visitor from another country, Ricco hardly spoke at all and gave the impression that he wanted to keep to himself. This kind of suited Les in a way, although he wouldn't have minded jumping behind the controls for a while; but he left him alone. After a while Laverne came down and got a pair of binoculars from one of the carry-bags. She saw Les watching her and reached over.

'I use these to watch out for dolphins. They're cool.'

'Yeah,' yelled Les, over the throbbing of the Evinrudes. 'We get them back in Australia. I sometimes see them off the beach where I live.'

'They're lovely. I don't like what the Japanese do to them though.'

'Yeah. I got to agree with you there, Laverne. The low bastards need a good kick up the date the way they slaughter them.'

Laverne got back up next to Ricco and began watching for dolphins as they continued to blast on. It was nice to know Laverne had a kind spot in her heart for some of the ocean's most beautiful and harmless creatures. But something did have Norton guessing just a little: if she's on the watch for dolphins, how come she keeps looking up at the sky all the time? I didn't think dolphins flew. I thought they swam.

They sped further out into the gulf as the approaching clouds got blacker and thicker, taking up almost the entire sky now as they swirled and tumbled menacingly into each other. Distant flashes of gold among the grey and black showed lightning was cracking and Norton didn't have to be some smartarse, drunken Australian, posing as a meteorologist, to know there was a bad, flash storm approaching. He'd seen things like this before along the Diamantina and other parts of the Australian outback. This could even be a cyclone. Or a hurricane. Oh well, thought Les, turning to the two Evinrudes throbbing away behind him. If this thing couldn't outrun

240

it, nothing would. A mile or two further on and Norton's curiosity as to why Laverne kept looking at the sky for dolphins was satisfied. Ricco cut the throttle back and a plane flew over them at no more than a hundred feet, if that. It was white with a blue and yellow trim, single wing and engine with extra fuel tanks slung under the wings and the latest Kevlar pontoons instead of wheels. The plane wiggled its wings twice as it went over the boat, then twice again, and if Les was any judge kept going on full throttle towards the Main Pass, which was now just a smear of high-rises in the distance.

Despite the roar of the outboard motors Les distinctly heard Ricco curse. 'Jesus goddamn Christ! Sonofa-fuckin-bitch!'

Ricco gave Laverne a tight look; she was expression-less. A few seconds later they had more company. A white helicopter with a wide orange band around it went belting and clattering overhead and if it wasn't in hot pursuit of the plane it was definitely going flat out in the same direction. Norton didn't say a word; he hardly had time to even think of one. Ricco shoved the throttle full forward, spun the big boat around and took off after the plane and the helicopter. In a few seconds he must have been doing close to eighty mph. Laverne turned to Les and gave him a weak smile. Les smiled back naively and raised his beer.

Despite his supposed naivety Norton was starting to get a bit toey. It wasn't hard to tell what was going on. Ricco had come out to meet the plane for some sort of a drop and had brought Les along for the ride. Unfortu-nately the coastguard must have got onto it. Probably it wasn't supposed to have worked out like this. Probably it was supposed to have gone over as smoothly as normal then when the job was done a nice day would have been spent out on the gulf having a good time. Now the shit had hit the fan and Les was stuck right in the middle of it. But not only that. It had completely blackened over now and streaks of lightning lit up the entire sky accompanied by crashing explosions of thunder. They moved on another couple of miles when a burst of cold wind buffeted the boat. Above them it looked like millions of gigantic plastic bags of coal were swirling and tumbling in the air. There was another streak of lightning accompanied by an almost deafening clap of thunder, then the wind and rain hit the boat at the same time. Norton had never experienced anything like it. At first it blew the boat sideways but Ricco got it back on course as the rain came down in sheets along with a dramatic drop in temperature. It was now becoming somewhat of a hairy situation. If they didn't get hit by lightning first the boat could sink or get flipped over. There was no time to be worrying about the coastguard, they had to reach land and in a hurry. The obvious thing to do would be to turn south and go with it, but Ricco, for some reason, was speeding across it in the direction of the Main Pass. No matter what he was doing it was all hands to the pumps. Norton tossed his drink over the side and got to his feet; there was that much noise he had to get about two inches from Ricco's ear.

'What do you want me to do?' he yelled.

'Just keep an eye on those doors underneath. Make sure they don't pop.'

'Nothing else?'

Ricco shook his head grimly and stared ahead into the storm. 'I'll ride this out. Christ!'

Les settled up against the doors beneath the cockpit and kept an eye on them and anything that looked like it might come loose as the full fury of the storm lashed the boat; it was even worse with Ricco belting the thing along as fast as he possible could. The only good thing was that Norton's teeth were chattering and he enjoyed feeling freezing cold for a change. Laverne settled down opposite Les; from somewhere she'd found a white plastic jacket. Ricco was still lashed to the wheel in his designer T-shirt and shorts. Norton had to give it to him, he had balls and he handled the boat admirably under the circumstances; of course a bad result if you blow things, like getting shot or going to gaol, certainly gives you a bit of incentive. Although you could hardly see ten feet, Norton looked up at the pitch black sky and hoped the bloke upstairs wasn't that dirty on him to leave him floating in the murky warm waters of the Gulf of Mexico.

Ricco made it to the Main Pass as the flash storm continued. Although the thunder and lightning was just as horrendous as ever and he was cold and soaked to the skin, Les felt a noticeable sense of relief. They turned left and seemed to be heading north towards downtown; although visibility was still atrocious Les thought he could make out some tall buildings in the gloomy distance. Ricco slowed the boat down. There were no other boats around and certainly no sign of either the plane or the helicopter. You could bet they'd be halfway to Louisiana by now. Norton decided to get to his feet and see what Ricco was up to now. Ricco still had his eyes peeled across the rain-lashed water then he switched on some sort of a scanner in front of the wheel. It looked like a spider's web of white lights and one bright red dot. Les noticed Ricco smile as he picked up the red dot and turned the boat in the direction it was showing up on the scanner. They went about two miles and Ricco began slowing down the boat some more. The light on the scanner got stronger and despite the wind and rain still howling around them Ricco managed to bring the boat to almost dead slow and keep it steady on course.

'Hey Laverne,' he yelled. 'Get your ass up here and take the wheel.'

Laverne was on her feet now also. 'I'm there, Ricco. I'm there.'

'And keep it steady. Dead steady.'

'Okay.'

Laverne took over the wheel, Ricco grabbed a boat hook and stood on the right hand side of the boat, one hand on the rail, the other holding the boat hook as the wind threatened to blow him overboard.

Les thought for a second then walked unsteadily over to him. 'You need a hand?'

Ricco looked at Les impassively for a moment then nodded his head. 'Yeah. Get ready to open those two doors for me.'

243

'Righto.'

Les got ready next to the two doors beneath the cockpit. A minute or so later Laverne yelled out to Ricco. He reached over the side with the boat hook and dragged in a thick, green, canvas bag; flotation rings were attached to the side and there was a waterproof red light blinking on top. It was about a metre and a half long by about a metre square. Ricco hit a switch and the light stopped blinking. As soon as he did that, he slung it to Les who had the doors open, Les slung it straight inside and quickly locked them again. Laverne handed the wheel over to Ricco, who wheeled the boat straight around in the direction of the marina and motored along with the storm now running behind them. Les heard Ricco laugh and saw him rough up Laverne's rain-splattered hair in a friendly fashion. He sensed Les watching him, turned around with a grin on his face and winked.

With the storm running behind them it was much smoother now. They travelled on, not going too fast, then of all things the storm seemed to disappear as quickly as it came up. The further they went the calmer it got till eventually the wind died away completely, the water in the keys glassed over and the sun came out again. Next thing Norton was almost sweating. He was about to say something to Ricco when three dolphins began circling the boat. Ricco was travelling at the speed limit of eight mph and one came right up alongside the boat, so close that Laverne was able to reach over and pat it as it 'whooshed' air and water up at them. Laverne squealed with delight, even Ricco laughed and Norton laughed too as he looked straight down the dolphin's mouth at its big pink tongue, its row of tiny white teeth and the pink fleshy mouth almost like a duck's bill. If Les wasn't mistaken, the way the dolphin had its mouth open and the look in its eye it was almost as if it was laughing back at them. Then the dolphin joined the other two and they started leaping up and down in the calm waters, almost as if they were putting on a display especially for the visitors. This went on for a while till a motor cruiser went past, going faster than it should, and they moved off further up the key.

There was an all-round sense of relief in the boat now. Not only had Ricco retrieved whatever was in the bag, but they'd come home safely through the eye of a violent mini-cyclone and in a sense were lucky to be alive. Les had half an idea what was in the bag and was entitled to start calling Ricco a bit of a dropkick for getting him involved. But right now he was happy to be heading back to dry land and into some dry clothes. So for the time being Norton opened the ice-box and proposed a toast to both Ricco's seamanship and the dolphins. This was readily accepted and from there it was a merry drink all the way back to the marina. There was no sign of cops or anything, no helicopters, no one at all really. Ricco berthed the boat, Les and Laverne moored it and they proceeded to get off.

'What would you like me to carry, Ricco?' asked Les, a hint of sarcasm in his voice. 'The canvas bag with the light or the ice-box?'

Ricco kind of smiled. 'You can bring the ice-box.'

'Aye-aye, skipper.'

Although the coast appeared clear it barely took five minutes to have everything off the boat and into the boot of the Mercedes, including the green canvas bag. Norton figured it was going to be a fairly quick getaway because Ricco didn't bother to comb his hair, neither did Laverne. Ricco dropped the boat's keys in at the office and they drove off.

They didn't appear to be heading back towards the highway, instead Ricco went left at the marina back along the water's edge. The road was fairly narrow but the houses, set among trees and landscaped estates on either side, were impressive, especially the ones overlooking the ocean. Every now and again they'd splash through huge puddles of water, so the flash storm must have dumped plenty of rain on this part of town too as it passed over. Ricco and Laverne weren't saying a great deal, though they certainly seemed happy enough about

245

something. Norton had a fair idea what and he was going to have to say something or Ricco would think he was a complete and utter goose. He was also going to have to be a little diplomatic and give Ricco an out. Les thought for a moment before catching the Mafia man's eye in the rear vision mirror.

'Okay, Ricco. I think we'd better get something straight between us, and don't bullshit me, either. The least you could have done was told me you went out there to do a bloody dope deal. Thanks a lot — mate.'

'Hey,' Ricco sounded genuinely offended. 'What are you talking about? Dope deal?'

'Well, what are you going to tell me's in that bag? Your bloody laundry?'

Ricco and Laverne looked at each other and it was all they could do to stop from bursting out laughing. 'Well, in a way, Les, you could say that. Yeah, you could say that.'

Now it was Norton's turn to look and act offended. 'Anyway, whatever it is, it's none of my business. So don't worry about it. But next time, just bloody tell me — alright?'

Ricco had to concede that Les had a point. Les also hadn't panicked and he'd done the right thing. 'Hey, Les, don't sweat it. Things just went a big wrong, that's all. I'm sorry. But I said I'd take you boating. And I got you back alive, didn't I?'

'Yeah,' nodded Les. 'You're a regular Indiana Jones. So where are we going now?'

'Round to my buddie Angelo's house. I gotta call in for a moment.'

And odd look flashed across Laverne's eyes when Ricco mentioned his buddie Angelo. 'Angelo?' inquired Les.

'Yeah. Angelo Licavoli. You heard of him in Australia?'

Les looked at Ricco for a second then turned to the window. Yeah. Just a bloody bit. If it was who Les was thinking of, he'd been on the news just about every night for the last two weeks before Les left Australia. Angelo 'Big Lick' Licavoli. He was the biggest Mafia Godfather in New York and controlled everything. They also called him the 'Teflon Don' because the cops could never make anything stick to him. But now the FBI had him on conspiracy, tax evasion and a whole host of other charges, mainly through an informant taking witness protection, and this time it looked like they had him. This was his last appeal and if he lost he'd get thirty years to life. The media had turned the trial into a bit of a circus because his daughter kept bobbing up on TV to say what a great man her father was and how all the cops were 'nuttin' but doity finks'. Plus all the people in Licavoli's neighbourhood were rioting outside the courthouse, turning over cars and punching up TV cameramen and journalists, etc.

Les turned back to the rear-vision mirror. 'No. I never heard of him.'

'I didn't think you would,' replied Ricco.

Ricco didn't bother to turn the radio on so they drove, not quite in air-conditioned silence, because Ricco was happy enough rabbiting on to Laverne about what a good skipper and how clever he was; Laverne agreed wholeheartedly. Les got sick of the air-conditioning again, flicked the power button and wound his passenger side window down behind Ricco. They were driving right along the water's edge now, Les could quite clearly see the Keys through the now very lavish houses. Then Ricco slowed the car right down as they approached a monster on their left. It seemed to take up an entire block and looked almost like a Spanish fortress painted green on white. There were brick arches and parapets all over the mansion built up over a surrounding ten foot brick wall that looked thick enough to stop a tank. Every ten feet along the wall was a TV security monitor and although it was completely walled off Les noticed a private jetty with a monstrous white cruiser moored to it out the back. Ricco pulled up in a driveway set off the road in front of two massive wooden and iron gates. He reached out his window and pushed a button on an intercom set in the wall.

'Yeah?' a throaty voice crackled over the intercom.

'Is that you, Tony? It's Ricco.'

'No it's Frankie. Stay there, Ricco. I'll be right out.'

Ricco looked at Laverne for a moment, then got out of the car and leant against the front. Les seemed to sense another odd vibe in the air, so he sat back, not looking at Ricco, not saying anything, but keeping his wits about him. A smaller door set in the massive double gate opened and out stepped a man in a white shirt and slacks smoking a cigar. He looked like a shorter, stockier version of Vinnie. He didn't say anything to Laverne and he didn't seem to notice Les in the back seat. Whoever it was had a worried look on his face that was more than just worry and, looking at him, Les somehow figured the guy wasn't all that bright.

'Hey, Frankie,' said Ricco. 'What's the matter? You look like shit. Where's Tony?'

Frankie squinted his piggy eyes at Ricco. 'What are you talkin' I look like shit? Ain't you heard?'

'Heard? What the fuck would I hear? I been out the fucking gulf in a hurricane half the fucking day.'

'Ohh yeah, I didn't think for a minute.' Frankie's face dropped further. 'Angelo went down. That sonofabitch judge gave him thirty years.'

Ricco was speechless. Laverne gave a double, triple blink. Norton made out he didn't hear anything, but the big Queenslander's hearing was good at any time and after sitting next to two pounding Evinrudes coming through a storm, he was now picking everything up crystal clear.

'Jesus Christ!' exclaimed Ricco. 'Thirty fucking years. You're bullshitting me.'

'I wish to Christ I was,' replied Frankie. 'Tony flew out to New York before lunch with Henry. Anyway where's ...?'

Ricco seemed to hesitate for a moment but Norton could sense his brain tap-dancing at about a hundred miles an hour. 'Well that's what I was about to tell you. We got fucked over too. A coastguard helicopter arrived so the plane kept going. Then that fucking storm hit us like you wouldn't fucking believe. I managed to get back and I been searching up and down the Keys for hours. Look at me. I'm half drowned already.'

'You don't mean...?'

'Yeah. It wasn't there. The fucking coastguard then the fucking storm fucked everything up.'

'Oh Christ!' Frankie threw his hands up in the air. 'That's all we fucking need on top of that other shit.'

'Hey!' Ricco looked helpless. 'What the fuck could I do?'

Frankie took a heavy puff on his cigar. 'Yeah, you're right. Anyway you'd better split.'

'Yeah. I'll call Tony in New York and give him the rest of the bad news. Shit! That's bad, really bad about Angelo.'

'Yeah. Everything seems to fuck up at once, don't it? Okay. I'll see you, Ricco.'

Frankie disappeared back through the door, Ricco got back in the car and looked at Laverne who was staring back at him. Then they drove off. Les just looked out the window like he was miles away, before catching Ricco's eye again in the rear-vision mirror.

'So where to now, Ricco?'

'Huh? Oh yeah, right. I'll take you straight home, Les. I got a few things I got to take care of.'

'Suits me,' answered Norton nonchalantly. 'I'm dying to get out of this wet gear.'

Not a great deal was said on the ride home. Ricco put the radio on this time but seemed to be driving a lot more carefully than before, obeying all the traffic laws, though at times he looked like he was going to lay an egg. Laverne looked at him every now and again as if she was getting ready to lay it for him. Norton kept his thoughts to himself. However, he did thank Ricco for the ride in the boat, made a comment about how nice his buddie Angelo's house looked and half pie apologised for blowing up a bit earlier. Ricco said that was okay and to make sure he came down the coffee shop at lunchtime tomorrow. Trying his best to sound enthusiastic, Norton reluctantly agreed. Before long they were at the condo.

'Okay Ricco. Thanks for the day,' said Les, closing the car door behind him. 'I'll see you around twelve tomorrow.'

'Yeah. See you then.' Ricco was fairly abrupt at the best of times. This time he was starting to reverse the car as he spoke.

'Goodbye, Les.' Laverne pressed the automatic switch, the window hissed back up and they were gone.

Back inside the condo Les got out of his wet clothes and had a shower, then, with a towel still around him, got a Corona from the fridge and sat on the lounge drinking it steadily while he had a think. You didn't need to be a Rhodes scholar to work out what was going on.

Ricco had gone out in the gulf to pick up a bag full of mob money, probably to pay wages and bribes or do deals with back in America. It could have been laundered money or it could originally have been counterfeit to be exchanged overseas for the real thing. The plane had pontoons on the bottom so normally it would have been a smooth transaction and Les, the dumb Australian tagging along, would have been fed some bullshit and expected to be none the wiser. Plus Ricco and Vinnie considered him a fairly cool-headed guy, who'd keep his mouth shut anyway. This time round though the coast-guard had got onto the plane — it was more than likely just a routine patrol — and picked it up, because there was no back up. On top of that, the storm came up out of nowhere. They would have had some sort of contingency plan or code in case the plane couldn't land because of rough seas or such. They wouldn't use a radio so the code was more than likely the pilot waggling his wings twice as he went over. The pilot, knowing the helicopter couldn't stick around in a storm like that, dumped the bag with the homing beacon on it in the Keys, fairly confident Ricco would be able to find it, then kept the helicopter on his tail. When and if they did pull the plane over or land next to it the pilot would say he was just running from the storm. With visibility as bad as it was and the distance between the plane and the helicopter, the coastguard wouldn't have seen the pilot throw anything over, so when they searched the plane what would they find? I understand your concern, officers, but are you sure you've got the right person? Les swallowed more beer. Ricco, being on the ball as well as having some, and despite the mini-hurricane, had found the bag then delivered it as usual like a good little mafioso. But when he'd found out the Godfather in New York was in the slam he had taken advantage of the situation, the storm, the confusion in the mob, half of them out of town, and clouted on the loot. And who would dispute him? Frankie? Frankie would probably think Levi jeans was a Jewish folk singer. He looked like pure muscle and nothing else, plus he'd witnessed the storm and seen Ricco arrive half drowned. Ricco would ring Tony, or whoever it was in New York he was supposed to deliver the money to, tell him what happened then say he went out again in the afternoon and he'd have another look all day tomorrow. But the dough's gone. *Arrivederci denaro*. It would be the first time it had happened, plus Ricco already had money so he could splash some more around if he wanted to and still cover his shifty arse without attracting any attention. Then one fine day he and Laverne could just go and do their thing anywhere in the world and live happily ever after. How much was in the bag? Les shook his head. Millions — at least. But stealing money from the mob? Les swallowed some more beer, shook his head again and reflected into the bottle. He'd heard, and seen, enough things with the mini versions of the mob back in Australia. No, Ricco. I'm glad it's you and not me, old son. Maybe it was a good thing that bloody storm did come up. When I think back about some of the things Lori baby said, and didn't say, you can bet he's under some sort of surveillance. And I've got to go and have a cup of coffee with him tomorrow. Oh well. It's only for an hour or so. Christ! I hope he doesn't still want to go out for dinner tomorrow night.

Norton finished that beer, got another one then sat back down and reflected some more on the day's events. It had certainly been different, even with Ricco pulling the stroke that he did. Les had never been out at sea and seen or been in a storm as fierce or treacherous as that, especially the way it just came and went. He looked out across the verandah to where it was quite sunny outside now and about half a dozen people were splashing around in the pool. And what did Laverne say when they were coming back up the Key after the dolphins had gone? Florida was due for a big cyclone any time now. It had been over ten years and they generally came in ten-year cycles. Well, if that's a small quick one, I'd sure hate to see the real thing. Norton's second beer was that good he decided to have another one and listen to the radio for a spell while he figured out what he was going to do that night. There would have to be some action in Sepposota on Thursday night: and it's certainly good drinking weather. Then Norton started to cackle into his beer. I should give Hank a ring, see what he's doing. Norton's cackling turned into a horrible laugh. I wonder if he's still home?

Three quick beers on an empty stomach kind of bowled Les a little so he thought he might grab forty winks before he went out. He turned off the radio and ended up sleeping for around two hours. When he got up he had a swim followed by a shower and a close shave. Although his stomach was rumbling a bit by now, Les still didn't feel all that much like eating because of the heat. But a good feed of vegetables wouldn't do any harm, and there was still plenty left. By a stroke of luck Les discovered that what he first thought was some sort of a mini-dishwasher was in fact a microwave oven; all the buttons and gauges on the front were different from the one back home that Warren had snookered off some advertising job. This didn't deter Norton from peeling too many potatoes, onions and carrots, etc. Half he put back in the fridge, the other half he put in the microwave then heaped butter and cajun dressing all over them. All up, not too bad at all. One can't go out pouring piss down one's throat on an empty stomach, mused Les, as he washed another piece of cauliflower down with some more orange juice. He followed this with a cup of coffee then a large delicious and more country and western after he'd cleaned up.

After he finished his first bourbon, Les poured another bigger one, then thought a little more on where he might go that night. He wasn't necessarily out to meet another girl; after coming across Hank then putting up with Ricco, Les just felt like finding a laugh somewhere and listening to a band; and having a few drinks of course. Club BandBox would definitely not be the place to be seen; if it was still open. Gator Man's could be okay. But what about that little place over at St Almonds Circle? Reggae Mambo's. The band there was good, so were the drinks and the punters. Plus, with the front open, you could go outside and get a bit of fresh air. Still sipping his bourbon Les looked at the card sitting next to the phone then dialled.

'Hello? Is Joey there please?'

'This is Joey.'

'G'day, Joey. Do you fancy running a poor, lonely Australian tourist over to St Almonds Circle?'

Joey started chuckling into the phone. 'Les, my man. Hey, how are you doin'?'

'I'll be doin' it on foot if you don't get your arse over here in say . . . thirty minutes.'

'Thirty minutes? You got it, big guy.'

'See you then, mate.'

Well that's that, smiled Les, putting down the phone. Now it's time to frock up and rev up. He finished his drink while he pressed a clean pair of jeans, a blue button-down collar shirt and ran a wet sponge over his sneakers. There was another milkshake container under the cupboard so Les made another gigantic, travelling delicious. He was test driving it while John Anderson drawled and twanged his way through 'Steamy Windows' when there was a knock on the door. Les picked up what he needed, turned off the lights and opened the door. Joey had pretty much the same jacket and driver's gear on as before.

'G'day, Joey,' smiled Les. 'How are you goin', mate?'

'Hey Les,' beamed Joey, as they started walking to the limo. 'Look at you, baby. You look like a million dollars.'

'Yeah. All green and wrinkly. You know how to get to a place called Reggae Mambo's, over at St Almonds Circle?'

'Hey. Are you kiddin'? I can take you anywhere you want and get you anything your little aussie heart desires — mate.'

'Good. Well get me over there in one piece and I might even let you bring me home afterwards. And there might even be a drink in it for you.'

Joey pointed to the drink in Norton's hand as he opened the back door. 'I thought that might have been for me.'

'Not tonight, Josephine.'

Norton climbed in the back and they cruised off towards town. Joey gave Les the old mates treatment on the way — good to see you again, how have you been, etc, thought he probably meant it. Les didn't let on too much. He remembered when he first met Ricco and how Ricco had said Joey Hubcaps had told him about Les and Lori number one. He told Joey he'd hired a car and that was why he hadn't needed the limo. But tonight he was out on the town again and he'd be needing a ride home or whatever at closing time, which was midnight. Joey was keen and said he'd be waiting out the front. Before Les knew it they were there and Joey had pulled up right outside. The punters drinking out the front and a few others coming and going gave an interested glance when Joey came round and opened the back door; possibly they were expecting Madonna or MC Hammer and didn't quite know what to think when Norton climbed out holding the last of his travelling delicious. Les didn't know what the fare was. He just handed Joey two twenties and the empty milkshake container, said he'd see him later and stepped through the crowd. The same solid bloke in shorts was on the door; he gave Les a smile and a very approving once up and down as he walked in.

Reggae Mambo's was bopping away just nicely. It wasn't quite packed but close enough, with pretty much the same kind of casually well-dressed crowds as before and a number of good sorts standing around. The same band was down the back finishing the last portion of their 'attitude check' before slipping into a more up tempo version of Garth Brooks's 'Nobody Gets Off In This Town'. Les found a space at the bar next to two spunky black girls in blue bum-huggers that hugged their solid little bums delightfully, and had no trouble at all ordering a margarita and a Wild Turkey highball. The margarita went down in about four swallows; the highball took a little longer. Clutching his drink Les found another spot at the bar, not far from the front door, where he sipped his highball and thought some more about his trip to America while he checked out the punters. It was a good spot to stand, a bit of fresh air was coming in from the front and the music was drifting down from the back while the crowd sort of milled around him, ebbing and flowing and having a good time. It was kind of odd in a way, being in a strange bar on the other side of the world, not knowing a soul. But Les, a little revved up from the drinks, was enjoying it. He would have enjoyed it more, however, with a couple of mates; the heads on some of the seppos and their mannerisms were nothing short of amazing at times. Norton was checking out some bloke with a black crewcut and hornrim glasses, wearing the most atrocious pair of green and pink shorts he'd ever seen, worse than anything in *Revenge of the Nerds*, when he heard a voice slightly to his left.

'Well, if it isn't the emu man from down under.' It was Terri, the boozy little Texan girl he'd met when he was in there before with the late Captain Rats.

'Hello, good-looking,' smiled Les. 'How are you tonight?'

Calling Terri good-looking was definitely giving her a giant rap; she looked just as dumpy as before, her face just as shiny and her blue shorts just as baggy.

'I'm just fine,' she replied, before slopping down some more beer. 'So what brings you here tonight?'

'The moon, the music and beautiful girls like you,' smiled Norton, raising the last of his drink.

Terri knew Les had to be joking; the music maybe. Then again, she accepted Norton's statement and smiled back without saying anything.

Norton downed his highball and was about to turn to the bar. 'I'm going to have another drink. Can I get you something?'

'Sure. I'll have a Millers Draught.'

'One "Genuine Millers Draught" coming right up.'

Les only had to turn around and in a couple of minutes he had a beer for Terri and the same again for himself. Terri mumbled thanks then swallowed about a third of her plastic mug of beer in one go. Although she was sort of alright, and probably just a battler doing her best, Les didn't particularly wish to be in Terri's company. But it was someone to talk to while he looked around and listened to the music. So Les chatted away to her over their drinks about absolutely nothing that remotely interested him, except that she agreed it certainly had been hot during the day and the storm was bad. Finally she said, 'Say, why don't you come over and have a drink with my friends over there?'

Norton looked towards where Terri had nodded her head. It was the three English blokes he'd noticed when he was there before. They were talking to three of the same pretty-looking girls that were there before as well in their shorts and the T-shirts with the funny-looking parrot wearing sunglasses on the front. The girls looked as if they'd just arrived; a waitress was standing next to their group and one of the English blokes had just paid her for some drinks which he was handing around.

'Yeah, righto,' said Les, figuring Terri wanted to drag him over to show she could get herself a bloke. At least over there he could politely get rid of her and they looked like much more interesting company. 'Why not?' He downed one drink and holding the other followed her over. The team were all nattering and drinking away but stopped as they approached.

'Hey, everybody. This is my buddy from Australia, Les.'

Norton smiled a little self-consciously and raised his glass. 'Hello. How's things?' Several smiles and muted greetings rippled around the table.

'From Australia, old boy?' smiled one of the three blokes. He had dark hair and a fullish sort of face, wearing jeans and a black vest over his white U2 T-shirt. Up closer he didn't sound so English. 'You're not a union man by any chance are you?'

'Yeah,' answered Les. 'I used to play union at school.'

'Same as us, old chap. Which school?'

'Dirranbandi Boys' Grammar. I played breakaway.'

'Splendid,' beamed the bloke in the vest. 'I played for Eton. These two oafs played for Cambridge.'

'Go — Cambridge,' said one his friends.

'Did you get to see the world cup this year?' asked Les.

'Certainly did,' acknowledged Vest. 'Your chaps went rather well.'

'Yes, you could say that,' winked Norton. 'Waderyerwannabe. A walla-wallaby.'

'Anything but a froggy,' said the same friend.

'Agreed,' nodded Les.

The waitress reappeared and Les noticed the boys didn't mind a drink; they'd just about demolished the previous round. 'Can I buy you fellahs a drink?'

'Okay, old chap,' replied Vest. 'That would be absolutely splendid.'

'What about you, girls?'

'Sure,' smiled one. 'Thanks.'

Les made a gesture towards the waitress and they ordered everything from draught beer to Pina Coladas to a Corona for Les this time as well as a margarita. The drinks arrived promptly, Les paid the waitress, giving her a ten dollar tip: which didn't go unnoticed. Norton's shout seemed to break the ice and from then on a jolly time was had by all.

The bloke in the vest was Marlow, his two mates with brown and sandy hair dressed pretty much the same were Vaughn and Teague. They had a lot of style about them and their handshakes were warm. The three girls were Duena, Roxy and Moya and looked almost identical. Blondish brown hair, wide eyes set in pixie faces on whippy little bodies and up closer they looked even more attractive in their shorts and T-shirts. Duena was about two inches taller then the others. Les judged them to be in their early twenties and the blokes all around thirty going on sixteen: a bit like himself. Norton told them the same lie he'd told Lori number one; he owned a bar back in Australia with his brother and he was on a holiday in America looking for ideas to take back home. This went over quite well. It turned out the boys weren't actually English, they were Irish, but had all been educated in England. They were marine engineers and all worked in London for the same firm, which was owned by Teague's father. They too were on a kind of working holiday selling hovercrafts to the yanks and were going back the following Monday. Les said he still had two weeks or so to go. The three girls worked round the corner as waitresses, as did Terri. Les tipped the owner would have the three little spunks working on the tables to get the male punters in, which was how they'd all met. Terri's date was too big and her attitude not quite up to it to get the blokes in so she'd stay out in the kitchen. The girls all liked Norton's accent as well as the others' and Norton liked theirs. They all enjoyed each other's company and the drinks went down just as enjoyably.

It appeared to be catch and kill your own with the three spunks, nobody seemed to be with anyone in particular. But they all seemed to be getting around to it and the English blokes were there first so Les didn't try to monster his way in. As it was, Norton was quite happy just to find someone to have a laugh and a drink with, and with this team he'd hit the jackpot; the lads certainly liked a laugh and they loved a drink. So did the girls; although for some reason Moya seemed a little more reserved than the others. Norton bought another round of drinks. The boys were obviously well heeled and weren't going to be outdone so they reciprocated in kind. The waitress who'd zeroed in on them just kept going backwards and forwards to the bar, either with their empties or to bring more back, and as they got progressively drunker she made herself a small fortune on the night. So they drank up, they sang, they all finished up on the dancefloor at different times and it was one of the funniest nights Les had ever had. It was that good he was wishing it would never end, especially when one of the waitresses told him he was a good dancer. Unfortunately it did end; at twelve o'clock.

The band had stopped, the lights were turned up and they were finishing their last round of drinks while the punters started drifting out into the night. Norton was in a great mood and so were the others, even Terri. They were laughing about nothing in particular when Marlow spoke.

'Well, what do you think we should do now?'

There was a bit of a mumbled, shrugging reply as they all looked at each other waiting for suggestions. Norton didn't know whether he should have said it, but before he knew it, he did.

'I got a good idea.'

'What's that?' said Marlow.

'Why don't we have a party back at my place?'

'Jolly good idea,' said Vaughn, giving Les a friendly slap on the back. 'Where's your place?'

'Just out on Manatee. About fifteen minutes from here.'

'You got anything to drink?'

'Heaps.'

'What about music?'

'Music? Mate, the music I got would make the blind see, the lame walk and the deaf and the dumb hear and talk.'

'Sounds alright to me,' said Roxy. 'But how are we going to get there? You guys have only got that little sports car. And there's eight of us.'

This was Norton's big moment, and no one would ever be able to take it away from him. 'Hey, no worries,' he grinned. 'I got a limo waitin' out the front.'

A little mystified the others finished their drinks and followed Les out onto the sidewalk. He waved one arm over his head and whistled. Seconds later Joey cruised up in the shiny blue stretch limousine. He got out, walked around and opened the back door. As Joey stood there he looked at the three spunks, shook his head and winked at Norton.

'You've done it again.'

Norton just smiled drunkenly. 'We're talkin' *Great Gatsby* here, son.'

Everybody was suitably impressed, especially Terri; Norton was everything he said he was and more. He was the true messiah. The arrival of the limo easily worked out the travelling arrangements and who was going to finish up with whom also. Les, Marlow, Terri and Moya bundled into the back of the limo, the others went round and got the sports car. Joey knew where to go, he waited a minute or two for the others to follow, as soon as they pulled up behind he drove off. Les mentioned that this could turn out to be a good night, he had plenty to drink and there was plenty of music. Then Moya mentioned that she had to be home by three at the latest, which was when her boyfriend arrived back from Tampa where he worked as a musician. The others would all be paired up by now so it would be left to Les and Marlow to fight it out for the affections of the fair Terri. Norton figured he'd lose on a TKO in the first round. He wasn't all that mad keen to do any porking that night in the first place, especially with Terri, no matter how drunk he was. She'd been pitching up to him a bit back at the bar and when Les would play her a little wide she'd start pitching up to Marlow, thinking it would make Les jealous. Now she was doing it again in the back of the limo and looking over at Les to see what his reaction would be. But Norton kept looking at Marlow. He was starting to piss in Terri's pocket now, lying to her about how lovely she was, yet all the time he had this weird look in his eye. Before long they arrived at the condo.

The little sports car turned out to be some kind of a green Nissan convertible. Les gave Joey a fifty and said to keep in touch. He'd probably be needed later on to ferry some drunks home. The driver said not to worry one bit, just ring any time, he wouldn't be far. Joey pocketed the money and drove off smiling then the happy little gathering bowled inside.

When he turned on the lights Norton explained that the condo belonged to some friends; have all the fun you want, but don't smash anything and no stubbing cigarettes out on the carpet. As it turned out, all the three waitresses were into aerobics and the boys still played rugby union, so nobody smoked and besides that nobody was a complete party animal so they treated the place with some respect. Les showed them where all the booze and ice and that was in the kitchen, making himself a rather large bourbon while he was at it. Teague had brought a bottle of Moët and some Irish whiskey in from their sports car so between them they managed to open the bottle of shampoo, find enough glasses and get whatever drinks they wanted together. While this was going on Les dropped a tape in the stereo. It was another of the ones he'd got a DJ pal to make up for him before he left, some more Oz music to remind him of home. A bit of old, a bit of new, just as long as it moved along. The first track was 'Shanghai in the Kitchen', by Scrap Metal. This cut into Cold Chisel's 'Home and Broken Hearted', and by the time that slid into 'Once Bitten Twice Shy' by the Angels, everybody was bopping around quite happily with a cool one in their hand.

'Hey, this is absolutely splendid!' said Vaughn, slipping a drunken arm around Norton's shoulder.

'Yeah,' agreed Roxy, who was hanging off Vaughn's arm. 'Thanks for having us around. It's great.'

'My pleasure,' replied Les, just as drunkenly. 'I'm glad to see you're all having a good time.' He raised his glass. 'I know I am.'

More booze flowed, more music played, Warumpi Band, Hunters and Collectors, even a chestnut by Scattered Aces — 'Highway 61 Revisited'. So the party, small as it was, cruised along splendidly. The stereo wasn't all that big, but it had a good sound so you could still dig the music and talk okay without shouting. Norton threw more tapes on and the night progressed. Les played the perfect host, topping up drinks while he nattered away about Australia and listened to stories about England, Ireland and America, and if Les said he was having a good time he was telling the truth. It was so good to meet some other people just out to have a good time that weren't either in the Mafia, undercover cops or gun-crazy morons. It was like a breath of fresh air. One thing Les had to notice: Terri had decided to lavish her attentions on Marlow, right under Les's nose, just to let him know what he was missing out on. Norton was shattered.

Eventually the three waitresses got into a huddle; Moya had to get home. This suited Teague and Vaughn, they could drive the other two back to their place, or wherever, and drop Moya off on the way. No sweat, said Les. Thanks for coming, the limo was at his disposal so the others would get home safely and in comfort. So it was a boozy farewell at the door, with Norton promising he'd catch up with them again tomorrow night down at Reggae Mambo's. Goodbye, drive carefully. This left Les, Marlow and the beautiful Terri to continue the party. Terri appeared pretty pissed and Marlow still had this weird look in his eye, so Les thought he'd leave them to their own devices for a while before ringing Joey. In the meantime he put another tape on and made himself another drink.

The two lovers were sitting on the lounge opposite Les and Marlow was starting to go to work. He was tongue kissing Terri and squeezing her tits and Terri was kissing him back. Every now and again she'd look out the side of her eye to see if Les happened to be watching, and if he thought she was she'd get into it a bit harder. Good heavens, thought Norton. Do I get the impression this woman is trying to nark me? Isn't that dreadful. And on top of all my generosity and hospitality. He had another mouthful of bourbon and shook his head sadly. Whatever did I do to deserve such abysmal treatment? Finally Marlow had his hand up Terri's shorts and Terri had her knee in his groin. Conduct like this definitely could not go on forever right before Norton's very eyes. He was going to have to do something about it.

'Hey, Marlow!'

Marlow looked up from what he was doing, somewhat startled. 'Les. I'm terribly sorry. What...?'

Terri just gave Les a dirty, supercilious kind of look, as if to say, Hah! Couldn't handle it could you? Now you've got the shits. Good. I got you, you asshole.

'Listen, Marlow,' continued Les, 'my bedroom's just down the hall.' He nodded his head in the general direction. 'Why don't you both go in there and finish the job off? I'll sit here and listen to some music. Go on, you're sweet.'

If the look in Marlow's eyes had been a bit weird earlier, the grin that suddenly spread across his face was purely diabolical. 'I say, Les, what an absolutely splendid idea. Jolly good. Come on Terri, old fruit. Let's go.'

With the weights dropped right on her, Terri looked a little surprised. But before she knew it Marlow had dragged her off down the hall. Oh well, mused Norton. I wonder how long that'll take. Marlow looks like a bit of a stropper, but I'd say — thirty minutes max. Then I'll ring Joey. Les raised his glass in the direction of the bedroom. So stick it in an extra inch or so for me, Marlow old fruit, cause I'm bloody sure I don't want to.

Norton settled back on the lounge with his drink while the tape played, and closed his eyes. Before long grunts and groans accompanied by much moaning and gasping were coming from his bedroom. Oh well, he smiled to himself, they're getting into it, and going well by the sound of things. Shouldn't be too much longer now and they'll be finished with my bed. My bed! Shit! I think I'd better give the sheets a drink tomorrow. They'll be like bloody tar-paper by the morning. Les switched off to the sexual whatevers that were going on in his bedroom and concentrated on the music. After a while it seemed to quieten down momentarily and he was half dozing off thinking about home when he was slightly startled by a tap on his shoulder.

'Marlow! What the fuck do you want? And get that fuckin' thing out of my face.'

Marlow was standing next to him stark naked with a wet, shiny-looking horn poking out perilously close to Norton's nose. 'Sorry about that, old chap,' he whispered, then crouched down next to Les. 'I say, Les. How would you like to be in a bit of a lark, old boy?'

Norton screwed up his face. 'A lark? What...?'

'Look. All I'm saying is this, old chap.' Marlow nodded his head in the direction of the bedroom. 'That yank bird's a bit slack what. A bit off. And I'd like to play a trick on her.'

'A trick?'

'Yes yes, exactly. And what I propose is this...'

Norton listened to what Marlow had to say. What he suggested definitely appealed to Norton's sense of humour if not quite his good taste or sense of ethics. But what Marlow said about Terri was true. She was a bit of a pain in the arse and playing a trick on her would liven up the evening and be something to have a laugh about when he got home. Les thought for a moment or two more then nodded his head.

'Okay, Marlow, I'll be in it. But there's no way in the world I'm going to root her. But get back to work and I'll be waiting by the door in about five minutes.'

Marlow rubbed his hands together gleefully. 'Jolly good, Les.' He tiptoed back into the bedroom and before long the sound of heavy breathing and porking again filled the air.

Norton waited a minute or so then went into the kitchen. He opened the fridge, took out one of the carrots he'd peeled earlier and held it in his hand. Yes, he mused, that ought to do the job, though it's a bit on the cold side. But. Smiling drunkenly Les turned to the microwave oven. I reckon about seven inches of carrot set at medium-high for two minutes should do the job. He put the carrot in the microwave and set the controls. Two minutes later a 'ding' said it was ready. Norton got it out, checked it in his hand again and gave a nod of grudging approval. Yes, not quite the old pulsating rod, but close enough. He smeared it with a bit of olive oil then with the carrot in his hand Les tiptoed down the hall and waited outside the bedroom door.

Marlow had Terri on the bed in the missionary position going for his life. His well-bred, white Irish arse was pumping away as he licked her sweaty neck while she grunted and farted and oohed and ahhed. She wasn't throwing her backside around much or kicking her legs up and impressed Norton as being as dud a root as she looked. Les watched indifferently outside the partly open door for a minute or so until Marlow spoke.

'Terri, my darling,' he panted, 'this is fantastic. But I wish to do something different. Something . . . a little kinky.'

'Kinky?' puffed Terri. 'Like what?'

'Hop up for a moment, my dear. Bend over and put your hands on the windowsill and close your eyes, while I have you from behind.'

'What?'

Before Terri knew quite what was going on, Marlow had her off the bed and bent over against the half-open window, her head facing outside with her hands resting on the windowsill. He spread her legs apart a little more then started humping her from behind, dog fashion. Terri went along with it; she even seemed to be enjoying it. Every now and again Marlow would put a couple of good ones in and she'd squeal and give a little grunt of delight.

'Now promise me you won't open your eyes until I tell you,' said Marlow.

'No. I promise,' grunted Terri.

Marlow pumped away a bit longer with Norton still watching from the door, till he saw Marlow give him the signal. Les tiptoed inside and stood next to Marlow, who had his hands gripped around Terri's backside as he pumped away. Les got ready with the carrot, got another signal from Marlow and as Marlow's dick came out slipped the carrot in beautifully, not breaking the rhythm by so much as a half-beat; if anything it slid in easily. Les put his hand where Marlow had his, got between Terri's legs and started working away. Terri didn't seem to notice the difference, in fact she seemed to liven up a little. Marlow stood next to Les with this fiendish grin on his face that horrible it almost glowed white in the darkened room.

Norton kept pumping away with the carrot. It was funny at first then after a while he was starting to wish he was back outside enjoying his drink while he listened to the music. Terri had a fat, white arse with red blotches all over it sitting on top of some rust-coloured pubic hairs that were all matted and sweaty. Her flaps gripped around the carrot reminded Les of two small stingrays jammed together and her date looked just like a mouldy Egyptian date, only one that had been deep fried in bad oil. None of it smelled too good either. Les was about to tell Marlow, okay you've had your fun, now take over again so I can get out of here and back to my drink. But when Les turned round, he was gone. What the . . .? Where is the pommy bastard? Les cursed to himself. It wasn't quite supposed to work out like this. Marlow said he just wanted Les to jump on for a few minutes to they could have a laugh behind Terri's back when he took her home and next time they saw her. Being half pissed, Norton agreed. Now he was standing there on his own. On top of that, over the sound of the music still drifting in from the loungeroom, Norton thought he heard the flyscreen door on the back verandah open and close. Christ, Les cursed to himself again. I hope he hasn't posted me. If Terri turns around and sees me here she'll have a bloody stroke.

'How long before I can open my eyes, Marlow?' Terri's voice painted.

'Huh? Oh, any moment now, old girl,' replied Les. 'Any moment.'

'Mmmhh. It feels good though, Marlow.'

'Splendid. Splendid, my dear,' said Norton, giving the carrot an extra twist.

Suddenly Norton thought he saw a movement among the shadows outside the window. Next thing Marlow's evil, grinning face came into view. Marlow inched carefully forward till he was about two feet away from the window and Terri's face. A bit of nervous adrenalin hit Les in the stomach and he unconsciously started going faster with the carrot. Terri gave an audible squeal of delight and pushed down on the windowsill; then Marlow called out.

'Okay, Terri. Now open your eyes.'

Terri blinked her eyes open and there was Marlow right in front of her leering at her from the darkness outside the window. To make matters worse, he put his thumbs on the side of his head, stuck his tongue out and wiggled his fingers. Terri didn't do or say anything at first because Norton was still pumping frantically away with the carrot. Then she screamed this awful, wailing scream of absolute horror before jamming her eyes shut again. Les gave the carrot a few more quick shoves to keep her occupied before she opened her eyes and screamed again. Marlow disappeared about the same time as Les slipped the carrot out and bolted out the bedroom door. He was in the hallway wondering what to do when Marlow came bolting out of the loungeroom. He ran straight past Les into the bedroom where Terri was frozen to the windowsill in horror still screaming these pitiful, muffled screams. Marlow didn't muck around, he ran straight in and got straight up her again.

'Terri, my dear,' he puffed. 'What's the matter? Did you just orgasm?'

'No, I didn't orgasm,' said Terri, sobbing and now gasping at the same time. 'I saw a face at the window.'

'At the window? I say, are you sure?'

'Yes, I'm positive,' squawked Terri. 'It was you.'

'Me? Absolutely impossible, my dear. I've been here all the time. You don't think I'd leave this do you?'

'It was you. It was you.'

'Absolutely impossible, my dear. You must have had a bad dream.'

'Ohh God,' moaned Terri. 'What's going on? I'm so confused.'

'Possibly you had a little too much to drink. Anyway, why didn't you wait till I told you to open your eyes?'

'You did tell me to open my eyes,' insisted Terri. 'And you were outside the window.'

'Couldn't have been, old girl. I'm not jolly Houdini you know.'

'Oh God, I'm so confused. I don't know what to think.'

'Maybe it might be best if you don't. Come on, my dear. Let's get back on the bed. This time you can keep your eyes open.'

'Oh God!'

Well, that's enough for me. Norton tiptoed down the hallway, tossed the carrot in the sink and went back to his drink in the loungeroom where the tape was still playing. The sounds of heavy porking resumed from the bedroom. Les gave it another ten minutes then made himself another drink and rang Joey, telling him to be there in fifteen minutes. Ten minutes later the racket died down and five minutes after that Marlow was dressed and standing in the loungeroom; looking sweaty, dishevelled and much like any bloke who's just had a session in the cot on a steamy summer night in Florida. He still had that weird look in his eye and down the end of the hall Les heard the light being switched on in the bathroom.

'I say, Les,' grinned Marlow. 'Jolly good show or what?'

'Yeah terrific, Marlow. You got a great sense of humour. What other good ideas have you got?'

'It works better if you're in an upstairs flat, then you run down into the street and call up to them. Hello up there! How's it going?' Marlow almost started to go into paroxysms of laughter. 'You should see the looks on their faces.'

'Yeah,' nodded Les. 'I can just imagine.' Christ! Can I find them. Anywhere in the bloody world. 'So did you finish the job?'

'Yes. Miss Lone Star State is all taken care of.'

'Good. Now when you get home have a couple of penicillin shots and take a Dettol bath.'

Marlow's face dropped slightly. 'Yes,' he agreed. 'Come to think of it, that might not be a bad idea actually.'

Norton was about to say something else when Terri drifted into the loungeroom. Her hair was matted, her clothes were a mess and she looked more than a little ashen faced.

'Terri,' smiled Les. 'How are you, matey? Shit! You look like you've seen a ghost.' Despite it all Norton couldn't help himself. 'Nyehh! What's up, doc?'

'I don't feel very well,' mumbled Terri. 'Something strange happened.'

'Yeah?' Les looked thoughtful. 'Maybe the earth moved for you. I hear Marlow's the last of the red-hot lovers.'

'That's me,' nodded Marlow. 'Back home they call me Marlow the Magnificent.'

Terri didn't reply. Marlow simply gave her an odd look. Les was going to ask them if they wanted another drink or something then changed his mind and started towards the door.

'Well, the limo's waiting outside, Marlow. You may as well get going.'

'Yes,' agreed Marlow. 'It is getting rather late.'

'You got enough money to get you home?'

'No problems at all, old boy. Anyway thanks for an absolutely splendid evening,' he said, as Les opened the door. 'Do catch up with us down at Reggae's tomorrow night. What do you say?'

'Yeah okay. Sounds good to me. See you then, Marlow.'

'Cheers, Les.'

'Goodnight Terri.' Terri muttered something as she walked past. Norton caught her eye, winked and gave her a little wave. 'Va-ver-va-va-ver. That's all, folks.' He closed the door and they were gone.

Bleary eyed, Les surveyed the mess in the flat as he finished his drink. There wasn't that much, but there was enough. Nothing he couldn't do tomorrow. With one great cavernous yawn he turned everything off, cleaned his teeth and crawled into bed. Before he did, however, he kicked the sheets off and slept on the bare mattress.

Norton wasn't exactly feeling one hundred per cent when he got up later that morning to face the brand new day. His mouth was furry and he had a reasonable sort of hangover; though no splitting headache. However he felt, it didn't make him any better when he walked into the loungeroom and surveyed the mess from the previous night. So he shook his head, got into his Speedos, grabbed a towel and went for a swim. Outside it was another blistering hot day and the water in the pool was the same as usual, but at least it cleared most of the cobwebs away again. Back in the condo, he had a large orange juice with ice and thought a bit about the previous night's festivities and remembered what he had to do today. Not a great deal except coffee with good bloke Ricco at twelve o'clock. I should ring him and say I can't make it, Les mused over his orange juice. No. I said I would and I don't want him getting the shits. I also don't want to be hanging around there too long either. Although that food he offered me sounds pretty good, I got a feeling I should just have a cup of coffee and hit the toe. Which means I'll make myself some breakfast before I leave. Norton's stomach was rumbling a little as he had another look at the mess in the kitchen; he was going to have to clean most of that up before he started. Then he spotted the carrot still sitting in the sink. Ohh poo! Les got a knife, skewered the carrot and dumped it in the kitchen-tidy. The heat had sent it off and it smelled like it was ready to blow up. In fact the whole flat needed a good clean. Ahh stuff it, thought Les. I know what I'll do. I'll go and have an all-American breakfast on the way to Ricco's and clean up all this shit this afternoon. He got into a pair of blue shorts, his blue Roosters T-shirt, got some money and left the flat as it was.

It was the same horror show outside in the car; Les had forgotten the windows again and was almost half dead with heat exhaustion and dehydration before he managed to find the buttons to get them all down, get the radio going and the air-conditioner set at warp ten. Some hillbilly song was twanging away as he turned right outside the flats and headed south. Ricco's shouldn't be too hard to find, thought Les and there has to be one of those roadside diners, or whatever they call them, on the way. The guitars and fiddles wafted easily out of the speakers as he drove along. Might even get myself a big ol' mess of crawdads, grits and sourdough flapjacks. Norton gobbed revoltingly out the window. And a plug of chewin' tobaccy as well. He drove past chicken shacks, pizza parlours, Mexican restaurants, McDonald's and others before he spotted it. A fairly big, cream-coloured brick restaurant with tinted windows and a sign out the front saying 'Howdy Neighbours Pancake Inn' next to the usual brace of American flags barely moving in the light breeze. It took up the whole corner, with parking for about six hundred cars plus the entire United States Polaris submarine fleet. Norton fish-tailed the T-bird into the parking lot, locked it up and stepped inside.

Howdy Neighbours was clean and modern in the usual American foodchain style, with seating for about eighty or more. Brown vinyl booths, chunky wooden tables in the middle and old iron or copper cooking utensils hung on the wall gave it a bit of chuck-wagon, old-homestead-out-on-the-prairie atmosphere. The place was about half full of fat arsed, black or white seppo families and retired couples shovelling food down their screeches with both hands. Les sat down in one of the booths and looked at the menu. It was on the table like a big paper serviette

271

with all the sloppy junk food for breakfast imaginable. Extra tender buttermilk pancakes, yeasty buckwheat, southern cornmeal, etc. Short stack and eggs, a western breakfast, one egg toast and grits, three little pigs in blankets. Everything from a Reuben to a Neighbours burger. A smiling blonde waitress wearing pigtails and a brown shirt and skirt, who looked like she'd just come from a square dance, drifted over. She had a glass of iced water in one hand a percolator full of coffee in the other.

'Well, hi there,' she beamed, placing the glass of water in front of Les. 'May I help you?'

'Yeah,' Norton smiled back. 'I'll have eggs benedict, hash browns and a Neighbours steak with mashed potatoes and gravy, thank you.'

'Alright,' beamed the waitress, sounding like a game-show host and Les had just answered a $5000 question. 'And how would you like your steak.'

'Medium rare, thanks.'

'Any toast with that?'

'Yeah, righto.'

'What kind of bread? Wholemeal, wheatmeal, cracked-grain, white French...'

'I don't really give a stuff,' cut in Norton. 'Just some that ain't got any mould on it'll do.'

The waitress looked at Norton for a moment then gestured with the percolator. 'Coffee?' Les shook his head. 'Okay then. This'll be up soon.'

'Thanks.'

Norton waited about five minutes and the first course arrived with a flurry of smiles. It was on a tray. Two fat, buttered muffins with an egg and a thick slice of ham sitting on each and then it looked as if someone had poured a forty-four-gallon drum of yellow glossmaster paint all over the lot. The hash brown was about as big as a manhole cover, only a couple of inches thicker. Christ, thought Les. How am I going to get through all this? And I had to go and order a steak as well. He picked up his knife and fork and dived in. Actually it didn't taste too bad; only there was just that much of it. Les ordered some orange juice to help wash it down and looked around him while he was eating. There were families knocking down the same size meals only with chips, Coca-Cola, ice cream and pancakes drowning in maple syrup, chocolate sauce and God knows what else. Christ! no wonder half these yanks look like Sumo wrestlers on steroids, thought Les, as he spooned some more Taubmans Daffodil Wallpamur down his throat. Then came the pièce de résistance. The Howdy Neighbours, all-American, cut on the premises, US prime steak. It was a piece of boneless sirloin, with a bowl of instant mashed potato swimming in gravy and a bowl of salad with a couple of cherry tomatoes sitting on top.

'Hey! How good does that look?' beamed the waitress.

'Yeah,' replied Norton, giving it the once over. 'Like a gangrened foot.' The he thought he heard the waitress say, 'I-went-away-to-get-some-four-seven-eleven.'

'What was that?' said Norton, looking from the steak to the girl.

'A-1-A or Heinz 57?' Les just looked at her and slowly shook his head. 'I think I'd better give you A-1-A,' said the waitress.

'You haven't got any A-1-B, have you?' said Les. 'Low-cal, sodium free, anti-cholesterol, have you?'

'I'm sorry sir. We don't.'

'Okay then, sweetheart. Hit us with the A-1-A.'

The waitress came back with a small white-labelled bottle full of some black shit that looked like octopus ink and tasted like concentrated Worcester sauce. Les slopped some over his Neighbours all-singing, all-dancing, all-American steak and got into it even though he was almost full. It wasn't too bad, as far as steaks go, just that Les was flat out getting it down on top of the other. But he forced down as much as he could, figuring a bit of protein wouldn't go astray. They could stick the mashed potato, however. It tasted like dog shit that had gone white after lying out in the sun. A nice coffee to go with the toast wouldn't have gone amiss, but Les decided to save himself for Ricco's. All up the bill didn't even come anywhere near twenty dollars with tax. Les figured Annie Oakley deserved a few extra dollars for putting up with him being a smartarse, so he left the US equivalent of a rock lobster on the table and split for Salmo.

The drive down to Salmo took Les about twenty-five minutes and was fairly pleasant despite the midday heat. He wasn't thinking about a great deal as he cruised along listening to country and western music and dropping the odd reprehensible fart now and again. Only how much Marlow and his mates reminded him a bit of his other 'Hooray Henry' mate Sir Peregrine Normanhurst the third, and whether Joey Hubcaps had shelfed him to Ricco yet about taking a team of drunks back to the condo and having a party. But stuff him anyway. If Ricco could swipe a big bag of money from the Mafia and knowingly involve Les, then expect him to keep his mouth shut, he could put up with one small turn back at his flat.

Norton slowed down when he saw Ricco's Rendezvous approaching on the right. There were no people around again and the same number of empty chairs and tables out the front. As he pulled in he noticed Ricco's blue Mercedes out the front of the coffee shop and if Les wasn't mistaken Vinnie's monstrous green Cadillac was parked next to it. For some reason Les parked right on the corner, keeping some distance between his car, the other two and the coffee shop. When he locked the T-bird and walked around he stood next to the boot for a moment, half joking with himself as to what scene out of what movie he'd be playing in today. For some other strange reason three came to mind: *Prizzi's Honor*, *Crossing 54th Street* and *The Getaway*. Shaking his head slightly Les started walking over; it was only about fifty feet or so but he was sweating before he got there.

The glass door had a sign on it saying OPEN. Norton stepped inside to find the place wasn't all that big but nicely air-conditioned with soft lighting. There were about a dozen chairs and tables to seat four, the walls were mainly black with murals of beach and boating scenes on them. On the left was a small counter with an espresso machine and a till sitting on it, next to several glass jars full of biscuits or chocolates, some artificial flowers and a stack of magazines. Behind the counter was a small alcove that was obviously the kitchen. Tinted windows faced the streets, and a door with EXIT above it in the back wall probably led to the toilets. The place was empty except for Ricco, Vinnie and Laverne sitting at a table near the back wall drinking coffee and a bloke behind the counter in a white shirt and black trousers standing with his arms folded. Ricco and the others were dressed designer casual as usual and Vinnie was smoking another monstrous cigar. The bloke behind the counter had thinning black hair and a sallow, pock-marked face, and looked like every Mafia heavy in every Mafia movie Les had ever seen on TV or at the movies. He looked at Norton suspiciously as Les came in with a smile on his face and walked straight over to the three against the wall who looked up from their coffee and stopped whatever they were talking about. There was no smiling greeting nor 'good to see you, Les, glad you could get here'. Nothing. If Norton wasn't mistaken there was a distinct air of tension hanging above the table.

'G'day, Ricco,' said Les. 'How's things? Hello, Laverne. G'day Vinnie.'

They kind of stared at him for a moment then Ricco spoke. 'Hey Les. How are you doin'?' he said quietly.

'Hi, Les,' said Laverne.

'Les. Nice to see you again,' said Vinnie impassively, before almost disappearing in a cloud of blue cigar smoke.

Les wasn't quite expecting a red carpet or twenty vestal virgins waiting out the front waving palm fronds and throwing frangipanis. But the reception so far made him feel as if they didn't give a stuff much whether he was there or not. There was definitely something in the wind and Norton had half an idea what; nevertheless, he batted on regardless.

'Well,' said Les, rubbing his hands together. 'You said to come down for a cup of coffee. So here I am.'

'Ohh yeah. That's right,' replied Ricco, sounding a little vacant. 'I ahh . . . it slipped my mind.' He looked at Les for a moment then turned to the man behind the counter. 'Hey, Sammy. Make this guy a straight white. A good one.'

Just a good one? mused Les. What about the 'Ricco special' and all the grouse food? 'Listen, if you've got business to discuss or that, don't worry about it. I can come back some other time.'

Ricco put a hand up. 'No. You came for coffee. You should have coffee.'

'I can't stay all that long anyway,' lied Norton. 'I met some Australian blokes last night and I arranged to have lunch with them today. I got to be back in town at one o'clock.'

'You met some buddies from Australia, did you?' nodded Ricco. 'That's good.'

'Anyway, sit down, Les,' said Laverne.

'Okay, thanks.' There was a kind of mumbled reception from the others as they moved their chairs around slightly when Les sat down. 'Hey, thanks for the meal the other night, Vinnie,' said Les, still attempting to make polite conversation. 'It was real good of you.'

'My pleasure,' said Vinnie. 'That was a nice-looking broad you had with you. Did you make out?' His face disappeared again in another cloud of cigar smoke.

'What was that?' asked Les.

Vinnie caught Laverne looking at him a little soberly. 'Did you enjoy yourself?'

'Yeah. I bit her on the ted a couple of times, threw her up in the air then kicked her khyber out the George Moore.'

'Excuse me?' said Vinnie.

Les noticed the others looking at him oddly as well. 'Yeah. I enjoyed myself.'

Norton attempted to make more polite conversation while he waited for his coffee, talking about nothing in particular and saying that he hadn't been doing much, just taking it easy and keeping quiet. He waited for a reaction to this from Ricco; there was none, so Les figured Joey the limo driver hadn't said anything yet. Les let Ricco lead with the trip out on the boat and only mentioned about the cyclone in reply. He made no mention of the bag full of money. The way Ricco and Vinnie looked at each other Vinnie was more than likely in on the scam too, or at least he knew they'd been out on Ricco's boat. Laverne added briefly to the conversation by mentioning the dolphins. But the way Ricco was almost forcing out the words, and judging from the unmistakable set of dark rings under his eyes, it was obvious he had more on his mind than the lack of lunchtime clientele.

Norton's coffee arrived. Les smiled up a thank you and got a lingering, expressionless look in reply. The coffee was good, though nothing special and definitely not worth over half an hour's drive across town and back for. Of course this didn't stop Les from saying how good it was after he'd stirred his sugar in and that he was sorry he didn't have time to stay for another one. The thought that Les would be pissing off soon seemed to please Ricco and the others more than his comments about the coffee. So they all sat there having a great time. Les sipped his coffee, Laverne stared into hers, Ricco said nothing and Vinnie puffed on his cigar. Sammy stood behind the counter with his arms folded. All that was missing was an old wooden clock ticking on the wall.

Les was down to his third-last sip when the door opened and a dark-haired girl wearing blue overalls with 'Salmo Linen Service' written across the front in white walked in carrying what looked like a bundle of table-cloths and serviettes. She wore sunglasses beneath an Elmer Fudd cap sitting on her head; dangling round her neck was a set of Walkman headphones, and a lump of chewing gum ground from one side of her mouth to the other.

'Linen service,' she drawled. 'Where you want it?'

Sammy looked at her impassively. 'On the counter.'

'Alrighty.'

'You're two hours late.'

'Yeah,' chewed the girl. 'We're flat out after the storm yesterday.'

'Where's Jenny?'

'Doin' two runs east. I gotta do the whole friggin' southside. We're up to our asses in dirty linen.' She dropped a piece of paper and a biro on the counter. 'You wanna sign this?' she chomped.

Sammy looked at the docket then signed it. The girl smiled a quick thanks and walked back out, adjusting her headphones under her cap as she went through the door. Les took another sip of coffee and watched Sammy place the parcel of linen under the counter. The others didn't say anything, hardly even bothered to give the girl a second glance, and went back to talking about absolutely nothing, managing to leave Les completely out of the conversation while they did. Norton reflected into his coffee for a few seconds. There was enough left for two good sips; he swallowed the lot in one go then wiped his mouth on a paper napkin.

'Well that was great, Ricco. I'd love another one but I got to get going and meet these blokes for lunch. I hope you don't think I'm rude pissing off like this.'

'Don't sweat it,' replied Ricco. 'You gotta go meet your buddies. That's fine.'

'We'll catch up again, Les,' said Laverne, as Les got to his feet.

'Yeah. I, ah . . . I'll probably give you a ring over the weekend.'

'Yeah. Do that,' nodded Ricco.

'Nice talking to you again Vinnie.'

'Yeah, you too, Les. You take care on the roads, huh?'

Norton winked goodbye at Vinnie, gave the others a smile then left. He gave Sammy a short wave as he got to the door and got an expressionless, slow nodding reply.

After the dim lights and the air-conditioning the sun and heat temporarily dazzled Les as he stepped outside. He walked over to the T-bird, not noticing that a few plain-looking cars had parked on either side of the coffee shop and another plain-looking grey car had parked almost opposite his.

Well, that was a nice fuckin' waste of time, he cursed to himself as he dug his car keys out of his shorts pocket. I should have rung up like I was going to. They would have told me not to bother coming over and I would've saved half the morning driving around. Plus I wouldn't be filled up with all that Howdy Neighbours shit either. When he arrived at the car another thought occurred to him and he didn't know whether to curse again or laugh. Not thinking fully on what he was doing he'd unconsciously walked to the wrong side of the car to get in and drive off. Bad luck there was no steering wheel. He was about to walk round to the correct side when Les heard a familiar voice behind him.

'Leave your hands right where they are, Les. Don't move them and turn around slowly. Very slowly.'

Norton winced and closed his eyes for a second. He knew who that voice belonged to and he knew exactly what to expect when he turned around. Nonetheless, when he did, he managed a look of complete surprise which turned to mild joy then mystified innocence.

'Lori,' he blinked. 'What are you doing down here?' Then Les pretended to notice the gun pointing at his face. 'Lori, what's the gun for? What have I done? Was it the meal? Did I give you a dud root? If I did I'm sorry. It won't happen again.'

Les was stalling for time; but all he was doing was wasting his time and hers. It was no good one way or the other. Lori, or Special Agent Benshoff from the Department of Justice literally had Norton right in her sights and if he tried anything cute she'd shoot him; and being a seppo she'd probably love it. Behind her six men got out of the plain-looking cars either side of the coffee shop wearing sunglasses, shirts and jeans the same as Lori. Three of them were carrying shotguns as well as pistols and all looked very grim and determined as they walked carefully towards the front door. Oh shit, Les groaned to himself. This is fuckin' it. I'm gone. Now I know what the movie is we're in today. *Midnight* bloody *Express*.

279

Lori might have been a cop to the core, but she did show a modicum of decorum towards Norton. As she spoke a tiny smile did flicker round the corner of her eyes. 'Lover. I don't know how to tell you this. But...'

Lori would have continued and her colleagues would have moved in on the coffee shop except that the next second Ricco's Rendezvous erupted in a boiling cloud of orange flame and a violent explosion that shook the whole neighbourhood. The windows disintegrated, showering broken glass everywhere, along with the windowsills and the door frame, and all the awnings flew up in the air, taking the neon sign with them in a spiralling cloud of black smoke and more roaring orange flames. Being cornered off a bit from the coffee shop Les missed the full blast of the explosion as it angled off left and right flinging wreckage everywhere. It didn't help Lori much though, who spun around just as the shop went up. Les, normally the perfect gentleman, would have flung himself on top of Lori to protect her; this time he got behind and held her in front of him. She missed most of the broken glass and other flying debris, but the force of the explosion scattered all the chairs and tables outside the coffee shop in all directions. One chair came rocketing across the carpark and smacked straight into Lori, the chrome bar at the back hit her flush on the forehead, the seat part thumped into her stomach. She gave a groan of pain, dropped her gun and fell back against Les, out like a light. Les grabbed her and held her up in front of him as more bricks, splintered wood and other junk came flying down around them.

'Holy bloody shit!' he cried. 'What the...?'

Les was dazed, partly deafened and shocked as the explosion died away and he stared at the carnage in front of him. Lori might have been knocked silly, but her colleagues were a lot worse off. They'd unexpectedly walked straight into it and those that weren't dead or unconscious were lying on the ground moaning with pain. Ricco's Rendezvous was no more. All that was left was a pile of smouldering rubbish, full of small fires everywhere, and a thick cloud of black smoke billowing up into the bright blue sky. Half the shop next door was gone, several waterpipes in the coffee shop had buckled, sending water and steam up into the air as well, and the blast had shattered the windscreens and blown off the bonnets of both the Mercedes and the Cadillac parked out the front. What was left of those inside the coffee shop wouldn't be worth looking for. Les looked at the mess then looked at Lori still lying in his arms, blood starting to ooze down from her forehead. Carefully he laid her against the wall of the carpark. He looked at her colleagues still lying on the ground, had another quick look around him then drew back his fist and punched Lori right on the jaw about as hard as he could, smiling to himself as he felt the bones break and several teeth come loose. Like going through her handbag it definitely wasn't the gentlemanly thing to do, but Lori literally never knew what hit her.

Blood now bubbling out of her mouth as well, Les left her propped against the wall and got in the car. A few stunned people had now started to emerge as he kicked the motor over, wondering what the hell had happened. Norton reversed the T-bird out of the parking lot, just like Grandma Duck, and if it had of been Grandma Duck driving he would have turned right and proceeded on slowly and carefully. But Les wasn't Grandma Duck and he was used to driving on the wrong side of the road. There was a slight break in the traffic, he gunned the T-bird across the highway and straight over the median strip. Whether there was a break in the traffic on the other side of the highway he didn't know. But a lot of cars had slowed down to geek at the fire and smoke. Les found a small space in front of an oncoming truck and went for it, fish-tailing the T-bird and burning rubber for about two hundred yards up the freeway. The car radio was blaring and the DJ had announced the track playing as 'Papa Loved Momma' by Garth Brooks. It was a howler and Norton vaguely heard the words. 'He never hit the breaks and he was shifting gears.' Somehow it seemed appropriate.

Les slowed down about a mile further on and casually mingled in with the other traffic. Nevertheless, it was a drive home full of trepidation and he kept his mind on the road and not much else for the time being; especially when a fire engine and two cop cars went screaming past about two miles south of the Siestasota Shopping Mall. Les made it back to the condo. When he pulled up and turned off the engine he noticed his hands were shaking a little and his adrenalin was still pumping; the sweat down the middle of his back wasn't entirely from the heat either. Still stunned and somewhat incredulous he locked the car and went inside. This time, for some reason, Norton found he couldn't see the funny side of things at all.

The smell inside the condo hadn't improved any since he left. But it was home so to speak and there had to be something left to drink in the fridge. There was; several bottles of Coors Cutter. Which suited Les in a way, he'd need to keep his head together and right now wasn't exactly the time to be getting half pissed. He opened the bottle, took a mouthful then went out and sat on the enclosed verandah, away from the mess, resting his feet up on the cross-bar of the old pushbike. Outside two or three people were splashing around in the pool and he thought he saw Jerome shuffle past the cabana carrying a hose. Les closed his eyes for a moment, wiped some sweat from his face then stared grimly out the verandah window.

That was just too close for comfort. Too close. If he'd stayed at Ricco's for another cup of coffee... If he'd stopped for a few minutes longer at Howdy Neighbours... If he'd got held up at a set of lights, left a few minutes later than he did... If, if, if. If what bloody ever, he'd have been blown all over Salmo, along with the other four in the coffee shop. Norton moved his gaze up to the sky for a moment. What could he say? Thanks again? He started to surmise what was going on and it wasn't that hard, especially when one of those three movies he'd been joking about came to mind. Ricco had probably got sprung keeping the money he was supposed to pick up or, with the Godfather in New York getting thirty years gaol, there was a power play in the mob and some other family wanted to take over. Maybe a bit of both. But more than likely Ricco got sprung, which was why they all seemed to be shitting themselves in the coffee shop. The bomb arrived in that bundle of linen. It was two hours late, the usual girl was doing another run. You can bet the girl with the Walkman was a female killer for the mob. *Prizzi's Honor* was today's movie alright. And I must have bloody ESP, thought Les, taking another mouthful of Coors. Then there was Lori and her little team turning up. Probably they were under surveillance all along and now was the time to swoop and get Ricco along with the money. Or it could have been part of a big FBI, Department of Justice bust to get the mob off-guard with the goaling of Licavoli. Bad luck about their timing and the fact that they chose to play Elliot Ness just as the place got blown up. Which unfortunately was why Les had to put one on Lori's chin. The other cops were either dead or close enough to it. But Lori, being only slightly injured, would be able to give a statement when she came to in which she would undoubtedly mention Les, where he lived and to go bring him in for questioning. However, with her jaw wired up, a few teeth missing and full of sedatives for the pain she wouldn't be saying too much. Not even for a woman. This, along with her other injuries, would be put down to the force of the explosion and it would also give Les breathing space to make his next move. Anyway, serve her fuckin' right, scowled Norton. It's not as if I did anything and she would have shot me for sure, the low moll. On top of half a good root and a grouse feed too. See how the cunt likes eating her meals through a straw for the next few months. He took another long swallow of Coors. No, Florida was getting too hot; even for summer. Apart from all this Mafia shit, his footprints were all over the floor back at Hank's. Not counting failing to report a murder and indirectly destroying a nightclub with considerable loss of life and limb

283

to the various customers. It was only a matter of time before there'd be a knock at the door. So even though there was no immediate need to panic, it was definitely time to get going. But where? Back to Australia? That would be the best idea, except he'd only been away about a week. New Orleans? Las Vegas? LA? Les shook his head, finished his beer and got another, then sat out on the verandah again. No. Somehow Les was starting to get a bit sick already of the land of the free and the home of the brave. He got into the second bottle and had a think. It didn't take long to both finish the bottle and make up his mind. Les looked at his watch, put the empty bottle in the kitchen and changed into a clean white T-shirt. With his VISA card, passport and other ID tucked in the back pocket of his shorts he locked the condo and walked out to the car.

There were three women in the little travel agency just across from the Amish restaurant. One look hispanic, the others had brownish blonde hair. They were all around thirty and well groomed, wearing double-breasted, orange cotton jackets with 'Manatee Keys Travel Agency' written across the breast pocket in black. There was a desk with a computer on it and a chair sitting in front when Les walked in. One of the blondes was working there. On the right was a small room with a lounge and a coffee table full of travel magazines, something like a doctor's waiting room. Behind another desk and computer the hispanic woman was talking into the phone. The third woman sat behind her and behind her another area was partitioned off with bamboo walls covered in travel posters. The girl at the front desk was fairly attractive except for this horrible Tammie Bakker kind of hairstyle. Les approached her and almost fainted when he looked at the name-tag on her jacket and it said Lori. On closer inspection it said Loni. Thank Christ for that, he thought. I don't think I could handle another one of those.

'Good afternoon,' Loni smiled up at Norton. 'Can I help you?'

'Yes,' replied Norton, sitting down. 'I'd like to book a flight to Jamaica, direct to Montego Bay. When's the next one leave?'

'Just one moment.' Loni hit the computer, looked at the screen then punched the keys a few more times. 'There's a North West flight leaves Tampa at 1.30 tomorrow afternoon direct to Montego Bay. Arriving 5.30 in the afternoon, Jamaican time.'

'That'll do me,' said Les.

'Do you have somewhere to stay?'

Les shook his head. 'Can you get me into the Rose Point Resort?'

Loni consulted some travel manual then clattered away at the computer again. 'How many nights?'

Les thought for a moment. 'Can I take two, with an option on another week or more if I want to?'

'That shouldn't be any trouble when you get there. It's the off-season.' Loni hit the computer again. 'I can get you a deluxe room for two nights, at $110 US a night. How's that sound?'

'Absolutely sensational, Loni,' smiled Les. 'And one more thing, I have to take my car back today. What's the best way to get to Tampa from here?'

'Unless you want to take a taxi, the airport shuttle service. That drops you right at the airport. Where are you staying?' Les told her. 'There's one calls in that way at 8.30 tomorrow morning.'

'Can you arrange for me to be on that?'

'No problem at all,' smiled Loni. 'It's a good idea to leave a little early too. Now. How do you wish to pay for all this?'

'VISA,' replied Les, placing his passport and the rest of his ID and travel documents on the desk. 'My American entry stamp gets me into Jamaica, doesn't it?'

'No problem at all.' Loni checked Norton's passport and his Qantas ticket. 'Yep, no problem at all.'

Les sat back in the chair and his smile widened. 'Terrific.'

Between the phone ringing, Loni having to help the

other girls now and again and other customers arriving demanding this that and the other, it took a good hour to get everything together. While he waited, Les drank two cans of soft drink from the nearby supermarket and thought out his plan of attack, or retreat, before he got out of Florida. There were two ways he could go about it. By the time Loni had his accommodation and his flight to Jamaica stapled together and his Qantas ticket re-arranged Les was certain he'd chosen the right one. He picked up his travel documents and thanked Loni. She wished him a good holiday then after saying goodbye Les walked out to the car and headed back to the condo. All he had to do now was sort a couple of things out, keep his head down and with a bit of luck he'd be on his way to Jamaica at 8.30 in the morning. Goodbye Sepposota, Hello Montego Bay. No matter what, the first thing Les did when he got back to the condo was have another bottle of Coors and a long, probably last, swim in the pool.

After he'd towelled off and had a shower, Les left his Speedos on and started cleaning up the condo. He didn't really have to; the chances of the present owner complaining about the mess were minimal to say the least. But if the place was left reasonably neat and tidy and the police did dome after he'd left, it wouldn't look so much as if he'd galloped out of the place like some fugitive on the run. After working at the Kelly Club and being involved with Price for some time Norton had a reasonable idea of how the police mind worked, and they wouldn't be all that much different over in this neck of the woods. Besides, the place stunk anyway and he didn't fancy sitting around in the mess and smell all night. He could have packed his gear and moved into a motel for the night. But why bother? Besides, the woman at the travel agency had arranged for the shuttle to pick him up at that address in the morning, he'd have to change all that and he'd probably stuff things up over the phone anyway. One thing did occur to Les, as he shoved more rubbish into a plastic garbage bag. He hadn't taken into account what would happen when Lori came to. Although she wouldn't be able to talk, she could still write out some sort of a statement or whatever. If Les had thought of that at the time he'd have broken all her fingers as well. The way things were, though, he figured he had about twenty-four hours up his sleeve from the time of the explosion.

As for the car? Well, he could leave it out the front. But there was a chance some concerned citizen might have got the number. Even in a nuthouse like America that scene at Ricco's Rendezvous would have to make it on the news, and there'd have to be a few concerned citizens living on the estate. It was only a chance. But at this stage why leave anything to chance? No. The best place for the car would be to rip up all the documents then take it back to Vinnie's and leave the keys in the glove box. A thin smile formed around Norton's mouth and a shitty, evil gleam emanated from his eyes. And leave a present on the back seat for someone too.

It took Les a bit longer than he thought to clean the flat up. He found where the dump-masters were out the back and a vacuum cleaner in a closet; however, he didn't bother to vacuum, just gave the place a good sweep. Even with the air-conditioners on it was hotter than he thought, so he ended up going for another swim. Then he started on his room.

He began by sorting out his gear and travel documents. While he did, he listened to his cassettes and not the radio, figuring the explosion would probably be on a news bulletin and what he didn't know wouldn't hurt him. Les also could have rung home for free, but he figured they might trace the calls back to Australia or something so why take another risk, small as it might be, for the sake of saving a few lousy dollars. There was junk and clothes, some dirty, scattered from one end of the room to the other and it was getting dark when he finally had everything packed except for a pair of jeans, joggers and a T-shirt to wear on the plane. Merv Hughes was gone, but he still had Dean Jones and David Hookes. I'll arrive in the Dean Jones, thought Les. Nothing like making a good impression with the cricket-loving natives. Apart from that there was nothing left except his shower kit and one awfully stained sheet lying on the bedroom floor. Les took it out to the kitchen, slopped a little cajun dressing on it just to give it some more colour then folded it up and put it in another plastic bag with the top tied. In one of the drawers he found a black texta-colour and wrote on the light grey garbage bag: To Special Agent Lori Benshoff, C/- US Department of Justice. In another drawer Les found an envelope. He put the same address on the front, put a short note inside and taped it to the garbage bag. It read: Dear Lori, I'll never forget the night you held this against me in evidence. Promise me you won't stain my reputation as well. Love Vinnie. Satisfied, he took the bag out and placed it on the back seat of the T-Bird, then went inside and arranged over the phone for a taxi to pick him up at the caryard. Les got into a pair of shorts and a T-shirt and checked Vinnie's address against his map of Siestasota. It was only a few blocks north of the estate and should be easy enough to find. He locked the condo and drove off.

The drive to Vinnie's was easier than Les thought. So easy in fact that he drove round the block a couple of times and sussed the place out. There was no one about, the coast looked clear enough so he pulled up in the driveway. There was a chain across the gate so he couldn't drive into the yard, though he was well off the main road. He locked the car, gave the parcel on the back seat a last smile and then stood out the front and waited for the taxi. The taxi was five minutes early and Les jumped straight in the back.

'4701 Manatee, mate. Greenwood Gardens Estate.'

'You got it, buddy,' said the driver.

They drove along in silence. Then the driver caught Norton's eye in the rear vision mirror.

'Say, where are you from, buddy?' he asked.

'Scotland,' replied Les vacuously.

'Oh.'

288

That was the entire conversation until they arrived at the estate. Les told the driver to drop him off out the front and paid him without leaving a tip.

Les didn't particularly feel like a walk in the hot, humid night air. But it did give him half a chance to stretch his legs and he also figured the fewer people knew where he lived the better. Les found the estate to be bigger than he imagined as he strolled beside the speed bumps in the semi darkness. There was a fair-sized tennis court at this end and another well-kept garden area. It was fairly dark, especially out on the driveway. There didn't seem to be anybody around and most of the condos at this end seemed either in darkness or unoccupied. But there was enough light coming from around to see where you were going. Les sensed he was approaching the caretaker's shed. He was, and as he got closer he heard voices; they were trying to keep subdued but dripped of anger and malice. For some reason Les slowed down a little and a tiny squirt of adrenalin hit him in the stomach along with a slight bristling up and down his spine. In the gloom from the one light outside the caretaker's shed he could see Jerome pushed up against a wall, surrounded by four men in their early twenties wearing baseball caps and boots, T-shirts and jeans. They weren't just a bunch of skinny kids, two looked white, one appeared to be hispanic, the other asian, and they looked as if they meant business. One white had a switch-blade knife and so did the asian. The white had the blade of his knife pressed under Jerome's chin. Les could distinctly see it glinting an evil silver in the darkness, the same as he could distinctly see Jerome's eyes bulging a sickly, terrified white.

'I say we cut the fuckin' nigger's throat,' said the white holding the switch-blade.

'Yeah,' hissed the hispanic. 'Cut the stinking fuckin' nigger. He don't want to talk. He don't want to live.'

'I can't help you, man,' pleaded Jerome. 'I's tellin' you the truth.'

'Bullshit! You lying, black nigger sonofabitch!!' The white with the switch-blade pressed it harder against

Jerome's chin. 'Half these condos are empty, and you got the fuckin' master key. You lying stinken nigger fuck!' Switch-blade's voice rose and he almost screamed out the last sentence. Watching silently Les figured either he was high on something or he needed it bad.

'The nigger's holding back,' cursed the asian. He brandished the knife he was holding and it too gleamed sinisterly in the dull light. 'Let me have him. I'll make the sonofabitch give us the keys.'

'I ain't lyin', man,' Jerome pleaded again. 'I's tellin' you the truth. I's just a janitor. I just sweeps and pushes a broom. I don't got nobody's keys. Oh God! Don't kill me.'

'You're bullshitting, you black sonofabitch,' snarled the other white.

'I'm not, man.' Jerome was almost begging on his knees. 'Please don't hurt me, man. I ain't done nothin'. And I don't know nothin'. Any other night and I wouldn't even be here, man. I swear.'

'Cut his lying nigger tongue out,' said the hispanic.

'Yeah, stick the mother,' urged the asian.

Norton watched from the shadows a moment or two longer then started to slowly shake his head. This was absolutely none of his business and, besides, he was in enough trouble as it was. But what could he do? Jerome didn't seem like a bad bloke and he did do Les a nice favour. Apart from that, though, he couldn't just stand there and let some poor, inoffensive cleaner get stood over and probably sliced up by a team of lowlife, junkie dropkicks. Maybe if he just made his presence felt they might piss off. Yeah, *might*. Les shook his head again, sucked in a lungful of air and moved out from the shadows into the half light.

'Hey, Jerome. How're you goin' there, mate?' Les sounded as if he was surprised to see him. 'Everything alright?'

The four hoods spun round and stared at Les. Their faces registered absolutely no fear, a little surprise maybe, but mostly annoyance.

'What the fuck do you want — asshole?' demanded the white holding the switch-blade.

'Nothing,' shrugged Norton. 'I was just on my way home and I saw my old mate Jerome here having some sort of multicultural get together. So I thought I'd put my Rocky Ned in and say hello. Any harm in that?'

The asian's face screwed up. 'What is he? Some kind of limey?'

'Who gives a fuck what he is,' said the hispanic. 'Stick the fucker.'

'Yeah, stick the mother,' said the other white.

The white holding the switch-blade advanced towards Les with the knife in his left hand. He was almost as tall as Les with a vicious, pock-marked face and crazy sunken eyes. Les moved his head slightly to one side as the hood brought the knife up and started making short, menacing movements with it an inch or two in front of the big Queenslander's face.

'You like to bleed do you, limey?' leered the hood. 'You ever been stuck, huh? You dumb ass sonofabitch.'

Norton shrugged again. 'I've been stuck in traffic. Been stuck for a crap. Even got stuck in a lift once. Can't say I've ever been stuck by one of those things though.'

'Well, ain't that cool,' sniggered the hood, turning to his mates for a second. 'I guess there's a first time for everything. And this is just your lucky day.'

'Go on,' said Norton, returning the hood's shitty smile. 'That must be why they call me Lucky Les.'

Norton had a quick look around him and at the other three hoods. He had the white with the switch-blade almost in front of him. Behind him Jerome was still standing against the wall shitting himself; although a little colour had drained back in his face since Les arrived. On Jerome's right was the asian holding the second knife. In front of the asian was the hispanic and in front of the hispanic to Norton's left was the other white, who looked enough like the other one to be his brother. If Les was going to do something he'd have to move pretty smartly, and the first one to go would have to be the white

291

hood holding the switch-blade in front of him. It was moments like these Les was glad he and Billy Dunne had got to know Manny Kramer — Kelvin's equally shifty brother and ex-lieutenant in the Israeli paratroopers. They'd gone on a number of training runs together and on several occasions, Manny being an expert knife fighter, he'd taken them back to the surf club and shown the boys a few dirty tricks that would come in handy up the Cross or wherever if some nutter comes at you with a knife. This was definitely one of those moments.

Les shuffled back a pace or so to let the hood in front of him think he was scared; the hood sneered and brought the knife up to make a thrust at Norton's face. This was all the momentum Les needed to pull off a double-handed-wristlock-leg-drop-elbow-break. At least that was what Manny called it. Les slapped his left hand down on top of the hood's left wrist, slapped his right hand underneath, gripped hard then twisted the hood's wrist up and his arm round in almost the same motion. The hood barely had time to grunt with pain and surprise as Les forced his arm down then stepped his right leg over it jamming the hood's elbow the wrong way round under his crutch. The rest was easy. Les just squatted down, pulling the hood's knife arm up a bit tighter at the same time. The hood screamed and there was an audible crack in the darkness as his elbow joint snapped like a stick of celery. Les gave another quick, but solid, twist and broke the hood's wrist this time. The hood gave another scream of pain, the knife clattered to the ground and Les stood up to face the other hood on his left, leaving hood number one curled up on the ground sobbing with pain as he grabbed at his shattered arm.

The second white hood had kind of shaped up to Les, but Norton's movements so far had been that quick the hood didn't quite know what was going on. Les didn't have time for any fancy stuff, half of which only looks good in the movies anyway, so he simply fired off a right snap kick, sinking the toe of his jogger in hood number two's solar-plexus. He gasped with pain and doubled

over as all the air was slammed out of his lungs. Les
grabbed the hood's hair and rammed his knee hard into
his face, mashing his nose all over it. Norton pulled his
arm back to give him a lazy backfist or two behind the
ear, but saw he needn't bother. He let go and the hood hit
the ground oozing blood, hardly able to breathe, hardly
able to see.

This left the hispanic and the asian with the other knife.
Les paused for a second, just a little bit toey. If he went for
the hispanic, the asian would probably have time to blade
him from behind. If he went for the asian, the hispanic
could jump on his back and the asian would still have
time to blade him. There's no rules in a knife fight and it
only takes one in the heart or the kidneys, especially with
the stiletto type of switch-blades these hoods were using,
and that's it. You hardly feel it at first, then a few seconds
later you don't feel anything at all, ever.

'Okay, Jerome,' Les called out to the cleaner. 'You grab
the spick. I'll take care of the dingbat with the knife.'
Jerome never moved an inch; Les didn't think he would.
But at least it stopped the hispanic for a moment while he
waited for Jerome to do something. This gave Norton a
few seconds clear to take on the asian hood with the
switch-blade.

The asian hood came at Les, crouching a bit lower
than the other guy and holding the knife in his right
hand. This time Norton went for a palm heel-strike-leg
sweeping-elbow break. He shaped up something like a
boxer as the hood lunged the knife at his chest. Les
knocked the hood's knife arm up with his left hand then
slammed the heel of his right palm up under his chin,
snapping his head back. Now he grabbed the hood's left
arm, straightened it out then stepped behind him and
banged his right leg behind the asian's right knee, effectively sweeping his legs from under him with enough
force to send him sprawling on his back. Les still had
hold of the hood's right arm, the knife still gripped in the
hood's hand. He squatted down beside him and
stretched his right leg out, grabbing the hood's wrist with

his left hand and clamping his right hand around his throat while he levered the hood's arm across his knee. The rest of this was relatively easy too. Les pushed the hood's arm down and moved his knee up at the same time; there was another audible 'crack', another awful scream and Les broke the asian hood's arm. This left a very worried-looking hispanic facing a very nasty-looking Les with nothing between them but fresh air. On the ground around him his mates were either out cold or howling with pain.

'Well, Jose,' said Norton, 'it looks like just you and me now, eh? How do you feel, you fuckin' hero?'

At least the hispanic had a bit of a go; probably hoping to stun Les for a moment then leg it. He swung his right leg and tried to kick Les in the groin. Les moved easily to one side and let the leg slip past. In the same movement he hooked his right arm up and under the hispanic hood's knee and banged his left forearm across his throat. The hood's legs went from under him and he slammed down backward, splitting his head open on the concrete as he landed, Les grabbed him by the front of his Florida Gators T-shirt and slammed three short rights into his face, smashing his nose, most of his front teeth and pulping his mouth into an awful-looking red mess. Les dropped him back onto the concrete and left him there, the blood bubbling out of his nose and mouth quickly joining the blood seeping from the back of his head. Norton stood up, glanced at the wreckage around him then turned to the caretaker.

'Well, come on Jerome,' he said, trying to sound serious. 'Don't stand there like a stale bottle of piss. Give me a hand to finish them off.'

Jerome looked at the four battered and bloody hoods lying on the ground either snoring or whimpering with shock and pain. 'What you talkin' 'bout, man? Finish them off? They is finished off. Man, they's about as finished off as they's ever gonna be.'

'Ahh bullshit! Come on, get into the cunts. They were gonna give it to bloody you.'

294

'Man, I'm from Alabama. I ain't ever hit no one in my life.' Jerome looked at the first hood with the knife. 'Sho nuff no white man.'

'Jerome, it doesn't matter whether these cunts are black, white, red or green with yellow dots. They're just cunts. And they need a good serve. Look, I'll show you.' Les stepped over to the first hood he dealt with and kicked him in the face: hard. The hood grunted with more pain as several teeth came loose, and tried to cover up. 'Go on, Jerome. Have a go. You'll love it.'

Jerome suddenly got a funny glint in his eye. He looked at Les for a second, looked at the hood on the ground then walked over and kicked him in the face too. The hood grunted with pain once more. 'Hey,' Jerome turned to Les, 'I dig this shit.'

'Good on you. Now give him another couple.'

Jerome kicked the hood again. 'Hey. How you like that, honky?' The hood howled again as Jerome sunk another one in. 'So, you was gonna stick old Jerome, was you? You white trash.' The caretaker reefed the hood again. 'How you like that bad news goin' down, huh? You white motherfucker.' Jerome sunk a couple of solid ones into the hood's ribcage. 'You mess wit the rest, now mess with the best — turkey.' *Thump!* In went another one.

Les watched contentedly as Jerome went round all four hoods and did a soul brother's version of some Balmain folk-dancing on their heads and ribcages. The four hoods just had to lie there, cover up as best they could and cop it. While he was watching, Les picked up one of the switchblades and had a good look at it. It was a vicious, deadly looking thing and he could just imagine the damage the hoods would have done to Jerome with it. Poor, inoffensive Jerome. Just a battling caretaker going about his job, not harming anybody, and these four bastards would have carved him up and thought nothing of it. More than likely laughed their heads off. A small well of hatred suddenly bubbled up inside Norton and for a moment he felt like going round and slitting all their throats. Instead, he walked over to the first hood, shoved the blade up his nose and sliced open his nostrils. Then he shoved the knife in the hood's thigh, right up to the hilt. He was still howling when Les went over and did the same to the asian hood. By now Jerome looked as if he'd had enough fun and was standing back looking at his blood-spattered handiwork.

'Hey, Jerome,' said Les, 'you reckon you can take these four turds and dump them somewhere?'

'Sho nuff, man. I'll ring my brother-in-law. He's got a pick-up. He'll call round and we'll dump these suckers out by Crab Keys.'

'You won't bother getting the cops, will you?'

'No suh. Ah don't wants no hassles with the po-lice.'

'Good,' replied Les. 'Well, I'm going to bed. I'm knackered. I'll probably see you tomorrow.'

'Okay. Hey, listen. You saved my ass here tonight. Thanks, brother.'

'Ahh, that's alright. Don't worry about it.' Les smiled and gave the caretaker a wink. 'You're not a bad bloke — for a nigger. See you later, mate.' Norton turned to walk away.

'Yeah, see you later. Hey, Les, before you go, there's something I got to ask you.'

Norton stopped and turned around. 'Yeah. What's that?'

'Les, just what kind of man are you, brother?'

Norton thought for a moment then shrugged. 'Just call me a digger with attitude. See you tomorrow, Jerome. And remember, no cops. Okay?'

'No suh. Ah swear.'

Back inside the condo Les had sworn earlier he wouldn't have a drink that night. But after that little incident... Fuck it. There was enough Diet Pepsi in the fridge and enough bourbon left in a bottle for several delicious: or delicioui. He poured one, finished it fairly smartly then made another. Bloody hell! Does it ever stop in this joint? Bombings, suicides, shootings, riots. I go to drop a car off and finish up in a knife fight. Norton shook his head and reflected into his drink. Boy, will I ever be glad to get out of this rathouse. I don't know nothing about Jamaica, but it couldn't possibly be any crazier than this. Les sipped his drink and tried to figure out what to do. He didn't want to watch TV, he didn't feel like turning on the radio or listening to any more cassettes. It wasn't getting any earlier and he should try to get some sleep. Finally he decided to read some more of his book about Jamaica and have another look through Elizabeth Norton Blackmore's book of poems. Les read for a while until his eyes started to flicker then close. He turned out the light and dozed of. But Les had a fitful night's sleep, tossing and turning, having to get up a couple of times for glasses of water. When he did drop off he'd start dreaming there was a bomb in the kitchen or the cops were coming through the door, or another bunch of hoods were driving round the estate with a car full of Uzis looking for him.

Before Les knew it the sun was up, it was eight o'clock and he was dressed and standing in the kitchen, looking at the kettle through grainy eyes as he tried to organise some coffee and toast. He felt more tired than if he'd never gone to bed at all. Les yawned his way through his coffee and toast when he heard noises out the front. A minute or so later there was a knock on the door. Les opened it to find a big, beefy man about sixty with thinning brown hair.

'You der person Norton going to Tampa airport?' he asked in a slightly guttural accent.

'Yeah, that's me, mate,' yawned Norton. 'You're right on time.'

'That is your bag?' Les nodded. Before he had a chance to say or do anything, the big man had picked it up effortlessly. 'I see you out in the bus.'

'Yeah righto,' blinked Les.

Les had a last, slightly nostalgic look around the condo and the old pushbike sitting out on the verandah. Well, he mused, looks like I made it, and we're out of here. It's certainly been a funny one. But at least I'm still alive. He rattled the keys in his hands for a second then dropped them on the bar next to the phone. 'See you, Ricco. See you, Laverne. Say hello to Hank for me if you see him.' Les picked up his overnight bag, closed the door quietly behind him and walked out the front.

The shuttle was an old, bulky-looking kind of brown and red minibus that seated about a dozen. So far Les was the only passenger. He climbed in the door, sat behind the driver and next thing they were on their way. Les didn't say a great deal at first, content to sit back and uninterestedly let the suburbs and dead flat roads of southern Florida roll past as they headed north towards Tampa. The driver wasn't saying much either; he just puffed on a cigarette while the old bus lurched and rolled along through the light, morning traffic. Eventually Les started to forget his tiredness and began to pick up at the thought that he was leaving Siestasota, so he got a bit of a mag on with the driver. He originally came from Austria and had migrated to Florida around forty years ago when he joined the circus as a strong man. The way he picked up Norton's bag like it was a packet of Sao biscuits Les didn't dispute that. The driver waffled on about how Florida had been developed to death over the last twenty years and soon they'd be in all sorts of trouble because the water plain couldn't take the pressure of all the housing and high-rises. Now where have I heard that before? mused Les. Florida was still nice but nowhere near as nice as it used to be with nowhere near the wildlife and fish life. I think I've heard that one too, thought Les. They turned off the main road and onto some back streets near a small bridge and another expanse of water, the driver saying he had to pick up one more passenger. The driver checked the streets and began to slow down, then Les gave a double, triple blink. Just when he thought he'd left behind all the movie and TV scenes, he found himself in the cartoons. Standing on the corner, outside a small white house with a small white fence and with three small suitcases next to her was Minnie Mouse.

Minnie was a little over five feet tall with her dark hair

stacked in two buns on either side of her head, and looked to be in her late sixties. She had on a dark grey, chalk-striped, dress suit, from which poked two skinny little legs in black stockings and a huge pair of white, high-heeled shoes. The best part, though was a pair of huge white glasses with these enormous heart shaped frames sitting on her chubby little face. The driver got out and took Minnie's bags. Les helped her in the door and as she sat down behind him he looked over at the house, half expecting Pluto, Goofy and Mickey to start waving from the window. They didn't however, and the driver got back behind the wheel and they proceeded on their way again.

Minnie intrigued Les in her monstrous white glasses so he got a bit of a mag going with her. It turned out her name was Mrs Conaghan, she was a sweet, chirpy old thing and when Les introduced himself Mrs Conaghan had a handshake as good as most men Les had met. She was a military widow and she was flying up to a naval base in Indianapolis for a ceremony where her son was to be made chief surgeon. She'd more or less been involved with the military all her life, at least since she married her officer husband when she was nineteen. She told Les about living and bringing up a family on army bases in Tokyo, Korea, West Germany and England, as well as America, and made it sound interesting as well as how much she enjoyed it. Her husband was older than her and died a few years back after he retired; she took a photo of him from her wallet and in his army uniform and neatly trimmed moustache he reminded Les of Robert Taylor in *Waterloo Bridge*. Christ, mused Les, as he handed Mrs Conaghan back her photo. I've got to stop equating everything I see over here with either the movies, TV or bloody cartoons. Les just said he was in America on a holiday and now he was on his way to Jamaica then back home. Like most Americans Mrs Conaghan knew bugger all about Australia but she was interested. The driver joined in the conversation and the trip up to Tampa was a regular beano, it wouldn't have surprised Les if they'd have all got a singalong going. Before Norton knew it they were climbing up some massive, arched bridge over an equally massive expanse of water, which he suddenly remembered from the night Hank picked him up, and the next thing they were outside the terminals at Tampa airport. Les paid the driver, shook Minnie Mouse's hand again, but she was that much of a sweetie he couldn't help himself and gave her a kiss on the cheek which Minnie thought was lovely. She wished Les a happy holiday and a safe trip back to Australia, Les picked up his travel bag, slung his backpack over his shoulder and walked through the terminal doors up to the North West Airlines counter. Although the terminal was huge Les was the only customer at the counter. The brown-haired man who took his bag had a bit of a twinkle in his eye and of all things a fairly thick Scots accent.

'So Aussie. Off to Jamaica are we, mon?' he said, as he attached the luggage ticket.

'Yeah,' nodded Les. 'For a couple of weeks or so.'

'Holiday?'

'Yeah. Just another tourist.'

'You ever been there before, laddie?'

Les shook his head. 'No. Don't even know much about the place.'

The clerk flicked across Norton's ticket with his biro. 'I suppose you'll be having plenty of "how's your father" with the local ladies?'

'I dunno,' shrugged Les. 'If it's on, why not?'

'I'll give you some advice, digger. If you do, make sure you wear enough rubber to bungee jump halfway back to Australia.'

Les stared at the clerk. 'It's that bad, is it?'

'Haiti's just down the road and you're heading into the tropics. It's just one big incubator for all sorts of things down there.' The clerk dropped Norton's bag on the conveyor belt and handed him his ticket. 'So have a good holiday, Aussie. But just make sure your next one isn't your last.'

'Yeah righto. Thanks,' replied Les blankly. He put his ticket in his bag and walked off.

Shit! How about that? thought Norton, as he stepped onto an escalator that took him upstairs to the terminal shuttles, the shopping area and the departure lounge. I remember Warren saying something to me before I left too. And when I come to think of it, I didn't give a stuff one way or the other when I was pissed back in Sepposota. Les was half shaking his head when he stepped off the escalator. Though it's not as if I was hanging out with any low molls in Sepposota. And I reckon that jock might have been taking the piss just a little. They've got a very dry sense of humour, the Scots. Norton stopped for a moment and got his bearings. Still, even though I doubt very much whether I'll be sharing needles or hanging around any gay bars copping it up the Ford V8 while I'm in Jamaica, I don't think I'll be doing any bareback riding while I'm there either.

There were plenty of shops, restaurants and bars in the airport terminal, but Les couldn't quite believe it when he found the duty-free shop and it was closed until 2 p.m. Which meant he'd have to buy another Walkman in Jamaica. They'd probably be cheaper there anyway. He had plenty of time before his flight left so he had a bit of a look around. He didn't need any Tampa Bay Buccaneers T-shirts or souvenirs and he didn't feel like getting on the piss. What he could do with was something else to read on the trip over and while he hung around. Les roamed around past gift shops, flower shops, coffee lounges till he found a bookshop along one of the walkways. He was browsing through the magazines and books when something caught his eye and brought a smile to his face. Hello, what's this? Les chuckled to himself. Something for the mug tourists just like me. Two books with green, yellow and black covers. The *How To Be a Jamaican* handbook, and *Understanding Jamaican Patois*. The price was a typical airport rip-off, but Les bought both of them, walked back to a coffee lounge and ordered a coffee and a toasted ham-on-rye, then sat down and started boning up on a bit of Jamaican culture. P.J. O'Rourke didn't help him all that much with American

301

culture and he doubted if these would either. However, by the time he was on to his second bottomless cup of coffee Norton was pleasantly surprised.

The first book, *How To Be a Jamaican*, was a bit of a send up and whoever wrote it didn't mind taking the piss out of Jamaica and the Jamaicans. It explained about Boops and Boopsies, Rankins and Higglers. Everything from Hard Cards to Sunsplash. Rasta Queens to Drug Barons. The book then went on about other things, including running with the posse and how to look like a Rankin, which was a kind of Jamaican gang boss or hood. You wore a big, funny-looking leather cap, mirror sunglasses and a plain shirt hanging out over a pair of cammies, along with a lot of flashy jewellery, and you always looked cool. You don't walk, you bop, and you never smile, except when you're displaying your Uzi or AK-47 or are about to fire it. Another part said what kind of people drove what kinds of cars in Jamaica. Ganja barons and reggae stars drove Benzes or BMWs. BMWs were considered extra cool mon because the initials stood for Bob Marley and the Wailers. Rankins and ganja runners drove rentals. The book also stated that Jamaicans had their own standard of time. 'I'll be deh in a few minutes, mon' meant about an hour to an hour and a half. 'I'll be deh soon, mon' meant anything from five to ten hours.

The other book on Jamaican patois was a different thing altogther. Jamaica is an English-speaking country, but the natives have a lingo all of their own. A blend of Afro-Jamaican-English-Creole. A kind of Pidgin-English, except they drop letters, shorten words a lot then cross vowels with peculiar diphthongs while using the third person plural pronoun after the noun to indicate the plural. Which can all be very confusing. Especially if some Jamrite Rankin bops up to you and says, 'Ire mon, respect. So no bada fas wid mi. Yai I nung. Ongle one dege dege piece dem gi mi. I'm say. Im gooda all tief dem.' And you have to very diplomatically reply, 'Cool runnin' mon. He no tief dem. Dat deh a fi uno. Yu waan sum? No muss mon. No muss. So keep a cool head, mon.' Which basically means, 'Okay, mate, you know who I am so don't stuff me around. He only gave me one lousy piece of that and I reckon he pinched the lot anyway.' To which you say, 'Everything's okay. He didn't nick anything. And that there's for you anyway. You want some, don't you? Of course you do. So take it easy, everything's sweet.' Les read on, avidly figuring out expressions like, 'Im nen dwi.' 'A ja so dem deh?' 'No dunza no deh.' He was getting into it and thinking maybe a knowledge of patois might help him solve this so-called buried treasure thing, when before Les knew it his second cup of coffee had gone cold and it was time to make a move.

He got on the shuttle with about five others; this brought them out onto a landing then down another escalator to where the plane waited, which was like most airline departure areas anywhere in the world. While he boarded, Les checked out the other punters and tourists around him; there weren't all that many. Mostly business-looking types in shirts and ties, a few young college kids, some big blacks in their tracksuits with X all over them and a number of smaller, flashier blacks that Les tipped were Jamaicans going home. They filed onto the plane which was barely half full. Norton thought this a little odd, then remembered the girl at the tourist agency said this was the off-season. With the help of a toothy, American air hostess Les found his seat and sat down; the other two alongside were empty so Les had the row to himself. He spread himself around, stared vacantly out the window for a while, next thing he had his seat-belt on, the flight attendants were in the aisle giving escape procedures and they were on their way. Les didn't know quite what to think as he watched Florida falling away while the plane climbed steadily into the clouds. It was a funny feeling of empty nostalgia and incredulity. Suddenly Les brightened up, he could feel some sort of a vibe in the air. Yeah. Jamaica was going to be alright. There was a good vibe. It be cool runnin' all deh we tru. Yassah.

Les spread out all three books he had on Jamaica, plus

303

the book of Blackmore's poems. Shit, he chuckled to himself, I'll be talking like a native after two weeks of this. He got into it, browsing mainly, but taking things in; and it was good even if he didn't know what he was talking to himself about half the time. Les was still curious as to what a manse was though. Norton's concentration was only broken twice on the journey. Once when he was served a feed of tuna salad slopped with mayonnaise and an orange juice, and a second time when the pilot said they were approaching the outer limits of Cuba and nobody was allowed to take photos. Which meant every tourist immediately jumped up and started firing away out the nearest window with their instamatic. Which also made Les think of something. He had a brand new camera in his bag, full of film, ready to go, and he hadn't taken one photo in Florida. Maybe it's just as well, he shrugged. Who'd want to be reminded of that rathouse? But I'll be taking plenty in Jamaica. The pilot's voice came on saying they were expecting some turbulence and to remain seated and put your seat-belt back on. Les buckled up as the plane began to buck and lurch about. Outside the window now was nothing but grey-brown clouds.

The clouds went all the way to Jamaica. Norton kept reading away till the pilot's voice came on again to say they would soon be landing at Montego Bay. Still buckled up, Les put his books away and looked out the window as the plane began to bank. It was still very cloudy. There was a quick break in the clouds and Les got a glimpse of blue ocean, a low, brown mountain range dotted with greenery and a few houses. Then rain spattered against the window. Les checked his bag and made sure his passport and everything else was in order as the plane banked a couple more times. He placed his bag under the seat in front of him, the plane banked again, then, to the usual accompanying cheers of the American students to let everyone know it was an American pilot at the controls, the plane landed. Norton had made it. He was in Jamaica. He eased back in his seat and smiled. Two weeks of sun, sand and snorkeling. A bit of good tucker, a bit of whatever and look up a few dearly departed ancestors. Norton's smile turned into a grin. Jamaica baby. Tuan Norton is back in town.

Everybody filed leisurely off the plane and Les was thinking what a breeze Sir Donald Sangster Airport was compared to the mad stampede at Los Angeles. They walked along a dusty, green wooden corridor, which looked like it needed a hit with a broom and a bit more paint on it, before arriving at the baggage claim. There wasn't a great deal to look at while Les waited for his one bag — so he watched the other passengers, the Jamaican airport staff shuffling around in brown or blue uniforms, and a sprinkling of skinny, expressionless cops in their blue pants with a red trim, army shirts and red peaked caps with a wide red and blue checked band. The one thing Les did seem to notice was as well as looking pretty laid-back, the Jamaicans were about a third the size of the blacks in America.

Norton's flight was the only one landing so the luggage didn't take long to start coming round on the carousel; he picked up his bag and followed the others over to the customs area. There appeared to be four counters open, the lane was barely a third full and there was absolutely no crush at all. However, they seemed to be standing there for ages. Les looked ahead of him and noticed that the customs officers were giving everybody but the Jamaican nationals a good going over, opening up all their bags, making them pull just about everything out and taking their own sweet time while they went about it. They didn't appear to be looking for anything, it was more like they had some sort of a chip on their shoulder and they enjoyed fucking people over; especially tourists arriving with pockets full of money to spend in their country. Christ, thought Les, as he watched the sour-faced customs officers ratting through everybody's belongings. What the fuck would you smuggle into the place? According to those books I've been reading, nobody's got any money in the joint anyway. He shook his head and shuffled in behind what looked like some kind of businessman wearing a white shirt and brown trousers. Where Norton's face reflected a kind of curious disbelief, the businessman's was a mask of sullen aversion. He turned round and caught Norton's eye.

'Jolly good fun, isn't it?' he said, in a polite English accent that dripped sarcasm.

'What was that, mate?' replied Les.

'Good fun, isn't it? Standing around while the bastards sit on their black arses annoying you.'

'Annoying you?'

'Yes, the little shits. They love it.'

Les had another bit of a look around. 'Yeah. I suppose they are a bit slow,' he nodded.

'Slow? Hah! Wait till you leave. They queue you up in the heat for a bloody eternity, till everybody's half dead from dehydration.'

'What are they looking for?'

The businessman gave a bit of a shrug. 'Nothing really. They just like to annoy you. Let you know who's boss. Or rip you off.' He half smiled at the look on Norton's face. 'I suppose you're here on holiday?'

'Yeah. Couple of weeks.'

'First time?'

Les nodded. 'What about yourself?'

'Work.' The businessman shook his head. 'I wish to God I wasn't. They couldn't have picked a worse time to send me either.'

Les was somewhat curious at the man's last remark. 'What kind of work do you do?'

'I'm with an importing firm in London. We bring in Jamaican rum.'

'Oh. So I suppose you come here a fair bit, do you?'

'Yes,' the businessman seemed to nod and sigh at the same time. 'That's one thing about the place. The rum here is absolutely superlative.'

'I've heard that,' said Les. 'I'll have to give it a go.'

They shuffled forward a bit in the queue. There was

one woman in front of the Brit staring embarrassedly at her clothes and underwear spread out in front of her while the female customs officer dawdled through her passport.

'Say, mate?' said Les.

'Yes?' replied the Brit.

'You wouldn't happen to know what a manse is, would you?'

The Brit screwed up his face. 'A manse?'

'Yeah. M-A-N-S-E. Manse.'

The businessman seemed to think for a moment. 'It's a residence built for a clergyman. You know, like a vicarage.' The man stared at Norton's expressionless face. 'To be precise, it's a modest house provided by the parishioners for the minister.'

'Oh.'

Norton was still expressionless when the Brit dropped his bags on the counter. For a whingeing pom he seemed to get through quicker than anyone so far. Norton was still thinking about this explanation of the word manse when it was his turn.

The blue uniformed customs officer appeared to be in her mid-twenties, petite compared to the black women Les had seen in Florida, but completely unsmiling. She gave Norton's Dean Jones T-shirt a slow once up and down, looked at his passport, then made a brief gesture with her fingers that could have been either graceful elegance or sullen contempt.

'Open your bags.'

'Sure,' nodded the big Queenslander, knowing more or less by now what to expect.

Norton was thinking of trying out a bit of his newly acquired patois on her to see how clever he was but the look on her face made him change his mind. He opened his bags then the woman gestured for him to start unpacking them. Les got out his jeans, socks, trainers, towels, etc, till he came to his T-shirts. He placed them on the counter and the customs officer started flicking through them till she came to one with Craig McDermott on the front.

'These yu T-shirts?'

'Yeah,' said Les.

'I'd like one.'

Les gave a double blink. 'What?'

'I want one. Give me one.'

Les stopped blinking and handed her the Craig McDermott T-shirt. 'There you are, officer. It's all yours. Be my guest.'

'Sign it.' The woman glanced briefly at the look on Norton's face and handed him a biro. 'Sign it.'

Norton took the biro and wrote, 'All Jamaicans are dropkicks' across the front. 'Love, Craig Norton.' Then handed it to her again. 'There. That do you?'

The customs officer folded the T-shirt and put it under the counter, then stamped Norton's passport and waved him on without looking at him. Les pushed his bag along the counter and started repacking it. As he did, he turned back to the customs officer.

'Daht be wun gud bandulu you gon deh 'oman. Tanks for all deh chaka chaka. Dropkick.'

The customs officer looked around and stared quizzically at Les as the next passenger dumped his bags down in front of her; for a second it looked as if a puzzled half smile was going to flit across her face. Whether it did or not, Les didn't bother to smile back.

Norton got his bag packed then walked a short distance towards a set of stairs that led down to the arrival lounge. Set against the wall, just before the steps was a small, one man, money-changing office. Les figured it might be a good idea to cash a traveller's cheque and get some Jamaican money. A hundred bucks should do for a start. He walked up to the window, got out a book of traveller's cheques, signed one and pushed it under the glass without noticing a sign behind the cashier saying, $US.1 . . . $J.24. The cashier had short cropped hair, a cheap tie, a cheap white shirt and a sour face, pretty much like the customs officer. He looked at the traveller's cheque and pushed it back under the glass.

'Sign it again, mon.'

Les took his biro, squeezed his hand awkwardly against the small counter and signed the traveller's cheque again.

The cashier looked at it for a second and pushed it back. 'Sign it again,' he said bluntly.

Les screwed his face up slightly. 'Yeah righto,' he muttered quietly and again signed the traveller's cheque.

The clerk had another look at it and pushed it back. 'Sign it again,' he said.

Les stared at him. 'How do you want me to sign it? In bloody Ethiopian?'

'Same as in deh corner,' ordered the cashier.

The cashier pointed to Norton's original signature on the cheque. Cramped against the counter he'd scrawled the last two letters on his name slightly. Les felt like telling the cashier to shove his money up his arse. That bloke wasn't wrong about them getting their jollys by annoying you, he thought, as he shook his head and had another go. The cashier looked at the traveller's cheque like Les had poked a rotten fish under the glass. Next thing Norton had $2400 in Jamaican dollars in front of him that looked like a lot of red and blue monopoly money that had gone through several washing machines. He packed it into his wallet, jammed the almost bursting wallet into the back pocket of his jeans then picked up his bag and followed a couple of other passengers down the stairs into the arrival area. Les was about two-thirds of the way down the stairs when he stopped dead and gave a double, triple blink. Below and in front of him was a scene of hot, smoky, absolute pandemonium.

It looked as if every higgler, hustler, rankin, rorter, taxi driver, pickpocket or just plain dropkick for miles was there waiting to fleece every poor mug arriving that looked like they might have had a few dollars in their kick. To make matters worse, the airport wasn't all that big and what there was was being rebuilt or bodgied up so the rabble swarming around were almost cheek by jowl. Among the melee a few impassive-looking cops drifted or stood around looking as if they were trying to avoid as much work as possible. To top it off there weren't all that many people arriving and those who were a bit slow getting away were being attacked by the mob like piranhas. Les had barely got his foot off the bottom step when the first wave hit him.

'Hey, mon.'

'Hey, mon.'

'Hey c'mere, mon.'

'Taxi, mon.'

'Ire mon. I got something for you, mon.'

'Hey, mon. I look after you.'

'Hey, mon. Taxi. Cheapest in Mo' Bay.'

Norton looked at the sea of black faces in front of him and a few thoughts suddenly struck him. He was about the only honky in sight. He had $2400 Jamaican on him, about a grand or more in US dollars, plus all his traveller's cheques. And he had 'mug tourist' written all over him. He had to get to the resort and he knew if he didn't get robbed, stabbed or hit over the head on the way out he was going to get ripped off in a taxi anyway. Anything could happen. He only had to turn left at the airport, follow the main road along the ocean and Rose Point was two bays and a couple of other resorts away; he'd have to find it. Les spotted what he was looking for behind the howling rabble. He elbowed his way through the mob and a pod of backpackers getting into some rum-punch some higglers were flogging, and dropped his bag in front of the counter, with his foot through the strap, while keeping his other bag over his shoulder and his eyes open. The young lady in the Hertz uniform was quite pleasant with a nice bright smile.

'I'd like to hire a car please,' said Les.

'Certainly sir. May I see your driver's licence and some other ID please?'

'Yeah, sure.'

Les carefully slid his licence out, plus any other documents the girl might need, and handed it to her. She smiled and went to the computer. While she was doing that some bloke, not wearing a Hertz uniform, handed him some papers to fill in, saying he was getting a Honda Starlet and also gave him a map with Jamaica on one side and Montego Bay and its surrounds on the other. Les took his time filling in the paperwork while he switched off to the noise around him as best he could. Before long it was all done and the man and woman led him out to the carpark.

Outside it was overcast, steamy, dusty, with a blustery wind blowing after the rain, and it was hot; hotter even than Florida. By the time Les had walked a hundred yards or so to the carpark his T-shirt was soaked and sweat was dripping off his chin. The Honda Starlet turned out to be a reasonably clean, blue-grey Honda Accord. While the man checked it for any dings against a clipboard he was carrying the girl explained to Les he was up for the first 1000 dollars worth of damage. US, not Jamaican. Which wasn't a bad rort, mused Norton. The crate would be flat out bringing $750 at Auto Auctions on Saturday morning. Les signed one more paper, then the girl left, leaving Les and the bloke. He looked a little like Jerome only with thinner features.

'There you are, mon,' he said, handing Les the keys. 'You know where you're goin'?'

'Yeah,' nodded Les. 'Rose Point Resort. Up there, turn left on the main drag and it's about fifteen clicks.'

'Ire mon. But let me jus say something.' The bloke came a little closer. 'Any ting you want while yu here, mon, you come see me.'

'Anything, eh?'

'Sure, mon. You know what me sehin.'

'Alright. So what's your name anyway?'

'You jus ask for I'roy Darcy.'

'Okay Elroy. If I need anything, I'll keep you in mind. No worries yah seh.'

'Cool runnin', mon.'

Elroy left and Les crammed himself into the Honda, which after the Thunderbird felt like a box on a roller-skate. But it had a little T-bar automatic on the floor, it started okay, one scratchy speaker worked in the front and, best of all, you drove on the proper side of the road. With some unknown reggae song playing, Les spread the map out across his knees. It was bigger than the one in the travel book and there was Rose Point Resort, just past Umbrella Point, Mahoe Bay and some other resorts. Les folded the map up and had a bit of a look around him. The airport was just as big a shit fight outside as it was inside. Heaps of small battered Japanese cars and old rusty trucks and vans going everywhere. People wandering around among the dust, rubble and excavations and a sign above the front of the terminal saying, 'Jamaican Tourist Bureau Building a Better Airport'. I don't know, mused Les. Nothing wrong with the old one. Except for some of the cunts working there. Ahead of him was the main road and behind that a sparse slope of low mountains that didn't appear to hold too many trees or much vegetation. To the right old, low-rise buildings and houses led to central Montego Bay and behind him was the Caribbean. All up, nothing to get a horn over; though it wasn't much of a day. He slipped the Honda into drive and took off.

The streets behind the airport were narrow, edged with low stone walls and stunted trees and looked as if they hadn't seen a council repair gang since slavery was abolished. Les reached the main road and a sign saying Dredmouth and Ocho Rios; he turned left, put his foot down and started climbing up a narrow winding hill dotted with houses set among the scrubby-looking trees. The road levelled off and for its size the little car didn't go too bad. But for a main road it was pretty ordinary. No kerbs or guttering, no shortage of potholes and street signs were virtually non-existent. Les kept going, concentrating mainly on the odometer to see how far he'd come. After a while he settled down and started to have a bit of a look around. The countryside out of town was definitely nothing to get excited about although the ocean off to the left did look nice; though no nicer than the north or south coast of New South Wales. Other traffic rattled past and now and again jam-packed buses, which looked so old and battered that in Australia you'd have to have them resprayed and straightened up just to get them put off the road. All the time Jamaicans, with funny-looking eyes and strange hairstyles would jump out and yell at Les, trying to get a lift; they were that keen they almost dived in the front window. There didn't seem to be any wildlife except for a few goats wandering around the side of the road and a few more lying in the middle of it gathering flies and spreading guts until someone dragged them off and turned them into stew. The houses scattered along the side of the road now were nice though. They looked like wooden boxes about ten feet square with a slightly sloping tin roof and nailed together with any pieces of wood you could find. Walls would be blue, green, brown, black or unpainted wooden planks; anything went. Outside, a few skinny poles stuck in the ground formed a fence and around these tribes of ragged, dreadlocked kids would be playing in the dust. Les had never been in a third world country before, but already he could sense a feeling of poverty and deprivation. Keeping his bearings, Les noted a garage on the left, a small shopping centre, mainly full of tourist traps, on the right, a couple of resorts then he came up a hill to a crossroad that overlooked the ocean and there it was, Rose Point Resort. It was all cream coloured and resort looking, set on about ten acres of estate going back to the water, walled and wired off with a private beach at the rear. There were boomgates and guardhouses out the front and at first it reminded Les of a well-appointed prison. The reason was probably right across the road. Waiting round the intersection was another regiment of higglers and hustlers pouncing on anybody unlucky enough to fall into their clutches. Les slowed down for a quick look then drove down to the boomgates.

The security guard and his partner, in their grey uniforms and NY-cop style hats, took one look at Les and his rental car and waved him through. Les drove up to a palm tree lined front where a big lump of a man in a white outfit and matching pith helmet opened the door for him. Les got out and opened the boot, the man handed Les's bag to a smaller staffy in a blue uniform then parked the car for him a few metres away and brought back the keys. Les thanked him, slipped him some monopoly money and walked into the foyer behind the bloke with his bag. Inside was cool and like most international resorts or good hotels. Thick carpet, well lit, mirrors, murals and indoor plants everywhere with an indoor shopping arcade to the left and a long currency-exchange counter on the right hand side of the stairs leading up. There was no shortage of staff roaming around in white or blue uniforms and behind the reception desk were attractive women in brown and yellow dresses and men in blue DB jackets. Les thought he'd check it all out later, walked over and placed his reservation ticket and other ID on the counter. The girl was pleasantly efficient with a polite if practised smile.

'Hello,' smiled Les. 'I've got a booking here for two nights. Mr Norton.'

'Certainly, sir,' replied the girl, looking at Les's ticket. 'Just one moment.' She went to a computer, tapped around for a few seconds then came back. 'Yes, that's confirmed, sir.'

'Unreal,' smiled Norton, relieved there was no stuff-up.

Les signed the register, the porter took his bag and led him to his room, which was on the same floor. They turned right at the foyer and through a kind of entertainment area that overlooked the pool and the beach where a few people were sitting around on plush furniture watching some sports show on a giant screen TV. From there, Norton's room was right again, past an ice machine and almost at the end of the hallway. The porter opened the door, let Les in then placed his bag on the bed; Les slipped him some more of the monopoly money, not sure how much, but the bloke seemed happy enough as he closed the door behind him. Norton gazed around and decided to check out his deluxe suite. It was big enough, all white with green floral furniture and a small balcony at one end that gave a view of the ocean on the left, the sloping hills beyond the carpark on the right and the other balconies above and next to his. There were two double beds, no TV, no fridge and no mini-bar. The bathroom was nothing flash, all white with a shower, a dunny, the usual soap and towels. Les poured himself a glass of water, went back out and sat on a bed. Between the two beds was the phone and a small clock radio; Les turned it on and got some more reggae that sounded a bit clearer than in the car. Oh well, thought Les, taking a sip of water. It's clean enough, the beds are comfortable and the air-conditioner works. This'll do me for the next few days or whatever then I might go and check the rest of the place out. In the meantime, a scrub and some fresh clothes wouldn't go astray then I'll check this place out. You never know. There might be something happening here on Saturday night. Ire mon.

It was around six and, apart from the clouds blowing across the sky, still broad daylight when Les stepped out of his room, clean-shaven and smelling good in his blue shorts and red T-shirt with a white aboriginal crocodile motif on the front. He'd stuffed some money in his pocket, planted everything else and locked up as best he could and was thinking a nice cold beer or three wouldn't go astray as he strolled down the hall. He stopped in the TV lounge and was gazing out over the pool, banana lounges and bars below and thinking maybe he should have gone for a swim, when he sensed some sort of commotion at the bottom of the stairs down past the foyer. People were coming and going, a lot of them wore waiters' and chefs' outfits and seemed to be carrying either rolled up documents tied with red ribbon or medals. Curious, Les walked over then down the stairs, coming out into a smaller foyer or lobby in front of a hallway full of stalls covered in white tablecloths. Pinned to the foyer wall was a white banner that said 'Welcome to Jamaica Cultural Development Commission Culinary Arts Exposition'. There was a security guard in a grey uniform and blue tie at the door, Les asked him what was going on and got told it was some kind of exhibition and awards presentation for the best cook, cocktail waiter, staff, etc from hotels and resorts all over Jamaica. Les showed the guard his key, told him he was staying there and would it be alright if he had bit of a look around. The guard smiled and waved him through. When Les walked into the hallway he gave a double, quadruple blink and his jaw nearly hit the floor.

Most of the stalls had rum-punch, the rest food, and smiling company employees were handing out samples. Very healthy samples. With his mouth watering for a local version of a delicious, Les was about to attack when he thought he might have a look around first before he started making a pig of himself. He walked down past the stalls and the people to a double door at the end, opened it and stepped inside. It was a huge banquet or reception hall full of people crowded around more stalls and up on a stage at one end employees from different hotels were receiving awards from various dignitaries while their fellow employees and everybody else clapped and cheered their effort. Les watched for a little while then walked back outside and joined the people strolling around the stalls sipping glasses of whatever. He walked up to one stall that said 'Sangsters Olde Jamaican Spirits' and asked a man in crisp white if it was okay if he had a sample. The barman handed him a large glass, pointed to a sizeable esky full of ice and told him to help himself. A minute later Les had close to a schooner glass full of Sangsters Passionfruit Rum, ice and Guava Fruit Punch in his hand. Les took a sip and could scarcely believe what his tastebuds were telling him; it tasted like nothing on earth. Sweet, fresh, absolutely delicious, no noticeable bite and extremely easy to drink; the proverbial angels crying on your tongue. He took a swallow, then another, while he perused the stalls and checked out the people. Some soft reggae music started playing in the background and it started shaping up as one fantastic Caribbean party.

By the time Les reached one end of the stalls the schooner glass was empty and he felt like the top of his head was going to blow off. Christ, he thought happily. That bloke at the airport was right again. The rum here is superlative. Better than that — it's bloody beautiful. And how easy does it go down? A huge grin spread across Norton's face. And even better: it's bloody free. He looked out a window and smiled up at the sky. Fancy lobbing in the middle of this. I always knew you loved me, boss. And when didn't you ever? Les went back to the Sangsters stand and helped himself to some mango rum this time. No one said a word; if anything they encouraged him so there'd be less for them to pack up. By the time Les had downed another three schooners his face looked like a big, scarlet, medicine ball and if someone had shoved a light bulb in his mouth it would have lit up. On top of that, Les couldn't remember ever feeling so happy, or drunk. He filled another schooner glass and with the deck moving slightly beneath his feet ambled back into the reception area to watch the awards and do a bit of cheering for the local team himself. However, it was all over now bar the shouting and everybody was packing up getting ready to leave. Any food lying around inside was either help yourself before it got ditched or somebody beat you to it. What was still lying around looked good and smelled good, and pissed and all as he was, Les knew that a bit of food on top of all the booze wouldn't go astray at all. With the utmost decorum, the big, red-headed Queenslander attacked.

Rather than stumble drunkenly around from table to table, bumping into people and probably dropping food everywhere, Norton chose to rape and pillage the table closest to him. It was some catering firm from Ocho Rios, the staff were clearing things away and didn't seem to mind at all when Les put down his drink, got a plate and fork and got stuck into what was left. First up was white fish fillets marinated in ortanique; a kind of orange and tangerine. The first bite almost brought tears of joy to Norton's eyes. He had five pieces. Next was peppered shrimp with red beans and a ginger and coconut sauce. Les had two plates, but left room for some crab balls in chilli and naseberry. These did bring a tear to his eye and Les was a bit worried they'd ignite the rum roaring through his body so he had a bowl of Matrimony to cool off a little, which was orange segments and star apple pulp in cream. That was more than enough. Les belched quietly, wiped his mouth on the tablecloth then picked up his drink and went back outside.

It was considerably more crowded now with the over-flow from the banquet hall. Les found a spot at the end near a stall for the Negril Commodity Company, staffed by three pretty girls in white, gold and red dresses and enormous pink and green straw hats. Apart from them, however, it was all fairly conservative. Most of the women wore plain, pastel dresses, the men either coloured or white shirts tucked into their trousers with maybe the odd safari or sports jacket. Apart from Les and a couple of wide-eyed Japanese tourists holding a mango someone had given them like it was the Hope Diamond, the people were all Jamaicans. A reggae track came on that Les recognised, Bob Marley's 'Exodus', and Norton felt like singing and getting down he was in that good a mood, then thought maybe it was best he didn't; he was horribly drunk. But not that drunk that he couldn't get another mandarin rum and fruit punch. With his fresh delicious clutched firmly in his hand Les went back to where he'd been standing and gazed happily into the crowd, still not believing his luck landing in the middle of a do like this and still not believing how drunk he'd got in such a short space of time. He took a large swallow and was smiling contentedly to himself when he heard a familiar English voice just to his right.

'I see you managed to clear customs alright.'

Les turned and blinked. It was the bloke from the airport. He'd freshened up noticeably and changed into a pair of neat, light blue trousers and a mauve silk, button-down collar shirt; round his neck a thin gold chain glinted in the light.

'Oh, g'day mate,' smiled Les. 'How are you goin' there? Hey, you needn't talk about customs. You got through okay. I got stiffed for a bloody T-shirt.'

'I thought you might have,' smiled the bloke. He looked at Les curiously. 'Have you been out in the sun or something?'

'Out in the rum'd be more like it. Have a look at me, I'm marinated! Christ! You weren't wrong about the local brew. It's unbelievable.'

The bloke shook his head slightly. 'You're stewed to the gills,' he said.

'Pissed as a fart,' agreed Norton. 'And it's partly your fault. You sell the bloody stuff.' Les winked and raised his glass. 'You ever thought of sending a tankerload to Australia? Fill the Exxon Valdez and wreck it just off Bondi. Where I love. Left. Live. Shit! I'm nice 'n' drunk.'

'Do tell! One would never have guessed.'

Les introduced himself and said he was staying at the resort for a while and he'd be in Jamaica for a couple of weeks. The bloke said his name was Nigel, he was in the hotel on business and he was staying on the other side of Montego Bay at the Royal Caribbean Hotel and Beach Club.

'So you don't mind the local rum?' said Nigel easily. He had a kind of half smile on his face when he spoke to Les, as if he found him likeable enough, no rocket scientist, yet not your average yobbo Australian tourist.

'Oath!' said Norton emphatically.

'Have you tried the local dacca?'

'The 'erb, mon?' said Les.

'That's the one,' nodded Nigel.

'No I haven't.'

'Do you want to?'

Les blinked for a moment then looked evenly at Nigel. 'Yeah, righto. Why not?'

'You got ten bucks US on you?'

Even in his drunken state Norton was a little dubious. Nigel didn't seem the type to be hanging around places, flogging ten dollar deals of pot. 'Yeah,' nodded Les.

'Well give it to me, and I'll send someone over.'

'You'll send someone over.'

'That's right. Hey Les, I'm no dealer. But I know a chap here who's got some. I'll fix it up for you.'

'Okay,' shrugged Les, he slipped a ten out of his pocket and gave it to Nigel.

'Stay here. He'll be over in about five or ten minutes.'

'You coming back?'

'Maybe,' said Nigel. He gave Les a wink. 'I do have to work, you know. Not like some.'

Nigel disappeared through the banquet hall doors, leaving Les staring at the floor. Well, what's going on? Have I scored some puff, or have I been conned for a broody hen by some shit-pot, pommy hustler? More than bloody likely. Oh well, who gives a stuff? I reckon I've had a hundred and ten dollars worth of food and drink here this arvo. Les took another slurp of his drink and swayed a little to the music.

About five or six minutes ticked by and a skinny Jamaican about thirty drifted out of the crowd and up to Les. Apart from a goatee beard he didn't look like a rankin or a hood. He wore a blue peaked cap, a white Bonds type of T-shirt with 'Marlin Club' on the pocket, and baggy, stone-washed jeans. With his hands in his pockets and this dreamy expression on his face he looked like a Jamaican Maynard Krebbes.

'Hey mon,' he said quietly. 'I got suntin' for you.'

Les held his hand out in front of him like he was going to shake the Jamaican's. The bloke palmed something into it and by the time Les emptied his hand into his own pocket and took it out again the bloke had disappeared into the crowd. Well, how about that, thought Les, taking another sip of rum. Looks like I got a bit of puff after all.

The crowd was starting to thin out now and most of the stalls had packed up, taking what was left with them. Not that Les needed any more to drink for the time being; as well as the rum hitting him, now he was starting to notice he'd had hardly any sleep the night before, and if he was going to have a sniff around later on he'd better ease up. Les also didn't want to be walking around with a pocketful of dacca either. He finished his drink and went back to his room.

The face staring back at Norton in the bathroom

mirror looked like it was going to explode any minute and should be sitting on a park bench with either a bottle of metho or a flagon of cheap brown muscat; definitely not tarting it up in some classy hotel. Christ, he thought, as he slopped some water over his face then swallowed a glassful. Another two bloody weeks of this and I'll go back home embalmed from the inside out. Les slopped some more water on his face. Anyway, let's see what I got for my ten bucks. He walked into the bedroom, flopped clumsily on the bed and emptied out his pocket.

It looked like three squashed up licorice allsorts bound in Gladwrap, only a dark, almost chocolate brown. Les opened one up and the sweet, pungent smell hit him straight away, and when he rubbed some between his fingers it was almost as sticky as tree sap. Well, well, well, Les smiled to himself. It looks like pot, feels like pot, and it sure smells like pot. In fact, I'd say if it ain't, it's that close it don't make no bloody difference. Les rubbed his fingers again and sniffed them. In fact, I don't remember ever seeing stuff like this. Close maybe. Still, there's only one way to find out if it's any good. Smoke it. Les sat on the bed thinking for a moment and then rolled the ganja back up and planted it under one bed. Well, if I'm going to organise that, I can have a walk and maybe a swim at the same time. He got a towel from the bathroom, locked his room and wandered off down the hallway.

The sun was setting and it was almost dark now. There was a door on the right past the TV lounge, Les took it and came out onto a fairly spacious entertainment area. There were white chairs and tables, a bar set against the wall to the right and a dais with a small stage in front. The speakers and musical instruments suggested it was set up for a band. Soft lighting played through the palm trees, indoor plants and flowers and everything overlooked the pool and beach below. Apart from some of the staff roaming around it was empty. Les took a set of stairs to his left, which led down through more flowers and palm trees to the pool area.

The pool was about fifty metres square at the shallow

end then angled off to a deep end about the same size; built out into the shallow end was a bar and concrete stool where you could swim up and have a drink if you so desired. All around this were white banana lounges and chairs and tables with what looked like huge, thatched umbrellas above them made from palm trees. Everything was set among manicured lawns, tropical flower gardens and more palm trees. A food servery, which was closed, sat on one side of the pool. Les had a quick look around. There was no one about except for a few staff cleaning things or tidying up. Les followed the pool to a set of sandstone steps leading onto the private beach. There were two security guards standing next to some chairs and tables at the top of the stairs having a cigarette; Les gave them a smile and a wave, they nodded slowly back.

The beach was no great shakes. About 150 metres of coarse sand running either side of the steps to a couple of manmade headlands with a few small waves washing over a reef a couple of hundred metres out from the shore. It was overcast, with a blustery on-shore breeze; Les decided to brush the beach till the morning and have a swim in the pool. On the way back up the steps he thought he might ask the security guards if it was okay to use the pool now and what was going on upstairs? Sorry, mon. The pool's closed till the morning. And upstairs was a band and a female singer. But the two guards were alright, one even asked where Les came from and seemed a little interested when Les said Australia. Norton even got a laugh out of them when he assured them he wasn't an American and started taking off a whining, mid-west American accent almost to perfection. They enjoyed Les bagging seppos and it wasn't hard to see where the locals' sentiments lay when it came to American tourists. Les was almost tempted to start up a conversation with them about reggae music and cricket, but between his drunken slurring and their patois he thought he might just say goodnight and quit while he was in front. The two guards said they'd probably see him tomorrow night, there was another band and an open-air banquet in the gardens next to the beach over to the right. Les thanked them and wandered off to the shopping arcade.

Apart from the staff, there was hardly anybody in the foyer when Les came up the stairs, especially for a Saturday evening. The shopping arcade, which held the usual shops full of rip-off clothes, jewellery and souvenirs, was completely empty. Only one shop was open and it was getting ready to close; the girl doing up the cash register didn't quite give Les a big cheerio when he walked in. The shop was a kind of chemist-papershop, selling chocolate, magazines, booze, aftershave, etc. Les was able to buy six cans of Diet 7-Up, a bottle of Sangsters Passionfruit Rum and a Bic lighter. Les had the right money so the girl didn't have to do too much; she still didn't smile, however, even if Les did. Fair enough though, mused Norton, as he walked out with his purchases. I suppose I am just another late-night drunk. They can be a pain in the arse at times.

Back in his room Les put the cans of 7-Up in the bath and the rum on a small table opposite the two beds. There was an ice container sitting on the table, he took it down to the ice machine and filled it to the brim. Back in his room again, Les thought it might be an idea if he had a long, cold shower and freshened up a little before he had another drink. The cold shower did the trick and feeling noticeably better he changed into his clean Emu Bitter T-shirt, turned on the radio and made himself a small rum and 7-Up, which tasted very, very nice indeed. With some reggae music playing softly in the background Les emptied the can of 7-Up in the sink, got a hanky from his bag and a safety pin from his shower kit, thinking if he was going to smoke that shit with no papers he was going to have to make a machine.

The bloke that showed Les how to make a machine was a country bloke called Lockie, who came to Sydney to play football and ended up doing two years over a truckload of hot bourbon. When he got out of the nick he stayed at Norton's place for a couple of days before he went back to Tamworth. One night Lockie got hold of some hash and showed Les and Warren how they used to make machines in gaol for smoking dope. All they really were were throwaway bongs or chillums, and they weren't the most pleasant way of smoking pot or whatever; just a super quick way of getting out of it and which left nothing much lying around. But they definitely worked, as Lockie proved to both Les and Warren that night back at the house. Norton twisted the ring-pull off the can, flattened the can out a little so it wouldn't roll around then put an indentation at one end of the can opposite the hole you drank from. With the safety pin he made several small holes in the indentation then wet his hanky, wrapped it round the end of the can where the hole was, something like you would a jar, and tied it loosely underneath. And that was it. The idea was you sprinkled the dacca or whatever you had over the holes, lit it and sucked like mad through the straw hole, where the wet hanky cooled the smoke down slightly so you didn't quite cough your lungs up all over the place. When he'd finished Les looked at his handiwork sitting on the table next to the bottle of rum and give it a nod of grudging approval. Yep. I reckon that ought to do. Now, where's the 'erb, mon? He groped around under the bed, got it out and started crumbling some up into a saucer. Shit! This stuff is bloody stickier then I thought. I hope it'll burn alright.

Before long Les had a small pile of ganja sitting on top of the holes in the can; he held it up to his mouth and picked up the lighter. Les was about to thumb it when he stopped and looked at himself in the mirror. Shit! What am I doing? I'm not a mull head. I'm just a poor silly drunk. In fact, I'm that drunk, I don't know what I am. The face in the mirror suddenly grinned back. Yes I do. I'm a Norton. And this is my turf. Let's go. Les thumbed the lighter and sucked through the hanky.

The first toke didn't go down too bad; it never burnt his lungs, he didn't start coughing everywhere and the ganja tasted okay, quite sweet, not unlike the hash Lockie had that night. Nothing much happened as far as getting stoned, though. Oh well, shrugged Les and loaded the machine again. Bong number two was a little livelier, but definitely no great hosanna. Elvis didn't come floating down out of the sky and Mickey, Donald and Goofy didn't start dancing round the room. Les waited a few moments then loaded up again. The third one did the trick. Les took a sip of his drink, sat back and the first things he noticed were his body currents and the electricity inside him starting to vibrate and the music picked up, then it all went weird, like he was looking at everything through a prism. Not realising how drunk and tired he was, Les hadn't given the first two tokes a chance to sink in. One probably would have been enough. Now he had three good ones rocketing around inside his brain like a nuclear reaction and it had barely just been detonated over ground zero. Oh yes, Norton nodded to himself. This stuff works alright. And I think it's a bloody creeper too.

The Jamaican ganja crept up on Les alright. His fingers and toes looked to be miles away and everything appeared to intensify and slow down; just to open and close his hand seemed to take five minutes. Everything was now some kind of virtual unreality and it was all happening in slow motion. He slowly swivelled his head around towards the tiny radio between the beds that was now starting to sound like a pair of Bose speakers. Some reggae track faded out and the DJ's deep voice rolled in, announcing the next track as 'Name Dem Out' by Daddy Shark. The singer started rabbiting away at a hundred miles an hour in a rap-patois that was totally incomprehensible and undecipherable, but Les was certain he could understand every word he was saying.

'Name dem out. Daddy Shark name dem out.'

'Remember Charlie Chaplin name dem Rastafarah.'

That was enough for Norton. Next thing he was on his feet and boogying around the room with his drink in his hand like a man possessed.

He danced his way down to the balcony, stepped outside and stood in the dark, moving loosely to the music coming through the curtains behind him while the nuclear reaction in his brain sent thoughts and ideas spinning everywhere. There was no moon or stars and not much to see except one massive grey cloudbank being blown towards the low silhouette of the mountains to his right. Then the weirdest thought hit Les. It was like he'd been there before; this bizarre feeling of déjà vu. Les could see the pirate ships, the slaves in the sugar fields, the women walking round in their crinoline dresses, holding parasols above their heads to shade their faces. Les knew he was drunk and well and truly out of it, but this feeling was too strong to be imagination. There was something there for sure. Some kind of bond going back hundreds of years. A funny little tingle went up and down Norton's spine and goosebumps began to pepper his arms. He stared into the darkness for a while as more wondrously crazy thoughts exploded through his mind then went back inside.

The reggae coming from the radio seemed to be filling the room and sounded pretty good. Yet Les couldn't help but think. Shit! How would a good stereo go now and a few of my tapes? Absolutely sen-bloody-sational. He took a sip of rum and 7-Up and stared at the funny-looking bloke in the mirror as more fascinating thoughts and perceptions swirled round inside his head. Well, it's all very nice grooving around in here thinking as if I'm the Dalai Lama. But. There's a band playing right on my doorstep and this pot and booze has got me just about knackered. I reckon I ought to go check out Mo' Bay on Saturday night because in about two hours I'm going to crash. Les took another sip of drink and winked at the bloke in the mirror. The bloke nodded back. Yes, a jolly good idea. He rolled himself into a pair of jeans, got some money and things together then laughing away at absolutely nothing drifted out the door.

Norton cruised up the hallway then took a left into the TV lounge on one leg, almost like Charlie Chaplin. Whether Les was paranoid about people looking at him didn't make any difference, they were anyway; it was a while since anyone had seen an entrance like that. He opened the door and floated out into the entertainment area landing softly among the chairs and tables like Peter Pan. There weren't that many people around, twenty at the most, mostly Americans in casual gear with their wives and girlfriends or whatever. Naturally they all stopped what they were doing and looked at Les. Norton didn't take that much notice. All he knew was that if he didn't sit down soon he was likely to drift off into the night sky and start singing 'The Banana Boat Song', thinking he was Harry Belafonte. There was an empty table almost in front of the small stage set up in front of the bandstand. He drifted over to it and sat down, dropping his room key on the table. Some sort of light, reggae-disco music drifted out of the speakers. It sounded pleasant enough and seemed to melt in with the surroundings. Les sat staring ahead as the ganja spread through him some more and thought that any second now and he was going to melt into the chair. From out of nowhere an apparition in black and white appeared at his table. Hello, thought Les. This is it. I'm being asked to leave. The T-shirt and joggers. I knew it was too good to be true.

'Good evening, sir. May I get you something?'

Completely Chinese-eyed, Les looked up at the waiter. It was bloody Harry Belafonte. No, his young brother. 'Banan... banana. Banana daiquiri please.'

'Certainly, sir.'

The waiter left with Norton staring blankly after him. What did I just do? Order a bloody banana daiquiri? I'm not a yank. I'm an Australian. I want a Vegemite one. I do? No, I don't. Shit! I don't know what I want. Les sat staring in front of him trying to figure out what he was thinking about, when the waiter returned and placed a huge, fluffy, white drink in front of him full of tiny pink umbrellas, pieces of fruit on toothpicks and other junk. He looked at Norton's room key and offered him the receipt and a biro. Hello, what's this? thought Les. He wants an autograph. He thinks I'm an aussie cricketer too. Hang on a minute. Norton began to sense this giant, enormous brainstorm arriving and forming in his mind. I can charge the drinks to my room. I'm a bloody genius. He took the biro and hesitated for a second. How many Ts in Norton? There's only one, isn't there? Yeah, right there is. Les signed the receipt and the waiter smiled. As he was about to move off Les handed him some monopoly money.

'Thank you, sir,' he smiled again.

Well, what about that? How clever am I? Charge it to my room. I'll bet there's not too many people round here would have known how to do that. Les glanced around at the other drinkers, convinced they were all staring at him. Probably the lot of them. Christ! That shit's worse than I thought.

Norton settled back in his chair and mellowed out into the music and the night and took a sip of his drink. It was unbelievably sweet and delicious. He took another sip, a bigger one, and started thinking again and laughing to himself. Bloody hell! What's wrong with this? I'm pissed, stoned, sitting back in a top hotel waiting for a band to come on, and I got two weeks or more to go. I got plenty of pot, all the grouse rum I can get my hands on and a heap of chops to spend. He took another slurp of his drink. Shit! I could think of worse places to be. Like freezing to death back in Sydney. In a Florida gaol. Stuck with Captain Rats back at Swamp Manor. Instead, I'm in Jamaica drinking daiquiris. I think I'm in front somehow. Les was sipping his drink, laughing and thinking to himself how lucky he was, when there was movement on stage. Four men in white tuxedos got behind some drums, guitars and an electric piano. The lead singer on bass guitar eased up to the mike and smiled out over the small crowd.

'Good evening, ladies and gentlemen,' he crooned. 'We're the Tego-Tones. We'd like to play for you for a while, before our lovely singer comes on to entertain you. Jamaica's own princess of song, Melanni Mystique. Thank you.'

The lead singer nodded to the others and they slipped

easily into some well-rehearsed, middle of the road, West Indian type of music. It was nothing spectacular, but it sounded pretty good to Les and if he closed his eyes he could imagine there were twenty up on stage instead of four. The music surrounded him, some notes hung in the air, others just seemed to drift off into the night sky. He ordered another two daiquiris and mellowed out some more, not thinking about a great deal in general; any thoughts he did have seemed to drift off into the night along with the music. After all the shit that went down in Florida Les couldn't believe how peaceful and relaxed he now felt.

Eventually the band stopped and the lead singer started up on some spiel that ended with, '... and now would you please welcome on stage, our very own Melanni Mystique.'

There was a ripple of applause and a slender woman, somewhere in her mid-twenties, stepped out onto the small stage. She wore white slacks, gold high-heels and a red, black and gold lame top. Her hair was bobbed short over a pretty face with full red lips and a pearly white smile that seemed to sparkle in the light.

'Good evening, ladies and gentlemen,' she beamed, as if she was playing a packed Sands at Las Vegas instead of twenty mildly interested American tourists and one drunk, stoned, but very enthusiastic Australian, 'I'd like to welcome you to the Rose Point Resort at Montego Bay on my beautiful island of Jamaica.' Melanni then went into her spiel about how wonderful it was to be here and entertain you, and how one visit to Jamaica wasn't enough and everybody always came back, etc, etc. Then she nodded to the band and cut into some song about Montego Bay, palm trees, beaches and love. She sounded good.

Les sat back and enjoyed the show and tried to think who the girl reminded him of. A whippy Dionne Warwick; she sang and held the notes almost exactly like her. It was a typical resort type show; fairly laid-back and don't excite the guests too much. But no matter what,

Melanni could warble like there was no tomorrow. The way she delivered the songs and held the notes almost brought tears to Norton's eyes. Any thoughts Les had about Dionne Warwick were justified when Melanni cut into 'Always Something There To Remind Me'. If the other songs almost brought tears to Norton's eyes, this one actually did. The big Queenslander couldn't help it. The high notes seemed to cut into him like a knife and he brimmed over. She did 'The More I See You', 'The Look of Love', 'Easy Skankin'', and more. All middle of the road stuff, but Les clapped like mad, dragging the other guests along with him. She finished the night then came on for an encore with 'No Woman No Cry' and brought the small house down. Les was a shot duck after that.

The band played a few more numbers but nobody got up and danced, and outside the night wasn't doing much except starting to drizzle. Les stared out into the night and at the lights flickering above the beach through the raindrops. Just like the rain, everything started to come down around him too. Les was stuffed. But what a night it had been. What a day, for that matter. That morning he'd been in America, now he was in Jamaica. And it was time he put his head down. He finished his last drink and left some money on the table. He was going to ring for a taxi but decided to walk home, it wasn't all that far. Norton weaved his way through the tables and back to his room.

The room wasn't quite spinning when he walked in, but it was certainly changing directions a bit. He climbed out of his clothes then poured himself a 7-Up and ice and took it out on the balcony; there wasn't much to see except light rain and darkness so he went back inside. The radio was starting to crackle and fade, Les decided to switch it off, along with the lights, and throw the towel in. He climbed into bed, pulled a sheet over him and lay back with his eyes closed staring into nothing except what looked like coloured, hexagonal snowflake patterns bursting over mountains behind his eyelids as he drifted off into the cosmos. Well, here I am, thought Les.

Jamaica. I've found my spiritual roots. Nirvana. I've finally reached a higher plain of consciousness. I am the bloody Dalai Lama. Norton thought for a moment. Shit! What would I do if I *was* the Dalai Lama? He yawned and burrowed his head further into the pillow. Probably walk into the nearest Pizza Hut and say 'make me one with everything'. Buggered if I know.

Norton didn't feel all that bad when he surfaced the following morning. He didn't feel all that good either; but at least the face staring at him in the bathroom mirror didn't look like a supernova this time round. Christ! What a landing that was, mused Les, wiping a towel over his face. Talk about 'work all night on a drink of rum'. Reckon. And what about that Bob Hope? I think I'll be keeping that in the bottom drawer for special occasions only. He got a glass of water and went out onto the balcony. It was grey and overcast outside with the same blustery wind blowing, but still as oppressively hot and humid as ever. Les went back inside into the cool, sipped his water and plotted what he was going to do. Norton had given up on the idea of leaving the air-conditioners off by now. Heat was heat. But this humidity was almost enough to drown you, and whether or not air-conditioning gave you the flu, pneumonia or legionnaires' disease, it was staying on. He didn't have to pay the power bill anyway. Well, a swim in the pool would be okay. Or even better, a snorkel round that reef in the warm, blue Caribbean. Then breakfast. And if it's not too early in the day I might even make another decision later on. I'm a live wire.

Feeling in a pretty good mood Les climbed into a pair of shorts and a T-shirt and cleaned up last night's evidence, in case the cleaner should come in. Still whistling softly to himself Les got his snorkeling gear, and with his sunnies on his face and a towel under his arm headed for the hotel beach.

Part of the previous night's entertainment area had been converted into a breakfast buffet. An elderly lady in a black maid's uniform opened the door for Les and he stepped out to where about ten yanks and a couple of Japanese were sitting around eating. It all looked good and it certainly smelled good. Don't worry gang, smiled Les, his stomach starting to rumble as he walked down the stairs to the pool area. I'll be back shortly. With a vengeance. He walked past the pool and down the sandstone steps onto the beach. There were barely half a dozen guests there, and about as many staff, standing around a few catamarans and windsurfers, their flags and cables fluttering or rattling in the on-shore breeze. A row of banana lounges went off to the left, Les had a quick look around and trudged off in that direction. The tide was right up and what sand there was seemed gritty and coarse. The water swirling round his ankles felt warm and looked like weak Lime Kooler after someone had tipped milk into it. The choppy windswell, washing over the reef about two hundred yards out, looked murky and chunderous also. Definitely not an inspiring sight. So much for the sparkling blue Caribbean, grimaced Norton. Still, it was raining fairly steadily last night. Anyway, I'm here now. A few more metres past the last banana lounge, he got into his snorkeling gear and plunged in.

The ocean temperature was the same as in Florida, but the water absolutely filthy; you could barely see five feet because of the run-off from the rain. Les swam on, bumping into rocks and lumps of dull brown coral; the water was hardly a metre deep in parts, but you wouldn't know how deep it was till you swam into something. Les put his head down and ground on till he finished up washing against the granite headland at one end. So far he'd seen absolutely nothing except murky, swirling water; he didn't even see the headland until he banged into it. Ohh fuck this, he cursed, pushing himself away from the rocks. It's like a shithouse. Somewhat disgruntled, he swam straight in, walked back along the beach and picked up his gear, then went back to the hotel.

Except for a couple of Japanese and a few kids, there was hardly anybody in the pool; Les dumped his stuff on a nearby banana lounge and dived straight in. After the salty, choppy mess on the beach it was delightful. He did a few laps, swam into the deep end and duck dived up and down, even lay on his back and spurted water up in the air like a whale. It wasn't hard to take and Les flopped around for quite a while, thinking he'd definitely spent worse mornings. His spirits restored and his hunger starting to mount, Les finally climbed out, towelled himself off and went back to his room to tidy up.

The same smiling woman, old enough to be Norton's mother, opened the door for him when he returned, making Les feel a little self-conscious; he felt like telling her he was big and ugly enough to open a door without some poor old lady opening it for him. But it was probably her job and even if it didn't feel right he just smiled back and said nothing. There was a new scrum of about ten diners now, all yanks, stuffing themselves with the glurpiest food they could find while their loud, whiny accents seemed to ricochet from table to table. It was punishing, but Les was that hungry now he wouldn't have been distracted from his food even if he'd landed in the middle of a Hitler youth rally. He went up to the girl on the till, showed her his key and signed the chit.

'So what do I do now, miss?' asked Les, looking at the tables full of food. 'Start here and just work my way along?'

'That's right, sir. Just help yourself.'

'Thank you,' smiled Les.

He picked up a plate then changed his mind and got a bowl, thinking he might go for a big feed of fresh fruit first washed down with chilled juice. By the time Les sat down his bowl was overflowing with sliced melon, pink banana, mango, star fruit and anything else that was peeled and colourful, along with two large glasses of guava and orange juice. There was that much fruit he had to get another two glasses of juice to wash it down. Next, Les got a plate and found the Jamaican spicy sausages, the scrambled eggs with gungo peas and shallots, fried tomatoes and heaps of other tasty little morsels. Les ripped into this with more fruit juice and finished off with three bammie cakes and two strong cups of Jamaican coffee thick enough to bog a duck. Well, thought Les, belching delicately into his serviette, I think that might do me for the time being. One certainly can't complain. He left some money on the table for the waiter who'd been clearing away his mess, then strolled over to the balcony and gazed contentedly out over the ocean. He was only standing there a few moments when a bit of a rumble went through his stomach. Mmmhh. Those gungo peas don't take long to get moving. S'pose I may as well leave another tip for someone before I go. As Les walked past a table of four, revoltingly dressed seppos doing their utmost to let everyone in the hotel know they were from Pocatello, Idaho, he dropped his key. When he bent down to pick it up, Norton silently and discreetly, like a true gentleman, slid out a long, withering fart that could only be described as inhumane. As the elderly lady opened the door for him again, Les smiled and stopped. That's funny, he thought. Am I getting another sense of déjà vu? He turned round to where the team from Pocatello, Idaho, were choking and gagging into their hash browns and pancakes as if a mustard gas shell had burst next to their table. I wonder how my old mate Peregrine's going? He'd be enjoying his breakfast this morning, a bit better than those seppos, I'd reckon.

Back in his room Les poured himself a glass of 7-Up, took it out onto the balcony and stared out over the countryside, thinking what he should do. There was no reggae coming down from the radio, only church music. That's right. It's bloody Sunday. I almost forgot. Praise the Lord or jah rastafarai, as the locals might say. More church music played, causing Les to think. Yes, if I was any sort of a decent bloke I'd go to church on a Sunday myself. But I'm not a decent bloke and I don't know where I'd find a church. But I think I know where there's something close to a church. A manse. According to that book, the Nortons have got one not far from here. He got the book on Jamaica and his map and spread them out on the bed. According to the map Dredmouth was about thirty or so kilometres along that same coast road in a kind of bay. And the book told you just about exactly where the manse was; down the end of Holding Street, past the post office, west of the town square fountain. Les stared at the book and map for a moment then clapped his hands together. That's what I'll do. I'll go check out the Norton Manse. Let's make a move.

He got his backpack, threw his camera in it, plus a few other things, and walked out the door. After leaving his key at the desk, the same bloke in the pith helmet got his car for him and brought it round the front. Les tipped him, squeezed in behind the wheel of the Honda then drove through the boomgates and swung left towards Dredmouth. The drive out was easy enough, the road, though narrow and in need of repair, was flat and fairly straight, with the same scrubby bush on either side. A low, stone wall ran along part of the ocean side of the road where, considering how overcast it was, the water over the seemingly endless reefs running out to sea was now a deep, iridescent blue. The same crazy-quilt houses dotted the countryside along with a few bigger ones. There were more resorts, golf clubs, light traffic and people jumping out at the car, hoping to get a lift, to keep you occupied. Les drove steadily on past some rundown-looking zoo where a sign said, 'Scenes From James Bond Movie Shot Here'. Might have a look in there one day before I go back and take some photos, mused Les as the road turned inland and the sign disappeared in the rear vision mirror.

A smattering of ramshackle houses, semis, the odd shop and several narrow streets running off the road he was on appeared out of the scrub now, telling Les he was approaching town. If he was right, this road should lead right into the village square. More people began to appear, walking or standing around, the houses got more congested till they became two-storey jobs or shops with rickety wooden balconies sitting on splintery wooden poles set into concrete footpaths crumbling away beneath. Everything looked old and rundown with the predominant colour either dull brown or faded dark blue. A sign above one balcony said, 'Red Stripe Beer — Club 500'. Lounging about underneath was a group of shabbily dressed, morose-looking men with odd-looking eyes and dreadlocks either tumbling all over the place or tucked up under huge, coloured beanies. They all gave Norton a heavy perusal as he drove past, some started yelling things out at him. Hello, thought Les, the natives are friendly. Yeah, too fuckin' friendly if you ask me, and despite the heat Les wound both front windows up. A bit further on he passed a corner with what looked like a small supermarket on it that said William Lee Shung and he was in the village square.

A dirt-stained, bone dry fountain with a few pieces of rusting, wrought-iron around it sat in the middle and the surrounding area looked like scenes Les had seen on TV in documentaries from places like Haiti or Guatemala. Old Japanese rust buckets parked or spluttering around, ramshackle wooden shops, men and women strolling about or lounging beneath the balconies trying to escape the heat. Dogs and goats wandering around among the dirt, smoke and dust, and if everyone was wearing their Sunday best, Sunday was definitely too far away. An old, faded, blue wooden building on the left had Post Office painted on it in white and not far from that a sign said Holding Street; Les swung a quick left, almost clipping several people, an old car and a couple of two-strokes that were a bit slow, and headed west. The road was fairly wide and considering the number of people in the village square quite deserted. On the left were a few old wooden houses and vacant blocks of scrubby land. On the right just open land dotted with palm trees and a few others and the blue-green ocean lapping the shore about two hundred yards away. A little further on were several rows of thick, somewhat strange-looking sandstone walls, very much the worse for wear. The road went for another couple of hundred yards past a couple more old houses and another vacant block of land and there it was, facing

336

the ocean on a corner where Holding Street ended in an old sandstone wall that angled into another street running off to the left.

Les pulled up for a moment and had a look; it definitely wasn't quite what he expected. But there was no mistaking it. A sign nailed high up on the wall facing him said Norton House Restoration Project, with some smaller lettering painted underneath. The scrubby, barren block of land had a few splintery poles on it for a fence. Les parked the car next to it and got out. There was no wind now, the sun wasn't casting any shadows and it was quite still and silent, making it all seem a little eerie as well as totally unexpected. With his hands on his hips, Les stared at the old building and slowly shook his head.

The manse was no cottage. It was a towering, two-storey building, at least fifty metres square, and took up the whole corner. A yard with a crumbling orange brick wall round it ran to some houses at the rear that had to be over a hundred metres long also. The bottom storey was built from thick sandstone slabs, and the top storey was all solid wooden panelling that jutted out a good five metres over the footpath and was propped up by six massive white wooden columns about five metres high. The roof was built in two sections, in what looked like either orange tiles or slate. Four double windows faced up Holding Street and five huge doors above the columns looked out over the harbour. There were no windows in the sandstone wall alongside the vacant block, but six more double windows were set in the sandstone wall facing the harbour downstairs with a massive wooden door in the middle. The footpath out the front was five metres wide and was all cobblestones, right up to the kerb. Norton stood next to the car, still shaking his head. What did that Nigel bloke say a manse was? A modest house provided by the parishioners. Modest fuckin' house? This place is built like St George bloody Leagues Club. It's a mansion. That, however, was the good news. Unfortunately the place also looked like it had been through every one of the Darwin air raids.

337

Most of the roof was missing, exposing the greying beams and rods underneath and what tiles remained were in clusters, sitting alongside where someone had tried to patch up the roof with sheets of galvanised iron, now twisted and rusting away. All the upstairs windows at the side were gone, leaving only the white frames sitting in the faded brown panelling, and the upstairs doors were gone also, leaving just the frames and empty spaces staring out over the harbour. The windows downstairs were all gone and the spaces boarded up; the massive front door remained, but it was cracked or splintered in parts with most of the white paint faded away. At one time the sandstone looked to have been stuccoed with white lime, now it was all crumbling away as well and the towering columns out the front were chipped and faded and had weeds growing up round the bases. For such an impressive structure it was quite a poignant sight really. As well as suffering from obvious neglect, the old building looked all sad and forlorn standing on its own at the end of the street with nothing to keep it company but the surrounding walls opposite and the overcast sky above. Les shook his head again and had another look at the sign nailed to the wooden panelling upstairs. 'Restoration Project'. Christ, he thought. How would they bloody restore that? From what I've seen it'd take the country's entire budget. He got back in the car, drove it down a bit further and parked right out the front.

Up close, the manse looked even bigger again. Les got out and stood next to one of the wooden columns; it was closer to seven metres high and when he put his arms around it his fingers barely met. He looked up to where the columns supported the equally massive beams that held the front of the manse above the footpath and noticed that, although the beams looked solid and secure enough, parts of the flooring were gone or splintering away. Everything seemed as if it was built by, or to accommodate, giants. More huge beams ran over his head, the sandstone blocks were a metre square, the double front doors were both close to twelve feet high;

even the cobblestones beneath his feet were as big as coconuts. The front doors had been boarded up in parts with a heavy chain and padlock securing them; Les walked over for a closer look and to see how solid they were. There was a sandstone arch built into the wall above them with a bigger, fan-shaped keystone in the middle. Chiselled into the keystone was a date: Les stepped back to see what it was and his jaw dropped. 1761.

'Holy bloody shit!' he said out loud.

He had another look then stepped back out onto the road and stared up at the old building in astonishment. 1761. This bloody joint was built before Australia was even discovered. It's hundreds of years old. Well, what must it have been like in its day? And in a spot like this right across from the water. Norton's eyes narrowed slightly. Modest bloody residence, eh? Yeah, pig's fuckin' arse. Something Les had been thinking about earlier began to tick over in his mind, but for the moment he couldn't figure what it was. He stood in the deserted street, staring at the manse for a while, shaking his head very slowly and unconsciously picking at his chin. Well, I wonder what it's like inside? he finally thought. Only one way to find out. He got his backpack off the front seat and locked the car.

There was no chance of getting in the front way. Les walked round the columns and turned left where the side of the manse ran along a quiet, wide street with not much in it except several trees, some old houses and shabby stone walls, several cracks in the uneven road, and a couple of women walking away in the distance. A high sandstone wall opposite the manse angled into the street and through a couple of gaps Les could see about 200 metres of more sandy scrub and palm trees before the harbour. It had to be a harbour, because a battered metal sign bolted to the sandstone wall said West Harbour Street. This side of the manse was much the same as the other; empty window frames in the panelling above and the lime stucco crumbling away from the sandstone blocks below. Les strolled past for about fifty metres to a high gateway and the start of a brick wall that ran part of the way round the yard before the wall became sandstone like the one across the road. Parts of the brick wall were falling away; Les was about to step through the empty gateway when he stopped and pulled a brick from one of the gaps. It was about half the size of a normal house-brick, softer and the most beautiful pinky-orange. Les juggled it in his hand. Look at this, he thought. These bricks are as old as the house. Handmade and hand baked. Imagine having a ton of these old colonials back in Australia. They'd be worth anything. Instead they're sitting here crumbling into the ground. He placed the old brick back with the others that the now powdery white mortar was still managing to hold together and stepped into the backyard.

It was overgrown with waist-high weeds and shrubs. One solitary tree, thick with branches and some kind of yellow fruit, jutted up in the middle and at the back were the remains of a dozen or so cubicles and a couple of horse troughs that suggested they were once stables. The back wall of the manse had four empty window frames in the panelling above but only two small ones in the sandstone below. Both were boarded up, but a big green wooden door between them, splintered and hanging off its hinges, was open; Les had a quick look around and stepped inside.

It was one long wide room, full of nothing but rubbish, broken furniture and hundreds of old books covered with dirty water and mud. Les picked one up: *Welsh Farming Procedures 1903*. He threw it back with the others then squinted momentarily and sniffed at the unmistakable odour of crap and stale piss. About four metres in front was a sandstone wall and two doorways that led to another room. Several chipped white gables, which were probably from the window frames round the side of the house, were stacked between the doors. A dilapidated staircase with half the steps missing and rusty nails sticking out everywhere went along one wall, then doglegged upstairs. Norton left it, walked across to the left doorway in the sandstone wall and stepped into the other room.

It was huge, at least thirty metres by ten, completely empty and reminded Les more of a ballroom than anything else. Apart from a few more soggy books scattered round the corners there was hardly any rubbish; just dirt and a few pieces of wood lying around the floor. There was enough light entering from the gaps in the roof and the flooring above to see, although at one end of the room where the ceiling was still intact it was somewhat darker. Les noticed the massive double doors with the chain plus the boarded-up windows and figured this must be some sort of main room that ran along the street outside. The sandstone walls in here were thickly stuccoed a lovely pale aquamarine; there was no graffiti, very little damage and they'd managed to retain their beauty over the years. Shit, thought Les. I wonder if the walls outside were once like that? If they were, this place would have looked sensational. Beneath the dirt the floor was solid marble tiles, now filthy after years of neglect. There was a small patch of water near his foot; Les rubbed it with the toe of his trainer and it didn't take long to come up white. But the most imposing and striking thing of all was four absolutely magnificent mahogany pillars running lengthways down the centre of the room about five metres apart. They were a deep, lustrous brown, at least fifteen feet tall and propped up a monster beam that supported the floor above. They were narrower at the top, where they'd been turned and carved, and the bottoms were bolstered up from the marble floor by about a metre of smaller sandstone blocks. Les walked over and rubbed one of the pillars with the sweaty tail of his T-shirt; almost immediately it began to shine an intense, reddish black, something like those plump Yass cherries you get at Christmas. Les wrapped his arm around the pillar. It wasn't quite as thick as the ones outside, but just by the feel of it Les could tell it would be twice as heavy. He stepped back from the columns and looked up to where

341

they met the crossbeam, then back to the sandstone blocks below. Bloody hell! Wouldn't you have some fun bevelling those bastards in? Especially in this heat. Les strolled along the columns to the far wall, where it was darker and noticeably cooler. The wall at this end was in the best shape of all of them. Les looked up at it and wasn't quite sure in the gloom if he could make out something painted neatly on the wall directly behind the last column. Was it an X? Yes it was, about a metre across. And there were two names painted alongside it in letters the same size. They weren't painted, they were neatly formed in the stucco and painted over and you could just make them out in the semi-darkness. Les stared for a moment then his eyes lit up.

'Look at bloody that!' he called out, loud enough for his words to echo round the large room.

Les could make out NORTON. The X was clearer now and on the left side of it was EDUARDO. Les banged his fist into his hand. EDUARDO X NORTON. Father Eduardo Xavier. The priest who owned this place. Elizabeth Norton Blackmore's brother. He's put his name up on the wall. Well good on you, Ed old mate, smiled Les. If I owned a joint as grouse as this I'd probably do the same thing. Les looked at the letters for a few more moments then decided to check it out upstairs.

If Les had been a filmstar he would have hired a good stuntman to go up the stairs for him. They were fucked. What wasn't rotting away was full of rusty nails with a few pieces of loose bannister left where it angled off the wall. Shit! Doesn't that look lovely? Oh well, I hope I don't ruin my handbag. Les put his backpack over his shoulders and carefully climbed up on to the first loose piece of staircase. It wasn't all that bad and by going slow, watching what he was doing and keeping to the sides, Les made it safely to the top floor.

Up closer the roof was certainly stuffed alright and half the floor was missing with at least a seven-metre drop to the floor below. The wall frames were mostly intact. There were four huge rooms at the top of the stairs, the remains of some hallways, and the front of the house was two monstrous rooms that looked out over the harbour. Les began moving carefully around the floors and beams. All the rooms were around fifteen feet high with arched doorways over six feet across and the remains of Adam fireplaces set in the walls. Round the arched doorways were dainty angels and chains of flowers carved as delicately as lace, the white paint still intact. God. What sort of a place must this have been? mused Les. Unbelievable. He had another look up at the gaping roof and around him and noticed the floors were a little wet. Good thing it didn't rain too bad over this way last night. Then again, I reckon if a good blow ever hit here it'd be the finish of the top half of this joint. What a shame. Les shook his head and walked across to the front room on the right, watching out for some massive iron bolts, almost countersunk into the giant beam supporting the floor.

The room had an absolutely magnificent view across the calm, safe waters of the harbour. The ocean was a little murky in close before it turned blue, there were houses for a while then nothing but coastline and palm trees with two or three small beaches in the distance. From above, the walls across the street began to take shape now. They'd been some kind of buildings in the past and the roofs were missing; the remains of a few blackened beams suggested there might have been a fire at one time. The walls were quite thick and Les could see they'd been strengthened with lumps of quartz and granite cemented among the sandstone. There were square holes in the walls, with thick iron bars set into them, some even had rusting metal shutters still hanging from the sides. Near the rocks down at the water's edge Les could see the remains of an old wooden jetty now rotting away and sinking into the water. Jesus, what a spot for a house. Imagine if this was Watsons Bay or Vaucluse. The place'd be worth millions. Les looked at the harbour for another minute or two then went into the other room and looked out from the doorway in there for a slightly different perspective.

Norton was leaning against the door frame, staring vacantly out at the ocean. The manse had taken him completely by surprise and he didn't quite know what to make of it; it was all too weird. But there was something else bugging him too, something he'd read somewhere and it wasn't in that book about Jamaica. Then the thought he'd had earlier kicked in. Next thing he flashed onto something he'd been thinking about in the plane when they'd just left Australia. Les looked around him at the huge old house with its massive rooms, marble floors, mahogany pillars and aquamarine walls. Cobblestones out the front, Adam fireplaces, the workmanship on the doors and just the stuff that was left. The labour that would have gone into building this place. The money it would have cost to build it. The money. Norton's jaw dropped slightly and he slapped his hand against the door frame.

'This is it!' he said out loud again. 'This is bloody it!'

That book. *The Holy Blood and the Holy Grail*. The poor priest living in the chateau he built in the French countryside, with its own separate library. Plus the roads, the gardens and every blood thing else. All on about twenty bucks a year and whatever he could scrounge from about the same number of parishioners. Father Eduardo Xavier Norton. Another poor priest doing his best in his modest residence? Have a look at it. It might be stuffed, but it's like that joint in *Gone With the Wind*. That monstrous entertainment room downstairs and the room alongside almost as big. That was the kitchen. All these beautiful rooms upstairs with the hand-carved doors and fireplaces. Stables down the back for a dozen horses or more. Christ! The upkeep alone would cost you an arm and a leg. Yes, Ed me old mate. For a poor, struggling vicar you sure knew how to live. Les looked up and down the street and at the solid stone walls of the buildings across the road with the iron bars and metal shutters set among the stone. Like a flash of light it hit him, almost sending a shiver up his spine. It could have been déjà vu, it could have been ESP, it could have been something subliminal in Norton's bloodline going back all the years. It could have been a flashback to the ganja last night. It could have been anything. But the whole thing was falling together right in front of Norton's eyes.

Holding Street. An apt name if ever there was one. That's what those old buildings across the road were. Holding pens for slaves. Prisons. You don't put iron bars and heavy metal shutters on windows to keep chickens and pigs. An unexpected gust of hot air swept up from the harbour and rattled several loose pieces of corrugated-iron on the roof. As they scraped across the broken nails it sounded like a clutch of screams hanging in the air. This did send a shiver up Norton's spine. He could see the ships and hear the screams of the slaves as they were whipped off the jetty and herded into the holding pens to be left in the heat. Then auctioned off at the town square and sent out to work in the sugar plantations or wherever. That's where kindly Father Eduardo was making all his money. He was a slave-trader posing as a priest. Okay, so slavery might have been legal in those days. But definitely not the done thing for a compassionate and caring man of the cloth. And if he wasn't? How come he let it go on right outside his front door? The front door of his shit pot, fibro weekender at The Entrance. Because according to that book, all that land across the road belongs to the church. It's church land. And everything on it. Oh Ed, Les laughed to himself. You shifty bludger. You had it all sewn up. But I'll bet you weren't no racist, Ed. I'll bet you whipped both the black ones and the brown ones and anything in between. Les smiled around the old building again. What else did it say in that book? You had a fallout with the family. And it seemed funny how the 'notoriously tight-fisted Nortons' would put up the money to build you a manse. You didn't need their money. You had plenty of your own. Plus free labour. Ed, old mate, you might have been a dropkick, but, shit, I like your style.

Family. Tight-fisted. The words hung in Norton's mind as clear as a bell. Like a cash register would be more like it. His eyes narrowed, he turned away from the window and suddenly looked at the manse with a different perspective again. Eduardo was family alright; he was a Norton. And if he was, he would have had a family trait that probably went back to the bronze age. As well as being tight, Eduardo would have planted money or valuables somewhere. All the Nortons did it. Fathers, mothers, sisters, brothers, aunts, uncles, cousins, whatever. They all planted something and always not far from where they lived. Les was no exception. He had cash and some other goodies he'd accumulated buried in the backyard of his house at Bondi. Eduardo would have been the same, no risk. And you could bet slaves weren't the only thing he was flogging in Jamaica. A quiver went through Les this time; from the soles of his size ten feet to the top of his rugged red head. Like a human divining rod. This was family. The Norton bloodline, thick as ever, even over centuries. There was treasure buried here, Les could feel it in his blood. In his bones. Forget what it said in the book about mysteries and buried treasure. It was no mystery. There was something buried in here alright, not far from where he was standing. And the clue was in one of Elizabeth Norton Blackmore's poems. Yeah, but which one? Crumbs! Les grinned as he looked around the old manse. Who gives a stuff which one? I got plenty of time to work it out. His grin got bigger. And I've got a couple of things in my favour. Family. Plus I know it's in here that bad I can almost taste the bastard. Les rubbed his hands together gleefully. I'm starting to like this Jamaica more and more. Especially now there's a chance for an earn. In the meantime, there's no hurry to leave and I ain't got nothing planned. I don't think old Eduardo would mind if I had a bit more of a look around the place. Les took his camera out of his backpack, pressed the automatic shutter button and started popping off photos from all over the manse, exploring the whole area, sussing it out and surmising where he might bury a big stack of loot if this was his place.

Les wandered around the old ancestral manse, taking

photos and exploring the area in general. A few people strolled past, some rag-mop kids with wonderfully cheeky smiles stopped for a look; Les was almost tempted to take their photos they looked that good, but played everyone wide, preferring to concentrate on doing his thing. Les got fully involved in what he was doing and the time flew by; exploring the manse was more fun and more interesting than anything he'd done in ages. After a while he'd discovered one or two things and figured out others that confirmed his theories about the late Father Eduardo Xavier Norton.

The old building was bigger and grander than ever, the size of the material used and the workmanship left inside looked almost impossible without power tools and heavy equipment. What was left of the stables down the back would have accommodated more like twenty horses than a dozen, there were even a few pieces of an old carriage or coach in one corner. At one time there'd been a fountain and gardens, and scattered among the weeds were the remains of a marble sundial. Les couldn't help but ponder what the place must have been like when it was fully furnished and Eduardo had a party going with his stereo on full blast. Which probably would have been a ten-piece band and over a hundred guests, and you still wouldn't have filled the main room. Les walked across the road and explored what was left of the slave pens. He surmised Eduardo probably built them away from the house, both for security reasons in case they tried to break out and peace; their moaning and wailing might have disturbed his sleep. This was also probably why Les didn't notice any slave quarters over at the manse. Why bother when he had a constant supply on tap almost across the road? It looked as if the slaves got even in the end, however. All the pieces of charred beams poking out of the walls suggested they either revolted at some time or came back and burnt the buildings down when slavery was abolished in Jamaica in 1843. Christ! Can't say I blame the poor bastards, thought Les. Even empty, with the roofs missing and some of the walls knocked down, the rooms were still oppressively hot. Shit! What would it have been like packed in here with the doors locked in the middle of summer? And no air-conditioning and lumping chains around as well? No worse than the poor bloody convicts back home, I suppose. And at least the slaves didn't have to put up with whingeing bloody abos. Les poked around the buildings for a while but there wasn't much to see. Just rubbish and gutted buildings that were little more now than monuments to people's pain and misery. He wandered over to the water's edge and was reminded a little of Rose Bay in Sydney, only instead of an enclosed harbour it was more a narrow bay and open sea with a patch of dark blue ocean that was probably a safe passage through the reefs. He strolled along the rocks and over the remains of the old jetty, taking some more photos and prodding things here and there. It was kind of sad in a way to see everything so rundown and going to ruin. Though according to that keystone, Eduardo had had around eighty years of fun and profit before all the rich plantation owners legged it both to save their hides from the freed slaves and the collapse of the sugar industry. But Eduardo died in a storm according to the book. Anyway, no matter how sad or melancholy it might have been to see everything crumbling away, if it was to free thousands of people from a lifetime of cruelty and suffering, it was unquestionably all for the best.

Les roamed around some more. In the end he more or less had Eduardo's psyche worked out. But he was still stuffed if he knew where Eduardo planted the loot. One thing for sure; it definitely wasn't in the roof. Les had some ideas, but the place to look was in that book of Elizabeth Norton Blackmore's poems. Anyway, no need to rush into it today. There was plenty of time. But shit, it had been fun, and Les couldn't wait to get back and start poking around again. He tossed his backpack on the front seat of the Honda and headed back to the hotel. Before he left, Norton wrote down the name and phone number written on the sign nailed to the side of the manse. It was the Laurecian Society of Jamaica in collaboration with the

348

Jamaican National Heritage Trust. Earl Street, Kingston, Jamaica. Looks like I might be taking a drive over to Kingston, mused Les. There could even be some clues over there. Old charts, books, manuscripts, etc. Les was that engrossed in thoughts of treasure, what he'd just seen and other things, he drove straight past the turn-off to Rose Point Resort.

'Hey! What the fuck?' Norton was driving down some hill with trees and houses on either side of the road that seemed vaguely familiar. Next thing Sir Donald Sangster Airport loomed up below on the right. Shit! Where the fuck am I? I'm heading into Montego Bay. Oh well. Why not have a look around. I'm not doing much else today. Les followed the traffic along the narrow road to some intersection, then a roundabout with a park behind it, hemmed with what looked like small Moreton Bay figs and behind that the harbour. He went left at the park then came down into what looked like a mini Calcutta with a two-storey high-rise limit. It was old buildings, crumbling streets and walls, one great congestion of smoke and traffic and swarms of people going in every direction. Les continued with the traffic flow, losing it as he drove into some wider part of the road. Almost immediately all these wild-eyed Jamaicans came running at him, shouting and waving their arms around. Shit! What's this? I'm caught in a race riot or something. These cunts are gonna drag me out of the car and kill me. Les didn't notice he'd blundered up a one-way street. Behind the howling mob Les did see a one-way street going right past the post office. He tromped it through the mob, across a short clearing, and forced his way into the swarm of noisy traffic going past the post office, just as it all choked to a smoky, horn-blowing bottleneck of seething chaos. Shit! What have I got myself into? Les was definitely, positively the only honky in town and the looks he was getting from the locals swarming past his car were more than just curiosity. Les knew smouldering resentment, if not outright hatred, when he saw it. He pulled his cap down over his white, honky face as far as he could and stared straight ahead through his sunglasses. 'You ain't been round till you been down Montego Bay.' Yeah. Pig's fuckin' arse, scowled Les, wiping some sweat from the back of his neck.

Eventually the traffic began to grind forward. Les followed it through a couple of narrow streets full of rickety wooden buildings and crowds of people either buying or selling. The road came out at what looked like some kind of open-air market, with more people flogging food and drinks from stalls along what passed for the footpath, then another chaotic intersection turned left or right into more traffic. Les went right. The wide, straight boulevards of Siestasota it wasn't. It was a shit fight and every car was packed with crazy-looking Jamaicans driving with only their accelerator and car horn. Les swung right at some roundabout to try and lose some of the traffic while he sorted out where he was. He went a bit further, the traffic thickened and next thing he was heading back into town again. Les chucked a left past some shops and houses, put his foot down, and four streets later he was halfway up some hill, completely lost. Christ! Where the fuck am I now?

Les had a look around him then got going again; playing it more or less by ear. He drove up a hill, past some reasonably tidy houses and trees and down the other side of the hill. The trees thinned out, the nice houses disappeared and he was in some kind of ghetto. It was absolutely ghastly. Narrow dirty streets full of rubbish, gutted car bodies, mangy dogs, burning garbage and the most miserable-looking people Norton had ever seen. The people walking or loafing around looked up when they saw the Honda and any semblance of a smile on any of their faces quickly evaporated when they saw what was behind the wheel. Oh oh! thought Les. Something tells me this poor lost tourist better not stop and ask the smiling locals directions. Not if he wants to drink Fourex and swim at Bondi again. He did a screeching U-turn and got out of there as quickly as he could. He drove up more hills and along narrow, unkerbed roads, past more houses and a few more skinny trees and hoped he was heading in the right direction. The roads were a shambles, if there were any street signs Les couldn't see them. After about five minutes he found himself driving back into the ghetto again. Shit! Les swore to himself. A scruffy-looking kid about ten walked past, carrying a plastic shopping bag half full of bottles; Les pulled up alongside him, wound the window down and waved a hundred dollars Jamaican.

'Hey, mon. You know how to get to Rose Point?'

The kid looked at the money, took it and said, 'Open de door, mon. Wi ungo deh soon time.'

'You're a lifesaver, pal,' said Les, opening the door. 'Hop in.'

The kid piled in the Honda and placed his precious bag of bottles carefully at his feet. He didn't smell but he had to be the greatest chat Les had ever seen in his life. Norton never wore Ermenegildo Zegna when he went to school, but if he'd turned up looking like this poor little kid they would have either sent him back home or had him working at the incinerator all day. He had on a pair of shorts that had been hacked from a pair of men's grey pants and which were tied round the waist with a piece of cord. His sandshoes were several sizes too big, had no laces and were more holes than canvas, and round his scrawny shoulders were the remains of a shirt that could have been white at one time. He had close-shaved hair and brown, artful dodger eyes set in a world-weary sort of face, and although he didn't look as if he'd been eating too many T-bone steaks lately, he had a ballsy presence for his size and Les wouldn't have fancied trying to steal his bottles off him.

He pointed Les back towards town then just before they got to that one-way street again made him take a steep, hairpin left that climbed up and away from the town centre. The kid directed him left and right past more houses and trees and some old white hotel with a sign out the front saying Badminton Club, then onto another street and before long they were on the Queens Drive then the A1 back towards Rose Point. Les told the kid he was okay now, but the little Jamrite said he'd go with him all the way. Fair enough, thought Les, I think I can handle him if he pulls a knife on me, and got a bit of a mag on. The kid's name was I'rold, he was eleven and lived in Mo' Bay with his ten brothers and sisters. Les didn't ask Harold who his tailor was, but out of curiosity he asked how much the bag of bottles was worth. It was about twenty-nine cents and almost his second haul for the day. By the time Les calculated it all in Australian dollars and took a quick time and motion study, on a good week, working seven days dawn to dusk, Harold would net around $3.85. Norton couldn't help but laugh. Yet at the same time something inside him wasn't laughing at the poor little kid doing his best.

A little further on, not far from the garage Les had noticed on Saturday, were two young girls hitchhiking. 'Hey, I'rold,' said Les. 'Why don't we stop and give 'em a lift? What do you reckon, mon?' Harold gave a noncommittal shrug and Les pulled up. The girls came running up alongside. 'I'm going as far as Rose Point Resort.'

'Ire mon. Tenk,' said the taller one, and they jumped in the back.

Les swivelled round and gave them a quick perusal. They both had short crimped hair, reasonable bodies and faces, though they were definitely no oil paintings. One wore a white Yellowman T-shirt, the other a blue Sugar Minott. Both girls were into supertight black shorts with their teds poking out that far you could have hung clothes pegs on them. Neither would have been a day over fifteen and both looked very, very streetwise.

'So where have you been, girls?' asked Les, taking off again.

'Mo' Bay,' replied the one in the Yellowman T-shirt.

No sooner had she said that than they got into a conversation with Harold. Norton would need more than his one book on patois to understand what was going on, they were just too fast. But by picking up a word or two here and there Les figured they were asking the kid about Les and how big a mug was he? The kid said Les was a tourist and he was just getting a lift. They rattled off some more patois and a bit further on Harold turned to Les.

'Hey, mon. De girls a nen nuf danza. You got, say... twenty Jam?'

Twenty Jam, thought Les. What's that, about a dollar? Not much of an ask. 'We'll see what happens,' he smiled back at Harold.

A bit further on the one behind Les in the Sugar Minott T-shirt caught his eye in the rear vision mirror. 'Hey, mon,' she crooned. 'Yu lik some swedyang Jamaican tunti? Tri hundrit Jam. Bot us.'

Les smiled back at her. It wasn't a bad offer. An afternoon's porking with two little fifteen-year-old girls for about fourteen dollars US. Wouldn't you have a great time, and wouldn't you feel proud of yourself afterwards. Not counting all the creepy-crawlies you'd probably finish up with as well. Sick wid heetch and full a fassy. And going by the way the girls' sweedyang tuntis were poking out from their shorts, Les conceded they might only root for their friends. But wouldn't have an enemy in Jamaica.

'We'll see what happens when we get back to the resort,' he said.

Young Harold's ears pricked up. He was probably in on the earn and had just pictured himself as Mo' Bay's number one pimp with a nice sideline in bottles as well.

They arrived back at the intersection in front of the resort. Les leant over and opened the back door. As he did, he handed the two junior hookers a fistful of monopoly money.

'Here you are, girls. Get yourselves an answering service and a new pimp.' They took the money and mumbled a kind of disdainful thanks. Les handed Harold some more money too. 'Here you are, I'rold. Get yourself some shares in ICI.' Les scrabbled the kid's frizzy head and winked. 'See you later, mate. Thanks for your help.' Before they could say anything Norton left them and drove through the boomgates.

Back in his room Les tossed his sweaty T-shirt on the bed, got some more ice from the machine then poured himself a glass of 7-Up and took it out on the balcony. Happily he gazed out at the ocean and the hills behind the resort and thought what an amazing old day it had been. He had plenty of time and there was a lot more of Jamaica to see, but he couldn't wait to get back to the manse and start sniffing around again. Even discounting the buried treasure it was still interesting and a lot of fun. And what an old villain Eduardo must have been. I wonder what the full SP on him would be, mused Les. I wonder what else he got up to? It'd be interesting to find out, that's for sure. In the meantime, it's still bloody hot and my air-conditioned room is quite pleasant. But I think a nice long swim and a few beers would be well in order. He got a towel and his sunglasses and strolled down to the pool.

It still wasn't all that crowded; a couple of Japanese and pockets of motormouth Americans. There were plenty of empty banana lounges; Les dropped his gear on one and dived in the deep end. Again the water was delightful and Les did pretty much what he did that morning; swam a few laps, dived up and down and generally just splashed around on his own enjoying himself. After a while he towelled off and decided to attack the pool bar. Part of the bar was at the edge of the pool and the other part was built out into the shallow end where you sat on these stools with your legs in the water and ordered your drinks. Norton found an empty seat, ordered a bottle of Red Stripe and charged it to his room. Whether the local brew was any good or not Les wasn't sure. But the first one slid down his throat like chilled honey, barely touching the proverbial sides. The barman hardly had time to ring it up on the till when Les ordered another one. He settled down a little with number two and had a look around.

There were only about six people sitting round the dry part of the bar; all yanks and all boring the tits off the barman about how wonderful life was in Slop Bucket,

Iowa, or Brucellosis, Idaho. In the pool, some more seppos had strung a net across part of the shallow end and were playing some kind of water netball as if their lives depended on it. There were two teams of around seven a side and every time someone scored they'd scream their lungs out, jump up and slap each others' hands in typical 'we're Americans and we're not gonna enjoy ourselves we're gonna win at all costs' style. The only things missing were two all-girl cheer squads waving pom-poms and a twenty-piece Marine band waving half a dozen American flags. For a muck round in a pool it was all 'hey, ho, whoa, yeah, right on, alright, wow, yo'. One particular Chucky boy stood out from the others. He was about six foot one, with a big fleshy face and his blond hair braided into tourist dreadlocks at the back. He was about sixteen stone and looked like a bodybuilder starting to go to fat. Somehow he managed to be louder than the rest, but what made him stand out was the gold-coloured G-string he was wearing that went right up his arse, as if he was trying to show the world, especially the smaller Jamaicans, what a hunk he was. Every time he'd score he'd wave to his girl sitting on a banana lounge and she'd clap back and whistle. Paradoxically, she was as skinny as a rake, with tits like two rusty bottletops and no arse. A pair of round-framed glasses were perched on her nose under a bush of mousy blonde hair and she reminded Les of that anorexic hen Miss Prizzy, who's always trying to pull Foghorn Leghorn. Lucky boy, thought Les. Lucky girl, for that matter. Four beers later Norton decided to go over and lie on his banana lounge, get away from the noise, catch a few rays and check out what other punters were in the hotel.

About five minutes after Les sat down the World Series finished in the pool. Muscles dragged his arse out and with a great flexing of pectorals and biceps swaggered over and sat down about two seats away from Les, where his dutiful wife started wiping his back. After that he started snapping his fingers at the waiters both for drinks and to let them know he was around. Norton avoided eye contact as if his life depended on it. But it wasn't too bad sitting where he was, a bit of shade had come over plus the outdoor kitchen was open and looking for customers and Norton was sorely tempted. However, he remembered what those two guards said about the band and the banquet later that night so he thought he'd save himself. The food smelled pretty good too; mostly Jamaican tasties with heaps of local fresh fruit and vegetables. Muscles snapped his fingers for a menu. A waiter brought one over and Muscles looked at it like he'd been offered dog shit cooked fifteen different ways instead of the succulent local cuisine. He gave it several very disapproving once up and downs while the waiter stood there in the sun like a stale bottle of piss, before dumping the menu in his girl's lap.

'You know what I could go right now?' he bellowed. 'A good burger deluxe and a root beer.'

'Yeah, me too,' replied his girl. 'And a plate of fries with ketchup.'

That was enough for Norton; he got up and left. Before he went back to his room he strolled around for a while and checked out where the night's festivities were being held. They were a few hundred yards away from the pool on the right. The band area was set up under some palm trees with quite a number of long tables and chairs about fifty yards away on the grass. It looked like a nice setting and Les was looking forward to it. Shit, he smiled to himself. How would another smoke of that rubbish go before I came down? I reckon it'd give you the munchies in a big way. Yeah, that's what I'll do. I'll get zonked again before I come down and go through that banquet like a school of Bronze Whalers. Les had one more Red Stripe, watched the ocean for a while then walked back to his room.

After the heat and the punishing seppos it was quite pleasant lying back on his bed with the air-conditioner going. Les poured himself a lazy delicious and pondered what to do. There was no TV and the radio was still pumping out gospel. It was an ideal time to go through some more of Elizabeth's poems and see if he could work something out. It was getting dark, Les was cutting into the Sangsters and 7-Up and was none the wiser when he put the book down. He'd marked a few with biro he thought might mean something, but by and large they were all too obscure. Christ! If old Betty baby wanted to make it hard for anybody to find the loot she sure did a good bloody job. You'd have to be Einstein. Look at some of these I've marked.

Gold and diamonds cast their shadow in my heart,
To measure the chrisms of love beyond meed.

That could be a clue though. Maybe when the sun's at a certain angle it points to somewhere in that joint and there's the treasure. Yeah, but where? And what time? What about this one?

I stand upon the glistened cobblestones where eternity
lies unreproved,
How deep does measured time sink its jewelled troth.

That could be it. The treasure's buried under the cobblestones out the front. Yeah, but whereabouts again? And you'd need half a ton of TNT and a front-end loader to move those bloody things. Forget about home made jelly and a pick and shovel. They weigh a fuckin' ton. Ahh, stuffed if I know. I reckon what I'm gonna have to do is take a run over to Kingston and see that heritage mob. The Laurecian or whatever they call themselves. That's where I reckon I'll get some clues. And I can forget about hiring a metal detector. According to that book, someone from the *National Geographic* went over the place and all he found was an old clay jar with a copper bracelet in it and a voodoo doll. Les took another sip of his drink. Maybe I was wrong. Maybe I just got a sudden rush of brain to the head and there's nothing there. Norton shook his head vehemently. No! It's there alright. I know it is. In the meantime I have to ring home.

Les sat up on the bed and blinked around the room. Now what made me think of that? I rang the oldies just before I left. Shit! I've only been gone about a week. It's not a bad idea though. Les rubbed his hands together.

Heh heh! Wait till I tell them what I've found in Jamaica. They'll shit themselves. He picked up the phone and booked a call to Dirranbandi. Ain't it funny how things just come to you out of the blue? A few minutes or so later the phone rang back and the operator connected him.

'Hello?'

Les loved that familiar digger voice at the other end. He could just picture his father, old Joe, sitting there in his moleskins, having a cup of tea or reading the paper. Lillian, his mother, wouldn't be too far away either, shelling peas or baking lamingtons for the CWA.

'G'day, Dad. How are you, mate? It's Les.'

'Oh. Oh hello, Les. How are you, son?'

The smile quickly evaporated from Les's face. Something was up. Generally it was 'how are you, you big goose,' or 'hello woodenhead'. Whenever Dad referred to him or Murray as 'son', something was wrong. Either that or they were going to get a good boot up the arse or a clip under the lug like when they were kids and got a bit too clever.

'I'm . . . alright, Dad,' hesitated Les. 'What about you? Is everything okay?'

'Where are you ringing from, Les?'

'Jamaica. Dad, is everything alright?'

'I'm okay, Les. But there's been a bit of an accident.'

'Ohh shit!' Les knew it. 'Christ, Dad. What's happened?'

'Aunty Daisy's been killed and Mum's in hospital.'

'Ohh, Christ almighty!'

Les felt as if someone had just ripped his stomach out and filled it with cold, wet sand. Aunty Daisy lived in Adelaide where she was married to a builder. She was Mum's sister and looked just like her; same brown hair, same bony face. She was the life of the party and everybody in the family used to call her Crazy Daisy. She used to like to drive up from Adelaide two or three times a year to see the family and it was always a big event, especially if Uncle Stan came with her. Now she was dead and Mum was in hospital. Les couldn't hide the grief in his voice.

'Shit Dad. What happened? How's Mum? Is she alright?'

'You needn't worry too much, mate. Lil's okay. But poor old Dais' is gone.'

Joe went on to say how Daisy had driven up on her own from Adelaide to see the family. She and Lil had gone out to see Murray and on the way back the car hit a wild pig of all things and rolled. Daisy was killed instantly, Lil broke her arm and got a fair bit of bruising. The pig got up and walked away. Mum was okay, but the whole family was in shock. The whole town, for that matter, because Daisy originally came from Dirranbandi. Mum would be out of hospital by Thursday, the funeral was on Sunday. Naturally the funeral and wake would be a monster turn-out. The Nortons were a big family on both sides so there'd be a giant gathering of the clan as well as almost the entire district. Les didn't need his father to tell him that if you were kin you got there no matter where you were. Jamaica, Tibet or living in a plastic bubble on the moon. And in your Sunday best too.

'I'll get the first plane out tomorrow morning, Dad. I reckon I should be there Wednesday. Thursday at the latest.'

'Good on you, Les. Jeez, it's a proper bastard ain't it, mate?'

'Yeah, is it what. But at least Mum's... well, you know.'

'Yeah. I s'pose that's one way of looking at it. You know it's funny, Les. It's gettin' on for eleven, Murray's comin' round soon and we're all goin' out to see Mum. And I was just thinkin' about you when you rang.'

'Yeah,' answered Les. 'It's funny alright, ain't it?'

They talked for a little while longer, but there wasn't a great deal either could say over the phone. Les didn't say anything about what he'd found in Jamaica or what happened in Florida. It wasn't the time or place. It was just a bummer all round. Eventually it was time to hang up.

'Alright, Dad. Well, I'll see you by the weekend. You look after yourself. And say hello to Mum and everyone for me till I get there.'

'I'll do that, Les. See you when you get here, mate.'

Norton stared at the phone in bitter disbelief. What a bastard of a thing to happen. And right in the middle of the best part of the trip. Suddenly Les found himself caught in a rotten bind. It was bad enough getting the awful news from home. Lovable Aunty Daisy was gone and his mother was banged up in hospital lucky to be alive. On the other hand, it couldn't have come at a worse time. He'd just found the manse and figured out there was a definite earn there, as well as all the fun finding it. He was staying in a top hotel, he had a bag of unbelievable pot, a giant pocketful of chops and the best rum he'd ever drunk in his life was about six bucks a bottle. Not counting all the grouse food and snorkeling he was going to get into. But blood was thicker than any holiday and Jamaica would always be here if he wanted to come back.

Les poured himself another rum and took it out on the balcony. He took a solid sip then let out a loud sigh of exasperation and had a look around. Well, here it is, my last night in Jamaica. Wasn't that bloody quick? Still, maybe it's all for the best in a way. It's stinken bloody hot, I'm sick of seppos, I wouldn't say the natives here are the friendliest in the world and there's something building up in the air here besides humidity. I keep getting this feeling that something I said when I was drunk is going to come back to haunt me. What's that old saying? Many a true word said in jest. Yeah, it'll be good to get back home. Catch up with the family and all that. Despite his blues Les had to smile into his drink. Aunty Daisy might be gone but I reckon there'll be a few yarns about Crazy Daisy at the wake. Christ! What about the time she put the cane toad down the front of Mum's draws at Murray's wedding anniversary? Silly old bastard.

Les went inside and made himself another rum. Seeing as he was leaving first thing in the morning he figured it wasn't much good sitting around moping; the only thing coming out of the radio was gospel music and that wasn't helping things. He switched it off and got his arse into gear. He rang the desk and said he'd be booking out at 7 a.m. could they have his bill ready. Certainly, sir. No problems. He had three attempts at ringing the airport, but each time the line was engaged. No big deal there, though. They probably took the phone off the hook on Sunday night. Just lob down in the morning and get on the next flight out. He started getting his travel documents together and packing his bags, including the books on Jamaica and the one of Elizabeth Norton Blackmore's poems. Guess I won't be needing these any more. S'pose they'll make good souvenirs though. This gave Les the shits a bit. Packing and unpacking was a drag at any time. Especially when you've just settled into some place and next thing you're leaving again. He looked at the Glad-Wrap foils of dacca and his machine. No, I don't think I'll be needing that tonight. Roaming around, zonked off my head the mood I'm in. He took the foils into the bathroom and flushed them down the toilet. Christ! Imagine what some of those heads I know in Bondi would give for that, thought Les, as he watched them disappear. They'll cry when I tell them what I did. No, just a few drinks and a feed'll do me tonight. He picked up his camera; there were six shots left. May as well take my camera with me, take a few photos of the band or whatever and burn them up. Before long Les had everything packed except for a pair of brown shorts and a black Midnight Oil T-shirt he'd wear that night and on the plane in the morning. Satisfied, but not all that happy, he had one more drink and with his camera over his shoulder walked down to the outdoor banquet.

The band had started when Les got there. It was a seven-piece calypso outfit, banging away on various-sized instruments made from cut-down, forty-four-gallon drums. The reverberating notes seemed to hang melodiously in the night air and beneath the palm trees with a small bank of spotlights over them and the Caribbean as a backdrop they certainly looked and sounded the part.

361

There was room for a dancefloor and with the rows of tables set up on the grass seating for about a hundred, although there wouldn't have been thirty there and most of these looked like Jamaicans on a freebie. There was a bar to the side, waiters and waitresses, and the food, opposite where Les was standing, was a help-yourself smorgasbord of hot and cold dishes with a chef standing behind a carvery at one end. Les propped for a few moments, figuring which way to jump, when the two security guards from the previous night walked past. They recognised Les and smiled and despite it all Les winked and smiled back. Oddly enough Norton wasn't all that hungry. The news from Australia had sunk in a bit more and he now found himself feeling tired and empty. Still, it was no good letting it get you down. It was Norton's last night in Montego Bay so he'd have a couple of beers, a feed, listen to the band for a while then hit the sack. He threaded his way around the seats and tables, paid the girl and had a look at what was on offer.

It was fairly standard buffet food. A dozen or so different salads, corn on the cob, vegetables, fruit, rice dishes, etc. There were cold meats and sausages, some kind of chicken goulash, stews, curries, plus the carvery. Les piled some salad and rice onto his plate and went for the carvery, getting mainly the hot smoked ham. There was no shortage of room. Les found a spot near where he'd been standing, ordered a beer and started eating. The food was quite nice, the salads were crisp and fresh, the ham lovely and tender. But Les picked more than he ate and when he finished he didn't bother to back up. Normally at a smorgasbord Les would wear a path through the carpet he'd back up that many times, and George Brennan reckoned he had rubber pockets for stealing soup. But tonight the big Queenslander's heart wasn't quite in it. Still, it was nice enough sitting out in the open with the sweet sound of the metal drums ringing in the air. He ordered another beer and was sipping it quietly when who should lob and sit almost in front of him but Muscles from the pool and Miss Prizzy.

The big seppo had squeezed himself into a skimpy white singlet, a couple of sizes too small to show off the muscles in his back, and a pair of red, rayon, jogging shorts, also a couple of sizes too small to show off his cut lunch, bulging out in the front like a big bunch of Waltham Cross grapes. Miss Prizzy had a red mu-mu draped over her sensational body and looked like the inside of a thermometer. Muscles sat down with his back to Les in a great grunting and farting and snapping of fingers for service. Miss Prizzy was a little more subdued, but Muscles was talking loud enough to let the staff and the world know that Captain America and his glamour had arrived. Muscles ordered two beers for himself and some fluffy green drink full of paper umbrellas and lumps of fruit for his girl. He knocked the beers off pretty smartly, belched loud enough to momentarily drown out the band then swaggered over to the smorgasbord. Miss Prizzy was a picker and Les might have gone easy, but Muscles made up for both of them.

He came back with two plates in his hands, stacked with that much food you couldn't have so much as fitted a business card on either one. Watching him eat fascinated Les almost as much as it repulsed him. Muscles didn't eat his food, he seemed to grind his way through it like some kind of human tree-mulcher. Bits of rice or lettuce would fall from his mouth onto the table and he'd grind away remorselessly, Miss Prizzy even cut up some of his food for him and pushed it in his mouth. He demolished the first two plates then came back with two more, plus bread rolls and four pieces of corn on the cob, and away he went again. Chomp, grind, snort, slurp; washing it down with another two beers. Les noticed some of the staff watching Muscles with looks of amused satisfaction. They saw Les looking at them and had to turn away when Les nodded towards Muscles and started scratching under his arms like a gorilla. Captain America snapped his fingers for more beers. One of the waiters brought them over and it was all the poor bloke could do to keep a straight face with Les looking at him and bobbing up and down on his seat making more monkey gestures. It was funny enough for a while then just as quickly the whole scene began to turn Norton off. It just didn't seem right. Les was no socialist or communist, but here at this luxury resort everybody was pigging into all this food till it was coming out their ears — what they didn't eat would probably get tossed in the garbage — and just outside the front gates people were living in little more than boxes made out of driftwood. Some poor, battling little kid was working seven days a week to make about four bucks picking up bottles, and two fifteen-year-old girls were selling their bodies for about another five bucks each. Yeah, it's a funny old world alright, thought Les. He had another mouthful of Red Stripe, left his camera case on the table and walked down to take some photos of the band.

There were one or two Jamaican couples dancing and it was quite pleasant down the front with the breeze coming in off the sea. Les took a couple of photos from directly in front, fiddled around with the zoom lens and took a couple from the side and another from behind a palm tree. He hung down the front for a while, enjoying the breeze, then went back to his table.

Les was sitting there, quietly sipping his beer and looking at his camera. There were three shots left and three black American girls sitting a couple of tables away. They were wearing baggy shorts and college T-shirts and baseball caps round the wrong way, and even though they were all horribly overweight they somehow reminded Les of three fat Supremes. They were definitely worth a photo and maybe Les'd take one of the staff. The zoom lens brought the three girls into focus and Norton fired off two photos. The girls didn't seem to notice Les taking photos. But Muscles did. He had more plates of food in front of him and was at them while he slurped more beer. He turned around at the flash.

'Hey buddy! What are you doin' there?' he bellowed

'Just taking a couple of photos,' replied Les, a little reservedly.

'Hey! You want some tourist photos?' slobbered Muscles. 'Take a photo of me and my gal.'

Les shook his head. 'No. I only got a couple of shots left and I want to get some more of the band.'

'Screw the band. Take a photo of me and Lori.'

Les winced, hardly able to believe what he'd just heard. 'No thanks, mate.'

Muscles scowled at Les. 'What's this, "no thanks — mite"? Come on, limey. Take a photo.'

Norton shook his head slowly, impassively and looked directly at Muscles. 'No.'

Captain America's chest started to rise. He looked at his girl then glared at Norton. 'Who do you think you are, you limey sonofabitch. Ain't we good enough for you to take our photo?'

'That's right,' nodded Les. 'You're too ugly. Especially your rotten skinny sheila. She looks liked a baked rabbit and I wouldn't waste the film on her.'

Miss Prizzy's jaw dropped. No one had ever spoken to her like that; especially not in front of her boyfriend. Muscles was absolutely outraged. His face coloured and his chest rose. No one had ever spoken to him like that either. Not since he started pumping iron and especially not at the hotel where all the Jamaicans were forced to kiss his big yank arse. He grunted something then lumbered to his feet and charged round the table up to Les.

'You sonofabitch!' he roared. 'You can't talk to me like that. I'm a goddamn American!'

Norton decided it was time to leave. A few of the staff had stopped what they were doing, sensing something was wrong, and Les didn't wish to cause a scene. He put his camera back in its case and stood up.

'No you're not,' he said evenly to Muscles. 'You know what you are — mate? You're a big fat fuckin' pain in the arse.'

Saying that, Les swung his right leg back and kicked Muscles straight up his massive cut lunch. There was no way Les could miss it. Muscles went cross-eyed with shock; he grabbed at his groin and howled with pain at the same time. Les bent his knees slightly and belted Muscles with a withering left hook, which only travelled about a foot, but which hit him on the jaw hard enough to lift him off his feet and send him crashing over Norton's table. Plates and cutlery went everywhere and the table split in half with a crack as Muscles landed at Miss Prizzy's feet with the tablecloth tangled up round one leg. Blood was starting to bubble out of his mouth and he was out cold but still clutching his cods and moaning. It was a good thing he got into all that food earlier, because from the look of his jaw the only things he'd be eating for the next couple of months would be through a straw. Miss Prizzy stood up, too blown out at the sight of Captain America lying on the deck like a big sack of rotten potatoes to start screaming. The staff looked on in silence, though it wasn't hard to see they were all secretly stoked. The two security blokes arrived, looked at Muscles lying on the deck among the plates and cutlery then looked at Norton. Les wasn't quite sure what they were going to do and he didn't give a stuff all that much either. With that awful Norton look on his face he walked through the broken table to where Muscles had been sitting. There were two plates of goat stew, or something Muscles hadn't finished eating, still left on the table. Les smiled at the horrified look on Miss Prizzy's face and scooped up the two plates of food, then turned to the staff, the security guys and anybody else looking.

'And de fun don't done,' grinned Norton.

Les dumped the two plates of stew in Muscles' face and what didn't splatter all over Muscles Les pushed into his mouth with the heel of his trainer. Poor Muscles. He looked like shit. Satisfied, Les walked back to where his camera had fallen among the stuff from the broken table. He picked it up and looked at the two security guards. They both grinned.

'Ire, mon,' said one. 'And de fun don't done. Respec, mon.'

'Respec, mon,' said the other, shaking his head. 'Respec.'

'Exactly,' nodded Les. 'Respec. Especially if you're an I'orton. Goodnight, everybody,' Les flicked a bit of dirt from his camera and walked back to his room.

Well, wally. When you leave a place, you certainly leave in style, don't you? Norton had turned off the light and was lying back in bed, half awake, half asleep, staring up at the ceiling. Almost as bad as when I left bloody Florida. Ahh, serves the big-mouthed seppo prick right, anyway. The overblown fat dope. He yawned and scrunched his head into the pillow. To tell you the truth I'll be glad to be back home. And the sooner the bloody better. I'm sick of this. Les yawned again and smiled. But jeez that felt good. You can't talk to me like that, I'm an American. Yeah righto ... mite. And I'm not a limey. Les yawned again; deeper this time. Before long his thoughts were of Sydney, Bondi and Dirranbandi. Next thing he was snoring peacefully.

It was closer to eight o'clock by the time Norton woke up the following morning, had a shower and got ready to make a move. He didn't dwell too much on the previous night's events. The main thing on his mind, apart from having to leave unexpectedly, was that after the few beers and not much to eat at last night's smorgasbord, he was starving hungry. He'd probably get fed on the plane. But stuff waiting that long for a sandwich or eating the usual, greasy rip-off stuff they give you at airports when there was a super nosh just outside the door. There wasn't all that mad a hurry and there'd be plenty of planes leaving that morning. Les had a final, slightly nostalgic look around his room before he closed the door. Oh well. So much for Jamaica. He left his bags at the desk and said he was having breakfast, could they have the bill ready and his car waiting when he finished. No problem, sir. Thank you for staying at Rose Point Resort.

The food was the same excellent fare as before. The girl at the cash register didn't say anything when he paid and nobody appeared to be pointing, or recognising him from last night's effort. There were only about a half a dozen people there and Captain America and Miss Prizzy weren't among them. Les filled his plates and sat near the balcony overlooking the ocean and away from everyone else just the same. There was barely a breeze coming in off the sea and it was unbelievably hot for so early in the morning. The sky was an odd, hazy violet colour with strips of gunmetal grey clouds out on the horizon, and the air was that thick with humidity you almost needed to get round with an aqualung. Sweat was dripping from Les while he ate and he drank almost two pitchers of cold fruit juice. Which wouldn't hurt anyway, Les surmised, because all he'd get on the plane would probably be Dr Pepper or some other horrible soft drink or soda pop or whatever the yanks call it. Full to the brim he left a tip, fixed things up at the desk, then, after giving the bloke on the door some monopoly money for putting his bags in the boot, climbed behind the wheel and headed for Sir Donald Sangster Airport.

The air terminal was just as big a shit fight as the last time Les was there, if not more so. Tour buses were pulling up, along with cars and taxis, all disgorging people and passengers weighed down with luggage. He paid some woman sitting in a little tin shed and found a spot down the back of some dusty, rock-strewn parking area, got out and locked the car. He took his bags with him but decided to leave the car until last just in case there was some delay and he could then take a bit of a drive round the harbour and maybe get a souvenir T-shirt or something rather than sit around the terminal getting annoyed by pests. Inside the departure area there were very few hustlers, but crowds of tourists, in complete contrast to when Les arrived. Mainly Americans, with what sounded like a scattering of Germans or Scandinavians. Euro-trash backpackers seemed to be fairly thin on the ground. Whatever they were, they were either queued up at the check-out counters ten deep, surging towards the departure gates or sitting in a lounge above, drinking either coffee or beer, and all seemed to have an air or relief about them that they were leaving. Les got behind a queue of unmistakable Americans wearing shorts almost as loud as their voices and got his travel documents from his overnight bag. Les had expected he might have to stand around for a while again, so before he left the resort he'd grabbed a copy of the *Daily Gleaner* from the front desk. He opened it up and glanced across the headlines. They didn't mean all that much. RICHARD EXPECTED POSSIBLY BY THE WEEKEND. MORE PROBLEMS TO HIT FARM WORK PROGRAM. HEALTH SERVICES STILL CRIPPLED. Something else caught his eye. COPS HELD ON DRUGS. 'Four policemen attached to Corporate Area stations, along with a civilian, have been detained by the St Ann's Bay police after a drug related incident in that parish on Sunday,' the police information centre said. Almost alongside that was WARDER NOW CHARGED WITH HELPING PRISONERS ESCAPE. 'A correctional officer at the general penitentiary has been arrested and charged with aiding and abetting two inmates at that penal institution to escape.' Well, there you go, smiled Les. And all the time I thought I'd left Australia. One part of the paper was a memorial section. Photo after photo of grim-faced Jamaican men, some of whom were cops. Under each one was their name and address, a little about his family and the words, 'Died under tragic circum-stances'. On another page was a small headline: TEN MEET VIOLENT DEATHS. Six were hacked to death with machetes. Two were shot. One got run over then doused with petrol and set on fire. The last was shot by the police. So much for love my black brother and oh island in the sun, mused Les. Next it was his turn at the counter.

'Hello,' Les said pleasantly, 'I'd like to change my ticket. I'm booked for two weeks or so, but I want to take the next flight out. Then on to Los Angeles and Australia. I just have to change the dates, that's all.'

The girl in the blue and white checked uniform looked about the same as the one at customs, only possibly a little politer. She looked quizzically at Norton then flicked through his reservations and passport. 'You've got two weeks left on your ticket.'

'That's right,' nodded Les. 'I want to take the next flight out to America. I want to change it.'

'No seats available till Wednesday.'

Norton gave her a slow blink. 'No seats till Wednesday?!!'

'That's right.' She looked behind Les at the rest of the queue.

'What?... I mean, how come?'

'De hurricane, mon. Hurricane Richard. It's building up in the gulf. It might get here Friday, we don't know. Everybody's getting out.' The girl pointed to the *Gleaner* under Norton's arm. 'Don't you read the newspapers? Listen to the radio, watch TV?' She flicked a long fingernail through Norton's passport again. 'Australian. I should have known.'

Les continued to stare at her. 'So...?'

'Seven-thirty next Wednesday evening. North West to Miami. Economy. You want a ticket?'

'Yeah. Yes, I'll take it.'

The girl started pushing buttons on the computer and rewriting Norton's ticket. That's when it dawned on him what had been going on. Carrying on like a mug in Florida when he was drunk, telling that sheila he was a meteorologist and there was a cyclone building up. Many a true word said in bloody jest alright. Not many people on the plane when he flew in. The resort barely a quarter full. That pommy Nigel saying his firm couldn't have sent him here at a worse time. Ricco and Laverne saying they were due for a big one after that mini one they got through. All this non-stop, stinken humidity. Then this. Les had another look at the headline in the *Daily Gleaner* before tossing it in a nearby dustbin. Christ! Talk about can't see the forest for the bloody trees. Les caught his reflection in a glass sign behind the counter. Not much mug in you, is there? He was still thinking on this as he trudged back across the airport in the heat with his bags and his new ticket and sat in the car.

Well, hasn't that thrown a nice fuckin' dampener on things? I'm stuck here till fuckin' Wednesday. Shit! He banged his fist on the steering wheel. So I suppose I'd better find a bloody joint to stay. I don't fancy going back to the resort. They can stick it up their arse. He had a look at the map the car company had given him. There was some street called Gloucester Avenue that ran up along the water's edge. There'd have to be hotels or something there. And it's handy to the airport if something else stuffs up. Les started the car and headed in that direction. It was easy enough to find, all he had to do was stick by the sea. Les found the start of it okay. But when he did, it was blocked off with barricades and swarming with traffic; mainly utilities and small trucks. He ground to a halt among all the other cars, next to two young cops trying not to do anything, especially direct traffic.

'Excuse me, officer,' Les called out the driver's window.

The cop glanced at Les. His partner took no notice at all. 'Ya, mon?'

'What's goin' on? Why all the barricades and that?'

'Mardi Gras. Monday night be Mardi Gras night. De whole street blocked off till morning.'

'Mardi Gras? Ohh shit!'

The cop looked at Les the way he did with every dumb tourist he met and made a gesture with his thumb. 'Move de car, mon.'

Les looked at him for a second then got going again. He couldn't quite believe what was happening. Now bloody what? he fumed. Les joined the smoky, noisy crawl of traffic, not knowing where he was going. Before long he found himself going past a park he recognised, then the roundabout. Beyond that was the one street into town and the hairpin bend that went up the hill. There was something up there if he remembered right. Les hung a quick right at the roundabout, zapped through the other cars and took the hairpin bend up the hill. By watching the trees and streets and other things as he climbed steadily, he found the one he was looking for; and there it was. Overlooking Montego Bay in all its faded glory. The Badminton Club.

An uneven, tarred parking area faced the street with a boomgate and a small shed on the left. At the back was an office and on its left were four empty, netted-off badminton courts with no shortage of weeds sprouting up through numerous cracks in the concrete; a sign next to the shed out front, two racquets and a shuttle in faded yellow said Badminton Club Hotel. Les pulled up at the boomgate, gave a double blink and shook his head. A skinny Jamaican in an ill-fitting, unpressed uniform and cap appeared from the shed. I've got to stop equating everything I see with movies or cartoons, blinked Les. I have to. But the bloke was that slow and gangly the only comparison Les could think of was that dopey mouse in the Bugs Bunny cartoons that Speedy Gonzales is always saving from the cat; the only thing missing was a sombrero. With his shoulders hunched and only the lower part of his body moving, he ambled over and fell on one end of the boom, then looked at Les through half-closed eyes as he drove through.

'I're mon,' he drawled.

'Si senor,' replied Les. 'Watch out for el pussy-cato.'

There were a couple of old Toyotas outside the office; Les pulled up alongside and went in. It too was in a state of disrepair — an almost-white laminex and bamboo reception desk with an old iron safe behind it, a cash register at one end, a yellow vinyl lounge and a couple of indoor plants surrounded by streaky white walls with a few dog-eared, Jamaican tourism posters clinging to them. Les rang a bell on the desk and a few minutes later a woman about thirty appeared from behind a brown floral curtain on the left. She was kind of dumpy, wearing a green dress with her hair stacked up on her head, and had this shifty, morose look about her. Instead of welcoming Les as a potential customer she peered at him as if he'd come in to rob the place or try to sell her something.

'Yes?' she muttered.

'I'd like a room for the night please. I might stay tomorrow. I'm not sure.'

The woman nodded something and handed Les a form to fill in, explaining tiredly as she watched him that the first night was in advance. Les nodded an okay, paid with his VISA and a few minutes later had the key to Number 27. She said the porter was busy for the moment and pointed out how to get to the room; which meant she sussed that Les was big and silly enough to lump his own luggage. Les half thanked her and got his bags from the car.

Behind the office a crumbling concrete path meandered through gardens of surprisingly lovely flowers. On the left was some sort of open restaurant or dining area then the path curved away from a kidney-shaped swimming pool that looked murky enough to hide the Creature from the Black Lagoon and all his immediate relatives. Behind this, however, was a walled area dotted with plastic chairs and tables that gave a sensational view across Montego Bay and the hills beyond. There was a bar and TV lounge to the left, then the path turned into stairs leading to the rooms spread out over two flat storeys. Everything was in need of more white paint and maintenance, especially where the rusting air-conditioners set next to the rooms had dripped, leaving pools of dirty brown water. When he opened the door, Norton's room was no exception.

It was one big white room with a bathroom on the left as you walked in. The double bed looked tidy enough with a red floral cover, but the rest of the room was just old and sparse, like something you'd expect in some outback New South Wales or Queensland town in 1950. There was a sideboard, chair and table along one wall then an orange curtain drew back over a skinny balcony that might have given a view over the bay except for a hilly block of land fully of scrubby trees fenced off with cyclone wire. Les had a quick, uninterested look around then checked out the bathroom. The toilet seat was half off, the sink was stained and the almost-white enamel was flaking from the bath. The shower nozzle was loose and the water dribbled out feebly. There was no fridge, no TV and no radio. But the phone was fairly new and appeared to work. Welcome to home sweet home, Les mumbled to himself. Still, it's only till bloody Wednesday. I hope.

There was a clean towel in the bathroom. He splashed some water over his face and neck, dried off, then flopped down on the bed with his hands behind his neck and scowled up at the ceiling. Now fuckin' what?

Norton's cup of happiness was definitely not flowing over. One minute he was on his way back to Australia with thoughts of home on his mind, now he was stuck in some flop till Wednesday, ready to dissolve and lucky to be away by then. What do they say in this bloody joint? Shit happens, mon? Does it bloody ever. Oh well, at least I got a roof over my head and transport. And I'm not short of dough. It could be a lot fuckin' worse. Les brooded up at the ceiling some more. Well, I can sit around here feeling sorry for myself or I can find something to do to take my mind off things. There must be somewhere round here I can go snorkeling in some clear water. And there's that Mardi Gras tonight. I wonder what sort it is? Les gave a bitter laugh. The way my luck's going I'll probably have to buy a pair of black leather jeans and cut the arse out of them just to get a look in. Or, for about seven bucks a day, I could get on the piss and blot the whole thing out. Bad luck I shot all that dacca down the brascoe. I could have really done a job on myself. Or? Norton suddenly found himself tap-dancing a bit quicker and in a different direction. Why don't I play Sherlock Holmes and see if I can find that loot old Eduardo's snaffled away? He looked at his watch. By the time I take the car back, sort things out and get to the airport, I've got till Wednesday afternoon. Roughly two and a half days. That'd keep me occupied. Yeah. Why don't I get my arse into gear and have a bloody go? I know it's there. Les looked at his watch and let ten seconds tick by, then swung himself off the bed and took a deep breath. Starting right bloody now. And if I don't find it, it won't be for lack of trying. But the first thing I'm going to need is some clues.

Les got the phone number of the Laurecian Society out of his backpack plus one or two other things. A quick trip over to Kingston and back wouldn't take all that long, thought Les, as he pushed the numbers on the phone. And I'll get a chance to see some more of the island. It rang for a while then a woman answered.

'Hello? Jamaican Heritage Trust.'

'Good morning. My name is Norton. Mr Les Norton. I'm over here from Australia and I'm trying to trace the Norton family around Montego Bay. And I'm after some information regarding the old Norton manse at Dredmouth. Would it be possible for me to come over and see some old books and documents and that?'

There was silence for a moment. 'You say your name is Mr Norton?'

'That's right, ma'am. Norton. N-O-R-T-O-N. As in Sweet Ginger Hill and Rose Hill Great House in Montego Bay. And the manse at Dredmouth.'

There was more silence. 'Just one moment please, sir. I will put you through to someone.'

'Thank you very much, ma'am' replied Les.

Les tapped his biro on the notebook he had open on the bed. I hope I don't get some bloody public service runaround. That sheila didn't sound too bright. There were a couple of clicks and a beep then a smooth, deep voice came on the line.

'Hello? Winston Glover.'

'Hello? Mr Glover is it? Mr Glover, my name is Norton, Mr Les Norton, and I'm over here from Australia.' Les went into the same spiel he gave the woman, only with a little more detail, and adding that the main reason he was interested in the manse was because two of his family back in Australia were in the priesthood. Mr Glover seemed to think for a short while.

'I understand perfectly what you're talking about, Mr Norton. Unfortunately, I'm more involved in the administration side of things. Restoration and all that. Do you understand?'

'Yes ... I think so, Mr Glover.' Here it is, thought Les. The old public service standby. Sorry, that's not my department.

'The person you need is Professor Eyres. Unfortunately

Professor Eyres is away at the moment lecturing in Antigua and won't be back till Thursday. He keeps all the historical data concerning that sort of thing locked in his office. How long are you here for, Mr Norton?'

'I leave on Wednesday.'

'Oh. Pity.'

'Yeah. Ain't it?' said Les glumly.

'Where are you ringing from, Mr Norton?'

'Montego Bay.'

'Montego Bay,' repeated Mr Glover slowly. He seemed to think for a few moments. 'There could be someone over that way who may be able to help you with your research.'

'Yeah?' Norton's voice rose a little.

'Yes. A Mr Millwood Downie. He's a schoolteacher and he's also a part-time historian. A dilettante, so to speak. He and Professor Eyres are good friends. I'm sure he could assist you in some way.'

'Fantastic. So how do I get in touch with Mr... Downie?' Les glanced at his notebook where he'd been writing all these names down.

'I don't know his home number and he teaches mainly at night. But during the day he works at the Autumn Moon Golf Club at Montego Bay. You'll find the number in the phone book and you should be able to contact him there.'

'That's great.' Norton was rapt. This Downie bloke might know something and at least he didn't have to drive over to Kingston. 'Well, thank you very much, Mr Glover. I appreciate your help.'

'My pleasure, Mr Norton. And I hope you find what you're looking for.'

'Thanks again, Mr Glover. Goodbye.'

'Goodbye.'

Well, there you go, smiled Les. Why did I write all Jamaicans are dropkicks on that T-shirt? He seemed like a pretty good bloke. Let's hope this Downie rooster's got his Jamaican shit together. Les looked through the phone book and there it was: 26 Spring Water Road, just off the

A1 and not far from Rose Point Resort. Les pushed the numbers, writing them and the address down while he waited. A younger woman's voice answered this time.

'Good morning. Autumn Moon Golf Club.'

'Could I speak to Mr Millwood Downie, please?'

'Yesss. May I say who is calling?'

'A Mr Norton, from Australia.'

'Just one moment, Mr Norton.'

Les waited and crossed his fingers. A switch clicked in his ear, there was silence for a while, another phone rang then a curious voice answered.

'Hello? Milton Downie?'

'Hello, Mr Downie? My name is Norton. Les Norton. I'm out here from Australia and I was told to contact you by a Mr Winston Glover at the Jamaican Heritage Trust.'

'Oh yes.'

'I was hoping to talk to Professor Eyres, but he's lecturing in Antigua at the moment. I believe you're a friend of Professor Eyres?'

'That's right. Yes.'

'Anyway, the reason I'm ringing you, Mr Downie, is...'

Les went into the same spiel, adding this time that he only had till Wednesday as he had to be back in Australia by Monday and he was leaving early to beat the hurricane. He also emphasised the bit about the manse and Father Eduardo Norton because of the two priests in the family.

'So what I was hoping, Mr Downie, is, seeing that I'm a bit strapped for time, could I call out to see you today and just introduce myself? Then when it's convenient for yourself, we could get together before I leave and you could tell me a few things about the family. Mainly Father Eduardo. Would that be alright?'

Downie seemed to think for a second or two. 'Oh yes. I don't see why not.'

'Well I'm staying just over in Montego Bay. Would some time today be alright?'

'Yes. I'm here till five. But I could be held up later on this afternoon. How about two o'clock?'

'Okay, Mr Downie. I'll see you at two o'clock.'

'I look forward to meeting you, Mr Norton. Goodbye.'

'Goodbye, Mr Downie. And thanks.'

Well there you go again, beamed Les, looking at the phone. One door closes and another one opens. He doesn't sound like a bad bloke either. But I don't think I'd better race out there and start coming on too strong about the manse. Like, come on, Millwood, I only got two days, where's the fuckin' loot stashed? Why don't I have a swim, take a few photos of the harbour from up here and read a bit more of that book on Jamaica so I sound as if I know what I'm talking about. Yes. Good idea. Les got into his Speedos, picked up his backpack and walked down to the Badminton Club's version of a swimming pool.

Except for a plump woman in a white uniform pushing a broom around, the pool area was deserted. It was still oppressively hot, completely still, with a thin cloud cover blocking out the worst of the sun. But the view from where Les stood certainly was sensational. It wrapped right around the harbour and the hills beyond and in the distance Les could see beaches and bays and a majestic white ocean liner moored to a wharf alongside some high-rise hotel. The hazy sun had turned the Caribbean almost turquoise across the bay and where the water deepened it was an intense, cobalt blue. It certainly was the postcard view of Jamaica. Les used the last shot in the camera, reloaded, and shot off a few more; he took some of the view and some of this funny-looking lizard with a big head and pink eyes crawling up the white-washed wall. Happy with that, Les found a chipped white table and chairs in the shade, put his gear down and fell in the pool.

The water wasn't all that bad; no worse than the Barrone back in Dirranbandi when it sometimes looks like it's flowing upside down, and it didn't look as if there'd been too many people around pissing in it. Les flopped around for a while, cooling off, did a few crooked laps then towelled off and sat in the shade with his book. After a while he was none the wiser about buried treasure, but he'd learnt a few more things about Jamaica. Eventually he looked at his watch and closed the book. Well, I reckon that might do. By the time I get there and sort a couple of other things out it'll be time. Even Jamaican style. He strolled up to his room, got into a light green T-shirt with a Koori drawing of a goanna on the front, and the same brown shorts, then after giving himself a quick detail drove to the Golf Club.

Just by watching the roads going downhill and keeping an eye on the ocean Les had no trouble finding the A1. Once on it, he ignored the hitchhikers and drove slowly. The same mob of higglers were ensconced on the corner opposite Rose Point Resort. Les swung left and the guards let him straight through the boomgates again. There was a parking space not far from the main entrance. Les was in and out with another pile of monopoly money and a few hundred more in US bills. After showing the clerk his receipt, proving he'd stayed there and he was coming back, he had no problems changing a traveller's cheque. With the money tucked into his wallet he drove back out through the boomgates and turned left for Spring Water Road.

At first Les thought it was an apparition. But no, it was a near-new street sign on the right with the name of the club underneath. He turned right up a slight hill then further on drove through two white-washed, sandstone pillars with copper lamps on top and a white and green sign above saying Autumn Moon Golf Club Resort. Past the sign was about half a kilometre of crunchy white gravel driveway surrounded by trees, with about another half a kilometre of golf links on either side. Everything looked green and lush and landscaped or manicured to within an inch of its life and very exclusive looking. Several golfers were buzzing around in electric golf buggies, others were strolling across the greens, pulling golf carts. The driveway stopped at a kind of island full of flowers then half circled past a red and white concrete restaurant on the left, a pro shop and clothes store in the middle and the resort proper on the right. It was built in the fashion of a small, white stuccoed castle with turrets on top and a number of steps out the front. Red and yellow bougainvilleas meandered round the turrets and the front was all plate glass and once again very exclusive looking. Les drove round the island, stopped in front of the steps and got out to see if he could find the office. Off to his right a Jamaican man about thirty was hurrying towards the stairs with a clipboard under his arm. He looked up from whatever he was preoccupied with and seemed to notice Norton.

'Excuse me, mate,' called out Les, pointing to the plate glass front. 'Is the office up there?'

The man slowed down and walked over, a cautious yet at the same time amused expression on his face. 'You wouldn't happen to be Mr Norton, would you?'

'Yeah. How...?'

'Oh we get a few Australian golfers in here at times. Mate.'

'Oh. I slipped one out, did I?'

The man returned Norton's smile. 'I'm Millwood Downie.'

'Les Norton. Pleased to meet you, Mr Downie.'

'Call me Mill. Everybody else does.'

'Les suits me too, Mill.'

Millwood had a good handshake and smile, was about five-seven, slim, with short hair in a kind of angular crew cut. He had high cheekbones on a thin, yet thoughtful face and two mercurial brown eyes that seemed to radiate life. He was wearing grey trousers and a white shirt with the name of the resort above the front pocket in red. Despite himself Les found he was being reminded of someone in the movies again.

'So you're out here looking up your long lost relations, Les? The Norton family tree, so to speak.'

'Yeah. Particularly Father Eduardo and the manse over at Dredmouth. That's why I'm hoping you might be able to help me.'

380

'I'll certainly do what I can. But you must remember this is more like a hobby with me. I'm not like Professor Eyres.'

Les thought it might be an idea to swing the conversation around for the moment before he started sounding too avaricious by honing straight in on the manse. Besides, he'd taken an instant liking to Millwood and was impressed not only by his genial nature, but the timbre in his voice and the precise way he spoke.

'Mr Glover told me you're a teacher and you only work here part time?'

'Part-time teaching and work here all the time would be more like it,' said Millwood. 'What the government pays me as a teacher would scarcely feed a budgerigar. And I give nearly all of it back to the children and the school. This is my bread and butter. And I wouldn't go so far as to describe the owners of the place as being generous to a fault.'

'Whereabouts is your school?'

Millwood pointed to the wooded slopes behind the golf club. 'Up there on the Hill of Zion. It's small, it's old, it's rundown. And we call it Spring Water Primary.'

Les smiled. 'Sounds nice. And it sounds like you've certainly got your work cut out for you.'

'You can say that again.' Millwood looked at his watch almost apologetically. 'And, to be honest, Les, you couldn't have called at a worse time. I've got a resort half full of whingeing seppos who can't make up their minds whether to go back to America or ride this goddamn hurricane out. Yee — hah!'

'You do get a few Australians in here, Mill,' chuckled Les.

'Yes. Most of them are pretty good — better than the chucky boys,' Millwood added with a wink. 'In the meantime, I'm going to be flat out all day with these gum-chewing rednecks. And I have to teach tonight.'

'Yeah. And I imagine you'll be busy again all day tomorrow?' said Les. 'What about tomorrow night?'

'I'm not doing anything tomorrow night.'

'Okay. How about I shout you a nice dinner in Mo' Bay tomorrow night? We'll have a few drinks and you might be able to fill me in on a few things. And if you want to bring your wife or your girlfriend along, that's alright.'

'No. My fiance's over at Port Antonio visiting her family. I'll just bring some documents and that.'

'Terrific. Well, I'll ring you here at, say, ten tomorrow morning, and make arrangements?'

'That would be excellent. In the meantime, Les, may I suggest you go and have a look at Rose Hill Great House? It's not far from here.'

'Yeah. But I was thinking more of having a look at Sweet Ginger Hill. Where Eduardo and Elizabeth were born.'

'I doubt if you'll get in there, Les. It's privately owned now.'

'That's right. It is too.'

'Anyway, Les, I must get going. I'll hear from you tomorrow morning.'

'For sure,' nodded Les. 'Before you go though, Mill. Would you mind coming over to the car for a minute?'

'Okay,' shrugged Millwood.

Les stood near the door and, rather than make a big display on the steps, discreetly slipped $300 US out of his pocket and handed it to Millwood Downie.

'Take that, Mill. My family back in Australia aren't short and your school sounds like it could do with some help. And please don't take it the wrong way, either. It's just my way of showing . . . the family's appreciation. And that we're fair dinkum. I think you know what that means, Mill.'

Millwood looked at the money, shook his head for a moment then put it in his pocket. 'Thank you very much Les. You're very generous. To a fault, I suppose you could say.'

'Don't worry about that,' winked Les. 'There's worse people around than us Nortons.'

'I'll hear from you tomorrow morning, Les.'

'Till tomorrow, Millwood.'

They shook hands once more then Les watched Millwood slowly walk towards the office; it was obvious he'd been moved. At the bottom of the steps he jumped slightly in the air, clicked his heels together and ran up them. It was an awkward, knock-kneed kind of run with his elbows all out of plumb. That was when Les knew what movie star Millwood reminded him of and which movie. It was Jerry Lewis in *The King of Comedy*. When he was running down the street trying to get away from Robert de Niro and his ugly ratbag girlfriend. Les shook his head and got in the car. I'm gonna have to turn this up. Equating everyone I see with either some cartoon or a movie. A schoolteacher and an historian becomes Jerry Lewis a comedian? This is madness. They'll finish up putting me in the rathouse. He started the car, slowly motored back down the white gravel driveway and through the sandstone gates. At the A1 he stopped and looked at his watch. It was too early to go back to the hotel. Why not take another look at the manse? See what turns up. Les hung a right and headed towards Dredmouth.

On the way to the manse Les mulled a few things over in his head about Millwood Downie and what he'd just done. Like giving three hundred bucks to some bloke he'd only just met. It was questionable if he could help him anyway and leaving it until Tuesday night was cutting it a bit fine also. But there was something about the skinny Jamaican teacher Les liked. He was genuine; and you didn't often see that in people these days. As for the lousy three hundred bucks, Les wouldn't even miss it, and it would go to a good cause anyway. Spring Water Primary. It had a nice sound to it. Les also couldn't help but think Millwood Downie, with his funny Jerry Lewis run, had another string to his bow besides teaching and a part-time interest in Jamaican history.

Les spent the rest of the afternoon at the manse. He walked all over it, banged his fist against walls looking for hollow spots, had a good look upstairs just in case, stubbing his toe on a big bolt half sticking out of the crossbeam. He waded through the weeds and shrubs in the backyard, checked the remains of the old sundial and the stables. He paced out the old building's measurements front and sides and around the cobblestones, took notes, even checked the alignments of the manse with the sun. After a while he found a spot in the shade across the road and went through Elizabeth Norton Blackmore's book of poems looking for clues.

There were references to a manse in four of her poems, one containing something even more obscure about an old fruit tree. Treasure was mentioned in six poems and gold and diamonds bobbed up in a couple of others. And to Les it was all gibberish. Ye olde seventeenth-century English speak, with its thees and thous and doths and dothn'ts, didn't go down well at all with the big Queenslander. In the end Norton was half convinced that whatever was there, if there *was* anything there, was either hidden in among the sandstone blocks or buried under the cobblestones out the front. That's where Les would have put it if he owned the joint. And if it was there, how was he going to get it out if he found it? Les gazed from the book of poems across to the manse and shook his head. Father Eduardo and his sister Elizabeth had certainly left him, and everybody else, a puzzle alright. The hot Jamaican sun had sizzled down into the blue waters of the Caribbean and it was quite dark when Les got back to the Badminton Club.

Well, didn't the day go quick, Les thought, as he stood under the dribbling, lukewarm water of the shower and washed away the dirt and dust he'd gathered crawling around and over the manse. I knew this was a good idea and it would keep my mind off things. Better than sitting around picking your arse and feeling sorry for yourself. The heat takes the edge off your appetite too; especially after that monster breakfast this morning. Though I'm a bit peckish now. I'll grab a bit of something down at the Mardi Gras. Hope to Christ it's not only fairycakes and queen pudding that they're selling. Mardi Gras in Montego Bay, Les chuckled to himself as he towelled off in front of the balcony. And I simply haven't got a thing to wear. Not long after, he was in his blue shorts, green Wallabies T-shirt and Nikes, and in the Honda heading down towards the waterfront.

Les knew that skinny hairpin bend coming up from town looked out over the harbour and the park next to where Gloucester Avenue began; he stopped about two-thirds of the way down, did a U-turn and parked facing back up. A few shifty-looking types were standing around talking or smoking cigarettes, Les locked the car, ignored them and started walking down. There were no buildings, only a low fence on the right side of the road and everything was spread out below him. Traffic and taxis were flowing towards town, it looked like some kind of reggae band was playing in the park and across the road behind the park were the inky-blue waters of the bay. More traffic was slowly moving down the road alongside the park, and to the right, barricades, cops and crowds of people swarming in that direction said the Mardi Gras was in full swing. Les got to the bottom of the hill, ducked across the traffic to the corner where the park met the intersection and the short road down to Gloucester Avenue. There were plenty of people around, all Jamaican men and women. A couple of blokes tried to sell him something, some women higglers selling drinks along the footpath called out to him. Les ignored them and stopped to look at the crowded park.

It was circular in shape with trees here and there, about a hundred metres across and built like an amphitheatre with tiers of seats facing down. The rows of seats were packed with people of all ages, the women in long dresses wearing red, gold and green belts, sandals and coconut shell earrings. The men mainly in jeans and T-shirts, with great mops of dreadlocks tumbling out all over the place and all looking gaunt and stringy. They were all avidly watching a stage set up below where a bunch of men were lounging around in front of two banks of speakers, out of which was coming this deep, slow beat from a bass and drum. In the middle of the stage some wild-looking bloke appeared to be preaching into a hand-held microphone. He had the mike and a clipboard in one hand and in the other a joint about as big as a Darwin Stubbie, which he was attacking with relish. Norton's reggae band in the park was a full-on Rastafarian meeting. Jah Rastafarai, mon. All the straight and righteous waiting it out away from the immoral peel-heads. Les was fascinated. More than a few punters along the footpath were giving him odd looks. But Les was expecting that, being one of the few honkys walking around. He also wasn't expecting any favours either, so he'd left everything at home, except some of his money, which he'd spread into all the pockets of his shorts so if he did get a tickle they wouldn't get the lot in one go. The street sloped down past the park towards Gloucester Avenue, Les followed the footpath to the end of the park and moved in among the crowd standing in front of the stage for a better look at the boys in the band.

Midnight Oil it wasn't. There were about a dozen stringy-looking dreads lolling about near the speakers. A couple of yabbahs were going around, glowing in the dark, some bloke was plunking out two notes on an electric bass and some other bloke was thumping out one monotonous note on a drum. Les arrived just in time to see the head rasta with the mike pull a massive toke on his spliff that made almost the top half of his body disappear in a cloud of thick blue smoke. Shit a brick, thought Les. I had three small tokes of that shit last night and I thought I was rollerblading through the rings around Saturn with Elle Macpherson. That ratbag just burnt off enough to jam a reaper and binder. Where must his head be? The rasta let some more smoke out and started crooning into the mike with this strong, melodious voice that crackled through the speakers in a rich vibrant bass. It was John Laws eat your heart out; about five octaves lower and twice as rich. The head rasta was in the middle of some giant spiel about Haile Selassie.

'Ire mon,' he crooned into the microphone. 'In nineteen tirty-tree, Haile Selassie broke de drought in Africa, stopped de war in de homeland and gave all de banks back to de people. Did you know dahhhhttt?'

Behind and around Les the crowd clapped and cheered. 'Ire mon. Jah rastafah!' they all yelled, in between toking on their spliffs.

'Ay. Jah Rastafarai,' echoed the rasta on stage. 'And in nineteen tirty-seven,' he continued, 'Haile Selassie saved all de peoples from starveershun, stopped de exploiteershun of children and gave women de vote. Did you know dahhhttt?'

'Ya woo! Ire mon. Jah Rastafah. Jah Rastafah,' howled the crowd, as another half a ton of ganja went up in smoke and hung over the park.

'Ire. Jah Rastafarai. Jah Rastafarai,' repeated the dread with the mike, and took another horrifying toke on his spliff that would have made a Nimbin hippy buy a grey flannel suit and get a job flogging life insurance in Melbourne. 'And in nineteen tirty-nine,' he crooned, 'Haile Selassie built twenty new dams, gave edjookeershun and 'lectricity to de peoples and beat de forces of imperialism. Did you know dahhhttt?'

'Ya roo! Ire. Jah Rastafah. Jah Rastafah,' howled the mob.

'Ire. Jah Rastafarai,' said the dread up on stage.

By the time he'd had another two tokes while continuing his rap, about the only things Haile Selassie hadn't done was invent the wheel, discover penicillin and beat Armstrong to the moon. The rasta was just about to load up again when Les noticed the bloke on stage wasn't the only centre of attention. Norton looked around and there were all these odd-looking, pinky brown eyes staring at him from the darkness. It was then that Les also noticed he was the only slice of white bread at the rastas' picnic; and from the looks he was getting it was giving most of the gathering a bad case of indigestion. Oh well, thought Les. I think it might be exit stage right for the goyen. Slowly and smiling Les eased his way through the crowd,

387

jogged across the street and around the barricade, winked at a cop, then joined the crowds of people swarming past the waterfront along Gloucester Avenue.

There were hundreds of people crowding along the street, mainly Jamaicans in their early twenties and a smattering of Euro-trash backpackers. The seaward side of the street was fenced off and open with a few restaurants, the other side mainly held small hotels and shops. Les passed another smaller park then above the crowds of people something caught his eye. It was a small, white, two-storey hotel with a parking area out the front for about a dozen cars and a sign near the street that said Biltmore Hotel, same as the one at Bondi. Norton's face broke into a grin, then a thought struck him. He wasn't all that rapt in where he was staying and was thinking of brushing it; the only reason he was there was because he'd been a bit confused and in a hurry and it was the only place he could think of. He could have stayed at the best hotel there was in Montego Bay. But why not get a room at the Biltmore just for a gag? It was only for another night. Yeah, bugger it. Why not? Les laughed to himself. I'll see if they've got any rooms. There was a vacant building on the right side and an open-front bar on the other. Les skipped through the crowd and into the parking lot.

It was full of small cars and led to a very plain-looking hairdressing salon at the rear, left of a set of stairs. A security guard in a white shirt and black bowtie was leaning against the wall next to the bottom step. He seemed about as energetic as the one at the Badminton Club but about a foot taller. He looked at Les sleepily.

'I'm after a room,' said Les. 'Okay if I go up?' The man mumbled something that sounded and looked like yes and stood aside. 'Thanks, mate,' winked Les, and jogged up the steps.

The stairs went up one storey to the foyer and office set just to the left. Right of the office a door led to what looked like a bar or restaurant and in the left corner from the office another set of stairs went to the floor above. On either side of the office the rooms angled off along two long balconies looking down on the carpark and at the top of the stairs was a small dining area scattered with black and white chairs and tables that overlooked the carpark and the darkness of the ocean behind. The reception desk was a wooden counter with a bell and the usual things found on hotel counters, a wall and a glass door led to the safe and office behind. A girl sitting on a chair behind the bell looked up as Les approached. She was plain and dumpy in a yellow uniform but appeared to be about a thousand times more pleasant than Lucretia Borgia up at the Badminton Club.

'Good evening, miss,' said Norton, returning her smile. 'I'd like a room for two nights if I could?'

'No problem, mon.' She pointed to the balcony behind Norton on his left. 'There's one over there. When did you want to move in?'

'Tomorrow morning.'

'No problem, mon.'

Les explained his position to the girl about being in the other hotel and not liking it, how he was walking past, saw this place but the only ID he had on him was his room key at the Badminton Club. Would $50 US as deposit be okay? No problem, mon. The girl gave him a receipt and Les said he'd fix the rest up when he came down in the morning with his bags to pick up the key. He wouldn't bother to check the room; he was certain it would be alright. Les pocketed the receipt, thanked the girl and said he'd see her tomorrow. Thank you, sir. Have a good night at the Mardi Gras. Les jogged down the stairs, told Sleepy on the door he was moving in and rejoined the noisy throng milling along Gloucester Avenue.

Les got about two hundred yards or so when things began to change. All along the sides of the road now was stall after stall of people trying to sell pretty much the same stuff. Jamaican T-shirts, beanies, scarves, etc. Jewellery, carvings, shells, dope pipes, etc. The usual tourist junk you find in any tourist trap anywhere in the world. Others that didn't have a stall were walking along the road, trying to flog stuff to any luckless tourists strolling along. As soon as they saw a white face they zeroed in like heat-seeking missiles.

'Hey, mon.'

'Hey, mon.'

'Hey come here, mon. I don't want to sell you nothing. I just wan to talk wit yu.'

After a while Les was wishing them to the shithouse and starting to think he wasn't a human being, just a walking dollar bill sign. A few higgler women selling fruit got a bit of Norton's business. He bought some beautifully sweet, chopped-up pineapple, some bananas and a bunch of what looked like huge yellow grapes that were more like berries with a big stone in them and reminded him of a cross between a plum and a paw-paw.

It was about now Les began to notice he was getting lots of smiles from young girls in bunches of twos and threes. Like a mug Les began smiling back. Next thing he knew he had five girls on his arm; two on his left, three on his right. They were all about twenty, wearing jeans, short dresses and T-shirts. No oil paintings and not quite as swedyang tunti as the two he picked up in the car. But takeaway tunti, nonetheless. In which Norton was not the slightest bit interested. Not having access to three, industrial strength, East German condoms and a hose-down with detoxicant afterwards. Les laughed along with the girls though and was sorry he hadn't brought his camera. It would have made a good photo; if someone could have taken one without running off with it. Les was pretty certain the young ladies weren't after him for his good looks and it didn't take them long to put their spiel on. First was, give them twenty bucks to get into the Mardi Gras. You didn't have to be a Rhodes scholar to know it was free and you were already there. Then it was, fifty bucks to get some beef jerky — they were hungry and hadn't eaten. Back in Australia three of the girls could have done with fifty bucks to join Jenny Craig.

Strolling along with the five young chicks having a yahoo was fun and they liked him even more when they realised he wasn't an American. But some of the looks he was getting from the local lads weren't so funny. Some of them seemed to know the girls and when they spoke Les could pick up parts of the conversation that were along the lines of, what are you girls doing with that prick just because he's got money when you should be porking your own kind for free. Les walked along with them a bit further before slipping each girl some monopoly money, saying he'd meet them later outside the hotel they were standing in front of. Once he was rid of them Les disappeared into the crowd.

It was a big night at the Mardi Gras, heaps of people, bustle and noise and a few reggae bands here and there; even if it did appear to be put on mainly for the tourists and the stallholders. Les couldn't make out much from the surrounding buildings because of the crowds, but it seemed to be mainly hotels and restaurants, a little like Manly Corso or St Kilda maybe. He found a bank, the post office and a chemist shop and that in a kind of mall near a park, but thought he'd check it out in more detail when he moved in tomorrow. Not that there was all that much need; he'd be leaving the next day.

Les was strolling along, looking around, avoiding the pricks running at him trying to flog something, when the crowd parted and a marching band about fifteen strong came down the street. Silver uniforms and hats, cymbals crashing, drums banging, brass blaring as they wound their way through the people who were dancing all these funny steps to the music they were playing. The band leader was a skinny little bloke with a baton and whistle. He'd blow his whistle, toss the baton and jump up in the air, and another little bloke next to him would do the same thing with a huge pair of cymbals. He'd jump up, spin around and crash the cymbals together in mid-air while behind him the band would kick their legs up, bob up and down or do something dazzling in time to the music. They were the best thing on the night and got a great reaction from the crowd. Les watched them till they moved on and once again wished he'd brought his camera.

The reggae bands sounded alright, but no one was nodding their heads, let alone getting up and having a bit of dance or a jig around. It was very subdued. In fact, apart from the marching band the whole scene was fairly average for a Mardi Gras. The higglers and the other rats weren't doing much of a trade because tourists were pretty thin on the ground, and the locals weren't buying anything because they were probably all too broke. Les also began to notice he was getting some dirty looks and muttered remarks from different bunches of blokes walking past. Les thought it best to avoid too much eye contact and kept in among the crowd. I suppose if I turned around and told some of them to get fucked, he thought, I'd be up for racial vilification.

There were a number of small stands selling rum-punches, which weren't bad, for around a dollar each so he had two. Another stand was selling some kind of flat bread with curried vegetables and a few stringy bits of meat on it, which didn't smell too bad either, so Les had a couple of these too. Standing back, eating and watching the punters, was okay. But there was something about the whole third-world scene that made him wary and took the edge off it. In fact, a few young blokes, as well as giving him dirty looks, were openly gobbing off at him. It definitely wasn't a good place to be on your own. Les got some more pineapple and started walking back to the car.

Past the Biltmore the crowd was starting to thin out a little and there were some blokes in battered cars touting as taxis. Yes, nodded Les. That could be an idea. Rather than walk past that park then up the hill on my own I might catch a cab. I can handle the rort to a certain extent. But a local posse of about half a dozen hungry nutters carrying knives and probably off their faces? Leave that to the Bruce Lee movies. Les bundled into some Japanese rustbucket with black carpet across the dash, told the drive he was German so he wouldn't have to talk to him and got a lift to his car. The bloke wanted five dollars US, rather than haggle Les gave him a handful of monopoly money, got in the Honda and drove back to the penthouse suite at the Badminton Club.

Speedy's mate opened the boomgate and Les parked in front of the office next to four other cars. Although he hadn't done a great deal all day, Les was looking forward to hitting the sack as he followed the path alongside the swimming pool. The sound of reggae music coming from closeby made him look up and Les was a little surprised to see the lights on and the bar open. It looked like a big night too. There was a blonde couple and two young Jamaican girls seated at tables in front of a tired-looking barman polishing glasses who could have been the bloke on the gate's brother. Ohh yeah, thought Les. Why not a couple of little nightcaps before I climb in the cot? Glad it was open in a way, he strolled over to the bar.

The Badminton Club cocktail lounge was about twice as big as your average loungeroom, with stone walls at one end and wooden ones at the other. It was painted a light mauve and dotted with orange light fittings. The bar was varnished wood, the chairs and tables the same, though they were just as much wood as they were varnish. There was a mirror behind the bar crossed with shelves full of bottles and edged in with tourist posters of Jamaica plus one of the Jamaican soccer team and another of Eartha Kitt. There was a TV set that wasn't on, and the music was a tape playing through the speakers set at either end of the bar. It was still quite hot so Les thought he might have a nice cold beer and ordered a Red Stripe, which he charged to his room.

'No problem, mon,' said the barman, placing the bottle in front of him. Les left the glass on the bar, took a good long pull and had a look around.

The couple were two Nordic Germans in shorts and T-shirts eyeing each other off very Teutonically and correctly over their bottles of Red Stripe. The two girls looked about twenty and were definitely no glamours, although their figures weren't too bad. One had on a pair of cheap, grey cord jeans and a white V-neck T-shirt. The other wore tight black shorts with red polka-dots and a white T-shirt with a pastel-coloured drawing of a reggae band on the front. They both had thick, short, bushy hair, big lips, and solid, bony features, and as far as being Jamaicans went, they could have both just paddled a canoe down the Sepik River in New Guinea. The one in the jeans's eyes were that far apart they were almost on the side of her head like a goldfish. But looks aside, they were the two most sorrowful, miserable, hangdog-looking excuses for women Norton had ever seen. They were both sitting staring into space, absolutely dejected, with nothing in front of them but an empty table top; no drinks, no purse, no keys, nothing. Just a plastic shopping bag under the table. Bloody hell, thought Les, looking at their pathetic faces. I know this place is a dump, but surely it's not that bad.

The one in jeans caught Les staring at them and said something to the barman in patois which Les didn't quite catch.

'Hey mon,' said the barman. 'Deh girls want to know would you buy dem a drink. Deh naa no dunza.'

Hello, here we go a-bloody-gain, thought Norton. I must have MUG written across my forehead in letters three feet high. 'Yeah, righto,' he replied wearily. 'Give them whatever they want. And put it on my tab.'

'Ire, mon,' said the barman. He poured two glasses of orange juice and placed them on the bar.

The one wearing jeans got up, took the drinks, mumbled a kind of shy thanks to Les then sat back down. As she did, the other one motioned for Les to join them. Les thought for a moment. Yeah, why not? he sighed to himself. It's someone to talk to, I suppose. He picked up his Red Stripe and walked over to their table.

'Hello, girls. How's things?' he said as he sat down.

They both mumbled something and continued to stare into space. Then the one in shorts pointed to Norton's T-shirt. 'A wa daht?' she asked.

'It's a wallaby,' replied Les. 'It's an Australian animal. Like a kangaroo.'

'Australian,' said the one in jeans. 'You no 'merican?'

394

Les smiled and shook his head. 'No. Australian.'

'Oh. Daht's good.'

Les nodded. 'Yes. Exciting, isn't it?' Though I reckon you pair wouldn't care if I was in the Khmer Rouge as long as I bought you a drink, thought Les. 'So what's your names anyway, girls? I'm Les.' The one in jeans was Delta. The other was Esme. Then they went back to staring mournfully into space. 'So what's doing anyway, girls? Are you staying here? And how come you're so miserable? You look like you've just shit yourselves.'

The girls stared at Les for a moment, exchanged glances, then Esme started up.

No. They weren't staying there. They'd both caught a bus over from Kingston, expecting to get work at the hotel. When they arrived there was none. Maybe next Thursday. In the meantime they were stone, motherless broke, had nowhere to stay and all their worldly possessions were in the plastic bag under the table. Part of the deal with the job was that along with the princely sum of $400 a week Jamaican they got a small room to share. But seeing as they weren't working there yet the woman Les met at the desk wouldn't let them stay there. So along with being broke and homeless, they were tired, hungry, thirsty and killing time till the bar closed so they could go and sleep in the park or the gutter or wherever. And it looked like being three long, hungry days till Thursday. Esme's bony face was pretty long at any time, but as she spoke it seemed to get longer and longer till it was almost hanging between her knees. Christ, thought Les. No wonder the poor bastards aren't laughing. And I thought I had it tough. Four hundred bloody bucks a week. And to think I just gave that to five sheilas down the road I'd never met just to get rid of them. It's a funny old world.

'Well,' Les said sympathetically, as Delta and Esme resumed staring morosely into space, 'I've heard some tales of woe in my time, but that's a pisser. You're the original. Fragged and far from home.' They stared at Les. 'You're knackered.' They looked at each other, then stared at Les again. 'You're doing it a bit tough.'

'Tuff?' said Esme.

'Yeah,' nodded Les.

'Ya. Tuff, mon,' said Delta gloomily.

Christ! Haven't I cracked it for a couple of nice drones to have a drink with? How am I ever gonna get a laugh out of these two? Forget the shout. But what a low bind to be in. Having to sleep in the park and no chops. I can't see that happening somehow. Norton winced slightly inside. He knew he was going to end up giving the girls some money. But, shit, he was getting sick of it. He didn't arrive in town to take over from the Department of Social Security. Then if he did give the girls some money they might take it the wrong way — or take it the right way. And Les wasn't at all keen. Though up closer they weren't all that bad. Esme, the older of the two, didn't have a bad pair of legs — except for where she'd given them a rough shave and the hairs were sticking up like broken tooth-picks. Les was going to have to work something out. In the meantime, just a few drinks and talk Edgar. The bus ride over from Kingston must have been sensational.

'Anyway, don't worry about it too much, girls. Brer Wallaby's in town. So come on, drink 'em up and I'll get you another one. Then I might tell you about what a good bloke I am.' Delta and Esme looked at each other, shrugged, then instead of sipping their orange juices got into them like they'd just finished a triathlon. Les ordered the same again for them, plus a rum-punch for himself; leaving some monopoly money on the bar when he picked them up.

Les told them he was a farmer back in Australia, he was on holidays and had just spent two weeks in America. He got here Saturday, but had to cut his holiday short and was leaving Wednesday. He was also moving into the Biltmore in the morning as this place didn't turn him on all that much. He was sorry he had to go so soon because he liked Jamaica; especially after meeting two sweet young girls like them. Les even kissed Esme's fingertips and was surprised to find her fingers underneath were soft and pink, almost like a baby's. Esme giggled and the girls smiled at Norton's innocent joke and, when they did, their lovely white smiles lit up their faces momentarily and their true beauty shone through. Les ordered some more drinks while he bullshitted away and somehow between their patois, English and Australian slang they got a conversation going. Les even asked them what some of the reggae songs were coming over the speakers, and got told names like Shaggy Wonder, Dignitary Stylish, Yellowman. They could have been a trifecta at Bulli Dogs for all Les knew, but the music wasn't too bad and the more rum-punches he sunk the better it got. The night cruised along and Les didn't even notice the Hitler Youth Movement had left when he got up for what were going to be the last drinks for the night. The barman hinted politely that he was going to have to shut shop. Fair enough, thought Norton. He was starting to feel a bit stuffed anyway. He placed the last drinks on the table, knowing the girls had been in a fairly earnest discussion while he was up. Well, here it comes. Now what? I can't see them coming back to my room. Not with me half pissed.

'Well, girls,' he said, raising his glass, 'looks like these are the last. Then it's off to . . . wherever.'

It looked like Esme was going to be the sacrificial lamb. If not her, Delta. 'So yu just got de room on you own, Les?'

'Yes Esme, that's right,' replied Les.

'Yu want tik me wit yu?'

Les smiled and shook his head. 'No. Not tonight, Esme. Thanks.'

Esme's face dropped a little. 'Yu don't lik me?'

'No, you're wrong, Esme. You're unreal. I haven't been able to keep my eyes off you all night. Anyway, what about Delta?'

Esme's eyes dropped again. 'Yu want Delta?'

'No,' smiled Les. 'I was just wondering what happens to her?'

'She be okay.' Esme's eyes widened. 'Yu want bot us?'

'No,' laughed Les. 'I don't want either of you. I'm

knackered. I just want to go to sleep.' Les cradled his head against his hands and closed his eyes for a second. The girls' faces went back to abject misery and dejection again. They'd played both their bowers to no avail. It looked like the park was coming up. 'But I'll tell you what I will do,' said Les. Suddenly their faces lit up just a little.

Through the night, Les had been checking out their jewellery. They wore cheap, but pretty, bead necklaces, leather bracelets in yellow, black and green, and these junky rings on their fingers. They weren't super tacky; even nice in a way. On their index fingers they wore a pewter and a copper ring with some kind of design in the metal. Even at Paddy's Markets they wouldn't have been more than a dollar each, tops.

'I'll tell you what I'll do,' said Les. 'I'll buy those two rings off you.' They fitted loosely and before they knew it Les had hold of their fingers and the rings off. 'How much do you want for them?' Like a miserable Bondi landlord Les looked at the two rings on the table and pulled out what money was in one pocket; there was a little over $200 Jamaican. 'Is that enough?' Delta and Esme blinked at the money then at each other, not quite believing what they were seeing. Les narrowed his eyes. 'Alright,' he said, going for his kick again. 'I'll throw in some more.' He dropped $50 American on the table. The two girls nearly fainted. 'And that's my final offer. What do you reckon?' Wide-eyed, Esme and Delta looked at Les, looked at each other, then scooped up the money. Les slid the rings on both his little fingers like he was a mug. But a happy one. 'And that's not all I'll do,' he said, 'seeing as you've got nowhere to stay for the night. Do you want to sleep in my car?'

'In your car?' said Esme.

'Yeah,' shrugged Les. 'I know it's not much. But . . .'

The two battlers looked at Les like he'd just offered them the Sir Robert Helpmann Suite at the Sebel Townhouse, and nodded their heads in disbelief. 'Well, come on. Finish these and I'll unlock it for you.' They finished their drinks and Les picked up their plastic shopping bag.

'I'll even give you a hand with your Giani travel case.' He gave the barman a wink, who winked back, and Les walked the girls out to the Honda.

Speedy's mate was leaning against the office wall smoking a cigarette. Half drunk Les told him what was going on and what he didn't understand the girls filled him in on with patois. He was too tired or uninterested to give a stuff one way or the other. He nodded something as Les unlocked the car.

'There you go, girls. You've got the flat till the morning. Now come here.' Les pulled Delta over and gave her a peck on the cheek. 'There you go, Del, me old mate. Sleep tight.' She tensed at first then relaxed. 'You too, Es, my little Jamaican princess.' Les did the same to her and she looked at Norton with the Caribbean splashing around in her eyes. 'Happy dreams, mate. I'm just sorry I can't give you one of my pillows.' Esme climbed in the back, Delta got in the front and Les closed the doors. The last he saw of them was their faces staring back through the windscreen as he waved a smile behind him and walked off.

Fair dinkum! The things you do when you're half drunk, Les mumbled to himself as he lay back on the pillows with just his jox on. The room felt like all the air-conditioner had done was make a noise and drip more slimy water out the front. Les turned it off and was staring up at the ceiling through half-closed eyes. Fifty bucks for those two rings I tossed on the dresser. They wouldn't be worth a zac. But I s'pose they'll make a funny souvenir. Anyway, what could you do? Poor little bastards. Wouldn't it be lovely sleeping in the park around here? And what a low dropkick that sheila must be, not letting them stay here. There's no one in the fuckin' joint. Oh well. At least I did someone half a favour. He yawned and closed his eyes. I got a big day tomorrow too. I got to visit that big house. Probably have another look at the mosque again. I mean the manse. Move into the Biltmore. Meet Millwood and do lunch. Have dinner. Whatever. Les let out one last, long yawn. Yeah, whatever.

Les knew he was going to be robbed when he checked out; from what he'd seen so far of the dropkick in the office it was inevitable and he wasn't even going to argue. He was more curious than anything else as to how the rob would come about and how strong it would be.

Despite the heat Les had slept in a little, but now he had his bags packed once more, the same clothes on as last night and was ready to go. Breakfast was two Hershey Bars he'd bought in Florida and thrown in his bag at some time, washed down with a glass of water. There was a dining room at the hotel; however, Norton was determined not to spend a cent more in the place than he had to. After a quick look around to make sure he hadn't left anything he picked up his bags and walked down to reception.

Lucretia Borgia wasn't in the office and there was no sign of Esme or Delta. Sleepy was seated out in his guard box. Les rang the bell and a minute or so later Lucretia appeared from behind the floral curtain, scowling and miserable as ever. She saw Norton's bags and looked at him.

'I'd like to check out please,' said Les.

Lucretia nodded and began making up the bill. She pushed some buttons on a battered-looking computer, wrote a couple of things down then pushed the bill across for Les to sign. Les looked at it, and there was the rob. Straight up. The drinks and phone calls were all kosher. But she'd charged him for two nights. It was a blatant rob because all Les had said was he might take an extra night. *Might*. He'd booked an extra night at the Biltmore just in case there was trouble with the planes. But here? No, it was a full-on rob and no amount of begging, pleading or arguing would change a thing. Not that Les intended to beg, plead or argue. But Price always said, if you get robbed and there's nothing you can do, cop it sweet and don't let on you know. Let the robber think that, although they've dudded you and got their earn, they've dudded themselves at the same time and could have got more. It takes the edge right off the rob. Like if some team of mugs break into a place and steal a half a million dollars then find out in the papers the next day there was another million in a drawer they missed. It does tend to sour things.

Norton stared at the bill for a moment, wrinkled his brow and looked at Lucretia. 'Are you sure you haven't made a mistake here?'

'You said two nights,' she replied stonefaced.

Norton looked at the bill and his face wrinkled even more. 'This is for two nights? It can't possibly be.'

'You said two nights.' Lucretia was adamant.

Norton made a dismissive gesture with his hands. 'I'm not worrying about that. It just seems so cheap.'

'Cheap?' Lucretia gave a double blink.

'Yes. All those drinks I had last night. The phone calls. That magnificent view by the swimming pool. My room was absolutely fabulous. And huge. I had one of the best night's sleep I've had for years.' Les shook his head in dismay. Lucretia's miserable face got even more miserable. 'If I'd only known you had such bargain rates here I'd never have moved out. I'm paying twice as much where I'm going and it's not half as good. And the only reason I'm going is to meet up with a friend.' Les shook his head and sighed. 'Dear oh dear. I don't know.'

'You want to ring up and cancel your booking? I can get you an even better room.' She moved the phone across to Les.

'No, it's too late now,' Les sighed again. 'I might come back though.' Les signed the bill cheerfully and pocketed his VISA card. 'Well, thank you very much. And I'm really sorry I'm leaving. Goodbye.' He had a last, wistful look around. 'I love it here.'

Les picked up his bags and walked out to the car, leaving Lucretia looking like she'd just swallowed Draino. Yeah, and stick it fair in your tunti, you poxy-lookin' moll, Les mumbled to himself as he put the key in the ignition. I'm only sorry I didn't shit in the bath. But some other poor bastard'd only have to clean it up. Speedy staggered out and opened the boomgate; Les gave him a wink and drove through. Well, so much for my one night at the Badminton Club. I could have had a suite at the Hilton for that. He sniffed around him. Oh well. At least Delta and Esme didn't piss in the car.

Getting from the hairpin bend across to Gloucester Avenue was a little tricky because Les didn't feel like driving through town again. So he waited until there was a break in the traffic then fanged the little Honda across the one-way street and down the side of the park into Gloucester Avenue, keeping his white honky head down and playing the dumb tourist at all the abuse and horn blasts he got from the other drivers. The Biltmore Hotel wasn't hard to find and there were only three other cars in the parking lot; Les pulled up alongside what looked like another rental, got his bags from the boot and walked up the stairs.

'Good morning, Mr Norton,' said the girl at the office, recognising him from the previous night.

'Hello, miss,' replied Les, returning her smile. 'How are you today?'

There were about half a dozen people eating breakfast on the balcony and enjoying the view over Montego Bay. Les watched them for a few moments while he picked up his key and filled in the usual paperwork. It certainly was another nice view. The weather was the same as yesterday, the water across the bay its usual smooth turquoise blue with a bit of a cloud build-up towards the horizon. The girl called for the tall security bloke; he picked up Norton's bag and took him over to number 14.

Norton's room was as big as the one at the Badminton Club and was in roughly the same condition. There were two single beds this time with white covers and a phone sitting next to a bed lamp in between. The shower looked better, as did the brasco, a window next to the door looked out over the balcony, there was a chair and table and another rusty air-conditioner jammed up in the wall next to the bathroom door. Les looked at a couple of paintings of tropical fish hanging on the plain white walls and turned to Long-Tack.

'Yeah, righto, mate,' he said. 'Looks alright to me.'

'Ire mon,' said the guard, and placed Norton's bag on the nearest bed.

Les pulled some money from his shorts and handed it to the guard. 'There you are, mate. What's your name anyway?'

'I'rol.'

'Nice to meet you, Errol. I'm Les.'

'Ire, Les. Respec mon.' Errol pocketed the money and closed the door softly behind him.

Well there you go, smiled Les. My new digs. It ain't too bad and it's only for one night. Now what to do? I suppose I'd better unpack a bit of gear. Les put his shower kit in the bathroom and was about to get some other stuff out when, heat or no heat, hunger pangs hit him; two bars of chocolate and a glass of water wouldn't go far. Some breakfast was definitely in order. He locked his room and walked out to the balcony.

A couple of people had left so Les had no trouble getting a table with a view across the carpark and out over the bay. Shortly after, he caught the waiter's eye. The waiter had on the usual white coat, bowtie and black trousers. But he was covered in grease and shit from head to foot and sweat was running down his face and dripping from his chin. He pulled a crumpled order-book and biro from his pocket.

'Ire mon.'

'Yes. Could I have scrambled eggs on toast, please? With tomato, extra toast, coffee and a large orange juice. And a bowl of fruit too. Is that okay?'

'No problem, mon.' The waiter wrote down Norton's order, more sweat dripped off his chin and he vanished out the back.

Les settled back against his chair, feeling quite contented. The view was truly delightful, the surroundings were pleasant and he wasn't pushed for time. He'd finish breakfast, ring Millwood, then go for a snorkel over in the bay and visit Rose Hill Great House after. Although Les had this feeling he should be checking out Sweet

Ginger Hill, where Elizabeth and Eduardo grew up. He was mulling on this when the girl from the office brought over his cutlery and orange juice. She explained breakfast might be a bit delayed as the cook hadn't turned up and the waiter was doing the cooking. That was perfectly alright, replied Les. It was quite enjoyable and relaxing just sitting there. The girl smiled and left. A bit delayed? thought Les, taking a sip of the beautifully chilled orange juice. In Jamaica that could mean anything. And here, at Montego Bay's answer to Fawlty Towers, with Manuel doing the cooking, I could get breakfast at midnight. Les decided to check out the bar or whatever it was through the door near the office.

One step led up into a large room split into two by a walkway, with a bar on the left side and a seated area on the right. The walls and floor were all polished wood except where part of the seated area was covered in dark blue carpet. The bar was solid wood with a split bamboo front facing a row of bamboo stools topped with padded blue leather. Several framed posters and one or two paintings sat on the wall alongside a sizeable mirror with JAMAICA frosted across it in blue and gold; beneath this the bottles were arranged neatly along a bench. Indoor plants sat round the walls and hung off the ceiling, the light fittings were blue and so was the padding on the seats by the tables. It was dark and empty but had a kind of olde worlde charm about it and Les surmised that at one time they probably called it the blue room or something. Another set of steps led up from the lounge to a rockery with a small, kidney-shaped swimming pool. Flower gardens stepped up into the surrounding walls and flowering vines meandered back down behind some indoor palms and other native trees and shrubs. There were a few banana lounges around the pool and it was all quite pleasant, though taking another look at the pool Les didn't think it would take Neil Brooks long to do a couple of laps. Les had another look around inside and gave it a grudging nod of approval. The lounge definitely had some sort of character and would be a good place to drag Millwood back to later on that night for a few drinks and a mag. Pleased with what he'd found Les walked back to his table.

Les had a few things to occupy his mind while he took in the view, though it didn't seem all that long before the Biltmore's answer to Manuel arrived with his breakfast. Two fried eggs on toast, no tomato and no fruit. But the extra toast was there plus a pot of coffee. Norton looked at the two fried eggs, which seemed to be staring back at him from the plate. That was all he needed in this heat. Manuel's face was absolutely expressionless.

'Look, mate,' said Les, 'I know you're on your own, but I ordered scrambled eggs.'

'Scrambled, fried. Same ting, mon.'

Les nodded thoughtfully. 'Yes, you're right. I never thought. And the fruit?'

'Fruit's finished, mon.'

Les looked at his watch. 'Yes, it is getting late. What about the tomato?'

'Tomato's not on today, mon.'

Les nodded again. 'Yes, of course. I should have realised. My humblest apologies, sir, for my appalling manners and totally unforgivable lack of discretion. Thank you very much. You've been more than generous.'

'No problem, mon.' Manuel looked oddly at Norton for a moment then disappeared back into the kitchen.

Les shook his head and speared one of the eggs with his fork. Ahh, who gives a fuck? Fair dinkum. But if I spew this up all over the place, too bloody bad. However, Manuel hadn't done too bad a job on the eggs and before long Les was kicking himself up the arse for whingeing. And any grease that did happen to be on the eggs would soon get eaten away by the Jamaican coffee. It was fabulous. Thick and strong, almost like chocolate. Les lingered over breakfast, finishing off the pot while he reminisced about some things and concentrated on various others. Before long it was time to make a phone call and the water across the street was starting to look more inviting than ever. Les drained the last drop from his cup and in appreciation of the marvellous service left a generous tip.

Back in his room the phone worked alright and Les had no trouble getting through to Millwood Downie at the golf club.

'Hello, Millwood? It's Les. How're you goin'?'

'Les. Good morning. How are you?'

'Pretty good, mate. How's yourself? And how was school last night?'

'School? School was very good. Very good indeed Les. And thank you for asking.'

'That's okay, mate.'

Les explained how he'd moved into the Biltmore and was everything still sweet for tonight? Did he know where the place was or did he need Les to come out and get him? Millwood replied that that was alright. His brother was using his car tonight, but a friend, who worked in a bar along Gloucester Avenue, would drive him in and pick him up at twelve. That suited Les to the ground and he arranged to meet Millwood in the back bar at the Biltmore around seven.

'Righto, Millwood,' said Les. 'You're probably busy so I'd better let you go. I'll see you tonight around seven. Make sure you're hungry.'

'You bet. I'll see you tonight, Les.'

'See you then, Millwood.'

Well how cosy's that? smiled Les. Don't know if I'll pick up any clues, but I reckon Millwood'll be a good bloke to have a drink with anyway. Les gave a bit of a chuckle. Not that it won't cost me. Besides the food and piss you can bet I'll end up buying a few more school books for Spring Water Primary. But like Price always says, it's only money. It's not an arm or a leg. Now, let's go snorkeling in the Caribbean again. Les got his snorkeling gear together and changed into his old running gear, figuring if they stole that while he was in the water, along with a hotel towel, they could have the lot. He locked the door behind him, left his key and a few other things with the girl in the office and trotted down the stairs, giving Long-Tack a wink as he walked across the carpark.

There wasn't that much traffic outside the hotel but more than enough pricks trying to sell him shit he didn't want as he jogged across Gloucester Avenue. A small park fenced off with cyclone-wire faced the hotel; near some trees was a set of concrete steps that led down to some sandy scrub then the beach. It wasn't all that big, a little smaller than Bronte with two small granite headlands at either end and a few boats bobbing up and down on the other side. It was nothing special. But it was dead calm and the water appeared blue and compared to the soup outside the resort it looked like Heron Island. There was one young prick on the beach with no front teeth and a pair of pants cut down into shorts who tried to sell him something. Les smiled wearily as he walked up one end of the beach to get away from him, got his diving gear on and plunged in.

The water was beautiful, warm but refreshing, not that salty, tepid shit like when he went diving with Hank in Florida. It was kind of murky clear, though not too bad at all considering it was right outside a main road in the middle of town. There was mud on the bottom, plenty of tiny colourful fish, rocks, coral, a boot, a pair of old trousers and a few other odds and ends sitting in the muddy sand on the bottom. It reminded Les a little of Clovelly when he'd gone snorkeling around there a few times in the summer. Les dived up and down, had a hit out with the webs and jet fins and enjoyed himself in general; it shit all over the dive he had outside the resort. He churned up and down a few times then floated on his back, looked over at the hotel and chuckled into his facemask. To think I've travelled halfway across the world and finished up in the Biltmore. And loving it. Les did a few more laps, wallowed around for a while longer then got out and walked back to the hotel.

After his sumptuous breakfast and the swim, Norton was feeling pretty good as he switched on the air-conditioner in his room. He got out of his wet gear and was about to climb under the shower when he heard loud reggae music pounding in through the bathroom window. He climbed up on the sink and saw that his room was right above the bar next door. Oh well, shrugged Les, climbing back down. Saves me buying a Walkman, I s'pose. And I ain't got deh reerdio, mon. Les slipped into the shower as Hopeton Lindo slipped into 'Gun Ting'. Not long after, Gregory Isaacs was bopping into 'Sound Bwoy' as Les stepped out the door wearing the same shorts, a plain white T-shirt plus an old sweatband, his Easts cap and sunnies and his backpack slung over his shoulder. He left his key at the desk again, got in the Honda and turned right down Gloucester.

The traffic was a little heavier now, taxis, buses, etc, people walking around and no shortage of pricks almost jumping in the car window they were that keen to flog something. After the surging crowds at the Mardi Gras it was now a little easier to see what was around and it was mainly hotels and shops on the right hand side and restaurants and bars on the harbour side. But Les wasn't interested in a tourist's guide of the area. He had a bit of a peruse before he found what he wanted in the mall opposite the post office; a place that developed film, right next to a bank. Les parked on a bus stop and went in. The shop sold T-shirts, drinks and other odds and ends and was run by a polite family of Pakistanis. His film would be ready in two hours but they stayed open late. Les got four cartons of fruit juice and some more film and went back to the car. There was an unhappy-looking bloke in a white uniform carrying a shotgun outside the bank. He gave Les half a once up and down when he walked in and another half a one when Les walked out with some more US and Jamaican money. Les wasn't sure why he got so much, he just had a feeling he might need it. He avoided another swarm of pricks yelling at him trying to flog stuff, although he honestly felt like booting a couple of them fair up the date, got back in the car and headed south for Rose Hill Great House; to find what, Norton wasn't quite sure. The A1 wasn't hard to find and neither was the

Great House. It was only about three kilometres past the golf club. Les swung right at a sign saying Kenilworth Road and followed it for about half a kilometre before coming to another gravelly drive overhung with trees. A few hundred metres more and there it was, Rose Hill Great House.

It looked much the same as the photo in the book, the massively built three-storey building with the sandstone balustrades and steps underneath, only now that Les was here he could see the entire property. He drove the car down a little further, pulled over to the left and got out. Rose Hill stood majestically in about five acres of well-kept fields and gardens that edged off into the surrounding trees and hills. The road stopped about fifty yards before the front steps, then circled around, evidently to allow coaches and tourists direct access. The area was dotted with trees, four men sat in the shade beneath a cluster to Norton's left and behind, and to his left was thick bush and a pathway that seemed to lead to a clearing about three hundred yards away. Les had a good view of the great house and could see a sign near the bottom step saying TOP HALF CLOSED TO RENA-VAITION. NO ENTRANCE WAY. That's nice, thought Les. Looks like I'll only get to see the bottom half of the joint anyway, and a bit of the backyard. Mmmhh. Terrific.

The four blokes under the tree seemed to notice Les and he was about to walk over when there was a rumbling, crunching and revving of motors, along with the sound of squealing brakes, and two tour buses came down the driveway. They were both forty-seaters and rolled noisily past Les to pull up in front of the Great House with more squealing of brakes and tyres crunching on the gravel. About two minutes later the doors on both buses hissed open and out poured at least sixty fat-arsed American tourists in mu-mus and shorts of equally revolting colours. Probably getting in for their last tourist bit before they flew back to Skunk Flats, Utah, or wherever they came from. Ahh shit! cursed Les. Isn't this going to be nice? I got one lousy floor to look at and I have to do it with eight million cigar smoking, blathering seppos. The blokes under the tree rose slowly to their feet with the arrival of the two buses so Les walked over.

There was a security guard in a brown uniform with a holstered gun on his belt, two young blokes in overalls and old hats, who looked like gardeners, and an older, dapper little bloke in a straw hat and sunglasses, wearing a yellow Bonds type T-shirt with 'Rose Hill' across the chest pocket in red and a pair of white trousers. He was the only one looking at Les and seemed as if he might be some kind of figure of authority, if not actually in charge, so Les thought he'd front him; just as another idea formed in his mind.

'Excuse me, mate,' said Les. 'Are you in charge?'

The little bloke poked his chest out slightly and looked at Les from behind his sunglasses. 'Ire, mon. I'm deh head groundsman,' he said, extending his hand. 'Deh name's Joshua.'

The two gardeners shuffled off, probably to look as if they were doing something. And the guard shuffled off, probably to make sure no Arab terrorists shot the American tourists; or anybody else repulsed enough by their accents and clothes. Les could feel Joshua preening a little; he shook his hand warmly then pointed a finger at him as if in recognition.

'I thought that's who you might have been,' he smiled. 'My name's Les. Les Norton. I'm a friend of Millwood Downie's. He said if I was up this way I should introduce myself to you.'

'Millwood Downie deh teacher?'

'That's right.'

'Yu friend of Millwood's?'

'Yup. I'm also a relative of the people who built the great house. The Nortons.' Les opened his wallet and showed Joshua his driver's licence. 'I'm out here from Australia.'

Joshua looked at the photo and name on the licence and touched the front of his straw hat. 'Ire mon. Norton. Respec mon. Respec.'

'Thank you very much, Joshua. Millwood said you were a good man.'

Joshua seemed to take to Les as the big Queenslander went into a spiel about knowing Millwood from Australia and he was out here looking up his family tree. He knew all about Spring Water Primary, his family had donated some money and he was having dinner with Mr Downie tonight before he flew back to Australia tomorrow. Joshua was suitably impressed.

'The thing is, Joshua,' said Norton, giving the little groundsman a bit of an Arthur Daley arm around the shoulders, 'I don't particularly want to see the great house with all those punishing yank tourists. What I'd really like to see is Sweet Ginger Hill. Where Elizabeth and Eduardo Norton grew up.'

Joshua shook his head sadly. 'Sorry, mon, but dat place private property. No one goes deh.'

Les nodded sagely. 'Millwood explained all that to me, Joshua,' he said, extracting an American fifty dollar bill from his wallet, folding it and placing it between his fingers. 'But if I get to see Sweet Ginger Hill that's yours. And if I get back okay there's another one in it for you. What do you say, Joshua? Old mate?'

The little groundsman looked at the fifty like it was a snake hypnotising him. Les was also a good friend of Millwood's and a Norton. Respec mon. 'Les,' he said, 'I have to take care of de Chucky Bwoys for tirty minutes, mebbe till dem gaan. I meet yu back here at yu car. Den I take yu up Sweet Ginger Hill.'

'Thank you, Joshua. I appreciate it.' Les handed him the fifty, which disappeared in a blink.

'While yu waiting, Les, why yu don go visit yu family graves?' Joshua pointed behind Les to the trail leading into the bush. 'No far tru deh.'

'Okay,' nodded Les. 'I'll do that.'

'I see yu back here at deh car, Les. Soon time.' The little groundsman adjusted his straw hat and walked off towards the babbling Chucky Bwoys and their horrible fat wives.

411

Well how about that? beamed Norton. I get to see Sweet Ginger Hill after all. See, I give that little bloke a bit of respec mon. And he gave me some. Of course the lazy fifty helped, I'd reckon. But maybe these Jams have got something deh mon. Anyway, now I've got thirty minutes to kill. Which would be closer to an hour, Jam time. And what better way to do it than going through all the old graves. Fancy Joshua tipping me into that. I was hoping to get a look at them. But I was buggered if I knew where they were. Didn't that little French priest in that other book find the buried loot by deciphering old graves? Les rubbed his hands together gleefully. Only one way to find out. Les locked the car, put some fresh film in his camera and with his backpack slung over his shoulder walked across to the thick bush. The old sun-bleached sign pointed up the trail and simply said NORTON BURIAL GROUND.

The trail was barely a metre of dry, dusty sand pushing through the shrubbery about fifteen feet overhead. It was dead still and almost crushingly hot and Les was glad he'd wrapped a thick sweatband round his head. The trail veered slightly then ran alongside a small sandstone watercourse full of cool, clear water a couple of feet deep. Les remembered from the book that these must be the canals they built in the sixteenth century to bring rain and springwater down from the mountains to irrigate the sugar plantations. Bubbling slowly past in the heat it looked good enough to bottle as Evian. Les wasn't too sure about drinking any, but he knelt down, splashed some over his face then soaked his sweatband in it and slopped more water over his neck and down his back. How good's this? thought Les, splashing more water over his face and in his hair. He gave one of the sandstone blocks a push with his foot; it felt solid and heavy and even after sitting there for three hundred years didn't even look like budging. Though I don't think I'd have fancied being one of the poor bastards putting the things in. Especially in this heat. They weigh a bloody ton. And especially not for the pay my loving relations were paying them back then. Les rung his sweatband out, wrapped it back round his head and continued along the trail.

The trail meandered on, sometimes it would run alongside a canal, other times cross over one then nothing but scrub. Les was sweating again when the pathway came out onto a level green something like a golf course. About a hundred yards across the green a few stumpy trees were dotted round a sandstone wall about five feet high, fifty yards long and twenty-five wide. There were one or two gaps in the wall and at the right hand end was a splintery, white picket fence and an old wrought-iron gate. Behind the far wall the hill sloped away again and Les could see the ocean horizon and further to the right the high-rise of some resort. He walked across the level green to the picket fence and looked through the open gate. Inside were rows and rows of old tombstones and vaults. Les stopped where he was and took off his cap and despite his earlier flippancy shook his head slowly almost in a state of reverent wonder. He'd found a lost Norton graveyard going back to the 17th Century. And that was definitely something you didn't do every day.

'Respec mon. Respec,' he whispered. 'Respec.' After a second or two Les put his cap back on and stepped through the gate.

The only comparison Les could make was those old Count Yorga films on latenight TV and he was glad it was daytime. There was row after row of ancient graves and tombstones. Granite ones, marble ones, black ones, white ones, grey ones. Most were built up on sandstone blocks, others had rusting, wrought-iron fencing round them, a lot of it starting to fall down. There was no shortage of Nortons and it appeared that when they went, they went out in style. Some of the graves had rows of a metre-square sandstone blocks stepped up six feet before you got to the marble cross or angel. Scattered here and there were crypts with great slabs of marble or blackened granite that had broken away from the sides lying crumbled and smashed around the bases and pathways. Weeds and shrubs were growing around the graves and

413

along the paths, among the dead leaves and small branches that had fallen down from the few surrounding trees. It was all in an advancing state of deterioration and neglect. Though after three hundred years of wind, rain, blazing sun and salt air blowing straight in off the Caribbean there wasn't much else to expect. But the Norton graveyard was starting to crumble. It was an eerie feeling for Les, walking around the old graves and seeing his surname on each one. It was also a strange feeling of belonging, as if he was entitled to be there. It was one of the weirdest feelings Les had ever experienced and although he wasn't really expecting apparitions or spirits to appear in crinoline dresses or three-corner hats, he was still glad it was daytime. Les wandered around a bit more then after drinking one of the cartons of fruit juice he'd brought with him got his camera out and started taking photos.

All the graves had inscriptions carved on them, most of them illegible from where the stone had been blackened or stained after centuries of exposure to the weather. One was a massive granite slab sitting up on four beautifully carved, marble legs. There were two squares carved into one end of the slab. Inside one was chiselled, 'Life How Short'. In the other it had, 'Eternity How Long'. Les peered into the dirt-caked inscription at the other end. Josephine Clementina Norton, June 1730–September 1816. Josephine didn't have a bad run, thought Les, taking a photo. I wonder who she was? Sarah Goodin Johanna Norton, 1707–1769. There were dozens more names and dates and rambling religious inscriptions across the stone, but the caked-in dirt made them too difficult to decipher. Les figured if you cleaned them up you'd be able to read them a lot better... but you'd be there a month. And almost that long if you wanted to write them all down. Isobelle Cordelia Norton Plummer, 1788–1861. Brigadier General Edward Wescott Moulton Norton, 1803–1883. As you were, General. Les took a photo and snapped off a quick salute. There were heaps of graves and old tombstones. Literally. Piled side by side, tumbling into each other. Les roamed up and down, clicking away, and although it might have been a little odd, perverse even, he was again having the time of his life.

Les climbed up the steps of some graves, walked across the slabs of others, shook some of the wrought-iron fencing to see how solid it was. A stiff breeze whipping in from the ocean blew across the sweat on his face and arms, taking the edge off the humidity and making things a little cooler. But after searching all over the tombstones and vaults Les was flat out finding anything he could decipher let alone make something out of. He did discover one thing — the oldest, but not necessarily the biggest, graves seemed to be in one corner of the graveyard closest to the ocean. Les knew he wouldn't find Elizabeth's grave, she died in Scotland. And Eduardo the priest disappeared. But among the oldest graves Les did find two other Eduardos. One was solid marble and granite built up on massive sandstone blocks. Over the years it had copped the full blast of the sun and ocean and although the script across the blackened slab was beautifully engraved, Les could just make out the words: 'Blessed Are the Dead ... Belief and Hope Through Jesus ... Rest From Their Labours and Their Works Will Follow.' The words on the top of the slab were a bit bigger. Stanley Moulton Eduardo Norton of Sweet Ginger Hill, 1641–1727. Les stepped back and took a photo. Stanley Norton of Sweet Ginger Hill, thought Les. That'd be Eduardo and Elizabeth's father. There was another crypt alongside. Les could make out the name Kathleen Loudivine Elinor Norton. I wonder if that was his wife, thought Les. He couldn't make out the dates. The one right in the corner was built up with a granite cover over the top, almost like a roof. The engraving this time was down the side, away from the ocean. It must have been the original Norton who started the dynasty. Moulton Eduardo Darius Norton of Rose Hill Great House, 1605–1692. The first inscription read, 'To the Memory of M.E.D. Norton. Whose remains rest beneath

415

until the sound of the last trumpet when this corruptible must put on incorruption and this mortal must put on immortality.' There were hearts and angels then the second inscription read, 'Sacred to the Memory of M.E.D. Norton. He represented the borough of Feruleshire for two successive parliaments in the British Senate and was a member of the council of this island when he died. He was benevolent to the poor, kind and generous to his servant — and attached and attaching to his friends. He died through the grace of God in the faith of Him. Who is the resurrection and the life.' Well, there you go, smiled Les, stepping back to take another photo. Benevolent to the poor. That's me since I've been here. I guess I'm just a chip off the old block Moulton. Les looked at the oldest grave for a few moments more, took another photo and the film started to automatically rewind so he reloaded the camera and wandered quietly around, taking more photos. Then a thought struck Les and his original elation began turning into melancholy. In a few days' time he'd be standing around another grave in Queensland, halfway across the world, among other Nortons. And there would somehow be this weird link back to this old graveyard in Jamaica that overlooked the ocean. The wind suddenly seemed to get cooler. Yes, it was weird alright. Weirder than Les had previously thought.

Les hung around for a little longer, finding absolutely nothing as far as clues to buried treasure went. But it was going to be a buzz showing all the folks back home the photos once they were all pissed at the wake. He opened the other carton of fruit juice then looked at his watch. Shit! By the time I finish this and walk back it'll be time to pick up young Joshua and visit Sweet Ginger Hill. Where I hope to find a clue of some description. Buggered if I know what, though. Les had one last look round the Norton graveyard, put his rubbish and the camera back in his bag then picked up a small piece of broken marble for a souvenir. At the old wooden fence he took off his cap again in a mark of respect, and with more than a touch of sentiment farewelled the resting place of his ancestors. Well, see you later, folks. Don't know when though. But RIP, as they say. Rest In Peace. Or is it Rise If Possible? Whatever: At least you've got a nice view from up here. Les put his cap back on and trudged off across the field to the trail.

He stopped briefly along the trail to splash some more water from one of the canals across his face and by the time he got back to the Honda it was all happening. The tour buses were pulling out and Joshua was walking briskly towards him. The security guard was coming down the steps in the same direction and the two gardeners were heading that way too; probably to take up their original positions beneath the trees. Les had just opened the car up to let the heat out and thrown his bag on the back seat when Joshua arrived almost on the trot.

'Ire, Les,' he said, closing the door as he climbed in the front seat. 'Let's go, mon.'

Norton looked at him for a second. 'Yeah, righto,' he replied, getting in and starting the engine. 'I wasn't quite expecting a Le Mans start.' Les nodded to his right; if he remembered Sweet Ginger Hill was behind and to the right of the great house.

Joshua shook his head. 'This way, Les. I show you de school.'

'School?'

'Ya, mon. Spring Water Primary. Where Millwood teaches. I show you.'

'Joshua. I don't . . .'

'C'mon, Les. This way, mon. Yu like de school. Meet de piccnys.' Joshua glanced over Norton's shoulder at the others coming along the path and earnestly pointed left.

Les looked at the little groundsman for a moment then slipped the car into drive. 'Yeah righto,' he said astutely.

It wasn't hard to tell what was going on. Joshua was legging it from his workmates as quickly as possible. Sweet Ginger Hill was out of bounds so he'd probably told them Les was a friend of Millwood Downie's and he was taking him up to show him the school. You could bet he'd never told his black brothers he'd zipped the honky from Australia for fifty dollars, and you could also bet the brothers weren't in the whack for the other fifty either. Which was why he wanted Les out of the road before they arrived and he said something in front of them. So it looked like Les was getting the grand tour around the Hill of Zion and Spring Water Primary before they doubled back to Sweet Ginger Hill. And being a supposed friend of Millwood's Les not only had to cop it sweet but look interested as well.

The great house faded in the background as under Joshua's directions they climbed up hills along dusty, bumpy, one-lane roads that would put the wind up a rally driver. There were monstrous potholes half hidden by rocks as big as TV sets and Les hoped and prayed the little Honda's sump didn't get torn out. They climbed on and on, crossing other roads, slightly wider but in the same condition. Passed a pretty little waterfall splashing down from under a huge old tree, a couple of caves in the side of the hill and an ancient sandstone bridge. It was all scrubby bush or low forest with clearings every now and again where the bush had been levelled for sugar fields or whatever and the trees had started to grow back. There were no birds and no wildlife. The closest thing to an animal Les saw was a notice saying STRAY GOATS WILL BE SHOT. S'pose I'd better keep in the car, he thought as they bumped and rattled along. The higher they climbed and the further they got from the great house, the more Joshua started to relax. Before long he started letting Les know he was a bit of a man about town and began giving him the *National Geographic* tour of the area. He told Les about Jenny the white witch, who had another property near Rose Hill, and how she had a tunnel connecting the home to a cave near the old bridge where she used to bring different slaves for a bit of discreet porking, and when she was sick of them she used to neck them. Until some slave ended up necking Jenny. Now her ghosts roams the old mansion and some nights appears on the bridge, etc, etc. Les was ecstatic. Joshua

418

told him about the pirates that used to anchor just off Rose Point and how they used to come ashore and steal the female slaves. A trio of curious workers walked past as they crossed onto another road near a clearing and Joshua pointed out that that was a remote part of a golf course where they shot scenes for a James Bond movie. Fabulous, nodded Les as they climbed higher again.

They seemed to have gone miles into the wilderness before coming onto another slightly wider, steeper road that climbed a bend to the right, then levelled out, and suddenly there was a scattering of ramshackle houses and dwellings. The road stopped on a plateau that overlooked the ocean on the right, and on the left was a deep valley that rolled into smaller valleys dotted with houses just like the ones along the road between Montego Bay and Dredmouth. It reminded Les of documentaries he'd seen on TV about the peasants living in the hills of Peru or Bolivia. Whatever it reminded Les of, it definitely wasn't Bellevue Hill or Toorak. Standing apart from the houses at the top of the road was a slightly larger building made out of sandstone, wood, brick and pieces of concrete. It had a warped timber roof and the smallest steeple at the front imaginable. A short set of stairs ran up to the front door, which was locked, and above the front door was a wooden plaque with Spring Water Primary School stencilled on it in green. Sitting on what passed for a lawn out the front were several wooden seats and desks, freshly painted and drying in the sun, and it looked like someone had just put a new bannister down one side of the steps and started to install a couple of new windows. So that's where my bloody money's going eh? smiled Les. Well, at least I know. Les made a comment about the school to Joshua then they pulled up a little further, on top of a high, gently sloping mountain that gave a panoramic view of the ocean. Joshua switched off the motor and they got out.

Before Les was the Caribbean, turning bluer and bluer as it stretched across countless white caps to a massive cloud bank on the horizon. To the left Les could see

Montego Bay and to the right the narrow harbour of Dredmouth. The breeze was wondrously refreshing as it swept up from the ocean below, cutting across the sugar fields and forests; Les stood there for a while, letting it flick through his hair and thinking it would be a while before he'd ever see a view like this again. Although he didn't want to at first, Les was glad now he'd come up here and it would be something worth mentioning to Millwood when he saw him that night. Joshua leant against the front of the car and seemed to be leaving Les to his thoughts. The little groundsman was probably alone with his own thoughts as well; like, how he was going to spend the hundred dollars. Whatever their thoughts were, they were abruptly shattered by the screaming and yelling of very young voices. Les turned around and ten of the wildest, feral children he'd ever seen in his life came charging out of the valley towards him. Shit! What's this? blinked Les. I'm about to be mugged by the local Munchkins. They were just about to swarm all over Les when Joshua stepped out and put his hand up. He rattled off something in patois that was too fast and too raw for Les to understand. But Joshua must have had some sort of respec, because whatever he said worked; the kids screeched to a halt and stood near the car, looking at Les with inquisitive, pinky-brown eyes.

If these were the local piccnys, for their size they were a ferocious-looking bunch. The boys all wore ragged blue singlets and baggy shorts, the girls wore thin blue dresses or pinafores; none of them wore shoes. Joshua said something else and the kids settled down even more, actually giving Les some respec. Les smiled, said g'day, offered his hand and by watching some blokes at the Mardi Gras and mucking around with Delta and Esme managed to pull off a couple of Jamaican handshakes where you make a fist and brush knuckles and fists in four brisk movements. The kids warmed up to Les, pulling at his shorts and T-shirt, two of the girls cuddled up against his legs. They were probably a mob of little horrors yet Les couldn't help but like them.

He scrabbled the boys' bristly heads, pulled the blue ribbons in the girls' pigtails, pointed a stern finger at each one of them and told them they were the cheekiest tribe of monsters he'd ever come across and if ever he was in town again he'd boot them all up the khyber; and that's not all. But the more Les scolded and hair-raided the kids, the more they laughed and giggled. Les took a couple of photos, gave the camera to Joshua, got him to take a couple then put his camera away, knowing it was both time to get going and time for the ask.

Les gave Joshua a wink and extracted about $400 Jamaican from his pocket. He gave half to the biggest boy and half to the oldest girl, then stood back. The kids literally exploded; whatever noise they made before was like a few whispers compared to now. The two kids with the money leapt straight off the starting blocks with the rest of the piccnys howling at their heels. They whooped and shrieked up and down the valley like banshees as they all tried to get in on the chop up. Norton had never seen anything like it; they left a pack of vultures or hyenas for dead. He watched them disappear into the valley, their voices still echoing around the mountain top and across the plateau, then turned to Joshua.

'Well what do you reckon, Joshua? Sweet Ginger Hill?'

'Ire Les,' nodded the little Jamaican. 'Back daht way, mon.'

Les filled his chest with another lungful of crisp mountain air, had a last look around the unique little town high up in the middle of nowhere then wheeled the Honda around and past the school. About half a kilometre back down the road Joshua directed him left onto a smaller one. They lurched and bumped over more potholes and rocks for a couple of miles then onto another narrow road that seemed to climb back up the mountain. They turned right again onto another road through the scrub. Les didn't have a clue where they were and was about to say something to Joshua when the road scalloped in on the left, forming a short, wide driveway set against an old sandstone wall and two sandstone pillars with an equally old bronze lamp sitting on each. Bolted between the two pillars was a beautifully embossed, double wrought-iron gate about ten feet high. Behind the gate was a driveway edged with more sandstone blocks and overhung with leafy cedar and mahogany trees that obscured the view of the house behind. Aloe Vera and other flowering cactus plants pushed up against the wall, bougainvillea and several colourful vines full of bigger flowers hung over the top. Fastened into one of the white-washed pillars was a solid slab of white marble and painstakingly chiselled into it in old-fashioned script was 'Sweet Ginger Hill'. Les gave a couple of double blinks through the windscreen. The place had a charm and old-fashioned beauty about it that almost took his breath away. It was like being transported back in time, into another era, another part of history. In a way Les was reminded of one of those old Southern mansion he'd seen in films or on TV and surmised that that was one of the reasons the American singer from Kentucky bought it. No matter what his reason, if Les had been a millionaire and found the place on the market he would have bought it too. It looked fabulous. He turned to Joshua.

'So what do we now, mate?'

'Just wait here, mon.'

Joshua got out of the car, walked over to one of the pillars and pushed a button. Les turned off the engine and waited, taking in all he could see so far. A few minutes later a beefy Jamaican woman came ambling up the driveway. Ohh no, Les groaned to himself. Not again. Please. She had some kind of yellow slippers on her feet, a red floral dress stretched over her ample behind and a blue and white polka dot scarf sitting on her head, and was a swap for that black woman who's always chasing Tom around the kitchen in those Tom and Jerry cartoons. Les shook his head as she waddled over to Joshua standing at the gate. They had some sort of a confab, so while they did Les put Tom and Jerry out of his mind and continued to take in the unexpected beauty of Sweet Ginger Hill. A minute or two later they finished whatever it was they were talking about; the woman unlocked a chain on a gate, opening it slightly, and Joshua walked over to the car window.

'Move de car over by de gate, Les. It be safe deh and we walk down.'

'Okey doke,' agreed Norton. He moved the Honda closer to the gate, got his backpack out and locked the doors.

'Les,' said Joshua quietly, 'de 'oman at de gate. Yu have to . . .'

'Of course, Josh,' beamed Les. 'Christ, mate, I'd be wondering what was going on if I didn't have to.' Les walked over to the woman, smiled at her as if she was long-lost kin, and flicked $150 Jamaican out of his wallet. She stuck it down her dress and motioned Les through the gate.

'Les,' said Joshua again, 'dis be Trishet.'

'Hullo, Trish,' said Les, offering his hand. 'Absolutely delighted to meet you. And I can't thank you enough for letting me in.'

Trishet shook Norton's hand then locked the gate again and ambled back down the drive with Les behind her and Joshua bringing up the rear. The driveway was all white quartz gravel; as they crunched along a bit further Les tapped Trishet on the shoulder.

'Alright if I take a few photos, Trishet?' The woman nodded so Les stopped, took his camera out of his bag and had a closer look.

Compared to Rose Hill Great House, Sweet Ginger Hill didn't look all that big, thought the old home was certainly big enough. About twenty metres of cleared lawn, dotted with more colourful trees and cactus. A stone fountain that wasn't working faced the home from where the driveway ended. The building was two storeys high with a tiled verandah around the front spaced with solid wooden beams that supported a slate roof above. The left half of Sweet Ginger Hill was solid timber, a double oak door in the middle, the right half stuccoed white sandstone with a wood-tiled roof, spaced here and there with tiny sandstone turrets. The main colour was white, although the tiles on the verandah were red and white in an old-fashioned, Italian-Pompeii design. Wooden beams jutted out from the bottom of the roof, ivy and vines flourished along the top of the verandah and the way the old home sat rather grandly in the clearing, it reminded Les of a rambling Spanish hacienda more than anything else. Lizards baked in the heat among the vines along the verandah and Les distinctly heard the chirping of small birds. He took a photo while Trishet waited by the front door, took another one, then walked over, wiped his feet and stepped inside.

There was a tiled foyer flanked with heavy wooden beams and solid wooden panelling; a few roughly hewn wooden chairs sat round the walls beneath some old paintings and carved wooden pegs to hang your clothes on. A corridor ran off to the main room on the left, a set of stairs faced the front door and another corridor on the right ran past several closets and what could have been pantries to the kitchen. The rooms and hallways inside were wide and high and Sweet Ginger Hill's interior was much bigger than it looked from the driveway. Les was getting a bit thirsty again and figured that for $150 Jamaican a glass of water wouldn't be too much of an ask. He followed Trishet into the kitchen and she got him one from the fridge. There were two people in the kitchen. A tall, solid bloke, who was probably a gardener and minder, and a young girl, who was probably some other part of the staff that looked after the place when Dollar wasn't there. Joshua introduced Les as Mr Norton, a friend of Millwood Downie's, from Australia, an ancestor of the original family and a benefactor of the school. They courteously shook hands and showed Les some respec. Les sipped his glass of water and looked around. The kitchen had just about been fully modernised with a stainless steel sink, porta-gas stove, electric oven and other modern conveniences. But Dollar, or whoever he bought the home from, had left the rough sandstone floor, a huge old cabinet full of willow pattern crockery

424

and soup tureens plus an equally old fuel stove with a copper tap in front still in its original position set under a sandstone chimney. There was also a log of wood standing upright with a marble bowl set in one end. A long pole with a weight at one end suggested this was originally for grinding corn or maize. A microwave oven, sitting on a mahogany table underneath a row of ancient copper pots and pans, didn't look all that incongruous, more an unusual blending of the old and new. The main room was a little different.

Les finished his glass of water and followed Trishet back through the foyer where a massive door opened up into a wide, spacious room full of floor-to-ceiling bay windows that overlooked the grounds outside. It was all exquisite period furniture of velvet and tapestry, mostly pink or maroon. Ornate gold mirrors and old paintings were set into the walls and heavy blue velvet curtains covered the windows. Rows of thick wooden beams supported the ceiling and in between hung delicate crystal chandeliers. There were beautifully carved oak and mahogany sideboards and shelves running round the walls full of seventeenth-century bric-a-brac, like porcelain statuettes and shell and butterfly displays set in glass domes. It was just like stepping back in time again. Except that at the far end, next to a piano, was a quadruple-decked stereo system crammed with boosters, faders and a graphic equaliser. It stood beneath two monstrous Bose speakers hanging from one of the beams. a teak sideboard was packed with CDs and vinyls and several gold records were pinned to the wall. Les didn't bother going through Dollar's holiday music collection, but he did ask Trishet about some of the paintings on the wall. There was a woman in a crinoline dress about thirty with long dark hair and an attractive if somewhat triste face. A man about fifty, of Mediterranean appearance, in a black coat and wide floppy tie. A severe-looking woman about the same age in a blue bodice and white bonnet, and a young boy about twelve, in a high, lace-collared, cream vest outfit. Both males had reddish hair.

Trishet began to come to life when she realised Les wasn't just some mug tourist looking for something different, and began pointing different things out to him; she probably wanted to show she was in charge here, knew a bit about the place and was no mug either. The younger woman in the paintings was Elizabeth. The man was Stanley Norton and the other woman his wife Kathleen. The boy in the breeches was Eduardo when he was young. Les stared at the paintings, slowly rubbing at his chin. Stanley looked a lot like Uncle Frank, who the whole family always joked had a bit of wog in him. And young Eduardo was almost a swap for Murray's eldest boy Wayne. Even Elizabeth looked like cousin Judy when she'd go a bit quiet and they'd call her 'Moody Judy'. It was uncanny. Les took a couple of photos and Trishet took him over to the staircase that wound upstairs past where Dollar had managed to bolt a monstrous alligator skin to the wall.

A French window let in light at the top of the stairs where it split into two more corridors. Trishet explained how she couldn't show Les Mr and Mrs Dollar's room and their private studies, but the kids' rooms would be okay. Which was fair enough, thought Les, and followed her along to Dollar's daughter's room, which was Elizabeth's old room. The biggest wooden four-poster bed Les had ever seen sat against one wall almost in the middle of the room; it was that high off the floor it had a small set of cushioned steps alongside it to climb up. There was a marble fireplace with an iron grate and more bric-a-brac displayed on the shelves and the cornice above. A thick square of brown carpet covered part of the floorboards, an oak wardrobe sat against one wall near a mahogany dresser with a marble top and shiny bronze candlesticks that caught the light streaming in from the French windows. It was a typical kid from the seventeenth century's room, right down to the wooden bidet in one corner. All except for a framed poster of the Munsters on one wall and a small stereo and TV set in another corner. Les took another photo.

Dollar had two boys and their room, Eduardo's old room, was down the other end of the hallway. The room was slightly bigger yet entirely different from Elizabeth's. Where Elizabeth's had a definite woman's touch about it, this one had a nautical influence and looked like the aft cabin on an old Spanish galleon. The windows were shaped like portholes, ancient wooden trunks with heavy iron locks stood against the walls or in the corners, black and white paintings of sailing ships and pirates hung on the walls and several carved wooden ships sat on shelves round the walls. Two smaller four-poster beds faced each other from opposite sides of the room among much the same kind of hand-tooled wood and marble furnishings as in the other bedroom. Dollar's two sons had added their own touch. Another small stereo, a TV computer game, toys, plus baseball and basketball posters on the wall and one of their father on stage in Nashville with his guitar. The room had a nice feel about it. In fact, the whole place so far had a nice feel about it. Dollar was a devoted family man and probably brought his family down here every now and again to get away from the American rat race and soak up a few old-fashioned values among the secluded peace and quiet of Sweet Ginger Hill. Les took a couple more photos.

The bathroom was all the original sandstone and copper with the same red tiles as the front verandah, except the plumbing and toilet were brand new. Trishet showed Les a few closets, another study with more old furniture in it and pointed out a few other things before taking him back down the stairs, through the kitchen, down a set of sandstone stairs and into the grounds at the rear of the house; or hacienda as Les had pictured it by now.

The grounds were much bigger than out the front and well landscaped up to where they edged off into the surrounding trees and scrub. In the middle was a swimming pool and near it was an old brass and sandstone sundial that had been well cared for over the centuries and looked almost brand new. Behind the pool was a solitary tree, thick with branches and some kind of yellow fruit at the top. Les snapped off a couple more photos then got Trishet to take one of him and Joshua standing next to the sundial with the fruit tree in the background. There were palm trees and other trees where the grounds led up to another verandah at the rear of the house; Les followed Trishet up. It was made of the same red and white Pompeii-style tiles as the front one, beams jutted out of the white stuccoed walls and other beams supported the roof above. There were several bamboo chairs and tables but a good part of the verandah was taken up by bursts of beautiful flowers kept in small sandstone beds. Along the front of the verandah were five shiny brown ceramic containers; three were about a metre and a half high and half a metre or so thick, the other two were closer to a metre long and about half as thick as the others. They reminded Les a little of a Greek amphoras, only they were straight with a round lip formed over the top for a stopper and had lugs formed into the sides for carrying instead of handles. Joshua said they were Spanish jars and were used to carry spices and oils back in the pirate days. Whatever they were, each had more flowering vines of all colours growing out of them and looked quite beautiful with the old tiles in the background, so Les took a couple more photos. Out of curiosity Les asked Trishet how the old home got its name. She reached over to one of the beams with a blue and green vine growing on it and small red berries about the same size as a pea. She picked one off, squashed it between her fingers and held it under Norton's nose. It smelled like ginger. Les picked one off and took a nibble. It tasted like ginger, only with a bitter-sweet, chocolate taste as well. Trishet said another couple of weeks and they sweetened right up. Les thought they tasted pretty good as they were.

Les wandered round a little longer, taking photos till the film began to automatically rewind itself and he felt Trishet and Josh were giving him the hint he'd got his money's worth. Les wasn't sure if he'd discovered anything, but it

428

was well worth the effort; the old home, besides dripping with character, was just plain beautiful and how often do you come across something like that? He envied Billy Ray Dollar's good fortune. Trishet led him back round the grounds to the front gate, where Les gave her hand a squeeze and thanked her again for showing him around. Trishet said it was her pleasure, Mr Norton. Joshua said something to her in patois, too fast for Les to understand, then they got back in the car as Trishet locked the gate again and ambled back down the driveway.

The roads were no better, but it was definitely easier going back down. Joshua gave Les a bit more of a travelogue on the way; Les didn't say much, preferring to concentrate on the rocks and potholes again to make sure he didn't pull the diff out of the car. Before long they'd criss-crossed their way over other roads and were back at Rose Hill Great House, not far from where Joshua's workmates were still sitting on their backsides beneath the trees. Joshua told Les to pull up where he was, the A1 was straight ahead. Les knew what was going on and slipped Joshua the other fifty dollars in the car so the others couldn't see. They shook hands again, Les thanked Joshua once more, even if it was the easiest hundred bucks the little groundsman had ever earned in his life, said goodbye and slowly drove back along the driveway into Kenilworth, then turned left towards Montego Bay.

Well there you go, mused Norton, moving the little Honda around the frantic hitchhikers and the other cars on the A1. That was Sweet Ginger Hill. So what did I find out? Les absently turned the radio on to hear Blood Fire Posse coming out of some station, doing a pretty good cover of 'Do You Remember', as he cruised along, deep in thought. Yeah, what do I know? Not much really. Except the old home was drop dead beautiful and there's some sort of Spanish influence in the family. And Eduardo was some kind of boat nut when he was a kid. As for clues? There might have been something in Dollar's room or those other rooms that were out of bounds. But stiff shit there. And after hundreds of years of different people

429

living there, everything would be changed around or damaged to a certain extent. Though I saw something there that reminded me of something somewhere else. But I can't think what it is. Anyway, we'll see what Millwood's got to say tonight. One thing I do know, by the time he gets there and we get to a restaurant and order some food it'll be after eight. I couldn't wait that long. Not on two lousy fried eggs this morning. I'm that hungry I'd eat a dead rat and make soup out of the trap. I'll get a hot dog or something when I drop these films off.

Les turned off the A1 to find the back way along Gloucester. He drove through some sort of gully with hills full of trees on one side and some kind of park with a crumbling concrete bus shelter, and couldn't quite believe what he'd just driven past. The road was wide, Les did a U-turn and pulled up near the bus shed. Across the road was a battered old blue van with a servery cut into the side. Most of the paint was chipped away or missing, the rest was bare metal tinged with rust. Across the top was written in white, 'Meals on Wheels'. I don't believe it, smiled Les. I've got to have a feed there. Hope they don't give me food poisoning. No, not a chance, he thought, as he locked the car and crossed over. Knowing these bastards they'd charge you extra for that too.

There was a bloke in a white singlet and a faded pair of jeans at the counter; Les heard him order chicken jerky and a bottle of sweet sap. The maître d, in a grease- and sweat-stained T-shirt, took his order then turned to Norton.

'Yah, mon?'

Les nodded to the bloke in the singlet. 'I'll have the same, thanks.'

'Yah, mon.'

The maître d moved across to the gourmet chef and gave him the orders; Les poked his head over the small counter for a look. Sitting just behind the driver's cabin was an old fuel stove with a blackened piece of grate over the top. Along a bit was an old wooden table with a block of ice covered by a sack on it, and some drawers and

430

shelves covered in food, spices, plates, etc. and other junk. There was no refrigeration. The gourmet chef tossed some small pieces of bone in chicken on the grate, slopped some reddish-orange sauce over the top, then proceeded to scorch the shit out of it while the maître d got a rusty Phillips-head screwdriver and started banging lumps of ice from the block on the table. By the time he'd hacked off enough to fill two paper cups, the gourmet chef had nuked the chicken to waste and it arrived on the counter in a little cardboard carton on a bed of rice with some tiny nuts and shreds of cabbage or something in it. The sweet sap arrived in a Stone's Green Ginger Wine bottle, and, going by the condition of the label and the chips around the neck, young Harold had probably been collecting it for the last two years. All up, it came to the outrageous price of a little less than two dollars Oz; Les paid him cheerfully and walked back to the car.

There were about half a dozen people sitting around the shelter, some were eating, a plumpish woman was drinking a bottle of Red Stripe and an old bloke in a funny little leather cap was trying to light up a roach. Rather than upset the locals with his disgusting table manners Norton chose to eat on the bonnet of the car; the thought that someone might try to steal it or stab him in the back and roll him while he sat round the shelter never occurred to him. The chicken jerky wasn't all that bad, especially at the price. It tasted exactly like something you'd get at a surf club barbecue where the cook's blind drunk and slops tomato sauce, tabasco and mustard over everything before he burns the shit out of it then goes and has a chunder somewhere. The sweet sap was something else, however. It was pale green, a little thicker than milk and tasted something like liquid banana, only sweeter. It was absolutely delicious and Les demolished the bottle without even bothering to put it in the cup with the ice. There was no garbage tin, just a pile of rubbish on a slope near the bus shed; Les ate what he could and dumped his rubbish on top of the rest. Well, so much for dining al fresco on authentic Jamaican cuisine, he burped as he got

431

back behind the wheel of the Honda. I could go another gallon of that drink though. I've never tasted nothing like that before.

Les picked up his photos from the Pakistanis and dropped the other film off. The boss said there was a chance it would be ready in about an hour or so, maybe. On the way out Les bought six T-shirts with Ire Jamaica, Reggae Sunsplash and Montego Bay on the front for the kids back home. As he paid, the owner gave him a smile oilier than a hurricane lamp and told him his photos would be ready in an hour; and not a Jamaican one. Les thanked him and walked out to the car. On the way back to the Biltmore Les wasn't thinking about a great deal, only where he'd eat that night and how the photos would turn out. He certainly wasn't expecting anybody to be waiting for him at the bottom of the stairs next to the security guard. He parked the Honda, got his stuff off the back seat and walked over.

'Esme? Delta? What...?' Les didn't mean to sound abrupt, but even though he'd told the girls where he was moving to he was a little surprised at them showing up, and he didn't particularly feel like putting them back on the drip; along with just about everybody else he'd met so far in Jamaica. However, the smiles on the girls' faces seemed genuine and although they were wearing the same jeans and shorts, they'd changed into clean white T-shirts and did look a lot brighter than when he'd first met them.

'Hi Les,' said Esme. 'Wi just hangin' bowt, so wi tort wi come by see yu.'

'Ya, mon,' said Delta. 'Wi jus wan sai hello, Les. See how be de big Brer Wallaby.'

What could Les do? They were probably pitching up to sleep in the car again and bum some more money and orange juice. But they weren't bad, poor sheilas, and a few more lousy dollars wouldn't kill him. 'Yeah, Brer Wallaby's okay,' he smiled back at Delta. 'Couldn't be creamier.' Les gave the security guard a wink. 'It's okay, I'rol. They're friends of mine.'

'Ire, mon.'

'Come on.' Les led the girls up the stairs, plonked them down at the same table where he had breakfast and pulled up a chair himself. 'So how have you been? Did you get a good night's sleep in the car?'

Yes, the girls did have a good night's sleep, for which they were grateful. They'd been hanging around the beach all day, but at least they had money for food, for which they were grateful also. Les told them about Lucretia ripping him off when he left and he was glad it was them going to work for her and not him. He also told them about his movements that night and how he was having a kind of business dinner with Millwood Downie. But the girls were welcome to hang about the hotel, the bar looked like it was open and, yes, they could have a few more drinks and put it on his tab. Why bloody not?

Esme reached across and placed her hand softly on Norton's arm; her soft brown eyes looked like they were going to melt and run down her face. 'Les, mon. We din come by fo yu danza. We come by jus see yu, mon. And daht tru, Les.'

'Ya, tru mon,' agreed Delta. 'A no lie wi a lie, Les. Wi still got de danze yu give night time.'

'Oh. Well, that's ... good.'

Les felt a little embarrassed. The girls' honesty had caught him off guard, mainly because it was the first time since he'd been there that somebody hadn't tried to put a snip on him first up. In fact, even though Delta was a bit breezy Esme was giving Les all kinds of looks from across the table and he probably could have put the snip on her and got his money back; with interest. Whatever their intentions, the girls seemed okay, and at least it was nice to have two friends he could talk to in town.

'Anyway, that's the truth, girls. I have to meet this bloke at seven. But if you want to have something to drink or a bite to eat, I'll shout you. Brer Wallaby don't mind.' The girls continued to stare at Les; especially Esme, who still had her hand on his arm. 'In the meantime, I'm going for a snorkel across the road then I'm going to get cleaned up and change into my tux.' Norton

433

stared back at the girls. 'Hey, you wouldn't like to do me a favour — would you?' Esme and Delta exchanged glances then shrugged. 'There's a sort of camera, souvenir shop down opposite the post office.'

'Yah mon,' said Delta. 'Run by deh coolies. Wi know im.'

'Whatever. I've got some photos down there be ready in about an hour. If I give you the money, will you pick them up for me?'

'Sure, Les,' said Esme.

'Beauty!' Les handed Esme the docket and enough US dollars to pay for the developing, then pointed a stern finger at her. 'And don' laas i money. And don' tief dem either. Yu know what I sayn, 'oman.'

'A wa yu say, mon?' said Esme, definitely affronted. 'Yu a deestant smadi, Les. Mi no a tief dem. No way, mon.'

Les smiled and blew her a little kiss. 'Esme, my little sugar glider, I never doubted you for a minute.'

Les stood up and said he'd see them back here in an hour; have a feed and a drink or whatever if they wanted to. He went to the office and sweetened it up with the girl, gave Esme and Delta a smile and a wave and went to his room. Norton wasn't quite ready for 'Slavery Let I Go' by Dr Alimantado coming from the bar downstairs, but he got it as soon as he opened the door; all seven minutes of wailing saxophone interspersed with crashing cymbals and thumping bass lines. With that ringing in his ears, Les got out of his sweaty clothes, splashed some water over his face and spread the photos across the bed.

Les probably shouldn't have laughed, but he did. The first photos he looked at were of the banquet and the band at the resort. Along with the three girls at the table, he'd caught Captain America stuffing himself with food. I wonder how he's feeling right now, Les chuckled to himself. Onya — mite. The photos he'd taken at the manse turned out perfect too. With the newest automatic cameras it is hard to go wrong, but somehow Les had fluked all the right angles and shadows and had managed to capture the old building in all its decaying splendour and beauty. The sandstone blocks, the wooden columns and the cobblestones outside. The aquamarine walls and the wooden columns inside, the massive beams supporting the ceiling, the views out across the bay, some of it was almost postcard material. The weed-choked backyard, the stables, what was left of the sundial, the slave barracks across the road, everything had turned out perfect. Even the lizard on the wall at the Badminton Club turned out great and the views from the balcony made it look like the Waldorf Astoria. Les looked at the photos spread out across the bed for a while longer. Was there something there to give him some sort of clue? Who knows? But they were top photos and he'd compare them with the other ones when the girls returned. Les climbed into his old pair of shorts, got his diving gear and headed for the beach across the road, managing to make it to the water with only about twenty pests jumping at him trying to flog him stuff he didn't need.

The water in the bay was just as pleasant as before, probably even better. The water was dead calm, with the sun almost getting ready to set, and although a cloud bank stopped most of it enough orange and gold washed through the grey to coat the turquoise waters of Montego Bay with a soft rubescent sheen. Les dived up and down, powering now and again with the webs and jet fins and just enjoying himself in general, thinking there could be worse places to be stuck in while waiting for a plane. He thought about a few other things as well; what, he wasn't quite sure. But there was something. No matter what, it had been a top day and maybe it would come to him later on. By the time he finished his swim, got back to the hotel and cleaned himself up, it was time for Esme and Delta to come back. After a close shave and a splash of Tabac, Les climbed into a pair of light green shorts and a white, Eumundi Lager T-shirt, and walked out the front. There were the two girls seated at the same spot with the photos on the table between them. Les strolled over, all smiles.

'Hello, ladies,' he said. 'I see you got the photos. Thanks. Did you have enough money?'

'More danuf,' said Esme handing Norton his change.

Les shook his head. 'No, keep it. Get yourself something to eat. You got enough money for a feed or whatever?'

'Sure we do mon,' said Esme, still a little starry eyed.

'Hey Les, mon?' said Delta, looking up from the table. 'Why yu so good wid wi?'

'Why?' replied Les, giving her a tickle under the chin. 'Because you're both good girls and I'm a bloody good bloke. Right?'

'Ire mon,' nodded Delta.

'And talking about blokes, I've got one coming around to see me soon time, and I want to have a good look at these photos before he gets here. So . . .'

'So yu want wi to piss off,' said Esme, a bit dejected.

'Well, if you wish to put it like that, yes. No, not really, Esme. You Boofhead.'

Les sat down and gave the girls' hands a little squeeze and a gentle piss in their pockets. But he did have to see this man on very important business. However, if they wanted to come back later on they were welcome to. And if they wanted to lease the Honda townhouse for the night again, that was alright too; he'd sweeten it up with Errol down the front. Again, you would have thought Norton had offered them the world, and the stars immediately returned to Esme's soft brown eyes. They both reached over and kissed him, then got up, saying they'd get a meal in town and go watch a band or something. They'd be okay. But if they got stuck or something they'd come back here, and they wouldn't get in the way. Les farewelled them down the stairs then went back to his room.

Whether it was safe to drink the local water or not Les wasn't quite sure. But he had two glasses while Jr Cat's 'Trailer Load of Guns' came howling up from the bar downstairs. He spread the photos out across the bed, separating the manse, the graves and Sweet Ginger Hill. Once again the little camera had done a perfect job. The photos of the old graves were as clear as a bell, you could make out the inscriptions on some of the tombstones and

436

with a magnifying glass you'd almost be able to read the lot. Sweet Ginger Hill was the same. The trees, the flowers, the colours, Les had captured all of the beauty of the old home again. The bedrooms, the old Spanish jars with the vines growing out of them, the Roman tiles on the verandah, the sandstone turrets. It all looked sensational. Even the photos of him and the kids at Spring Water Primary, and the one of him standing with Joshua next to the sundial and the fruit tree looked good. In fact, they were the two best happy snaps of the lot. Les was pretty rapt. He went over the photos for a while longer, looking for an angle. There was something there that reminded him of something and that was about all. Though for the moment he couldn't figure that out either. Maybe he'd go through them later on with Millwood. Who, incidentally, would be there before long. Norton put the photos back in their folders then thought he'd wait for the schoolteacher out on the balcony and watch the sun go down over Montego Bay while he had a bit of a think.

It was quite a pleasant view looking out across the beach and harbour from the front of the hotel. In the carpark below Les could see Errol talking with some other bloke in overalls who must have been the caretaker. He was taking down an old wooden gate at the side and putting in a new one. Errol was leaning on a pinch bar, near them was a broom, a shovel and a few other tools. Les watched them bumbling around for a while then switched his gaze back to the harbour and the street outside. Gloucester Avenue wasn't all that busy. A few cars went past, an old red bus, a truck or two; nearly all bombs. There were some pedestrians, and a couple of young cops were walking down the opposite side of the road towards the bottom end of town.

Out the front of the hotel the road curved a little to the right down a slight rise. Les watched absently as three Jamaicans came along the rise pushing a battered white Datsun 1600 that must have run out of petrol or something. There was another bloke behind the wheel. They

437

were all scruffy and dreadlocked and definitely weren't
breaking any records pushing the little car, it was hardly
moving and they were flat out getting it up the slight rise
in the road. Les watched in astonishment. It was hard to
think a bunch of men could be so pathetically slow and
lethargic, even in this heat. Useless, lazy bludgers, he
smiled derisively to himself. You're lucky slavery's been
abolished. Or old Moulton Eduardo Norton'd be out
there whipping your black arses. He'd soon get you
moving.

They'd just about got the Datsun round the crest in
front of the hotel when another Jamaican man started to
cross the road; head down, sunglasses, his dreadlocks
bundled up under a big green, yellow and red beanie. He
was shuffling along, even slower than the other three
snails. He made it to the middle of the road, shuffled a few
steps further then walked in front of the Datsun and got
run over by the blokes pushing it. Les gave a double blink
as his beanie flew off and he hit the road in a great burst of
dreadlocks and the contents of an old cotton sling bag he
had draped over his shoulder. The bloke behind the wheel
hit the brakes, the blokes pushing all went on their arse as
well, then got up and started abusing the bloke lying on
the road half sticking out from under the car, who in turn
started abusing them. It was one of the most lamentable,
ridiculous things Les had ever seen, yet it looked like a
major road accident. Next thing the cops came running
over from across the road and everybody started abusing
everybody else, while the 'accident victim' still lay on the
road, either too lazy, too stupid or too stoned to get up.
The cops started to get a bit heated and Les was watching
the shambles almost in disbelief when a blue-grey Toyota
pulled up across the road, driven by a young bloke who
seemed to fill the entire front seat of the car. The passenger door opened and out stepped Millwood Downie in
a pair of neat grey trousers, black shoes and a light blue
shirt; in his hand was a thin, tan briefcase. He tapped on
the roof and the car drove off. Norton figured that by the
time Millwood crossed the road and negotiated his way

438

through the rattle out the front, which was increasing all the time, he could meet him at the bottom of the stairs. Les walked back along the balcony and arrived at the front steps the same time as Millwood came walking across the carpark, half looking behind him, half looking where he was going.

'Hello, Millwood,' smiled Les. 'You got here alright?'

The schoolteacher turned around. 'Oh! Hello Les. How are you? What's...' He turned back to the crowd out the front where even I'rol and the caretaker had walked over to stick their heads in.

'Nothing much, Millwood. Just a motor accident out the front. That's all.'

'Good Lord. Did anybody get hurt?'

'Yes. A Jamaican pedestrian got knocked conscious.'

Milton screwed his face up a little. 'He what?'

'Millwood,' said Les, 'I don't know much about voodoo and zombies over here, but I'm convinced Jamaica is the proof of reincarnation. No other people could be that dumb in one lifetime.'

The schoolteacher shook his head. 'I...?'

'Come on, mate. Let's go upstairs and have a drink. It's good to see you again.' Les shook Millwood's hand then led him upstairs to the bar.

There were about six or eight people in there, a young Canadian couple wearing faded red, maple leaf T-shirts, a couple of white feral aunties around forty in floral frocks, who slewed around heavily when Les and Millwood walked in, the rest were Jamaicans having a quiet beer after work, or whatever. Two were seated on stools talking to the barman in his white shirt and black bowtie, who turned out to be Manuel the waiter from earlier in the morning. Christ, thought Les. They sure get their pound of flesh out of him. Les suggested a table away from the others and let the schoolteacher sit down.

'Well, what would you like, Mill? Or do you want to go and eat first? Whatever suits you, mate. You're my guest.'

'No. A drink would be fine, Les.'

'Suits me. What'll you have?'

439

'A Jack Daniel's and Coke? Is that alright?'

The way Millwood was a bit hesitant, Les surmised he didn't get to drink too much Jackies and had probably developed a taste for it by scrounging a bit at the golf club now and again. 'Coming right up. In a tall glass with plenty of ice — and I think we might make it a double.' Les walked over to the bar, where Manuel immediately recognised him with a smile, and got a tab going. Les ordered the bourbon for Millwood and a papaya rum and pineapple juice for himself, then took them back to the table and sat down. Another look of surprise registered on the thinnish schoolteacher's face. After being bossed around by punctilious, loud-mouthed Americans at the golf club, it was probably the first time any white person with money had not only bought him a drink, but got it for him as well then treated him as both a friend and equal. 'Cheers, Mill,' said Les, raising his glass. 'Thanks for coming over.'

'Cheers, Les. Thanks very much.'

'My pleasure — mate,' Les added with a wink, and they both took a decent slurp. 'So how was work today, Mill? Alright?'

Millwood closed his eyes and nodded his head. 'Yes. It was alright. I suppose.'

Millwood explained that normally the golf club was tolerable enough, but at the moment with Hurricane Richard in the air, so to speak, he had Germans, British and mainly Americans running around everywhere, not knowing what they wanted to do. As well as being catering officer, he was also in charge of the staff and the complaints department; and the last few days he'd been getting plenty of them, mostly from the Americans. Not counting trying to teach the kids at night. Still, he couldn't complain too much, jobs were hard to get and he managed to put a little aside each week and with a bit of luck he was hoping to get married next year. Millwood took out a battered wallet and showed Les a photo of his girlfriend Adriana. Her head was reasonable, but she wouldn't miss losing about three stone, and Les figured that if that was her at twenty-two, after five years of marriage she'd look like a baby rhinoceros. Nonetheless, he told Millwood he was a lucky man.

Les told Millwood he drove out to Rose Hill Great House but the top half was closed for repairs and it was swarming with American tourists so he brushed it. He met Joshua, saw the Norton graveyard, then finished up at Sweet Ginger Hill; which was very interesting. He admitted he slung Joshua a few dollars to get there and just happened to mention Millwood's name so he got to see the school as well. But that and the plateau it stood on were interesting too, and Les was pleased to see that his money was going to a good cause; like new windows and stairs and maybe a whip, a chair and a gun for the pupils, Les added with a wink. Millwood smiled and admitted they were a wild lot, but once you got to know them they were alright, and Les had only seen half of the crew. Les winked at Millwood over his glass and said that you never know, towards the end of the night there might even be a few dollars more floating around to finish the stairs and maybe get some more desks for the little monsters. The likeable schoolteacher tried, but couldn't hide his embarrassment when Les said that, and it didn't take the big Queenslander long to figure that Millwood Downie was one of those honest, appreciative types of people who were fast becoming an endangered species these days. They got through another two stiff drinks and Les was thinking of getting down to the nuts and bolts of their meeting. But they had plenty of time yet and he was more than enjoying Millwood's company as they swapped yarns about Jamaica and Australia.

'There is something I do have to ask you, Mill,' said Les, talking a hefty slurp of rum and pineapple juice.

'Sure, Les. What is it?'

'Well, you speak excellent English, Mill. Much better than me. How come...?'

'A wah yu say, mon?' replied Millwood, rising up in his chair. 'Yu a sayn mi no talk lik de dreads and de braas? Yu sayn mi sum cubbitch peelhead, mon? Huh? Yah I nung,

441

mon. No bada fas wid mi, Les. Yu know where mi stand from. Mi a wan bad leggo beas' eenai place.'

'Ire mon,' grinned Les. 'I no bada fas wid yu. I no tek smadi mek poppy show. I no com de bakra stoosh wid yu, mon.'

'Hey, Raatid, mon. Mi no mik cut yai.'

'Ya mon. No trace. Yu mik I flat on I feece. Mik I tie I shoe leece.'

Millwood threw back his head and laughed. 'Hey, Les, you're not bloody bad. Des words riv by yu. Or yu tief dem?'

'Respec mon. Respec,' protested Les. 'I no tief dem. I got a book I bought at the airport and I read it on the plane. Not bad for an Aussie bakra, eh?'

'Not bad at all.' Millwood laughed and tipped some more bourbon down his throat. 'To be honest, Les, the jambo's okay — it's cute, it's tricky and the tourists love it. But after a while it does tend to get a bit naff.'

'Yeah I can dig that, Mill. It's a bit like aussie slang. It can get a bit punishing at times when they lay it on too thick.'

'I try to teach the kids at school to speak English properly. A good command of the English language won't hurt them. And they're not going to get far in life running around talking like a mob of Red Hills ganja barons.'

'Or semi-literate Australians.'

'Yeah. I can dig that too — cobber.'

'Hey. Respec, mon. Respec.'

Les chuckled into what was left of his third rum and could feel that familiar rosy glow starting to spread across his face. There wasn't a real lot of Millwood and by the way his eyes were starting to get that glazed over, soft boiled egg look, it appeared the three double delicious on an empty stomach had hit the spot with him also.

'Well, what do you want to do, Mill? Have another cool one? Or will we go and have a bite?'

'I wouldn't mind eating, to be honest, Les. Another one of these and I'll go into Harry Belafonte mode.' Millwood closed his eyes and threw back his head. 'Daaayyy-Oh. Da-a-a-Oh.'

'Yeah, I know how you feel, Mill,' nodded Les. 'Another one of these rum things and I'll get a pair of maracas, lie back on the bar and start up with "When my baby, when my baby smiles at me I go to Rio..." And believe me, Mill, Peter Allen I definitely ain't.'

'Do you have a place in mind?'

'Yeah. There's a joint about three doors down called Calico Jack's looked alright.'

'It's very stoshus, Les.'

'Good,' nodded Les. 'Just what a couple of talawa gents like us deserve. Do you want to leave your briefcase in my room?'

'No. There's a couple of things in it I can show you over dinner.'

'Okey doke, Mill. Then we'll come back here, have a few more cool ones and I'll show you the photos I took. And a couple of other things I got.'

They got up, Les signed the tab, giving Manuel a few dollars, then managing to avoid eye contact with the two feral aunties walk out the front with Millwood.

Not a great deal was happening in Gloucester Avenue on Tuesday night. There were a few people in the bar next door, drinking Red Stripe and nodding their heads to some reggae song. Alongside was a restaurant called Willie's that looked more like a beer garden. A dozen or so people, mostly Germans, were sitting around, either drinking beer or eating hamburgers and chips off plates. A bit of traffic crawled past, a number of Jamaicans were walking around, ready to pounce on any tourists and try to flog them the usual rubbish they didn't want. Oddly enough, when the rats saw Les walking along with another Jamaican they left him alone. It was only a few minutes' walk to the restaurant.

Calico Jack's had evidently been named after some notorious pirate and was painted mainly white with a ye olde pirate touch about it. A concrete wall, with balustraded gaps to see in or out, ran across the front and two small brass cannons sat at the entrance. There was a dining room and bar inside and an open area in front spaced with heavy concrete seats and tables. A full-size mural of a bearded pirate with a brace of muskets across his chest and a wooden leg stood on one side of the dining room door and a skull and crossbones was draped on the other. The waitresses wore white dresses beneath black aprons with a skull and crossbones on them and were getting it easy because there wouldn't have been ten customers in the place. Les suggested they eat out in the open, Millwood agreed and they chose a table near a gap in the wall to watch the passers by. Millwood dropped his briefcase on a seat and said he'd be back in a minute; Les sat down facing the street. A smiling young waitress brought two menus over and while she was there Les ordered two bottles of Heineken. He was absently going over the menu when a small posse of Jamaican men somewhere in their twenties sauntered past and noticed Les sitting on his own.

'Enjoying de meal are you, mon?' said one, in a slow, sarcastic sneer.

'Everything just nice is it, mon?' hissed another.

'Yeah,' nodded Les stiffly. 'Couldn't be creamier.'

'Daht's good, mon,' muttered another. 'We so fucking happy for you.'

With three rums under his belt, Norton was about to tell them all to get well and truly fucked, but thought maybe it best if he kept his mouth shut. Millwood arrived back and sat down; walking over he'd heard what the posse said before they slouched off.

'I was thinking of inviting your mates in for a feed, Mill,' said Les, nodding to the street. 'But I changed my mind.'

'Yes, I heard what they just said, Les. I'm . . . sorry. But, that's the poor and downtrodden that they sing about in the songs.'

'Well, it ain't my fault, Millwood old son. I didn't kick the British out.'

'You noticed, Les,' smiled Millwood.

'Noticed? Millwood, I've never come across so many people filthy on the fuckin' world.'

'Of course,' smiled Millwood.

'You hate everybody. You even hate the other blacks in America.'

'Of course,' smiled Millwood.

'You got independence and black rule in 1962. And put in a shonky government that couldn't run a choko vine over a shithouse.'

'Of course,' Millwood smiled again.

'So you kicked all the evil whites out and took over the place like it was yours. But you weren't even here in the first place?'

Millwood's smile turned into a grin. 'Les, what are you? Some kind of racist?'

'Oh of course,' nodded Les. 'Though I think the correct word is realist.'

Norton's arse was still burning at being abused for doing no more than shout a Jamaican a meal in a half decent restaurant when the waitress arrived with the beers. She put them on the table then waited to take their orders. Millwood raised his bottle and smiled at Les.

'Just remember, Les. You're white. And even if you're right, you're still wrong.'

Norton clinked his bottle against Millwood's. 'Yeah, you can say that again, Millwood, me old China. So here's to you anyway. The white man's burden.'

'That's me, Les. But I ain't heavy. I'm your brother.'

'Yeah. And you'll miss ol' Brer Les when he's gone.' Les took a hefty swallow of beer and looked at the menu again. 'I'll tell you what, mate. The food doesn't look too bad.'

Les ordered a bowl of conch chowder and peppered shrimp with wild rice. Millwood went for red perch fillets in coconut and avocado for an entree and garlic crab for a main. They looked like they were going to knock the first beers off pretty smartly so Les ordered two more.

'Anyway, Millwood. So what have you got in the briefcase?'

'Not a great deal, to be honest, Les. Nearly all the documentation is over in Kingston with Professor Eyres. But I did my best.'

'Oh. Oh well ... I'm sure you did,' nodded Les, trying not to sound too disappointed.

Millwood moved some of the plates across and placed three books on the table plus a blue folder with four foolscap pages in it. Les took a look at the books: *A Brief History of Jamaica 1650–1800* by Zachary Esquemeling; *Tales of Olde Jamaica 1603–1874* by Edith Nettleford; and *Montego Bay. Its History, Politics and Heritage* by Dr Donald Cumper MBE. Written in 1950. Les could have two of the foolscap pages. Millwood had typed them up at the golf club when he got a chance, then photo-copied and put them in his briefcase before he left. Les glanced through them. There was roughly what he already knew about the family, plus a lot more names and dates that he recognised from some of the old tomb-stones, and Millwood had also explained who were the different aunties, uncles, grandparents, etc. Millwood had also typed out the names of the three books on the table, as well as some others Les's family might be interested in. Anything else they might need they could get by contacting the Jamaican National Heritage Trust whose shield and logo were on the top of the page along with the address and phone number in Kingston. The books he couldn't let Les have. But Les could go through them and take a few notes before he left. They were mainly snippets here and there about his family and others, plus some photo plates of portraits and paintings of the old houses. The only two portraits of Eduardo were over in Kingston. Centuries ago, the Nortons were the main family around Montego, with the biggest planta-tions, the most slaves and the most employees. Over the years they interbred with the slaves, who adopted the name and died off, then when slavery was abolished the Nortons that were left drifted off; some went to America, most went back to England then on to the colonies or wherever. Millwood had obviously gone to some trouble

446

in the short space of time he had and the papers were exactly what you would give some decent type of person hoping to trace their family tree. Nothing much to interest an avaricious intrigant trying to find a swag of buried loot in an equally short space of time.

'Yeah. Well, that's real good, Millwood,' said Les. 'Thanks very much for all the trouble you've gone to, considering me just bowling in out of the blue like this.'

'I did what I could on such short notice, Les.' Millwood shrugged and took a sip of beer. 'It's unfortunate you have to leave so soon, because if you went over to Kingston and spoke to Professor Eyres, I know you'd find a lot more.'

'Yeah. Yeah, I suppose I would.' Les glanced across the two pages then looked at the teacher. 'What about you, Millwood? You must have come across a few things about Eduardo and Elizabeth, rumours, anecdotes, old tales. What do you know yourself?'

Millwood stared back at Les over his bottle. 'You're very interested in those two, aren't you, Les?'

'Well . . . in a curious sort of way, yes. Mainly for my brother Edward back home who's a priest. And . . . cousin Judy. She's a schoolteacher too.'

A tiny smile seemed to flicker around the corners of Millwood's eyes. 'I do know a couple of things about them. There's references in Edith Nettleford's book. But I think I should tell you back at the hotel, over a few drinks.'

'What's wrong with now?'

'It'll be better back there. We'll have more time.'

Les was about to say something when the food arrived; and it looked and smelled good.

Norton's conch chowder was thick and spicy, tasted a little like abalone or Tasmanian scallops and had just enough chilli in it to make him sweat. Millwood's fish looked alright and it must have been okay because he was chomping away like there was no tomorrow. He'd smack his lips, take a sip of beer then look around him every now and again as if Scotty had beamed him down to the wrong planet. Even though he was paying for it, Les was rapt the little schoolteacher was enjoying the spoil and at times it was hard for Norton not to burst out laughing. They just had time to finish the entrees, wipe their chins and order more beer when the mains arrived. Norton's prawns were fat and juicy and there was plenty of them in a rich, peppery sauce. Millwood had to wrestle four medium-size crabs to death. But fortunately they were all drowned in a delicious garlic, ackee and red onion sauce and the shells were that soft he could bite straight through them. It was no contest. The only thing left on Millwood's plate at the end of the bout was the pattern. Neither felt like sweets, but they had a Jamaican coffee each to finish that almost blew the top of Norton's skull off. Despite all the booze they'd consumed so far, Millwood seemed keen to get back to the hotel and attack a few more Jackies; which suited Les. He paid the bill, left the girl a nice tip then they headed back to the Biltmore. As they stepped out of the restaurant, Millwood stopped to tie his shoelaces. Les hoped the posse wasn't around; he wasn't in the mood for any more shit and he wasn't in the mood for any heroics either. If it came to a pinch he'd grab Millwood and they could sprint back to the hotel in a few seconds; it wasn't far.

Les was strolling casually along. It was quite dark now, what street lights there were just worked and there weren't many people about. Between Calico Jack's and Willie's was a wide, angular set of steps running up off the road about fifty feet to some buildings above. Les noticed a movement about halfway up the steps on his left, and this pest, about twenty, in a pair of raggy army pants and a Bob Marley T-shirt with a cotton sling bag over his shoulder spotted Les the mug tourist on his own and came charging down the stairs.

'Hey mon, hey, mon!' he yelled. 'Hey wait deh, mon. I got sometin' for yu, mon.'

Ohh no, Norton groaned to himself. Not again. Does it ever fuckin' end? He was definitely going to tell this one to piss off and shove whatever he was hustling fair up his arse. However, the poor higgler was that frantic to get to Les he missed his footing and tumbled down the last dozen steps arse over head, landing on the footpath almost at Norton's feet grabbing at his ankle and yelping with pain; even through the bloke's filthy trainers Les could see he'd completely stuffed it. Being a good bloke, Norton immediately did the right thing. He stood there and burst out laughing. It was the best thing he'd seen since he got off the plane. Millwood stood up and walked over to Les who was almost in tears with the bloke lying on the footpath rolling around in agony.

'Good Lord! Les. What happened?'

'What happened? This prick just tried to mug me with a knife. But he fell over.'

'Right here on the main street?! My God! What's the town coming to?'

'Yeah. It's a dangerous place alright. Especially if you're a poor bloody white.'

'I can't believe it.' The schoolteacher was visibly shocked.

'No. Neither can I.' Les gave Millwood a quick once up and down. 'Millwood. Would you excuse me for a second?'

'Sure Les...?'

Norton turned around to where the higgler was lying on the ground in a foetal position, whimpering and clutching at his throbbing ankle. Les drew back his foot and booted the bloke right up the backside: hard. The higgler yelped with more pain and let go of his ankle with one hand to grab his arse.

'Thanks, Millwood.' Les draped a bit of an Arthur Daley arm round the schoolteacher's shoulders. 'I don't quite know how to explain this to you, Millwood, but Jesus that felt good.' Taking their time, they strolled on to the Biltmore.

Apart from two other Jamaicans at the bar they had the place to themselves. They sat at the same table and Les got his tab going again. Manuel said he'd have to close at twelve. That suited Les and seeing as it was quiet he asked Manuel if he'd mind bringing the drinks over? No problem, mon. Les got the same shout as before and placed them on the table. They had a good slurp each, commented on the nice meal, for which Millwood thanked Les again, then Les went to his room and returned with his backpack. He handed Millwood the photos, placed his book of poems on the table, plus the one he had on Jamaica, and flicked through the books Millwood had brought along. Millwood commended Les on the photos; he appeared to have a flair for photography. It was truly sad the way the old manse was slowly deteriorating, truly a shame. But didn't Sweet Ginger Hill look great? He laughed out loud at the photos of Les and the kids and the one of him standing with Joshua. He pointed to some of the kids and told Les their names and how old they were. It was hard to believe Joshua was close to eighty and had eleven kids himself and just as many grandchildren. Joshua was a very good boxer when he was young too. Millwood picked up Norton's book on Jamaica then the book of Elizabeth Norton Blackmore's poems. He flicked through them, then it seemed as if he was laughing at some private joke. Again Les had this feeling that the skinny schoolteacher was holding something back. He waved to Manuel and primed them up again then decided to get things going.

'Okay, Millwood. What's these stories about Eduardo and his sister you were going to tell me? I'm keen to hear them.'

'Father Eduardo Xavier Norton.' Millwood smiled at Les over the top of his latest Jack Daniel's. 'Man of the cloth.' Millwood smiled boozily again. 'Well, your dearly departed ancestor might have been a priest, Les, but he was also . . . a bit of a dropkick. Is that the expression you Australians like to use?'

'Careful there, Millwood,' said Les evenly. 'We're talking family here, son.'

'Exactly, I think,' replied Millwood, giving Les a quick once up and down. 'As well as preaching absolute rubbish on very rare occasions, Father Eduardo made a fortune slave trading, smuggling and doing a lot of business with pirates. When he wasn't doing that he was having a high old time and threw some of the best parties on the island back at the manse, until he vanished in that storm off Dredmouth in ... the date's on one of those pages you put in your bag.'

'Father Eduardo a slave trader and a shonk.' Les shook his head and tried to look shocked. 'Poor Edward back home will be shattered. I suppose that was what caused the break-up in the family?' Les nodded to his book on Jamaica.

'That ... amongst other things.'

'Mmmhh.' Les stared at Millwood. 'And when did Elizabeth go back to England?'

'About five years before Eduardo drowned. Which wasn't long after he completed building the manse. The date's there with the others.'

'Yeah, right.' Les matched Millwood's eyes for a moment then decided it was time to get to the nitty gritty, while the schoolteacher could still talk. 'So what's this story about buried treasure, Millwood? And Elizabeth leaving the clues to where it is in one of her poems or whatever? Is there any ...?'

Millwood threw back his head and laughed. 'That old chestnut. God! That's been going around for years.' He took another healthy slurp of Jack Daniel's. 'There's no treasure, Les.'

'There isn't?'

'No. They've been over the great house. The manse. All the Norton homes. It doesn't exist. Elizabeth never left any clues about buried treasure in her poems. She left a lot of little allegorical and paradoxical messages in her poems about different things. A bit like Nostradamus. But most of the messages were about something else.'

'Something else, Millwood? Like what?'

'The relationship between her and her brother. They were very close.'

'Close?'

'Yes. Possibly because unlike most families in those

451

days there was just one brother and sister, when there would usually be up to a dozen. So they were … close.'

Les looked evenly at the teacher. 'Exactly what are you trying to say, Millwood?'

'Oh alright, Les.' Millwood tried not to smile drunkenly. 'Eduardo and Elizabeth were getting it off together.'

'Getting it off?'

'Yes, Les. Jiggy-jig. You know. Humbo bumbo.' Norton shook his head. 'Elizabeth and Eduardo were screwing each other like mad.'

The way the schoolteacher said it, it seemed like it only happened yesterday, instead of hundreds of years ago. Les was a little astonished.

'Incest in my family? You're kidding, Millwood. I'm shocked.'

'Sorry, Les.'

'Christ! I come over here, I get ripped off, almost get mugged, have racial slurs slung at me. I find out we've got a slave trader and crook in the family. Now this. Bloody hell! What am I gonna tell the folks back home?'

Millwood shrugged. 'I'm sorry, Les. But it's all there in Edith Nettleford's book. Okay, she was a bit of an old gossip, but it's been the best-kept secret going around for years.

'Shit!'

'I'll quote you Elizabeth's poem "Love at the Manse". That's the one. Professor Eyres has gone over it a hundred times. I've been over it time and again myself.' Millwood put his drink down and picked up Norton's book of poems, then thumbed through it till he found what he was looking for. 'Here it is, Les. I'll read it to you as best I can in my state and explain what she meant.' Millwood took at slurp of Jackies to moisten his vocal chords and began reciting.

How do I love thee? Let me count four ways.
Confronting you directly, my beloved, I see all four
  at once,
Yet 'tis for this very reason I canst see the ten.
Norton shook his head.

'See, what she means there, Les, by let me count four ways, is they made love in four different places. Rose Hill Great House. Sweet Ginger Hill. The manse. And Pear River Great House, their Uncle Bigmore Moulton Norton's place, which you didn't see.'

Norton continued to shake his head.

'Then she says, "Confronting you directly, my beloved, I see all four at once, etc, etc. Yet I canst see the ten." That means they were doing it for ten years. Before she went to England.'

Les sipped his rum and stared at Millwood.

'Then she says, "A heartbeat to the left or right and I see all four again. Though the last love may be obscured." See, you must remember, Les, she was writing about affairs of the heart from memory and the memory is obscure. As with the passage of time. You with me, Les?'

Norton nodded slowly. 'Sort of.'

'And the last bit. "And 'tis indeed the last love I treasure most, my dearest. This is love we both did share and shall ever treasure. Our laboured love. The last love at the manse." The best loving they had was at the manse before he died. And "laboured love", Les, meant she was pregnant. The last screwing at the manse was good, but she got pregnant. So she went back to England to have the baby, where she met Davidson Blackmore the poet and married him almost as soon as she got there. He was penniless, she was rich and she supported him. They had three children altogether. But she died not long after she found out the news about Eduardo. Some say it was pneumonia. But Elizabeth died of a broken heart. She thought of coming back to Jamaica, but they never found Eduardo's body so there was little point. So she spent what was left of her life writing poetry.'

'What about the kid?'

'Ginger Loudivine Edwaina Norton Blackmore. Evidently she turned out looking just like her mother. But died when she was twenty. In a storm at sea, of all things.'

Les took a sip of rum and stared impassively across his glass at Millwood. 'Shit! This is bloody sad in a way.'

453

'Oh Les, it's tragic. Elizabeth was a tragic sort of woman. Read her poems. It's just that not many people know that she and her brother took sex off the streets in Montego Bay all those years ago. And kept it in the family where it belonged.'

'Tastefully put, Millwood.'

'I'm sorry, Les. But I have had a fair bit to drink.'

'Yeah.' Les continued to stare at Millwood Downie. Eduardo and his sister getting it on together? It just didn't seem right. And it didn't make sense. Why? Though they were very close. Too close maybe? But why would he bother? Eduardo had the pick of hundreds of young female slaves. He had heaps of money and he'd be the darling of the social set with all his parties. Still, stranger things happened in those days. Especially in a place like Jamaica. And there was that poem. Millwood and Professor Eyres had lived there all their lives, who was Les to dispute two experts? One an academic. Maybe Les was a little close because it was family and the booze had muddled his thinking. But something didn't seem right.

'Well, I suppose what you say makes sense, Millwood. Especially going by that poem. But do you think you might have interpreted it wrong? Sometimes you can't see the forest for the trees. She might have meant something else with her poems.'

'She might have,' shrugged Millwood. 'But get a copy of Edith Nettleford's book. Fair enough, she did romanticise a bit. But it's all there. Warts, trees, forests, the lot. Sorry it turned out like this for you and your family, Les. But...'

'Yeah, Millwood. But.'

'There is something else I can tell you about Father Eduardo, Les. And this is a hundred per cent true.'

'What? He was making porn videos as well?'

'He had a reputation as a man that would bonk a barber's floor.'

'A barber's floor?'

'Yes, Les. Anything with hair on it.'

Norton shook his head again. 'I think it must be my shout.'

454

Millwood grinned boozily and held up his empty glass. 'I'm ready to go again.'

Les caught Manuel's attention and fresh drinks arrived at their table shortly after.

They both took another hefty slurp while Les continued to study Millwood. He was getting good and drunk and had this impish kind of smile on his face. Not as if he was laughing at Les finding a couple of skeletons in the family closet. It was more like Millwood had played a harmless trick on a friend; pulled his leg, so to speak. Not that Les gave a stuff in that respect. The Jamaican Nortons had been dead for hundreds of years and if he hadn't left Australia Les wouldn't have known about them anyway. Yet at the same time Millwood had proved to Les that for a schoolteacher he had almost an expert knowledge of Jamaican history and knew what he was talking about. Norton didn't mind the little schoolteacher having a bit of a laugh at his expense; Millwood was still one of the most likeable people Les had ever come across. But the schoolteacher was definitely mistaken about something. Les wasn't quite sure what. But something he'd seen somewhere and something Millwood had said had set a loose cannon crashing around inside Norton's head. Millwood was wrong. He was right about one thing. But he was wrong about something else. Les was firmly convinced.

'So how long have you been a schoolteacher and an historian, Millwood?' he asked carefully.

'How long? Too bloody long. And too long at that golf club putting up with them honky chucky boys too.' Millwood leant across the table and fixed Les with a boozy, inimical leer. 'You know what I always wanted to be, Les?'

Hello. Here it comes, thought Les. The drunken, belligerent abo with a chip on his shoulder is finally coming out. Only this one'll have five hundred years of rape and torture. At least he can't accuse me of stealing his fuckin' country.

'Yeah, what, Millwood?'

'A stand-up comedian.'

'You? A stand-up comic? Get the fuck out of here.'

'That's it, Les. Exactly. A Jamaican Eddie Murphy.'

'A black Eddie Murphy? Shit!' said Les. 'I never thought of that.'

'Not as filthy as him, a bit more class. But in the same genre.'

'So what happened, Eddie? Why aren't I seeing you on Jamrite TV with your own show?'

'Ahh, how can I working two jobs?' wailed Millwood, taking another slurp of bourbon. 'I got up a few times, but all these hard cards and boopsies in the audience talkin' dread mon. I'm giving them the best patter ever gone down, all in perfect English, and the dumb hicks couldn't understand a word I was saying. I went over like a dead rat in a wedding cake.'

'That bad, eh?'

'The papers gave me a rap. They said my performances were very refreshing. The audience always felt better when they woke up. They said if I'd been a ventriloquist even my dummy would have quit and got a new partner. One gig was a success, though, they screamed for me to come back. But I was able to outrun the bastards.'

Les shook his head sagely. 'So it was back to Spring Water Primary while you still had your good looks?'

'Yeah. A brilliant career nipped in the bud.' Millwood seemed to brood for a second then he rose up in his seat and pointed a finger at Les. 'Les Norton. Tuan of Rose Hill Great House and heir apparent to the Norton Dynasty. Did you, or did you not, say I was your guest tonight?'

'My bloody oath I did, Millwood,' declared Les. 'And an honoured one at that, I might add.'

'Then in that case I will give you my genius routine. The one these peasants round here didn't appreciate.'

Ohh shit no, thought Norton. I'd rather he got drunk and wanted to fight me than bombard me with corny jokes. 'You don't have to, Mill. I'm quite happy just to sit here and have a drink.'

'No. I insist, Massah Les. So sit back and relax as Down Town Downie, AKA Mill the Thrill, takes the stage. And, before we start, I think it's my shout.' Millwood caught Manuel's eye and made a gesture with his fingers for the same again on Norton's tab then took a solid slurp on the one he still had. 'Okay, Les, here we go.'

Norton sucked in some more rum. So this is what Jerry Lewis has been holding back? He's a frustrated bloody comedian. And to think this has cost me a feed. Among other things.

'Why don't cannibals eat clowns?'

'You got me, Mill.'

'Because they taste funny.'

'Keep goin'.'

'Did I tell you about my dog that ate all the Christmas decorations?'

'No.'

'He finished up with tinselitis. How do you start a bear and a cat race?'

'How?'

'Ready Teddy. Go cat go.'

'I don't know what to say, Millwood.'

'Hey. I ain't even started yet.'

The drinks arrived and Millwood got going again. Norton wished there was some music.

'Two poofs in a lift, Les. One says to the other, "How's your bum?" The other says, "Shut up." The first poof says, "Yeah, so's mine. It must be the cold weather." I went to a doctor's the other day. He said, "Take off all your clothes." I said, "Where will I put them?" He said, "Just put them over there on top of mine." Two poof judges met in a bar, so they got drunk and tried each other. Hollywood are making a movie about a gay gangster. It's going to be called the Fairy Godfather. Personally, I've never screwed a poof. But I've screwed a guy that has. How am I going so far, Les?'

'Not enough Ts in terrific to describe you, Mill.' Christ, thought Les. I hope the bloke that's picking him up doesn't have to work back.

'I knew you'd like it.' Millwood took another monstrous slurp of Jack Daniel's. 'What about my girl, Les? I entered her in a contest on the weekend and she took out first prize. That was okay, but I'd have been happier if my dog had won it. I'm not saying she's ugly, Les. But I took her to the zoo and people starting feeding her broken biscuits. We walked past the gorilla cage and a zoo keeper ran out and shot her with a tranquilliser dart. When she takes her dog for a walk, people talk to the dog and pat her on the head. She was sitting in a bus the other day and said to the kid next to her, "Why don't you get up and give one of those old ladies a seat?" And the kid said, "Why don't you get up and the three of them can sit down?" She caught a jumbo jet to Miami and the plane had to stop at Cuba for a hernia operation. But I love her, Les. She found an ear at a soccer game and took it to a psychiatrist's. I said, "Why did you do that?" She said, "Because it was off its head." I bought her an electric toothbrush for her birthday but she took it back. She didn't know whether her teeth were AC or DC. She woke up the other morning with a headache and I told her she had a bad hangover. So she went and bought herself a bigger bra. I'm telling you, Les. She bought a parrot at an auction last week and paid five thousand dollars for it. It wasn't till she got home she found out the parrot was bidding against her. Even her canary hates her. It tried to commit suicide the other night. It broke out of its cage and threw itself in front of the cat. How good am I, Les?'

'Electrifying, Millwood,' said Les expressionlessly. Shocking would be fuckin' more like it.

'I told you I was good.' Millwood tipped some more bourbon down his throat. 'Did I tell you she was into drugs? She used to take Lo-Cal LSD. She wanted to expand her consciousness. But not too much. She's never been in trouble with the police. But she did get picked up by the fuzz once. She reckons it didn't half make her eyes water. Her uncle's a cop over in Kingston. He arrested an acid bath murderer then burnt both his arms off trying to pull the plug out of the bath. Her young brother was a

458

haemophiliac. He died trying to cure himself with acupuncture. One of her sisters went mad. She worked in a brothel for five years before she found out the other girls got paid. She was working up near the park the other night, a priest walked past and said, "What would your mother do if she saw you working here?" And she said, "Probably kill me. It's her corner." Her father was killed by a posse over in Kingston. Six hundred times they shot him. He had that much lead in him when he died they didn't bury him. They took him out and had him smelted. Her young brother . . .'

'Righto, Millwood. That's fuckin' it,' cut in Norton.

The schoolteacher blinked. 'Les, what's the matter?'

'Nothing's the matter, Millwood. I've just had enough. I don't want to hear any more gags.'

'You didn't like them?'

'No. They were great, Millwood. It's just . . .'

'I noticed you weren't laughing all that much.'

'Yeah, well . . .'

'Alright then. Let's hear you have a go.'

'Me?'

'Yeah you. Come on. What have you got to offer?'

'I'm not a fuckin' comedian.'

'I gathered that. But you must know something. You Australians are supposed to have a good sense of humour. Show me what you can do. Go on, massah 'orton mon. Strut your stuff, big dude from down under.'

Les had to think for a moment. 'Okay. Just a couple.'

'Many as you like, Les. If they're any good I'll steal them and start up a new act.'

It couldn't be any worse than your old one, thought Les. 'Righto Millwood, here we go.' Les took a giant slurp of rum, caught Manuel's eye and ordered another shout. 'What's black and white and red all over?'

'What?'

'A nun with stab wounds.'

'Not bad, Les. Not bad. What else have you got to offer?'

'You like that, Mill? Alright. How many Jamaicans does it take to eat a goat?'

459

'How many?'

'Three. One to eat the goat, and two to watch out for cars.'

'Hey. You're not bad on your feet, Les. Keep going.'

'What happens when a Vulcan woman's tampon fails?'

'What?'

'She gets Toxic Spock Syndrome.'

'Reasonable.'

'What's the difference between Rock Hudson and Saddam Hussein?' Millwood shook his head. 'Saddam's aides haven't killed him yet. What's brown and squishy and likes leather? A gay rights movement. How many poofs does it take to rape a lesbian? Four. Three to hold her down and one to gel her hair.'

'Oh go, Les, go,' said Millwood, taking another slurp as the next drinks arrived.

'You like me so far?' Norton slurped some more rum. 'Okay, Mill baby. What's a seventy-one?'

'You got me again.'

'A sixty-nine with two fingers stuck in your arse. What do you get when you cross an elephant with a prostitute? A hooker that fucks for peanuts and never forgets your name. How can you tell if a Jamaican woman's having her period? She's only wearing one sock. Why don't American negroes have to wear seat-belts? Because it's easier to put velcro on the headrests. Did you hear about the Jamaican abortionist who went broke? The piece of string split and somebody ate his rat. How many United States Marines does it take to change a light bulb? Fifty. One to change the bulb and the other forty-nine to guard him.'

'Oh beautiful, Les. Beautiful.'

'Thanks, Mill.'

'Alright, my turn. My turn!' cried Millwood.

'Ohh shit! Alright then.'

'Knock knock.'

'No. I refuse.' Norton shook his head. 'Definitely no knock knock jokes.'

'Come on, Les. Just a couple.'

Norton slurped some more rum and reluctantly nodded his head. 'Alright. Just a couple.'

'Knock knock.'

'Who's bloody there?'

'Sahara.'

'Sahara who?'

'Sahara ya goin', mate?'

'Ohh, Millwood. Gimme a fuckin' break.'

The little schoolteacher chortled with glee, spilling almost as much bourbon down his shirt as he got in his mouth. 'Knock knock.'

'Who's there?'

'Isobel.'

'Isobel who?'

'Isobel out of order?'

'Ohh, for Christ's sake.'

'Knock knock.'

'Who's there?'

'Sony.'

'Sony who?'

'Sony me.'

'God almighty.'

'Knock knock.'

'Yeah, who's there?'

'Mia.'

'Mia bloody who?'

'Mia again.'

Norton was about to reach across the table. 'Fair dinkum, I'll kill you. You little prick.'

Millwood ignored the threat. 'Knock knock.'

'Yeah, who's bloody there?'

'Hassan.'

'Hassan fuckin' who?'

'Hassan been that long since I seen you.'

'Alright,' roared Norton. 'Now it's my turn. Knock fuckin' knock.'

'Who's fuckin' there?'

'Howard.'

'Howard who?'

461

'Howard you like to go and get fucked?'

'Ahh, you're beautiful, Les. I love you.' Millwood gargled down more Jack Daniel's. 'Okay, Les. Doctor jokes.'

'Ohh, Millwood. For Christ's sake!'

The teacher ignored Les. 'I went to my doctor, Les. I said, "Can you give me something for wind?"'

'Yeah? What did he give you?' grunted Norton.

'A kite. I said to him, "Doctor, doctor. I've just swallowed a frog. Will it make me sick?" He said, "Sick? You could croak at any moment." I said, "Doctor, doctor. My brother the invisible man's waiting outside." He said, "I'm sorry, I can't see him right now." I said, "Doctor, doctor. My wife reckons I smell like a goat." He said, "Yeah. What about the kids?"'

Norton half rose from the table; his face florid. 'Alright, Millwood!' he almost screamed. 'I went to my fuckin' doctor. I said, "Doctor, fuckin' doctor. I feel like a curtain." He told me to pull myself together. I said, "Doctor, doctor. I'm living on a knife edge." He said, "Now cut that out." I said, "Doctor, doctor. I think I'm a billiard ball." And you know what he fuckin' said, Millwood?'

'No, Les. What did he say?'

'He told me to get back to the end of the fuckin' queue.'

'Ahhh! You're a genius, Les!' howled Millwood, spilling and drinking more bourbon. 'We're a team, Les. You and me. We'd be a sensation.'

'Yeah,' nodded Les, his eyes rolling as he shuddered at the thought. 'Bad luck I'm flying out tomorrow night.'

'What a waste, Les. What a waste. And we haven't even scratched the surface. Les, how much money do you get if you cross 200 female pigs with 200 male reindeer?'

'I honestly don't want to know, Millwood.'

'Four hundred sows and bucks.'

'Ohh shit!' Norton buried his face in his hands.

'Les, what do you get if you cross a gorilla with a pavlova? A meringue-utan.'

'Righto, Millwood!' roared Norton. 'That's fuckin' it!'

Les shook his two huge fists with rage and was about to reach across the table and start choking the little school-teacher when one of the biggest men he'd ever seen came lumbering into the bar. He was about six feet four and at least eighteen stone, wearing a pair of jeans and a white Tapper Zukie T-shirt. His hair was cut something like Millwood's on a big square head, under which jutted a big square jaw. Oddly enough he didn't look a day over fifteen. He seemed a little hesitant at first when he came in, then, spotting Millwood and Les, came over. When he saw the state Millwood was in and the look on Norton's face he appeared a little concerned.

'Are you alright, Mr Downie?' he asked, in a voice almost as deep as his shoulders were wide.

Les tipped this must be the bloke he saw in the car earlier who had brought Millwood in and was taking him home after work.

'Yeah, he's alright,' said Les. 'In fact you couldn't have timed it better, mate. He's just getting ready to leave.'

'Harvey, my boy,' garbled Millwood. 'How are you?'

'I'm fine thanks, Mr Millwood. We finished work a little early so I came straight round. But if you want to stay longer I can wait outside in the car.'

'No. That's okay,' said Les. 'Mr Downie's got ignition and he's just about ready for lift off.'

'Harvey, I want you to meet Mr Les Norton. Les, this is one of my star pupils, Harvey.'

'Hello Harvey,' said Les, half rising from the table. 'How are you, mate?'

'Good thank you, Mr Norton,' replied Harvey politely. He wrapped his hand around Norton's like a baseball mitt. 'Mr Millwood told me about you.'

'I hope it was all good, Harvey?' replied Les, settling back down with his drink.

'He's a big lad for sixteen, isn't he?' said Millwood.

'Sixteen!' Les gave Harvey an astonished once up and down. 'Shit, Harvey! If ever you want to come to Australia and play football, give me a yell.'

'Football, no,' said Millwood. 'Cricket, yes.'

463

'Yes, I like cricket, Mr Norton,' rumbled Harvey. 'Do you?'

'Do I like cricket, Harvey?' said Les. 'I don't like cricket. Oh no! I love it. Oh yeah! Shit! Sorry about that, Harvey. Mr Downie's got me a bit drunk.'

Harvey smiled good naturedly. There was a silence for a second or two as Les and Millwood looked at each other across the table. Where he was in a rage of frustration minutes before, Norton suddenly found himself chuckling away. The schoolteacher soon joined in.

'Well, Millwood,' said Les. 'It's been a funny old night, mate.'

'Oh Les, I've had such a good time. The drinks, the meal, everything. I have to thank you.' He reached across the table and shook Norton's hand warmly.

'Ahh, that's alright, Mill old mate,' replied Les. 'I've had a pretty good time myself. It's been a bottler. And,' Les held up a finger, 'I don't want you going away empty-handed either.' Les fumbled into his pocket and pulled out a wad of money. $500 US. 'There you are, Mill. Buy a few more things for the school. And anything left over, get yourself a new gag writer.'

Millwood looked at the money in his hands and blinked. Even Harvey's eyes bulged. 'Les, I . . . I can't take all this.'

'Ohh, get stuffed, Millwood. What are you talkin' about? Christ! It's only money. It's not an arm or a leg.'

'Yes, Les. But. I've done hardly anything. A few names and dates on some paper. Nothing.'

A strange gleam suddenly appeared in Norton's eyes, which was accentuated by the craggy, slightly boozy grin beginning to spread across his face. 'No, Millwood,' he replied, slowly shaking his head. 'You're wrong. You're wrong, mate. You've been more help than you can imagine.'

Millwood shook his head also. 'I . . .?'

'In fact, Millwood, I've got a feeling you should see me off tomorrow night before I catch my plane.'

'Oh, Les,' spluttered the teacher, 'I insist. I'm definitely coming down to say goodbye to my... my mate from Australia.'

'Thanks, Millwood. I'd appreciate that.'

'No problem, Les. It's the least, the very least, I can do.'

'I'll have to leave here at about six-thirty. The plane leaves at seven-thirty.'

'I shall be here, Les. No matter what.' Millwood finished the last of his drink and went to get up. 'Oh dear. Harvey, I think you'd best give me an arm, my boy.'

Harvey took another look at Millwood and a grin formed across his massive jaw also. 'Sure, Mr Millwood.'

Gently and effortlessly Harvey took Millwood by the elbow, lifted him up and walked him to the balcony. Millwood sucked in some fresh night air, smiled drunkenly at Les and they shook hands once more. Les shook Harvey's monstrous paw also, farewelled them from the top of the stairs, saying he'd see Millwood tomorrow night. Harvey had parked not far from the entrance, Les watched them get in the car under the slightly amused gaze of Errol standing at the bottom of the stairs, then walked back into the lounge, picked up his bag and walked across to the bar.

'Okay, Manuel. You'd better give me one for the road, son. A Jack Daniel's and Coke. Heaps of ice and make it a double.'

'No problem, mon.'

'Then tell me what I owe you and I'll settle up.' Les shook his head and blinked. 'Phew! De rum. Im junk yu.'

'Daht im do, mon,' smiled Manuel. 'Daht im do.'

Back in his room, Les put his drink on the phone table between the two beds, got down to his jox and splashed some cold water over his face and neck. It was bloody hot and about the only thing the World War One air-conditioner was doing was making noises; Les turned it off, opened his backpack and spread the contents out on one bed, separating the photos. Wha Do Dem's 'Eek-A-Mouse' came pumping up the wall from next door. A little annoying, but definitely not annoying enough to distract Les from the task at hand. Norton took a sip of

465

his delicious and figured he was a little drunker than he thought. But nowhere near as drunk as poor Millwood. Maybe it was all the fruit juice Les had downed along with the rum and he pondered for a moment whether switching to Jack Daniel's would pick him up or make him drunker? Who cared anyway. He moved the photos around the bed and checked some of the names and dates on the two papers the schoolteacher had given him, smiling at the Heritage logo on top of the page. Millwood had probably typed them up with official letterheads to give it a little extra touch and it would certainly make a good souvenir when he got back home. Despite his horrible jokes, Millwood certainly was a good little bloke to go to all the trouble he did, considering how busy he was at the moment. One thing for sure, you wouldn't say anything else about Millwood in front of young Harvey. But there was something that drunken schoolteacher had said that didn't make sense. Or maybe it made sense and there was a comparison to something somewhere. A comparison to something that didn't make sense. Les took another sip of bourbon. Doesn't that make a lot of fuckin' sense? Les took another sip and reached for the book of poems. Where's that poem Millwood read out to me? The one about Eduardo porking Elizabeth. Christ! Imagine if Hinch ever found out about this? 'Priest brainwashes poor defenceless sister and roots her against her will.' He'd go off his brain. Les thumbed through his book till he found the poem then read it several times before tossing the book back on the bed next to the photos. This just doesn't make sense, thought Les, shaking his head. Incest? Not even in my silly bloody family. I remember me and Murray trying to play doctors and nurses when we were kids and we got the shit kicked out of us. By everyone. Sisters, cousins, aunts, uncles, the lot. I didn't think I was ever going to sit down again after Mum and Aunty Daisy got through with me.

Les took another sip of bourbon and returned his gaze to the photos, his jaw now clenched with frustration. What is this fuckin's sheila trying to tell me? The loot's there. I know it is. But nothing makes sense. Norton scowled down at the photos, almost ready to let go a string of obscenities, when he started to blink. Then he began to blink some more. Wait a minute. Yes it does. Norton picked up one of the photos, stared at it for a moment then picked up the book of poems, read it, then tossed it back on the bed and picked up the photo again. My bloody oath it does. I was right and Millwood was wrong. In a paradoxical sort of way as he said. And what did I say to him? Sometimes you can't see the forest for the trees? Les stared down at the photos and grinned. Well, you can't, can you? Hah! No, you definitely canst not. Norton clapped his hands together hard and loud. Liz, baby, I think I know your little secret. Laughing now, Les pushed four of the photos together. And as for you, Eduardo, you shifty Spanish-named bludger who just happens to look like young Wayne. You're a lot shiftier than even I gave you credit for. But what a good idea. Les laughed and held up his drink. Well, here's to you, Eduardo old son. And you too, Elizabeth. You can fool some of the Nortons all of the time. And all of the Nortons some of the time. But you can't fool all of the Nortons all of the time. Not the Australian branch of the family anyway. And I think I know the whole story too. Les grinned triumphantly and sipped his drink. Then it dawned on him that if he was right he was going to need, if not quite earth-moving equipment, then at least something along those lines. Along with his jubilation Les began to ponder on this new development when there was a knock on the door. Hello, who's this? he frowned, and got up to open the door.

'Errol? How are you, mate?'

'Ire mon.'

'That's good. So am I. What's...?'

'De two 'oman, Delta and Esme. Dey waitin' down de front wan see yu. Suntin baht de car. I tell dem get laas?'

'No. No, that's okay, Errol. I'll come down and sort it out.'

'Ire mon.'

467

Les was about to close the door and stopped. 'Hey I'roll. Come inside for a minute. I want to see you about something, mon.'

Les closed the door behind them and had a quiet, friendly chat with the security guard dropping a bit of an Arthur Daley arm around his shoulders at the same time. A few minutes later Errol was $50 US in front, with the promise of another $50 later on.

'I'll be leaving early and I'll be back in the afternoon. I'm not sure when.'

'No problem, mon.'

'Good on you, I'rol. Okay, tell the two lovelies I'm on my way down.'

'Ire mon.' Errol closed the door behind him.

Beauty, Norton smiled to himself. That sort of settles that. Now I suppose I'd better throw a pair of shorts on and let the two Jamaican princesses have the home unit for the night. Then try and get a good night's sleep myself. Hah! Tony Rebel and Red Rose's 'No More Gun Talk' came ricocheting up the walls from next door. Don't like my chances.

Esme and Delta were standing with their valuables next to the Honda, under the steady gaze of Errol, when Les came down the stairs. They didn't look in too bad a shape. Fed, sober, they'd even shouted themselves a new plastic shopping bag from somewhere; and they were happy to see Les again.

'Hello, girls,' he smiled. 'How's things?'

'Hi Les,' chorused Esme and Delta.

Their night had been pleasant enough. They'd had a meal down the road, saw a band in a bar, had a few orange juices, walked around. Les told them about Millwood and himself. They'd had a nice meal too, but unfortunately they'd got a little drunk. Then he opened the car door.

'Listen, if you want any pillows or that see Errol and he should be able to scrounge you some up. He's alright. I'll be down around seven and we'll have breakfast. Then I have to go away for the day.'

Delta wasn't wasting any time. She put her arms around Norton's neck, gave him the sweetest little kiss then jumped in the front, leaving the door open for Esme. Esme stood there for a moment with this strange look on her face. She stepped across in front of Les and pushed her tunti right up against him.

'Les, why yu no take me upstairs wi yu? No danza. No bandulu. Jus bi wi yu.'

'Esme,' smiled Les, 'you're a sweetie. You really are. But I have to get some sleep. I've got a lot on again tomorrow.'

Esme's eyes narrowed a little. 'Deh suntin' wrong wi me? Mi no good nuff, Les?' She nodded her head slowly. 'Ya. Ya mon. Mi no good nuff for yu. Daht's it.'

'Ohh bullshit, Esme. You're the grouse. Fair dinkum, I'd swim across a beach full of bluebottles just to hear you piss in an old hubcap. But I want to be on my own. I have to think about something. Besides, I got a girlfriend back in Australia. What would she think?'

'A wa do yu,' protested Esme. 'She no heh. She ovah deh. No, Les. Mi no good nuff for yu. Tell trut, mon.'

'Oh arseholes! Come here.' Les put his hand around Esme's waist and gave her a kiss. It wasn't too bad either. Her lips were disgustingly soft and warm, with a little bit of spice, and her body firm; even if she didn't close her eyes. 'Goodnight, Ez. I have to go. I'll see you in the morning.' Les gave her one more on the cheek. Esme stood there for a moment, giving Les another strange look, before she climbed in the back of the Honda. 'See you later, Errol,' winked Norton and climbed up the stairs.

'Ire mon.'

Bloody sheilas, thought Les back in his room. It's alright for them to knock you back for a root. But knock them back and they carry on as if you're either a poof or there's something wrong with you. What are you supposed to do? Light candles round it, roll out a prayer mat, get down on your knees and worship it? Christ! Creepy-crawlies aside, I'm too drunk, too tired and it's too fuckin' hot. Les finished his drink and yawned. Next door decided to play another reggae track just for a change. 'Dirts Heart' by Coca Tea and Ninja Man. Bloody hell! Do they ever play any rock 'n' roll in this joint? Even some Col Joye, Bay City Rollers, ABBA, Duran Duran, techno funk, house music. Anything. Hang on. What am I saying? No, keep the reggae going. Ire mon. Norton yawned again and looked at his watch. It wasn't getting any earlier. He switched off the light, lay back on the bed and closed his eyes.

It wasn't easy trying to sleep. He'd doze off but the steady bass, the short, tinny rattle of drums now and again or bursts of laughter coming from below would keep waking him up. And there was nothing Les could do about it. He'd toss and turn and try to switch off, but to no avail. Oh well. I suppose I'll drift off sooner or later. I'll just feel buggered when I wake up in the morning, that's all. Les laughed bitterly to himself. I should have let Esme and Delta have the room. I'd be better off sleeping in the fuckin' car.

Reggae music continued to pump into the room. Before long it all began to sound the same; one continuous bass riff punctuated by drums and unintelligible lyrics. By now Les was half asleep, half awake, drifting in and out of consciousness, more buggered than anything else. One minute his mind would be in Australia, the next minute it would be in Jamaica as he'd toss and turn and sweat into the sheets. Les yawned and rolled over and the beat seemed to get closer. Then the beat sounded like a knock on the door. Les opened his grainy eyes. It *was* a knock on the door. What the . . .? Les looked at his watch in the half-light, swung his legs wearily over the bed then got up and answered it.

'Esme! What the . . .?'

Esme didn't look horny or doe-eyed or in love. She was pouty and shitty.

'Daht iez-haad, bugayaga I'rrol mon,' she smouldered. 'Him a one bad man dat. Let mi in, Les. Please mon.'

Before Norton had a chance to say yes, no, or maybe,

470

Esme was inside. He closed the door, switched on the light and looked at her through puffy eyes. 'What's wrong, Esme? What did Errol do?' Bloody hell, Les muttered tiredly to himself. He's probably tried to get her pants off. I'm fucked if I'm going down there to defend her honour, or her bloody chastity, or what bloody ever.

'I eenai biksit mi sleep im done i wuk...' Esme started blowing up.

Les held up a hand. 'Hey, hang on, Esme. Slow down. I can't understand a bloody word you're saying.'

'Ire mon. Mi bex. Sorry, Les.'

It turned out Errol hadn't tried to pork her or Delta. He hadn't even made so much as a sexist remark or a mild sexual innuendo. Esme would have been happier if he had. Les had slung Errol fifty dollars earlier to get him a loan of a pinchbar or a crowbar; with another fifty in his dook when Les returned them in the afternoon. Norton remembered seeing Errol helping the caretaker earlier with the gate and figured he might be able to get him a loan of some tools. For a hundred dollars US Errol would have choked the caretaker and torn them out of his hands; stuff the new gate. Evidently there wasn't much happening so Errol finished work early. He'd got the tools together on the sly, didn't want to have them lying around and didn't have a key to the boot of the Honda. So being the good, honest bloke he was, and not knowing when Les was leaving in the morning, he'd thrown them in the back, a pinchbar, crowbar, shovel and one or two other things, all over Esme; nearly busting her skull. Delta was alright in the front, but in the back you would have been more comfortable locked in an iron maiden. Errol's philosophy, however, was Esme wasn't giving him a hundred bucks and if she didn't like the idea she could fuck off. So here she was; tired, shitty, a lump on her scone and Norton had a spare bed. Fair's the go. Even his rotten ancestors wouldn't have been that bad back in the slave days. Les looked at her, closed his eyes and shook his weary head.

'Alright,' he said, clearing some stuff off the spare bed. 'But behave yourself. And no snoring or farting.'

'Sure Les,' answered Esme happily. 'No problem, mon.'

'You can leave that to me.'

'Wa yu say, mon?'

'Nothing. If you want a glass of water or whatever, it's in there.'

Esme had a drink, took her sandals off, but left the rest of her gear on and climbed on the bed, pleased as punch. Les turned off the light, pulled a sheet over him and said goodnight to Esme; she smiled the same back at him. Norton closed his eyes and resumed staring into the cosmos as more reggae continued to pump in from next door. Bloody hell, he thought. How am I ever gonna get to sleep? And I've got to be on the ball a bit tomorrow. Norton was about buggered now and another thought was running through his mind; worrying him. If he was right about what he was going to do tomorrow, and he stuffed it up, there was a good chance he could get badly hurt; more than likely killed. There was also a chance he could get sprung. A slim one, but a chance nonetheless, especially if he stuffed up. Les was lying on his back, drifting off, half thinking about different things, miles away at times, when instinct told him someone was watching him. Someone was. Esme. Les opened his eyes slightly and Esme was lying on her side, resting on one elbow, staring at him. In the gauzy darkness Les could see and feel these soft pink eyes boring into him like laser beams. His mind on other things he'd almost forgotten about her and got a bit of a start.

'Esme? What's the matter? Can't you sleep?'

'Mebbi sleep,' crooned Esme, her eyes never leaving Norton.

'Yeah, righto. Whatever.'

Les closed his eyes again and continued staring into the cosmos, trying to get some rest at least, and not get up feeling too shithouse in the morning. Try as he might, however, Les found it impossible to switch off from the beams Esme was scorching into him from about a metre away. Go to sleep will you, Esme? Les almost pleaded. For Christ's bloody sake. But Esme wasn't letting up.

'Les. Les.'

'Yeah whad?' mumbled Norton.

'Wa wrong wi mi?'

'Nothing's wrong with you. Esme, go to bloody sleep.'

'No. Suntin' wrong with me. Wa?'

'Esme. Go to sleep. You're enough to give anyone the shits.'

Norton tried to get to sleep as Esme continued to stare at him and more thumping reggae pounded in through the bathroom window.

'A hiry music deh pon i radio,' she said dreamily.

It was some old Bob Marley track Les vaguely remembered. 'Yeah. Some of it's alright,' he mumbled.

There was silence for a little while apart from the music. 'Les, wa wrong wi me?'

'Nothing. I can't afford you and you're too nice. Now go to sleep and stop being a pain in the arse.'

Even with his eyes closed Les could sense Esme slowly shaking her head. He yawned, settled back and again tried to ignore her. Next thing his bed moved. Esme was sitting on the edge staring down at him.

'Esme!!?'

'Les. Wa matter wi yu?'

'Oh Esme! Give it a bloody rest, will you? Go to sleep. Jesus!'

Norton lay back on the bed with his eyes closed, too tired and too buggered to argue any more. Anything for a peaceful life. There was silence, darkness and more reggae music.

'Ire mon,' Esme finally said. 'I think I understand.'

'That's terrific, Esme. Now goodnight.'

'But Les.' Esme placed her hand on his chest. 'Yu bin so good wi mi 'n Delta, I want do suntin for yu.'

'Esme,' protested Norton.

'Relax mon,' soothed Esme. 'I give yu Jameercan sno'stum.'

'Esme. For . . .'

But it was too late. Esme pulled the sheet back and started running her fingers across Norton's chest and stomach muscles, very much liking what she was finding. It wasn't long before her soft pink fingers were sliding gently down his midriff and under his jox. Shit! Isn't this nice? thought Les. All I wanted was some sleep, now I've got this bird attacking me with some monstrous tampering. I s'pose I'll just have to lie back and think of Australia. What else can a man do? Les let out a little sigh. I suppose it could be worse.

Norton might not have been all that keen for any porking, but Mr Wobbly was more than keen to get up and have a look around. Esme's hands were gentle, she gave him a rub, a stroke and a squeeze and Mr Wobbly got keener than ever and from where he was now standing, he didn't mind the view either. Then Esme got down to it. Her tongue and lips were soft and warm and her mouth moist and wide; a shiver went up Norton's back then down to his knees. Ohh yes, he sighed. It definitely could be worse alright. Even the music started to sound better. 'Stranger on the Shore' by Scotty and Johnny P. It was all bass and beat pumping up the wall with Mr Wobbly now pumping away in unison also. Les writhed on the bed, sweat pouring down his face and stinging his eyes as Esme's head bobbed up and down over his loins. In practically a dream-like state Les could make out some woman with a beautiful, crackling voice singing the lyrics and some bloke rapping out a chorus. 'Tell you where me stand, tell you where me stand. Tell you where me, tell you where me, tell you where me stand. Need a 'oman to keep me healthy and strong. To all 'oman dis is an invateershun.' Yeah, whatever, muttered Les. I ain't gonna argue. It was all he could do to stay on the bed. Esme knew what she was about. Then the Jamaican girl hit warp ten and Norton's erogenous zone or whatever at the same time, sending the big Queenslander cross-eyed. He gasped in some air, arched his back and Mr Wobbly exploded into what felt like a thousand pieces. Esme bit and chewed and, try as he might, Les couldn't help but howl like a werewolf that had just put one foot in a dingo trap and the other on a cigarette butt as Esme got square

474

for everything Norton's ancestors had done to hers back in the good old days. His back arched again, his bones rattled, then Les flopped back on the bed, completely drained, with his eyes spinning around like roulette wheels. After a moment or two Les dragged in some air, let it out and glanced up at Esme, who was looking down at him through the soft light and the music with this enigmatic, almost Mona Lisa like smile on her face.

'So that's a Jamaican Snow Storm, Esme?' Norton smiled dreamily back at her. 'Unreal.'

Esme shook her head slowly. 'N'Les,' she garbled. 'No daht. Di is. *Shhsplluuurrrshhphllwt! Phwt! Phut!'* Esme sprayed the lot all over Les.

'Ohh, you dirty, rotten low moll!' howled Norton. 'You prick!'

Les flopped back on the mattress with the Norton dynasty bloodline in his face, his eyes, all over his chest plus the sheets and pillows. He drew back his arm in a half-hearted attempt to belt Esme one, but he was too stuffed and now too weak to move. Esme had done a good job and all he could do was lie there and listen to her laughing as she went to the bathroom then came back and climbed on her own bed, still giggling. To make things worse again, Les found himself starting to laugh too. Naturally, like a typical woman, insouciant or otherwise, as soon as Esme's head hit the pillow she was asleep.

'Righto, Esme,' muttered Les, 'that's it. Get your gear and piss off.'

'Zzzz.'

'You heard me, Esme. Get. And you can forget about breakfast in the morning. You just had it and knocked it back.'

'Zzzz.'

Shit! What am I gonna do? Les was a beaten man. Too tired, too lazy and too whipped to move. He found a piece of sheet that hadn't got dragged up his arse in the finale, half wiped his face and eyes then flopped his arm back down by his side. Ahh, bugger it. I couldn't give a stuff. More reggae pumped in from next door, the humid

Jamaican night settled in further and for some reason Norton went out like a light.

Les didn't wake up feeling too bad in the morning, his eyes were a little bit grainy and he'd slept in a bit longer than he'd planned. But apart from that he felt alright. Esme was still snoring softly in the next bed with her back to him and her arse up in the air. Les climbed out of bed, looked at her for a moment and a nasty smile flickered round the corners of his eyes; Les couldn't miss. He raised his right arm, with his hand and fingers dangling loose, and flicked her right across the rump. She jerked her eyes open and mumbled something as she moved slightly on the bed. Les flicked her again and got a better reaction this time.

'Yeeooww!!'

'Morning, Esme. Have a good night's sleep, did you?'

Despite rubbing gingerly at her backside, Esme still had this insouciant smirk on her face. 'Hi Les. How are yu di maanin?'

'Fine, thank you Esme,' Les smirked back. 'You won't mind if I use the shower first?' Esme looked up at Norton and blankly shook her head. 'Thank you,' smirked Les.

Les climbed under the shower and got cleaned up. He didn't bother shaving — he didn't want to waste too much time — just freshen up, get rid of the sweat and anything else he didn't fancy clinging to him. When he came out, with a towel round his waist, Esme was sitting on the bed sipping a glass of water. She smile up at Les staring down at her pofaced, then jumped up off the bed, put her arms round his neck and kissed him. Despite himself Les kissed her back.

'Brer Wallaby sleep good?' she crooned, rubbing herself up against him.

'Yeah,' nodded Les. 'You beat the hell out of Serepax.' Les had his hands around her waist and the next thing he knew he was getting a horn. 'Now get in the shower and we'll have some breakfast.'

'Okay bebe.' Esme kissed him again.

Bloody sheilas, muttered Les, as he climbed into his blue shorts and half-clean Wallabies T-shirt. They make it hard for you, in more ways than one. By the time he'd got his bag packed with what he needed, Esme was cleaned up and looking and smelling more than half alright. Norton was sorely tempted. She gave him another big smile and a kiss, slipped her arm in his and they stepped out onto the balcony. It was cloudy, didn't quite look like rain, just unpredictable and, of course, hot, humid and no wind. Delta was sitting at the same table as before, sipping a glass of orange juice. She smiled up when they walked over and in her white T-shirt and shorts look fairly fresh considering.

'G'day, Delta,' smiled Les. 'How's things?'

'Fine, Les. How yu?'

'Pretty good.'

They sat down, Delta and Esme got into a quick, direct conversation that was too fast for Les to understand. But going by a few words here and there and the looks on their faces, everyone was happy enough. Les had a quick look around while they were talking. There was only another six people there, including the two feral aunties crushed into bicycle pants with baggy LA Gear T-shirts over the top. This time Les caught their eye, smiled and gave them a tiny wave; and this time they completely ignored him. Next thing Manuel hovered next to the table and going by the shit and grease all over him it looked like the cook hadn't shown up again.

'Ya mon?' he asked dully.

Les knew what to expect. 'Anything, mate,' he said. 'Anything. Whatever you can muster up for the three of us that's quick and easiest for you. Okay? With plenty of coffee.'

'Ire mon. No problem.'

Manual disappeared and Les turned to the two lovelies. 'Well, what do you reckon? Here I am, overlooking Montego Bay and having breakfast with two beautiful girls. It's like something out of a movie, isn't it?'

They both moved in a little closer. 'You one lucky man, Les,' said Esme.

'She right too,' smiled Delta.

Les thought for a second. 'Let's just hope you're right,' he said quietly.

It was quite pleasant again out on the balcony and they chatted away. The girls' faces dropped a little, especially Esme's, when Les mentioned again that he had to leave around six-thirty to catch the plane. Could they please come and see him off? Of course they could; in fact, Les wanted them to hang around as he needed a small favour done.

While they were talking Les thought he could hear raised voices coming from downstairs so he peeped over the balcony. The caretaker was having heated words with Errol. Errol had height, reach and age on the caretaker and was shrugging his shoulders indifferently. Oh well, surmised Les, I'd say my tools are still in the car. Next thing Manuel arrived with breakfast. All he brought was a pile of thick, crisp toast, pots of beautiful, sweet jam and two steaming pots of fresh, strong, Jamaican coffee. Plus a bowl of sliced fruit: pineapple, papaya, guava and bananas. Shit! What a bastard, grinned Les, and dived straight into the papaya. While they were eating, Les gave Delta and Esme a few instructions and filled them in on a couple of things. He wrote down Millwood's number and told them to ring him and make sure he was there to see him off tonight. Millwood would probably he hungover or busy. But keep ringing till they got through and say it was a message from a Mr Norton from Australia. Then ring back again later in the afternoon if Les was late getting back and make sure he was coming. He gave the girls the key to his room and a bit more money. The room was booked for tonight so they could both stay there. Esme and Delta were rapt. But be there this afternoon just in case he needed them. The girls were a little curious about this, but didn't say anything. That was about it. Les looked at his watch; it was time for him to get going. No, they couldn't come with him. In the meantime, have some more coffee, use the pool, throw their gear in the room, it was theirs till tomorrow. Les got his backpack from his room, fixed things up at the desk for Delta and Esme, said goodbye to the girls and walked down the front stairs.

Errol and the caretaker had moved their argument to the other side of where the new gate was supposed to be going up. Errol had thrown an old piece of green tarpaulin over the tools on the back seat; Les gave them a quick check. There was a pinchbar, a crowbar, a shovel and a yard broom with a broken handle. I suppose that'll do, shrugged Les. He started the car and got going without wasting any time.

Apart from the usual pests yelling out at him, the drive through Montego Bay was uneventful and before he knew it Les was past the airport and bumping along the A1 thinking about things. There was something else he hadn't taken into account, something else he hadn't thought of from the word go, and he couldn't figure out what it was. One thing Les did take into account, he'd used more petrol than he expected and you could bet the hire car mob would squeal like stuck pigs and rip him off unmercifully if he took the Honda back empty. There was a garage just near Mahoe Bay, Les filled up, found the water was down too and while he was there got three cartons of orange juice and some more film. This too was uneventful except for about a dozen different Jamaican kids with homemade spearguns trying to flog him strings of small, yet beautiful, tropical fish that people overseas would have paid a fortune for to put in their fishtanks or aquariums. Les climbed back in the Honda and continued on.

Les was still deep in thought and before he knew it he'd wound his way past the coastline, curved round the zoo and was heading along a scrubby, deserted stretch of road that led into Dredmouth. He wasn't speeding, just taking his time with his seat-belt on and the radio off when a fatter, older cop stepped out of the bushes about twenty metres on the left in front of him and waved him down. It was the last thing Les was expecting. What the fuck's this all about? he thought, as he pulled up a few metres along from the cop. I haven't done anything. Then something he'd read in one of those books he'd bought at Tampa airport dawned on him. Dope dealers drive rentals. Shit! What if this prick tries to bust me? But I haven't done anything. Uh-oh! What about the bloody tools in the back? And they're as corrupt as buggery over here. Fuck! How's my luck? The cop lumbered slowly over and Les could sense him checking things out. He was about sixty, with a neat moustache, in a neat blue uniform with a red stripe down the leg and a great big gun sitting in a holster on a white belt. He reminded Les of a Jamaican version of Jackie Gleason in *Smokey and the Bandit*, only this time Norton wasn't in the mood for silly bloody comparisons with yank movies. He didn't know which way this local walloper might jump and Les was more than a little concerned.

The cop rested an arm on the roof and stuck his head in the passenger window. 'Ire mon,' he said casually. Too casually for Norton's liking. 'Where you from, mon?'

'Montego Bay,' replied Les. 'I'm staying at the Biltmore Hotel.'

'Ire mon,' the cop nodded slowly. 'Who owns de car?'

'I hired it at the airport,' said Les. 'I'm here on a holiday.'

'Ire mon,' the cop slowly nodded again. 'Why you don't switch off de motor and step out?'

'Yeah, alright.' Les cut the ignition, got out and walked carefully round to the back of the car.

The cop gave Les an expressionless once up and down and stepped round to the back of the car also. 'Open de trunk, mon.'

'Sure,' answered Les.

Norton got the keys out of the ignition and opened the boot. The cop had a good look around, told Les to close it then walked to the back window. He had a look inside then opened the passenger side door and had a rummage round on the back seat. He left the door open and returned to Les.

'Why de tools, mon?'

'Why the tools?' echoed Les, staring blankly at the cop. 'Why the tools? Well . . . why wouldn't I need the tools?'

'Daht's what I'm sayin mon,' the cop nodded impassively. 'Why de tools?'

Norton blinked at the cop. 'Because . . . because I'm an official with the Australian Government Arts Council Foundation working in . . . conjunction with the Jamaican Heritage Trust in Kingston. We're fully restoring the Norton manse at Dredmouth.'

The cop blinked back at Les. 'What yu say, mon? Norton? De manse?'

'Yeah, hang on boss. I'll show you.'

Les showed the cop his driver's licence with his photo and ID, then got his backpack from the front seat and showed the cop the papers Millwood had given him with the Jamaican Heritage Trust letterhead on the top. He emphasised his story again, adding that his whole family was involved, along with both the Australian and Jamaican governments. He was going over to give the place a tidy up then take some notes and photos to get a proper idea of what they were going to need. Les also added he was involved with the church back in Australia and if there were any problems the cop could contact Professor Eyres or Mr Winston Glover over in Kingston. Bloody Hell! That's the best I can do, thought Les. He should buy that. The cop seemed to stare at Les in a strange kind of disbelief.

'Is there something wrong, officer?' asked Les politely.

The cop's attitude seemed to change. 'You're . . . a Mr Norton from Australia? With de government and de church?'

'That's right, officer. Why . . .?'

A sickly smile formed on the cop's face. 'I only selling de tickets, suh.' The cop seemed to unconsciously pull a book of tickets from his top pocket.

Les stared at the tickets. They were white with blue printing, very official looking and about twice as big as a playing card. They were for the Sommersby Police Sports Club Annual Ball to be held under the Distinguished

Patronage of the Hon. Rossiter Norton, Custos of Sommersby. At the Sommersby Beach Hotel Ballroom, Dredmouth. The tickets then had the date, the time and the number. Plus, Music by Sweet Seven. Dress Formal. Admission $100:00. Gate Prize, Weekend For Two at Grand Orchid Hotel, Negril. Then it dawned on Les what was going on. The fat bludger had been out hustling motorists, probably putting the heavies on them to buy a ticket for their rotten local wallopers' ball. He'd seen the rental, and a cop being a cop with a gun he'd pulled Les over and started giving him a bit of a hurry up and found out he'd hustled a government official. Who it appeared could have something to do with the rooster who was the distinguished patron of their ball. The Hon. Rossiter Norton, Custos of Sommersby. A sigh of relief went through Les. It looked like he was off the hook.

'I say,' beamed Les. 'How absolutely marvellous. I know the Hon. Rossiter Norton.'

'You do, suh?' said the cop.

'Yeah. Used to play two-up with him on Anzac Day.' Les went for his wallet just in case. 'I've got some friends back in Montego Bay who'd love to meet him. Give me ten tickets.'

The cop seemed awfully nervous as he took the fifty U.S. and gave Les his tickets. 'You're Mr Norton yourself? With de Australian government?' he repeated.

'That's correct, officer. Over here to finally restore the manse. And other things, of course.'

The cop touched the peak of his hat and seemed to draw himself to attention. 'And yu going over deh to work in de heat? On your own?'

'Oh yes.' Les rubbed his hands together sort of compassionately. 'When you're involved with the church, and the government, you're always prepared to make sacrifices.'

'No suh. No way,' said the cop, touching his hat again. 'I'll get someone to help you.'

'You'll what?'

'I'll get two officers to help you. We can't have you working in this heat on your own. Please, Mr Norton. In the car, suh. I'll show you where to go.'

Norton's face fell that far it looked like he'd need a building crane to pick it back up. 'Yeah...righto.'

They got in the car and the cop told Les where to go. Norton couldn't believe it. The cop was directing him to the police station to pick up two young cops that weren't doing anything who could give him a hand. Me and my big bloody mouth, Les gobbed out the window. By buying all those tickets and coming on a bit strong about the church and this other Norton, the cop had felt like he'd put the heavies on a government official who evidently had connections in Sommersby as well as Montego Bay and Kingston; which could mean repercussions. So for a square up he was getting Les some help. The cop introduced himself as Inspector Lewis Noonan and by the time they got to Dredmouth they were both on first-name terms and Les was wishing Lewis to the shithouse. Norton looked out the window and up at the grey Jamaican sky. Thanks mate. Terrific. You've been a great help.

Dredmouth Police Station was in the street on the left before the town square, three doors down on the same side of the road. It was pockmarked grey and white with two sets of barred windows out the front, a short set of concrete steps on the left, and POLICE painted across the top in faded blue. There were some equally daggy shops with battered awnings perched on splintery wooden poles on either side, a couple of light poles and a few vacant-looking punters lounging around or strolling past. Parked out the front was a blue and white Toyota and going by the condition it was in, pretty much like the police station, Les tipped it was a police car; he pulled up just behind it. Lewis said there was no need for Les to come inside, he'd only be a few minutes. Les smiled graciously and said he'd keep an eye on the car and the tools on the back seat. Norton stared absently at Lewis going up the stairs and at the punters walking by staring in at him. What bloody next, he scowled, cursing his alleged good luck. Les didn't have a clue what to do now or what to expect. Before long Lewis came back down the stairs, herding two young cops in front of him. They were about the same size as Millwood, only stockier, wearing blue, red-striped trousers, blue caps and khaki shirts. Each had a gun in a holster on a white belt and they both scowled inimically at Les sitting in the Honda before they climbed inside the Toyota. Lewis came round to Norton's side window.

'Follow us down to the manse, Les. It's not very far.'

'Yeah, righto Lewis,' smiled Les, as best he could.

Les started the engine and with the locals watching curiously the little procession wound down the back-streets of Dredmouth into Holding Street and along the waterfront. On the way half an idea formed in Norton's shifty red head, he was working on the other half when they pulled up next to the cobblestones and wooden columns in front of the manse. Les got out of the car and Lewis introduced him to the two cops. Their names were Coyne and Moylan and Les couldn't remember ever getting two lousier handshakes or filthier looks in his life. Coyne was a little taller than Moylan. Les smiled a syrupy smile, thinking if looks could kill he'd spend the rest of his Jamaican holiday planted with the rest of them out the front of Rose Hill Great House; starting this afternoon. He was also thinking he'd better put his plan into action and smartly as he didn't have all bloody day either.

'Alright, gentlemen,' he said, holding the crowbar and handing the two cops the rest of the tools, 'we'll have to go round the back. Professor Eyres is in Antigua at the moment and I don't have the key. Just follow me,' he smiled, receiving another two filthy looks for his trouble.

'Come on, has'e up,' ordered Lewis. 'And no fiesty either. Show de mon some respec.'

Les turned to Lewis and smiled. 'This is so good of you, Lewis. I honestly don't know how to show my appreciation.'

'My pleasure, Les. No problem at all, suh.'

They trooped round the corner, down the side then through the gap in the wall into the backyard; Les stopped near the back door and waited for them, all smiles. Inspector Noonan was okay, all pumped up with his own importance at being able to display some authority. The two young cops were screaming. They'd probably both been sitting on their arses in the station out of the heat, now they were going to spend the rest of the day shovelling shit in an old ruined building for nothing and being ordered around by some stinken, white bastard as well. Les nodded for them to follow him through. Norton walked straight into the main ballroom, dropped his backpack against the wall and took out his notebook and biro. With a look of rapture and reverence on his face Norton gazed around the inside of the manse and went into this pious spiel about how absolutely marvellous the old building was and how enlightening it would be to be able to restore the manse to its original splendour and do something fitting for the Jamaican people. Lewis beamed while the two young cops leant against their tools and sulked. You know, thought Les, I might even be able to have a bit fun with these two palookas. They're both at my disposal. Okay boys, let's see how you like a bit of honest toil in the name of the Lord. And just hope Eduardo hasn't left one of his whips lying around or you'll get it right across your black arses.

'Okay,' Les said to Coyne, holding the broom, 'if you'd like to sweep up in here, around these columns and along the walls. Then push all the rubbish in the corner near the door and we'll take it out later.' Coyne snarled something under his breath and removed his cap as Les turned to Moylan. 'Now, what I had in mind was this . . .' Les led Moylan out near the kitchen where all the muddy, water sodden books were slowly pulping themselves on the floor. 'If you'd like to shovel those into that corner, that would be great. I'll be along to help you shortly.' Moylan removed his cap and gave Norton a look even more diabolical than his mate.

'Ire,' snapped Inspector Noonan. 'You heard de mon. Mik movin'.'

'Absolutely marvellous,' beamed Norton. 'Now, Lewis. Tell me a bit about yourself while I take some notes.'

Les loaded his camera and walked Lewis round the bottom floor of the manse while he took photos, wrote meaningless scrawls in his notebook and talked about absolutely nothing. Nothing Les was interested in anyway. Lewis waffled on about how long he'd been in the force, his family and what a good turn the ball should be on the weekend. Les said he couldn't wait to be there with his friends and he was going to have at least one dance with Lewis's wife. Les was also ringing Kingston and Australia the following morning and he'd make sure he mentioned Inspector Noonan and the trouble he'd gone to for him. Lewis beamed like a lighthouse as Norton continued to piss in his pocket. Behind them, Coyne and Moylan were toiling away, getting shit all over them and getting more sour by the minute. Les and Inspector Noonan wandered out into the backyard, Les got the fat cop to strike an authoritative pose near the back door and took his photo then they wandered back inside again with Les still making notes.

'You know, Lewis,' Norton said sincerely, 'I don't think it's going to take as much as we thought to restore this building.'

'It won't?'

Les shook his head. 'No. We budgeted for half a million dollars. My family's putting up one half, the other half comes from the Australian government.' Les looked at his notebook again. 'We'll get out of it for a lot less than that.'

Noonan's eyes lit up at the phone number Les was tossing around. 'You will?'

'Easy. And you've been such a help and so friendly, Lewis, I don't know why we wouldn't be able to do something for your people. Could the Sommersby Police Sports Club do with a little help in some way?'

Noonan started to fluster. He'd stumbled across a walking, talking Australian pot of gold. 'Well. If you . . .'

'Excellent,' smiled Les. 'We might even organise it all through you.'

'I can assure you, Les, I'm the right man for the job there.'

'Do you think I ever doubted that for a minute, Lewis? In the meantime,' Norton draped an arm over Lewis's shoulder and went into Arthur Daley spiel about warp nine, 'I know what a busy man you are Lewis. With the ball coming up and all that. Plus the police station's running a couple of men short. You may as well go on about your business. I can organise things here.'

This pretty much suited Inspector Noonan. He could get back on the road, hustling motorists and putting half the money in his kick. 'Okay, Les. But only if you're sure.'

Norton removed his arm, made a magnanimous gesture and, out of sight from the other two cops, pulled a fifty from his wallet and offered it to the inspector. 'Take this, Lewis. Share it around up the station or whatever. With the Australian government's thanks. And mine too.'

Lewis tipped his cap again. 'Thank you, Les. I shall see that it goes to the right place.' Like my false bank account over at Ocho Rios.

'I'm sure you will, Lewis. Now, come on, mate, I'll walk you out to your car.'

Inspector Noonan gave Coyne and Moylan a goodbye blast as he was leaving, then let Norton piss in his pocket some more all the way out to the battered Toyota. Les shook his hand as Lewis got behind the wheel, thanked him profusely again and said if he didn't see him tomorrow he'd be in touch by the weekend. See you, Lewis. Thanks again. Les waved the inspector off up Holding Street, watched the little car disappear out of sight then walked back round the corner.

Coyne and Moylan were barely going through the motions as Les walked inside and Les was certain he could still detect the echo of obscenities hanging in the air as he entered the main ballroom. They picked up the pace slightly at the sight of the white bastard. Les gave them a thin smile each, went to his backpack, took out a carton of orange juice and drank it in front of them.

'You're doing a good job,' he said. 'Keep it up.'

Apart from two more sour looks there was no reply.

Les glanced at his watch, finished his orange juice and went upstairs.

From the top floor Les looked out over Dredmouth Harbour. It was still cloudy and crushingly humid, a couple of large brown birds hung in the air and a slight breeze drifted in from the bay, on which Les could smell the ocean and seaweed drying on the beach. He thought about a couple of things then started walking across the floorboards and beams, watching for gaps and loose nails. The ceiling was in a lot worse condition than Les had first thought. A lot of the floor was on the way out, and even though the beams supporting it were huge slabs of some local hardwood, they couldn't be expected to last forever. Not with most of the roof missing and rain constantly pouring in rotting them, then the sun streaming in and warping what was left when the rain stopped. Les walked slowly around some more. Through the gaps and the broken floorboards Les could see Coyne shuffling around below with the broken yard broom. Even doing very little he'd still managed to bring the marble tiles up in one area and Les could see just how opulent the old building must have been in its day. He could just picture Father Eduardo and hundreds of people whirling and dancing away while slaves in breeches and powdered wigs walked around with trays full of champagne or punch. Les could just picture it. But that wasn't what he was there for. He had one last look around then went back downstairs.

Moylan was still shovelling away at the books near the kitchen. Les called for him then nodded for him to follow him into the ballroom where he called Coyne over. They dropped their tools and sullenly walked across to Les standing at the kitchen door.

'Listen, you two wombats,' said Les. 'You're both about as much use as tits on a bull. You may as well hit the toe.' The two young cops looked at each other, then back at Les. Yeah, you pair of monkeys, thought Les. You're alright with your bloody patois. But you're not so good when it comes to a bit of good old, north corner,

488

Jack Lang, are you?' 'Go on, stall, you pair of dropkicks. Do a Harold. Before I give you a size ten St Louis right up both your abo khybers.' The two cops blinked at Norton as if he was from another planet. Les smiled another syrupy smile. 'Moylan. Coyne,' he said. 'This is no job for two fine young officers like you. Go. You can leave. With my blessing.' This got a response. 'And before you go, tch-tch-tch! Look at the state of your uniforms. Here, take this for dry cleaning. And don't tell Inspector Noonan.' Les handed Coyne $10 US. This got a response too. Les couldn't tell if it was gratitude or contempt. But they didn't need to be told twice. They picked up their caps and Les walked them out to the gap in the wall, where he shook their hands again and thanked them just to sweeten the pot some more; the handshakes were no better but at least the looks this time weren't so bad. Les watched them vanish around the corner into Holding Street and breathed a sigh of relief.

Les had a look around then walked over to the old fruit tree in the middle of the backyard. It reminded him of the one up at Sweet Ginger Hill and he thought of the happy snap of him and Joshua standing next to it and the sundial. For some reason Les suddenly felt himself badly in need of a leak; he didn't think anybody would mind if he piddled up against the tree. Why he wanted to piss against the old tree, Les didn't know. He just did. When he finished, Les stared absently up at the yellow fruit for a moment then slowly nodded his head. Righto. Let's go treasure hunting. Les turned around and walked straight into the great hall of the manse.

Maybe it had been the presence of the police, maybe it was the shadows playing tricks in the muted light, but suddenly it seemed quite eerie standing alone in the huge old room. Thick shafts of hazy sunshine were slicing down from the gaps in the ceiling, and the four massive wooden columns seemed even more prominent now where Coyne had swept around their sandstone bases, casting vague, slightly intimidating shadows across the marble-tiled floor and the aquamarine walls. It was very seventeenth century. Les checked his watch then went to his backpack and took out his book of Elizabeth Norton Blackmore's poems. He opened it and flicked to the one Millwood had read to him in the bar the previous night. Arguably her most famous poem.

'Well, Betty baby,' he said out loud, 'I haven't read any poetry since I left school. But seeing as there's no one around — I hope — I might have a go. Now, what's it say here?' Les looked at the book again. '"How do I love thee? Let me count four ways."'

Still holding the book of poems, Les walked over and stood directly in front of the four brown mahogany columns where they ran along the huge ballroom to the far wall that faced Holding Street. He started reading again.

Confronting you directly, my beloved, I see all four
*   at once,*
Yet 'tis for this very reason I canst see the ten,
A heartbeat to the left or right and I see all four again,
Though the last love may be obscured.

Norton stared up at the huge wooden pillar in front of him to where it met the ceiling above, then back to its sandstone base. Betty, he pondered, you weren't talking about these four columns inside the manse, were you? Because standing right in front of them I can see all four at once. Though I can't, or canst, see no ten. I can't see any bloody thing. Les stepped half a pace to the left. Yes, now I can see all four again. Les stepped across to the right. Same thing here. And the last one's certainly obscure, ain't it? Norton stepped back to the left hand side and began slowly walking along the wooden columns. But this ten you're talking about, Betty? This ten I canst see. Les kept walking, then stopped next to the end column and looked up to where Father Eduardo had embossed his name on the wall. That wouldn't happen to be the X up there, would it? As in Eduardo, X for Xavier, Norton. And isn't an X ten in Roman numerals? It was when I went to school. And you definitely canst see it standing up the other end of the columns. Les opened the book and started reading again.

And tis indeed the last love I treasure most, my dearest,
This is a love we both did share and shall ever treasure,
Our laboured love. The last love at the manse.

Betty, pondered Les again, closing the book. This last love you're talking about? The one you treasure most. You wouldn't happen to mean the last column, would you? The one at the end in front of the X? It's definitely the last one from the other end, ain't it? And it's pretty bloody obscure looking from up there. Les tapped the book against his hand and smiled. Betty, I've got this feeling that's what you're talking about. Norton shifted his gaze from the last column back to the end wall. And as for you, Eduardo X Norton. Les's smile got broader. I think I've twigged to your modus operandi too. Norton switched his gaze back to the end column. The thing is, though, if I have, there's still one burning question: If there is something in there. How the fuck do I get it out?

Les gave the end column several intense once up and downs. Well, I don't know exactly what is in there, though I've got a sort of an X-ray picture, if you'll pardon the pun, Father Eduardo. One thing for sure, if there is anything in there you wouldn't pick it up on a metal detector. But how do I get it out without that dirty great beam crashing down and squashing me or wrecking what's left of the place? That's the thing. If that column came down, it'd shake the whole town. Les absently rubbed the right toe of his trainer against his left calf muscle. With a bit of luck, though, I don't think it will. Les had one more look and shook his head. Well, only one way to find out. He walked up to where the pinchbar was standing near the inside door.

If what Les thought was in there, the last part of the poem would all fall into place. But for the time being getting it out was the problem. Les surmised, however, that when Eduardo stashed his loot he hadn't intended burying a time capsule; it just happened that way. If there was some sort of trouble and he had to leg it, he'd want to be able to get it out without too much trouble. Les tapped the hammer end of the pinchbar against the sandstone blocks supporting the wooden column; they appeared solid enough. He swung the pinchbar back and gave it a good, hard hit. The noise kind of boomed across the room and off the walls. Les walked up to the next column and did the same thing. This time what noise there was was more of a dull thud. The sandstone blocks at the end definitely weren't as dense. Les walked back to the end column and stared at it for a while, trying to picture himself in Eduardo's shoes, then decided to take a punt. He walked around and stood with his back to the X on the far wall, so he faced all the doors and entrances to the manse, jammed the pinchbar near the left hand corner of the sandstone blocks and heaved. Nothing happened or felt like happening. Les moved the pinchbar to the middle and tried. Same result. He moved the pinchbar to the right corner and heaved again, keeping up the strain. There was nothing at first, then a faint movement. Les sweated and strained some more; this time the sandstone blocks definitely moved. This is it, panted Les. There's some sort of a key stone or balance. He stopped, took a deep breath then jammed the pinchbar underneath as far as he could and heaved again, keeping up the pressure. The whole column seemed to creak and groan mournfully through the great hall as the sandstone blocks lifted about an inch. There was a crunching, grating sound of wood on stone and a horrible, dry scraping sound of metal against metal and the sandstone blocks swung round to the left as one, pivoting to a stop with one corner pinned beneath the base of the column diagonally across from where Les had stuck the pinchbar. Norton wiped a hand across his forehead then stepped back for a look.

Set into the marble tiles where the sandstone blocks had been were the tips of half a dozen bronze cannonballs sticking up like several partially buried Easter eggs. Les knelt down and stuck his fingers as far as he could beneath the sandstone blocks and felt the edge of a metal plate. He surmised the inside of the blocks would have been hollowed out to a certain extent and the metal plate set over the cavity. He stood back up and noticed the top of the sandstone blocks had been smoothed off, almost like marble, and was the same as the bottom of the massive wooden column, which was still suspended in mid air with one small edge resting on the sandstone blocks. Three of the cannon balls at the edge were loose, something like a set of ballbearings, and Les guessed these would be the balance or counterweight. There'd probably be indentations in the plate beneath the sandstone blocks, you hit it on the sweet-spot, it lifted, clicked out then swung across. Very ingenious Eduardo, commended Les. And I'll bet you had the slaves killed too after they built it. Les looked up at the mahogany column hanging in the air again and gave it a bit of bump. It shook slightly, but held firm. That's what Les had been counting on. Because now he had to crawl under it, and if it came down while he was there, Les would end up flatter than a cane toad after a week on the Pacific Highway; that's if they could scrape enough of him up. Les gave the wooden column one more tap, put down the pinchbar and crawled underneath over the cannonballs.

They were hard and cold and dug into his back. Shit! What I need is a bloody mechanic's trolley, cursed Les as one dug into his hip and another his elbow, making him curse again with discomfort. He felt round the bottom of the column and looked up. There was some sort of a wooden dowel sunk into it, something like the stopper on a hot-water bottle, only this was about eighteen inches across and the lug in the middle was about two inches thick and a foot across where it was carved out. Les gripped it and gave it a wrench anti-clockwise, but after sitting there all these years it wasn't about to budge. Les grunted and wrenched again. Nothing. He climbed back out and picked up the pinchbar. Les squatted down, held the hammer end of the pinchbar about two feet away from the wooden stopper, and swung. It hit the wooden lug with a dull thump and maybe a tiny crunch. Les swung the pinchbar again. This time there was a definite crunching sound and movement. Les gave the lug a few more taps and climbed back underneath.

The wooden stopper was loose now. Les gripped it and twisted and it started coming out just like the plug in a hot-water bottle. Les kept twisting. Would stuff start pouring out once he removed it? Norton didn't think so. The stopper was about six inches thick with a solid, wooden thread; Les got it out and placed it on the tiles. Inside the column was a cavity wider than the stopper with a lip running around the bottom. Les placed his hand inside and felt something cold, hard and heavy sitting at an angle against the hole. Les gave it a push and a shove and figured it wouldn't be hard to jam the tips of your fingers getting it out, so he went and got the crowbar. He levered the crowbar under the object till it was right on the edge of the hole, gave it one last twist, pulled the crowbar away and out fell a Spanish jar about a yard long and a bit over a foot wide. Les took the weight on his chest and rolled out from under the column. I thought so, grinned Les, as he got to his feet and stood the Spanish jar on its end. I bloody well thought so. In the light from above, the shiny, brown, ceramic container looked almost like a small version of one of the mahogany columns. Look at that, smiled Les. He shook his head in admiration and his gaze moved back to the name on the far wall. You're not bad, Eduardo. Not bad at all. That's about as perfect a fit as you can get. Now, though, what's in the bloody thing? Les got a towel from his backpack, placed it on the ground near the last column and laid the Spanish jar on its side with the neck over the towel.

Getting the wooden stopper out of the Spanish jar was a snack compared to the column. It was the same thing, only this time Les only had to give it a couple of light taps with the crowbar and it came away easily. He twisted it round a few more times, there was a muffled, rattling sound and as Les removed the stopper hundreds of gold coins began pouring from the neck of the jar. Les lifted the container up and screwed the stopper back in before any more fell out. Les looked at the pile of coins sitting on the towel, glistening and shining before his eyes. There

494

would have been three or four hundred piled on the towel and who knows how many more still in the Spanish jar; and the only word to describe them would be beautiful.

'Holy bloody hell!' Les shook his head again and called out loud. 'Have a look at that.'

Les picked up one of the coins. Between his fingers he couldn't tell exactly how big it was; it was about the same size as an Australian dollar, only thicker, heavier and a little rougher in the moulding. A sudden burst of sunshine came through the ceiling, causing the coins to glisten and shine even more. Norton didn't have a clue what they were, but you didn't have to be Albert Einstein to know they weren't ferry tokens. He held one up in the light and examined it in more detail. On one side was a profile of a square-jawed man with a big nose, solid chin and long hair tumbling over the shoulder of his breast plate. Running clockwise round the rim was 'Phillip V. D.G. Rex', beneath the breast plate was a date, 1729. Les turned the coin over. On the other side was a circle of flowers or a garland with a crown at the top and in the middle was a shield divided into four parts. Les could faintly make out what looked like a hand in one corner and some kind of engraving in the others. The printing on this read, 'S. Initium Sapientia Timor Domini'. Les looked at it for a moment then dropped it among the rest and picked up a couple of others. They were all the same, only with different dates. Les was still none the wiser as to what they were. But they were obviously gold and just the weight of them alone would have made them worth a fortune. There had to be four or five kilograms, or more, lying on the towel. Not counting their historical value as collector's items. Les ran his hand through the money and something caught his finger and glinted up through the gold coins. Les moved the coins aside and picked up the most beautiful gold necklace he had ever seen. It was at least a couple of feet in diameter with thick, chunky links as thick as a pencil. Set at the bottom was a gold cross about three inches by two inches and a good half an inch thick. But it was like no other cross or crucifix Norton had ever seen. The ends of the crucifix weren't squared off, they were split into three and turned out and around, something like the design on the ace of clubs in a deck of playing cards. Set at the ends of the arms of the cross were two rubies as big as pencil heads, and set at the ends of the cross were two emeralds the same size. The centre of the cross was thicker and crafted in a hexagonal design and set in the middle was a diamond as big as a fingernail. The sun had gone back behind the clouds but the exquisite cross still dazzled and shone in Norton's hands. Its weight or value Les couldn't even hope to guess. Oddly enough, from the rough, hand-crafted workmanship you would think it was one of those junk things you pick up in a flea market or Woolworths. But this was the real McCoy. Les looked at it for a while before putting it back among the coins. He sat back and looked at what he had found and a few things began to fall into place. Including the one thing he'd overlooked in his haste. But he was a bit dry. He got another carton of orange juice and sipped it while he sat on the floor and stared at the coins and the necklace lying on the towel in front of the Spanish jar.

Les wasn't sure what put him onto it at first; it just all seemed to come together at once when he was half drunk. When he lined the photos up the Spanish jars sitting on the verandah looked a lot like the wooden columns in the manse. The red, Pompeii tiles they were sitting on made him think briefly of ancient Rome. Then Millwood reading the poem out to him at the hotel, giving his explanation, only convinced Les even more that he was wrong. Les kept reflecting back to that old saying, 'You can't see the forest for the trees.' Like he'd done with the hurricane. Only this time it was 'you canst see something else'. The ten. Next thing Les thought of Eduardo's Spanish name on the wall, last love, treasure, and, bingo! There it was. The other clue though was Norton's toe. He'd stubbed it on a protruding bolt when he was walking around upstairs at the manse. It hadn't hurt enough to worry him, even though part of the nail went blue, but as he walked around upstairs he was on the lookout for more bolts sticking out. There weren't any. Which made Les a little curious as to why he found four sticking up from the beam above the column at the end. Eduardo had bored them into the column for extra support. Which, paradoxically, was the thing that had Les worried. He wasn't sure whether the inside of the beam was full of dry rot over the years or the rain had got to it. Evidently not. They built them to last in those days. Getting it out was elementary common sense. When the time came for Eduardo to remove his loot, he wouldn't have his back turned. He'd be watching the doors and entrances to the manse to make sure he was on his own. As for cleaning up afterwards, the sandstone blocks would swing back into place alright, thought probably not as neat as before. But whoever came into the manse would be looking for Eduardo, not a loose-fitting column down one end of the ballroom. Bad luck he drowned in a storm and never got a chance to retrieve his swag. Though it was nice to think one of the family finished up with it. And that was probably the bottom line. Norton was family. He knew there was something stashed in the manse from the first time he went upstairs and looked around. The bloodline and the family traits were just too strong — even over the centuries. As old uncle Harry always says, a Norton is a Norton. Whether they're baked, boiled or fried.

As for Eduardo porking his sister? That was pure bullshit. Malicious gossip fostered over the years by the likes of that old bag Mother Nettleford. Eduardo and Elizabeth would have been close. They would have loved each other deeply and probably been the best of mates. They would have danced together, dined together, got drunk together. If there was any ganja around in those days, you could bet they would have packed a few ping-pongs together. They were more than likely almost inseparable. As for the laboured love where she fell pregnant to Eduardo, that was another clue. The labour was helping her rotten, slave-trading brother get the column together and stash the loot. Part of it was probably Elizabeth's. You could bet your life she was halves in the whack with

Eduardo; or she'd at least have done his bookwork for him. She had plenty of money. The whole family was loaded. Look at the places they lived in. She probably felt like a break from Jamaica, so all cashed up she sailed over to England for a while. Which was no big deal; ships came and went all the time in those days. In England she teamed up with Blackmore the poet, supported him, found out she was a dab-hand at poetry herself and sort of lived happily ever after. The news of her brother's death obviously affected her and brought on her own premature death. She probably thought about going back to Jamaica, but apart from her family, there wasn't that much there now. The loot? She didn't particularly need it at the time. But being a woman she had to tell someone about it. So she wrote the secret into one of her most beautiful poems. How did the rumour start? When she took ill suddenly, she probably garbled it on her deathbed. No one, not even her immediate family, knew what she was talking about and it just became rumour and folklore from there. And that was about it. 'How do I love thee? Let me count four ways.' I wouldn't fancy counting those coins, thought Les, still staring at the ones on the towel and in the Spanish jar. There's probably thousands of them. Not counting any other Tom Foolery that might be sitting in the jar. Then Les began to laugh. A scornful, bitter laugh that echoed off the surrounding walls and the marble tiles as the last thing he'd over-looked dawned on him.

Norton had plotted, schemed, paid out a fortune in slings, driven all over the place, almost got arrested, not counting stubbing his toe, to find this loot. Now what was he going to do with it? Yeah, what? Take it with him? Hah! If he went within cooee of those metal detectors at the airport they'd start going off like New Year's Eve in Brazil. Plus it weighed a ton, and the customs department was red hot in Jamaica. It wouldn't last five minutes in his travel bag. If they didn't find it with X-rays, imagine some baggage handler picking it up. He'd get a few coins out among the dimes and quarters he still had from Florida, plus the Jamaican ones he was keeping and the coins he still had from home. But that was about it. Forget it, Les. Well done, nice try, but you blew it. Les stared at the coins lying on the towel and in the Spanish jar. Maybe it wasn't meant to be, after all. Maybe it was a secret between a brother and sister that was supposed to be left in the grave. Les had a bit of a think for a minute. Yeah. I'll put it all back where I found it. And just leave things as they were. At least I know where it is if I want it. Les looked up at the name embossed on the wall and at the massive, mahogany column, still hanging from the ceiling like a monstrous, chocolate-coloured stalactite. So back it all goes, Eduardo and Elizabeth. Well, not quite all of it.

Getting the Spanish jar back into its hiding place was a monumental pain in the arse. Les packed the coins back in easy enough then took his last few photos, after that it was like lying on a pile of half housebricks, trying to do bench presses with your hands in the middle of your chest. Les grunted and strained, cursed and sweated as he slipped across the cannonballs and banged his knees and elbows trying to get the heavy ceramic container back into the mahogany column. Finally, with the help of the crowbar, he was able to heave it in, lever it around then get the stopper screwed on; ending up with three bleeding knuckles and bruises all over his back. After that, Les had a quick breather and drank his last carton of orange juice, then picked up the pinchbar and jammed it back under the sandstone blocks, only on the opposite side. After being loosened, they moved easier this time. Without too much trouble Les was able to jemmy them across the cannonballs with some more crunching and grating before they rumbled and clunked down into place. The only difference this time was a gap between the sandstone blocks and the bottom of the column where the sandstone blocks had been dislodged. But if you didn't know it was there, you probably wouldn't notice it. Well, that's the best I can do, thought Les. At least it's back in there and I doubt if anyone will ever find it. Unless maybe the place caught on fire. Les stood back and was admiring his afternoon's work when there was a groaning, rumbling, slow crack from the ceiling. Les slowly raised his eyes. The huge beam above the columns seemed to quiver for a moment, dust and bits of debris fell to the floor then the end column slammed down onto the sandstone blocks with a dull thump that shook the floor. It wasn't hard enough to smash the blocks. But if they had been pivoted to the side, with just the edge of the column resting on them instead of right underneath them, the whole thing more than likely would have come crashing down. Five tonnes of solid, milled hardwood rolling and banging round the ballroom. The four bolts were holding the column now with the sandstone blocks underneath. But the huge old beam above had more dry rot inside than Les first thought. Norton gave one giant blink then stared at where the massive column had jammed itself against the sandstone blocks, wide-eyed as more dust hung in the hazy shafts of light surrounding him.

'Oooohhh! Ooohhh!' Les shook his head slowly. 'I don't think I like this.'

Strange thoughts began to fill Norton's head. If he'd spent some more time drinking his orange juice, if he'd gone for a leak, if he'd had some more film in the camera. Just a few minutes either way ... Les decided to stop thinking. It wasn't a good idea. One thing was for sure though, Les thought. The Spanish jar would be a lot harder to get out next time. After that, it didn't take Les long to get his stuff together, the tools rolled up in the sheet of tarpaulin and back in the car. He didn't stay for any final, nostalgic farewells to the old manse. Something weird was going on, Les could feel it in his bones, and he wanted out of the place before he started hearing strange voices and seeing luminous outlines amid the shadows.

Seconds later Norton was in the Honda, taking a short cut up Harbour Street behind the police station then back onto the main road leading out of Dredmouth. If Inspector Noonan appeared out of the bush trying to sell tickets

500

to the policemen's ball, Les would have driven straight over the top of him.

Back at the hotel Errol was standing in his usual place at the bottom of the stairs when Les swung the Honda into the carpark and pulled up almost next to him. There was no sign of the caretaker, so Les motioned for Errol to come over to the car, where Les handed him the tools, plus his other fifty dollars, thanking him again for his trouble. Errol seemed happy as a clam and carried the tools off down the side passage. Les watched him for a moment then got the rest of his stuff from the car and trotted up the stairs to the office. There was no sign of Esme or Delta. But his key was at the desk with a message. They had rung Millwood Downie three times. They'd gone for a walk and would be back by six. Short and to the point, thought Les. Though they didn't say whether Millwood would be at the hotel by six-thirty.

There was definitely a woman's touch in his room when Les opened the door. Two plastic bags on the neatly made spare bed, the whiff of cheap, yet sweet, perfume in the air and a couple of bottles plus some knickers and other odds and ends in the bathroom and two girlie magazines near the phone. Besides that, all his clothes were neatly folded and placed on his bed, his towels, sock and shoes were all together and someone even had the audacity to iron his blue, button-down collar shirt and a clean pair of jeans and hang them on the wardrobe. Nothing was missing, not even the change he'd left by the phone. In fact, even that was stacked into four neat piles. The cheeky little bastards, thought Les, dumping his backpack on the bed. How's their form? They're bloody lucky I'm leaving tonight or they'd both get a piece of my mind. Not that I've got that much to spare. Whistling happily, Norton climbed out of his dirty, sweat-sodden clothes and got under the shower. He took his time and had a good close shave, got all the crap out of his hair then spruced up with several dabs of Jamaica Island Lyme he'd bought at the resort.

Before long Les was looking pretty chic in his freshly

501

ironed jeans and shirt with a plain white T-shirt underneath. Packing his gear was easy, everything was all
neatly laid out and he had time for a think. There wasn't a
great deal to think about now, just one or two things. But
mainly Indiana Norton had scraped through again, made
some more friends and got out in front. He was thinking
of getting another bottle of Sangsters Rum and going out
in style, but Les had a feeling the drink might finish up a
bit melancholy. They say parting is such sweet sorrow
and this was shaping up as no exception to the rule. There
was something about Esme and Delta tidying up his
clothes for him that touched Les, and Millwood, corny
jokes or not, was one of the most decent blokes he'd ever
come across. He was a destant smadi, alright. Then
finding his roots going back all those years was something else again. Weird, uncanny; spooky even. And right
on top of that bizarre, crazy experience in America. For a
first trip away from Australia it hadn't been a bad one.
Les was reflecting on all this when there was a knock on
the door.

'Well, well, well. If it isn't the two best sorts in Jamaica.
How are you, girls?'

'Fine Les,' chorused Esme and Delta. 'How are yu?'

'Tops,' grinned Norton. 'Couldn't be creamier. No pun
intended of course, Esme.' This went over Esme's head,
but she kept smiling as Les closed the door. 'So what's
been happening?'

They sat on the beds, facing each other, and Les sorted
out what the girls had been up to and what was happening
with Millwood. The girls had spent a lovely day hanging
round the hotel and the beach and resting up in the room.
They'd rung Millwood three times. He got to work late
and he was busy, but he should be at the hotel by six-
thirty. If not, he'd see Les at the airport.

'At the airport?' frowned Norton.

'That's what he say,' nodded Esme. 'We ring back
twice. But he busy and de 'oman not put us through.'

'Mmmhh.' Les picked at his chin for moment. 'Oh well,
it's not half past six yet. He'll probably get here. Come on,

502

let's go and have an orange juice or something while we're waiting.'

'Okay,' smiled Esme.

'Hey. And thanks for tidying up the room and ironing my shirt for me,' said Les, returning Esme's smile. 'No wonder I love the both of youse.'

'We know you do,' said Delta. 'You're our Brer Wallaby.'

They had a bit of a laugh and a muck around then walked out onto the balcony.

The Caribbean sun was starting to set behind the clouds, filling the sky with streaks of violet and gold while it turned the still waters of Montego Bay a shimmering mauve. Considering the threat of an approaching hurricane it was quite a beautiful evening. There were only two other couples on the balcony so they sat down at the same table again and Les got two orange juices and a bottle of Red Stripe from the bar. Les was going to stick to orange juice, but it was a kind of celebration and he figured a couple of beers wouldn't hurt him. They clinked glasses then sat around talking while they waited for Millwood. Les was in a fairly jubilant kind of mood, which would have been even heightened if Millwood had been there. The girls were a little down. Besides being genuinely sad at seeing Les go, they had to be out of the room in the morning, then they had to go and start working for Lucretia Borgia at the Badminton Club in the afternoon. Not something to make you want to start doing handstands. But it would have been a lot worse if it hadn't been for Les. They almost brightened up a little when Les told them not to worry. Happy up. Things could only get better. Wait and see. Les told them a bit about Australia and his trip to Florida. He'd drop them a line when he got home. All the time he was talking Les kept checking his watch and looking out at the street. But there was still no sign of the schoolteacher. Where is the bastard? frowned Les. It's not getting any earlier. He bought another bottle of beer and drank that. Before Les knew it, time had run out.

'Righto, girls,' he said, finishing his beer. 'I got to make a move. By the time I fix up my bill it'll be time to get to the airport and check the car in. Millwood did say he'd be here, didn't he?'

'If not here, the airport,' shrugged Esme.

'Shit!' Les waited another minute, peering over the balcony just in case.

'What the crosses, Les?' asked Delta. 'Why you so screw face?'

'Why? Cause I want to bloody see him. That's why.'

'Okay, Les. I know he yu friend. I only asking.'

'I mean he's a good bloke,' said Les. 'And I'd like to say goodbye to him, Delta. That's all. Sorry. Anyway, we might catch him at the airport. I know I gave him my flight number. Righto.'

Les went to his room, had a last look around and gave himself a last detail. Some reggae track came belting up the wall from downstairs; Les didn't know what it was and he didn't particularly care. He made sure all his travel documents were in his backpack, checked to see that everything he'd need was in order, had one quick think for a moment then picked up his travel bag and walked out to reception. While the girl was fixing his bill, Les got her to ring the golf club; the number was engaged both times. The girl sorted out Norton's bill and hoped he had a pleasant stay at the hotel. Les smiled and said it was great. Esme and Delta got what they wanted from their room now and they walked down to the car. Errol was standing in his usual spot, so Les shook his hand and said goodbye. Errol was cool and he'd been a big help — though from the look on Esme's face you wouldn't think so. As they got in the car Les thought she was going to kick him fair in the nuts. Next thing they were on their way to Sir Donald Sangster Airport with Esme sitting in the front, her hand resting gently on Norton's knee.

The traffic wasn't heavy and the short drive out was uneventful. Les didn't say much. Most of the time he was looking in the rear vision mirror as if he expected Millwood to zoom up behind him with Harvey at the wheel and start honking. Next thing they were there. It wasn't anywhere near as hectic as last time and Les was able to drive straight into the rental area without any trouble and they got out of the car. Esme offered to carry Les's backpack; it looked heavy and he had a sore hand. Les said that it was quite alright. He could manage. The departure lounge didn't seem any busier than normal either. There were the usual crowds of tourists, passengers and staff walking around or whatever. But for a place expecting a hurricane at any time it seemed all very casual. Les decided to check his bag in first. There was a middle-aged couple in front of Les and he was patiently waiting his turn when he was surprised slightly by some bloke in a blue suit carrying a walkie-talkie who approached him from out of the crowd. He asked if that was Norton's bag, did he pack it and did he know that it would be X-rayed and sniffer dogs would go over it before it went on the plane? Les told the bloke it was his bag and they could do what they liked with it for all he cared. Spray graffiti on it, raise goats in it, fire a gun through it; anything they wanted. Just as long as it finished up in Australia. The bloke gave Les a miserable once up and down and drifted off into the crowd.

'What was that all about?' asked Esme, when Les came back from the counter.

'Buggered if I know,' replied Norton, a little mystified. 'Come on, I'll get rid of the Rolls then we should have time for a couple of drinks before I go.' Les scanned the crowd again then led the girls over to the Hertz counter. Maybe that's why the bloke from customs came over, mused Les. I haven't stopped looking around since I got here.

Les didn't know whether the car hire turned him over or not and he didn't care, he just kept looking at his watch and searching the crowd. But although they went over the car with a fine tooth comb and he ended up paying gratuity and tax and God only knows what else, they were pleasant enough and it didn't take long. Les paid with his VISA and they walked up to the departure lounge.

The lounge was up two short flights of stairs, not far from and above the check-in counters. It seated about fifty and was almost two-thirds full. The bar was down one end to the left, Les found a table to the right of the stairs with a view over the departure area and sat down facing the stairs with Esme on his right and Delta on his left. There was the usual throng of people coming and going, the hubbub of voices around them and the occasional, crackling din of the PA system paging passengers and staff throughout the terminal. A waiter in a white shirt and bowtie appeared from among the other tables and Les ordered two more orange juices and another Red Stripe. The two girls didn't say a great deal while they sat and waited for their drinks; they seemed more intent on watching Les, who was watching everyone walking round the airport and checking his watch about every half-minute. The drinks arrived, Les paid the waiter and left his wallet on the table.

'Well girls,' he said, holding up his bottle. 'Here's to Jamaica.'

'Ire mon. Jamaica,' said Delta.

'I Island,' said Esme, smiling right into Norton's eyes.

'Yeah. Island in the sun,' nodded Les, and took a swig of beer. Les paused for a moment and stared at the two girls while a poignant silence seemed to settle in around them. Then Norton seemed to click into second gear. 'Alright, Esme and Delta,' he said, looking at his watch again, 'I haven't got much time left and it looks like Millwood isn't going to make it. So here's what I want you both to do.' Les took most of the money out of his wallet, gave it a quick count then put his wallet back in his jeans. 'There's the best part of a grand US there,' he said, handing the money to Esme. 'I've also written down Millwood's phone number again. Plus the name of the school he teaches at.'

Both girls blinked at the money in Esme's hand. 'Les,' she said, screwing her face up a little, 'why yu do all this? Yu something else, mon.'

'I told you,' replied Les, 'because I love the both of you. Now listen.'

506

'He does too,' smiled Delta, her eyes widening. 'Look.' She reached across the table and took Norton's hand. 'Yu wearing our rings. I ony jus notice.'

'He is too,' said Esme excitedly, reaching across the table to take Norton's other hand.

'Yeah, well why wouldn't I?' shrugged Les, a sheepish grin on his face as he looked at the two, cheap, junky rings he'd bought from the girls jammed on both his little fingers. 'I just didn't want to make a big thing of it. That's all.'

Esme's eyes started to swim. 'Oh Les. Yu so sweet.' Both girls put their arms around Norton's neck and kissed him tenderly.

'Yeah, alright,' said Les. 'That's nice. But listen, because this is important. When you leave here and go back to the hotel, get a phone book. Then...'

Delta cut in and pointed towards the stairs. 'Is that...?'

Les looked over at an awkward, spindly movement near the stairs. Some bloke had just run up them, elbows and knees going everywhere, now he was standing at the top in a white shirt and blue trousers, a briefcase in one hand, his other arm resting on his head something like a chimpanzee, as he peered round the lounge through a pair of black-rimmed glasses. Les knew he'd seen that face before somewhere. Another bloody American movie: *The Nutty Professor*. Without thinking, Les jumped to his feet.

'Jerry! Over here,' he yelled out.

Millwood Downie saw Les and came gangling through the chairs and tables, knocking people with his briefcase and bumping their seats with his knees. 'Les,' he puffed. 'Thank God I made it.'

'You can say that again,' said Les, his face lighting up like a Christmas tree as he pumped Millwood's hand. 'Here, grab a seat.' Les pushed a chair out and Millwood sat down next to Delta with his briefcase on his lap. Les quickly introduced him to the girls then sat down himself. 'Hey, thanks for coming out, Millwood. Do you want something to drink?'

The skinny schoolteacher nodded his head gingerly. 'I might have a soda water.'

Norton gave him a wink. 'Wasn't a bad night, was it?'

'Terrific Les. Except for when I had to get up this morning. Why do you think I'm wearing my glasses?'

Les caught the waiter's eye and ordered another round of drinks. 'So what happened? I didn't think you were bloody well going to get here.'

'Well, apart from a monumental hangover, there was that hurricane again.'

'Hurricane!!?' said Les. 'Don't tell me the bloody thing's on its way?'

'No, it's changed direction. It doesn't look like it's coming now.'

'It's not? What the . . .?'

'Don't yu read de newspaper, Les?' said Delta. 'Listen to i radio?'

'What yu do all day today?' asked Esme.

'Went down the beach,' said Les.

'So instead of everyone cancelling,' continued Millwood, 'they've all changed their minds at once and decided to stay. Plus about another two million chucky bwoys have booked in. And there's more coming. Honestly, Les, I went that close to telling them to shove it today. I'm absolutely stuffed.'

A smile flickered around Norton's eyes. 'You never know yet, Mill. You might be able to.'

'I wouldn't mind.' The teacher closed his eyes and shook his head for a second.

The drinks arrived and Les paid. 'Well, here's to you, Millwood,' said Les, raising his bottle. 'You're something else, old mate.'

Millwood raised his soda and smiled. 'You're not bad yourself, Les. Just bad luck you haven't got any sense of humour.'

'Haven't got a sense of humour!' howled Norton. 'Millwood, your jokes'd turn a baked dinner cold.'

'Get out, you big red-headed buguyaga. I'm a killer.'

'Hey. Not so fiesty there, mon.'

Whatever was going on between Les and Millwood seemed to slip straight over Esme and Delta's heads. They seemed more mystified than anything else. All this money and concern over a skinny little bloke with glasses and a dud crewcut carrying an old briefcase.

'Listen, Millwood,' said Les urgently. 'We haven't got much time.'

'I know,' cut in Millwood, 'which is why before we go any further I want you to have this souvenir of Jamaica.'

'Souvenir? What . . .?'

'I got you a T-shirt, Les.'

Millwood opened up his briefcase and pulled out a white T-shirt big enough for two people. Printed across the front in green, yellow and black was 'Spring Water Primary School, Jamaica'. Underneath was a funny drawing of three young faces; a boy and two girls. The boy wore dreadlocks. The girls wore pigtails and bows. It was all bright, squiggly colours, yet had an abstract, childlike innocence about it that stood out.

Les stood up and held the T-shirt in front of him for all to see. Even Esme and Delta were impressed. 'Shit! Thanks Millwood. That's terrific.'

'It's one of Harvey's. He painted it with natural dye from berries up in the hills. That won't come out.'

'It's unreal, Millwood. Gee, thanks mate.'

'The children said to say hello. And so did Harvey. He can't come in. He's waiting outside in the car.'

'Tell him thanks.' Les looked at the T-shirt across his chest and started to laugh. 'You're not going to believe this, Mill, but I've got a T-shirt for you too.'

'You're kidding?'

'No.' Les folded up his present, put it on the table and sat down. 'Millwood,' he said sincerely, 'I've got bugger all time. And so much I want to tell you. But before I go any further, do you know what this is?'

Les dipped into the fob pocket of his jeans and pulled out one of the coins he'd found at the manse and handed it to Millwood. The schoolteacher's forehead knitted, he moved his glasses and started examining the coin. The way it sparkled in the light caught Esme and Delta's eye and they moved in closer for a look too. While they were all staring at the coin Les took the T-shirt he got for Millwood out of his backpack and placed it on the table. It was Norton's white Emu Bitter one that was a size too big for him. Where the one Millwood brought for Les was folded flat, Norton had folded Millwood's present up rather lumpily, so it looked something like a loaf of bread. He then placed the one Millwood had brought him in his backpack and resumed sipping his beer. A few seconds later Millwood looked up at Les and his eyes were starting to get that boiled egg look again.

'Les, do you know what this is?' he said incredulously.

'If I knew what it was, Millwood, you Dubbo, I wouldn't be asking you. Would I?'

'It's an eight-escudo piece.'

'A what?'

'It's an old Spanish coin. Eight escudos.' Millwood pointed to one side of the coin. 'That's Phillip the Fifth of Spain. He was the first monarch for hundreds of years to start having his likeness on the coins again.' Millwood turned the coin over. 'My Latin's not what it should be, but, "Timor" is fear of. "Domini" means rule or ruler. "Sapientia". That's ... wise, or something. And "initium ...".'

'Yeah, alright, Millwood,' interjected Les. 'I haven't got time for a bloody lesson in Latin right now. Is it worth anything?'

'Worth anything? You're joking! It's solid gold. Old, old gold. The finest there ever was. That's not counting its other value as a collector's item. Coins like this can be worth up to a thousand dollars or more. US.' Millwood stared at Les through his glasses. 'Where did you get this?'

'Don't worry where I got it. Just put it in your pocket.'

'What!!?'

'Put it in your pocket. There's people around.'

Millwood stared at Les, stared at the coin and put it in his trouser pocket. 'I ... don't understand, Les.'

'I don't expect you to. Now, there's your T-shirt. Don't open it up, put it in your briefcase.'

Millwood reached across to pick up his T-shirt and it didn't move. Millwood's face went all funny. 'Les, this weighs a ton. What's in it?'

Norton stared right into the little schoolteacher's puzzled eyes. 'At the last count, about three hundred and ten of those eight-piece escudos. Now stick it in your briefcase. Hurry up.'

Millwood picked up his T-shirt with both hands and placed it as carefully as he could in his briefcase, then put it down on the floor with a dull thump. 'Les,' he said nervously, 'this is all getting a bit weird for me.'

'Don't worry about it, Millwood. It's all sweet.' Les took a sip of beer and looked Millwood in the eye. The girls just sat there and blinked. 'Millwood, I've got about two minutes. But all I say is this. You were wrong about that poem.'

'Poem?'

'Yeah. That one you were reading me last night.' Les took his book of Elizabeth Norton Blackmore's poems from his backpack and handed it to Millwood. 'I want you to have this too as a souvenir. Have a good read and forget about old Edith Nettlefart, or whatever her name is. There's no incest in my family, son. I don't mind you calling one of my ancestors a thief and a slave trader. But brush the incest.' Millwood just sat there blinking. 'One of these days I'll tell you, Millwood. Now there's a fortune there in your briefcase. You'll know how to cash those coins in. Do up the school, set yourself up in business or whatever up there at Spring Water. You'll know what to do. And give Esme and Delta a job up there. They could teach. They're good girls and I want you to look after them. Okay?'

'Yeah,' replied Millwood faintly. 'No problem.'

'They've got my old room for the night. Give them a lift back with you after I leave and you can sort things out at the hotel. But everything's alright now, Millwood. You can tell the chucky bwoys and the golf club to get stuffed.' Les turned to Delta and Esma. 'And you two don't have to start work at that sleazy Badminton Club. You're now on Millwood's payroll. You're social workers.'

Esme and Delta both shook their heads. 'Social workers?'

'Yeah. Millwood'll explain it all to you back at the hotel. You're TAFE teachers.'

'Tief?' said Delta.

'No. Not thief. TAFE.' Norton looked at his watch. 'Shit! I got to go.' He stood up and offered his hand to Millwood. The schoolteacher shook it as warmly as he could. 'See you, Millwood. Old mate,' smiled Norton. 'Don't bother coming down to see me off. If you come near those metal detectors down there you'll blow the place up. Stay here, then take the girls back in to the hotel.'

Millwood sat there motionless. It looked as if someone had punched him hard in the stomach. 'I . . . I don't know what to say, Les.'

'Goodbye'll have to do for the time being. See you, Millwood. You take care. Come on, girls. You can see me off at the gate.'

Les picked up his backpack, left Millwood staring into space and walked down to the departure gate with Esme and Delta. There weren't that many people going through; some backpackers, an English couple, a few Americans. Les looked at the girls and smiled.

'Well, this is it girls. Uncle Les is off.'

'We gonna miss yu, Brer Wallaby,' said Delta. The girls didn't look like they were going to burst into tears, but they weren't laughing all that much and it wouldn't have taken a great deal to set them off.

'I'm going to miss you too, Delta. Come here.' Les gave her a nice kiss. 'Goodbye, Delta. Have a good time up at Spring Water Primary.'

'Goodbye, Les.'

'As for you, Esme,' grinned Norton. 'Come here.' Les bent her over and gave her the full Rhett Butler–Scarlett O'Hara. Right in front of all the other passengers. She didn't seem to mind at all. 'See you, Esme.'

'I see yu too, Les,' said Esme.

Norton shuffled in behind some other tourists in the queue. 'I'll write to you care of the school.'

'You promise, Les?' said Esme.

'Yeah. I promise.'

Next thing it was Norton's turn. He placed his back-pack on the conveyor belt to go through the X-ray machine as a woman in a blue uniform came over to him, holding a portable metal detector and a small plastic bowl for him to put his watch in, and any jewellery he might have, while he walked through the main metal detector. Les gave the girl a smile, removed his old silver Timex and placed it in the bowl, then took off the two junky rings he'd bought from Esme and Delta and placed them next to his watch. While the girl in the blue uniform watched indifferently, Les undid the top two buttons of his blue shirt, reached under his white T-shirt, removed the junky gold chain with the jewel-encrusted Spanish cross from round his neck and dropped that in the bowl with his watch and the two rings, then walked through the metal detector. Round the other side, the woman quickly ran the portable metal detector over him then handed him back his things. Les put them on in exactly the same order as he had taken them off. After doing up his shirt, Les picked up his backpack and got ready to walk towards his plane. He'd just turned when he heard a girl's voice call out.

'Hey, Les!'

Norton turned around slowly. 'Yes Esme?' he smiled.

'And de fun don't done?'

Les thought for a moment then blew her a kiss. 'You never know, Esme. You just never know what might happen. See you, mate.'

Les slung his backpack over his shoulder, melted in with the other passengers and walked towards his plane.

Robert G. Barrett
You Wouldn't Be Dead For Quids

You Wouldn't Be Dead For Quids is the book that launched Les Norton as Australia's latest cult hero.

Follow Les, the hillbilly from Queensland, as he takes on the bouncers, heavies, hookers and gamblers of Sydney's Kings Cross, films a TV ad for Bowen Lager in Queensland and gets caught up with a nymphomaniac on the Central Coast of New South Wales.

In one of the funniest books of the past decade you will laugh yourself silly and be ducking for cover as Les unleashes himself on Sydney's unsuspecting underworld.

Robert G. Barrett
The Real Thing

Les Norton is back in town!

It all began in *You Wouldn't Be Dead For Quids*... And now there's more of it in *The Real Thing*.

Trouble seems to follow Les Norton like a blue heeler after a mob of sheep.

Maybe it's his job.

Being a bouncer at the infamous and illegal Kelly Club in Kings Cross isn't the stuff a quiet life is made of.

Maybe it's his friends.

Like Price Galese, the urbane and well-connected owner of the Kelly Club, or Eddie Salita who learnt to kill in Vietnam, or Reg Campbell, struggling artist and dope dealer.

But, then again, maybe Les is just unlucky.

Robert G. Barrett's five stories of Les Norton and the Kelly Club provide an entertaining mix of laughter and excitement, and an insight into the Sydney underworld; a world often violent and cynical, but also with its fair share of rough humour and memorable characters.

Robert G. Barrett
The Boys From Binjiwunyawunya

Les Norton's back in town!

There's no two ways about Les Norton — the carrot-topped country boy who works as a bouncer at Sydney's top illegal casino. He's tough and he's mean. He's got a granite jaw, fists like hams, and they say the last time he took a tenner from his wallet Henry Lawson blinked at the light.

Lethal but loyal, he's always good for a laugh. In this, the third collection of Les Norton adventures, Les gets his boss off the hook. But not without the help of the boys from Binjiwunyawunya.

Having got over that, Les finds himself in a spot of bother in Long Bay Gaol then in a lot more bother on a St. Kilda tram in Melbourne...

Robert G. Barrett's Les Norton stories have created a world as funny as Damon Runyon's. If you don't know Les Norton, you don't know Australia in the eighties.

Robert G. Barrett
The Godson

'I wonder who that red-headed bloke is? He's come into town out of nowhere, flattened six of the best fighters in Yurriki plus the biggest man in the valley. Then he arrives at my dance in an army uniform drinking French champagne and imported beer like it's going out of style. And ups and leaves with the best young sort in the joint... Don't know who he is. But he's not bloody bad.'

Les Norton is at it again!

Les thought they were going to be the easiest two weeks of his life.

Playing minder for a young member of the Royal Family called Peregrine Normanhurst III sounded like a deadset snack. So what if he was a champagne-guzzling millionaire Hooray Henry and his godfather was the Attorney General of Australia? Les would keep Peregrine out of trouble... So what if he was on the run from the IRA? They'd never follow him to Australia...

Robert G. Barrett's latest Les Norton adventure moves at breakneck speed from the corridors of power in Canberra to the grimy tenements of Belfast, scorching the social pages of Sydney society and romping through the North Coast's plushest resorts to climax in a nerve-shattering, blood-spattered shootout on a survivalist fortress in the Tweed Valley. *The Godson* features Les Norton at his hilarious best, whatever he's up against — giant inbreds, earth mothers, Scandinavian au pair girls, jealous husbands, violent thugs and vengeful terrorists.

If you thought Australia's favourite son could get up to some outrageous capers in *You Wouldn't Be Dead For Quids*, *The Real Thing* and *The Boys from Binjiwunyawunya*, until you've read *The Godson*, you ain't read nothin' yet!

Robert G. Barrett
**Between the Devlin and the
Deep Blue Seas**

Okay, so it looks like the Kelly Club is finally closing
down — it had to happen sooner or later. And it isn't
as if Les Norton will starve. He has money snookered
away, he owns his house, and his blue-chip
investment — a block of flats in Randwick — must be
worth a fortune by now. Except that the place is falling
down, the council is reclaiming the land, there's been
a murder in Flat 5, and the tenants are the biggest
bunch of misfits since the Manson Family. And that's
just the good news, because the longer Les owns the
Blue Seas Apartments, the more money he loses.

This time Les Norton's really up against it.

But whilst he's trying to solve his financial problems, he
still has time to fight hate-crazed roadies, sort out a
drug deal after fighting a gang of bikies, help a
feminist Balmain writer with some research she won't
forget in a hurry, and get involved with Franulka,
super-sexy leadsinger of an all-girl rock band, The
Heathen Harlots.

And with the help of two ex-Romanian Securitate
explosive experts, he might even be able to sort out
his investment.

But can Les pull off the perfect crime? Of course —
and why not throw the street party of the year at the
same time?

Robert G. Barrett's latest Les Norton novel is probably
no more outrageous than his previous ones.

But then again...

Robert G. Barrett
White Shoes, White Lines and Blackie

All Norton wanted was a quiet coffee and Sacher cake at the Hakoah club in Bondi, and to be left alone to sort out his troubled love life. How he let notorious conman Kelvin Kramer talk him up to Surfers Paradise for five days, Les will never know. Supposedly to mind KK and his massively boobed girlfriend, American model Crystal Linx, in Australia to promote her latest record. Though it did seem like a good idea at the time. Apart from the President of the United States arriving and Norton's domestic problems, there wasn't much keeping him in Sydney.

Norton went to the Gold Coast expecting some easy graft in the sun, an earn and possibly a little fresh romance. Les definitely got the earn. He certainly got the girl. But what Norton got in Surfers Paradise was trouble. In a size 40 Double-D cup.

Robert G. Barrett
Davo's Little Something

All easy-going butcher, Bob Davis, wanted after his divorce was to get on with his job, have a few beers with his mates, and be left alone. But this was Sydney in the early eighties. The beginning of the AIDS epidemic, street gangs, gay bashings, murders.

When a gang of skinheads bashed Davo's old school friend to death simply because he was gay, and left Davo almost dead in an intensive care unit, they unleashed a crazed killer onto the city streets. Before the summer had ended, over thirty corpses had turned up in the morgue, leaving two bewildered detectives to find out where they were coming from.

Robert G. Barrett's latest book is not for the squeamish. Although written with lashings of black humour the action is chillingly brutal — a story of a serial killer bent on avenging himself on the street tribes of Sydney. *Davo's Little Something* proves conclusively why Robert G. Barrett, author of the Les Norton series, is one of Australia's most popular contemporary writers.